War Stories

War Stories

Edited and with an Introduction

by Lamar Underwood

LYONS
PRESS

Guilford Connecticut

An imprint of Globe Pequot, the trade division of The Rowman & Littlefield Publishing Group, Inc.
4501 Forbes Blvd., Ste. 200
Lanham, MD 20706
LyonsPress.com

Distributed by NATIONAL BOOK NETWORK

British Library Cataloguing in Publication Information Available

Library of Congress Cataloging-in-Publication Data Available

ISBN 978-1-4930-2961-7 (hardcover)
ISBN 978-1-4930-2962-4 (e-book)
ISBN 978-1-4930-6200-3 (paperback)

♾™ The paper used in this publication meets the minimum requirements of American National Standard for Information Sciences—Permanence of Paper for Printed Library Materials, ANSI/NISO Z39.48-1992.

CONTENTS

Contents

INTRODUCTION

"THIS IS A SIMPLE STORY OF A BATTLE; SUCH A TALE AS MAY BE TOLD BY A SOLDIER WHO is no writer to a reader who is no soldier."

The very first sentence of the first story comprising this gigantic volume sets the exact tone I believe will result in great reader reward in the pages ahead. The opening line jump-starts the story "What I Saw of Shiloh" by Ambrose Bierce, who in fact was a writer of prodigious talent. Bierce, like many of the other authors of the thirty-seven tales presented here, knew that the art of storytelling went far beyond the accounting of raw "facts" and brought to life the deepest emotions of all those involved. While the "facts" may hold the interest of war buffs and scholars for a considerable time, the average reader needs more. The books they turn to again and again reveal life laid bare, the moments of terror and heartbreak, of victory and exhalations. Such moments form the heart and soul of great war stories—the Classics.

It is the pursuit of such stories that has brought this editor to the tales worthy of comprising this volume. The final collection is composed mostly of stories gleaned from three previously published Lyons Press anthologies: My own *Classic War Stories*, Lisa Purcell's *Classic Civil War Stories*, and Stephen Vincent Brennan's *Classic American Hero Stories*. Also included are tales of the modern era: World War II, Vietnam, and the Iraq/Afghanistan operations.

From ordinary citizens describing their war experiences to the most distinguished writers of their generations, these stories comprise a diverse treasury of voices, eager to describe what they saw and felt in war.

Consider this gem from Rudyard Kipling's enduring poem "Recessional":

> The tumult and the shouting dies;
> The captains and the kings depart;
> Still shines Thine ancient sacrifice,
> An humble and contrite heart.
> Lord God of Hosts, be with us yet,
> Lest we forget—lest we forget!

Even though he wrote "Recessional" before the death of his son in the First World War, Kipling knew a thing or two about the pain of war and the drama of war stories. He knew, for instance, that the "captains and kings" would command center stage as much as the troops who fought the battles, and that afterwards the bloodshed and losses would be horrible to contemplate without linking them to some Almighty purpose.

Today, such reflections continue, just as the battles themselves continue, followed by the accounts and journals of what happened on the fields where victories and defeats were forged. News of the outcomes is not enough. The details, the exact history, the stories of the men in uniform—these accounts go on for decades, or, as in the case of some battles, for centuries. It would seem from the popularity of war literature that once a certain amount of interest is created by a particular battle or campaign, there will always be readers on the hunt for accounts and stories that put them in the very flames of the battle itself. They search to know and feel: What was it like?

What was it like at Waterloo, or Gettysburg, or the Marne? What was it like to maneuver the armies, carry the weapons, and face the enemy? What was it like to feel the pain and loss?

So many of mankind's most talented authors have tackled this amazing subject so many times for the simple reason that for many, many people the material is endlessly fascinating. When it comes to war, whether the scenes depicted are of bravery and glory or tragedy and defeat, many of us avid readers are drawn irresistibility to the pages, like rubber-neckers staring at the site of an accident.

The war stories I personally feel qualify for the exalted title "Classic" have earned their way onto my list by being sources of great reading reward for many years. In my mind they are not Classics because the gurus and high priests of literature have deemed them so, but because they are enduring as great pleasures to read. Considering the authors who have penned these tales, one can hardly be surprised by their quality and staying power. Hugo, Tolstoy, Crane, Kipling . . . several others . . . are not exactly one-book celebrities. These gentlemen were drawn to war as a colossal canvas because they had plenty to say about the subject and the talent to back up their ambitions. We readers are truly blessed by their efforts.

In rereading many of these tales, I am often struck by the vividness and intensity of the scenes the prose evokes. The great writers did not settle for dry reportage of facts and events. Their pages instead capture mood and atmosphere, while crackling along with the pace and exhilaration of action unfolding. The pages of Victor Hugo on Waterloo, or Tolstoy on Borodino, or Stephen Crane on a Civil War battle become some kind of magical wide-screen film in my mind. I can see, hear, and feel the tumult of the battle. It is the best way to go to war.

In preparing this book, I resisted the temptation to present the stories in any sort of chronological time line, either by the dates the action occurred or in the sequence in which the works were published. That sort of thing may seem tidy, but in my mind the book becomes more exciting by a random presentation, tale after tale jumping across the ages, each story a unique experience.

Obviously, there are many, many stories that could have been included. No doubt, some readers will feel a stab of disappointment on not seeing a favorite among these tales. Being an editor is, I think, rather like being a quarterback in football. You call the play, then run it, hoping for the best.

On behalf of myself, Lisa Purcell, and Stephen Vincent Brennan, I would like to thank you for your attention.

—Lamar Underwood
January 2017

CHAPTER ONE

What I Saw of Shiloh
By Ambrose Bierce

As no other war, the Civil War has captured the American imagination. This is not surprising: It had great leaders, such as Abraham Lincoln, Robert E. Lee, Ulysses S. Grant, Stonewall Jackson, and William T. Sherman. It had great battles, too, such as Shiloh, Chickamauga, Antietam, and Gettysburg. This war—the only war fought on American soil, between Americans—was surely one of the most heroic and the most horrific. During the four years of this brutal, bloody conflict, Americans killed each other in greater numbers than in any war before or since. The Civil War left the Southern Confederacy defeated and the Union intact, and it ended slavery, all at the cost of nearly 1,100,000 casualties and more than 620,000 lives.

Between the first shots fired at Fort Sumter on April 12, 1861, and Lee's surrender to Grant at Appomattox on April 9, 1865, the nation was irrevocably changed. Homes were transformed into headquarters; churches and schools into makeshift hospitals. Marauding armies decimated the once-peaceful landscape, pillaging farms, burning towns, and killing each other wherever they met. And whether soldier or civilian, the lives of those who lived through the war were irrevocably changed, too.

Newspaper columnist, satirist, essayist, short-story writer, and novelist Ambrose Bierce was a veteran of the war, fighting for the Union at several major battles, including Shiloh and Chickamauga, before he was severely wounded in the head at Kennesaw Mountain.

In contrast to the romanticism of most turn-of-the-century writers, the work of Ambrose Bierce is far more realistic, whether he was writing short stories or nonfiction pieces. Bierce wrote gritty, often disturbing tales of wartime experience. His "What I Saw of Shiloh" is an idiosyncratic account of this famous battle, which in two days claimed a greater number of American lives than all previous wars combined.

*—*LISA PURCELL

I

THIS IS A SIMPLE STORY OF A BATTLE; SUCH A TALE AS MAY BE TOLD BY A SOLDIER WHO
is no writer to a reader who is no soldier.

The morning of Sunday, the sixth day of April, 1862, was bright and warm. Reveille
had been sounded rather late, for the troops, wearied with long marching, were to have a
day of rest. The men were idling about the embers of their bivouac fires; some preparing
breakfast, others looking carelessly to the condition of their arms and accoutrements,
against the inevitable inspection; still others were chatting with indolent dogmatism
on that never-failing theme, the end and object of the campaign. Sentinels paced up
and down the confused front with a lounging freedom of mien and stride that would
not have been tolerated at another time. A few of them limped unsoldierly in deference
to blistered feet. At a little distance in rear of the stacked arms were a few tents out of
which frowsy-headed officers occasionally peered, languidly calling to their servants to
fetch a basin of water, dust a coat or polish a scabbard. Trim young mounted orderlies,
bearing dispatches obviously unimportant, urged their lazy nags by devious ways amongst
the men, enduring with unconcern their good-humored raillery, the penalty of superior
station. Little negroes of not very clearly defined status and function lolled on their stomachs, kicking their long, bare heels in the sunshine, or slumbered peacefully, unaware of
the practical waggery prepared by white hands for their undoing.

Presently the flag hanging limp and lifeless at headquarters was seen to lift itself spir-
itedly from the staff. At the same instant was heard a dull, distant sound like the heavy
breathing of some great animal below the horizon. The flag had lifted its head to listen.
There was a momentary lull in the hum of the human swarm; then, as the flag drooped
the hush passed away. But there were some hundreds more men on their feet than before;
some thousands of hearts beating with a quicker pulse.

Again the flag made a warning sign, and again the breeze bore to our ears the long,
deep sighing of iron lungs. The division, as if it had received the sharp word of command, sprang to its feet, and stood in groups at "attention." Even the little blacks got up.
I have since seen similar effects produced by earthquakes; I am not sure but the ground
was trembling then. The mess-cooks, wise in their generation, lifted the steaming camp-
kettles off the fire and stood by to cast out. The mounted orderlies had somehow disappeared. Officers came ducking from beneath their tents and gathered in groups. Headquarters had become a swarming hive.

The sound of the great guns now came in regular throbbings—the strong, full pulse of
the fever of battle. The flag flapped excitedly, shaking out its blazonry of stars and stripes
with a sort of fierce delight. Toward the knot of officers in its shadow dashed from somewhere—he seemed to have burst out of the ground in a cloud of dust—a mounted aide-
de-camp, and on the instant rose the sharp, clear notes of a bugle, caught up and repeated,
and passed on by other bugles, until the level reaches of brown fields, the line of woods
trending away to far hills, and the unseen valleys beyond were "telling of the sound," the

farther, fainter strains half drowned in ringing cheers as the men ran to range themselves behind the stacks of arms. For this call was not the wearisome "general" before which the tents go down; it was the exhilarating "assembly," which goes to the heart as wine and stirs the blood like the kisses of a beautiful woman. Who that has heard it calling to him above the grumble of great guns can forget the wild intoxication of its music?

II

The Confederate forces in Kentucky and Tennessee had suffered a series of reverses, culminating in the loss of Nashville. The blow was severe: immense quantities of war material had fallen to the victor, together with all the important strategic points. General Johnston withdrew Beauregard's army to Corinth, in northern Mississippi, where he hoped so to recruit and equip it as to enable it to assume the offensive and retake the lost territory.

The town of Corinth was a wretched place—the capital of a swamp. It is two days' march west of the Tennessee River, which here and for a hundred and fifty miles farther, to where it falls into the Ohio at Paducah, runs nearly north. It is navigable to this point— that is to say, to Pittsburg Landing, where Corinth got to it by a road worn through a thickly wooded country seamed with ravines and bayous, rising nobody knows where and running into the river under sylvan arches heavily draped with Spanish moss. In some places they were obstructed by fallen trees. The Corinth road was at certain seasons a branch of the Tennessee River. Its mouth was Pittsburg Landing. Here in 1862 were some fields and a house or two; now there are a national cemetery and other improvements.

It was at Pittsburg Landing that Grant established his army, with a river in his rear and two toy steamboats as a means of communication with the east side, whither General Buell with thirty thousand men was moving from Nashville to join him. The question has been asked, Why did General Grant occupy the enemy's side of the river in the face of a superior force before the arrival of Buell? Buell had a long way to come; perhaps Grant was weary of waiting. Certainly Johnston was, for in the gray of the morning of April 6th, when Buell's leading division was en bivouac near the little town of Savannah, eight or ten miles below, the Confederate forces, having moved out of Corinth two days before, fell upon Grant's advance brigades and destroyed them. Grant was at Savannah, but hastened to the Landing in time to find his camps in the hands of the enemy and the remnants of his beaten army cooped up with an impassable river at their backs for moral support. I have related how the news of this affair came to us at Savannah. It came on the wind—a messenger that does not bear copious details.

III

On the side of the Tennessee River, over against Pittsburg Landing, are some low bare hills, partly inclosed by a forest. In the dusk of the evening of April 6 this open space, as seen from the other side of the stream—whence, indeed, it was anxiously watched by thousands of eyes, to many of which it grew dark long before the sun went down—would have appeared to have been ruled in long, dark lines, with new lines being constantly drawn across. These lines were the regiments of Buell's leading division, which having moved from Savannah through a country presenting nothing but interminable swamps and pathless "bottom lands," with rank overgrowths of jungle, was arriving at the scene of action breathless, footsore and faint with hunger. It had been a terrible race; some regiments had lost a third of their number from fatigue, the men dropping from the ranks as if shot, and left to recover or die at their leisure. Nor was the scene to which they had been invited likely to inspire the moral confidence that medicines physical fatigue. True, the air was full of thunder and the earth was trembling beneath their feet; and if there is truth in the theory of the conversion of force, these men were storing up energy from every shock that burst its waves upon their bodies. Perhaps this theory may better than another explain the tremendous endurance of men in battle. But the eyes reported only matter for despair.

Before us ran the turbulent river, vexed with plunging shells and obscured in spots by blue sheets of low-lying smoke. The two little steamers were doing their duty well. They came over to us empty and went back crowded, sitting very low in the water, apparently on the point of capsizing. The farther edge of the water could not be seen; the boats came out of the obscurity, took on their passengers and vanished in the darkness. But on the heights above, the battle was burning brightly enough; a thousand lights kindled and expired in every second of time. There were broad flushings in the sky, against which the branches of the trees showed black. Sudden flames burst out here and there, singly and in dozens. Fleeting streaks of fire crossed over to us by way of welcome. These expired in blinding flashes and fierce little rolls of smoke, attended with the peculiar metallic ring of bursting shells, and followed by the musical humming of the fragments as they struck into the ground on every side, making us wince, but doing little harm. The air was full of noises. To the right and the left the musketry rattled smartly and petulantly; directly in front it sighed and growled. To the experienced ear this meant that the death-line was an arc of which the river was the chord. There were deep, shaking explosions and smart shocks; the whisper of stray bullets and the hurtle of conical shells; the rush of round shot. There were faint, desultory cheers, such as announce a momentary or partial triumph. Occasionally, against the glare behind the trees, could be seen moving black figures, singularly distinct but apparently no longer than a thumb. They seemed to me ludicrously like the figures of demons in old allegorical prints of hell. To destroy these and all their belongings the enemy needed but another hour of daylight; the steamers in that case would have been doing him fine service by bringing more fish to his net. Those of us who had the good fortune to arrive late could then have eaten our teeth in important rage. Nay, to make his victory sure it did not need that the sun should pause in the heavens; one of many random shots falling into the river would have done the business had chance directed it into the engine-room of a steamer. You can perhaps fancy the anxiety with which we watched them leaping down.

But we had two other allies besides the night. Just where the enemy had pushed his right flank to the river was the mouth of a wide bayou, and here two gunboats had taken station. They too were of the toy sort, plated perhaps with railway metals, perhaps with boiler-iron. They staggered under a heavy gun or two each. The bayou made an opening in the high bank of the river. The bank was a parapet, behind which the gunboats crouched, firing up the bayou as through an embrasure. The enemy was at this disadvantage: he could not get at the gunboats, and he could advance only by exposing his flank to their ponderous missiles, one of which would have broken a half-mile of his bones and made nothing of it. Very annoying this must have been—these twenty gunners beating back an army because a sluggish creek had been pleased to fall into a river at one point rather than another. Such is the part that accident may play in the game of war.

As a spectacle this was rather fine. We could just discern the black bodies of these boats, looking very much like turtles. But when they let off their big guns there was a conflagration. The river shuddered in its banks, and hurried on, bloody, wounded, terrified! Objects a mile away sprang toward our eyes as a snake strikes at the face of its victim. The report stung us to the brain, but we blessed it audibly. Then we could hear the great shell tearing away through the air until the sound died out in the distance; then, a surprisingly long time afterward, a dull, distant explosion and a sudden silence of small-arms told their own tale.

IV

There was, I remember, no elephant on the boat that passed us across that evening, nor, I think, any hippopotamus. These would have been out of place. We had, however, a woman. Whether the baby was somewhere on board I did not learn. She was a fine creature, this woman; somebody's wife. Her mission, as she understood it, was to inspire the failing heart with courage; and when she selected mine I felt less flattered by her preference than astonished by her penetration. How did she learn? She stood on the upper deck with the red blaze of battle bathing her beautiful face, the twinkle of a thousand rifles mirrored in her eyes; and displaying a small ivory-handled pistol, she told me in a sentence punctuated by the thunder of great guns that if it came to the worst she would do her duty like a man! I am proud to remember that I took off my hat to this little fool.

V

Along the sheltered strip of beach between the river bank and the water was a confused mass of humanity—several thousands of men. They were mostly unarmed; many were wounded; some dead. All the camp-following tribes were there; all the cowards; a few officers. Not one of them knew where his regiment was, nor if he had a regiment. Many had not. These men were defeated, beaten, cowed. They were deaf to duty and dead to shame. A more demented crew never drifted to the rear of broken battalions. They would have stood in their tracks and been shot down to a man by a provost-marshal's guard, but they could not have been urged up that bank. An army's bravest men are its cowards. The death which they would not meet at the hands of the enemy they will meet at the hands of their officers, with never a flinching.

Whenever a steamboat would land, this abominable mob had to be kept off her with bayonets; when she pulled away, they sprang on her and were pushed by scores into the water, where they were suffered to drown one another in their own way. The men disembarking insulted them, shoved them, struck them. In return they expressed their unholy delight in the certainty of our destruction by the enemy.

By the time my regiment had reached the plateau night had put an end to the struggle. A sputter of rifles would break out now and then, followed perhaps by a spiritless hurrah. Occasionally a shell from a far-away battery would come pitching down somewhere near, with a whir crescendo, or flit above our heads with a whisper like that made by the wings of a night bird, to smother itself in the river. But there was no more fighting. The gunboats, however, blazed away at set intervals all night long, just to make the enemy uncomfortable and break him of his rest.

For us there was no rest. Foot by foot we moved through the dusky fields, we knew not whither. There were men all about us, but no camp-fires; to have made a blaze would have been madness. The men were of strange regiments; they mentioned the names of unknown generals. They gathered in groups by the wayside, asking eagerly our numbers. They recounted the depressing incidents of the day. A thoughtful officer shut their mouths with a sharp word as he passed; a wise one coming after encouraged them to repeat their doleful tale all along the line.

Hidden in hollows and behind clumps of rank brambles were large tents, dimly lighted with candles, but looking comfortable. The kind of comfort they supplied was indicated by pairs of men entering and reappearing, bearing litters; by low moans from within and by long rows of dead with covered faces outside. These tents were constantly receiving the wounded, yet were never full; they were continually ejecting the dead, yet were never empty. It was as if the helpless had been carried in and murdered, that they might not hamper those whose business it was to fall to-morrow.

The night was now black-dark; as is usual after a battle, it had begun to rain. Still we moved; we were being put into position by somebody. Inch by inch we crept along, treading on one another's heels by way of keeping together. Commands were passed along the line in whispers; more commonly none were given. When the men had pressed so closely together that they could advance no farther they stood stock-still, sheltering the locks of their rifles with their ponchos. In this position many fell asleep. When those in front suddenly stepped away those in the rear, roused by the tramping, hastened after with such zeal that the line was soon choked again. Evidently the head of the division was being piloted at a snail's pace by someone who did not feel sure of his ground. Very often we struck our feet against the dead; more frequently against those who still had spirit enough to resent it with a moan. These were lifted carefully to one side and abandoned. Some had sense enough to ask in their weak way for water. Absurd! Their clothes were soaked, their hair dank; their white faces, dimly discernible, were clammy and cold. Besides, none of us had any water. There was plenty coming, though, for before midnight a thunderstorm broke upon us with great violence. The rain, which had for hours been a dull drizzle, fell with a copiousness that stifled us; we moved in running water up to our ankles. Happily, we were in a forest of great trees heavily "decorated" with Spanish moss, or with an enemy standing to his guns the disclosures of the lightning might have been inconvenient. As it was, the incessant blaze enabled us to consult our watches and encouraged us by displaying our numbers; our black, sinuous line, creeping like a giant serpent beneath the trees, was apparently interminable. I am almost ashamed to say how sweet I found the companionship of those coarse men.

So the long night wore away, and as the glimmer of morning crept in through the forest we found ourselves in a more open country. But where? Not a sign of battle was here. The trees were neither splintered nor scarred, the underbrush was unmown, the ground had no footprints but our own. It was as if we had broken into glades sacred to eternal silence. I should not have been surprised to see sleek leopards come fawning about our feet, and milk-white deer confront us with human eyes.

A few inaudible commands from an invisible leader had placed us in order of battle. But where was the enemy? Where, too, were the riddled regiments that we had come to save? Had our other divisions arrived during the night and passed the river to assist us? Or were we to oppose our paltry five thousand breasts to an army flushed with victory? What protected our right? Who lay upon our left? Was there really anything in our front?

There came, borne to us on the raw morning air, the long weird note of a bugle. It was directly before us. It rose with a low clear, deliberate warble, and seemed to float in the gray sky like the note of a lark. The bugle calls of the Federal and the Confederate armies were the same: it was the "assembly"! As it died away I observed that the atmosphere had suffered a change; despite the equilibrium established by the storm, it was electric. Wings were growing on blistered feet. Bruised muscles and jolted bones, shoulders pounded by the cruel knapsack, eyelids leaden from lack of sleep—all were pervaded by the subtle fluid, all were unconscious of their clay. The men thrust forward their heads, expanded their eyes and clenched their teeth. They breathed hard, as if throttled by tugging at the leash. If you had laid your hand in the beard or hair of one of these men it would have crackled and shot sparks.

VI

I suppose the country lying between Corinth and Pittsburg Landing could boast a few inhabitants other than alligators. What manner of people they were it is impossible to say, inasmuch as the fighting dispersed, or possibly exterminated them; perhaps in merely classing them as non-saurian I shall describe them with sufficient particularity and at the same time avert from myself the natural suspicion attaching to a writer who points out to persons who do not know him the peculiarities of persons whom he does not know. One thing, however, I hope I may without offense affirm of these swamp-dwellers—they were pious. To what deity their veneration was given—whether, like the Egyptians, they worshiped the crocodile, or, like other Americans, adored themselves, I do not presume to guess. But whoever, or whatever, may have been the divinity whose ends they shaped, unto Him, or It, they had builded a temple. This humble edifice, centrally situated in the heart of a solitude, and conveniently accessible to the super sylvan crow, had been christened Shiloh Chapel, whence the name of the battle. The fact of a Christian church—assuming it to have been a Christian church—giving name to a wholesale cutting of Christian throats by Christian hands need not be dwelt on here; the frequency of its recurrence in the history of our species has somewhat abated the moral interest that would otherwise attach to it.

VII

Owing to the darkness, the storm and the absence of a road, it had been impossible to move the artillery from the open ground about the Landing. The privation was much greater in a moral than in a material sense. The infantry soldier feels a confidence in his cumbrous arm quite unwarranted by its actual achievements in thinning out the opposition. There is something that inspires confidence in the way a gun dashes up to the front, shoving fifty or a hundred men to one side as if it said, "Permit me!" Then it squares its shoulders, calmly dislocates a joint in its back, sends away its twenty-four legs and settles down with a quiet rattle which says as plainly as possible, "I've come to stay." There is a superb scorn in its grimly defiant attitude, with its nose in the air; it appears not so much to threaten the enemy as deride him.

Our batteries were probably toiling after us somewhere; we could only hope the enemy might delay his attack until they should arrive. "He may delay his defense if he likes," said a sententious young officer to whom I had imparted this natural wish. He had read the signs aright; the words were hardly spoken when a group of staff officers about the brigade commander shot away in divergent lines as if scattered by a whirlwind, and galloping each to the commander of a regiment gave the word. There was a momentary confusion of tongues, a thin line of skirmishers detached itself from the compact front and pushed forward, followed by its diminutive reserves of half a company each—one of which platoons it was my fortune to command. When the straggling line of skirmishers had swept four or five hundred yards ahead, "See," said one of my comrades, "she moves!" She did indeed, and in fine style, her front as straight as a string, her reserve regiments in columns doubled on the center, following in true subordination; no braying of brass to apprise the enemy, no fifing and drumming to amuse him; no ostentation of gaudy flags; no nonsense. This was a matter of business.

In a few moments we had passed out of the singular oasis that had so marvelously escaped the desolation of battle, and now the evidences of the previous day's struggle were present in profusion. The ground was tolerably level here, the forest less dense, mostly clear of undergrowth, and occasionally opening out into small natural meadows. Here and there were small pools—mere discs of rainwater with a tinge of blood. Riven and torn with cannon-shot, the trunks of the trees protruded bunches of splinters like hands, the fingers above the wound interlacing with those below. Large branches had been lopped, and hung their green heads to the ground, or swung critically in their netting of vines, as in a hammock. Many had been cut clean off and their masses of foliage seriously impeded the progress of the troops. The bark of these trees, from the root upward to a height of ten or twenty feet, was so thickly pierced with bullets and grape that one could not have laid a hand on it without covering several punctures. None had escaped. How the human body survives a storm like this must be explained by the fact that it is exposed to it but a few moments at a time, whereas these grand old trees had had no one to take their places, from the rising to the going down of the sun. Angular bits of iron, concavo-convex, sticking in the sides of muddy depressions, showed where shells had exploded in their furrows. Knapsacks, canteens, haversacks distended with soaken and swollen biscuits, gaping to disgorge, blankets beaten into the soil by the rain, rifles with bent barrels or splintered stocks, waist-belts, hats and the omnipresent sardine-box—all the wretched debris of the battle still littered the spongy earth as far as one could see, in every direction. Dead horses were everywhere; a few disabled caissons, or limbers, reclining on one elbow, as it were; ammunition wagons standing disconsolate behind four or six sprawling mules. Men? There were men enough; all dead apparently, except one, who lay near where I had halted my platoon to await the slower movement of the line—a Federal sergeant, variously hurt, who had been a fine giant in his time. He lay face upward, taking in his breath in convulsive, rattling snorts, and blowing it out in sputters of froth which crawled creamily down his cheeks, piling itself alongside his neck and ears. A bullet had clipped a groove in his skull, above the temple; from this the brain protruded in bosses, dropping off in flakes and strings. I had not previously known one could get on, even in this unsatisfactory fashion, with so little brain. One of my men whom I knew for a womanish fellow, asked if he should put his bayonet through him. Inexpressibly shocked by the cold-blooded proposal, I told him I thought not; it was unusual, and too many were looking.

VIII

It was plain that the enemy had retreated to Corinth. The arrival of our fresh troops and their successful passage of the river had disheartened him. Three or four of his gray cavalry videttes moving amongst the trees on the crest of a hill in our front, and galloping out of sight at the crack of our skirmishers' rifles, confirmed us in the belief; an army face to face with its enemy does not employ cavalry to watch its front. True, they might be a general and his staff. Crowning this rise we found a level field, a quarter of a mile in width; beyond it a gentle acclivity, covered with an undergrowth of young oaks, impervious to sight. We pushed on into the open, but the division halted at the edge. Having orders to conform to its movements, we halted too; but that did not suit; we received an intimation to proceed. I had performed this sort of service before, and in the exercise of my discretion deployed my platoon, pushing it forward at a run, with trailed arms, to strengthen the skirmish line, which I overtook some thirty or forty yards from the wood. Then—I can't describe it—the forest seemed all at once to flame up and disappear with a crash like that of a great wave upon the beach—a crash that expired in hot hissings, and the sickening "spat" of lead against flesh. A dozen of my brave fellows tumbled over like ten-pins. Some struggled to their feet only to go down again, and yet again. Those who stood fired into the smoking brush and doggedly retired. We had expected to find, at most, a line of skirmishers similar to our own; it was with a view to overcoming them by a sudden coup at the moment of collision that I had thrown forward my little reserve. What we had found was a line of battle, coolly holding its fire till it could count our teeth. There was no more to be done but get back across the open ground, every superficial yard of which was throwing up its little jet of mud provoked by an impinging bullet. We got back, most of us, and I shall never forget the ludicrous incident of a young officer who had taken part in the affair walking up to his colonel, who had been a calm and apparently impartial spectator, and gravely reporting: "The enemy is in force just beyond this field, sir."

IX

In subordination to the design of this narrative, as defined by its title, the incidents related necessarily group themselves about my own personality as a center; and, as this center, during the few terrible hours of the engagement, maintained a variably constant relation to the open field already mentioned, it is important that the reader should bear in mind the topographical and tactical features of the local situation. The hither side of the field was occupied by the front of my brigade—a length of two regiments in line, with proper intervals for field batteries. During the entire fight the enemy held the slight wooded acclivity beyond. The debatable ground to the right and left of the open was broken and thickly wooded for miles, in some places quite inaccessible to artillery and at very few points offering opportunities for its successful employment. As a consequence of this the two sides of the field were soon studded thickly with confronting guns, which flamed away at one another with amazing zeal and rather startling effect. Of course, an infantry attack delivered from either side was not to be thought of when the covered flanks offered inducements so unquestionably superior; and I believe the riddled bodies of my poor skirmishers were the only ones left on this "neutral ground" that day. But there was a very pretty line of dead continually growing in our rear, and doubtless the enemy had at his back a similar encouragement.

The configuration of the ground offered us no protection. By lying flat on our faces between the guns we were screened from view by a straggling row of brambles, which marked the course of an obsolete fence; but the enemy's grape was sharper than his eyes, and it was poor consolation to know that his gunners could not see what they were doing, so long as they did it. The shock of our own pieces nearly deafened us, but in the brief intervals we could hear the battle roaring and stammering in the dark reaches of the forest to the right and left, where our other divisions were dashing themselves again and again into the smoking jungle. What would we not have given to join them in their brave, hopeless task! But to lie inglorious beneath showers of shrapnel darting divergent from the unassailable sky—meekly to be blown out of life by level gusts of grape—to clench our teeth and shrink helpless before big shot pushing noisily through the consenting air—this was horrible! "Lie down, there!" a captain would shout, and then get up himself to see that his order was obeyed. "Captain, take cover, sir!" the lieutenant-colonel would shriek, pacing up and down in the most exposed position that he could find.

O those cursed guns!—not the enemy's, but our own. Had it not been for them, we might have died like men. They must be supported, forsooth, the feeble, boasting bullies! It was impossible to conceive that these pieces were doing the enemy as excellent a mischief as his were doing us; they seemed to raise their "cloud by day" solely to direct aright the streaming procession of Confederate missiles. They no longer inspired confidence, but begot apprehension; and it was with grim satisfaction that I saw the carriage of one and another smashed into matchwood by a whooping shot and bundled out of the line.

X

The dense forests wholly or partly in which were fought so many battles of the Civil War, lay upon the earth in each autumn a thick deposit of dead leaves and stems, the decay of which forms a soil of surprising depth and richness. In dry weather the upper stratum is as inflammable as tinder. A fire once kindled in it will spread with a slow, persistent advance as far as local conditions permit, leaving a bed of light ashes beneath which the less combustible accretions of previous years will smolder until extinguished by rains. In many of the engagements of the war the fallen leaves took fire and roasted the fallen men. At Shiloh, during the first day's fighting, wide tracts of woodland were burned over in this way and scores of wounded who might have recovered perished in slow torture. I remember a deep ravine a little to the left and rear of the field I have described, in which, by some mad freak of heroic incompetence, a part of an Illinois regiment had been surrounded, and refusing to surrender was destroyed, as it very well deserved. My regiment having at last been relieved at the guns and moved over to the heights above this ravine for no obvious purpose, I obtained leave to go down into the valley of death and gratify a reprehensible curiosity.

Forbidding enough it was in every way. The fire had swept every superficial foot of it, and at every step I sank into ashes to the ankle. It had contained a thick undergrowth of young saplings, every one of which had been severed by a bullet, the foliage of the prostrate tops being afterward burnt and the stumps charred. Death had put his sickle into this thicket and fire had gleaned the field. Along a line which was not that of extreme depression, but was at every point significantly equidistant from the heights on either hand, lay the bodies half buried in ashes; some in the unlovely looseness of attitude denoting sudden death by the bullet, but by far the greater number in postures of agony that told of the tormenting flame. Their clothing was half burnt away—their hair and beard entirely; the rain had come too late to save their nails. Some were swollen to double girth; others shriveled to manikins. According to degree of exposure, their faces were bloated and black or yellow and shrunken. The contraction of muscles which had given them claws for hands had cursed each countenance with a hideous grin. Faugh! I cannot catalogue the charms of these gallant gentlemen who had got what they enlisted for.

XI

It was now three o'clock in the afternoon, and raining. For fifteen hours we had been wet to the skin. Chilled, sleepy, hungry and disappointed—profoundly disgusted with the inglorious part to which they had been condemned—the men of my regiment did everything doggedly. The spirit had gone quite out of them. Blue sheets of powder smoke, drifting amongst the trees, settling against the hillsides and beaten into nothingness by the falling rain, filled the air with their peculiar pungent odor, but it no longer stimulated. For miles on either hand could be heard the hoarse murmur of the battle, breaking out nearby with frightful distinctness, or sinking to a murmur in the distance; and the one sound aroused no more attention than the other.

We had been placed again in rear of those guns, but even they and their iron antagonists seemed to have tired of their feud, pounding away at one another with amiable infrequency. The right of the regiment extended a little beyond the field. On the prolongation of the line in that direction were some regiments of another division, with one in reserve. A third of a mile back lay the remnant of somebody's brigade looking to its wounds. The line of forest bounding this end of the field stretched as straight as a wall from the right of my regiment to Heaven knows what regiment of the enemy. There suddenly appeared, marching down along this wall, not more than two hundred yards in our front, a dozen files of gray-clad men with rifles on the right shoulder. At an interval of fifty yards they were followed by perhaps half as many more; and in fair supporting distance of these stalked with confident mien a single man! There seemed to me something indescribably ludicrous in the advance of this handful of men upon an army, albeit with their left flank protected by a forest. It does not so impress me now. They were the exposed flanks of three lines of infantry, each half a mile in length. In a moment our gunners had grappled with the nearest pieces, swung them half round, and were pouring streams of canister into the invaded wood. The infantry rose in masses, springing into line. Our threatened regiments stood like a wall, their loaded rifles at "ready," their bayonets hanging quietly in the scabbards. The right wing of my own regiment was thrown slightly backward to threaten the flank of the assault. The battered brigade away to the rear pulled itself together.

Then the storm burst. A great gray cloud seemed to spring out of the forest into the faces of the waiting battalions. It was received with a crash that made the very trees turn up their leaves. For one instant the assailants paused above their dead, then struggled forward, their bayonets glittering in the eyes that shone behind the smoke. One moment, and those unmoved men in blue would be impaled. What were they about? Why did they not fix bayonets? Were they stunned by their own volley? Their inaction was maddening! Another tremendous crash!—the rear rank had fired! Humanity, thank Heaven! is not made for this, and the shattered gray mass drew back a score of paces, opening a feeble fire. Lead had scored its old-time victory over steel; the heroic had broken its great heart against the commonplace. There are those who say that it is sometimes otherwise.

All this had taken but a minute of time, and now the second Confederate line swept down and poured in its fire. The line of blue staggered and gave way; in those two terrific volleys it seemed to have quite poured out its spirit. To this deadly work our reserve regiment now came up with a run. It was surprising to see it spitting fire with never a sound, for such was the infernal din that the ear could take in no more. This fearful scene was enacted within fifty paces of our toes, but we were rooted to the ground as if we had grown there. But now our commanding officer rode from behind us to the front, waved his hand with the courteous gesture that says apres vous, and with a barely audible cheer we sprang into the fight. Again the smoking front of gray receded, and again, as the enemy's third line emerged from its leafy covert, it pushed forward across the piles of dead and wounded to threaten with protruded steel. Never was seen so striking a proof of the paramount importance of numbers. Within an area of three hundred yards by fifty there struggled for front places no fewer than six regiments; and the accession of each, after the first collision, had it not been immediately counterpoised, would have turned the scale.

As matters stood, we were now very evenly matched, and how long we might have held out God only knows. But all at once something appeared to have gone wrong with the enemy's left; our men had somewhere pierced his line. A moment later his whole front gave way, and springing forward with fixed bayonets we pushed him in utter confusion back to his original line. Here, among the tents from which Grant's people had been expelled the day before, our broken and disordered regiments inextricably intermingled, and drunken with the wine of triumph, dashed confidently against a pair of trim battalions, provoking a tempest of hissing lead that made us stagger under its very weight. The sharp onset of another against our flank sent us whirling back with fire at our heels and fresh foes in merciless pursuit—who in their turn were broken upon the front of the invalided brigade previously mentioned, which had moved up from the rear to assist in this lively work.

As we rallied to reform behind our beloved guns and noted the ridiculous brevity of our line—as we sank from sheer fatigue, and tried to moderate the terrific thumping of our hearts—as we caught our breath to ask who had seen such-and-such a comrade, and laughed hysterically at the reply—there swept past us and over us into the open field a long regiment with fixed bayonets and rifles on the right shoulder. Another followed, and another; two—three—four! Heavens! Where do all these men come from, and why did they not come before? How grandly and confidently they go sweeping on like long blue waves of ocean chasing one another to the cruel rocks! Involuntarily we draw in our weary feet beneath us as we sit, ready to spring up and interpose our breasts when these gallant lines shall come back to us across the terrible field, and sift brokenly through among the trees with spouting fires at their backs. We still our breathing to catch the full grandeur of the volleys that are to tear them to shreds. Minute after minute passes and the sound does not come. Then for the first time we note that the silence of the whole region is not comparative, but absolute. Have we become stone deaf? See; here comes a stretcher-bearer, and there a surgeon! Good heavens! a chaplain!

The battle was indeed at an end.

XII

And this was, O so long ago! How they come back to me—dimly and brokenly, but with what a magic spell—those years of youth when I was soldiering! Again I hear the far warble of blown bugles. Again I see the tall, blue smoke of camp-fires ascending from the dim valleys of Wonderland. There steals upon my sense the ghost of an odor from pines that canopy the ambuscade. I feel upon my cheek the morning mist that shrouds the hostile camp unaware of its doom, and my blood stirs at the ringing rifle-shot of the solitary sentinel. Unfamiliar landscapes, glittering with sunshine or sullen with rain, come to me demanding recognition, pass, vanish and give place to others. Here in the night stretches a wide and blasted field studded with half-extinct fires burning redly with I know not what presage of evil. Again I shudder as I note its desolation and its awful silence. Where was it? To what monstrous inharmony of death was it the visible prelude?

O days when all the world was beautiful and strange; when unfamiliar constellations burned in the Southern midnights, and the mocking-bird poured out his heart in the moon-gilded magnolia; when there was something new under a new sun; will your fine, far memories ever cease to lay contrasting pictures athwart the harsher features of this later world, accentuating the ugliness of the longer and tamer life? Is it not strange that the phantoms of a blood-stained period have so airy a grace and look with so tender eyes?—that I recall with difficulty the danger and death and horrors of the time, and without effort all that was gracious and picturesque? Ah, Youth, there is no such wizard as thou! Give me but one touch of thine artist hand upon the dull canvas of the Present; gild for but one moment the drear and somber scenes of to-day, and I will willingly surrender another life than the one that I should have thrown away at Shiloh.

CHAPTER TWO

The Sword of the Lord and of Gideon
By Theodore Roosevelt Jr.

American troops were not in the actual fighting in World War I for very long—only five months in 1918—but that was long enough for many acts of gallantry, including one massive display of fortitude that made the name Alvin York a legend. The husky redhead from the remote Tennessee valley called "Three Forks of the Wolf"—one of eleven children raised with scant "book l'arnin'"—killed 20 German soldiers and captured 132, including a battalion commander and 35 guns, virtually single-handedly.

Roosevelt's account of the action is my favorite. It first appeared in Rank and File, *published by Scribner's in 1928, and was later collected in the anthology edited by Ernest Hemingway,* Men at War, *published by Crown.*

A SCANT HUNDRED AND FIFTY YEARS AGO THE UNITED STATES WAS BUT A FRINGE OF settlements that clung to the skirts of the Atlantic. A few miles inland from the seaboard the "backwoods" stretched unbroken from north to south. The restless pioneer spirit that built our country was astir, and hardy men and brave women were pushing westward, ever westward. The rush was starting over trackless mountain and tangled forest, turbulent river and wide, shimmering plain, which never faltered until the covered wagons jolted over a crest and the broad Pacific stretched horizon-far.

To the north the stream westward flowed along the lake-shore by the Wilderness Trail. By the wagons walked the men. When there was a halt for the night children tumbled out over the tail-board like mud-turtles from a log in a pond. The families carried their scant household goods. At Oyster Bay, we have in our library a Windsor rocking-chair that went with my wife's great-great-grandparents over this trail from Vermont to the settlement of Ohio.

To the south the pioneers struck the Appalachian Mountains as the first great barrier to their advance. These ranges stretch like a bulwark down the mid-eastern part of our country. Though not high, they are rugged and very beautiful. In spring they are cloaked in green, save where some gray shoulder of rock has thrust through. In autumn they are painted by the purple pomp of changing foliage gorgeous as a columbine.

Into these mountains tramped the wilderness hunters. They were lean, silent men, clad in coonskin caps and homespun. Around their necks were slung powder-horns. They carried the heavy, smooth-bore flint-lock guns. Such men were Daniel Boone and Simon Kenton.

These lone hunters carried more than their rifles over their shoulders; they carried the destiny of a nation. They were stout fighting men. Under Braddock they were all that stood between the British regulars and massacre. During the Revolutionary War they fought notably for the colonies and independence. Morgan's rifles were composed of them. Under General Clarke they beat the Indians time and again, and won Kentucky and Ohio for the colonists.

In the closing years of the eighteenth century one of these wilderness hunters worked his way over the Cumberland Mountains. He wandered south along the western slope until he came to the lovely little valley now known as the "Three Forks of the Wolf." The country looked so friendly and fertile that he settled there, cleared his fields, and travelled no more. His name was Conrad Pile.

The land attracted other settlers, and soon a little community was nestling between the rugged slopes of the mountains. It was christened Pall Mall, though no one knows why. After many years of uncertainty it was assigned to the State of Tennessee.

Like most of the other settlements in these hills the people were isolated, and had but little contact with the men and women of the lowlands. They were poor, for the valley yielded a scanty living. Most of them left but rarely the mountains that surrounded their log and board cabins. Schools were almost unknown. Children worked, not as training for life, but because it was necessary to work to live. The fiery spirit still flamed, and it was from the men of the Tennessee and Kentucky Mountains that "Old Hickory" drew the raw levees that beat the pick of the veteran British regulars at New Orleans.

Perhaps the strongest force in shaping these men and women was their religion. Their faith was of the deep-rooted, zealous type that carried the Roundheads to victory under Cromwell. Their ministers were circuit-riders, who travelled weary miles to carry the gospel to their widely scattered flocks. It was the religion of the Bible, hard and narrow at times but living, and was brought into the occurrences of every-day life, not kept as a thing apart. It was not merely for Sunday consumption in a padded pew. The citizens were the spiritual as well as probably the physical descendants of the Covenanters. For their general, when forming them for battle, to ride down their lines with a sword in one hand and a Bible in the other, would not have struck them as strange but as natural.

Next to their religion they were perhaps most influenced by the wilds. Hunting or trapping in the wooded hills was the recreation of the men. The youth of the mountains were learned in woodcraft. They could shoot rapidly and accurately and were toughened by life in the open.

During the Civil War these mountains formed an isolated island of loyalty to the Union in a sea of secession. Though the majority of the people were Federals some were Confederate sympathizers, and bitter bloody feuds tore the little hill settlements.

At the dawn of the twentieth century more than a hundred years had passed since old Conrad Pile halted from his wandering in the valley of the Three Forks of the Wolf, but Pall Mall was not greatly changed. The men wore homespun, the women calico. The houses were but little improved. Indeed, the log cabin Conrad built was still in use. The people spoke a language which was not, as many believe, a corruption of English, but an old form. They used "hit" for "it," which is the old neuter form of he or him. They spoke of "you'uns," which is an old colloquial plural of you. Over their sewing the girls sang early English ballads, long forgotten by the rest of the world. Their recreations were husking-bees and log-rolling parties. This little valley in the mountains seemed a changeless back-eddy in the march of progress. The Reverend Rosier Pile, the great-great-grandson of Conrad, was preacher. Full 80 per cent of the people were descendants of the first half-dozen settlers.

Among these were William York and his wife. They had eleven children, one of whom was a strapping, red-headed young mountaineer named Alvin. The family lived in a little two-room board cabin. William York was a blacksmith by profession, but loved hunting and spent much of his time wandering over the hills.

Alvin was much like the boys of his acquaintance. His education was scant. The little mountain school he attended was open only for three months during the summer. For the rest of the year it was closed, because the children had to work, or were winter-bound in their scattered homes on the hillsides. All young York got of "book-larnin'" was a foundation in the "three Rs." There was other training, however, that stood him in good stead. When he was not working on the farm or at the school, he was hunting. At an early age he had been given a rifle and it was his most valued possession.

The men of Pall Mall had cleared a rough rifle-range for themselves and had competitions on Saturdays. They used the old muzzle-loading, ball-powder-and-patch rifles handed down by their forefathers. Such rifles are very accurate for perhaps seventy-five yards. Turkeys and beeves were the usual prizes. In a turkey contest they did not use a target, but the turkey itself. In one competition the turkey was tethered by its foot to a stake some hundred and forty yards from the competitors. In another it was tied behind a log forty yards distant in such fashion that only its head showed. In both instances the turkey was given freedom of action, so that the target was constantly on the move. A turkey's head is not large, and a man who can hit it when it is bobbing about is a real marksman.

John Sowders, young York's principal rival at these matches, used to "limber up" by sticking carpet-tacks in a board and driving them home with his bullets at a range of twenty-five yards.

When Alvin York and two of his brothers were well grown, their father died. The mother, however, with their aid and the small farm, managed to keep the family together. There was no money for trimmings, but everyone had enough to eat. Her tall, red-headed son for a time had a mild "fling"—drank his corn whiskey and went on parties with his contemporaries among the boys. In the mid-twenties his stern religion gripped him and he stopped drinking. He took a deeper interest in church affairs and became an elder.

Early in the spring of 1917, word came to the little mountain community that the United States had declared war on Germany. They were such a back-eddy of the country that they had heard very little of the cumulative causes. Indeed, I have been told that the men who came to enlist in the army from some of the more isolated spots in these mountains believed that we were again at war with England, and were deeply suspicious when told we were her ally. At the Three Forks of the Wolf the War was not popular. Memories of the Civil War, with its bitter interfamily feuds, were still alive in the community. Few of the young fellows volunteered. At last the draft came.

Alvin York was a husky six-footer nearly thirty years old. He did not believe in war. He felt that the New Testament definitely stood against the killing of man by man. "For all they that take the sword shall perish with the sword." He was engaged to be married and was the principal support of his mother. Pastor Pile, of whose church he was a member, firmly believed that the tenets of his church forbade war. All York had to do was to state his case. He had clear grounds on which to claim exemption, but he was made of sterner stuff. Though he believed it wrong to kill, he believed it necessary to serve his country. He refused to claim exemption or let any one make such application in his behalf.

Down to Jamestown, the county-seat, he rode on one of his two mules. He registered, was examined and passed. Back at Pall Mall he told his womenfolk the news. They grieved bitterly, but they knew that a man must seek his happiness by following what he believes to be right.

His blue card reached him in November. In a few hours he said good-by and drove in a buggy to Jamestown. He was sent to Camp Gordon near Atlanta, Ga. It was the first time he had ever been out of sight of his beloved mountains. In his diary he wrote: "I was the homesickest boy you ever seen."

After nearly three months' training he was assigned in February, 1918, to Company G, 328th Infantry, 82nd Division. This division was really a cross-section of the country. Its men were drawn from every State of the Union. They were of every racial stock that goes to make up our nation, from the descendants of colonial English to the children of lately arrived Italian immigrants. Every trade and occupation was represented among its personnel.

Now began his battle with himself as to what course it was right for him to follow. His mother had weakened at the thought that he might be killed, and together with Pastor Pile had written to the officers stating that York's religion forbade war. York himself was deeply troubled, for Pastor Pile in letters pleaded with him not to jeopardize his eternal salvation by killing man.

He turned, in his distress, to his immediate superiors, Major G. E. Buxton and Captain E. C. B. Danforth, Jr. Fortunately both were men of high principle and broad vision. They realized at once that here was no yellow-streaked malingerer but a sincere man seeking guidance.

Late one evening the three men met in the little tar-paper shack that served Buxton for quarters. There, in the hard light of the single unshaded electric bulb that dangled from the ceiling, the officers reasoned with the lanky, red-headed private. The causes that led to the War were explained in detail. Then they turned to the Bible, and by text and teaching showed that while peace was desirable it must not be a peace at any price. Though we are in the world to strive for righteousness, justice, and peace, if one of these has to be sacrificed in order to obtain the other two, it must be peace.

They read him the thirty-third chapter of Ezekiel, and told him that he and all Americans were as "the watchman" in the Bible. On them was laid the charge of guarding humanity. To fail in the task would be traitorous.

York was absolutely honest. He strove for light. Gradually he became convinced, as had his spiritual ancestors the Covenanters, that right and war were bedfellows in this instance. Once his mind was clear, there was no faltering or hesitation. If it was right to fight at all, then it was right to fight with all your might. He flung himself into the drill and training with every ounce of energy he possessed. He soon showed that his days of shooting at the Three Forks of the Wolf were not ill spent. The Enfield rifle with which the division was equipped was the best firearm he had ever used. In rapid firing at moving targets he easily outdistanced the other men.

Some months passed. The American troops had reached Europe. Instead of a division or two scattered through the line that stretched like a dike across the north of France, the Americans now had over two million men. The United States had an army in the field and was prepared to carry her share of the battle. The tide had turned, and the Allies were crushing the gray lines back. The Germans had lost the initiative.

Our army was attacking as a unit. The battle of the Argonne was raging. Through the shell-torn woods and fields, over hills and valleys, the American troops were fighting their way forward. Then came a check. The 1st Division had gone through, but the divisions on its right and left had encountered severe resistance. As a result the Regulars were thrust out in the enemies' lines, and were swept with fire from three sides. It was imperative that the lines on the right and left be advanced. The 82nd Division was selected for this mission. On October 6th they were assigned a position on the left of the 1st Division, with orders to attack on Chatel Chehery Hills.

All day on October 7th the 328th Infantry lay in shell-holes and ditches on the slopes of Hill 223, and along the road that stretched to its rear. All day long the German shrapnel and high explosive burst along their lines. Behind them and in front were the wooded slopes of the rough Argonne hills. The ground was heavy with rain, the soldiers were mud-caked and sodden with wet.

Beyond Hill 223, the farthest point of their advance, was an open valley about five hundred yards wide. On the other side of this valley rose three hills, the central one steep and rugged, the other two gently sloping. The crest of the ridge formed by these was held by a division of veteran German troops, hard-schooled by years of war.

The position was of great importance, for behind these hills lay the narrow-gauge railroad, which supplied the Germans in the forest where they had checked the advance of the American battle line.

Late in the afternoon of October 8th York's battalion, the 2nd, received its orders. It was to relieve the 1st which had seized the hill, and then to thrust due west into the German flank. The attack was to start at six next morning from Hill 223, and the final objective was the railroad.

Through the black of the night the troops stumbled up the wooded slopes and took their position. Dawn came with gray reluctance; a heavy mist drifted through the tree-tops and choked the valley below. Gradually it lifted and shredded off. Zero hour had come.

The Americans started down through the tangled undergrowth. The sun rose and swallowed the last remnants of mist, giving the Germans a fair view of the attacking troops. Immediately from all sides the hostile fire burst. High explosives shrieked through the trees, filling the air with scraps of iron and flying splinters. Shrapnel exploded in puffs of smoke and rained down its bullets on the advancing men. Through it all machine-guns spattered our advance with a rattling hurricane of lead.

When they had descended the long wooded slope they started across the open country. The flanking fire was so ferocious that the American lines melted like snow in a spring thaw. To advance was impossible. The companies lay frozen to the ground while bullets whipped over them like sleet in a northeaster.

Lieutenant Stewart, a splendid young giant from Florida, commanded a platoon in York's company. He jumped to his feet and called to his men to follow. So great was their confidence in him that they struggled up and started ahead, though it looked certain death. He had not gone ten yards before a bullet struck him shattering his right thigh, and he crashed to the ground. Though his leg was shattered his manhood was not. By a supreme effort he shoved himself erect on the one leg left, and started to hop forward. A couple of yards farther he pitched on his face. A bullet had struck him in the head and his gallant spirit had joined the hero-dead of the nation.

The platoon dropped to the ground again and lay flat. It was clear that no advance could be attempted until the guns that were sweeping the plain with flanking fire were silenced. Captain Danforth decided to send a detachment from York's platoon on this mission.

Raising his head from the ground he turned to the platoon. Sergeant Harry Parsons, an ex-vaudeville actor from New York, was commanding it. Like a well-trained soldier he was watching his company commander for orders.

The roar of the artillery drowned all sound of his voice, so Danforth pointed to the hill on the left and motioned in its direction. Parsons understood at once. Quietly but quickly he chose three squads of his platoon. The German fire had taken its toll, a third of the men were wounded or dead. Of the twenty-four who had composed these squads when they left the hill-crest half an hour ago, only sixteen remained.

The make-up of this detachment was in itself a mute comment on our country and our army. Of the sixteen soldiers, eight had English names; the other eight were men whose parents had come from Ireland, Italy, Poland, Germany, and Sweden. One of the members of this patrol was Alvin York of Tennessee, lately promoted corporal.

Sergeant Early was placed in command. He was told to outflank in any fashion possible the machine-guns that were causing the damage, and beat down their fire or destroy them.

On their bellies the men wormed their way to the woods, hitching themselves along below the bullets that swept scythelike across the field.

When they reached the cover of the trees they rose and, crouching, threaded their way to the left. Stealing from stump to stump, taking cover wherever possible, they reached the far end of the valley without casualties. Here fortune favored them, for they found a thicket that concealed them until they were nearly half-way across.

Suddenly bullets began to rattle around them, passing with the crack of a whip. They were under fire from the right flank. They must either retreat and abandon their mission or quickly pass on. Sergeant Early's decision was made without hesitation. They moved forward. In a few seconds they were clambering up the steep hillside beyond the valley. The boldness of this move protected them. The Germans were watching the hills opposite and the valley, but not the slopes on which their own guns rested. For a moment the Americans were sheltered. The soul-satisfying relief that comes to a soldier when he finds himself defiladed from fire is like waking after a severe illness to find the pain gone.

Stumbling through the brush and dead leaves they came to a wood path that led in rear of the crest. Here they halted for a moment to get their bearings and decide on the next move. To their left stretched unbroken woodlands from which no sound of firing came. To their right crackled the machine-guns they were to silence. They had succeeded in reaching a position in rear of the Germans.

While they were standing breathless, listening for any sound that might give a further clew, they caught faintly the guttural sound of Germans talking in the valley on the reverse slope of the hill. Just at this moment a twig snapped, and right ahead of them they saw two German stretcher-bearers. There was no time to be lost, for these men might give the alarm to the machine-guns, and the Americans opened fire at once. Both Germans escaped into the woods, though one was wounded. The time for discussion had passed. It was now or never. Quick as a flash Early called: "As skirmishers, forward!"

Down the bank of a small stream they plunged, and up the other side. Here the woods were thinner. Suddenly they saw just above them about fifty Germans gathered near a small board hut. The surprise of the Americans was nothing to that of the Germans, who knew themselves to be well in rear of their own lines. They had been getting their orders for a counterattack when out of the bush had burst the Americans, ragged, unshaven, with fierce eyes and gleaming bayonets.

A couple of Boches tried to reach for their rifles, but the crack of the Enfields halted them. Up went their hands, and "Kamerad!" echoed through the grove.

It was the battalion headquarters of the machine-guns. Among the group were a major and two junior officers. The Americans formed a crescent and moved toward their prisoners, who were on high ground just above them. On the left flank was Alvin York. As he approached the group the bushes became sparser. Right above him, not forty yards away, he saw German machine-guns. The Boche gunners had got the alarm. They were trying frantically to turn their guns to the rear. A few of them picked up rifles and fired at York, who stood in plain sight. The bullets burnt his face.

A command in German was shouted. At once the prisoners dropped flat on their faces. York and six of his comrades, who were now close to the Germans, did the same. Sergeant Early, with the other Americans, did not understand what was happening and remained standing. A burst of fire swept the grove.

Six of our patrol fell dead and three were wounded, including the sergeant. The surviving Americans were now among their prisoners. Probably on this account the hail of bullets was held two or three feet above the ground. There were no more casualties.

York was a comparatively green soldier. He was fighting not for the love of fighting, but for a firm conviction of the righteousness and justice of our cause. The shadows of the men who fought at Naseby and Marston Moor stood at his elbow. The spirit that inspired Cromwell and Ireton, Hampden and Vane, stirred in him. He saw "enfranchised insult" in the persons of the German soldiers, and, like the Covenanters, with a cold fury he "smote them hip and thigh."

He was in the open. Calling to his comrades, who were cloaked by the bushes and could neither see nor be seen, to stay where they were and guard the prisoners, he prepared to take the offensive. Crawling to the left through some weeds, he reached a point from which he got a clear view of the German emplacements. Just as he got there the German fire ceased. Several rose and started down the slope in the direction of the Americans to investigate. Quick as a flash York's rifle spoke. One pitched forward on his face and the rest scuttled back. Again a hail of bullets swept through the grove.

In a few minutes it slackened. York sat up and took the position used by hunters since rifles were first invented. The range to the gun-pits was that at which he had so often shot in those seemingly distant days, in his far-off home in the Tennessee mountains. This time, however, he was not shooting for sport but "battling for the Lord." He saw several German heads peering cautiously over the emplacements. He swung his rifle toward one and fired; the helmet flew up and the head disappeared. Four times more he fired before the Germans realized what was happening and ducked back.

Bullets spattered around him, splintering the tree at his elbow and covering him with slivers of wood and dust. Heedless of the danger, he watched the ridge until another head appeared. Again his rifle cracked and again the head disappeared. Hitting German heads at forty yards was easy for a man who had hit turkey heads at the same range, and whose nerves were of iron because of his belief in his cause.

The battle rested entirely on his shoulders, for the rest of the Americans were so screened by the brush that they were only able to fire a few scattered shots.

The Germans could not aim at this lone rifleman, for whenever a head appeared it was met with a bullet from the mountaineer. York was not fighting from a passion for slaughter. He would kill any one without compunction who stood in the way of victory; but it was not killing but victory for which he strove. He began calling: "Come down, you-all, and give up."

The battle went on.

At times the Boche riflemen would creep out of their emplacements, take cover behind some tree, and try to get the American. The hunter from the Cumberland Mountains was trained to note the slightest movement. The man who could see a squirrel in the tree-top could not fail to observe a German when he moved. Every time he found them and fired before they found him. That ended the story.

The Germans by this time knew that the brunt of the battle was being borne by one American. They realized they were not quick enough to kill him by frontal attack, so they sent an officer and seven men around his left flank to rush him. These crawled carefully through the brush until they were within twenty yards of him. Then with a yell they sprang up and came at him on a dead run, their fixed bayonets flashing in the sun.

The clip of cartridges in York's rifle was nearly exhausted and he had no time to reload. Dropping his Enfield he seized his automatic pistol. As they came lunging forward through the undergrowth he fired. One after another the Germans pitched forward and lay where they fell, huddled gray heaps in the tangled woods. Not only had York killed them all, but each time he had shot at the man in rear in order that the others might not halt and fire a volley on seeing their comrade fall. The machine-gun fire had slackened during the charge. Again it burst forth and again York stilled it with his rifle.

The grim, red-headed mountaineer was invincible. Almost unaided he had already killed some twenty of his opponents. The German major's nerve was shaken. He could speak English. Slowly he wriggled on his stomach to where the American sat and offered to tell the machine-gunners to surrender. "Do it and I'll treat ye white," said York.

At this moment a lone German crawled close, jumped to his feet, and hurled a grenade. It went wide, but when the Enfield spoke its bullet did not. The German pitched forward on his face, groaning. The Boche major then rose to his knees and blew his whistle shrilly. All firing ceased. He called an order to his men. Instantly they began scrambling to their feet, throwing down belts and side-arms.

The American was alert for treachery. When they were half-way down the hill, with their hands held high over their heads, he halted them. With the eyes of a backwoodsman he scanned each for weapons. There were none. The surrender was genuine.

Corporal York stood up and called to his comrades. They answered him from where they had been guarding their first prisoners. The thick grove had prevented them from taking an active part in the fighting, but they had protected York from attacks by the prisoners who would otherwise have taken him from the rear.

Sergeant Early, the leader of the patrol, was lying in the brush desperately wounded in the abdomen. York called: "Early, are you alive?"

"I am all through," groaned the sergeant. "You take command. You'll need a compass. Turn me over. You'll find mine in my pocket. Get our men back as soon as you can, and leave me here."

York had well over a hundred prisoners, as sixty had come from the machine-gun emplacements. Some of the Americans doubted the possibility of getting them back to the lines. York paid no attention to this. He formed the Germans in column of twos, placing our wounded at the rear, with prisoners to carry Sergeant Early, who could not walk. Along the flanks he stationed his surviving comrades, with instructions to keep the column closed up and to watch for treachery. He himself led, with the German major in front of him and a German officer on each side.

Before they started York had had the major explain to the men that at any sign of hostility he would shoot to kill, and the major would be the first to die. They had seen enough of the deadly prowess of the mountaineer. Not one made the attempt. He marched his column around the hill to a point from which he could probably have taken them back safely, but his mission was to clear the hill of machine-guns. He knew that some still remained on the front slope.

Turning the column to the left, he advanced on the Boche garrisons. As he approached he had the German major call to each in turn to surrender. When they did he disarmed them and added them to his train of prisoners. In only one instance did a man attempt to resist. He went to join the long roll of German dead.

York's troubles were not over. Though he had cleaned up and destroyed the machine-guns, he still had to get back to our lines with the men he had captured. To do this he had to be very careful, for so large a body of Germans marching toward our lines might well be taken for a counter-attack and mowed down with rifle-fire. Bringing all his woodcraft into play he led his long column of gray-clad prisoners over the ridge and down through the brush, until he reached the foot of the slope up which his patrol had climbed earlier in the day.

Suddenly from the brush on the other side the command "Halt!" rang out. York jumped to the front to show his uniform, and called out that he was bringing in prisoners. He was just in time to prevent casualties. The lines of our infantry opened to let the party through. As the doughboys from left and right looked between the tree-trunks they saw gray form after gray form pass. A yell of approval rang out. Some one shouted: "Are you bringing in the whole German Army?" The lines closed behind the column. Corporal York had fulfilled his mission.

In a few minutes he reported at battalion headquarters. The prisoners were counted. There were one hundred and thirty-two, including three officers, one a major. With less than a year's military training a red-headed mountaineer, practically single-handed, had fought a veteran battalion of German troops, taken thirty-five guns, killed twenty men, captured one hundred and thirty-two and the battalion commander.

For three weeks more the Division hammered its way forward. The stubborn German defense was beaten back, the Allies drove on to Sedan. Even among the fighting troops rumors of peace became more persistent. One morning word came to the front lines where the tired men stood, ankle-deep in mud—an armistice had been signed.

York had become a sergeant. He was with his company. His feat, as he saw it, was merely a part of the day's work. The officers and men of the 82nd Division, however, were very proud of him. They had reported the facts to General Headquarters. The story had spread like wild-fire, and Alvin York was famous.

During his simple country life York had never met any of the great of the world. His nearest approach to a general had been when he stood stiffly at attention while the general inspected the ranks. Now he found himself honored of all, because physical courage, especially when backed by moral worth, commands universal admiration. General Headquarters ordered him from place to place in France. A brigade review was held in his honor. He was decorated not only by the United States but also by the Allies. At Paris Poincaré, the president of the French Republic, pinned the highest decorations to his coat.

In May, 1919, he came back with his regiment to our country. Here enthusiasm ran even higher. The streets of New York were jammed with people who cheered themselves hoarse. He went to see the Stock Exchange, where no visitors are allowed on the floor. Not only was he permitted to visit the floor but business was suspended and the stockbrokers carried him around on their shoulders.

In Washington, when he went to the gallery of the House of Representatives, the congressmen stopped debate and cheered him to the echo. Great banquets were given for him, which were attended by the highest ranking civil, military, and naval officials.

In his olive-drab uniform, with his medals and shock of red hair, he was a marked man. When he walked the streets enthusiastic crowds gathered. There were men and women to greet him at the railroad-stations as he travelled back to Tennessee to be mustered out.

He was offered a contract for $75,000 to appear in a moving-picture play on the War. He was approached by vaudeville firms, who suggested tours on which they agreed to give him a salary of $1,000 a week. Newspapers were willing to pay fabulous sums for articles by him.

He was taken up on a mountain and shown the kingdoms of the world. Ninety-nine men out of a hundred would have cracked under the adulation. Ninety-nine men out of a hundred who can bear the famine worthily will lose their heads at the feast. York did not. Though his twelve months in the army had greatly broadened him, his character was still as strong and unshaken as the rock of his own hills. He refused the offers of money or position, saying rightly that these were made him only because of his feat in the Argonne. To sell his war record would be putting a price on patriotism.

As soon as he could he made his way back to his home in the mountains, his family, and his friends. There he was met by his mother in her calico bonnet, his sisters and brothers, and Grace Williams, the mountain girl to whom he was betrothed.

In a few days there was an open-air wedding at Pall Mall. It was held on the hillside. A gray ledge of rock served as altar. The new leaves of spring danced in the sunlight, casting flickering shadows on the white starched "Sunday-go-to-meeting" dresses and blue serge "store clothes" of the mountain folk, who had driven in from the surrounding country. The governor of the State officiated, assisted by Pastor Pile. The bride and groom were Grace Williams and Sergeant Alvin York, late of the United States Army.

Though York refused to sell his service record, he knew his Bible far too well to have forgotten the parable of the talents. That which it would be wrong to use for his own benefit, it would be wrong not to use for the benefit of others. His experience in the world had made him bitterly conscious of his scanty education. He realized that "wisdom excelleth folly as far as light excelleth darkness." He decided to bend his efforts toward establishing proper schools for the children of the hills.

The people of Tennessee had been collecting an Alvin York Fund. He asked them to turn it into a foundation for building schools in the mountains. All he would accept for himself was a small farm.

CHAPTER THREE

Poker and Missiles: A Pilot's Life in Vietnam
By Craig K. Collins

"My uncle was a top-gun pilot before there were top-gun pilots. He was Tom Cruise before there was a Tom Cruise. In addition to his motorcycle, he drove a red MG convertible with silver-spoked wheels. I recall him on leave, roaring up to our house in the MG with his dark, wavy hair and aviator sunglasses. The entire neighborhood would step onto their porches and walk to their lawns to catch a glimpse. He was Hollywood handsome and a magnet for beautiful women. At five feet nine, he was the perfect size for a plane jockey. His vision was 20-15. He had the strength of a wrestler, the reflexes of an athlete, and the timing of a musician. His ego was as large as the planes he flew. He once told me, years hence, with matter-of-fact sincerity that he was the best fighter pilot in the world. I reflexively laughed. His eyes seethed. I then thought about it. Maybe there was some Russian MiG pilot who was better. Maybe another hotshot American. Maybe not. Regardless, there was a time when my uncle could make an authentic claim to be king of the sky."

That's how author Craig K. Collins introduced his uncle, Don Harten, in the book Midair, *published by Lyons Press in 2016. As a pilot in Vietnam, with incredible skills ranging from the cockpits of B-52 bombers to F-105 and F-111 fighters, Harten was the ultimate sky warrior. His adventures, with narrow escapes and lucky breaks, are captured with incredible realism in Collins's book, the source of this excerpt.*

—LAMAR UNDERWOOD

POKER WAS LIFE FOR THE AMERICAN PILOTS OF VIETNAM. BETWEEN MOMENTS OF white-knuckle, adrenaline-filled, Russian-roulette terror that was the average combat mission, there lay vast expanses of boredom—boredom that was partially assuaged by poker.

The men played poker in the Officers' Club. They played poker on base. They played poker off base. They played poker in the backrooms of bars and clubs in Bangkok.

Poker was a way to maintain camaraderie. To talk to each other candidly—man to man, emotionally even—with the macho buffer of a card table between them. To sustain a certain mental acuity. To compete. To win. To dominate.

Not lost on any of the men was how the game put the vagaries of chance on full display. Just as each of their lives was now fully subjected to the great spinning wheels of Fortune and Fate, so was each hand of poker. An ace of spades here. An inside straight there. All so random. All so essential to the game.

And, of course, poker was something in which Don reveled.

Like his uncle John Boyatt, it was a game at which he excelled.

Don had played cards—mostly family favorites like pinochle and bridge—from a young age and had an exceptional mind for calculating probabilities and tracking the remaining cards in each deck.

At the age of sixteen, Don was scheduled to spend the weekend at a church camp near Pocatello. His uncle instead took him on a road trip to a country club in Sandpoint in the state's far northern panhandle. It was ostensibly a golf outing but instead turned into a marathon game of poker with a group of well-to-do club members. Don and his uncle drove back to Pocatello with more money than Don could've earned in an entire summer of working at his father's business.

Don would later recall, "On that trip to Sandpoint, Uncle John told me, 'It's great that you can count cards and that you have a wonderful technical grasp of poker. But here's ten thousand dollars' worth of advice that I learned the hard way in World War II: if you got 'em, bet 'em. If you don't got 'em, fold. It's really that simple. Don't try to overthink.'"

It was advice Don would take to heart and later live by.

"I maybe bluffed three times in all the poker games I ever played in Vietnam. And when I returned stateside, I had enough from all my winnings—of which I saved every penny—to buy a brand new Corvette and a penthouse apartment."

⌐■━━■⌐

Whenever Billy Sparks was hungover, which was often, his fellow pilots would yell out, "Hey, Sparky, let me see that aerial map of Hanoi." Sparks would then oblige. He had the ability to pull down on one of his lower eyelids, flex a combination of facial muscles, and force his eyeball to bulge gruesomely from its socket. Though Billy's bulging, bloodshot eye the morning after a long night at Takhli's Stag Bar was unnerving, pilots viewed it as something of a good-luck talisman. And its resemblance to the air force's bombing maps of Hanoi was so uncanny as to be satirically hilarious.

In 1967, President Lyndon Johnson crowed, "They can't even bomb an outhouse without my approval."

Which, sadly, was true.

And it was clearly no way to run a war.

But that was the reality the pilots of Takhli found themselves in. And as good soldiers, they flew the missions they were told to fly, even though the strategy was so clearly unsound.

The F-105 pilots were all familiar with the aerial map of Hanoi. They'd all spent hours studying every statute mile, river, tributary, road, bridge, building, and landmark. Their lives depended on it. The map featured a solid red circle, five miles in diameter, encompassing the city center. No target within this circle could be engaged without direct approval from the Joint Chiefs of Staff. And of the approved targets, most likely were handed down from President Johnson himself. The pilots were essentially left to peck at their enemy, all at the whim of politicians and bureaucrats over eight thousand miles away.

Radiating from the solid red blotch encircling downtown Hanoi were thin, red, jagged lines representing railways, roads, and supply lines, essential for keeping the North Vietnamese war machine humming. These extended to the edge of another circle, extending ten miles from Hanoi's city center.

Viewed from a few feet back, the map, with its blood-red pupil and surrounding web of throbbing red veins, was indeed an eerie likeness of Sparky's eye.

Further complicating the map of Hanoi and the pilots' missions was the fact that the North Vietnamese had so readily adapted to the US playbook and highly predictable aerial intrusions. It would be akin to a football team running the exact same play over and over again and expecting success.

By 1967, downtown Hanoi bristled with the most sophisticated, jam-packed aerial defense system on the planet, courtesy of the Soviet Union. "Going downtown," for an F-105 pilot, meant flying directly into the blood-red circle of Sparky's eye. More than seventeen thousand Soviet missile men had been dispatched to Hanoi to operate more than 7,600 SA-2 electronically guided surface-to-air missiles. One particularly skilled Soviet SAM operator was Lt. Vadim Petrovich Shcherbakov, who by himself downed twelve American fighter jets over Hanoi. By the end of the war, some 205 US aircraft had succumbed to Soviet-made and mostly Soviet-launched guided missiles.

The missiles were typically fired in a series of three at an incoming jet. The amount of physical and mental energy required of each targeted pilot to avoid each missile was nearly overwhelming. If the pilot were able to jink away from the first missile, he then had split seconds to locate and jink away from the second. And if the second missile could somehow be avoided, the third missile almost always proved to be the deadliest. The slightest mistake, inattention, or fatigue would result in a fireball of death.

If a SAM operator had successfully locked onto your plane, it was fairly similar to three pulls of the trigger in a game of Russian roulette. Don's first encounter with a SAM came on February 22, 1968, during his sixth mission in an F-105 and on his first "downtown" run. He was tense in flight, and the sensation of fear—a sensation that clouded judgment and slowed reaction time—began to creep over him. He rarely flew while scared, but this time was different. He was flying into the maw of Sparky's eye, and it was inevitable that he'd encounter a SAM launch.

Don's squadron, dubbed Bison for this mission, was tasked with bombing a MiG airfield, called Hòa Lạc, on Hanoi's western outskirts. Flying in a four-plane finger formation, the Bison pilots streaked through clear skies at eighteen thousand feet as they approached Hanoi, which was shrouded beneath a thick undercast at ten thousand feet. This added to the pilots' unease. Should any SAM be fired at them, they would have only an eight-thousand-foot buffer in which they could visually locate the missile—which by then would be flying at nearly Mach 3—and attempt an evasive maneuver.

As the squadron prepared to dive toward their target, predictably, Don's radio crackled: "Valid launch at one o'clock."

It crackled again: "Valid at ten o'clock."

And again: "Valid at twelve o'clock."

Don hesitated. His mind froze. He could think only of incoming missiles. He checked his E-scope, but for whatever reason, it wasn't registering the SAMs.

Don's mind reflexively began to count.

"Seventeen seconds to die."

"Twelve seconds to die."

Don was unsure of what to do. Drop in elevation? Jink right? Jink left? Dive?

He was the number four plane in the formation, so he just stayed close to his wingman, Lt. Col. Larry Pickett, and continued to count.

"Ten seconds to die."

"Five."

"Three."

There is no sound other than radio chatter in the cockpit of a fighter jet. It's not like the movies with lush flourishes of audience-gratifying special effects: supersonic whooshes, thunderous explosions, and rat-a-tat machine-gun fire. If death were to come, it would come in a silent burst. The pilot would almost never live to hear it.

Don's cockpit lit up as though someone had flashed a camera bulb in his face. The SA-2 sliced between his wingman and him, only a few feet from taking down either of the planes, traveling at three-and-a-half times the speed of sound—over 2,600 miles per hour. The flame from its solid-fuel rocket motor lit the daytime sky. A trailing squadron reported that the missile had exploded about one thousand feet above the pair of jets, its timing off by only a split second.

Anticipating the second oncoming missile, Lt. Jim Butler swooped beneath the squadron, deploying a rudimentary radar-jamming device and using his plane as a decoy. The maneuver worked. The missile curved slightly before detonating to the left of squadron leader Capt. Erik Lunde, peppering the side of his plane with shrapnel and debris. None of the pilots had an answer for the third missile other than to hope and pray.

Don spotted it as soon as it burst from the undercast, slicing brilliant yellow against the gray backdrop, streaking laser-like from the clouds below, flying directly toward his jet.

Don braced for impact. There was another camera-bulb flash. And then it was over. Film from an automated camera mounted near the nose of Don's plane showed that the missile had skimmed just a few feet beneath his fuselage before detonating some yards past his tail. Don was well within the missile's "kill zone" as it exploded, leaving mission analysts wondering how he and his aircraft had escaped unscathed.

Don's hands shook uncontrollably as he followed his wingman into an attack dive. The Bison squadron flew into bursts of antiaircraft fire above Hòa Lạc; Don strained to push his fear aside and to focus only on acquiring his target and dropping his bombs. The squadron swooped above the airfield and dropped its bombs, leaving the tarmac and MiG hangars devastated beneath the fearsome rumble of ordnance.

Don pulled up and shot skyward. Though his hands still trembled from his SAM encounter, he was nearly overwhelmed with relief. As the squadron reassembled for the flight south, Don's radio again crackled.

It was Capt. Lunde: "Bison One. Seems Three hasn't come up with us. I've got him still flying north. Four, can you go get him? I think those SAMs messed with his head."

"Uh, Roger," replied Don, who banked hard, turned on his plane's afterburners, and raced north in search of Lt. Col. Pickett, a highly experienced combat pilot on his second F-105 tour.

Humans, like nearly all mammals, have evolved sophisticated mental and physiological responses to life-threatening danger. In simple terms, this is known as the fight, flight, or freeze response. The process, which can be entirely involuntary, begins with a huge surge of adrenaline triggered by a perceived threat. As it flushes through the body, adrenaline works almost instantly to increase heart rate and cardiac output as well as respiratory rate and blood pressure. This is designed to prepare muscles for a maximum burst of energy. Adrenaline also causes pupils to widen and the digestive system to shut down.

A person fleeing imminent danger will be primed by an adrenaline surge to run faster, jump higher, and be more cognitively attuned to the threat at hand than a person whose nervous system hasn't been sparked by fear.

In fight mode, however, an almost converse physiological reaction occurs. The body's vascular system contracts, especially at the extremities (arms, legs, hands, feet). This is nature's way of reducing the potential danger from cuts, bruises, or abrasions suffered from a fight. If blood vessels are constricted and an arm gets slashed, blood loss from the wound will be significantly diminished, and chances of survival will be increased. Of course, there is a tax from this process on other bodily functions. Fine motor skills will be impaired as the body places its bet on large muscle groups more useful for fighting. And subtle cognitive tasks will be difficult as the mind shoves away all sensations, sights, sounds, and thoughts that might distract from winning or surviving the battle.

Fighter pilots are trained to manage their heart and respiratory rates in an effort to maintain optimal use of their mental and physical abilities during flight. However, unlike combatants on the ground, pilots are strapped to their seats and confined to their cockpits. They can't run, jump, box, wrestle. Their large muscle groups can't be used to expend excess energy in order to shunt the effects of an adrenaline rush. And because of the nature of their work, pilots are required to maintain a high level of mental acuity and fine motor skill.

And for all those reasons, Don's mind thrived in an adrenaline-soaked environment. He'd learned to carefully manage and balance the multitude of mental and physiological inputs demanded of a fighter pilot.

Some pilots, no matter how experienced or skilled, however, are susceptible to a flood of adrenaline so intense that they ultimately "freeze." This typically occurs when the body shifts to fight mode, thus constricting vascular systems at the extremities. In the meantime, the heart begins to race, sometimes beating at over 185 beats per minute—as fast as or faster than a sprinter or distance runner at full exertion. But a fighter pilot is sitting still in the cockpit. This contrast between a racing heart and constricted blood vessels can lead to a catastrophic mental and physical breakdown. Muscles become starved for oxygen and stiffen. Cognitive abilities plunge and the ability to think rationally is lost. Respiratory rates soar, and hyperventilation occurs. Control of some bodily functions becomes impossible; bowels and bladders release. Simple tasks become exceedingly difficult. Complex tasks such as flying a plane become nearly impossible.

A SAM missile sizzling just past one's cockpit is certainly an event that can trigger such an involuntary adrenaline surge. Which is exactly the condition Lt. Col. Pickett found himself in.

⌒∿⌒

Don caught up with Pickett's jet as it cruised at three thousand feet, now well north of Hanoi. He was nervous about MiGs, more SAM missiles, and a flight path that would soon take them dangerously close to Chinese air space. However, he put all those considerations out of his mind and focused on getting Pickett's attention.

"Uh, Bison Three, this is Bison Four," Don radioed to the stricken pilot. "Do you read, Bison Three?

"Uh, Three, do you read?

"Three?"

It was clear that radio contact wasn't going to be sufficient to get Pickett's attention. So Don attempted a maneuver he'd read about but had never had been required to use. He had his doubts it would even work.

Don swung wide of Pickett's plane and began swerving back and forth in front of him like a highway patrolman running a traffic break on a freeway. On the third swerve, Don swooped so close he thought the two planes were in danger of colliding. Pickett was finally able to track Don's plane and put his jet into a bank just off Don's right wing. Don carefully banked east toward the ocean. He and Pickett followed the coast south, away from enemy territory, and eventually back to Takhli.

Of the incident, Don would later say, "Pickett was in such bad shape that I'm pretty sure he would've flown until he ran out of gas before finally crashing somewhere in central China."

———

Schlitz, according to its motto, was "The Beer That Made Milwaukee Famous."

But Milwaukee's international renown was of little concern to the pilots at Takhli, even though the US Air Force provided them with all the free Schlitz they could stomach.

Following his close encounters with the SA-2, Don, back on base, rushed through the doors of the Stag Bar like a gunslinger, striding straight to the bar, hopping on a stool, and promptly ordering a can of Schlitz, which was served to him cold, with rivulets of condensation dripping down its aluminum sides due to the perpetually thick tropical air. He tipped the can back, took three big gulps, set the beer on the bar, and belched.

"Schlitz does taste like piss water," he thought.

It was something every pilot agreed on. But it was free. He sat alone, staring at the word "Schlitz," written on the can in a white, florid script against a brick-red background.

Piss water or not, Don prayed into his beer. He thought of all the men he'd known who'd died. Good men, smart men, most better pilots than he was right now.

Slowly and solemnly, he bowed his head and spoke to the Schlitz can: "Dear Lord, I need your help. I need to get better as a pilot. I can't afford fear. Not now. Not ever. If you don't help me, I'm not going to make it. Amen."

With a few more quick swigs, he finished his beer, setting the empty can, which he began to study intently, back on the bar in front of him.

"Jos. Schlitz Brewing Co."

"Contents 12 Fluid Oz."

The bartender walked near, nodded in assumption that Don wanted another, and reached to take away the empty. Don gripped the can with both hands, waving the bartender off with a quick shake of his head.

Don resumed his silent study. He traced with his finger the word "Schlitz," which scrolled up at an angle across the can. He lifted the can a couple of inches off the bar to gauge its weight, swinging it back and forth like a dinner bell and detecting that there was still a half swig sloshing at its bottom. He threw his head back, drained the remnants fully into his mouth, set the can back on the bar, and proceeded to stare in vacant meditation for a full fifteen minutes. This time, the bartender knew not to come near.

Don would later explain, "I stared at that empty can and stuffed all my fear inside it. I vowed never again to be afraid when I flew. And I never was. From that point on in the war, flying was fun. I made it so. I vowed I would never again become unnerved by the death of a fellow pilot. And I never was. I simply pledged that I would save all my grief until after the war was done. Which I did. And, finally, I came to terms with all the killing I'd done and was about to do. I simply and plainly told myself that every single person I'd killed would have gladly killed me in a second, given the chance. It was my job to never give them that chance. It's something I still believe, something I still tell myself to this day."

⌐ ‿ ⌐

"Hey, Weeze," Maj. Jim Metz called out to Don as the two prepared to walk out to the tarmac and go on their separate missions.

Don's call sign was Weeze, as in Wild Weasel. Don liked to think he'd earned the name because he was renowned as a cunning, agile killer. But perhaps it had more to do with the fact that most of the men at Takhli had lost money to him at poker. Either way, it had become a term of endearment, such as it is among men in combat.

Don walked over to Metz.

"What time you got, Weeze?"

Don lifted his left wrist.

"Just about oh-nine-hundred on the dot."

A childish fraternity-like prank had broken out among the men on the base. They'd taken to breaking each other's crystal watch faces. No one was sure how it had started, but Don was one of the few men remaining with an unblemished wristwatch.

Like a viper, Metz snapped his right fist onto Don's watch, his bulky college class ring cracking the crystal face like an eggshell.

"Oh, you bastard," said Don. "You fucked up my watch."

Metz laughed. "Man, I've been planning this for a week. I figured the only time you'd fall for it was right before a mission. Welcome to the club of pilots with fucked-up watches."

"Okay," laughed Don. "This just means I'm going to go extra hard on you in poker tonight."

"Roger that, Weeze," laughed Metz. "But I'm feeling lucky, so you best come with some extra cash."

They slapped each other's backs—a nonverbal "be safe out there"—and strode toward their jets.

⌐ ‿ ⌐

The odds of being dealt a royal flush in five-card draw poker are about 650,000 to 1. Putting that in perspective, if a person played twenty hands of poker every day, that person could expect to be dealt only one royal flush in eighty-nine years. The odds of being dealt a four-card royal flush, discarding the unmatched fifth card and drawing the necessary card to complete the royal, are about 130,000 to 1. It would take a person playing twenty hands of poker per day about eighteen years to behold such a hand. For in poker, a royal flush is near mythical—a unicorn.

Having returned from his mission that day with nothing more severe than a broken watch face, Don sat with his fellow pilots at the Officers' Club to play poker. About an hour into the game, he was dealt a ten, jack, king, and ace of hearts, as well as an ace of spades. It was tempting and probably wise to keep the two aces and try for two pair or three of a kind. But Don had a feeling about this hand. Plus, the cards in the deck were getting low, and he was pretty sure the queen of hearts was still there to be had.

He tossed a dime chip in the pot, not too confident of his hoped-for outcome, and the three other players followed. The dealer spun a card, face down, toward Don. As he lifted it, a glow washed over him. Don fanned the four cards in his hand, tucked the newly acquired queen of hearts between his jack and his king, and paused to admire the symmetrical beauty. Ten, jack, queen, king, and ace of hearts. All in a row. Maybe a once-in-a-lifetime hand. Don's face remained vapid, his hands steady.

But the import of Fate's smile wasn't lost on him in the least.

"That's a quarter to anyone who wants to see whether the one card I drew was any good or not," said Don in a flat tone, kicking off that round of betting by tossing a blue poker chip into the pot at the center of the table.

"Fold," said the pilot to his left.

"I'm in," said the next pilot, tossing his chip into the small pile.

"In, too," chimed the next.

"Alright, Weeze, let's see 'em," said one of the pilots who hadn't folded.

Don chuckled, laid his cards elegantly in the center of the table, let out a gleeful laugh, and rubbed his hands quick together.

"Holy shit," said his poker mates in awe and near-unison.

The table then erupted with laughter as each man leaned close to inspect the regal hand. A crowd gathered, and soon more than a dozen men were slapping Don on the back, admiring his work.

Don reached with both hands across the table and scooped the chips in the pot toward him. After stacking his winnings, he announced: "One dollar, on the nose."

He added, "You'd think with a hand like that it'd be worthy of a king's ransom, but not with you cheap bastards at the table."

As the crowd laughed, Don had become fully aware of Maj. Metz's absence.

He lifted his left wrist to check the time, saw his cracked watch face, and knew.

—⌣—

Earlier, Maj. Metz flew his F-105 into a heavy barrage of flak and caught fire above a heavily populated area of Quảng Bình Province just north of the coastal provincial capital of Đồng Hói.

Metz banked his wounded plane, flames and smoke streaking behind it, toward open water in hopes of an ejection and safe rescue in the South China Sea.

Capt. Dick Rutan, who would later become the first pilot to fly an aircraft, the Voyager, nonstop around the globe without refueling, was aboard a nearby F-100 when he saw Metz and his flaming jet, first mistaking it for an SA-2 missile.

Rutan observed Metz ejecting just short of the beach and parachuting into a tree, where he was swarmed by enemy troops. Aerial recovery teams later came under heavy fire and were forced to abandon the search after they'd seen the North Vietnamese removing Metz's parachute. In 1973, 591 Americans were released from Vietcong prisons. Maj. Metz was not among them. The North Vietnamese denied that Metz had ever been a POW, holding that ruse until his remains were finally shipped home in 1977.

Back at the Officers' Club, Don looked again at his watch and made note that the hour was growing late.

In war, sometimes it's your lucky day. Until it's not.

There was nothing to do now but deal another hand.

CHAPTER FOUR

The Very Real George Washington
By Henry Cabot Lodge

Published in 1895 by the Century Company, the book Hero Tales from American History *teamed Republican senator and historian Henry Cabot Lodge with our 26th president, Theodore Roosevelt. The stories in the book alternate between those told by Lodge and those by Roosevelt. Lodge's portrait of George Washington is typical of the illuminating stories that fill the book.*

—LAMAR UNDERWOOD

THE BRILLIANT HISTORIAN OF THE ENGLISH PEOPLE[*] HAS WRITTEN OF WASHINGTON, that "no nobler figure ever stood in the fore-front of a nation's life." In any book which undertakes to tell, no matter how slightly, the story of some of the heroic deeds of American history, that noble figure must always stand in the fore-front. But to sketch the life of Washington even in the barest outline is to write the history of the events which made the United States independent and gave birth to the American nation. Even to give a list of what he did, to name his battles and recount his acts as president, would be beyond the limit and the scope of this book. Yet it is always possible to recall the man and to consider what he was and what he meant for us and for mankind He is worthy the study and the remembrance of all men, and to Americans he is at once a great glory of their past and an inspiration and an assurance of their future.

To understand Washington at all we must first strip off all the myths which have gathered about him. We must cast aside into the dust-heaps all the wretched inventions of the cherry-tree variety, which were fastened upon him nearly seventy years after his birth. We must look at him as he looked at life and the facts about him, without any illusion or deception, and no man in history can better stand such a scrutiny.

---

[*]John Richard Green

Born of a distinguished family in the days when the American colonies were still ruled by an aristocracy, Washington started with all that good birth and tradition could give. Beyond this, however, he had little. His family was poor, his mother was left early a widow, and he was forced after a very limited education to go out into the world to fight for himself. He had strong within him the adventurous spirit of his race. He became a surveyor, and in the pursuit of this profession plunged into the wilderness, where he soon grew to be an expert hunter and backwoodsman. Even as a boy the gravity of his character and his mental and physical vigor commended him to those about him, and responsibility and military command were put in his hands at an age when most young men are just leaving college. As the times grew threatening on the frontier, he was sent on a perilous mission to the Indians, in which, after passing through many hardships and dangers, he achieved success. When the troubles came with France it was by the soldiers under his command that the first shots were fired in the war which was to determine whether the North American continent should be French or English. In his earliest expedition he was defeated by the enemy. Later he was with Braddock, and it was he who tried to rally the broken English army on the stricken field near Fort Duquesne. On that day of surprise and slaughter he displayed not only cool courage but the reckless daring which was one of his chief characteristics. He so exposed himself that bullets passed through his coat and hat, and the Indians and the French who tried to bring him down thought he bore a charmed life. He afterwards served with distinction all through the French war, and when peace came he went back to the estate which he had inherited from his brother, the most admired man in Virginia.

At that time he married, and during the ensuing years he lived the life of a Virginia planter, successful in his private affairs and serving the public effectively but quietly as a member of the House of Burgesses.

When the troubles with the mother country began to thicken he was slow to take extreme ground, but he never wavered in his belief that all attempts to oppress the colonies should be resisted, and when he once took up his position there was no shadow of turning. He was one of Virginia's delegates to the first Continental Congress, and, although he said but little, he was regarded by all the representatives from the other colonies as the strongest man among them. There was something about him even then which commanded the respect and the confidence of every one who came in contact with him.

It was from New England, far removed from his own State, that the demand came for his appointment as commander-in-chief of the American army. Silently he accepted the duty, and, leaving Philadelphia, took command of the army at Cambridge. There is no need to trace him through the events that followed. From the time when he drew his sword under the famous elm tree, he was the embodiment of the American Revolution, and without him that revolution would have failed almost at the start. How he carried it to victory through defeat and trial and every possible obstacle is known to all men.

When it was all over he found himself facing a new situation. He was the idol of the country and of his soldiers. The army was unpaid, and the veteran troops, with arms in their hands, were eager to have him take control of the disordered country as Cromwell had done in England a little more than a century before. With the army at his back, and supported by the great forces which, in every community, desire order before everything else, and are ready to assent to any arrangement which will bring peace and quiet, nothing would have been easier than for Washington to have made himself the ruler of the new nation. But that was not his conception of duty, and he not only refused to have anything to do with such a movement himself, but he repressed, by his dominant personal influence, all such intentions on the part of the army. On the 23d of December, 1783, he met the Congress at Annapolis, and there resigned his commission. What he then said is one of the two most memorable speeches ever made in the United States, and is also memorable for its meaning and spirit among all speeches ever made by men. He spoke as follows:

"Mr. President:—The great events on which my resignation depended having at length taken place, I have now the honor of offering my sincere congratulations to Congress, and of presenting myself before them, to surrender into their hands the trust committed to me and to claim the indulgence of retiring from the service of my country.

Happy in the confirmation of our independence and sovereignty and pleased with the opportunity afforded the United States of becoming a respectable nation, I resign with satisfaction the appointment I accepted with diffidence; a diffidence in my abilities to accomplish so arduous a task, which, however, was superseded by a confidence in the rectitude of our cause, the support of the supreme power of the Union, and the patronage of Heaven.

The successful termination of the war has verified the most sanguine expectations, and my gratitude for the interposition of Providence and the assistance I have received from my countrymen increases with every review of the momentous contest.

While I repeat my obligations to the Army in general, I should do injustice to my own feelings not to acknowledge, in this place, the peculiar services and distinguished merits of the Gentlemen who have been attached to my person during the war. It was impossible that the choice of confidential officers to compose my family should have been more fortunate. Permit me, sir, to recommend in particular those who have continued in service to the present moment as worthy of the favorable notice and patronage of Congress.

I consider it an indispensable duty to close this last solemn act of my official life by commending the interests of our dearest country to the protection of Almighty God, and those who have the superintendence of them to His holy keeping.

Having now finished the work assigned me, I retire from the great theatre of action, and, bidding an affectionate farewell to this august body, under whose orders I have so long acted, I here offer my commission and take my leave of all the employments of public life."

The great master of English fiction, writing of this scene at Annapolis, says: "Which was the most splendid spectacle ever witnessed—the opening feast of Prince George in London, or the resignation of Washington? Which is the noble character for after ages to admire—yon fribble dancing in lace and spangles, or yonder hero who sheathes his sword after a life of spotless honor, a purity unreproached, a courage indomitable and a consummate victory?"

Washington did not refuse the dictatorship, or, rather, the opportunity to take control of the country, because he feared heavy responsibility, but solely because, as a high-minded and patriotic man, he did not believe in meeting the situation in that way. He was, moreover, entirely devoid of personal ambition, and had no vulgar longing for personal power. After resigning his commission he returned quietly to Mount Vernon, but he did not hold himself aloof from public affairs. On the contrary, he watched their course with the utmost anxiety. He saw the feeble Confederation breaking to pieces, and he soon realized that that form of government was an utter failure. In a time when no American statesman except Hamilton had yet freed himself from the local feelings of the colonial days, Washington was thoroughly national in all his views. Out of the thirteen jarring colonies he meant that a nation should come, and he saw—what no one else saw—the destiny of the country to the westward. He wished a nation founded which should cross the Alleghenies, and, holding the mouths of the Mississippi, take possession of all that vast and then unknown region. For these reasons he stood at the head of the national movement, and to him all men turned who desired a better union and sought to bring order out of chaos. With him Hamilton and Madison consulted in the preliminary stages which were to lead to the formation of a new system. It was his vast personal influence which made that movement a success, and when the convention to form a constitution met at Philadelphia, he presided over its deliberations, and it was his commanding will which, more than anything else, brought a constitution through difficulties and conflicting interests which more than once made any result seem well-nigh hopeless.

When the Constitution formed at Philadelphia had been ratified by the States, all men turned to Washington to stand at the head of the new government. As he had borne the burden of the Revolution, so he now took up the task of bringing the government of the Constitution into existence. For eight years he served as president. He came into office with a paper constitution, the heir of a bankrupt, broken-down confederation. He left the United States, when he went out of office, an effective and vigorous government. When he was inaugurated, we had nothing but the clauses of the Constitution as agreed to by the Convention. When he laid down the presidency, we had an organized government, an established revenue, a funded debt, a high credit, an efficient system of banking, a strong judiciary, and an army. We had a vigorous and well-defined foreign policy; we had recovered the western posts, which, in the hands of the British, had fettered our march to the west; and we had proved our power to maintain order at home, to repress insurrection, to collect the national taxes, and to enforce the laws made by Congress. Thus Washington had shown that rare combination of the leader who could first destroy by revolution, and who, having led his country through a great civil war, was then able to build up a new and lasting fabric upon the ruins of a system which had been overthrown. At the close of his official service he returned again to Mount Vernon, and, after a few years of quiet retirement, died just as the century in which he had played so great a part was closing.

Washington stands among the greatest men of human history, and those in the same rank with him are very few. Whether measured by what he did, or what he was, or by the effect of his work upon the history of mankind, in every aspect he is entitled to the place he holds among the greatest of his race. Few men in all time have such a record of achievement. Still fewer can show at the end of a career so crowded with high deeds and memorable victories a life so free from spot, a character so unselfish and so pure, a fame so void of doubtful points demanding either defense or explanation. Eulogy of such a life is needless, but it is always important to recall and to freshly remember just what manner of man he was. In the first place he was physically a striking figure. He was very tall, powerfully made, with a strong, handsome face. He was remarkably muscular and powerful. As a boy he was a leader in all outdoor sports. No one could fling the bar further than he, and no one could ride more difficult horses. As a young man he became a woodsman and hunter. Day after day he could tramp through the wilderness with his gun and his surveyor's chain, and then sleep at night beneath the stars. He feared no exposure or fatigue, and outdid the hardiest backwoodsman in following a winter trail and swimming icy streams. This habit of vigorous bodily exercise he carried through life. Whenever he was at Mount Vernon he gave a large part of his time to fox-hunting, riding after his hounds through the most difficult country. His physical power and endurance counted for much in his success when he commanded his army, and when the heavy anxieties of general and president weighed upon his mind and heart.

He was an educated, but not a learned man. He read well and remembered what he read, but his life was, from the beginning, a life of action, and the world of men was his school. He was not a military genius like Hannibal, or Caesar, or Napoleon, of which the world has had only three or four examples. But he was a great soldier of the type which the English race has produced, like Marlborough and Cromwell, Wellington, Grant, and Lee. He was patient under defeat, capable of large combinations, a stubborn and often reckless fighter, a winner of battles, but much more, a conclusive winner in a long war of varying fortunes. He was, in addition, what very few great soldiers or commanders have ever been, a great constitutional statesman, able to lead a people along the paths of free government without undertaking himself to play the part of the strong man, the usurper, or the savior of society.

He was a very silent man. Of no man of equal importance in the world's history have we so few sayings of a personal kind. He was ready enough to talk or to write about the public duties which he had in hand, but he hardly ever talked of himself. Yet there can be no greater error than to suppose Washington cold and unfeeling, because of his silence and reserve. He was by nature a man of strong desires and stormy passions. Now and again he would break out, even as late as the presidency, into a gust of anger that would sweep everything before it. He was always reckless of personal danger, and had a fierce fighting spirit which nothing could check when it was once unchained.

But as a rule these fiery impulses and strong passions were under the absolute control of an iron will, and they never clouded his judgment or warped his keen sense of justice.

But if he was not of a cold nature, still less was he hard or unfeeling. His pity always went out to the poor, the oppressed, or the unhappy, and he was all that was kind and gentle to those immediately about him.

We have to look carefully into his life to learn all these things, for the world saw only a silent, reserved man, of courteous and serious manner, who seemed to stand alone and apart, and who impressed every one who came near him with a sense of awe and reverence.

One quality he had which was, perhaps, more characteristic of the man and his greatness than any other. This was his perfect veracity of mind. He was, of course, the soul of truth and honor, but he was even more than that. He never deceived himself. He always looked facts squarely in the face and dealt with them as such, dreaming no dreams, cherishing no delusions, asking no impossibilities,—just to others as to himself, and thus winning alike in war and in peace.

He gave dignity as well as victory to his country and his cause. He was, in truth, a "character for after ages to admire."

CHAPTER FIVE

Waterloo
By Victor Hugo

A classic battle, described by the author of Les Misérables.

LET US GO BACK,—THAT IS ONE OF THE STORY-TELLER'S PRIVILEGES,—AND PUT OUR-
selves once more in the year 1815, and even a little prior to the period when the action
narrated in the first part of this book took place.

If it had not rained in the night between the 17th and the 18th of June, 1815, the fate
of Europe would have been different. A few drops of water, more or less, made Napoleon
waver. All that Providence required in order to make Waterloo the end of Austerlitz was a
little more rain, and a cloud crossing the sky out of season sufficed to overthrow the world.

The battle of Waterloo could not be begun until half past eleven o'clock, and that gave
Blücher time to come up. Why? Because the ground was moist. The artillery had to wait
until it became a little firmer before they could manœuvre.

Napoleon was an artillery officer, and felt the effects of one. . . . All his plans of battle
were arranged for projectiles. The key to his victory was to make the artillery converge on
one point. He treated the strategy of the hostile general like a citadel, and made a breach
in it. He crushed the weak point with grape-shot; he joined and dissolved battles with
artillery. There was something of the sharpshooter in his genius. To beat in squares, to pul-
verize regiments, to break lines, to destroy and disperse masses . . . for him everything lay
in this, to strike, strike, strike incessantly,—and he entrusted this task to the cannon-ball.
It was a formidable method, and one which, united with genius, rendered this gloomy
athlete of the pugilism of war invincible for the space of fifteen years.

On the 18th of June, 1815, he relied all the more on his artillery, because he had
numbers on his side. Wellington had only one hundred and fifty-nine guns; Napoleon
had two hundred and forty.

Suppose the soil dry, and the artillery capable of moving, the action would have begun at six o'clock in the morning. The battle would have been won and ended at two o'clock, three hours before the change of fortune in favour of the Prussians. How much blame attaches to Napoleon for the loss of this battle? Is the shipwreck due to the pilot?

Was it the evident physical decline of Napoleon that complicated this epoch by an inward diminution of force? Had the twenty years of war worn out the blade as it had worn the scabbard, the soul as well as the body? Did the veteran make himself disastrously felt in the leader? In a word, was this genius, as many historians of note have thought, eclipsed? Did he go into a frenzy in order to disguise his weakened powers from himself? Did he begin to waver under the delusion of a breath of adventure? Had he become—a grave matter in a general—unconscious of peril? Is there an age, in this class of material great men, who may be called the giants of action, when genius becomes short-sighted? Old age has no hold on ideal genius; for the Dantes and Michael Angelos to grow old is to grow in greatness; is it declension for the Hannibals and the Bonapartes? Had Napoleon lost the direct sense of victory? Had he reached the point where he could no longer recognize the rock, could no longer divine the snare, no longer discern the crumbling edge of the abyss? Had he lost his power of scenting out catastrophes? He who had in former days known all the roads to victory, and who, from the summit of his chariot of lightning, pointed them out with a sovereign finger, had he now reached that state of sinister amazement when he could lead his tumultuous legions harnessed to it, to the precipice? Was he seized at the age of forty-six with a supreme madness? Was that titanic charioteer of destiny now only a Phaëton?

We do not believe it.

His plan of battle was, by the confession of all, a masterpiece. To go straight to the centre of the Allies' lines, to make a breach in the enemy, to cut them in two, to drive the British half back on Halle, and the Prussian half on Tingres, to make two shattered fragments of Wellington and Blücher, to carry Mont-Saint-Jean, to seize Brussels, to hurl the German into the Rhine, and the Englishman into the sea. All this was contained in that battle, for Napoleon. Afterwards people would see.

Of course, we do not here pretend to furnish a history of the battle of Waterloo; one of the scenes of the foundation of the drama which we are relating is connected with this battle, but this history is not our subject; this history, moreover, has been finished, and finished in a masterly manner, from one point of view by Napoleon, from another by Charras.

For our part, we leave the historians to contend; we are but a distant witness, a passer-by along the plain, a seeker bending over that soil all made of human flesh, perhaps taking appearances for realities; we have no right to oppose, in the name of science, a collection of facts which contain illusions, no doubt; we possess neither military practice nor strategic ability which authorize a system; in our opinion, a chain of accidents dominated the two captains at Waterloo; and when it becomes a question of destiny, that mysterious culprit, we judge like the people.

～

Those who wish to gain a clear idea of the battle of Waterloo have only to place, mentally, on the ground, a capital A. The left leg of the A is the road to Nivelles, the right one is the road to Genappe, the tie of the A is the hollow road to Ohain from Braine-l'Alleud. The top of the A is Mont-Saint-Jean, where Wellington is; the lower left tip is Hougomont, where Reille is stationed with Jérôme Bonaparte; the right tip is the Belle Alliance, where Napoleon is. At the centre of this point is the precise point where the final word of the battle was pronounced. It was there that the lion has been placed, the involuntary symbol of the supreme heroism of the Imperial Guard.

The triangle comprised in the top of the A, between the two limbs and the tie, is the plateau of Mont-Saint-Jean. The dispute over this plateau was the whole battle. The wings of the two armies extended to the right and left of the two roads to Genappe and Nivelles; d'Erlon facing Picton, Reille facing Hill.

Behind the point of the A, behind the plateau of Mont-Saint-Jean, is the forest of Soignes.

As for the plain itself, imagine a vast undulating sweep of ground; each ascent commands the next rise, and all the undulations mount towards Mont-Saint-Jean, and there end in the forest.

Two hostile troops on a field of battle are two wrestlers. It is a question of seizing the opponent round the waist. The one tries to throw the other. They cling at everything; a bush is a point of support; an angle of the wall offers them a rest to the shoulder; for the lack of a hovel under whose cover they can draw up, a regiment yields its ground; an unevenness in the ground, a chance turn in the landscape, a cross-path encountered at the right moment, a grove, a ravine, can stay the heel of that colossus which is called an army, and prevent its retreat. He who leaves the field is beaten; hence the necessity devolving on the responsible leader of examining the smallest clump of trees and of studying deeply the slightest rise in the ground.

The two generals had attentively studied the plain of Mont-Saint-Jean, which is known as the plain of Waterloo. In the preceding year, Wellington, with the sagacity of foresight, had examined it as the future seat of a great battle. Upon this spot, and for this duel, on the 18th of June, Wellington had the good post, Napoleon the bad post. The English army was above, the French army below.

It is almost superfluous here to sketch the appearance of Napoleon on horseback, telescope in hand, upon the heights of Rossomme, at daybreak, on June 18, 1815. All the world has seen him before we can show him. The calm profile under the little three-cornered hat of the school of Brienne, the green uniform, the white facings concealing the star of the Legion of Honour, his great coat hiding his epaulets, the corner of red ribbon peeping from beneath his vest, his leather breeches, the white horse with the saddle-cloth of purple velvet bearing on the corners crowned N's and eagles, Hessian boots over silk stockings, silver spurs, the sword of Marengo,—that whole appearance of the last of the Cæsars is present to all imagination, saluted with acclamations by some, severely regarded by others.

That figure stood for a long time wholly in the light; this arose from a certain legendary dimness evolved by the majority of heroes, and which always veils the truth of a longer or shorter time; but to-day history and daylight have arrived.

That illumination called history is pitiless; it possesses this peculiar and divine quality, that, pure light as it is, and precisely because it is wholly light, it often casts a shadow in places that had been luminous; from the same man it constructs two different phantoms, and the one attacks the other and executes justice on it, and the shadows of the despot contend with the brilliancy of the leader. Hence arises a truer measure in the definitive judgments of nations. Babylon violated diminishes Alexander, Rome enchained diminishes Cæsar, Jerusalem murdered diminishes Titus. Tyranny follows the tyrant. It is a misfortune for a man to leave behind him the night which bears his form.

All the world knows the first phase of this battle; an opening which was troubled, uncertain, hesitating, menacing to both armies, but still more so for the English than for the French.

It had rained all night, the ground was saturated, the water had accumulated here and there in the hollows of the plain as if in tubs; at some points the gear of the artillery carriages was buried up to the axles, the circingles of the horses were dripping with liquid mud. If the wheat and rye trampled down by this cohort of transports on the march had not filled in the ruts and strewn a litter beneath the wheels, all movement, particularly in the valleys, in the direction of Papelotte would have been impossible.

The battle began late. Napoleon, as we have already explained, was in the habit of keeping all his artillery well in hand, like a pistol, aiming it now at one point, now at another, of the battle; and it had been his wish to wait until the horse batteries could move and gallop freely. In order to do that it was necessary that the sun should come out and dry the soil. But the sun did not make its appearance. It was no longer the rendezvous of Austerlitz. When the first cannon was fired, the English general, Colville, looked at his watch, and saw that it was twenty-five minutes to twelve.

The action was begun furiously, with more fury, perhaps, than the Emperor would have wished, by the left wing of the French resting on Hougomont. At the same time Napoleon attacked the centre by hurling Quiot's brigade on La Haie-Sainte, and Ney pushed forward the right wing of the French against the left wing of the English, which leaned on Papelotte.

The attack on Hougomont was something of a feint; the plan was to attract Wellington thither, and to make him swerve to the left. This plan would have succeeded if the four companies of the English Guards and the brave Belgians of Perponcher's division had not held the position firmly, and Wellington, instead of massing his troops there, could confine himself to despatching thither, as reinforcements, only four more companies of Guards and one battalion of Brunswickers.

The attack of the right wing of the French on Papelotte was calculated, in fact, to overthrow the English left, to cut off the road to Brussels, to bar the passage against possible Prussians, to force Mont-Saint-Jean, to turn Wellington back on Hougomont; thence on Braine-l'Alleud, thence on Halle; nothing easier. With the exception of a few incidents this attack succeeded. Papelotte was taken; La Haie Sainte was carried.

A detail is to be noted. There were in the English infantry, particularly in Kempt's brigade, a great many young soldiers. These recruits were valiant in the presence of our redoubtable infantry; their inexperience extricated them intrepidly from the dilemma; they performed particularly excellent service as skirmishers: the soldier skirmisher, left somewhat to himself, becomes, so to speak, his own general. These recruits displayed some of the French ingenuity and fury. These novices had dash. This displeased Wellington.

After the taking of La Haie Sainte the battle wavered.

There is in this day an obscure interval, from mid-day to four o'clock; the middle portion of this battle is almost indistinct, and participates in the sombreness of the hand-to-hand conflict. Twilight reigns over it. We perceive vast fluctuations in the midst, a dizzy mirage, paraphernalia of war almost unknown to-day, flaming colbacks, floating sabretaches, crossbelts, cartridge boxes for grenades, hussar dolmans, red boots with a thousand wrinkles, heavy shakos garlanded with gold lace, the almost black infantry of Brunswick mingled with the scarlet infantry of England, the English soldiers with great, white circular pads on the slopes of their shoulders for epaulets, the Hanoverian light-horse with their oblong casques of leather, with brass hands and red horse-tails, the Highlanders with their bare knees and plaids, the great white gaiters of our grenadiers; pictures, not strategic lines—what a canvas for a Salvator Rosa requires, but Gribeauval would not have liked it.

A certain amount of tempest is always mingled with a battle. *Quid obscurum, quid divinum.* Each historian traces, to some extent, the particular feature which pleases him amid this pell-mell. Whatever may be the combinations of the generals, the shock of armed masses has an incalculable ebb and flow. During the action the plans of the two leaders enter into each other and become mutually thrown out of shape. Such a point of the field of battle devours more combatants than such another, just as more or less spongy soils soak up more or less quickly the water which is poured on them. It becomes neces-sary to pour out more soldiers than one would like; a series of expenditures which are the unforeseen. The line of battle floats and undulates like a thread, the trails of blood gush illogically, the fronts of the armies waver, the regiments form capes and gulfs as they enter and withdraw; all these reefs are continually moving in front of each other. Where the infantry stood the artillery arrives, the cavalry rushes in where the artillery was, the battal-ions are like smoke. There was something there; search for it. It has disappeared; the open spots change place, the sombre folds advance and retreat, a sort of wind from the sepulchre pushes forward, hurls back, distends, and disperses these tragic multitudes. What is a battle? An oscillation? The immobility of a mathematical plan expresses a minute, not a day. To depict a battle, there is required one of those powerful painters who have chaos in their brushes. Rembrandt is better than Vandermeulen; Vandermeulen, exact at noon, lies at three o'clock. Geometry is deceptive; the hurricane alone is true. That is what confers on Folard the right to contradict Polybius. Let us add, that there is a certain moment when the battle degenerates into a combat, becomes specialized, and disperses into innumerable detailed feats, which, to borrow the expression of Napoleon himself, "belong rather to the biography of the regiments than to the history of the army." The historian has, in this case, the evident right to sum up the whole. He cannot do more than catch the principal outlines of the struggle, and it is not given to any one narrator, however conscientious he may be, to fix, absolutely, the form of that horrible cloud which is called a battle.

This, which is true of all great armed encounters, is particularly applicable to Waterloo.

Nevertheless, at a certain moment in the afternoon the battle came to a decided point.

—— ⸺ ——

About four o'clock the condition of the English army was serious. The Prince of Orange was in command of the centre, Hill of the right wing, Picton of the left wing. The Prince of Orange, wild and intrepid, shouted to the Dutch Belgians: "Nassau! Brunswick! Don't yield an inch!" Hill, having been weakened, had come up to the support of Wellington; Picton was dead. At the very moment when the English had captured from the French the flag of the 105th of the line, the French had killed the English general, Picton, with a bullet through the head. The battle had, for Wellington, two bases of action, Hougomont and La Haie Sainte; Hougomont still held out, but was on fire; La Haie Sainte was taken. Of the German battalion which defended it, only forty-two men survived; all the officers, except five, were either dead or taken prisoners. Three thousand combatants had been massacred in that barn. A sergeant of the English Guards, the foremost boxer in England, reputed invulnerable by his companions, had been killed there by a little French drummer-boy. Barny had been dislodged. Alten sabred. Many flags had been lost, one from Alten's division, and one from the battalion of Lunenburg, carried by a prince of the house of Deux-Ponts. The Scots Greys no longer existed; Ponsonby's great dragoons had been cut to pieces. That valiant cavalry had bent beneath the lancers of Bro and beneath the cuirassiers of Travers; out of twelve hundred horses, six hundred remained; out of three lieutenant-colonels, two lay on the earth,—Hamilton wounded, Mater slain. Ponsonby had fallen, pierced by seven lance thrusts. Gordon was dead. Marsh was dead. Two divisions, the fifth and the sixth, had been annihilated.

Hougomont attacked, La Haie Sainte taken, there now existed but one rallying-point, the centre. That point still held firm. Wellington reinforced it. He summoned thither Hill, who was at Merle Braine; he summoned Chassé, who was at Braine l'Alleud.

The centre of the English army, rather concave, very dense, and very compact, was strongly posted. It occupied the plateau of Mont-Saint-Jean, having behind it the village, and in front of it the slope, which was tolerably steep then. It rested on that stout stone dwelling which at that time belonged to the domain of Nivelles, standing at the crossroads—a pile of the sixteenth century, and so robust that the cannonballs rebounded from it without injuring it. All about the plateau the English had cut the hedges here and there, formed embrasures in the hawthorn trees, thrust the throat of a cannon between two branches, embattled the shrubs. There artillery was ambushed in the brushwood. This Punic task, incontestably authorized by war, which permits traps, was so well done, that Haxo, who had been despatched by the Emperor at nine o'clock in the morning to reconnoitre the enemy's batteries, had discovered nothing of it, and had returned and reported to Napoleon that there were no obstacles except the two barricades which barred the road to Nivelles and to Genappe. It was at the season when the grain is tall: on the edge of the plateau a battalion of Kempt's brigade, the 95th, armed with carbines, was concealed in the tall wheat.

Thus assured and buttressed, the centre of the Anglo-Dutch army was in a good position. The peril of this position lay in the forest of Soignes, then adjoining the field of battle, and intersected by the ponds of Groenendael and Boitsfort. An army could not retreat thither without dissolving; the regiments would have broken up immediately there. The artillery would have been lost among the marshes. The retreat, according to many a man versed in the art of war,—though it is disputed by others,—would have been a disorganized flight.

To this centre, Wellington added one of Chassé's brigades taken from the right wing, and one of Wincke's brigades taken from the left wing, plus Clinton's division. To his English, to the regiments of Halkett, to the brigades of Mitchell, to the guards of Maitland, he gave as reinforcements and aids, the infantry of Brunswick, Nassau's contingent, Kielmansegg's Hanoverians, and Ompteda's Germans. He had thus twenty-six battalions under his hand. The right wing, as Charras says, was thrown back on the centre. An enormous battery was masked by sacks of earth at the spot where there now stands what is called the "Museum of Waterloo." Besides this, Wellington had, behind a rise in the ground, Somerset's Dragoon Guards, fourteen hundred horse strong. It was the remaining half of the justly celebrated English cavalry. Ponsonby destroyed, Somerset remained.

The battery, which, if completed, would have been almost a redoubt, was ranged behind a very low wall, backed up with a coating of bags of sand and a wide slope of earth. This work was not finished; there had been no time to make a palisade for it.

Wellington, restless but impassive, was on horseback, and there remained the whole day in the same attitude, a little in front of the old mill of Mont-Saint-Jean, which is still in existence, beneath an elm, which an Englishman, an enthusiastic vandal, purchased later on for two hundred francs, cut down, and carried off. Wellington was coldly heroic. The bullets rained about him. His aide-de-camp, Gordon, fell at his side. Lord Hill, pointing to a shell which had burst, said to him: "My lord, what are your orders in case you are killed?" "Do as I am doing," replied Wellington. To Clinton he said laconically, "To hold this spot to the last man." The day was evidently turning out ill. Wellington shouted to his old companions of Talavera, of Vittoria, of Salamanca: "Boys, can retreat be thought of? Think of old England!"

About four o'clock, the English line drew back. Suddenly nothing was visible on the crest of the plateau except the artillery and the sharp-shooters; the rest had disappeared; the regiments, dislodged by the shells and the French bullets, retreated into the hollow, now intersected by the back road of the farm of Mont-Saint-Jean; a retrograde movement took place, the English front hid itself, Wellington recoiled. "The beginning of the retreat!" cried Napoleon.

——

The Emperor, though ill and discommoded on horseback by a local trouble, had never been so good tempered as on that day. His impenetrability had been smiling ever since the morning. On the 18th of June, that profound soul masked by marble was radiant. The man who had been gloomy at Austerlitz was gay at Waterloo. The greatest favourites of destiny make mistakes. Our joys are composed of shadow. The supreme smile is God's alone.

Ridet Cæsar, Pompeius flebit, said the legionaires of the Fulminatrix Legion. Pompey was not destined to weep on that occasion, but it is certain that Cæsar laughed. While exploring on horseback at one o'clock on the preceding night, in storm and rain, in company with Bertrand, the hills in the neighbourhood of Rossomme, satisfied at the sight of the long line of the English camp-fires illuminating the whole horizon from Frischemont to Braine-l'Alleud, it had seemed to him that fate, to whom he had assigned a day on the field of Waterloo, was exact to the appointment; he stopped his horse, and remained for some time motionless, gazing at the lightning and listening to the thunder; and this fatalist was heard to cast into the darkness this mysterious saying, "We are in accord." Napoleon was mistaken. They were no longer in accord.

He had not slept a moment; every instant of that night was marked by a joy for him. He rode through the line of the principal outposts, halting here and there to talk to the sentinels. At half-past two, near the wood of Hougomont, he heard the tread of a column on the march; he thought at the moment that it was a retreat on the part of Wellington. He said: "It is the rear-guard of the English getting under way for the purpose of decamping. I will take prisoners the six thousand English who have just landed at Ostend." He talked expansively; he regained the animation which he had shown at his landing on the 1st of March, when he pointed out to the Grand Marshal the enthusiastic peasant of the Gulf Juan, and cried, "Well, Bertrand, here is a reinforcement already!" On the night of the 17th to the 18th of June he made fun of Wellington. "That little Englishman needs a lesson," said Napoleon. The rain redoubled in violence; it thundered while the Emperor was speaking.

At half past three o'clock in the morning, he lost one illusion; officers who had been despatched to reconnoitre announced to him that the enemy was not making any movement. Nothing was stirring; not a bivouac-fire had been extinguished; the English army was asleep. The silence on earth was profound; the only noise was in the heavens. At four o'clock, a peasant was brought in to him by the scouts; this peasant had served as guide to a brigade of English cavalry, probably Vivian's brigade, which was on its way to take up a position in the village of Ohain, at the extreme left. At five o'clock, two Belgian deserters reported to him that they had just quitted their regiment, and that the English army meant to fight. "All the better!" exclaimed Napoleon. "I prefer to overthrow them rather than to drive them back."

At daybreak he dismounted in the mud on the slope which forms an angle with the Plancenoit road, had a kitchen table and a peasant's chair brought to him from the farm of Rossomme, seated himself, with a truss of straw for a carpet, and spread out on the table the chart of the battle-field, saying to Soult as he did so, "A pretty chess-board."

In consequence of the rains during the night, the transports of provisions, embedded in the soft roads, had not been able to arrive by morning; the soldiers had had no sleep; they were wet and famished. This did not prevent Napoleon from exclaiming cheerfully to Ney, "We have ninety chances out of a hundred." At eight o'clock the Emperor's breakfast was brought to him. He invited several generals to it. During breakfast, it was said that Wellington had been to a ball two nights before, in Brussels, at the Duchess of Richmond's; and Soult, a rough man of war, with the face of an archbishop said, "The ball will be to-day." The Emperor jested with Ney, who had said, "Wellington will not be so simple as to wait for Your Majesty." That was his way, however. "He was fond of a joke," says Fleury de Chaboulon. "A merry humour was at the foundation of his character," says Gourgaud. "He abounded in pleasantries, which were more peculiar than witty," says Benjamin Constant. These gaieties of a giant are worthy of comment. It was he who called his grenadiers "his growlers"; he pinched their ears; he pulled their moustaches. "The Emperor did nothing but play pranks on us," is the remark of one of them. During the mysterious trip from the island of Elba to France, on the 27th of February, on the open sea, the French brig of war, *Le Zéphyr*, having encountered the brig *L'Inconstant*, on which Napoleon was concealed, and having asked the news of Napoleon from *L'Inconstant*, the Emperor, who still wore in his hat the white and violet cockade sown with bees, which he had adopted at the isle of Elba, laughingly seized the speaking trumpet, and answered for himself, "The Emperor is quite well." A man who laughs like that is on familiar terms with events. Napoleon indulged in many fits of this laughter during the breakfast at Waterloo. After breakfast he meditated for a quarter of an hour; then two generals seated themselves on the truss of straw, pen in hand and their paper on their knees, and the Emperor dictated to them the order of battle.

At nine o'clock, at the instant when the French army ranged in echelons and moving in five columns, had deployed—the divisions in two lines, the artillery between the brigades, the music at their head; as they beat the march, with rolls on the drums and the blasts of trumpets, mighty, vast, joyous, a sea of casques, of sabres, and of bayonets on the horizon, the Emperor was touched, and twice exclaimed, "Magnificent! Magnificent!"

Between nine o'clock and half-past ten the whole army, incredible as it may appear, had taken up its position and was drawn up in six lines, forming, to repeat the Emperor's expression, "the figure of six V's." A few moments after the formation of the line, in the midst of that profound silence, like that which heralds the beginning of a storm, which precedes battle, the Emperor tapped Haxo on the shoulder, as he beheld the three batteries of twelve pounders, detached by his orders from the corps of Erlon, Reille, and Lobau, and destined to begin the action by taking Mont-Saint-Jean, which was situated at the intersection of the Nivelles and the Genappe roads, and said to him, "There are four and twenty pretty girls, General."

Sure of the result, he encouraged with a smile, as they passed before him, the company of sappers of the first corps, which he had appointed to barricade Mont-Saint-Jean as soon as the village should be carried. All this serenity had been traversed by but a single word of human pity; perceiving on his left, at a spot where there now stands a large tomb, those admirable Scots Greys, with their superb horses, massing themselves, he said, "It is a pity."

Then he mounted his horse, advanced beyond Rossomme, and selected for his coign of vantage a contracted elevation of turf to the right of the road from Genappe to Brussels, which was his second station during the battle. The third station, the one adopted at seven o'clock in the evening, between La Belle Alliance and La Haie Sainte, is formidable; it is a rather lofty mound, which still exists, and behind which the guard was massed in a hollow. Around this knoll the balls rebounded from the pavements of the road, up to Napoleon himself. As at Brienne, he had over his head the whistle of the bullets and canister. Mouldy cannon-balls, old sword blades, and shapeless projectiles, eaten up with rust, have been picked up at the spot where his horse's feet stood. *Scabra rubigine*. A few years ago, a shell of sixty pounds, still charged, and with its fuse broken off level with the bomb, was unearthed. It was at this station that the Emperor said to his guide, Lacoste, a hostile and timid peasant, who was attached to the saddle of a hussar, and who turned round at every discharge of canister and tried to hide behind Napoleon: "You ass, it is shameful! You'll get yourself killed with a ball in the back." He who writes these lines has himself found, in the friable soil of this knoll, on turning over the sand, the remains of the neck of a bomb, rotted by the oxide of six and forty years, and old fragments of iron which parted like sticks of barley sugar between the fingers.

Every one is aware that the variously inclined undulations of the plains, where the encounter between Napoleon and Wellington took place, are no longer what they were on June 18, 1815. On taking from this mournful field the wherewithal to make a monument to it, its real relief has been taken away, and history, disconcerted, no longer finds her bearings there. It has been disfigured for the sake of glorifying it. Wellington, when he beheld Waterloo once more, two years later, exclaimed, "They have altered my field of battle!" Where the huge pyramid of earth, surmounted by the lion, rises to-day, there was a crest which descended in an easy slope towards the Nivelles road, but which was almost an escarpment on the side of the highway to Genappe. The elevation of this escarpment can still be imagined by the height of the two knolls of the two great sepulchres which enclose the road from Genappe to Brussels: one, the English tomb, is on the left; the other, the German tomb, is on the right. There is no French tomb. The whole of that plain is a sepulchre for France. Thanks to the thousands of cartloads of earth employed in erecting the mound one hundred and fifty feet in height and half a mile in circumference, the plateau of Mont-Saint-Jean is now accessible by an easy slope. On the day of battle, particularly on the side of La Haie Sainte, it was abrupt and difficult of approach. The incline there is so steep that the English cannon could not see the farm, situated in the bottom of the valley, which was the centre of the combat. On the 18th of June, 1815, the rains had still further increased this acclivity, the mud complicated the problem of the ascent, and the men not only slipped back, but stuck fast in the mire. Along the crest of the plateau ran a sort of trench whose presence it was impossible for the distant observer to guess.

What was this trench? Let us explain. Braine l'Alleud is a Belgian village; Ohain is another. These villages, both of them hidden in hollows of the landscape, are connected by a road about a league and a half in length, which traverses the plain along its undulating level, and often enters and buries itself in the hills like a furrow, which makes a ravine of this road in certain parts. In 1815, as to-day, this road cut the crest of the plateau of Mont-Saint-Jean between the two highways from Genappe and Nivelles; only, it is now on a level with the plain; it was then a hollow way. Its two slopes have been appropriated for the monumental mound. This road was, and still is, a trench for the greater portion of its course; a hollow trench, sometimes a dozen feet in depth, and whose banks, being too steep, crumbled away here and there, particularly in winter, under driving rains. Accidents happened here. The road was so narrow at the Braine l'Alleud entrance that a passer-by was crushed by a cart, as is proved by a stone cross which stands near the cemetery, and which gives the name of the dead, Monsieur Bernard Debrye, Merchant of Brussels, and the date of the accident, February, 1637. It was so deep on the plateau of Mont-Saint-Jean that a peasant, Mathieu Nicaise, was crushed there, in 1783, by a slide from the slope, as is stated on another stone cross, the top of which has disappeared in the excavations, but whose overturned pedestal is still visible on the grassy slope to the left of the highway between La Haie Sainte and the farm of Mont-Saint-Jean.

On the day of battle, this hollow road whose existence was in no way indicated, bordering the crest of Mont-Saint-Jean, a trench at the top of the escarpment, a rut concealed in the soil, was invisible; that is to say, terrible.

On the morning of Waterloo, then, Napoleon was content.

He was right; the plan of battle drawn up by him was, as we have seen, really admirable.

The battle once begun, its various incidents,—the resistance of Hougomont; the tenacity of La Haie Sainte; the killing of Dauduin; the disabling of Foy; the unexpected wall against which Soye's brigade was broken; Guilleminot's fatal heedlessness when he had neither petard nor powder sacks; the sticking of the batteries in the mud; the fifteen unescorted pieces overwhelmed in a hollow way by Uxbridge; the small effect of the shells falling in the English lines, and there embedding themselves in the rain-soaked soil, and only succeeding in producing volcanoes of mud, so that the canister was turned into a splash; the inutility of Piré's demonstration on Braine-l'Alleud; all that cavalry, fifteen squadrons almost annihilated; the right wing of the English badly alarmed, the left wing poorly attacked; Ney's strange mistake in massing, instead of echelonning the four divisions of the first corps; men delivered over to grape-shot, arranged in ranks twenty-seven deep and with a frontage of two hundred; the terrible gaps made in these masses by the cannon-balls; attacking columns disorganized; the side-battery suddenly unmasked on their flank; Bourgeois, Donzelot, and Durutte compromised; Quiot repulsed; Lieutenant Vieux, that Hercules graduated at the Polytechnic School, wounded at the moment when he was beating in with an axe the door of La Haie Sainte under the downright fire of the English barricade which barred the angle on the Genappe road; Marcognet's division caught between the infantry and the cavalry, shot down at the very muzzle of the guns amid the grain by Best and Pack, put to the sword by Ponsonby; his battery of seven pieces spiked; the Prince of Saxe Weimar holding and guarding, in spite of the Comte d'Erlon, both Frischemont and Smohain; the flags of the 105th taken, the flags of the 45th captured; that black Prussian hussar stopped by the flying column of three hundred light cavalry on the scout between Wavre and Plancenoit; the alarming things that had been said by prisoners; Grouchy's delay; fifteen hundred men killed in the orchard of Hougomont in less than an hour; eighteen hundred men overthrown in a still shorter time about La Haie Sainte,—all these stormy incidents passing like the clouds of battle before Napoleon, had hardly troubled his gaze and had not overshadowed his imperial face. Napoleon was accustomed to gaze steadily at war; he never added up the poignant details. He cared little for figures, provided that they furnished the total, victory; he was not alarmed if the beginnings did go astray, since he thought himself the master and the possessor at the end; he knew how to wait, supposing himself to be out of the question, and he treated destiny as his equal: he seemed to say to fate, You would not dare.

Composed half of light and half of shadow, Napoleon felt himself protected in good and tolerated in evil. He had, or thought that he had, a connivance, one might almost say a complicity, of events in his favour, which was equivalent to the invulnerability of antiquity.

Nevertheless, when one has Bérésina, Leipzig, and Fontainebleau behind one, it seems as though one might defy Waterloo. A mysterious frown becomes perceptible on the face of the heavens.

At the moment when Wellington retreated, Napoleon quivered. He suddenly beheld the plateau of Mont-Saint-Jean deserted, and the van of the English army disappear. It was rallying, but hiding itself. The Emperor half rose in his stirrups. Victory flashed from his eyes.

Wellington, driven into a corner at the forest of Soignes and destroyed—that was the definite conquest of England by France; it would be Crécy, Poitiers, Malplaquet, and Ramillies avenged. The man of Marengo was wiping out Agincourt.

So the Emperor, meditating on this terrible turn of fortune, swept his glass for the last time over all the points of the field of battle. His guard, standing behind him with grounded arms, watched him from below with a sort of religious awe. He pondered; he examined the slopes, noted the declivities, scrutinized the clumps of trees, the patches of rye, the path; he seemed to be counting each bush. He gazed with some intentness at the English barricades of the two highways,—two large masses of felled trees, the one on the road to Genappe above La Haie Sainte, defended with two cannon, the only ones out of all the English artillery which commanded the extremity of the field of battle, and that on the road to Nivelles where gleamed the Dutch bayonets of Chassé's brigade. Near this barricade he observed the old chapel of Saint Nicholas, which stands at the angle of the cross-road near Braine-l'Alleud; he bent down and spoke in a low voice to the guide Lacoste. The guide made a negative sign with his head, which was probably perfidious.

The Emperor straightened himself up and reflected.

Wellington had withdrawn.

All that remained to do was to complete this retreat by crushing him.

Napoleon turning round abruptly, despatched an express at full speed to Paris to announce that the battle was won.

Napoleon was one of those geniuses from whom thunder issues.

He had just found his thunder-stroke.

He gave orders to Milhaud's cuirassiers to carry the plateau of Mont-Saint-Jean.

There were three thousand five hundred of them. They formed a front a quarter of a league in length. They were giants, on colossal horses. There were six and twenty squadrons of them; and they had behind them to support them Lefebvre Desnouettes's division,—the one hundred and six picked gendarmes, the light cavalry of the Guard, eleven hundred and ninety-seven men, and the lancers of the guard of eight hundred and eighty lances. They wore casques without plumes, and cuirasses of beaten iron, with horse pistols in their holsters, and long sabre swords. That morning the whole army had admired them, when, at nine o'clock, with blare of trumpets and all the music playing "Let us watch o'er the Safety of the Empire," they had come in a solid column, with one of their batteries on their flank, another in their centre, and deployed in two ranks between the roads to Genappe and Frischemont, and taken up their position for battle in that powerful second line, so cleverly arranged by Napoleon, which, having on its extreme left Kellermann's cuirassiers and on its extreme right Milhaud's cuirassiers, had, so to speak, two wings of iron.

The aide-de-camp Bernard carried them the Emperor's orders. Ney drew his sword and placed himself at their head. The enormous squadrons were set in motion.

Then a formidable spectacle was seen.

The whole of the cavalry, with upraised swords, standards and trumpets flung to the breeze, formed in columns by divisions, descended, by a simultaneous movement and like one man, with the precision of a brazen battering ram which is affecting a breach, the hill of La Belle Alliance. They plunged into the terrible depths in which so many men had already fallen, disappeared there in the smoke, then emerging from that shadow, reappeared on the other side of the valley, still compact and in close ranks, mounting at a full trot, through a storm of grape-shot which burst upon them, the terrible muddy slope of the plateau of Mont-Saint-Jean. They ascended, grave, threatening, imperturbable; in the intervals between the musketry and the artillery, their colossal trampling was audible. Being two divisions, there were two columns of them; Wathier's division held the right, Delort's division was on the left. It seemed as though two immense steel lizards were to be seen crawling towards the crest of the plateau. They traversed the battle like a flash.

Nothing like it had been seen since the taking of the great redoubt of the Moskowa by the heavy cavalry; Murat was missing, but Ney was again present. It seemed as though that mass had become a monster and had but one soul. Each column undulated and swelled like the rings of a polyp. They could be seen through a vast cloud of smoke which was rent at intervals. A confusion of helmets, of cries, of sabres, a stormy heaving of horses amid the cannons and the flourish of trumpets, a terrible and disciplined tumult; over all, the cuirasses like the scales on the dragon.

These narrations seemed to belong to another age. Something parallel to this vision appeared, no doubt, in the ancient Orphic epics, which told of the centaurs, the old hippanthropes, those Titans with human heads and equestrian chests who scaled Olympus at a gallop, horrible, invulnerable, sublime—gods and brutes.

It was a curious numerical coincidence that twenty-six battalions rode to meet twenty-six battalions. Behind the crest of the plateau, in the shadow of the masked battery, the English infantry, formed into thirteen squares, two battalions to the square, in two lines, with seven in the first line, six in the second, the stocks of their guns to their shoulders, taking aim at that which was on the point of appearing, waited, calm, mute, motionless. They did not see the cuirassiers, and the cuirassiers did not see them. They listened to the rise of this tide of men. They heard the swelling sound of three thousand horses, the alternate and symmetrical tramp of their hoofs at full trot, the jingling of the cuirasses, the clang of the sabres, and a sort of grand and formidable breathing. There was a long and terrible silence; then, all at once, a long file of uplifted arms, brandishing sabres, appeared above the crest, and casques, trumpets, and standards, and three thousand heads with grey moustaches, shouting, "Vive l'Empereur!" All this cavalry debouched on the plateau, and it was like the beginning of an earthquake.

All at once, a tragic incident happened; on the English left, on our right, the head of the column of cuirassiers reared up with a frightful clamour. On arriving at the culminating point of the crest, ungovernable, utterly given over to fury and their course of extermination of the squares and cannon, the cuirassiers had just caught sight of a trench or grave,—a trench between them and the English. It was the sunken road of Ohain.

It was a frightful moment. The ravine was there, unexpected, yawning, directly under the horses' feet, two fathoms deep between its double slopes; the second file pushed the first into it, and the third pushed on the second; the horses reared and fell backward, landed on their haunches, slid down, all four feet in the air, crushing and overwhelming the riders; and there being no means of retreat,—the whole column being no longer anything more than a projectile,—the force which had been acquiring to crush the English crushed the French; the inexorable ravine could only yield when filled; horses and riders rolled there pell-mell, grinding each other, forming but one mass of flesh in this gulf: when this trench was full of living men, the rest marched over them and passed on. Nearly a third of Dubois's brigade fell into that abyss.

This began the loss of the battle.

A local tradition, which evidently exaggerates matters, says that two thousand horses and fifteen hundred men were buried in the sunken road of Ohain. This figure probably comprises all the other corpses which were flung into this ravine the day after the combat.

Let us note in passing that it was Dubois's sorely tried brigade which, an hour previously, making a charge to one side, had captured the flag of the Lunenburg battalion.

Napoleon, before giving the order for this charge of Milhaud's cuirassiers, had scrutinized the ground, but had not been able to see that hollow road, which did not even form a wrinkle on the crest of the plateau. Warned, nevertheless, and put on his guard by the little white chapel which marks its angle of juncture with the Nivelles highway, he had put a question as to the possibility of an obstacle, to the guide Lacoste. The guide had answered No. We might almost say that Napoleon's catastrophe originated in the shake of a peasant's head.

Other fatalities were yet to arise.

Was it possible for Napoleon to win that battle? We answer No. Why? Because of Wellington? Because of Blücher? No. Because of God.

Bonaparte victor at Waterloo does not harmonise with the law of the nineteenth century. Another series of facts was in preparation, in which there was no longer any room for Napoleon. The ill will of events had declared itself long before.

It was time that this vast man should fall.

The excessive weight of this man in human destiny disturbed the balance. This individual alone counted for more than the universal group. These plethoras of all human vitality concentrated in a single head; the world mounting to the brain of one man,—this would be mortal to civilization were it to last. The moment had arrived for the incorruptible and supreme equity to alter its plan. Probably the principles and the elements, on which the regular gravitations of the moral, as of the material, world depend, had complained. Smoking blood, overcrowded cemeteries, mothers in tears,—these are formidable pleaders. When the earth is suffering from too heavy a burden, there are mysterious groanings of the shades, to which the abyss lends an ear.

Napoleon had been denounced in the infinite, and his fall had been decided on. He embarrassed God.

Waterloo is not a battle; it is a transformation on the part of the Universe.

⌒ ⌒

The battery was unmasked simultaneously with the ravine.

Sixty cannons and the thirteen squares darted lightning point-blank on the cuirassiers. The intrepid General Delort made the military salute to the English battery.

The whole of the flying artillery of the English had re-entered the squares at a gallop. The cuirassiers had not had even the time for reflection. The disaster of the hollow road had decimated, but not discouraged them. They belonged to that class of men who, when diminished in number, increase in courage.

Wathier's column alone had suffered in the disaster; Delort's column, which had been deflected to the left, as though he had a presentiment of an ambush, had arrived whole.

The cuirassiers hurled themselves on the English squares.

At full speed, with bridles loose, swords in their teeth, pistols in their hand,—such was the attack.

There are moments in battles in which the soul hardens the man until the soldier is changed into a statue, and when all flesh becomes granite. The English battalions, desperately assaulted, did not stir.

Then it was terrible.

All the faces of the English squares were attacked at once. A frenzied whirl enveloped them. That cold infantry remained impassive. The first rank knelt and received the cuirassiers on their bayonets, the second rank shot them down; behind the second rank the cannoneers charged their guns, the front of the square parted, permitted the passage of an eruption of grape-shot, and closed again. The cuirassiers replied by crushing them. Their great horses reared, strode across the ranks, leaped over the bayonets and fell, gigantic, in the midst of these four living walls. The cannon-balls ploughed furrows in these cuirassiers; the cuirassiers made breaches in the squares. Files of men disappeared, ground to dust under the horses. The bayonets plunged into the bellies of these centaurs; hence a hideousness of wounds which has probably never been seen anywhere else. The squares, wasted by this mad cavalry, closed up their ranks without flinching. Inexhaustible in the matter of grape-shot, they created explosions in their assailants' midst. The form of this combat was monstrous. These squares were no longer battalions, they were craters; those cuirassiers were no longer cavalry, they were a tempest. Each square was a volcano attacked by a cloud; lava combated with lightning.

The extreme right square, the most exposed of all, being in the air, was almost anni-hilated at the very first attack. It was formed of the 75th regiment of Highlanders. The piper in the centre dropped his melancholy eyes, filled with the reflections of the forests and the lakes in profound inattention, while men were being exterminated around him, and seated on a drum, with his pibroch under his arm, played the Highland airs. These Scotchmen died thinking of Ben Lothian, as did the Greeks remembering Argos. The sword of a cuirassier, which hewed down the bagpipes and the arm which bore it, put an end to the song by killing the singer.

The cuirassiers, relatively few in number, and still further diminished by the catastro-phe of the ravine, had almost the whole English army against them, but they multiplied themselves so that each man of them was equal to ten. Nevertheless, some Hanoverian battalions yielded. Wellington saw it, and thought of his cavalry. Had Napoleon at that same moment thought of his infantry, he would have won the battle. This forgetfulness was his great and fatal mistake.

All at once, the cuirassiers, who had been the assailants, found themselves assailed. The English cavalry was at their back. Before them two squares, behind them Somerset; Somer-set meant fourteen hundred dragoons of the guard. On the right, Somerset had Dornberg with the German light-horse, and on his left, Trip with the Belgian carbineers; the cuiras-siers attacked on the flank and in front, before and in the rear, by infantry and cavalry, had to face all sides. What did they care? They were a whirlwind. Their valour was indescribable.

In addition to this, they had behind them the battery, which was still thundering. It was necessary that it should be so, or they could never have been wounded in the back. One of their cuirasses, pierced on the shoulder by a ball, is in the Waterloo Museum.

For such Frenchmen nothing less than such Englishmen was needed. It was no longer a hand-to-hand mêlée; it was a shadow, a fury, a dizzy transport of souls and courage, a hurricane of lightning swords. In an instant the fourteen hundred dragoon guards numbered only eight hundred. Fuller, their lieutenant colonel, fell dead. Ney rushed up with the lanc-ers and Lefebvre Desnouettes's light-horse. The plateau of Mont-Saint-Jean was captured, recaptured, captured again. The cuirassiers left the cavalry to return to the infantry; or, to put it more exactly, the whole of that formidable rout collared each other without releasing the other. The squares still held firm after a dozen assaults. Ney had four horses killed under him. Half the cuirassiers remained on the plateau. This struggle lasted two hours.

The English army was profoundly shaken. There is no doubt that, had they not been enfeebled in their first shock by the disaster of the hollow road, the cuirassiers would have overwhelmed the centre and decided the victory. This extraordinary cavalry petrified Clin-ton, who had seen Talavera and Badajoz. Wellington, three-quarters vanquished, admired heroically. He said in an undertone, "Splendid!"

The cuirassiers annihilated seven squares out of thirteen, took or spiked sixty guns, and captured from the English regiments six flags, which three cuirassiers and three chas-seurs of the Guard bore to the Emperor in front of the farm of La Belle Alliance.

Wellington's situation had grown worse. This strange battle was like a duel between two savage, wounded men, each of whom, still fighting and still resisting, is expending all his blood.

Which will be the first to fall?

The conflict on the plateau continued.

What had become of the cuirassiers? No one could have told. One thing is certain, that on the day after the battle, a cuirassier and his horse were found dead among the woodwork of the scales for vehicles at Mont-Saint-Jean, at the very point where the four roads from Nivelles, Genappe, La Hulpe, and Brussels meet and intersect each other. This horseman had pierced the English lines. One of the men who picked up the body still lives at Mont-Saint-Jean. His name is Dehaye. He was eighteen years old at that time.

Wellington felt that he was yielding. The crisis was at hand.

The cuirassiers had not succeeded, since the centre was not broken through. As every one was in possession of the plateau, no one held it, and in fact it remained, to a great extent, in the hands of the English. Wellington held the village and the plain; Ney had only the crest and the slope. They seemed rooted in that fatal soil on both sides.

But the weakening of the English seemed irremediable. The hæmorrhage of that army was horrible. Kempt, on the left wing, demanded reinforcements. "There are none," replied Wellington. Almost at that same moment, a singular coincidence which depicts the exhaustion of the two armies, Ney demanded infantry from Napoleon, and Napoleon exclaimed, "Infantry! Where does he expect me to get it? Does he think I can make it?"

Nevertheless, the English army was in the worse plight of the two. The furious onsets of those great squadrons with cuirasses of iron and breasts of steel had crushed the infantry. A few men clustered round a flag marked the post of a regiment; some battalions were commanded only by a captain or a lieutenant; Alten's division, already so roughly handled at La Haie Sainte, was almost destroyed; the intrepid Belgians of Van Kluze's brigade strewed the rye-fields all along the Nivelles road; hardly anything was left of those Dutch grenadiers, who, intermingled with Spaniards in our ranks in 1811, fought against Wellington; and who, in 1815, rallied to the English standard, fought against Napoleon. The loss in officers was considerable. Lord Uxbridge, who had his leg buried on the following day, had a fractured knee. If, on the French side, in that tussle of the cuirassiers, Delort, l'Héritier, Colbert, Dnop, Travers, and Blancard were disabled, on the side of the English there was Alten wounded, Barne wounded, Delancey killed, Van Meeren killed, Ompteda killed, the whole of Wellington's staff decimated, and England had the heaviest loss of it in that balance of blood. The second regiment of foot guards had lost five lieutenant-colonels, four captains, and three ensigns; the first battalion of the 30th infantry had lost 24 officers and 1,200 soldiers; the 79th Highlanders had lost 24 officers wounded, 18 officers killed, 450 soldiers killed. Cumberland's Hanoverian hussars, a whole regiment, with Colonel Hacke at its head, who was destined to be tried later on and cashiered, had turned bridle in the presence of the fray, and had fled to the forest of Soignes, spreading the rout as far as Brussels. The transports, ammunition wagons, the baggage wagons, the wagons filled with wounded, on seeing that the French were gaining ground and approaching the forest, rushed into it. The Dutch, mowed down by the French cavalry, cried, "Alarm!" From Vert Coucou to Groentendael, a distance of nearly two leagues in the direction of Brussels, according to the testimony of eye-witnesses who are still alive, the roads were dense with fugitives. This panic was such that it attacked the Prince de Condé at Mechlin, and Louis XVIII at Ghent. With the exception of the feeble reserve echelonned behind the ambulance established at the farm of Mont-Saint-Jean, and of Vivian's and Vandeleur's brigades, which flanked the left wing, Wellington had no cavalry left. A number of batteries lay dismounted. These facts are attested by Siborne; and Pringle, exaggerating the disaster, goes so far as to say that the Anglo Dutch army was reduced to thirty-four thousand men. The Iron Duke remained calm, but his lips blanched. Vincent, the Austrian commissioner, Alava, the Spanish commissioner, who were present at the battle in the English staff, thought the Duke lost. At five o'clock Wellington drew out his watch, and he was heard to murmur these sinister words, "Blücher, or night!"

It was about that moment that a distant line of bayonets gleamed on the heights in the direction of Frischemont.

This was the culminating point in this stupendous drama.

— ⁓ —

The awful mistake of Napoleon is well known. Grouchy expected, Blücher arriving. Death instead of life.

Fate has these turns; the throne of the world was expected; it was Saint Helena that was seen.

If the little shepherd who served as guide to Bülow, Blücher's lieutenant, had advised him to debouch from the forest above Frischemont, instead of below Plancenoit, the form of the nineteenth century might, perhaps, have been different. Napoleon would have won the battle of Waterloo. By any other route than that below Plancenoit, the Prussian army would have come out upon a ravine impassable for artillery, and Bülow would not have arrived.

Now the Prussian general, Muffling, declares that one hour's delay, and Blücher would not have found Wellington on his feet. "The battle was lost."

It was time that Bülow should arrive, as we shall see. He had, moreover, been very much delayed. He had bivouacked at Dieu-le-Mont, and had set out at daybreak; but the roads were impassable, and his divisions stuck fast in the mud. The ruts were up to the axles of the cannons. Moreover, he had been obliged to pass the Dyle on the narrow bridge of Wavre; the street leading to the bridge had been fired by the French, so the caissons and ammunition-wagons could not pass between two rows of burning houses, and had been obliged to wait until the conflagration was extinguished. It was mid-day before Bülow's vanguard had been able to reach Chapelle Saint Lambert.

Had the action begun two hours earlier, it would have been over at four o'clock, and Blücher would have fallen on the battle won by Napoleon. Such are these immense risks proportioned to an infinite which we cannot comprehend.

The Emperor had been the first, as early as mid-day, to descry with his field glass, on the extreme horizon, something which had attracted his attention. He had said, "I see over there a cloud, which seems to me to be troops." Then he asked the Duc de Dalmatie, "Soult, what do you see in the direction of Chapelle Saint Lambert?" The marshal, looking through his glass, answered, "Four or five thousand men, Sire." It was evidently Grouchy. But it remained motionless in the mist. All the glasses of the staff had studied "the cloud" pointed out by the Emperor. Some said: "They are columns halting." The truth is, that the cloud did not move. The Emperor detached Domon's division of light cavalry to reconnoitre in that direction.

Bülow had not moved, in fact. His vanguard was very feeble, and could accomplish nothing. He was obliged to wait for the main body of the army corps, and he had received orders to concentrate his forces before entering into line; but at five o'clock, perceiving Wellington's peril, Blücher ordered Bülow to attack, and uttered these remarkable words: "We must let the English army breathe."

A little later, the divisions of Losthin, Hiller, Hacke, and Ryssel deployed before Lobau's corps, the cavalry of Prince William of Russia debouched from the Bois de Paris, Plancenoit was in flames, and the Prussian cannon-balls began to rain even upon the ranks of the guard in reserve behind Napoleon.

―⌣―

The rest is known,—the irruption of a third army; the battle broken to pieces; eighty-six cannon thundering simultaneously; Pirch the first coming up with Bülow; Zieten's cavalry led by Blücher in person, the French driven back; Marcognet swept from the plateau of Ohain; Durutte dislodged from Papelotte; Donzelot and Quiot retreating; Lobau attacked on the flank; a fresh battle precipitating itself on our dismantled regiments at nightfall; the whole English line resuming the offensive and thrust forward; the gigantic breach made in the French army; the English grape-shot and the Prussian grape-shot aiding each other; the extermination; disaster in front; disaster on the flank; the Guard entering the line in the midst of this terrible crumbling of all things.

Conscious that they were about to die, they shouted, "Long live the Emperor!" History records nothing more touching than that death rattle bursting forth in acclamations.

The sky had been overcast all day. All of a sudden, at that very moment,—it was eight o'clock in the evening,—the clouds on the horizon parted, and allowed the sinister red glow of the setting sun to pass through, athwart the elms on the Nivelles road. They had seen it rise at Austerlitz.

Each battalion of the Guard was commanded by a general for this final dénouement. Friant, Michel, Roguet, Harlet, Mallet, Poret de Morvan, were there. When the tall bearskins of the grenadiers of the Guard, with their large plaques bearing the eagle, appeared, symmetrical, in line, tranquil; in the midst of that combat, the enemy felt a respect for France; they thought they beheld twenty victories entering the field of battle, with wings outspread, and those who were the conquerors, believing themselves to be vanquished, retreated; but Wellington shouted, "Up, Guards, and at them!" The red regiment of English Guards, lying flat behind the hedges, sprang up, a cloud of grape-shot riddled the tricoloured flag and whistled round our eagles; all hurled themselves forwards, and the supreme carnage began. In the darkness, the Imperial Guard felt the army losing ground around it, and in the vast shock of the rout it heard the desperate flight which had taken the place of the "Long live the Emperor!" and, with flight behind it, it continued to advance, more crushed, losing more men at every step it took. There -were none who hesitated, no timid men in its ranks. The soldier in that troop was as much of a hero as the general. Not a man was missing in that heroic suicide.

Ney, bewildered, great with all the grandeur of accepted death, offered himself to all blows in that tempest. He had his fifth horse killed under him there. Perspiring, his eyes aflame, foam on his lips, with uniform unbuttoned, one of his epaulets half cut off by a sword-stroke from the horse guard, his plaque with the great eagle dented by a bullet; bleeding, bemired, magnificent, a broken sword in his hand, he said, "Come and see how a Marshal of France dies on the field of battle!" But in vain; he did not die. He was haggard and angry. At Drouet d'Erlon he hurled this question, "Are you not going to get yourself killed?" In the midst of all that artillery engaged in crushing a handful of men, he shouted: "So there is nothing for me! Oh! I should like to have all these English bullets enter my chest!" Unhappy man, thou wert reserved for French bullets!

The rout in the rear of the Guard was melancholy.

The army yielded suddenly on all sides simultaneously—Hougomont, La Haie Sainte, Papelotte, Plancenoit. The cry, "Treachery!" was followed by a cry of "Save yourselves who can!" An army which is disbanding is like a thaw. All yields, splits, cracks, floats, rolls, falls, collides, is precipitated. The disintegration is unprecedented.

Ney borrows a horse, leaps upon it, and without hat, cravat, or sword, dashes across the Brussels road, stopping both English and French. He strives to detain the army, he recalls it to its duty, he insults it, he clings to the route. He is overwhelmed. The soldiers fly from him, shouting, "Long live Marshal Ney!" Two of Durutte's regiments go and come in affright as though tossed back and forth between the swords of the Uhlans and the fusillade of the brigades of Kempt, Best, Pack, and Ryland; the worst of hand-to-hand conflicts is the defeat; friends kill each other in order to escape; squadrons and battalions break and disperse against each other, like the tremendous foam of battle. Lobau at one extremity, and Reille at the other, are drawn into the tide. In vain does Napoleon erect walls from what is left to him of his Guard; in vain does he expend in a last effort his last serviceable squadrons. Quiot retreats before Vivian, Kellermann before Vandeleur, Lobau before Bülow, Morand before Pirch, Domon and Subervic before Prince William of Prussia; Guyot, who led the Emperor's squadrons to the charge, falls beneath the feet of the English dragoons. Napoleon gallops past the line of fugitives, harangues, urges, threatens, entreats them. All the mouths which in the morning had shouted, "Long live the Emperor!" remain gaping; they hardly recognize him. The Prussian cavalry, newly arrived, dashes forward, flies, hews, slashes, kills, exterminates. Horses lash out, the cannons flee; the soldiers of the artillery train unharness the caissons and use the horses to make their escape; wagons overturned, with all four wheels in the air, block the road and occasion massacres. Men are crushed, trampled down, others walk over the dead and the living. Arms are lost. A dizzy multitude fills the roads, the paths, the bridges, the plains, the hills, the valleys, the woods, encumbered by this invasion of forty thousand men. Shouts, despair, knapsacks and guns flung among the wheat, passages forced at the point of the sword, no more comrades, no more officers, no more generals, an indescribable terror. Zieten putting France to the sword at his leisure. Lions converted into goats. Such was the flight.

At Genappe, an effort was made to wheel about, to present a battle front, to draw up in line. Lobau rallied three hundred men. The entrance to the village was barricaded, but at the first volley of Prussian canister, all took to flight again, and Lobau was made prisoner. That volley of grape-shot can be seen to-day imprinted on the ancient gable of a brick building on the right of the road at a few minutes' distance before you reach Genappe. The Prussians threw themselves into Genappe, furious, no doubt, that they were not more entirely the conquerors. The pursuit was stupendous. Blücher ordered extermination. Roguet had set the lugubrious example of threatening with death any French grenadier who should bring him a Prussian prisoner. Blücher surpassed Roguet. Duchesme, the general of the Young Guard, hemmed in at the doorway of an inn at Genappe, surrendered his sword to a huzzar of death, who took the sword and slew the prisoner. The victory was completed by the assassination of the vanquished. Let us inflict punishment, since we are writing history; old Blücher disgraced himself. This ferocity put the finishing touch to the disaster. The desperate rout traversed Genappe, traversed Quatre Bras, traversed Gosselies, traversed Frasnes, traversed Charleroi, traversed Thuin, and only halted at the frontier. Alas! And who, then, was fleeing in that manner? The Grand Army.

This vertigo, this terror, this downfall into ruin of the highest bravery which ever astounded history,—is that causeless? No. The shadow of an enormous right is projected across Waterloo. It is the day of destiny. The force which is mightier than man produced that day. Hence the terrified wrinkle of those brows; hence all those great souls surrendering their swords. Those who had conquered Europe have fallen prone on the earth, with nothing left to say nor to do, feeling the present shadow of a terrible presence. *Hoc erat in fatis.* That day the perspective of the human race was changed. Waterloo is the hinge of the nineteenth century. The disappearance of the great man was necessary for the advent of the great age, and he, who cannot be answered, took the responsibility on himself. The panic of heroes can be explained. In the battle of Waterloo there is something more than a cloud, there is something of the meteor.

At nightfall, in a meadow near Genappe, Bernard and Bertrand seized by the skirt of his coat and detained a man, haggard, pensive, sinister, gloomy, who, dragged to that point by the current of the rout, had just dismounted, had passed the bridle of his horse over his arm, and with wild eye was returning alone to Waterloo. It was Napoleon, the immense somnambulist of this dream which had crumbled, trying once more to advance.

CHAPTER SIX

David Crockett: The Frontiersman
By John S. C. Abbott

"I am that same David Crockett, fresh from the backwoods, half horse, half alligator, a little touched with the snapping-turtle. I can wade the Mississippi, leap the Ohio, ride upon a streak of lightning, and slip without a scratch down a honey-locust. I can whip my weight in wildcats, and, if any gentleman pleases, for a ten-dollar bill he can throw in a panther. I can hug a bear too close for comfort, and eat any man opposed to General Jackson." Those are the words of an American legend, describing himself to a group of politicians. This chapter from Stephen Brennan's Classic American Hero Stories *will acquaint you with this frontiersman in detailed, colorful prose you will find more engaging than reading the dry facts of history.*

—LAMAR UNDERWOOD

CROCKETT WAS VERY FOND OF HUNTING-ADVENTURES, AND TOLD STORIES OF THESE enterprises in a racy way, peculiarly characteristic of the man. The following narrative from his own lips, the reader will certainly peruse with much interest.

"I was sitting by a good fire in my little cabin, on a cool November evening, roasting potatoes I believe, and playing with my children, when some one halloed at the fence. I went out, and there were three strangers, who said they come to take an elk-hunt. I was glad to see 'em, invited 'em in, and after supper we cleaned our guns. I took down old Betsey, rubbed her up, greased her, and laid her away to rest. She is a mighty rough old piece, but I love her, for she and I have seen hard times. She mighty seldom tells me a lie. If I hold her right, she always sends the ball where I tell her. After we were all fixed, I told 'em hunting-stories till bedtime.

"Next morning was clear and cold, and by times I sounded my horn, and my dogs came howling 'bout me, ready for a chase. Old Rattler was a little lame—a bear bit him in the shoulder; but Soundwell, Tiger, and the rest of 'em were all mighty anxious. We got a bite, and saddled our horses. I went by to git a neighbor to drive for us, and off we started for the *Harricane.* My dogs looked mighty wolfish; they kept jumping on one another and growling. I knew they were run mad for a fight, for they hadn't had one for two or three days. We were in fine spirits, and going 'long through very open woods, when one of the strangers said, 'I would give my horse now to see a bear.'

"Said I, 'Well, give me your horse,' and I pointed to an old bear, about three or four hundred yards ahead of us, feeding on acorns.

"I had been looking at him some time, but he was so far off; I wasn't certain what it was. However, I hardly spoke before we all strained off, and the woods fairly echoed as we harked the dogs on. The old bear didn't want to run, and he never broke till we got most upon him; but then he buckled for it, I tell you. When they overhauled him he just rared up on his hind legs, and he boxed the dogs 'bout at a mighty rate. He hugged old Tiger and another, till he dropped 'em nearly lifeless; but the others worried him, and after a while they all come to, and they give him trouble. They are mighty apt, I tell you, to give a bear trouble before they leave him.

"'Twas a mighty pretty fight—'twould have done any one's soul good to see it, just to see how they all rolled about. It was as much as I could do to keep the strangers from shooting him; but I wouldn't let 'em, for fear they would kill some of my dogs. After we got tired seeing 'em fight, I went in among 'em, and the first time they got him down I socked my knife in the old bear. We then hung him up, and went on to take our elk-hunt. You never seed fellows so delighted as them strangers was. Blow me, if they didn't cut more capers, jumping about, than the old bear. 'Twas a mighty pretty fight, but I believe I seed more fun looking at them than at the bear.

"By the time we got to the *Harricane,* we were all rested, and ripe for a drive. My dogs were in a better humor, for the fight had just taken off the wiry edge. So I placed the strangers at the stands through which I thought the elk would pass, sent the driver way up ahead, and I went down below.

"Everything was quiet, and I leaned old Betsey 'gin a tree, and laid down. I s'pose I had been lying there nearly an hour, when I heard old Tiger open. He opened once or twice, and old Rattler gave a long howl; the balance joined in, and I knew the elk were up. I jumped up and seized my rifle. I could hear nothing but one continued roar of all my dogs, coming right towards me. Though I was an old hunter, the music made my hair stand on end. Soon after they first started, I heard one gun go off, and my dogs stopped, but not long, for they took a little tack towards where I had placed the strangers. One of them fired, and they dashed back, and circled round way to my left. I run down 'bout a quarter of a mile, and I heard my dogs make a bend like they were coming to me. While I was listening, I heard the bushes breaking still lower down, and started to run there.

"As I was going 'long, I seed two elks burst out of the *Harricane* 'bout one hundred and thirty or forty yards below me. There was an old buck and a doe. I stopped, waited till they got into a clear place, and as the old fellow made a leap, I raised old Bet, pulled trigger, and she spoke out. The smoke blinded me so, that I couldn't see what I did; but as it cleared away, I caught a glimpse of only one of them going through the bushes; so I thought I had the other. I went up, and there lay the old buck kicking. I cut his throat, and by that time, Tiger and two of my dogs came up. I thought it singular that all my dogs wasn't there, and I began to think they had killed another. After the dogs had bit him, and found out he was dead, old Tiger began to growl, and curled himself up between his legs. Everything had to stand off then, for he wouldn't let the devil himself touch him.

"I started off to look for the strangers. My two dogs followed me. After gitting away a piece, I looked back, and once in a while I could see old Tiger git up and shake the elk, to see if he was really dead, and then curl up between his legs agin. I found the strangers round a doe elk the driver had killed; and one of 'em said he was sure he had killed one lower down. I asked him if he had horns. He said he didn't see any. I put the dogs on where he said he had shot, and they didn't go fur before they came to a halt. I went up, and there lay a fine buck elk; and though his horns were four or five feet long, the fellow who shot him was so scared that he never saw them. We had three elk, and a bear; and we managed to git it home, then butchered our game, talked over our hunt, and had a glorious frolic."

Crockett served in the Legislature for two years, during which time nothing occurred of special interest. These were the years of 1823 and 1824. Colonel Alexander was then the representative, in the National Legislature, of the district in which Crockett lived. He had offended his constituents by voting for the Tariff. It was proposed to run Crockett for Congress in opposition to him. Crockett says:

"I told the people that I could not stand that. It was a step above my knowledge; and I know'd nothing about Congress matters."

They persisted; but he lost the election; for cotton was very high, and Alexander urged that it was in consequence of the Tariff. Two years passed away, which Crockett spent in the wildest adventures of hunting. He was a true man of the woods with no ambition for any better home than the log cabin he occupied. There was no excitement so dear to him as the pursuit and capture of a grizzly bear. There is nothing on record, in the way of hunting, which surpasses the exploits of this renowned bear-hunter. But there is a certain degree of sameness in these narratives of skill and endurance which would weary the reader.

In the fall of 1825, Crockett built two large flat-boats, to load with staves for the making of casks, which he intended to take down the river to market. He employed a number of hands in building the boat and splitting out the staves, and engaged himself in these labors "till the bears got fat." He then plunged into the woods, and in two weeks killed fifteen. The whole winter was spent in hunting with his son and his dogs. His workmen continued busy getting the staves, and when the rivers rose with the spring floods, he had thirty thousand ready for the market.

With this load he embarked for New Orleans. His boats without difficulty floated down the Obion into the majestic Mississippi. It was the first time he had seen the rush of these mighty waters. There was before him a boat voyage of nearly fifteen hundred miles, through regions to him entirely unknown. In his own account of this adventure he writes:

"When I got into the Mississippi I found all my hands were bad scared. In fact, I believe I was scared a little the worst of any; for I had never been down the river, and I soon discovered that my pilot was as ignorant of the business as myself. I hadn't gone far before I determined to lash the two boats together. We did so; but it made them so heavy and obstinate that it was next akin to impossible to do any thing at all with them, or to guide them right in the river.

"That evening we fell in company with some Ohio boats, and about night we tried to land, but we could not. The Ohio men hollered to us to go on and run all night. We took their advice, though we had a good deal rather not. But we couldn't do any other way. In a short distance we got into what is called the Devil's Elbow. And if any place in the wide creation has its own proper name I thought it was this. Here we had about the hardest work that I was ever engaged in in my life, to keep out of danger. And even then we were in it all the while. We twice attempted to land at Wood Yards, which we could see, but couldn't reach.

"The people would run out with lights, and try to instruct us how to get to shore; but all in vain. Our boats were so heavy that we could not take them much any way except the way they wanted to go, and just the way the current would carry them. At last we quit trying to land, and concluded just to go ahead as well as we could, for we found we couldn't do any better.

"Some time in the night I was down in the cabin of one of the boats, sitting by the fire, thinking on what a hobble we had got into; and how much better bear-hunting was on hard land, than floating along on the water, when a fellow had to go ahead whether he was exactly willing or not. The hatch-way of the cabin came slap down, right through the top of the boat; and it was the only way out, except a small hole in the side which we had used for putting our arms through to dip up water before we lashed the boats together.

"We were now floating sideways, and the boat I was in was the hindmost as we went. All at once I heard the hands begin to run over the top of the boat in great confusion, and pull with all their might. And the first thing I know'd after this we went broadside full tilt against the head of an island, where a large raft of drift timber had lodged. The nature of such a place would be, as everybody knows, to suck the boats down and turn them right under this raft; and the uppermost boat would, of course, be suck'd down and go under first. As soon as we struck, I bulged for my hatchway, as the boat was turning under sure enough. But when I got to it, the water was pouring through in a current as large as the hole would let it, and as strong as the weight of the river would force it. I found I couldn't get out here, for the boat was now turned down in such a way that it was steeper than a house-top. I now thought of the hole in the side, and made my way in a hurry for that.

"With difficulty I got to it, and when I got there, I found it was too small for me to get out by my own power, and I began to think that I was in a worse box than ever. But I put my arms through, and hollered as loud as I could roar, as the boat I was in hadn't yet quite filled with water up to my head; and the hands who were next to the raft, seeing my arms out, and hearing me holler, seized them, and began to pull. I told them I was sinking, and to pull my arms off, or force me through, for now I know'd well enough it was neck or nothing, come out or sink.

"By a violent effort they jerked me through; but I was in a pretty pickle when I got through. I had been sitting without any clothing over my shirt; this was torn off, and I was literally skinn'd like a rabbit. I was, however, well pleased to get out in any way, even without shirt or hide; as before I could straighten myself on the boat next to the raft, the one they pull'd me out of went entirely under, and I have never seen it any more to this day. We all escaped on to the raft, where we were compelled to sit all night, about a mile from land on either side. Four of my company were bareheaded, and three bare-footed; and of that number I was one. I reckon I looked like a pretty cracklin ever to get to Congress!

"We had now lost all our loading, and every particle of our clothing, except what little we had on; but over all this, while I was sitting there, in the night, floating about on the drift, I felt happier and better off than I ever had in my life before, for I had just made such a marvellous escape, that I had forgot almost everything else in that; and so I felt prime.

"In the morning about sunrise, we saw a boat coming down, and we hailed her. They sent a large skiff, and took us all on board, and carried us down as far as Memphis. Here I met with a friend, that I never can forget as long as I am able to go ahead at anything; it was a Major Winchester, a merchant of that place; he let us all have hats, and shoes, and some little money to go upon, and so we all parted.

"A young man and myself concluded to go on down to Natchez, to see if we could hear anything of our boats; for we supposed they would float out from the raft, and keep on down the river. We got on a boat at Memphis, that was going down, and so cut out. Our largest boat, we were informed, had been seen about fifty miles below where we stove, and an attempt had been made to land her, but without success, as she was as hard-headed as ever.

"This was the last of my boats, and of my boating; for it went so badly with me along at the first, that I had not much mind to try it any more. I now returned home again, and, as the next August was the Congressional election, I began to turn my attention a little to that matter, as it was beginning to be talked of a good deal among the people."

Cotton was down very low. Crockett could now say to the people: "You see the effects of the Tariff." There were two rival candidates for the office, Colonel Alexander and General Arnold. Money was needed to carry the election, and Crockett had no money. He resolved, however, to try his chances. A friend loaned him a little money to start with; which sum Crockett, of course, expended in whiskey, as the most potent influence, then and there, to secure an election.

"So I was able," writes Crockett, "to buy a little of the 'creature,' to put my friends in a good humor, as well as the other gentlemen, for they all treat in that country; not to get elected, of course, for that would be against the law, but just to make themselves and their friends feel their keeping a little."

The contest was, as usual, made up of drinking, feasting, and speeches. Colonel Alexander was an intelligent and worthy man, who had been public surveyor. General Arnold was a lawyer of very respectable attainments. Neither of these men considered Crockett a candidate in the slightest degree to be feared. They only feared each other, and tried to circumvent each other.

On one occasion there was a large gathering, where all three of the candidates were present, and each one was expected to make a speech. It came Crockett's lot to speak first. He knew nothing of Congressional affairs, and had sense enough to be aware that it was not best for him to attempt to speak upon subjects of which he was entirely ignorant. He made one of his funny speeches, very short and entirely non-committal. Colonel Alexander followed, endeavoring to grapple with the great questions of tariffs, finance, and internal improvements, which were then agitating the nation.

General Arnold then, in his turn, took the stump, opposing the measures which Colonel Alexander had left. He seemed entirely to ignore the fact that Crockett was a candidate. Not the slightest allusion was made to him in his speech. The nervous temperament predominated in the man, and he was easily annoyed. While speaking, a large flock of guinea-hens came along, whose peculiar and noisy cry all will remember who have ever heard it. Arnold was greatly disturbed, and at last requested some one to drive the fowls away. As soon as he had finished his speech, Crockett again mounted the stump, and ostensibly addressing Arnold, but really addressing the crowd, said, in a loud voice, but very jocosely:

"Well, General, you are the first man I ever saw that understood the language of fowls. You had not the politeness even to allude to me in your speech. But when my little friends the guinea-hens came up, and began to holler 'Crockett, Crockett, Crockett,' you were ungenerous enough to drive them all away."

This raised such a universal laugh that even Crockett's opponents feared that he was getting the best of them in winning the favor of the people. When the day of election came, the popular bear-hunter beat both of his competitors by twenty-seven hundred and forty-seven votes. Thus David Crockett, unable to read and barely able to sign his name, became a member of Congress, to assist in framing laws for the grandest republic earth has ever known. He represented a constituency of about one hundred thousand souls.

An intelligent gentleman, travelling in West Tennessee, finding himself within eight miles of Colonel Crockett's cabin, decided to call upon the man whose name had now become quite renowned. This was just after Crockett's election to Congress, but before he had set out for Washington. There was no road leading to the lonely hut. He followed a rough and obstructed path or trail, which was indicated only by blazed trees, and which bore no marks of being often travelled.

At length he came to a small opening in the forest, very rude and uninviting in its appearance. It embraced eight or ten acres. One of the humblest and least tasteful of log huts stood in the centre. It was truly a cabin, a mere shelter from the weather. There was no yard; there were no fences. Not the slightest effort had been made toward ornamentation. It would be difficult to imagine a more lonely and cheerless abode.

Two men were seated on stools at the door, both in their shirt-sleeves, engaged in cleaning their rifles. As the stranger rode up, one of the men rose and came forward to meet him. He was dressed in very plain homespun attire, with a black fur cap upon his head. He was a finely proportioned man, about six feet high, apparently forty-five years of age, and of very frank, pleasing, open countenance. He held his rifle in his hand, and from his right shoulder hung a bag made of raccoon skin, to which there was a sheath attached containing a large butcher-knife.

"This is Colonel Crockett's residence, I presume," said the stranger.

"Yes," was the reply, with a smile as of welcome.

"Have I the pleasure of seeing that gentleman before me?" the stranger added.

"If it be a pleasure," was the courtly reply, "you have, sir."

"Well, Colonel," responded the stranger, "I have ridden much out of my way to spend a day or two with you, and take a hunt."

"Get down, sir," said the Colonel, cordially. "I am delighted to see you. I like to see strangers. And the only care I have is that I cannot accommodate them as well as I could wish. I have no corn, but my little boy will take your horse over to my son-in-law's. He is a good fellow, and will take care of him."

Leading the stranger into his cabin, Crockett very courteously introduced him to his brother, his wife, and his daughters. He then added:

"You see we are mighty rough here. I am afraid you will think it hard times. But we have to do the best we can. I started mighty poor, and have been rooting 'long ever since. But I hate apologies. What I live upon always, I think a friend can for a day or two. I have but little, but that little is as free as the water that runs. So make yourself at home."

Mrs. Crockett was an intelligent and capable woman for one in her station in life. The cabin was clean and orderly, and presented a general aspect of comfort. Many trophies of the chase were in the house, and spread around the yard. Several dogs, looking like war-worn veterans, were sunning themselves in various parts of the premises.

All the family were neatly dressed in homemade garments. Mrs. Crockett was a grave, dignified woman, very courteous to her guests. The daughters were remarkably pretty, but very diffident. Though entirely uneducated, they could converse very easily, seeming to inherit their father's fluency of utterance. They were active and efficient in aiding their mother in her household work. Colonel Crockett, with much apparent pleasure, conducted his guest over the small patch of ground he had grubbed and was cultivating. He exhibited his growing peas and pumpkins, and his little field of corn, with as much apparent pleasure as an Illinois farmer would now point out his hundreds of acres of waving grain. The hunter seemed surprisingly well informed. As we have mentioned, nature had endowed him with unusual strength of mind, and with a memory which was almost miraculous. He never forgot anything he had heard. His electioneering tours had been to him very valuable schools of education. Carefully he listened to all the speeches and the conversation of the intelligent men he met with.

John Quincy Adams was then in the Presidential chair. It was the year 1827. Nearly all Crockett's constituents were strong Jackson-men. Crockett, who afterward opposed Jackson, subsequently said, speaking of his views at that time:

"I can say on my conscience, that I was, without disguise, the friend and supporter of General Jackson upon his principles, as he had laid them down, and as I understood them, before his election as President."

Alluding to Crockett's political views at that time, his guest writes, "I held in high estimation the present Administration of our country. To this he was opposed. His views, however, delighted me. And were they more generally adopted we should be none the loser. He was opposed to the Administration, and yet conceded that many of its acts were wise and efficient, and would have received his cordial support. He admired Mr. Clay, but had objections to him. He was opposed to the Tariff, yet, I think, a supporter of the United States Bank. He seemed to have the most horrible objection to binding himself to any man or set of men. He said, 'I would as lieve be an old coon-dog as obliged to do what any man or set of men would tell me to do. I will support the present Administration as far as I would any other; that is, as far as I believe its views to be right. I will pledge myself to support no Administration. I had rather be politically damned than hypocritically immortalized.'"

In the winter of 1827, Crockett emerged from his cabin in the wilderness for a seat in Congress. He was so poor that he had not money enough to pay his expenses to Washington. His election had cost him one hundred and fifty dollars, which a friend had loaned him. The same friend advanced one hundred dollars more to help him on his journey.

"When I left home," he says, "I was happy, devilish, and full of fun. I bade adieu to my friends, dogs, and rifle, and took the stage, where I met with much variety of character, and amused myself when my humor prompted. Being fresh from the backwoods, my stories amused my companions, and I passed my time pleasantly.

"When I arrived at Raleigh the weather was cold and rainy, and we were all dull and tired. Upon going into the tavern, where I was an entire stranger, the room was crowded, and the crowd did not give way that I might come to the fire. I was rooting my way to the fire, not in a good humor, when some fellow staggered up towards me, and cried out, 'Hurrah for Adams.'

"Said I, 'Stranger, you had better hurrah for hell, and praise your own country.'

"'And who are you?' said he. I replied:

"'I am that same David Crockett, fresh from the backwoods, half horse, half alligator, a little touched with the snapping-turtle. I can wade the Mississippi, leap the Ohio, ride upon a streak of lightning, and slip without a scratch down a honey-locust. I can whip my weight in wildcats, and, if any gentleman pleases, for a ten-dollar bill he can throw in a panther. I can hug a bear too close for comfort, and eat any man opposed to General Jackson.'"

All eyes were immediately turned toward this strange man, for all had heard of him. A place was promptly made for him at the fire. He was afterward asked if this wondrous outburst of slang was entirely unpremeditated. He said that it was; that it had all popped into his head at once; and that he should never have thought of it again, had not the story gone the round of the newspapers.

"I came on to Washington," he says, "and drawed two hundred and fifty dollars, and purchased with it a check on the bank in Nashville, and enclosed it to my friend. And I may say, in truth, I sent this money with a mighty good will, for I reckon nobody in this world loves a friend better than me, or remembers a kindness longer."

Soon after his arrival at Washington he was invited to dine with President Adams, a man of the highest culture, whose manners had been formed in the courts of Europe. Crockett, totally unacquainted with the usages of society, did not know what the note of invitation meant, and inquired of a friend, the Hon. Mr. Verplanck. He says:

"I was wild from the backwoods, and didn't know nothing about eating dinner with the big folks of our country. And how should I, having been a hunter all my life? I had eat most of my dinners on a log in the woods, and sometimes no dinner at all. I knew, whether I ate dinner with the President or not was a matter of no importance, for my constituents were not to be benefited by it. I did not go to court the President, for I was opposed to him in principle, and had no favors to ask at his hands. I was afraid, however, I should be awkward, as I was so entirely a stranger to fashion; and in going along, I resolved to observe the conduct of my friend Mr. Verplanck, and to do as he did. And I know that I did behave myself right well."

Some cruel wag wrote the following ludicrous account of this dinner-party, which went the round of all the papers as veritable history. The writer pretended to quote Crockett's own account of the dinner.

"The first thing I did," said Davy, "after I got to Washington, was to go to the President's. I stepped into the President's house. Thinks I, who's afeard. If I didn't, I wish I may be shot. Says I, 'Mr. Adams, I am Mr. Crockett, from Tennessee.' So, says he, 'How d'ye do, Mr. Crockett?' And he shook me by the hand, although he know'd I went the whole hog for Jackson. If he didn't, I wish I may be shot.

"Not only that, but he sent me a printed ticket to dine with him. I've got it in my pocket yet. I went to dinner, and I walked all around the long table, looking for something that I liked. At last I took my seat beside a fat goose, and I helped myself to as much of it as I wanted. But I hadn't took three bites, when I looked away up the table at a man they called *Tash* (attaché). He was talking French to a woman on t'other side of the table. He dodged his head and she dodged hers, and then they got to drinking wine across the table.

"But when I looked back again my plate was gone, goose and all. So I jist cast my eyes down to t'other end of the table, and sure enough I seed a white man walking off with my plate. I says, 'Hello, mister, bring back my plate.' He fetched it back in a hurry, as you may think. And when he set it down before me, how do you think it was? Licked as clean as my hand. If it wasn't, I wish I may be shot!

"Says he, 'What will you have, sir?' And says I, 'You may well say that, after stealing my goose.' And he began to laugh. Then says I, 'Mister, laugh if you please; but I don't half-like sich tricks upon travellers.' I then filled my plate with bacon and greens. And whenever I looked up or down the table, I held on to my plate with my left hand.

"When we were all done eating, they cleared everything off the table, and took away the table-cloth. And what do you think? There was another cloth under it. If there wasn't, I wish I may be shot! Then I saw a man coming along carrying a great glass thing, with a glass handle below, something like a candlestick. It was stuck full of little glass cups, with something in them that looked good to eat. Says I, 'Mister, bring that thing here.' Thinks I, let's taste them first. They were mighty sweet and good, so I took six of them. If I didn't, I wish I may be shot!"

This humorous fabrication was copied into almost every paper in the Union. The more respectable portion of Crockett's constituents were so annoyed that their representative should be thus held up to the contempt of the nation, that Crockett felt constrained to present a reliable refutation of the story. He therefore obtained and published certificates from three gentlemen, testifying to his good behavior at the table. Hon. Mr. Verplanck, of New York, testified as follows:

"I dined at the President's, at the time alluded to, in company with you, and I had, I recollect, a good deal of conversation with you. Your behavior there was, I thought, perfectly becoming and proper. And I do not recollect, or believe, that you said or did anything resembling the newspaper account."

Two other members of Congress were equally explicit in their testimony.

During Crockett's first two sessions in Congress he got along very smoothly, cooperating generally with what was called the Jackson party. In 1829 he was again reelected by an overwhelming majority. On the 4th of March of this year, Andrew Jackson was inaugurated President of the United States. It may be doubted whether there ever was a more honest, conscientious man in Congress than David Crockett. His celebrated motto, "Be sure that you are right, and then go ahead," seemed ever to animate him. He could neither be menaced or bribed to support any measure which he thought to be wrong. Ere long he found it necessary to oppose some of Jackson's measures. We will let him tell the story in his own truthful words:

"Soon after the commencement of this second term, I saw, or thought I did, that it was expected of me that I would bow to the name of Andrew Jackson, and follow him in all his motions, and windings, and turnings, even at the expense of my conscience and judgment. Such a thing was new to me, and a total stranger to my principles. I know'd well enough, though, that if I didn't 'hurrah' for his name, the hue and cry was to be raised against me, and I was to be sacrificed, if possible. His famous, or rather I should say his *infamous* Indian bill was brought forward, and I opposed it from the purest motives in the world. Several of my colleagues got around me, and told me how well they loved me, and that I was ruining myself. They said this was a favorite measure of the President, and I ought to go for it. I told them I believed it was a wicked, unjust measure, and that I should go against it, let the cost to myself be what it might; that I was willing to go with General Jackson in everything that I believed was honest and right; but, further than this, I wouldn't go for him or any other man in the whole creation.

"I had been elected by a majority of three thousand five hundred and eighty-five votes, and I believed they were honest men, and wouldn't want me to vote for any unjust notion, to please Jackson or any one else; at any rate, I was of age, and determined to trust them. I voted against this Indian bill, and my conscience yet tells me that I gave a good, honest vote, and one that I believe will not make me ashamed in the day of judgment. I served out my term, and though many amusing things happened, I am not disposed to swell my narrative by inserting them.

"When it closed, and I returned home, I found the storm had raised against me sure enough; and it was echoed from side to side, and from end to end of my district, that I had turned against Jackson. This was considered the unpardonable sin. I was hunted down like a wild varment, and in this hunt every little newspaper in the district, and every little pinhook lawyer was engaged. Indeed, they were ready to print anything and everything that the ingenuity of man could invent against me."

In consequence of this opposition, Crockett lost his next election, and yet by a majority of but seventy votes. For two years he remained at home hunting bears. But having once tasted the pleasures of political life, and the excitements of Washington, his silent rambles in the woods had lost much of their ancient charms. He was again a candidate at the ensuing election, and, after a very warm contest gained the day by a majority of two hundred and two votes.

Colonel Crockett, having been reelected again repaired to Washington. During the session, to complete his education, and the better to prepare himself as a legislator for the whole nation, he decided to take a short trip to the North and the East. His health had also begun to fail, and his physicians advised him to go. He was thoroughly acquainted with the Great West. With his rifle upon his shoulder, in the Creek War, he had made wide explorations through the South. But the North and the East were regions as yet unknown to him.

On the 25th of April, 1834, he left Washington for this Northern tour. He reached Baltimore that evening, where he was invited to a supper by some of the leading gentlemen. He writes:

"Early next morning, I started for Philadelphia, a place where I had never been. I sort of felt lonesome as I went down to the steamboat. The idea of going among a new people, where there are tens of thousands who would pass me by without knowing or caring who I was, who are all taken up with their own pleasures or their own business, made me feel small; and, indeed, if any one who reads this book has a grand idea of his own importance, let him go to a big city, and he will find that he is not higher valued than a coonskin.

"The steamboat was the *Carroll* of Carrollton, a fine craft, with the rum old Commodore Chaytor for head man. A good fellow he is—all sorts of a man—bowing and scraping to the ladies, nodding to the gentlemen, cursing the crew, and his right eye broad-cast upon the 'opposition line,' all at the same time. 'Let go!' said the old one, and off we walked in prime style.

"Our passage down Chesapeake Bay was very pleasant. In a very short run we came to a place where we were to get on board the rail-cars. This was a clean new sight to me. About a dozen big stages hung on to one machine. After a good deal of fuss we all got seated and moved slowly off; the engine wheezing as though she had the tizzic. By-and-by, she began to take short breaths, and away we went, with a blue streak after us. The whole distance is seventeen miles. It was run in fifty-five minutes.

"At Delaware City, I again embarked on board of a splendid steamboat. When dinner was ready, I set down with the rest of the passengers. Among them was Rev. O. B. Brown, of the Post-Office Department, who sat near me. During dinner he ordered a bottle of wine, and called upon me for a toast. Not knowing whether he intended to compliment me, or abash me among so many strangers, or have some fun at my expense, I concluded to go ahead, and give him and his like a blizzard. So our glasses being filled, the word went round, 'A toast from Colonel Crockett.' I give it as follows: 'Here's wishing the bones of tyrant kings may answer in hell, in place of gridirons, to roast the souls of Tories on.' At this the parson appeared as if he was stumpt. I said, 'Never heed; it was meant for where it belonged.' He did not repeat his invitation, and I eat my dinner quietly.

"After dinner I went up on the deck, and saw the captain hoisting three flags. Says I, 'What does that mean?' He replied, that he was under promise to the citizens of Philadelphia, if I was on board, to hoist his flags, as a friend of mine had said he expected I would be along soon.

"We went on till we came in sight of the city and as we advanced towards the wharf, I saw the whole face of the earth covered with people, all anxiously looking on towards the boat. The captain and myself were standing on the bow-deck; he pointed his finger at me, and people slung their hats, and huzzaed for Colonel Crockett. It struck me with astonishment to hear a strange people huzzaing for me, and made me feel sort of queer. It took me so uncommon unexpected, as I had no idea of attracting attention. But I had to meet it, and so I stepped on to the wharf, where the folks came crowding around me, saying, 'Give me the hand of an honest man.' I did not know what all this meant: but some gentleman took hold of me, and pressing through the crowd, put me into an elegant barouche, drawn by four fine horses; they then told me to bow to the people: I did so, and with much difficulty we moved off. The streets were crowded to a great distance, and the windows full of people, looking out, I suppose, to see the wild man. I thought I had rather be in the wilderness with my gun and dogs, than to be attracting all that fuss. I had never seen the like before, and did not know exactly what to say or do. After some time we reached the United States Hotel, in Chesnut Street.

"The crowd had followed me filling up the street, and pressing into the house to shake hands. I was conducted up stairs, and walked out on a platform, drew off my hat, and bowed round to the people. They cried out from all quarters, 'A speech, a speech, Colonel Crockett.'

"After the noise had quit, so I could be heard, I said to them the following words:

"'Gentlemen of Philadelphia:

"'My visit to your city is rather accidental. I had no expectation of attracting any uncommon attention. I am travelling for my health, without the least wish of exciting the people in such times of high political feeling. I do not wish to encourage it. I am unable at this time to find language suitable to return my gratitude to the citizens of Philadelphia. However, I am almost induced to believe it flattery—perhaps a burlesque. This is new to me, yet I see nothing but friendship in your faces; and if your curiosity is to hear the backwoodsman, I will assure you I am illy prepared to address this most enlightened people. However, gentlemen, if this is a curiosity to you, if you will meet me to-morrow, at one o'clock, I will endeavor to address you, in my plain manner.'

"So I made my obeisance to them, and retired into the house."

It is true that there was much of mere curiosity in the desire to see Colonel Crockett. He was a strange and an incomprehensible man. His manly, honest course in Congress had secured much respect. But such developments of character as were shown in his rude and vulgar toast, before a party of gentlemen and ladies, excited astonishment. His notoriety preceded him, wherever he went; and all were alike curious to see so strange a specimen of a man.

The next morning, several gentlemen called upon him, and took him in a carriage to see the various objects of interest in the city. The gentlemen made him a present of a rich seal, representing two horses at full speed, with the words, "Go Ahead." The young men also made him a present of a truly magnificent rifle. From Philadelphia he went to New York. The shipping astonished him. "They beat me all hollow," he says, "and looked for all the world like a big clearing in the West, with the dead trees all standing."

There was a great crowd upon the wharf to greet him. And when the captain of the boat led him conspicuously forward, and pointed him out to the multitude, the cheering was tremendous. A committee conducted him to the American Hotel, and treated him with the greatest distinction. Again he was fêted, and loaded with the greatest attentions. He was invited to a very splendid supper, got up in his honor, at which there were a hundred guests. The Hon. Judge Clayton, of Georgia, was present, and make a speech which, as Crockett says, fairly made the tumblers hop.

Crockett was then called up, as the "undeviating supporter of the Constitution and the laws." In response to this toast, he says,

"I made a short speech, and concluded with the story of the red cow, which was, that as long as General Jackson went straight, I followed him; but when he began to go this way, and that way, and every way, I wouldn't go after him; like the boy whose master ordered him to plough across the field to the red cow. Well, he began to plough, and she began to walk; and he ploughed all forenoon after her. So when the master came, he swore at him for going so crooked. 'Why, sir,' said the boy, 'you told me to plough to the red cow, and I kept after her, but she always kept moving.'"

His trip to New York was concluded by his visiting Jersey City to witness a shooting-match with rifles. He was invited to try his hand. Standing, at the distance of one hundred and twenty feet, he fired twice, striking very near the centre of the mark. Some one then put up a quarter of a dollar in the midst of a black spot, and requested him to shoot at it. The bullet struck the coin, and as Crockett says "made slight-of-hand work with it."

From New York he went to Boston. There, as the opponent of some of President Jackson's measures which were most offensive to the New England people, he was fêted with extraordinary enthusiasm. He dined and supped, made speeches, which generally consisted of but one short anecdote, and visited nearly all the public institutions.

Just before this, Andrew Jackson had received from Harvard University the honorary title of LL.D. Jackson was no longer a favorite of Crockett. The new distinguished guest, the renowned bear-hunter, was in his turn invited to visit Harvard. He writes:

"There were some gentlemen that invited me to go to Cambridge, where the big college or university is, where they keep ready-made titles or nick-names to give people. I would not go, for I did not know but they might stick an LL.D. on me before they let me go; and I had no idea of changing 'Member of the House of Representatives of the United States,' for what stands for 'lazy, lounging dunce,' which I am sure my constituents would have translated my new title to be. Knowing that I had never taken any degree, and did not own to any—except a small degree of good sense not to pass for what I was not—I would not go it. There had been one doctor made from Tennessee already, and I had no wish to put on the cap and bells.

"I told them that I did not go to this branding school; I did not want to be tarred with the same stick; one dignitary was enough from Tennessee; that as far as my learning went, I would stand over it, and spell a strive or two with any of them, from *a-b-ab* to *crucifix*, which was where I left off at school."

A gentleman, at a dinner-party, very earnestly invited Crockett to visit him. He returned the compliment by saying:

"If you ever come to my part of the country, I hope you will call and see me."

"And how shall I find where you live?" the gentleman inquired.

"Why, sir," Crockett answered, "run down the Mississippi till you come to the Obion River. Run a small streak up that; jump ashore anywhere, and inquire for me."

From Boston, he went to Lowell. The hospitality he had enjoyed in Boston won his warmest commendation. At Lowell, he was quite charmed by the aspect of wealth, industry, and comfort which met his eye. Upon his return to Boston, he spent the evening, with several gentlemen and ladies at the pleasant residence of Lieutenant-Governor Armstrong. In reference to this visit, he writes:

"This was my last night in Boston, and I am sure, if I never see the place again, I never can forget the kind and friendly manner in which I was treated by them. It appeared to me that everybody was anxious to serve me, and make my time agreeable. And as a proof that comes home—when I called for my bill next morning, I was told there was no charge to be paid by me, and that he was very much delighted that I had made his house my home. I forgot to mention that they treated me so in Lowell—but it is true. This was, to me, at all events, proof enough of Yankee liberality; and more than they generally get credit for. In fact, from the time I entered New England, I was treated with the greatest friendship; and, I hope, never shall forget it; and I wish all who read this book, and who never were there, would take a trip among them. If they don't learn how to make money, they will know how to use it; and if they don't learn industry, they will see how comfortable everybody can be that turns his hands to some employment."

Crockett was not a mere joker. He was an honest man, and an earnest man; and under the tuition of Congress had formed some very decided political principles, which he vigorously enforced with his rude eloquence.

When he first went to Congress he was merely a big boy, of very strong mind, but totally uninformed, and uncultivated. He very rapidly improved under the tuition of Congress; and in some degree awoke to the consciousness of his great intellectual imperfections. Still he was never diffident. He closed one of his off-hand after-dinner speeches in Boston, by saying:

"Gentlemen of Boston, I come here as a private citizen, to see you, and not to show myself. I had no idea of attracting attention. But I feel it my duty to thank you, with my gratitude to you, and with a gratitude to all who have given a plain man, like me, so kind a reception. I come from a great way off. But I shall never repent of having been persuaded to come here, and get a knowledge of your ways, which I can carry home with me. We only want to do away prejudice and give the people information.

"I hope, gentlemen, you will excuse my plain, unvarnished ways, which may seem strange to you here. I never had but six months' schooling in all my life. And I confess, I consider myself a poor tyke to be here addressing the most intelligent people in the world. But I think it the duty of every representative of the people, when he is called upon, to give his opinions. And I have tried to give you a little touch of mine."

Crockett returned to Washington just in time to be present at the closing scenes, and then set out for home. So much had been said of him in the public journals, of his speeches and his peculiarities, that his renown now filled the land . . .

Crockett's return to his home was a signal triumph all the way. At Baltimore, Philadelphia, Pittsburgh, Cincinnati, Louisville, crowds gathered to greet him. He was feasted, received presents, was complimented, and was incessantly called upon for a speech. He was an earnest student as he journeyed along. A new world of wonders were opening before him. Thoughts which he never before had dreamed of were rushing into his mind. His eyes were ever watchful to see all that was worthy of note. His ear was ever listening for every new idea. He scarcely ever looked at the printed page, but perused with the utmost diligence the book of nature. His comments upon what he saw indicate much sagacity.

At Cincinnati and Louisville, immense crowds assembled to hear him. In both places he spoke quite at length. And all who heard him were surprised at the power he displayed. Though his speech was rude and unpolished, the clearness of his views, and the intelligence he manifested, caused the journals generally to speak of him in quite a different strain from that which they had been accustomed to use. Probably never did a man make so much intellectual progress, in the course of a few months, as David Crockett had made in that time. His wonderful memory of names, dates, facts, all the intricacies of statistics, was such, that almost any statesman might be instructed by his addresses, and not many men could safely encounter him in argument. The views he presented upon the subject of the Constitution, finance, internal improvements, etc., were very surprising, when one considers the limited education he had enjoyed. At the close of these agitating scenes he touchingly writes:

"In a short time I set out for my own home; yes, my own home, my own soil, my humble dwelling, my own family, my own hearts, my ocean of love and affection, which neither circumstances nor time can dry up. Here, like the wearied bird, let me settle down for a while, and shut out the world."

But hunting bears had lost its charms for Crockett. He had been so flattered that it is probable that he fully expected to be chosen President of the United States. There were two great parties then dividing the country, the Democrats and the Whigs. The great object of each was to find an *available* candidate, no matter how unfit for the office. The leaders wished to elect a President who would be, like the Queen of England, merely the ornamental figure-head of the ship of state, while their energies should propel and guide the majestic fabric. For a time some few thought it possible that in the popularity of the great bear-hunter such a candidate might be found.

Crockett, upon his return home, resumed his deerskin leggins, his fringed hunting-shirt, his fox-skin cap, and shouldering his rifle, plunged, as he thought, with his original zest, into the cheerless, tangled, marshy forest which surrounded him. But the excitements of Washington, the splendid entertainments of Philadelphia, New York, and Boston, the flattery, the speech-making, which to him, with his marvellous memory and his wonderful fluency of speech, was as easy as breathing, the applause showered upon him, and the gorgeous vision of the Presidency looming up before him, engrossed his mind. He sauntered listlessly through the forest, his bear-hunting energies all paralyzed. He soon grew very weary of home and of all its employments, and was eager to return to the infinitely higher excitements of political life.

General Jackson was then almost idolized by his party. All through the South and West his name was a tower of strength. Crockett had originally been elected as a Jackson-man. He had abandoned the Administration, and was now one of the most inveterate opponents of Jackson. The majority in Crockett's district were in favor of Jackson. The time came for a new election of a representative. Crockett made every effort, in his old style, to secure the vote. He appeared at the gatherings in his garb as a bear-hunter, with his rifle on his shoulder. He brought 'coonskins to buy whiskey to treat his friends. A 'coonskin in the currency of that country was considered the equivalent for twenty-five cents. He made funny speeches. But it was all in vain.

Greatly to his surprise, and still more to his chagrin, he lost his election. He was beaten by two hundred and thirty votes. The whole powerful influence of the Government was exerted against Crockett and in favor of his competitor. It is said that large bribes were paid for votes. Crockett wrote, in a strain which reveals the bitterness of his disappointment:

"I am gratified that I have spoken the truth to the people of my district, regardless of the consequences. I would not be compelled to bow down to the idol for a seat in Congress during life. I have never known what it was to sacrifice my own judgment to gratify any party; and I have no doubt of the time being close at hand when I shall be rewarded for letting my tongue speak what my heart thinks. I have suffered myself to be politically sacrificed to save my country from ruin and disgrace; and if I am never again elected, I will have the gratification to know that I have done my duty. I may add, in the words of the man in the play, 'Crockett's occupation's gone.'"

Two weeks after this he writes, "I confess the thorn still rankles, not so much on my own account as the nation's. As my country no longer requires my services, I have made up my mind to go to Texas. My life has been one of danger, toil, and privation. But these difficulties I had to encounter at a time when I considered it nothing more than right good sport to surmount them. But now I start upon my own hook, and God only grant that it may be strong enough to support the weight that may be hung upon it. I have a new row to hoe, a long and rough one; but come what will, I will go ahead."

Just before leaving for Texas, he attended a political meeting of his constituents. The following extract from his autobiography will give the reader a very vivid idea of his feelings at the time, and of the very peculiar character which circumstances had developed in him:

"A few days ago I went to a meeting of my constituents. My appetite for politics was at one time just about as sharp set as a saw-mill, but late events have given me something of a surfeit, more than I could well digest; still, habit, they say, is second nature, and so I went, and gave them a piece of my mind touching 'the Government' and the succession, by way of a codicil to what I have often said before.

"I told them, moreover, of my services, pretty straight up and down, for a man may be allowed to speak on such subjects when others are about to forget them; and I also told them of the manner in which I had been knocked down and dragged out, and that I did not consider it a fair fight anyhow they could fix it. I put the ingredients in the cup pretty strong I tell you, and I concluded my speech by telling them that I was done with politics for the present, and that they might all go to hell, and I would go to Texas."

<hr />

A party of American adventurers, then called filibusters, had gone into Texas, in the endeavor to wrest that immense and beautiful territory, larger than the whole Empire of France, from feeble, distracted, miserable Mexico, to which it belonged. These filibusters were generally the most worthless and desperate vagabonds to be found in all the Southern States. Many Southern gentlemen of wealth and ability, but strong advocates of slavery, were in cordial sympathy with this movement, and aided it with their purses, and in many other ways. It was thought that if Texas could be wrested from Mexico and annexed to the United States, it might be divided into several slaveholding States, and thus check the rapidly increasing preponderance of the free States of the North.

To join in this enterprise, Crockett now left his home, his wife, his children. There could be no doubt of the eventual success of the undertaking. And in that success Crockett saw visions of political glory opening before him. I determined, he said, "to quit the States until such time as honest and independent men should again work their way to the head of the heap. And as I should probably have some idle time on hand before that state of affairs would be brought about, I promised to give the Texans a helping hand on the high road to freedom."

He dressed himself in a new deerskin hunting-shirt, put on a foxskin cap with the tail hanging behind, shouldered his famous rifle, and cruelly leaving in the dreary cabin his wife and children whom he cherished with an "ocean of love and affection," set out on foot upon his perilous adventure. A day's journey through the forest brought him to the Mississippi River. Here he took a steamer down that majestic stream to the mouth of the Arkansas River, which rolls its vast flood from regions then quite unexplored in the far West. The stream was navigable fourteen hundred miles from its mouth.

Arkansas was then but a Territory, two hundred and forty miles long and two hundred and twenty-eight broad. The sparsely scattered population of the Territory amounted to but about thirty thousand. Following up the windings of the river three hundred miles, one came to a cluster of a few straggling huts, called Little Rock, which constitutes now the capital of the State.

Crockett ascended the river in the steamer, and, unencumbered with baggage, save his rifle, hastened to a tavern which he saw at a little distance from the shore, around which there was assembled quite a crowd of men. He had been so accustomed to public triumphs that he supposed that they had assembled in honor of his arrival. "Strange as it may seem," he says, "they took no more notice of me than if I had been Dick Johnson, the wool-grower. This took me somewhat aback;" and he inquired what was the meaning of the gathering.

He found that the people had been called together to witness the feats of a celebrated juggler and gambler. The name of Colonel Crockett had gone through the nation; and gradually it became noised abroad that Colonel Crockett was in the crowd. "I wish I may be shot," Crockett says, "if I wasn't looked upon as almost as great a sight as Punch and Judy."

He was invited to a public dinner that very day. As it took some time to cook the dinner, the whole company went to a little distance to shoot at a mark. All had heard of Crockett's skill. After several of the best sharpshooters had fired, with remarkable accuracy, it came to Crockett's turn. Assuming an air of great carelessness, he raised his beautiful rifle, which he called Betsey, to his shoulder, fired, and it so happened that the bullet struck exactly in the centre of the bull's-eye. All were astonished, and so was Crockett himself. But with an air of much indifference he turned upon his heel, saying, "There's no mistake in Betsey."

One of the best marksmen in those parts, chagrined at being so beaten, said, "Colonel, that must have been a chance shot."

"I can do it," Crockett replied, "five times out of six, any day in the week."

"I knew," he adds, in his autobiography, "it was not altogether as correct as it might be; but when a man sets about going the big figure, halfway measures won't answer no how."

It was now proposed that there should be a second trial. Crockett was very reluctant to consent to this, for he had nothing to gain, and everything to lose. But they insisted so vehemently that he had to yield. As what ensued does not redound much to his credit, we will let him tell the story in his own language.

"So to it again we went. They were now put upon their mettle, and they fired much better than the first time; and it was what might be called pretty sharp shooting. When it came to my turn, I squared myself, and turning to the prime shot, I gave him a knowing nod, by way of showing my confidence; and says I, 'Look out for the bull's-eye, stranger.' I blazed away, and I wish I may be shot if I didn't miss the target. They examined it all over, and could find neither hair nor hide of my bullet, and pronounced it a dead miss; when says I, 'Stand aside and let me look, and I warrant you I get on the right trail of the critter,' They stood aside, and I examined the bull's-eye pretty particular, and at length cried out, 'Here it is; there is no snakes if it ha'n't followed the very track of the other.' They said it was utterly impossible, but I insisted on their searching the hole, and I agreed to be stuck up as a mark myself, if they did not find two bullets there. They searched for my satisfaction, and sure enough it all come out just as I had told them; for I had picked up a bullet that had been fired, and stuck it deep into the hole, without any one perceiving it. They were all perfectly satisfied that fame had not made too great a flourish of trumpets when speaking of me as a marksman: and they all said they had enough of shooting for that day, and they moved that we adjourn to the tavern and liquor."

The dinner consisted of bear's meat, venison, and wild turkey. They had an "uproarious" time over their whiskey. Crockett made a coarse and vulgar speech, which was neither creditable to his head nor his heart. But it was received with great applause.

The next morning Crockett decided to set out to cross the country in a southwest direction, to Fulton, on the upper waters of the Red River. The gentlemen furnished Crockett with a fine horse, and five of them decided to accompany him, as a mark of respect, to the River Washita, fifty miles from Little Rock. Crockett endeavored to raise some recruits for Texas, but was unsuccessful. When they reached the Washita, they found a clergyman, one of those bold, hardy pioneers of the wilderness, who through the wildest adventures were distributing tracts and preaching the gospel in the remotest hamlets.

He was in a condition of great peril. He had attempted to ford the river in the wrong place, and had reached a spot where he could not advance any farther, and yet could not turn his horse round. With much difficulty they succeeded in extricating him, and in bringing him safe to the shore. Having bid adieu to his kind friends, who had escorted him thus far, Crockett crossed the river, and in company with the clergyman continued his journey, about twenty miles farther west toward a little settlement called Greenville. He found his new friend to be a very charming companion. In describing the ride, Crockett writes:

"We talked about politics, religion, and nature, farming, and bear-hunting, and the many blessings that an all-bountiful Providence has bestowed upon our happy country. He continued to talk upon this subject, travelling over the whole ground as it were, until his imagination glowed, and his soul became full to overflowing; and he checked his horse, and I stopped mine also, and a stream of eloquence burst forth from his aged lips, such as I have seldom listened to: it came from the overflowing fountain of a pure and grateful heart. We were alone in the wilderness, but as he proceeded, it seemed to me as if the tall trees bent their tops to listen; that the mountain stream laughed out joyfully as it bounded on like some living thing that the fading flowers of autumn smiled, and sent forth fresher fragrance, as if conscious that they would revive in spring; and even the sterile rocks seemed to be endued with some mysterious influence. We were alone in the wilderness, but all things told me that God was there. The thought renewed my strength and courage. I had left my country, felt somewhat like an outcast, believed that I had been neglected and lost sight of. But I was now conscious that there was still one watchful Eye over me; no matter whether I dwelt in the populous cities, or threaded the pathless forest alone; no matter whether I stood in the high places among men, or made my solitary lair in the untrodden wild, that Eye was still upon me. My very soul leaped joyfully at the thought. I never felt so grateful in all my life. I never loved my God so sincerely in all my life. I felt that I still had a friend.

"When the old man finished, I found that my eyes were wet with tears. I approached and pressed his hand, and thanked him, and says I, 'Now let us take a drink.' I set him the example, and he followed it, and in a style too that satisfied me, that if he had ever belonged to the temperance society, he had either renounced membership, or obtained a dispensation. Having liquored, we proceeded on our journey, keeping a sharp lookout for mill-seats and plantations as we rode along.

"I left the worthy old man at Greenville, and sorry enough I was to part with him, for he talked a great deal, and he seemed to know a little about everything. He knew all about the history of the country; was well acquainted with all the leading men; knew where all the good lands lay in most of Western States.

"He was very cheerful and happy, though to all appearances very poor. I thought that he would make a first-rate agent for taking up lands, and mentioned it to him. He smiled, and pointing above, said, 'My wealth lies not in this world.'"

From Greenville, Crockett pressed on about fifty or sixty miles through a country interspersed with forests and treeless prairies, until he reached Fulton. He had a letter of introduction to one of the prominent gentlemen here, and was received with marked distinction. After a short visit he disposed of his horse; he took a steamer to descend the river several hundred miles to Natchitoches, pronounced Nakitosh, a small straggling village of eight hundred inhabitants, on the right bank of the Red River, about two hundred miles from its entrance into the Mississippi.

In descending the river there was a juggler on board, who performed many skilful juggling tricks. and by various feats of gambling won much money from his dupes. Crockett was opposed to gambling in all its forms. Becoming acquainted with the juggler and, finding him at heart a well-meaning, good-natured fellow, he endeavored to remonstrate with him upon his evil practices.

"I told him," says Crockett, "that it was a burlesque on human nature, that an able-bodied man, possessed of his full share of good sense, should voluntarily debase himself, and be indebted for subsistence to such a pitiful artifice.

"'But what's to be done, Colonel?' says he. 'I'm in the slough of despond, up to the very chin. A miry and slippery path to travel.'"

"'Then hold your head up,' says I, 'before the slough reaches your lips.'"

"'But what's the use?' says he: 'it's utterly impossible for me to wade through; and even if I could, I should be in such a dirty plight, that it would defy all the waters in the Mississippi to wash me clean again. No,' he added in a desponding tone, 'I should be like a live eel in a frying-pan, Colonel, sort of out of my element, if I attempted to live like an honest man at this time o' day.'"

"'That I deny. It is never too late to become honest,' said I. 'But even admit what you say to be true—that you cannot live like an honest man—you have at least the next best thing in your power, and no one can say nay to it.'

"And what is that?'"

"Die like a brave one. And I know not whether, in the eyes of the world, a brilliant death is not preferred to an obscure life of rectitude. Most men are remembered as they died, and not as they lived. We gaze with admiration upon the glories of the setting sun, yet scarcely bestow a passing glance upon its noonday splendor.'"

"'You are right; but how is this to be done?'"

"Accompany me to Texas. Cut aloof from your degrading habits and associates here, and, in fighting for the freedom of the Texans, regain your own.'"

"The man seemed much moved. He caught up his gambling instruments, thrust them into his pocket, with hasty strides traversed the floor two or three times, and then exclaimed:

"'By heaven, I will try to be a man again. I will live honestly, or die bravely. I will go with you to Texas.'"

To confirm him in his good resolution, Crockett "asked him to liquor." At Natchitoches, Crockett encountered another very singular character. He was a remarkably handsome young man, of poetic imagination, a sweet singer, and with innumerable scraps of poetry and of song ever at his tongue's end. Honey-trees, as they were called, were very abundant in Texas. The prairies were almost boundless parterres of the richest flowers, from which the bees made large quantities of the most delicious honey. This they deposited in the hollows of trees. Not only was the honey valuable, but the wax constituted a very important article of commerce in Mexico, and brought a high price, being used for the immense candles which they burned in their churches. The bee-hunter, by practice, acquired much skill in coursing the bees to their hives.

This man decided to join Crockett and the juggler in their journey over the vast prairies of Texas. Small, but very strong and tough Mexican ponies, called mustangs, were very cheap. They were found wild, in droves of thousands, grazing on the prairies. The three adventurers mounted their ponies, and set out on their journey due west, a distance of one hundred and twenty miles, to Nacogdoches. Their route was along a mere trail, which was called the old Spanish road. It led over vast prairies, where there was no path, and where the bee-hunter was their guide, and through forests where their course was marked only by blazed trees.

The next morning they crossed the river and pushed on for the fortress of Alamo. When within about twenty miles of San Antonio, they beheld about fifteen mounted men, well armed, approaching them at full speed. Crockett's party numbered five. They immediately dismounted, made a rampart of their horses, and with the muzzles of their rifles pointed toward the approaching foe, were prepared for battle.

It was a party of Mexicans. When within a few hundred yards they reined in their horses, and the leader, advancing a little, called out to them in Spanish to surrender.

"We must have a brush with those blackguards," said the pirate. "Let each one single out his man for the first fire. They are greater fools than I take them for if they give us a chance for a second shot. Colonel, just settle the business with that talking fellow with the red feather. He's worth any three of the party."

"Surrender, or we fire!" shouted the fellow with the red feather. The pirate replied, with a piratic oath, "Fire away!"

"And sure enough," writes Crockett, "they took his advice, for the next minute we were saluted with a discharge of musketry, the report of which was so loud that we were convinced they all had fired. Before the smoke had cleared away we had each selected our man, fired, and I never did see such a scattering among their ranks as followed. We beheld several mustangs running wild without their riders over the prairie, and the balance of the company were already retreating at a more rapid gait than they approached. We hastily mounted and commenced pursuit, which we kept up until we beheld the independent flag flying from the battlements of the fortress of Alamo, our place of destination. The fugitives succeeded in evading our pursuit, and we rode up to the gates of the fortress, announced to the sentinel who we were, and the gates were thrown open; and we entered amid shouts of welcome bestowed upon us by the patriots."

The fortress of Alamo is just outside of the town of Bexar, on the San Antonio River. The town is about one hundred and forty miles from the coast, and contained, at that time, about twelve hundred inhabitants. Nearly all were Mexicans, though there were a few American families. In the year 1718, the Spanish Government had established a military outpost here; and in the year 1721, a few emigrants from Spain commenced a flourishing settlement at this spot. Its site is beautiful, the air salubrious, the soil highly fertile, and the water of crystal purity.

The town of Bexar subsequently received the name of San Antonio. On the tenth of December, 1835, the Texans captured the town and citadel from the Mexicans. These Texan Rangers were rude men, who had but little regard for the refinements or humanities of civilization. When Crockett with his companions arrived, Colonel Bowie, of Louisiana, one of the most desperate of Western adventurers, was in the fortress. The celebrated bowie-knife was named after this man. There was but a feeble garrison, and it was threatened with an attack by an overwhelming force of Mexicans under Santa Anna. Colonel Travis was in command. He was very glad to receive even so small a reinforcement. The fame of Colonel Crockett, as one of the bravest of men, had already reached his ears.

"While we were conversing," writes Crockett, "Colonel Bowie had occasion to draw his famous knife, and I wish I may be shot if the bare sight of it wasn't enough to give a man of a squeamish stomach the colic. He saw I was admiring it, and said he, 'Colonel, you might tickle a fellow's ribs a long time with this little instrument before you'd make him laugh.'"

According to Crockett's account, many shameful orgies took place in the little garrison. They were evidently in considerable trepidation, for a large force was gathering against them, and they could not look for any considerable reinforcements from any quarter. Rumors were continually reaching them of the formidable preparations Santa Anna was making to attack the place. Scouts ere long brought in the tidings that Santa Anna, President of the Mexican Republic, at the head of sixteen hundred soldiers, and accompanied by several of his ablest generals, was within six miles of Bexar. It was said that he was doing everything in his power to enlist the warlike Comanches in his favor, but that they remained faithful in their friendship to the United States.

Early in the month of February, 1836, the army of Santa Anna appeared before the town, with infantry, artillery, and cavalry. With military precision they approached, their banners waving, and their bugle-notes bearing defiance to the feeble little garrison. The Texan invaders, seeing that they would soon be surrounded, abandoned the town to the enemy, and fled to the protection of the citadel. They were but one hundred and fifty in number. Almost without exception they were hardy adventurers, and the most fearless and desperate of men. They had previously stored away in the fortress all the provisions, arms, and ammunition, of which they could avail themselves. Over the battlements they unfurled an immense flag of thirteen stripes, and with a large white star of five points, surrounded by the letters "Texas." As they raised their flag, they gave three cheers, while with drums and trumpets they hurled back their challenge to the foe.

The Mexicans raised over the town a blood-red banner. It was their significant intimation to the garrison that no quarter was to be expected. Santa Anna, having advantageously posted his troops, in the afternoon sent a summons to Colonel Travis, demanding an unconditional surrender, threatening, in case of refusal, to put every man to the sword. The only reply Colonel Travis made was to throw a cannon-shot into the town. The Mexicans then opened fire from their batteries, but without doing much harm.

In the night, Colonel Travis sent the old pirate on an express to Colonel Fanning, who, with a small military force, was at Goliad, to entreat him to come to his aid. Goliad was about four days' march from Bexar. The next morning the Mexicans renewed their fire from a battery about three hundred and fifty yards from the fort. A three-ounce ball struck the juggler on the breast, inflicting a painful but not a dangerous wound.

Day after day this storm of war continued. The walls of the citadel were strong, and the bombardment inflicted but little injury. The sharpshooters within the fortress struck down many of the assailants at great distances.

"The bee-hunter," writes Crockett, "is about the quickest on the trigger, and the best rifle-shot we have in the fort. I have already seen him bring down eleven of the enemy, and at such a distance that we all thought that it would be a waste of ammunition to attempt it." Provisions were beginning to become scarce, and the citadel was so surrounded that it was impossible for the garrison to cut its way through the lines and escape.

Under date of February 28th, Crockett writes in his Journal:

"Last night our hunters brought in some corn, and had a brush with a scout from the enemy beyond gunshot of the fort. They put the scout to flight, and got in without injury. They bring accounts that the settlers are flying in all quarters, in dismay, leaving their possessions to the mercy of the ruthless invader, who is literally engaged in a war of extermination more brutal than the untutored savage of the desert could be guilty of. Slaughter is indiscriminate, sparing neither sex, age, nor condition. Buildings have been burnt down, farms laid waste, and Santa Anna appears determined to verify his threat, and convert the blooming paradise into a howling wilderness. For just one fair crack at that rascal, even at a hundred yards' distance, I would bargain to break my Betsey, and never pull trigger again. My name's not Crockett if I wouldn't get glory enough to appease my stomach for the remainder of my life.

"The scouts report that a settler by the name of Johnson, flying with his wife and three little children, when they reached the Colorado, left his family on the shore, and waded into the river to see whether it would be safe to ford with his wagon. When about the middle of the river he was seized by an alligator, and after a struggle was dragged under the water, and perished. The helpless woman and her babes were discovered, gazing in agony on the spot, by other fugitives, who happily passed that way, and relieved them. Those who fight the battles experience but a small part of the privation, suffering, and anguish that follow in the train of ruthless war. The cannonading continued at intervals throughout the day, and all hands were kept up to their work."

The next day he writes: "I had a little sport this morning before breakfast. The enemy had planted a piece of ordnance within gunshot of the fort during the night, and the first thing in the morning they commenced a brisk cannonade, point blank against the spot where I was snoring. I turned out pretty smart and mounted the rampart. The gun was charged again; a fellow stepped forth to touch her off, but before he could apply the match, I let him have it, and he keeled over. A second stepped up, snatched the match from the hand of the dying man, but the juggler, who had followed me, handed me his rifle, and the next instant the Mexican was stretched on the earth beside the first. A third came up to the cannon. My companion handed me another gun, and I fixed him off in like manner. A fourth, then a fifth seized the match, who both met with the same fate. Then the whole party gave it up as a bad job, and hurried off to the camp, leaving the cannon ready charged where they had planted it. I came down, took my bitters, and went to breakfast."

In the course of a week the Mexicans lost three hundred men. But still reinforcements were continually arriving, so that their numbers were on the rapid increase. The garrison no longer cherished any hope of receiving aid from abroad.

Under date of March 4th and 5th, 1836, we have the last lines which Crockett ever penned.

"*March 4th.* Shells have been falling into the fort like hail during the day, but without effect. About dusk, in the evening, we observed a man running toward the fort, pursued by about half a dozen of the Mexican cavalry. The bee-hunter immediately knew him to be the old pirate, who had gone to Goliad, and, calling to the two hunters, he sallied out of the fort to the relief of the old man, who was hard pressed. I followed close after. Before we reached the spot the Mexicans were close on the heels of the old man, who stopped suddenly, turned short upon his pursuers, discharged his rifle, and one of the enemy fell from his horse. The chase was renewed, but finding that he would be overtaken and cut to pieces, he now turned again, and, to the amazement of the enemy, became the assailant in his turn. He clubbed his gun, and dashed among them like a wounded tiger, and they fled like sparrows. By this time we reached the spot, and, in the ardor of the moment, followed some distance before we saw that our retreat to the fort was cut off by another detachment of cavalry. Nothing was to be done but fight our way through. We were all of the same mind. 'Go ahead!' cried I; and they shouted, 'Go ahead, Colonel!' We dashed among them, and a bloody conflict ensued. They were about twenty in number, and they stood their ground. After the fight had continued about five minutes, a detachment was seen issuing from the fort to our relief, and the Mexicans scampered off, leaving eight of their comrades dead upon the field. But we did not escape unscathed, for both the pirate and the bee-hunter were mortally wounded, and I received a sabre-cut across the forehead. The old man died without speaking, as soon as we entered the fort. We bore my young friend to his bed, dressed his wounds, and I watched beside him. He lay, without complaint or manifesting pain, until about midnight, when he spoke, and I asked him if he wanted anything. 'Nothing,' he replied, but drew a sigh that seemed to rend his heart, as he added, 'Poor Kate of Nacogdoches.' His eyes were filled with tears, as he continued, 'Her words were prophetic, Colonel,' and then he sang in a low voice, that resembled the sweet notes of his own devoted Kate:

But toom cam' the saddle, all bluidy to see,
And hame came the steed, but hame never came he.

He spoke no more, and a few minutes after died. Poor Kate, who will tell this to thee?"

The romantic bee-hunter had a sweetheart by the name of Kate in Nacogdoches. She seems to have been a very affectionate and religious girl. In parting, she had presented her lover with a Bible, and in anguish of spirit had expressed her fears that he would never return from his perilous enterprise.

The next day, Crockett simply writes, "*March 5th.* Pop, pop, pop! Bom, bom, bom! throughout the day. No time for memorandums now. Go ahead! Liberty and Independence forever."

Before daybreak on the 6th of March, the citadel of the Alamo was assaulted by the whole Mexican army, then numbering about three thousand men. Santa Anna in person commanded. The assailants swarmed over the works and into the fortress. The battle was fought with the utmost desperation until daylight. Six only of the Garrison then remained alive. They were surrounded, and they surrendered. Colonel Crockett was one. He at the time stood alone in an angle of the fort, like a lion at bay. His eyes flashed fire, his shattered rifle in his right hand, and in his left a gleaming bowie-knife streaming with blood. His face was covered with blood flowing from a deep gash across his forehead. About twenty Mexicans, dead and dying, were lying at his feet. The juggler was also there dead. With one hand he was clenching the hair of a dead Mexican, while with the other he had driven his knife to the haft in the bosom of his foe.

The Mexican General Castrillon, to whom the prisoners had surrendered, wished to spare their lives. He led them to that part of the fort where Santa Anna stood surrounded by his staff. As Castrillon marched his prisoners into the presence of the President, he said:

"Sir, here are six prisoners I have taken alive. How shall I dispose of them?"

Santa Anna seemed much annoyed, and said, "Have I not told you before how to dispose of them? Why do you bring them to me?"

Immediately several Mexicans commenced plunging their swords into the bosoms of the captives. Crockett, entirely unarmed, sprang, like a tiger, at the throat of Santa Anna. But before he could reach him, a dozen swords were sheathed in his heart, and he fell without a word or a groan. But there still remained upon his brow the frown of indignation, and his lip was curled with a smile of defiance and scorn.

And thus was terminated the earthly life of this extraordinary man. In this narrative it has been the object of the writer faithfully to record the influences under which Colonel Crockett was reared, and the incidents of his wild and wondrous life, leaving it with the reader to form his own estimate of the character which these exploits indicate. David Crockett has gone to the tribunal of his God, there to be judged for all the deeds done in the body. Beautifully and consolingly the Psalmist has written:

"Like as a father pitieth his children, so the Lord pitieth them that fear him. For he knoweth our frame; he remembereth that we are dust."

CHAPTER SEVEN

The Red Badge of Courage
By Stephen Crane

This excerpt from Stephen Crane's masterpiece, The Red Badge of Courage, *takes place during the climatic portions of the Civil War novel, when Crane's protagonist—identified throughout the story as "the youth"—faces the ultimate horrors of combat.*

Published in 1895, the novel brought to the general public of that time the most wrenching battlefield images since the photographs of Matthew Brady that had been taken and exhibited during the war. Brady's photographs and his own research, talent, and imagination were the creative impetus that led Crane to produce his stirring portrait of courage under fire. The popular writer Ambrose Bierce said of Crane, "This young man has the power to feel. He knows nothing of war, yet he is drenched in blood. Most beginners who deal with this subject spatter themselves with ink."

—LAMAR UNDERWOOD

THE YOUTH STARED AT THE LAND IN FRONT OF HIM. ITS FOLIAGE NOW SEEMED TO VEIL powers and horrors. He was unaware of the machinery of orders that started the charge, although from the corners of his eyes he saw an officer, who looked like a boy a-horseback, come galloping, waving his hat. Suddenly he felt a straining and heaving among the men. The line fell slowly forward like a toppling wall, and, with a convulsive gasp that was intended for a cheer, the regiment began its journey. The youth was pushed and jostled for a moment before he understood the movement at all, but directly he lunged ahead and began to run.

He fixed his eye upon a distant and prominent clump of trees where he had concluded the enemy were to be met, and he ran toward it as toward a goal. He had believed throughout that it was a mere question of getting over an unpleasant matter as quickly as possible, and he ran desperately, as if pursued for a murder. His face was drawn hard and tight with the stress of his endeavor. His eyes were fixed in a lurid glare. And with his soiled and disordered dress, his red and inflamed features surmounted by the dingy rag with its spot of blood, his wildly swinging rifle and banging accoutrements, he looked to be an insane soldier.

As the regiment swung from its position out into a cleared space the woods and thickets before it awakened. Yellow flames leaped toward it from many directions. The forest made a tremendous objection.

The line lurched straight for a moment. Then the right wing swung forward; it in turn was surpassed by the left. Afterward the center careered to the front until the regiment was a wedge-shaped mass, but an instant later the opposition of the bushes, trees, and uneven places on the ground split the command and scattered it into detached clusters.

The youth, light-footed, was unconsciously in advance. His eyes still kept note of the clump of trees. From all places near it the clannish yell of the enemy could be heard. The little flames of rifles leaped from it. The song of the bullets was in the air and shells snarled among the tree-tops. One tumbled directly into the middle of a hurrying group and exploded in crimson fury. There was an instant's spectacle of a man, almost over it, throwing up his hands to shield his eyes.

Other men, punched by bullets, fell in grotesque agonies. The regiment left a coherent trail of bodies.

They had passed into a clearer atmosphere. There was an effect like a revelation in the new appearance of the landscape. Some men working madly at a battery were plain to them, and the opposing infantry's lines were defined by the gray walls and fringes of smoke.

It seemed to the youth that he saw everything. Each blade of the green grass was bold and clear. He thought that he was aware of every change in the thin, transparent vapor that floated idly in sheets. The brown or gray trunks of the trees showed each roughness of their surfaces. And the men of the regiment, with their starting eyes and sweating faces, running madly, or falling, as if thrown headlong, to queer, heaped-up corpses—all were comprehended. His mind took a mechanical but firm impression, so that afterward everything was pictured and explained to him, save why he himself was there.

But there was a frenzy made from this furious rush. The men, pitching forward insanely, had burst into cheerings, moblike and barbaric, but tuned in strange keys that can arouse the dullard and the stoic. It made a mad enthusiasm that, it seemed, would be incapable of checking itself before granite and brass. There was the delirium that encounters despair and death, and is heedless and blind to the odds. It is a temporary but sublime absence of selfishness. And because it was of this order was the reason, perhaps, why the youth wondered, afterward, what reasons he could have had for being there.

Presently the straining pace ate up the energies of the men. As if by agreement, the leaders began to slacken their speed. The volleys directed against them had had a seeming windlike effect. The regiment snorted and blew. Among some stolid trees it began to falter and hesitate. The men, staring intently, began to wait for some of the distant walls of smoke to move and disclose to them the scene. Since much of their strength and their breath had vanished, they returned to caution. They were become men again.

The youth had a vague belief that he had run miles, and he thought, in a way, that he was now in some new and unknown land.

The moment the regiment ceased its advance the protesting splutter of musketry became a steadier roar. Long and accurate fringes of smoke spread out. From the top of a small hill came level belchings of yellow flame that caused an inhuman whistling in the air.

The men, halted, had opportunity to see some of their comrades dropping with moans and shrieks. A few lay under foot, still or wailing. And now for an instant the men stood, their rifles slack in their hands, and watched the regiment dwindle. They appeared dazed and stupid. This spectacle seemed to paralyze them, overcome them with a fatal fascination. They stared woodenly at the sights, and, lowering their eyes, looked from face to face. It was a strange pause, and a strange silence.

Then, above the sounds of the outside commotion, arose the roar of the lieutenant. He strode suddenly forth, his infantile features black with rage.

"Come on, yeh fools!" he bellowed. "Come on! Yeh can't stay here. Yeh must come on." He said more, but much of it could not be understood.

He started rapidly forward, with his head turned toward the men. "Come on," he was shouting. The men stared with blank and yokel-like eyes at him. He was obliged to halt and retrace his steps. He stood then with his back to the enemy and delivered gigantic curses into the faces of the men. His body vibrated from the weight and force of his imprecations. And he could string oaths with the facility of a maiden who strings beads.

The friend of the youth aroused. Lurching suddenly forward and dropping to his knees, he fired an angry shot at the persistent woods. This action awakened the men. They huddled no more like sheep. They seemed suddenly to bethink them of their weapons, and at once commenced firing. Belabored by their officers, they began to move forward. The regiment, involved like a cart involved in mud and muddle, started unevenly with many jolts and jerks. The men stopped now every few paces to fire and load, and in this manner moved slowly on from trees to trees.

The flaming opposition in their front grew with their advance until it seemed that all forward ways were barred by the thin leaping tongues, and off to the right an ominous demonstration could sometimes be dimly discerned. The smoke lately generated was in confusing clouds that made it difficult for the regiment to proceed with intelligence. As he passed through each curling mass the youth wondered what would confront him on the farther side.

The command went painfully forward until an open space interposed between them and the lurid lines. Here, crouching and cowering behind some trees, the men clung with desperation, as if threatened by a wave. They looked wild-eyed, and as if amazed at this furious disturbance they had stirred. In the storm there was an ironical expression of their importance. The faces of the men, too, showed a lack of a certain feeling of responsibility for being there. It was as if they had been driven. It was the dominant animal failing to remember in the supreme moments the forceful causes of various superficial qualities. The whole affair seemed incomprehensible to many of them.

As they halted thus the lieutenant again began to bellow profanely. Regardless of the vindictive threats of the bullets, he went about coaxing, berating, and bedamning. His lips, that were habitually in a soft and childlike curve, were now writhed into unholy contortions. He swore by all possible deities.

Once he grabbed the youth by the arm. "Come on, yeh lunkhead!" he roared. "Come on! We'll all git killed if we stay here. We've on'y got t' go across that lot. An' then"—the remainder of his idea disappeared in a blue haze of curses.

The youth stretched forth his arm. "Cross there?" His mouth was puckered in doubt and awe.

"Certainly. Jest 'cross th' lot! We can't stay here," screamed the lieutenant. He poked his face close to the youth and waved his bandaged hand. "Come on!" Presently he grappled with him as if for a wrestling bout. It was as if he planned to drag the youth by the ear on to the assault.

The private felt a sudden unspeakable indignation against his officer. He wrenched fiercely and shook him off.

"Come on yerself, then," he yelled. There was a bitter challenge in his voice.

They galloped together down the regimental front. The friend scrambled after them. In front of the colors the three men began to bawl: "Come on! come on!" They danced and gyrated like tortured savages.

The flag, obedient to these appeals, bended its glittering form and swept toward them. The men wavered in indecision for a moment, and then with a long, wailful cry the dilapidated regiment surged forward and began its new journey.

Over the field went the scurrying mass. It was a handful of men splattered into the faces of the enemy. Toward it instantly sprang the yellow tongues. A vast quantity of blue smoke hung before them. A mighty banging made ears valueless.

The youth ran like a madman to reach the woods before a bullet could discover him. He ducked his head low, like a football player. In his haste his eyes almost closed, and the scene was a wild blur. Pulsating saliva stood at the corners of his mouth.

Within him, as he hurled himself forward, was born a love, a despairing fondness for this flag which was near him. It was a creation of beauty and invulnerability. It was a goddess, radiant, that bended its form with an imperious gesture to him. It was a woman, red and white, hating and loving, that called him with the voice of his hopes. Because no harm could come to it he endowed it with power. He kept near, as if it could be a saver of lives, and an imploring cry went from his mind.

In the mad scramble he was aware that the color sergeant flinched suddenly, as if struck by a bludgeon. He faltered, and then became motionless, save for his quivering knees.

He made a spring and a clutch at the pole. At the same instant his friend grabbed it from the other side. They jerked at it, stout and furious, but the color sergeant was dead, and the corpse would not relinquish its trust. For a moment there was a grim encounter. The dead man, swinging with bended back, seemed to be obstinately tugging, in ludicrous and awful ways, for the possession of the flag.

It was past in an instant of time. They wrenched the flag furiously from the dead man, and, as they turned again, the corpse swayed forward with bowed head. One arm swung high, and the curved hand fell with heavy protest on the friend's unheeding shoulder.

When the two youths turned with the flag they saw that much of the regiment had crumbled away, and the dejected remnant was coming back. The men, having hurled themselves in projectile fashion, had presently expended their forces. They slowly retreated, with their faces still toward the spluttering woods, and their hot rifles still replying to the din. Several officers were giving orders, their voices keyed to screams.

"Where in hell yeh goin'?" the lieutenant was asking in a sarcastic howl. And a red-bearded officer, whose voice of triple brass could plainly be heard, was commanding: "Shoot into 'em! Shoot into 'em, Gawd damn their souls!" There was a mêlée of screeches, in which the men were ordered to do conflicting and impossible things.

The youth and his friend had a small scuffle over the flag. "Give it t' me!" "No, let me keep it!" Each felt satisfied with the other's possession of it, but each felt bound to declare, by an offer to carry the emblem, his willingness to further risk himself. The youth roughly pushed his friend away.

The regiment fell back to the stolid trees. There it halted for a moment to blaze at some dark forms that had begun to steal upon its track. Presently it resumed its march again, curving among the tree trunks. By the time the depleted regiment had again reached the first open space they were receiving a fast and merciless fire. There seemed to be mobs all about them.

The greater part of the men, discouraged, their spirits worn by the turmoil, acted as if stunned. They accepted the pelting of the bullets with bowed and weary heads. It was of no purpose to strive against walls. It was of no use to batter themselves against granite. And from this consciousness that they had attempted to conquer an unconquerable thing there seemed to arise a feeling that they had been betrayed. They glowered with bent brows, but dangerously, upon some of the officers, more particularly upon the red-bearded one with the voice of triple brass.

However, the rear of the regiment was fringed with men, who continued to shoot irritably at the advancing foes. They seemed resolved to make every trouble. The youthful lieutenant was perhaps the last man in the disordered mass. His forgotten back was toward the enemy. He had been shot in the arm. It hung straight and rigid. Occasionally he would cease to remember it, and be about to emphasize an oath with a sweeping gesture. The multiplied pain caused him to swear with incredible power.

The youth went along with slipping, uncertain feet. He kept watchful eyes rearward. A scowl of mortification and rage was upon his face. He had thought of a fine revenge upon the officer who had referred to him and his fellows as mule drivers. But he saw that it could not come to pass. His dreams had collapsed when the mule drivers, dwindling rapidly, had wavered and hesitated on the little clearing, and then had recoiled. And now the retreat of the mule drivers was a march of shame to him.

A dagger-pointed gaze from without his blackened face was held toward the enemy, but his greater hatred was riveted upon the man, who, not knowing him, had called him a mule driver.

When he knew that he and his comrades had failed to do anything in successful ways that might bring the little pangs of a kind of remorse upon the officer, the youth allowed the rage of the baffled to possess him. This cold officer upon a monument, who dropped epithets unconcernedly down, would be finer as a dead man, he thought. So grievous did he think it that he could never possess the secret right to taunt truly in answer.

He had pictured red letters of curious revenge. "We are mule drivers, are we?" And now he was compelled to throw them away.

He presently wrapped his heart in the cloak of his pride and kept the flag erect. He harangued his fellows, pushing against their chests with his free hand. To those he knew well he made frantic appeals, beseeching them by name. Between him and the lieutenant, scolding and near to losing his mind with rage, there was felt a subtle fellowship and equality. They supported each other in all manner of hoarse, howling protests.

But the regiment was a machine run down. The two men babbled at a forceless thing. The soldiers who had heart to go slowly were continually shaken in their resolves by a knowledge that comrades were slipping with speed back to the lines. It was difficult to think of reputation when others were thinking of skins. Wounded men were left crying on this black journey.

The smoke fringes and flames blustered always. The youth, peering once through a sudden rift in a cloud, saw a brown mass of troops, interwoven and magnified until they appeared to be thousands. A fierce-hued flag flashed before his vision.

Immediately, as if the uplifting of the smoke had been prearranged, the discovered troops burst into a rasping yell, and a hundred flames jetted toward the retreating band. A rolling gray cloud again interposed as the regiment doggedly replied. The youth had to depend again upon his misused ears, which were trembling and buzzing from the mêlée of musketry and yells.

The way seemed eternal. In the clouded haze men became panic-stricken with the thought that the regiment had lost its path, and was proceeding in a perilous direction.

Once the men who headed the wild procession turned and came pushing back against their comrades, screaming that they were being fired upon from points which they had considered to be toward their own lines. At this cry a hysterical fear and dismay beset the troops. A soldier, who heretofore had been ambitious to make the regiment into a wise little band that would proceed calmly amid the huge-appearing difficulties, suddenly sank down and buried his face in his arms with an air of bowing to a doom. From another a shrill lamentation rang out filled with profane illusions to a general. Men ran hither and thither, seeking with their eyes roads of escape. With serene regularity, as if controlled by a schedule, bullets buffed into men.

The youth walked stolidly into the midst of the mob, and with his flag in his hands took a stand as if he expected an attempt to push him to the ground. He unconsciously assumed the attitude of the color bearer in the fight of the preceding day. He passed over his brow a hand that trembled. His breath did not come freely. He was choking during this small wait for the crisis.

His friend came to him. "Well, Henry, I guess this is goodbye—John."

"Oh, shut up, you damned fool!" replied the youth, and he would not look at the other.

The officers labored like politicians to beat the mass into a proper circle to face the menaces. The ground was uneven and torn. The men curled into depressions and fitted themselves snugly behind whatever would frustrate a bullet.

The youth noted with vague surprise that the lieutenant was standing mutely with his legs far apart and his sword held in the manner of a cane. The youth wondered what had happened to his vocal organs that he no more cursed.

There was something curious in this little intent pause of the lieutenant. He was like a babe which, having wept its fill, raises its eyes and fixes them upon a distant toy. He was engrossed in this contemplation, and the soft under lip quivered from self-whispered words.

Some lazy and ignorant smoke curled slowly. The men, hiding from the bullets, waited anxiously for it to lift and disclose the plight of the regiment.

The silent ranks were suddenly thrilled by the eager voice of the youthful lieutenant bawling out: "Here they come! Right on to us, b'Gawd!" His further words were lost in a roar of wicked thunder from the men's rifles.

The youth's eyes had instantly turned in the direction indicated by the awakened and agitated lieutenant, and he had seen the haze of treachery disclosing a body of soldiers of the enemy. They were so near that he could see their features. There was a recognition as he looked at the types of faces. Also he perceived with dim amazement that their uniforms were rather gay in effect, being light gray, accented with a brilliant-hued facing. Moreover, the clothes seemed new.

These troops had apparently been going forward with caution, their rifles held in readiness, when the youthful lieutenant had discovered them and their movement had been interrupted by the volley from the blue regiment. From the moment's glimpse, it was derived that they had been unaware of the proximity of their dark-suited foes or had mistaken the direction. Almost instantly they were shut utterly from the youth's sight by the smoke from the energetic rifles of his companions. He strained his vision to learn the accomplishment of the volley, but the smoke hung before him.

The two bodies of troops exchanged blows in the manner of a pair of boxers. The fast angry firings went back and forth. The men in blue were intent with the despair of their circumstances and they seized upon the revenge to be had at close range. Their thunder swelled loud and valiant. Their curving front bristled with flashes and the place resounded with the clangor of their ramrods. The youth ducked and dodged for a time and achieved a few unsatisfactory views of the enemy. There appeared to be many of them and they were replying swiftly. They seemed moving toward the blue regiment, step by step. He seated himself gloomily on the ground with his flag between his knees.

As he noted the vicious, wolflike temper of his comrades he had a sweet thought that if the enemy was about to swallow the regimental broom as a large prisoner, it could at least have the consolation of going down with bristles forward.

But the blows of the antagonist began to grow more weak. Fewer bullets ripped the air, and finally, when the men slackened to learn of the fight, they could see only dark, floating smoke. The regiment lay still and gazed. Presently some chance whim came to the pestering blur, and it began to coil heavily away. The men saw a ground vacant of fighters. It would have been an empty stage if it were not for a few corpses that lay thrown and twisted into fantastic shapes upon the sward.

At sight of this tableau, many of the men in blue sprang from behind their covers and made an ungainly dance of joy. Their eyes burned and a hoarse cheer of elation broke from their dry lips.

It had begun to seem to them that events were trying to prove that they were impotent. These little battles had evidently endeavored to demonstrate that the men could not fight well. When on the verge of submission to these opinions, the small duel had showed them that the proportions were not impossible, and by it they had revenged themselves upon their misgivings and upon the foe.

The impetus of enthusiasm was theirs again. They gazed about them with looks of uplifted pride, feeling new trust in the grim, always confident weapons in their hands. And they were men.

Presently they knew that no fighting threatened them. All ways seemed once more opened to them. The dusty blue lines of their friends were disclosed a short distance away. In the distance there were many colossal noises, but in all this part of the field there was a sudden stillness.

They perceived that they were free. The depleted band drew a long breath of relief and gathered itself into a bunch to complete its trip.

In this last length of journey the men began to show strange emotions. They hurried with nervous fear. Some who had been dark and unfaltering in the grimmest moments now could not conceal an anxiety that made them frantic. It was perhaps that they dreaded to be killed in insignificant ways after the times for proper military deaths had passed. Or, perhaps, they thought it would be too ironical to get killed at the portals of safety. With backward looks of perturbation, they hastened.

As they approached their own lines there was some sarcasm exhibited on the part of a gaunt and bronzed regiment that lay resting in the shade of trees. Questions were wafted to them.

"Where th' hell yeh been?"

"What yeh comin' back fer?"

"Why didn't yeh stay there?"

"Was it warm out there, sonny?"

"Goin' home now, boys?"

One shouted in taunting mimicry: "Oh, mother, come quick an' look at th' sojers!"

There was no reply from the bruised and battered regiment, save that one man made broadcast challenges to fist fights and the red-bearded officer walked rather near and glared in great swashbuckler style at a tall captain in the other regiment. But the lieutenant suppressed the man who wished to fist fight, and the tall captain, flushing at the little fanfare of the red-bearded one, was obliged to look intently at some trees.

The youth's tender flesh was deeply stung by these remarks. From under his creased brows he glowered with hate at the mockers. He meditated upon a few revenges. Still, many in the regiment hung their heads in criminal fashion, so that it came to pass that the men trudged with sudden heaviness, as if they bore upon their bended shoulders the coffin of their honor. And the youthful lieutenant, recollecting himself, began to mutter softly in black curses.

They turned when they arrived at their old position to regard the ground over which they had charged.

The youth in this contemplation was smitten with a large astonishment. He discovered that the distances, as compared with the brilliant measurings of his mind, were trivial and ridiculous. The stolid trees, where much had taken place, seemed incredibly near. The time, too, now that he reflected, he saw to have been short. He wondered at the number of emotions and events that had been crowded into such little spaces. Elfin thoughts must have exaggerated and enlarged everything, he said.

It seemed, then, that there was bitter justice in the speeches of the gaunt and bronzed veterans. He veiled a glance of disdain at his fellows who strewed the ground, choking with dust, red from perspiration, misty-eyed, disheveled.

They were gulping at their canteens, fierce to wring every mite of water from them, and they polished at their swollen and watery features with coat sleeves and bunches of grass. For a time the men were bewildered by it. "Good thunder!" they ejaculated, staring at the vanishing form of the general. They conceived it to be a huge mistake . . .

Presently, however, they began to believe that in truth their efforts had been called light. The youth could see this convention weigh upon the entire regiment until the men were like cuffed and cursed animals, but withal rebellious.

The friend, with a grievance in his eye, went to the youth. "I wonder what he does want," he said. "He must think we went out there an' played marbles! I never see sech a man!"

The youth developed a tranquil philosophy for these moments of irritation. "Oh, well," he rejoined, "he probably didn't see nothing of it at all and got mad as blazes, and concluded we were a lot of sheep, just because we didn't do what he wanted done. It's a pity old Grandpa Henderson got killed yesterday—he'd have known that we did our best and fought good. It's just our awful luck, that's what."

"I should say so," replied the friend. He seemed to be deeply wounded at an injustice. "I should say we did have awful luck! There's no fun in fightin' fer people when everything yeh do—no matter what—ain't done right. I have a notion t' stay behind next time an' let 'em take their ol' charge an' go t' th' devil with it."

The youth spoke soothingly to his comrade. "Well, we both did good. I'd like to see the fool what'd say we both didn't do as good as we could!"

"Of course we did," declared the friend stoutly. "An' I'd break th' feller's neck if he was as big as a church. But we're all right, anyhow, for I heard one feller say that we two fit th' best in th' reg'ment, an' they had a great argument 'bout it. Another feller, 'a course, he had t' up an' say it was a lie—he seen all what was goin' on an' he never seen us from th' beginnin' t' th' end. An' a lot more struck in an' ses it wasn't a lie—we did fight like thunder, an' they give us quite a send-off. But this is what I can't stand—these everlastin' ol' soldiers, titterin' an' laughin', an' then that general, he's crazy."

The youth exclaimed with sudden exasperation: "He's a lunkhead! He makes me mad. I wish he'd come along next time. We'd show 'im what—"

He ceased because several men had come hurrying up. Their faces expressed a bringing of great news.

"O Flem, yeh jest oughta heard!" cried one, eagerly.

"Heard what?" said the youth.

"Yeh jest oughta heard!" repeated the other, and he arranged himself to tell his tidings. The others made an excited circle. "Well, sir, th' colonel met your lieutenant right by us—it was damnedest thing I ever heard—an' he ses: 'Ahem! ahem!' he ses. 'Mr. Hasbrouck!' he ses, 'by th' way, who was that lad what carried th' flag?' he ses. There, Flemin', what d' yeh think 'a that? 'Who was th' lad what carried th' flag?' he ses, an' th' lieutenant, he speaks up right away: 'That's Flemin', an' he's a jimhickey,' he ses, right away. What? I say he did. 'A jimhickey,' he ses—those'r his words. He did, too. I say he did. If you kin tell this story better than I kin, go ahead an' tell it. Well, then, keep yer mouth shet. Th' lieutenant, he ses: 'He's a jimhickey,' and th' colonel, he ses: 'Ahem! ahem! he is, indeed, a very good man t' have, ahem! He kep' th' flag 'way t' th' front. I saw 'im. He's a good un,' ses th' colonel. 'You bet,' ses th' lieutenant, 'he an' a feller named Wilson was at th' head 'a th' charge, an' howlin' like Indians all th' time,' he ses. 'Head 'a th' charge all th' time,' he ses. 'A feller named Wilson,' he ses. There, Wilson, m'boy, put that in a letter an' send it hum t' yer mother, hay? 'A feller named Wilson,' he ses. An' th' colonel, he ses: 'Were they, indeed? Ahem! ahem! My sakes!' he ses. 'At th' head 'a th' reg'ment?' he ses. 'They were,' ses th' lieutenant. 'My sakes!' ses th' colonel. He ses: 'Well, well, well,' he ses. 'They deserve t' be major-generals.'"

The youth and his friend had said: "Huh!" "Yer lyin' Thompson." "Oh, go t' blazes!" "He never sed it." "Oh, what a lie!" "Huh!" But despite these youthful scoffings and embarrassments, they knew that their faces were deeply flushing from thrills of pleasure. They exchanged a secret glance of joy and congratulation.

They speedily forgot many things. The past held no pictures of error and disappointment. They were very happy, and their hearts swelled with grateful affection for the colonel and the youthful lieutenant.

Having stirred this prodigious uproar, and, apparently, finding it too prodigious, the brigade, after a little time, came marching airily out again with its fine formation in nowise disturbed. There were no traces of speed in its movements. The brigade was jaunty and seemed to point a proud thumb at the yelling wood.

On a slope to the left there was a long row of guns, gruff and maddened, denouncing the enemy, who, down through the woods, were forming for another attack in the pitiless monotony of conflicts. The round red discharges from the guns made a crimson flare and a high, thick smoke. Occasional glimpses could be caught of groups of the toiling artillerymen. In the rear of this row of guns stood a house, calm and white, amid bursting shells. A congregation of horses, tied to a long railing, were tugging frenziedly at their bridles. Men were running hither and thither.

The detached battle between the four regiments lasted for some time. There chanced to be no interference, and they settled their dispute by themselves. They struck savagely and powerfully at each other for a period of minutes, and then the lighter-hued regiments faltered and drew back, leaving the dark-blue lines shouting. The youth could see the two flags shaking with laughter amid the smoke remnants.

Presently there was a stillness, pregnant with meaning. The blue lines shifted and changed a trifle and stared expectantly at the silent woods and fields before them. The hush was solemn and churchlike, save for a distant battery that, evidently unable to remain quiet, sent a faint rolling thunder over the ground. It irritated, like the noises of unimpressed boys. The men imagined that it would prevent their perched ears from hearing the first words of the new battle.

Of a sudden the guns on the slope roared out a message of warning. A spluttering sound had begun in the woods. It swelled with amazing speed to a profound clamor that involved the earth in noises. The splitting crashes swept along the lines until an interminable roar was developed. To those in the midst of it it became a din fitted to the universe. It was the whirring and thumping of gigantic machinery, complications among the smaller stars. The youth's ears were filled up. They were incapable of hearing more.

On an incline over which a road wound he saw wild and desperate rushes of men perpetually backward and forward in riotous surges. These parts of the opposing armies were two long waves that pitched upon each other madly at dictated points. To and fro they swelled. Sometimes, one side by its yells and cheers would proclaim decisive blows, but a moment later the other side would be all yells and cheers. Once the youth saw a spray of light forms go in houndlike leaps toward the waving blue lines. There was much howling, and presently it went away with a vast mouthful of prisoners. Again, he saw a blue wave dash with such thunderous force against a gray obstruction that it seemed to clear the earth of it and leave nothing but trampled sod. And always in their swift and deadly rushes to and fro the men screamed and yelled like maniacs.

Particular pieces of fence or secure positions behind collections of trees were wrangled over, as gold thrones or pearl bedsteads. There were desperate lunges at these chosen spots seemingly every instant, and most of them were bandied like light toys between the contending forces. The youth could not tell from the battle flags flying like crimson foam in many directions which color of cloth was winning.

His emaciated regiment bustled forth with undiminished fierceness when its time came. When assaulted again by bullets, the men burst out in a barbaric cry of rage and pain. They bent their heads in aims of intent hatred behind the projected hammers of their guns. Their ramrods clanged loud with fury as their eager arms pounded the cartridges into the rifle barrels. The front of the regiment was a smoke wall penetrated by the flashing points of yellow and red.

Wallowing in the fight, they were in an astonishingly short time resmudged. They surpassed in stain and dirt all their previous appearances. Moving to and fro with strained exertion, jabbering the while, they were, with their swaying bodies, black faces, and glowing eyes, like strange and ugly fiends jigging heavily in the smoke.

The lieutenant, returning from a tour after a bandage, produced from a hidden receptacle of his mind new and portentous oaths suited to the emergency. Strings of expletives he swung lashlike over the backs of his men, and it was evident that his previous efforts had in nowise impaired his resources.

The youth, still the bearer of the colors, did not feel his idleness. He was deeply absorbed as a spectator. The crash and swing of the great drama made him lean forward, intent-eyed, his face working in small contortions. Sometimes he prattled, words coming unconsciously from him in grotesque exclamations. He did not know that he breathed; that the flag hung silently over him, so absorbed was he.

A formidable line of the enemy came within dangerous range. They could be seen plainly—tall, gaunt men with excited faces running with long strides toward a wandering fence.

At sight of this danger the men suddenly ceased their cursing monotone. There was an instant of strained silence before they threw up their rifles and fired a plumping volley at the foes. There had been no order given; the men, upon recognizing the menace, had immediately let drive their flock of bullets without waiting for word of command.

But the enemy were quick to gain the protection of the wandering line of fence. They slid down behind it with remarkable celerity, and from this position they began briskly to slice up the blue men.

These latter braced their energies for a great struggle. Often, white clinched teeth shone from the dusky faces. Many heads surged to and fro, floating upon a pale sea of smoke. Those behind the fence frequently shouted and yelped in taunts and gibelike cries, but the regiment maintained a stressed silence. Perhaps, at this new assault the men recalled the fact that they had been named mud diggers, and it made their situation thrice bitter. They were breathlessly intent upon keeping the ground and thrusting away the rejoicing body of the enemy. They fought swiftly and with a despairing savageness denoted in their expressions.

The youth had resolved not to budge whatever should happen. Some arrows of scorn that had buried themselves in his heart had generated strange and unspeakable hatred. It was clear to him that his final and absolute revenge was to be achieved by his dead body lying, torn and gluttering, upon the field. This was to be a poignant retaliation upon the officer who had said "mule drivers," and later "mud diggers," for in all the wild graspings of his mind for a unit responsible for his sufferings and commotions he always seized upon the man who had dubbed him wrongly. And it was his idea, vaguely formulated, that his corpse would be for those eyes a great and salt reproach.

The regiment bled extravagantly. Grunting bundles of blue began to drop. The orderly sergeant of the youth's company was shot through the cheeks. Its supports being injured, his jaw hung afar down, disclosing in the wide cavern of his mouth a pulsing mass of blood and teeth. And with it all he made attempts to cry out. In his endeavor there was a dreadful earnestness, as if he conceived that one great shriek would make him well.

The youth saw him presently go rearward. His strength seemed in nowise impaired. He ran swiftly, casting wild glances for succor.

Others fell down about the feet of their companions. Some of the wounded crawled out and away, but many lay still, their bodies twisted into impossible shapes.

The youth looked once for his friend. He saw a vehement young man, powder-smeared and frowzled, whom he knew to be him. The lieutenant, also, was unscathed in his position at the rear. He had continued to curse, but it was now with the air of a man who was using his last box of oaths.

For the fire of the regiment had begun to wane and drip. The robust voice, that had come strangely from the thin ranks, was growing rapidly weak.

The colonel came running along back of the line. There were other officers following him. "We must charge'm!" they shouted. "We must charge'm!" they cried with resentful voices, as if anticipating a rebellion against this plan by the men.

The youth, upon hearing the shout, began to study the distance between him and the enemy. He made vague calculations. He saw that to be firm soldiers they must go forward. It would be death to stay in the present place, and with all the circumstances to go backward would exalt too many others. Their hope was to push the galling foes away from the fence.

He expected that his companions, weary and stiffened, would have to be driven to this assault, but as he turned toward them he perceived with a certain surprise that they were giving quick and unqualified expressions of assent. There was an ominous, clanging overture to the charge when the shafts of the bayonets rattled upon the rifle barrels. At the yelled words of command the soldiers sprang forward in eager leaps. There was new and unexpected force in the movement of the regiment. A knowledge of its faded and jaded condition made the charge appear like a paroxysm, a display of the strength that comes before a final feebleness. The men scampered in insane fever of haste, racing as if to achieve a sudden success before an exhilarating fluid should leave them. It was a blind and despairing rush by the collection of men in dusty and tattered blue, over a green sward and under a sapphire sky, toward a fence, dimly outlined in smoke, from behind which spluttered the fierce rifles of enemies.

The youth kept the bright colors to the front. He was waving his free arm in furious circles, the while shrieking mad calls and appeals, urging on those that did not need to be urged, for it seemed that the mob of blue men hurling themselves on the dangerous group of rifles were again grown suddenly wild with an enthusiasm of unselfishness. From the many firings starting toward them, it looked as if they would merely succeed in making a great sprinkling of corpses on the grass between their former position and the fence. But they were in a state of frenzy, perhaps because of forgotten vanities, and it made an exhibition of sublime recklessness. There was no obvious questioning, nor figurings, nor diagrams. There was, apparently, no considered loopholes. It appeared that the swift wings of their desires would have shattered against the iron gates of the impossible.

He himself felt the daring spirit of a savage, religion-mad. He was capable of profound sacrifices, a tremendous death. He had no time for dissections, but he knew that he thought of the bullets only as things that could prevent him from reaching the place of his endeavor. There were subtle flashings of joy within him that thus should be his mind.

He strained all his strength. His eyesight was shaken and dazzled by the tension of thought and muscle. He did not see anything excepting the mist of smoke gashed by the little knives of fire, but he knew that in it lay the aged fence of a vanished farmer protecting the snuggled bodies of the gray men.

As he ran a thought of the shock of contact gleamed in his mind. He expected a great concussion when the bodies of troops crashed together. This became a part of his wild battle madness. He could feel the onward swing of the regiment about him and he conceived of a thunderous, crushing blow that would prostrate the resistance and spread consternation and amazement for miles. The flying regiment was going to have a catapultian effect. This dream made him run faster among his comrades, who were giving vent to hoarse and frantic cheers.

But presently he could see that many of the men in gray did intend to abide the blow. The smoke, rolling, disclosed men who ran, faces still turned. These grew to a crowd, who retired stubbornly. Individuals wheeled frequently to send a bullet at the blue wave.

But at one part of the line there was a grim and obdurate group that made no movement. They were settled firmly down behind posts and rails. A flag, ruffled and fierce, waved over them and their rifles dinned fiercely.

The blue whirl of men got very near, until it seemed that in truth there would be a close and frightful scuffle. There was an expressed disdain in the opposition of the little group, that changed the meaning of the cheers of the men in blue. They became yells of wrath, directed, personal. The cries of the two parties were now in sound an interchange of scathing insults.

They in blue showed their teeth; their eyes shone all white. They launched themselves as at the throats of those who stood resisting. The space between dwindled to an insignificant distance.

The youth had centered the gaze of his soul upon that other flag. Its possession would be high pride. It would express bloody minglings, near blows. He had a gigantic hatred for those who made great difficulties and complications. They caused it to be as a craved treasure of mythology, hung amid tasks and contrivances of danger.

He plunged like a mad horse at it. He was resolved it should not escape if wild blows and darings of blows could seize it. His own emblem, quivering and aflare, was winging toward the other. It seemed there would shortly be an encounter of strange beaks and claws, as of eagles.

The swirling body of blue men came to a sudden halt at close and disastrous range and roared a swift volley. The group in gray was split and broken by this fire, but its riddled body still fought. The men in blue yelled again and rushed in upon it.

The youth, in his leapings, saw, as through a mist, a picture of four or five men stretched upon the ground or writhing upon their knees with bowed heads as if they had been stricken by bolts from the sky. Tottering among them was the rival color bearer, whom the youth saw had been bitten vitally by the bullets of the last formidable volley. He perceived this man fighting a last struggle, the struggle of one whose legs are grasped by demons. It was a ghastly battle. Over his face was the bleach of death, but set upon it were the dark and hard lines of desperate purpose. With this terrible grin of resolution he hugged his precious flag to him and was stumbling and staggering in his design to go the way that led to safety for it.

But his wounds always made it seem that his feet were retarded, held, and he fought a grim fight, as with invisible ghouls fastened greedily upon his limbs. Those in advance of the scampering blue men, howling cheers, leaped at the fence. The despair of the lost was in his eyes as he glanced back at them.

The youth's friend went over the obstruction in a tumbling heap and sprang at the flag as a panther at prey. He pulled at it and, wrenching it free, swung up its red brilliancy with a mad cry of exultation even as the color bearer, gasping, lurched over in a final throe and, stiffening convulsively, turned his dead face to the ground. There was much blood upon the grass blades.

At the place of success there began more wild clamorings of cheers. The men gesticulated and bellowed in an ecstasy. When they spoke it was as if they considered their listener to be a mile away. What hats and caps were left to them they often slung high in the air.

At one part of the line four men had been swooped upon, and they now sat as prisoners. Some blue men were about them in an eager and curious circle. The soldiers had trapped strange birds, and there was an examination. A flurry of fast questions was in the air.

One of the prisoners was nursing a superficial wound in the foot. He cuddled it, babywise, but he looked up from it often to curse with an astonishing utter abandon straight at the noses of his captors. He consigned them to red regions; he called upon the pestilential wrath of strange gods. And with it all he was singularly free from recognition of the finer points of the conduct of prisoners of war. It was as if a clumsy clod had trod upon his toe and he conceived it to be his privilege, his duty, to use deep, resentful oaths.

Another, who was a boy in years, took his plight with great calmness and apparent good nature. He conversed with the men in blue, studying their faces with his bright and keen eyes. They spoke of battles and conditions. There was an acute interest in all their faces during this exchange of viewpoints. It seemed a great satisfaction to hear voices from where all had been darkness and speculation. The third captive sat with a morose countenance. He preserved a stoical and cold attitude. To all advances he made one reply without variation, "Ah, go t' hell!"

The last of the four was always silent and, for the most part, kept his face turned in unmolested directions. From the views the youth received he seemed to be in a state of absolute dejection. Shame was upon him, and with it profound regret that he was, perhaps, no more to be counted in the ranks of his fellows. The youth could detect no expression that would allow him to believe that the other was giving a thought to his narrowed future, the pictured dungeons, perhaps, and starvations and brutalities, liable to the imagination. All to be seen was shame for captivity and regret for the right to antagonize.

After the men had celebrated sufficiently they settled down behind the old rail fence, on the opposite side to the one from which their foes had been driven. A few shot perfunctorily at distant marks.

There was some long grass. The youth nestled in it and rested, making a convenient rail support the flag. His friend, jubilant and glorified, holding his treasure with vanity, came to him there. They sat side by side and congratulated each other.

—⁓—

The roarings that had stretched in a long line of sound across the face of the forest began to grow intermittent and weaker. The stentorian speeches of the artillery continued in some distant encounter, but the crashes of the musketry had almost ceased. The youth and his friend of a sudden looked up, feeling a deadened form of distress at the waning of these noises, which had become a part of life. They could see changes going on among the troops. There were marchings this way and that way. A battery wheeled leisurely. On the crest of a small hill was the thick gleam of many departing muskets.

The youth arose. "Well, what now, I wonder?" he said. By his tone he seemed to be preparing to resent some new monstrosity in the way of dins and smashes. He shaded his eyes with his grimy hand and gazed over the field.

His friend also arose and stared. "I bet we're goin' t' git along out of this an' back over th' river," said he.

"Well, I swan!" said the youth.

They waited, watching. Within a little while the regiment received orders to retrace its way. The men got up grunting from the grass, regretting the soft repose. They jerked their stiffened legs, and stretched their arms over their heads. One man swore as he rubbed his eyes. They all groaned "O Lord!" They had as many objections to this change as they would have had to a proposal for a new battle.

They trampled slowly back over the field across which they had run in a mad scamper.

The regiment marched until it had joined its fellows. The reformed brigade, in column, aimed through a wood at the road. Directly they were in a mass of dust-covered troops, and were trudging along in a way parallel to the enemy's lines as these had been defined by the previous turmoil.

They passed within view of a stolid white house, and saw in front of it groups of their comrades lying in wait behind a neat breastwork. A row of guns were booming at a distant enemy. Shells thrown in reply were raising clouds of dust and splinters. Horsemen dashed along the line of intrenchments.

At this point of its march the division curved from the field and went winding off in the direction of the river. When the significance of this movement had impressed itself upon the youth he turned his head and looked over his shoulder toward the trampled and débris-strewn ground. He breathed a breath of new satisfaction. He finally nudged his friend. "Well, it's all over," he said to him.

His friend gazed backward. "B'Gawd, it is," he assented. They mused.

For a time the youth was obliged to reflect in a puzzled and uncertain way. His mind was undergoing a subtle change. It took moments for it to cast off its battleful ways and resume its accustomed course of thought. Gradually his brain emerged from the clogged clouds, and at last he was enabled to more closely comprehend himself and circumstance.

He understood then that the existence of shot and counter-shot was in the past. He had dwelt in a land of strange, squalling upheavals and had come forth. He had been where there was red of blood and black of passion, and he was escaped. His first thoughts were given to rejoicings at this fact.

Later he began to study his deeds, his failures, and his achievements. Thus, fresh from scenes where many of his usual machines of reflection had been idle, from where he had proceeded sheeplike, he struggled to marshal all his acts.

At last they marched before him clearly. From this present viewpoint he was enabled to look upon them in spectator fashion and to criticize them with some correctness, for his new condition had already defeated certain sympathies.

Regarding his procession of memory he felt gleeful and unregretting, for in it his public deeds were paraded in great and shining prominence. Those performances which had been witnessed by his fellows marched now in wide purple and gold, having various deflections. They went gayly with music. It was pleasure to watch these things. He spent delightful minutes viewing the gilded images of memory.

He saw that he was good. He recalled with a thrill of joy the respectful comments of his fellows upon his conduct.

Nevertheless, the ghost of his flight from the first engagement appeared to him and danced. There were small shoutings in his brain about these matters. For a moment he blushed, and the light of his soul flickered with shame.

A specter of reproach came to him. There loomed the dogging memory of the tattered soldier—he who, gored by bullets and faint for blood, had fretted concerning an imagined wound in another; he who had loaned his last of strength and intellect for the tall soldier; he who, blind with weariness and pain, had been deserted in the field.

For an instant a wretched chill of sweat was upon him at the thought that he might be detected in the thing. As he stood persistently before his vision, he gave vent to a cry of sharp irritation and agony.

His friend turned. "What's the matter, Henry?" he demanded. The youth's reply was an outburst of crimson oaths.

As he marched along the little branch-hung roadway among his prattling companions this vision of cruelty brooded over him. It clung near him always and darkened his view of these deeds in purple and gold. Whichever way his thoughts turned they were followed by the somber phantom of the desertion in the fields. He looked stealthily at his companions, feeling sure that they must discern in his face evidences of this pursuit. But they were plodding in ragged array, discussing with quick tongues the accomplishments of the late battle.

"Oh, if a man should come up an' ask me, I'd say we got a dum good lickin'."

"Lickin'—in yer eye! We ain't licked, sonny. We're going down here aways, swing aroun', an' come in behint 'em."

"Oh, hush, with your comin' in behint 'em. I've seen all 'a that I wanta. Don't tell me about comin' in behint——"

"Bill Smithers, he ses he'd rather been in ten hundred battles than been in that heluva hospital. He ses they got shootin' in th' nighttime, an' shells dropped plum among 'em in th' hospital. He ses sech hollerin' he never see."

"Hasbrouck? He's th' best off'cer in this here reg'ment. He's a whale."

"Didn't I tell yeh we'd come aroun' in behint 'em? Didn't I tell yeh so? We——"

"Oh, shet yer mouth!"

For a time this pursuing recollection of the tattered man took all elation from the youth's veins. He saw his vivid error, and he was afraid that it would stand before him all his life. He took no share in the chatter of his comrades, nor did he look at them or know them, save when he felt sudden suspicion that they were seeing his thoughts and scrutinizing each detail of the scene with the tattered soldier.

Yet gradually he mustered force to put the sin at a distance. And at last his eyes seemed to open to some new ways. He found that he could look back upon the brass and bombast of his earlier gospels and see them truly. He was gleeful when he discovered that he now despised them.

With the conviction came a store of assurance. He felt a quiet manhood, non-assertive but of sturdy and strong blood. He knew that he would no more quail before his guides wherever they should point. He had been to touch the great death, and found that, after all, it was but the great death. He was a man.

So it came to pass that as he trudged from the place of blood and wrath his soul changed. He came from hot plowshares to prospects of clover tranquilly, and it was as if hot plowshares were not. Scars faded as flowers.

It rained. The procession of weary soldiers became a bedraggled train, despondent and muttering, marching with churning effort in a trough of liquid brown mud under a low, wretched sky. Yet the youth smiled, for he saw that the world was a world for him, though many discovered it to be made of oaths and walking sticks. He had rid himself of the red sickness of battle. The sultry nightmare was in the past. He had been an animal blistered and sweating in the heat and pain of war. He turned now with a lover's thirst to images of tranquil skies, fresh meadows, cool brooks—an existence of soft and eternal peace.

Over the river a golden ray of sun came through the hosts of leaden rain clouds.

CHAPTER EIGHT

Sniper: American Single-Shot Warriors in Iraq and Afghanistan

By Gina Cavallaro with Matt Larsen

The Hindu Kush mountains of Afghanistan are far from the site of the attacks that left New York's World Trade Center in smoldering ruins on 9/11. However, the epic shock of the attacks was very much on the minds of an elite group of soldiers deployed in the rugged mountains six months later. They had unique skills, unique weapons. They were trained snipers, and they would begin writing a stirring new chapter in American warfare. Excerpted from the book of the same title, published by Lyons Press, 2010.

—LAMAR UNDERWOOD

IN THE FRIGID MOUNTAINS OF AFGHANISTAN SIX MONTHS AFTER THE SEPTEMBER 11, 2001, attacks on the United States, Sgt. Stan Crowder took a knee on the jagged top of an icy escarpment. Fierce gunfire had greeted his platoon upon landing, and he was already in the crude sights of an enemy fighter as the helicopter that took them there flew away in a riot of wind.

The soldiers had rehearsed. They were told to expect little resistance and were supposed to arrive before dawn, but it was later than planned and the light of a bright winter sun robbed them of the advantage of darkness.

Even before their Chinooks descended to the landing zone, the helicopters' door gunners were ripping through the belts of their M60 machine guns in full engagement with fighters on the ground who were shooting rockets and firing machine guns at the birds. An alternate LZ only two hundred meters away was hot, too, leaving the soldiers little choice but to brave the fire on either one and take covering positions as soon as their boots hit the ground.

Crowder and his partner, Staff Sgt. Jason Carracino, were snipers assigned to their battalion's scout platoon and had just hitched a ride with a rifle platoon with a plan to branch off after insertion. It was March 2002 at the start of a major U.S.-led offensive, and everyone had a role to play.

"A 240B machine gun crew got off just before us. Jason and I went off the back ramp with a ten-foot hover. We looked at each other and we're both like, 'Man! here we go!,'" Crowder said through an uproarious laugh, retelling the story years later from the comfort of a kitchen table back home and with obvious nostalgia for the hubris of the early days of the war.

He and Carracino each carried more than one hundred pounds of gear for what they calculated would be about a two-day stay-over, watching the rifle platoon and the back side of a mountain pass where Taliban fighters might escape as the offensive put the squeeze on their camp.

Just moments after they got to the ground, while the rifle platoon infantrymen lay prone, regaining their bearings and trying not to get killed, Crowder, from his kneeling position, took two shots at a man wielding an AK-47 assault rifle. The wounded man was jolted but kept firing. Crowder adjusted his aim, took a calculated breath, and finished him off on the third shot, his first kill on the battlefield.

For the next thirty-six hours, the sniper team would stay to help the platoon, getting an introduction to the fighting prowess of the armed men who lived and fought in Afghanistan's majestic and forbidding Hindu Kush.

On 9/11 Crowder didn't even know where the World Trade Center was.

As a kid in the rural town of Pound, deep in southwestern Virginia's mountainous coal country, Crowder led an uncomplicated life, revolving around family, guns, and hunting, not so terribly different from the lives of so many Afghans—except for such American amenities as running water, electricity, and schooling.

The denizens of New York, where terrorists had rained mayhem on the city, likely knew as much about the people of Pound and Afghanistan as the people of Pound and Afghanistan knew about them. But on that day, Crowder and every American in uniform learned exactly where the World Trade Center was and what the attack meant. For him, the excitement of going to war began to sink in.

He was an infantryman assigned to Second Battalion, 187th Infantry Regiment of the Rakkasan Brigade in the cradle of one of the Army's most storied divisions, the 101st Airborne Division, known as the Screaming Eagles, at Fort Campbell, Kentucky. The mobilization for the Screaming Eagles, the Marine Corps, and the rest of the military began almost immediately.

Armed National Guard soldiers were posted at American airports, and F-16 fighter jets flew sorties over the nation's capital. Aircraft carriers were steaming toward the Middle East, and people everywhere waved newly purchased American flags. Support for a war in Afghanistan was strong and widespread.

As it dawned on Crowder that his unit would be one of the first to step foot on the ground overseas, he weighed the implications of going to war, and though his stepfather, a Vietnam veteran who had raised him from the age of four, suggested he think hard about his options, he also answered the question in Crowder's mind about doing his part.

"It's your conflict, man," his stepfather told him. "I had mine, everybody has theirs. It's your turn."

"I kinda felt that way in the back of my mind, but once I heard him say it, I was like, 'Well, all right.' It kind of fell into place. I guess that was just the way it was supposed to be."

TRAINED AT SOTIC

During his three years in the Army, Crowder had been a fortunate soldier, too, one of only a very few from the conventional side of the Army who had the opportunity to be trained by Special Forces soldiers in the art of sniping.

The course is for Green Berets and other soldiers in the Special Operations community, but back when Crowder was at Fort Campbell, instructors at the Special Operations Target Interdiction Course, or SOTIC, rounded out its class by offering slots to units located near the school. In July 2001, Crowder, who had already been selected to be in his battalion's scout platoon where the snipers get assigned, received one of those slots. Though he expected to eventually be trained at the Army Sniper School at Fort Benning, Georgia, it wasn't a given.

"Back then," he said, "they would send forty guys [to Benning], and five would graduate. It was a heartbreaker and costly. SOTIC was attractive because it was right there at Fort Campbell."

Crowder eventually did go to the school at Benning in 2004, and he later became an instructor there after a tour to Iraq in 2006. But what he learned at SOTIC, he said, was what he took to war with him.

When his unit got orders to deploy to Afghanistan the week before Thanksgiving in 2001, the excitement level among his brothers in arms exploded. "I think I felt like I won the Heisman Trophy! I called everybody. I told them, 'I can't tell you what's going on, all I can say is keep watching the news,'" he said. "My dad said he knew what it meant. 'I got it,' he told me. 'Just don't do nothin' dumb.'"

ARRIVING IN KANDAHAR AND THE CRASH

The Kandahar air base in southern Afghanistan on January 18, 2002, the day Crowder arrived, was an austere smattering of living quarters—tents, mostly—and brutally cold.

Incredibly, to him, within a few short days of arriving at the compound, he and his partner at the time, Spc. Justin Solano, were given the job to work sniper missions for three months with a Special Forces team at a safe house in Khost.

Along with the enviable mission came the obligatory swagger of superiority. "Some guys who had been on the team longer, one guy in particular, were peeved," Crowder said.

Not one to let a good taunting go by, he smugly informed the peeved soldier that "tenure doesn't matter if you can shoot better."

But the elation of getting his first combat mission so quickly would be violently interrupted by one of those things that happen when you're just trying to get somewhere: The CH-47 Chinook helicopter taking the soldiers to Khost to their mission with the Army's elite Green Berets crashed on landing, leaving Crowder practically blind in his right eye and teetering on the edge of getting sent home for good.

The disaster happened in the moments before they were to make a running landing, a method of inserting troops quickly in which the helicopter pilot points the aircraft's nose skyward and angles the rear of the bird downward with the back ramp open during a skilled hover so everybody can run off onto the landing strip.

Crowder was sitting on the port side of the helicopter with his knees smashed against the fuel blivet, a giant rubber-like bubble cell filled with sloshing jet fuel that allows the pilots to refuel in flight and make fewer stops. The bird was packed with troops lining the benches on the sides of the aircraft, and everyone's stuff was piled loosely into the middle. About forty-five minutes out, he said, the door crew did a test-fire, and then the troops got their one-minute warning.

"It was like we'd done a million times in training at Fort Campbell. We were told they would do a running landing, which we had even practiced at Kandahar a few days before," Crowder said.

But the air crews stumbled on the landing order. Crowder speculated that it was because they had failed to perform a preflight commo check and were unable to talk on the radios with one another when the first helicopter landed in the wrong place. "When the chalk went to land, bird one landed in bird two's spot, and bird two landed in bird three's spot. I was on bird three," he said, suggesting that the crew flying the third Chinook suddenly had to execute an unplanned landing. "Even if they had an alternate plan, they had no way of communicating it to each other. Bird three, which had almost no visibility because of the sand and dust being blown around by the other two birds, landed on its nose while everyone was standing up."

Crowder was knocked out cold on the impact, and everybody's untethered gear tumbled down on top of him. The helicopter rolled as the rotors turned and the fuel blivet burst open.

When he came to, he remembered seeing the dim illumination from a half-moon, and he instinctively checked for his weapons. He still had his M4 slung across his chest, and his pistol was snug in its holster, giving him some assurance that he could fight back if the enemy was swarming the helicopter. He remembered lowering his NODs just before impact and saw stars in the sky through the back of the angled helo.

But no enemy fighters were approaching the bird just yet. A rescue was under way and people were injured, but no one was killed. Crowder was soaked with fuel, and the right side of his face was numb.

A young soldier on his first ride in a Chinook who was sitting to Crowder's left during the flight had the sense to escape through the door gunner's hatch, but Crowder couldn't move. He was pinned under the weight of the jumbled equipment, his helmet was gone, he was disoriented, and as he started to push through the weight on top of him, he saw lights darting around in front of his left eye, the only one that was working.

The eerie flickers were coming from the handheld flashlight of a Green Beret who pulled him out of the helicopter by the shoulder straps of his chest rig and patched him up before his evacuation to a U.S. field hospital in Uzbekistan.

Had the unidentified Special Forces soldier not taken care of him as expertly as he did, doctors told Crowder in Uzbekistan, he would have lost his right eye. Crowder never learned the name of the guy, but the guy remembered him when they met several months later. Crowder ate some humble pie when the guy reminded him how belligerent he'd been during the rescue.

In Uzbekistan, under the shock of bright hospital lights, his eye was irrigated and bandaged before Crowder was flown to Landstuhl Regional Medical Center in Germany.

The excitement of war had ended as quickly as it began, and his anxiety mounted as he realized he was getting farther and farther away from the unit and the mission with the Special Forces soldiers in Khost that he had been so pumped up to do.

In Landstuhl he was recuperating with about six other soldiers who had been wounded in the helicopter crash—some more critically than others—and while he was trying to figure out a way to avoid going back to Kentucky, he found a surprising ally in the Air Force surgeon who had tended to his eye wound.

The doc, a former pararescue jumper, not only said that he understood Crowder's desire to get back to the fight in Afghanistan, but he also tipped him off to a bar run by an Irish lady at the end of the road from the hospital and suggested he might check it out. "He knew that infantry guys wanted to stay with their units, could kind of speak the language and understood a lot of what I was talking about, the stuff at the crash site," Crowder said.

The doc and his young patient met daily for medical follow-up and sometimes ate together. Then one day Crowder got just the kind of tip he was looking for—with a little wink of the eye, the doc told him that two C-17s were headed to Afghanistan, leaving the door open for Crowder to make his own decision.

Crowder didn't even have a uniform to speak of. His had been cut off his body during the medical evacuation, and he had no gear, either. Plus, he was expected in the rear at Fort Campbell where the other wounded soldiers were going. Wearing his hospital-issued DCUs, Crowder showed up at one of the birds and asked the Third Special Forces Group soldiers loading up if he could hitch a ride with them to Kandahar. "They gave me some clothes, but I showed up in Kandahar with no weapon or gear," he said.

His gear—a drag bag, a chest rig, and a pair of mini-binos—had in fact been split up between the two guys, peeved soldier included, who took the mission in Khost after the crash.

OPERATION ANACONDA

What Crowder didn't know was that the mission to work in Khost with the Special Forces soldiers would pale in comparison to what he and some two thousand other U.S. and coalition air and ground troops would take part in just a few weeks later.

Operation Anaconda was launched on March 1, 2002, in the Shah-i-Kot valley in southeastern Afghanistan south of Gardez, and it remains one of the largest U.S.-led offensives to occur in Iraq or Afghanistan since operations began in each country.

The massive operation took place over a seventy-square-mile area in extremely frigid temperatures that dropped to as low as fifteen degrees Fahrenheit at night in fighting positions that had to be established in mountains with altitudes higher than ten thousand feet. Well-trained Taliban fighters numbered in the hundreds, a considerably higher number than U.S. planners were aware of, and their tenacity as warriors was compounded by their intimate knowledge and mastery of the terrain.

"We were told to expect like a pocket of one hundred or so hard-core fighters, and everybody else would be local to the area. It was the other way around," Crowder said. "There were big-wig hard-core fighters, hundreds of them. They were pretty smart about it; they were just waiting for us to come in."

The mission, he said, "went south really fast."

"We practiced going in at night, but when we got to the Shah-i-Kot valley for the mission, the sun had been out for about fifteen minutes; so we're flying in over villages where there were people outside waving at us."

He's nervous, too, he said, because the helicopter flight is only his second one in country since the night of the crash. And the guy sitting next to him is the same one who sat next to him during the crash.

But Crowder had a lot more on his mind than helicopter crashes when he took that knee on the icy mountaintop, moving solely on instinct to put down the enemy fighter most willing to close with them on the landing zone.

While members of the platoon engaged sporadic gunfire, firing the first live shots of their lives at human targets, Carracino was behind Crowder pulling his M24 rifle out of his bag and checking it over. Once organized and ready to move, the soldiers would march to a blocking position about five hundred meters up, even though it wasn't the plan envisioned by the sniper team.

The wind was wickedly erratic, and there were close shots all around. Crowder was looking south toward an area where he'd heard rounds coming out every few seconds. What he saw was more than rocks and boulders staring back at him.

"I saw an Afghani wearing like a pizza hat, those hats that are rolled up. At first I second-guessed myself because it was all boulders and rocks, I didn't know if it was the guy or not. Jason asked if I had something," Crowder recalled. "I could see more than half the guy and I thought, 'That's kinda dumb,' but then I thought, 'He's probably not alone.'"

With his M4 trained on the pizza-hatted shooter, Crowder took him on. "I put my red dot on him, acquired him as a target. I shot him twice, saw my rounds impact, and it kind of knocked him for a loop for a little bit, but he didn't actually ever go down. He kind of recomposed himself and continued moving forward. So I took another few seconds, went through my breathing pattern one more time and slowed down and shot again."

This time he had adjusted his hold from the enemy's high chest area and beamed his lethal red dot on the man's nose, squeezing the trigger that scored the kill.

"I saw it hit right on the base where the neck and the chest meet, and he went down. It was probably like 125 or 150 meters," Crowder said, speculating that the Afghani hadn't seen him because, as he points out himself, "I'm not a very tall man" and can easily disappear behind a boulder. But he may have seen Carracino, who is almost six feet tall, and the other platoon members behind him.

"It was kind of like really quick and to the point. On that last shot when I saw him go down, I double-checked to make sure he wasn't moving. I was still thinking, 'Why is that guy by himself?' So I was worried about a larger pocket of guys in the rocks," Crowder said.

As he would learn in the coming days, in Afghanistan there are lone fighters in remote positions as well as pockets of guys. The platoon was ready to move out, and there was no chance to answer Carracino's hunch that Crowder had been up to something while Carracino was busy checking maps and other gear.

"About four or five hours later, Jason's like, 'Hey, man, did you shoot a guy down there?' and I'm like 'yeah' and he's like, 'I saw you shooting and I thought I saw a guy down there and then I saw him fall,'" Crowder recounted. "I guess he only saw the third shot."

The rifle platoon started its move toward higher ground, and the Crowder-Carracino sniper team hung back about one hundred meters from the rest of the platoon to make sure no one closed with them. Their plan to branch off was fragged by the intensity of the contact they were all taking, and they decided to stick with the rifle platoon so they could mutually support one another. The men trekked and walked and climbed through low ground and dead space, through wadis and rocks and boulders on the way up from the LZ to the blocking position known as "Diane."

The snipers' planned mission was to stop fighters fleeing the Marzak Camp toward the Pakistan border and to block reinforcements or anyone who was able to get past the rifle platoon from heading to the mountain pass behind the blocking position and higher ground directly above.

The platoon would be the snipers' contingency security plan, the nearest friendly unit. They had expected to operate alone and stay for twenty-four to forty-eight hours. But they stayed with the rifle platoon for thirty-six hours, and ten days would go by before the battalion picked them up.

As the hours wore on, the platoon moved through Taliban country, the soldiers learning that they would have to adapt quickly and anticipate the enemy's movements if they were to survive the assaults of well-entrenched fighters, whose positions had been stationary for decades and who were as much a part of the landscape as the centuries-old rock formations.

"Their positions are so well built, they're not moving around as much or doing a lot of dumb things to let themselves get caught," Crowder said.

He was amused by their crazy fashion choices, a hodgepodge of ancient biblical-style man jammies layered with modern-day cold-weather gear and high-performance designer labels like North Face.

And he was impressed with the unexpected accuracy of their fires. The enemy had only to wait for the Americans to make a move before striking from their well-hidden big machine guns, mortars, and howitzers recessed into the sides of rock face. Wherever the Americans moved, Crowder said, they'd invariably get potshotted by the invisible Taliban.

"We used to find stacks of rocks. One day I pace-counted it. It was roughly one hundred meters from one stack to the next, all the same height and stacked in similar fashion. They weren't painted or anything. They probably had some guy with binos or optics watching, and that's how they figured out their range," he said.

Crowder said he and the platoon found a few positions where bedrock was chiseled in the shape of a base plate or mortar system so that when the enemy took a shot, they would be on target with the first round. "They don't have to set it at all, because it's in rock, not dirt," Crowder said.

THIRSTY PLATOON SERGEANT

The lessons of exposing themselves to the enemy were made startlingly clear early on, when a senior noncommissioned officer (NCO), apparently thirsty and not just a little bit complacent, took off his body armor and helmet during the platoon's first full day in the mountain.

Perhaps thinking he was at his favorite fishing hole back home, he casually approached a stream of water and within seconds he was nearly shredded by a DShK machine gunner.

"I can't for the life of me figure out why he did that. At this point we had been mortared and gazed quite a few times from the time we reached the blocking position, and the next morning when we came down and reached this position is where this happened," Crowder said. "We would hear rounds for a few minutes, and then you get hit by a few more just on top of each other."

Members of the platoon were on the inside wall of a wadi running east to west. The banks were about seven feet high, and the wadi was about one hundred meters wide. It was a giant riverbed, but only about a three-foot trickle of water ran down the center because the winter snow hadn't melted.

Crowder saw the platoon sergeant approach the water and admonished him against taking such a chance. He knew there was a hilltop just to the west of their position known as "the well" that was home to a couple DShKs (pronounced dish-kah), large-caliber Russian machine guns that could cut a man in half. As the sergeant bent over to scoop up some water in a cupped hand, Crowder said, he could hear the sound of those guns in the distance.

"Boom!Boom!Boom!Boom!Boom! and then I counted one thousand, two thousand, three thousand, and these bullets are coming in all around his feet, hitting the sides of the wadi, he's dancing around and comes running back," Crowder said. "They're all laughing, and then the sergeant told everyone to get their stuff on," but no one else had taken their equipment off because they were about to head out to the LZ to move to a new position.

As if to punctuate the display of terrain dominance, the enemy let fly a new barrage of heavy metal onto the platoon. While the troops were moving out, a mortar sailed in and hit the exact position where they had been sitting. That was followed by the "pop" of a rocket-propelled grenade (RPG), and a young corporal who was standing about fifty feet from Crowder got lucky.

"It hit right at his feet and blew his chest plate out the top of his plate carrier, shredded his magazines. He took shrapnel in his armpit, on the back of his legs and his butt and knocked him a few feet in the air," Crowder said. "The RPG was a dud."

A Ridgeline Shooter and Reading the Wind

Another early lesson for Crowder and Carracino was the difficulty of reading Afghanistan's wind at high altitude, a formidable foe that snaps and blows erratically. Short of channeling Aeolus, the mythological ruler of winds, they drew on their training and instincts to get the shot they wanted.

"The wind is insane between fifteen and twenty miles per hour, and it's crazy, too," Crowder said, describing the conditions on their first day at the blocking position. "The wind will come off the ridge, come down, come back up, hit you in the face. A lot of guys make the mistake of misreading that kind of wind because it's hitting them in the face and they're thinking it's coming straight at them. It's your basic stuff you learn."

Instead of branching off immediately from the platoon as planned, Crowder and Carracino agreed to stay a little longer to help the rifle platoon retain the advantage a two-man sniper team represents—and the benefit of their enhanced optics and weapons.

Crowder and Carracino also knew that minimizing their movement and exposure to enemy eyes after the heavy contact they had seen at the LZ would be smarter than launching on plan—and they could rest and eat. They would help the platoon pull some long-range observation of the vast landscape before them.

They didn't wait long for action. It started day one. A team of 240B machine gunners in a position above the platoon's outpost was receiving shots, inaccurate shots, every few minutes from a gunman somewhere on an adjacent ridgeline. The blowing wind likely kept him from succeeding, but it didn't stop him from trying.

"The way the terrain was, on the other side of the ridge was Khost and then on the other side was the Pakistan border. That ridge looked to be about six hundred meters away, and the top of the ridge looked about nine hundred meters," Crowder recalled.

But he knew distances could be deceiving. Because it all looked so enormous and prominent, he said, "everything looked closer than it really is, plus there was snow and the light reflected on it makes it seem even closer."

The machine gunners fired back across the ridge, but it did nothing to deter the shooter on the other side. At the request of the rifle platoon sergeant, Crowder and Carracino hiked up to a position near the machine gunners. Carracino set up his rifle, and Crowder positioned his scope. They told the gunners to stay back.

The snipers lay side by side, Crowder reading the wind, Carracino relaxing and getting his body position nestled comfortably into the earth. They scanned the ridge for about an hour, looking for all the possible nooks, ledges, cracks, and gaps where a shooter might hide and giving themselves a chance to get used to the wind.

"There was snow, places where snow had melted, there were spruce pines. I wondered where I'd be, what I'd be doing if the shoe were on the other foot. I wouldn't be on the ridgeline because behind it is a big blue sky to show everybody where you're at. I'd probably be a couple hundred meters below the ridgeline shooting down at us at a slight angle," Crowder remembered.

After scanning for at least another hour, the team saw no movement and figured the gunman had retreated. Then "Zip!" a shot whizzed past about five feet overhead. The enemy had refocused his sights on the American sniper team and came damn close, but Crowder was faster. With that one shot, he saw a quick muzzle flash, even though the sun was out, and adjusted his scope to as close to the spot as he could.

"I still wasn't exactly on top of the guy, I figured a little fifty-meter area, yeah he's right here," Crowder said, explaining how he adjusted the magnification on his scope to bring in everything from the area. After a short while he "saw the outline of the guy from the high chest to the top of the head and what looked like a stick out off to an angle. I kept Jason vectored in between a few boulders."

He focused a little more, "just like we do in training," and identified the stick as a rifle. He saw rocks piled up like sandbags. Carracino quietly said to Crowder that the shooter was at twelve o'clock, directly in front of them about fifty meters up, and said he had seen the flash and was on him.

In one of the only Hollywood moments of the mid-afternoon duel, the sun came across the ridgeline and exposed the shooter. Carracino waited for Crowder's last call to shoot. And now it was between Crowder and the wind, which was constant but with wildly varying speeds. He knew it would be hard to nail it, and they didn't want to miss.

"I asked the 240 guys to give me a three-round burst so I could see the behavior of the tracer. That wind took it for a ride. I told Jason to shoot when the wind was at its lowest so when I say 'go,' we need to go," Crowder said.

He figured out the range and had the scope dialed right around 750 at elevation. He said he didn't dial in for wind, but used scope hold off, a method of compensating for wind.

There are two methods of adjusting for windage and elevation. The first method is to estimate the range and the effect the wind will have on a bullet, then adjust the reticle by dialing the scope. This allows the shooter to aim directly at the target.

The second way to do it is to use the reticle's features, such as mil dots, to adjust the point of aim. This method is known as scope hold off.

"You use your crosshair to judge and the wind was coming from left to right at a constant so we're going to shoot to the left side, a heavy left."

So they waited a bit, saw the guy move slightly every once in a while as if to adjust his own position.

"Jason has no optics, and once the wind slowed down a bit, I told him to shoot immediately. . . . Then I was going to say 'fire' but he shot, which was good, he was right on the guy. It was three inches off his left shoulder. I said, 'Standby.' He did exactly what he was supposed to, he shot, breathed out, re-cycled the bolt, never lifted his head off the gun. The elevation looked good, but the wind needed to be played with so I gave him a correction to move slightly left," Crowder said.

The next shot hit the gunman just above the belly button, and he went down. Crowder considered the shot and wondered if the fight was over. "I thought in the back of my head, 'OK, that's a hydraulic wound, unless we hit him in the spine; he's going to die but it could be a half hour or two hours.' I looked at Jason and said, 'All right man, 750 feet in insane winds with all the climbing and all the stuff all morning, that's good stuff, man.'"

The wide-eyed machine gunners on the hill asked, "You got him?" And I said, 'Yeah, we got him.'"

But the snipers kept an eye on the place they'd sent the shot, and a couple of minutes later, they saw the wounded shooter hunched over the rocks that had been shielding him. He was weak and trying to hold himself up with one arm. Jason shot again and hit the rocks right in front of him. Then he shot one more time.

"That last shot hit the guy right on the right side of his high chest, and he fell straight back and never got back up. We hit him on the second round, and we hit him on the fourth round. "The actual shot was 745 or 746 meters. It wasn't quite 750. In Afghanistan with a 7.62, that's a long shot, especially in that region, it's really long," Crowder said.

CHAPTER NINE

The Parisian
By Alden Brooks

The murderous trench warfare that took place in World War I, with fixed positions of troops attacking each other over open ground, amid machine-gun and artillery firing, has been chronicled by many writers. Few, however, capture the intensity and feeling of the troops like this Alden Brooks story from his book, The Fighting Men, *first published by Scribners in 1917.*

—LAMAR UNDERWOOD

IT WAS A TERRIBLY DARK NIGHT, WET AND PIERCING COLD. THE PAVEMENTS WERE SLIPpery with a muddy slush. They tramped along in silence; not a word; each man his own thoughts, yet each man's thoughts the same. Slowly, however, their blood warmed a little, and their shoulder straps settled into place. The trenches were five kilometres away to the north. By the time they reached the field kitchens, the night was a little less dark; dawn was coming. There was a wee light burning. They halted beside it and wondered what was going to happen next. One or two went and knocked on the rough huts where the cooks slept. Perhaps there might be some chance of getting a little coffee.

"Coffee for us? You're crazy. Do you think they'd waste coffee on us?"

But it so happened that they had halted for just that reason. From the wee light there came a man with great buckets of hot coffee. They gathered about him and held out their tin cups. The man told them not to crowd around so, he could not see what he was doing, and there was plenty for everybody. Standing up, they gulped it down. It was hot. It warmed. Shortly afterward they were filing along the channels through the earth—the third trenches, the second trenches, then slowly into the first trenches. The watchers there rose stiffly and made room for them. A blue rocket shot up from the Germans opposite. It lit up the landscape with a weird light. The earth seemed to grow colder. Then the artillery began intermittently. Then it got to work in earnest, and for half an hour or more it tore the sky above into shreds. They became impatient. They wanted to know what they were waiting for. It was the captain.

"What in the hell is he fussing about now?"

"Oh, he's fussing about the machine-guns!"

"Oh, he's always fussing about something or other!"

"Hell, that's his business!"

Presently the captain came creeping along. He spoke in a low whisper to the young lieutenant in charge of De Barsac's section.

"Are your men ready?"

"Yes, all ready."

"You've placed your machine-guns the way I told you?"

"Yes."

"Good. Then, you understand, you attack right after us. Give me a few minutes, then come out and dash right up."

There was silence again. The captain moved off. Presently George snickered.

"That's all. Dash right up. Well, I'll promise you one thing, old whiskers," he murmured to a watcher by his side, "if I've got to rot and stink out here for the next month, I'll try and carry my carcass as near as I can to their nostrils rather than to yours."

"Shut up," growled Jules.

George looked around.

"God! you're not funking it, are you?"

"Oh, what do you lose? Nothing. Eh! What do you leave behind?"

"Old man, I leave behind more wives than you."

"Yes, I guess you do—yes, I guess you do—yes, I guess that's about it."

"Stop that noise," whispered the lieutenant.

The artillery fire ceased. A minute later they heard the shouts of the other company over to the left, and above the shouting, the rapid, deadly, pank-pank-pank of the German machine-guns. They stood up instinctively; they swung on their knapsacks; they drew out their bayonets and fixed them on their rifles, and while they did so, their breath steamed upon the cold, damp air. Then, standing there in a profound silence, they looked across at each other through that murky morning light and gave up now definitely everything life had brought them. It was a bitter task, much harder for some than for others; but when the lieutenant suddenly said, "At 'em, boys!" all were ready. A low, angry snarl shot from their lips. Like hunted beasts, ready to tear the first thing they met to pieces in a last death-struggle, they scrambled out of the trench. Creeping through the barbed wire, they advanced stealthily until a hail of bullets was turned upon them, then they leaped up with a mighty yell, ran some twenty paces, fell flat upon the ground, and leaped up once more.

Head bent down, De Barsac plunged forward. Bullets sang and hissed about him. Every instant he expected death to strike him. He stumbled on, trying to offer it the brain and nothing else. He fell headlong over shell holes, but each time picked himself up and staggered on and on. Hours seemed to pass. He remembered George's words. Not rot here—nor here nor here—but carry one's carcass higher and higher. Finally, he heard the young lieutenant yelling: "Come on, boys, come on, we're almost there." He looked up. Clouds of smoke, bullets ripping up the earth, comrades falling about him, a few hurrying on, all huddled up like men in a terrible rain-storm. Of a sudden he found himself among barbed wire and pit holes. The white bleached face of a man, dead weeks ago, leered at him. He stepped over the putrid body and flung himself through the wire. It tore his clothes, but failed to hold him. Bullets whizzed around his head, but they all seemed to be too high. Then, of a sudden, he realized that he was actually going to reach the trench. He started up. He gripped his rifle in both hands and let out a terrible yell. He became livid with rage. Up out of the ground rose a wave of Germans. He saw George drive his bayonet into the foremost; and as the bayonet snapped off, heard him shout: "Keep it and give it to your sweetheart for a hatpin!" A tall, haggard German charged full at him. He stood his ground, parried the thrust. The German's rifle swung off to one side and exposed his body. With a savage snort he drove his bayonet into the muddy uniform. He felt it go in and in, and instinctively plunged it farther and twisted it around, then heard the wretch scream, and saw him drop his rifle and grasp at life with extended arms, and watched him fall off the bayonet and sink down, bloody hands clasped over his stomach, and a golden ring upon the fourth finger. He stood there weak and flabby. His head began to whirl. Only just in time did he ward off the vicious lunge of a sweating bearded monster. Both rifles rose up locked together into the air. Between their up-stretched arms the two men glared at each other.

"Schwein!" hissed the German.

With an adroit twist, De Barsac threw the other off and brought the butt of his rifle down smack upon the moist red forehead. The fellow sank to his knees with a grunt and, eyes closed, vaguely lifted his hand toward his face. De Barsac half fell over him, turned about, and clubbed the exposed neck as hard as he could with his rifle. Bang! went the rifle almost in his sleeve. He swore angrily. But the bullet had only grazed his arm. He leaped on with a loud shout. Within a crater-like opening in the earth a wild, uproarious fight was going on. He caught one glimpse of George swinging the broken leg of a machine-gun and battering in heads right and left, then was engulfed in the melee.

A furious struggle took place—a score of Frenchmen against a score of Germans—in a cockpit of poisoned, shell-tossed earth. None thought of victory, honor. It was merely a wild, frenzied survival of the fittest, wherein each man strove to tear off, rid himself of this fiendish thing against him. Insane with fury, his senses steeped in gore, De Barsac stabbed and clubbed and stabbed; while close by his side a tall Breton, mouth ripped open with a bayonet point, lip flapping down, bellowed horribly: "Kill! Kill! Kill!"

They killed and they killed; then as the contest began to turn rapidly in their favor, their yells became short, swift exclamations of barbaric triumph; then, unexpectedly, it was all over, and the handful of them that remained understood that, by God and by Heaven, they ten, relic though they were of two hundred better men, had actually come through it all alive and on top. The lieutenant, covered with blood, his sword swinging idly from his wrist, staggered over and leaned upon De Barsac's shoulder. In his other hand he held the bespattered broken leg of the machine-gun. So George must be dead. De Barsac burst out laughing nervously. The lieutenant laughed until he had to double up with a fit of coughing. What a picnic! Others sat down, breathing heavily, and told the whole damned German army to come along and see what was waiting for them. But a bullet flew out of the heap of fallen. It burned the skin on De Barsac's forehead like a hot poker. In a twinkling all ten were on their feet again glaring like savages. The lieutenant reached the offender first. The broken leg of the machine-gun came down with an angry thud; then the rest of them turned about and swarmed over the sloping sides of the pit and exterminated, exterminated.

"He's only playing dead. Give him one just the same. Hell! Don't waste a bullet. Here, let me. There, take that, sausage!"

The lieutenant climbed up and took a cautious peep over the top of the crater. There was nothing to see. A dull morning sky over a flat rising field. A bit of communicating trench blown in. Way over to the left, like something far off and unreal, the pank-pank-pank of machine-guns and the uproar of desperate fighting. Behind, on the other side, a field littered with fallen figures in light blue, many crawling slowly away.

"What's happening?" asked De Barsac, still out of breath.

"Can't see. The fighting's all over to the left. Everybody seems to have forgotten us. As far as I can judge, this was an outpost, not a real trench."

· "Well, whatever it was, it's ours now," said someone.

"Well, why don't they follow us up?"

"Yes, by God, right away, or else—"

"Oh, they will soon!" said the lieutenant, "so get busy—no time to waste. Block up that opening, and fill your sand-bags, all the sand-bags you can find, and dig yourselves in."

But they stood there astonished, irritated. Yes, where were the reinforcements? If reinforcements did not come up, they were as good as rats trapped in a cage. The lieutenant had to repeat his command. Angrily they shoved the dead out of their way and dug themselves in and filled up the sand-bags and built a rampart with them along the top of the hollow. They swore darkly. No reinforcements! Not a man sent to help them! So it was death, after all. By chance they uncovered a cement trough covered with boards and earth, a sort of shelter; and down there were a great number of cartridge-bands for a machine-gun. The sight of them inspired the lieutenant. He went and busied himself over the captured machine-gun, still half buried in the dirt. Only one leg was broken off; that was all. Hurriedly he cleaned the gun and propped it up between the bags. Then he stood back and rubbed his hands together and laughed boyishly and seemed very pleased. The sun came up in the distance; it glittered upon the frost in the fields. But with it came the shells. Cursing furiously, the ten ducked down into the trough, and for an hour or more hooted at the marksmanship. Only one shell exploded in the crater. Though it shrivelled them all up, it merely tossed about a few dead bodies and left a nasty trail of gas. They became desperate savages again. Then the firing ceased, and the lieutenant scrambled out and peered through the sand-bags. He turned back quickly, eyes flashing.

"Here they come, boys!"

They jumped up like madmen and pushed their rifles through the sandbags. The lieutenant sat down at the machine-gun. De Barsac fed the bands. Over the field came a drove of gray-coated men. Their bayonets sparkled wonderfully in the new morning light; yet they ran along all doubled up like men doing some Swedish drill. They seemed to be a vast multitude until the machine-gun began to shoot. Then the ten saw that they were not so many after all.

"Take care she doesn't jam, old man," said the lieutenant to De Barsac.

"Oh, don't worry, she isn't going to jam!"

They were both very cool.

"Ah! now she's getting into them beautifully," said the lieutenant; "look at them fall. There we go. Spit, little lady, spit; that's the way—steady, old man."

As if by some miracle the gray line of a sudden began to break up. Many less came rushing on. They were singing some guttural song. The rifles between the sand-bags answered them like tongues aflame with hate; but the machine-gun answered them even faster still, a remorseless stream of fire. Finally, there were only some seven or eight left. The lieutenant did not seem to notice them.

"You see how idiotic it all is," he said nonchalantly. "These attacks with a company or two? Why, our little friend here could have taken care of a whole battalion!"

Only one man remained. He was yelling fiercely at the top of his lungs. He looked like some devil escaped from hell. He came tearing on. Bullets would not hit him. Then he was right upon them. But he saw now he was alone and his whole expression changed. Across his eyes glistened the light film of fear. The man with the torn lip jumped up.

"Here you are," he spluttered hideously, "all yours!"

A loud report in De Barsac's ears, smoke and the muddy soles of a pair of hobnailed boots trembling against the nozzle of the machine-gun.

"Do you see what I mean?" continued the lieutenant. "What is the use of it? Did I say a battalion? Why we could have managed a whole regiment—now, then, somebody shove those pig feet out of the way, so that I can finish off the whole lot properly."

The sun came up now in earnest and warmed them; but though they sat back in their little caves and ate some of the food they had brought and then rolled cigarettes and smoked them, they were very nervous and impatient. Every so often one of them would go up the other side of the pit and look back. Always the same sight through the tangle of barbed wire—a foreground heaped with dead, a field sprinkled with fallen blue figures, and three or four hundred yards away the trenches they had come from; otherwise, not a soul. Once they waved a handkerchief on a bayonet. It only brought a shower of bullets. So that was it. After they had accomplished the impossible, they were going to be left here to die like this. A little later the shells once more began to explode about them. The aim once more was very poor, but they knew it was the prelude to another attack. Death was again angling for them—and this time—

"Here they come!" shouted the lieutenant.

They stood up and, pushing their rifles well out through the sand-bags, glanced along the barrels. They swore furiously at what they saw—twice as many of the pig-eaters as before. De Barsac anxiously fed the bands to the vibrating machine before him. The lieutenant's face was very stern and set. It had lost its boyish look. Suddenly there was a terrific explosion, clouds of smoke, and a strange new pungent odor of gas. A man left his post and, eyes closed, turned round and round and went staggering down the slope and stumbled over a dead man and lay where he fell. They stopped firing and huddled against their caves until the lieutenant shouted out something and the machine-gun trembled again. Then there were two more frightful explosions right over their heads. Great God! It was their own artillery!

Through the fog of smoke De Barsac could only see the lieutenant, cringed up over the machine. His face became purple with rage as he hissed into De Barsac's ear his whole opinion of the matter. If he had not said anything before, it was because it was not fit that he should; but before dying now he wanted to tell one man, one other Frenchman, what he thought of a general staff who could first send men out stupidly to their slaughter, then abandon them in positions won, and finally kill them off with their own artillery. But De Barsac, now that the smoke had rolled away a little, was hypnotized by the huge gray wave roaring toward them nearer and nearer. The machine-gun seemed to be helpless among them. However many fell, others came rushing on. Then, unexpectedly, a shell skimmed just over the heads of the nine and exploded full among the advancing throngs. It was the most beautiful sight any of the nine had ever seen. The gray figures were not simply knocked over, but blown into pieces. And in quick succession came explosion after explosion. Priceless vengeance! The field seemed to be a mass of volcanoes. The ranks faltered, broke, plunged about blindly in the smoke, turned, and fled. Only a few came charging wildly on. But the trembling little machine-gun lowered its head angrily. One by one the figures went sprawling, just as if each in turn had of a sudden walked on to slippery ice. So ended the second attack. The third attack, following right after, was a fiasco. The artillery now had their measure to a yard. The shells blew up among them before they were half started. The nine along the crater top did not fire a shot. Shortly afterward they heard the roar of an aeroplane overhead. It must have been there all the time, head in the wind. Under the wings were concentric circles of red and white about a blue dot. The mere sight of it intoxicated them like champagne. And when it was all over for the moment, and the distant figure, moving off, waved his hand, they gave him a cheer it was a great pity he could not hear.

"You see, boys," said the lieutenant gayly, "he's telling us that it's all right now. Reinforcements will be up after dark."

They sat back once more and scraped the blood and muck off their uniforms and smoked and found another meal, and for want of a suitable oath mumbled abstractedly to themselves. Long, tedious hours followed. Little by little it grew colder; then, at last, the sun began to go down. A dreary, desolate landscape stretched out all around. But the thought that reinforcements would soon be coming cheered them. They rose up and got ready to go, then stood about impatiently. The lieutenant had to tell them to never mind what was going on behind them, but stick to their posts. It grew darker, and darker still. Now help would be here any minute. They heard voices; but they were mistaken. It became quite dark, night, half an hour, an hour, two hours, and still no one came, only an ever-increasing cannon fire all around them, shells whistling and screaming to and fro over their heads, red and blue rockets, cataclysms of sound ceaselessly belched into the hollow. At last they threw their knapsacks off in disgust and sat down and cursed and swore as they had never cursed or sworn before.

The night air became painfully cold. They had to stand up again and stamp about to keep warm and not fall asleep. The lieutenant told them to fire off their rifles from time to time. Jules came nearer to De Barsac.

"Ah!" grumbled De Barsac, "they're making monkeys of us."

"Yes—or else they don't know we've taken this place."

"Oh, they know that well enough. Look at the artillery. No; they don't want this hole. They never wanted it. We were never meant to get here."

"Yes," said a voice in the darkness, "it's like this: They went to Joffre and said: 'General, some damned fools have gone and taken an outpost over there.' 'The hell they have!' says Joffre. 'Why, the damned fools! Well, give them all the military medal.' 'Very well, General,' says the Johnny who brought the message, 'but they are rather hard to reach,' 'Oh, in that case,' says Joffre, 'just finish the poor devils off with a couple of shells.' "

"Look here, boys," said the lieutenant, "cut that talk out. You know, as well as I do, that Joffre had nothing to do with this—"

"Well, why the devil then doesn't he send some one up to reinforce us?"

"Well," said the lieutenant after a pause, "look at all those fireworks. There's enough iron in the air to kill ten army corps. They don't dare come up."

"Don't dare? Christ! we dared, didn't we?"

"Well, they may come up by and by."

But no one came; just the furious interchange of shells all night long. So dawn appeared once more and found them stiff, weary, half frozen, and in their dull, hollow eyes no longer a ray of hope. And soon the shells began to fall again upon the hollow. Heedlessly the young lieutenant stood up and took a long look back at those trenches from which help should come. A shell broke just above him. He was still standing upright; but the top of his head was gone, only the lower jaw remained. Blood welled up for a second, then the figure slowly sank into a heap. De Barsac took the revolver out of the clinched hand and removed the cartridge-belt. He went back and sat down at the machine-gun.

"Feed the bands, will you, when the time comes?" he said to Jules.

"Look here," said a man, "it's sure death hanging on here any longer. I'm going to make a dash back for it before it is too light."

"Stay where you are," growled De Barsac.

"No, I'm going to take my chance."

"Do you hear what I say? Get back where you belong, or I'll blow your brains out."

More shells exploded over them. They were caught unawares. They had barely time to crawl into the trough. In fact, some of them had not. The man, who at last wanted to run away, doubled himself up grotesquely and coughed blood until he slowly rolled down toward the bottom of the pit. And there amidst the smoke was the man with the torn lip, lying on one elbow, and both legs smashed off above the knees. De Barsac and Jules tried to haul him under cover.

"Don't bother, boys; no, don't bother—I'm done for now—my mouth was nothing—but this finishes me—no, you can't stop it bleeding—so get back quick—and I'm not frightened of death—I like it—really, I do—I've been waiting for it for a long time."

The bombardment continued. It soon became a tremendous affair. It was the worst bombardment any of them had ever experienced. It was as if they were trying to hide in the mouth of a volcano. They never could have imagined such a thing possible. Then it grew even worse still. The very inside of hell was torn loose and hurled at them. Sheltered though they were in the cement trough, they were slowly buried under earth and stones and wood and dead flesh. And so, while they lay there thus, suffocated by gas and smoke, blind, deaf, senseless, the bombardment went on hour after hour. In fact, it was a great wonder that any of them lived on. But they were only six. And it is always difficult to kill the last six among a crowd of dead; the very dead themselves rise up and offer protection. At last the French artillery once more began to gain the master hand, and the bombardment gradually weakened, and finally it ceased altogether. Slowly, very slowly, the six unravelled themselves. They did not recognize their surroundings. Most of the dead had disappeared, just morsels of flesh and bone and uniform, here and there. They did not recognize themselves. As for rifles, knapsacks, machine-gun, ammunition, they had no idea where any of these were. Should an attack come now, they were defenseless. But that was just the point. They had not come out to live, but to die. The bottom of the pit was more or less empty now. One by one they went and sat down there and stared stupidly at the ground. If another shell came into the crater, they would all be killed outright. But no shell came—just a nice, warm midday sun ahead. So, presently, for want of something better to do, they gathered about a blood-soaked loaf of bread, a box of sardines, a canteen full of wine, and in this cockpit of poisonous, shell-tossed earth, with only a blue sky overhead and a few distant melodious shells singing past, they ate their last meal together.

As they ate they slowly decided several things. First of all, they decided they were cursed; but that, such being the case and since it was their fate to die like this, forgotten in this bloodstained hole, they would die like men, like Frenchmen. Then they decided that this hole was their property. Back of them lay France and her millions of acres and her millions of men; but right here in the very forefront of the fighting was this sanguinary pit; it belonged to them, all six of them, and they would die defending it. Then, finally, as soldiers of experience, they decided many things about modern warfare that all the thousand and one generals and ministers did not know. They decided that knapsacks were useless, and rifles also. What one wanted was a knife, a long knife—look, about as long as that, well, perhaps a little longer—a revolver, bombs, and endless machine-guns, light and easy to carry. They agreed it was a pity none of them would survive to give these valuable conclusions to the others back there.

But after the six had finished their meal and had smoked up all the tobacco of the only man who had any left, they decided that death was not so hard upon them as they first thought. They could still meet it as it should be met. They rose stiffly and found here a spade, there a rifle, and eventually the machine-gun. Under De Barsac's direction they threw up once more a semblance of a bulwark along the top of the hollow, and to show that there was still some fight left in them, fired a few volleys at the Germans, that is to say, all the cartridges they had left, save a full magazine for that last minute when one goes under, killing as many as one can. But whether because the Germans had grown to be a trifle frightened of them, or for some other reason, they received no reply to their taunts beyond an occasional bullet—just a sweet little afternoon when people in cities flock about, straighten their shoulders, sniff the soft atmosphere, and inform each other that Spring is coming. After a time they slumped down where they were, all of them, and stretching out their wet, mud-soaked legs, fell asleep like tired children, and slept on and on until they were awakened in the dark by scores of mysterious figures who patted them on the back, told them they were all heroes, and explained how each time the German artillery had driven them back, and how all they had to do now was to take hold of the rope there and go home to Bray.

So they got up slowly and, hands upon the rope, wandered off. Once they stopped. They heard men digging away busily toward them. They said nothing. They wandered on.

But before the six could reach even the men digging toward them, the darkness was suddenly rent with stupefying explosions, and shell fragments slashed among them. They fell apart, tumbled into shell holes, rose up, fell down again, lost touch with each other, and what became of them all no one will ever know. One or two must have been killed outright; the others must have crawled about in the dark until Fate decided what she wished to do with them. It was rather a sad end; for they deserved better than this, and the Germans did not prevent reinforcements from coming up. But thus ended the six; who they were and what became of them the world will never know.

De Barsac fell flat upon his stomach and put his hands over his head. The ground shook under him. The darkness was a bedlam of endless explosions and death hisses. He rose up again and made a dash for it, a wild, frenzied dash for life and safety. But though he ran on some distance, it was blind work and the ground was littered with obstacles, and suddenly he was lying half buried under a pile of earth. He was in great pain; such that he moaned and moaned; yet he could not move, and now it was less cold and it was morning. Slowly he extricated his right arm, but his left he could not move, and he had to take the dirt away handful by handful, until the sun made his head ache. When his arm was at last uncovered, he could not move it. His whole sleeve was a mass of blood, and the sun had gone of a sudden and it was raining, and the wet ground was tossing him about again like a man in a blanket, and his leg was broken and blood was trickling into his eyes. He moaned upon his arm until the sun again made his head ache, and Jules and his father had disappeared. He asked them to stay there a little longer, but the man next [to] him was so repulsive he could not die thus beside him. Leaning on his right elbow and pushing with his left foot, he moved away inch by inch; only the dead man followed him, or it was his brother, and he was repelled as before, so he took the canteen away from the dead man across his path and drank the stuff down. Then he began to shout at the top of his lungs. A race of bullets swished by over his head. He fell back again on his side and cried weakly into his arm. But presently he crawled on, inch by inch, until even the sun got tired watching him, and he fell down into a sort of trench. There were a lot of dead men there, but all their canteens were empty except one, and he had a great loaf of bread strapped on his knapsack. It was very good inside under the crust.

He sat up and looked around slowly. Just an empty trench, not a living soul, just the dead. How he had got here he could not remember, except that it had taken days, weeks. If his leg were not broken, he might get up now and walk away somewhere. Ah, what dirty luck! As if his arm were not enough! He judged it was late afternoon. He wondered what had happened to the others—well, he would get the machine-gun into place all by himself and kill, kill, right up to the end. Then he remembered that, of course, that was over. Yes, of course.

"I'm out of my head."

He took some more cognac out of the canteen. He found his knife and his emergency roll. Slowly he cut off his sleeve, and slowly over the great bloody hole in his arm he wound the bandage; then he emptied the iodine bottle over it, and yelled and moaned with pain. But by and by he felt better. Some one spoke to him. It was a white face among the black dead men. He gave the fellow cognac. They sat up together and ate bread and drank cognac. They talked together. All the friend had was a bullet through his chest, just a little hole, but he said it hurt him every time he tried to breathe. He belonged to the 45th. The trench here had been taken by the Germans, only the Germans had to abandon it because they had lost a trench over there to the left.

"Yes," said De Barsac. "That was us."

By and by De Barsac asked the friend if he could get up and walk. The friend said he thought he could now. So he got up and fell down, and got up and fell down, until the third time he did not fall.

"Wait," said De Barsac, "my leg's broken."

They helped each other. They went along scraping the sides of the channel. De Barsac moaned in constant agony. But they saw two men with a stretcher in the fields above. De Barsac halloed feebly. The men turned around with a start; then one of them said, with a scowl: "All right, wait a minute." Then there was the ordinary explosion overhead. They saw nothing more of the two men; just a bit of broken stretcher and canvas sticking up out of the ground and a large cloud of dark smoke rolling away fainter and fainter. The trench was muddy. The trench smelled. The whole land smelled. The earth about was all burned yellow. The clay was red. There were boards in the bottom of the trench, but the boards wabbled and one could not hop along them. They slopped and twisted about.

"Here," said the friend, "lean on me some more."

But he only fainted. So they both lay huddled up in the mud of the channel, and death came down very near them both. But De Barsac's face was lying against a tin can in the mud, and he lifted himself up and saw that it was nearly dark and he shivered with cold. He remembered the cognac. He gulped it all down. It hurt his arm, made it throb, throb, throb; but it somehow also made him feel like laughing. So he laughed; then he cried; then he laughed; all because the friend at his side was dead and he loved him. He had not known him very long, but he loved him. He turned the head up and the friend's eyes opened. He was not dead, after all. Quickly De Barsac hunted for the cognac and at last he found it. He was horrified. He had drunk it all and not left the friend any. But there were just a few drops.

"Thanks, old camel," said the friend.

De Barsac slowly got up and, after he had got up, he helped the friend up.

"Come on."

"All right."

"Here, you get on my back."

"No, you get on mine."

But they both fell again. So they decided to crawl along. Only it was growing colder and colder, and the waits were awful. Finally, the white face said:

"I'm—I'm going to sleep a little—you go on—you see—then you call me—then I'll come along."

De Barsac wondered why they had not thought of doing it that way before. He crawled on and on. At last he stopped and called back. The friend did not come the way he said he would. He was asleep of course. De Barsac started back to fetch him, only some men came along and stepped on him until they suddenly stepped off.

"Yes, he's alive."

De Barsac pointed feebly up the channel.

"He's back there," he said.

"Who?"

"The friend."

"He's delirious," said a voice.

"Well, pass him back to the stretcher-bearers and look lively with those machine-guns."

The dressing-station was all under ground and lined with straw. It was very warm, only it was also very crowded. They gave him some hot soup with vegetables in it. He lay back on the stretcher and perspired; and though he was now in very great pain, he said nothing, because he had nothing to say. The surgeon, sleeves rolled up, bent over him. He set his leg and slapped plaster about. He swabbed his head and made him nearly scream. Then he unwound the bandage on his arm and swore and stood up and said: "Too late. Put on the tag, 'Operate at once.'" It was cold between the two wheels under the open stars amid the cigarette smoke, but the ambulances in Bray made a powerful noise, and through the darkness a sergeant looked at him under a lantern and said impatiently: "Well, I don't give a damn, there isn't an inch of space left. Fire him along to Villers-Bretonneux with that convoy that's starting." The ambulance rocked and bounced over the roads, and it was twice as cold as before. He had not enough blankets. The ambulance smelled so he knew the man to his left must be dead; yes, the man to his left, not the man above, for the man above from time to time dripped hot blood upon him, now upon his neck, now upon his face. In the big shed at Villers-Bretonneux it was warm again, and he lay there upon the straw with the others while crowds of peasant people stared at them. One woman came up and offered him half an orange. He did not take it. Another woman said: "He's out of his head, poor fellow." He said: "No, I'm not." After the man on the stretcher next him had told him he was wounded in the stomach, left shoulder, and both legs, the man on the stretcher next him asked him where he came from and how things were getting on there. He said: "All right." Then the man on the stretcher next him said weakly: "Well, you seem to have picked up all the mud there is up there." So he said: "Oh, there's plenty left!" and a neat little man in black, with a red ribbon in his buttonhole, shook his head and said to a large man staring with a heavy scowl: "They're all that way, you know; a joke on their lips up to the end."

They carried him out through the crowd, and when he was opposite the bloody table under the great arc-light, the men carrying him had to stop a second and the doctor said to the man holding the end of the leg: "Bend down, idiot, haven't you ever sawed wood?" And he saw that there were beads of perspiration upon the doctor's forehead, and he wondered why. In the train it was very, very warm, only it smelled dreadfully—that same smell. He knew now it was the man in the bunk next to him that was dead, and he wanted to tell the attendant so, only the shadows on the wooden ceiling danced about as the train rushed along over bridges and through tunnels. The shadows danced about, and sometimes they were horsemen on chargers and sometimes they were just great clouds flying out across the ocean, and all the time that the shadows danced about and the train rushed on and on a man in the other end of the compartment yelled and swore. But although he called the attendants all the names a man has ever called another, the attendants did not move. One said:

"Well, if they do shunt us over on to that other service, that'll mean we'll get down to Paris now and then."

And the first man answered:

"Oh, well, anything for a change—pass me the morphine again, will you, if you're through with it."

The train stopped, and every one wanted to know where they were. One of the attendants told them, "Amiens." He was taken out slowly and carried before a man with a glossy, black beard, smoking a pipe, who read the tag on his buttonhole and wrote something on a sheet of paper. They took him out into the cold, biting wind of a railway yard and carried him across railway tracks and set the stretcher down in pools of black mud, and argued whose turn it was, while a long freight-train rolled slowly by and a man blew a whistle. The ambulance bobbed lightly over cobbles amid the clang of street-cars and the thousand noises of a city. This ambulance also smelled that same smell; but it could not be the man next him, for he was all alone. Then the ambulance ran along a smooth drive and stopped, and the flaps were opened and he was lifted out and carried into a long hallway, where a small man in red slippers scampered about and told others to come, and a white-hooded woman bent over him.

"What's the matter with him?"

"Operation."

"Yes—his left arm—the smell is sufficient indication. George, tell the doctor not to go away."

The white-hooded woman again leaned over him. Her face was wrinkled and tired, but her eyes were very beautiful—they were so gentle and so sad.

"How do you feel?"

"Yes," he mumbled.

"Poor boy! What's your name?"

"Pierre De Barsac."

She took his hand gently and held it.

"Well, Pierre, don't worry. We are going to take care of you."

A little later she said:

"Poor fellow! Are you suffering?"

Tears came into his eyes and he nodded his head.

They carried him up-stairs. They went up slowly, very carefully, and as they turned the corners of the staircase the eyes of the little man with the red slippers glittered and strained over the end of the stretcher. They undressed him. They washed him. They put him to bed. They unwound his arm. Then they stood away and stopped talking. They left him alone with a great wad of damp cotton upon his arm until the doctor came and said:

"My boy, we've got to amputate your left arm at the shoulder."

"At the shoulder," he repeated mechanically.

"Yes, it's the only thing that will save you. What's your profession?"

"Lawyer."

The doctor smiled pleasantly.

"Oh, then you are all right! An arm the less will be a distinction."

They went away. He turned over a little and looked at his arm. He realized that this was the dead thing he had so often smelled. The arm was all brown. It crackled under his finger; then came the large cotton wad where there were strips of black flesh. The hand was crumpled up like a fallen leaf. He saw the scar on his forefinger where, as a little boy, he had cut through the orange too swiftly. What a scene that was, and his mother was dead now, and his father was very old, and the hand now was going to be taken away from him! He turned his head back and cried weakly, not on account of his hand, but because he was in such pain, his arm, his leg, his head, everything. They rolled him into another room. They fussed about him. They hurt him dreadfully; but he said nothing, because he had nothing to say. Then he was back there again, beside the lieutenant, only the machine-gun jammed and he had to break the leg off and use it against the hordes of pig-eaters, and smoke, more smoke, down one's nostrils, and then it was awful, awful, never like this, and he clutched the pig-eater by the throat and swore, swore, until now more smoke came rolling into his nostrils, and the white-hooded nurse was standing by his bed.

She went away; and when he woke up again, he was all alone. There was a bandage upon his left arm; no, his left shoulder. His arm hurt much less; he felt much better. By and by he moved his right hand over. The sleeve of the nightgown was empty.

He lay there quietly a long time and looked up into the sky through some pine boughs swaying in the wind. They reminded him of other trees he knew of—trees way back there in Brittany by the seaside where he was born. They swayed beautifully to and fro, and every so often they bent over and swished against the window-pane.

Presently he smiled, smiled quietly, happily. Life, when one can live it, is such a really wonderful thing.

CHAPTER TEN

General Custer

By Francis Fuller Victor

It's all here: The 7th Cavalry and its leader, General George Armstrong Custer, as they ride toward the Little Big Horn. Custer thought a glorious victory over the Indians would be his destiny. He was wrong.

—LAMAR UNDERWOOD

GENERAL TERRY LEFT FORT ABRAHAM LINCOLN ON THE MISSOURI RIVER, MAY 17TH 1876, with his division, consisting of the 7th Cavalry under Lieut. Col. George A. Custer, three companies of infantry, a battery of Gatling guns, and 45 enlisted scouts. His whole force, exclusive of the wagon-train drivers, numbered about 1,000 men. His march was westerly, over the route taken by the Stanley expedition in 1873.

On the 11th of June, Terry reached the south bank of the Yellowstone at the mouth of Powder River, where by appointment he met steamboats, and established his supply camp. A scouting party of six companies of the 7th Cavalry under Major M. A. Reno was sent out June 10th, which ascended Powder River to its forks, crossed westerly to Tongue River and beyond, and discovered, near Rosebud River, a heavy Indian trail about ten days old leading westward toward Little Big Horn River. After following this trail a short distance Reno returned to the Yellowstone and rejoined his regiments, which then marched, accompanied by steamboats, to the mouth of Rosebud River where it encamped June 21st. Communication by steamboats and scouts had previously been opened with Col. John Gibbon, whose column was at this time encamped on the north side of the Yellowstone, near by.

Col. Gibbon of the 7th Infantry had left Fort Ellis in Montana about the middle of May, with a force consisting of six companies of his regiment, and four companies of the 2d Cavalry under Major J. S. Brisbin. He had marched eastward down the north bank of the Yellowstone to the mouth of the Rosebud, where he encamped about June 1st.

Gen. Terry now consulted with Gibbon and Custer, and decided upon a plan for attacking the Indians who were believed to be assembled in large numbers near Big Horn River. Custer with his regiment was to ascend the valley of the Rosebud, and then turn towards Little Big Horn River, keeping well to the south. Gibbon's troops were to cross the Yellowstone at the mouth of Big Horn River, and march up the Big Horn to its junction with the Little Big Horn, to co-operate with Custer. It was hoped that the Indians would thus be brought between the two forces so that their escape would be impossible.

Col. Gibbon's column was immediately put in motion for the mouth of the Big Horn. On the next day, June 22d, at noon, Custer announced himself ready to start, and drew out his regiment. It consisted of 12 companies, numbering 28 officers and 747 soldiers. There were also a strong detachment of scouts and guides, several civilians, and a supply train of 185 pack mules. Gen. Terry reviewed the column in the presence of Gibbon and Brisbon and it was pronounced in splendid condition. "The officers clustered around Terry for a final shake of the hand, the last good-bye was said, and in the best of spirits, filled with high hopes, they galloped away—many of them to their death."

Gen. Terry's orders to Custer were as follows:

Camp at the mouth of Rosebud River,
June 22d, 1876.
Lieut. Col. Custer, 7th Cavalry.

Colonel: The Brigadier General Commanding directs that as soon as your regiment can be made ready for the march, you proceed up the Rosebud in pursuit of the Indians whose trail was discovered by Major Reno a few days ago. It is, of course, impossible to give any definite instructions in regard to this movement, and, were it not impossible to do so, the Department Commander places too much confidence in your zeal, energy, and ability to wish to impose upon you precise orders which might hamper your action when nearly in contact with the enemy. He will, however, indicate to you his own views of what your action should be, and he desires that you should conform to them unless you shall see sufficient reason for departing from them. He thinks that you should proceed up the Rosebud until you ascertain definitely the direction in which the trail above spoken of leads. Should it be found (as it appears to be almost certain that it will be found) to turn towards the Little Big Horn, he thinks that you should still proceed southward per-haps as far as the head waters of the Tongue, and then turn toward the Little Big Horn, feeling constantly, however, to your left, so as to preclude the possibility of the escape of the Indians to the south or south-east by passing around your left flank. The column of Col. Gibbon is now in motion for the mouth of the Big Horn. As soon as it reaches that point it will cross the Yellowstone, and move up at least as far as the forks of the Big and Little Big Horn. Of course its future movements must be controlled by circumstances as they arise; but it is hoped that the Indians, if up on the Little Big Horn, may be so nearly inclosed by the two columns that their escape will be impossible. The Department Commander desires that on your way up the Rosebud you should thoroughly examine the upper part of Tulloch's Creek, and that you should endeavor to send a scout through to Col. Gibbon's column with information of the result of your examination. The lower part of this creek will be examined by a detachment from Col. Gibbon's command. The supply steamer will be pushed up the Big Horn as far as the forks of the river are found to be navigable for that space, and the Department Commander, who will accompany the column of Col. Gibbon, desires you to report to him there not later than the expiration of the time for which your troops are rationed, unless in the meantime you receive further orders.

Respectfully, &c.,

E. W. Smith, Captain 18th Infantry,

Acting Assistant Adjutant General.

After proceeding southerly up the Rosebud for about seventy miles, Custer, at 11 p.m. on the night of the 24th, turned westerly towards Little Big Horn River. The next morning while crossing the elevated land between the two rivers, a large Indian village was discovered about fifteen miles distant, just across Little Big Horn River. Custer with characteristic promptness decided to attack the village at once.

One company was escorting the train at the rear. The balance of the force was divided into three columns. The trail they were on led down to the stream at a point some distance south of the village. Major Reno, with three companies under Capt. T. H. French, Capt. Myles Moylan, and Lieut. Donald McIntosh, was ordered to follow the trail, cross the stream, and charge down its north bank. Capt. F. W. Benteen, with his own company and two others under Capt. T. B. Weir and Lieut. E. S. Godfrey, was sent to make a detour to the south of Reno. The other five companies of the regiment, under the immediate command of Custer, formed the right of the little army.

On reaching the river Reno crossed it as ordered, and Custer with his five companies turned northerly into a ravine running behind the bluffs on the east side of the stream.

The supply steamer *Far West* with Gen. Terry and Col. Gibbon on board, which steamed up the Yellowstone on the evening of June 23d, overtook Gibbon's troops near the mouth of the Big Horn early on the morning of the 24th; and by 4 o'clock p.m. of the same day, the entire command with the animals and supplies had been ferried over to the south side of the Yellowstone. An hour later the column marched out to and across Tulloch's Creek, and then encamped for the night.

At 5 o'clock on the morning of the 25th (Sunday), the column was again in motion; and after marching 22 miles over a country so rugged as to task the endurance of the men to the utmost, the infantry halted for the night. Gen. Terry, however, with the cavalry and the battery pushed on 14 miles further in hopes of opening communication with Custer, and camped at midnight near the mouth of the Little Big Horn.

Scouts sent out from Terry's camp early on the morning of the 26th discovered three Indians, who proved to be Crows who had accompanied Custer's regiment. They reported that a battle had been fought and that the Indians were killing white men in great numbers. Their story was not fully credited, as it was not expected that a conflict would occur so soon, or believed that serious disaster could have overtaken so large a force.

The infantry, which had broken camp very early, now came up, and the whole column crossed the Little Big Horn and moved up its western valley. It was soon reported that a dense heavy smoke was resting over the southern horizon far ahead, and in a short time it became visible to all. This was hailed as a sign that Custer had met the Indians, defeated them, and burned their village. The weary foot soldiers were elated and freshened by the sight, and pressed on with increased spirit and speed.

Custer's position was believed to be not far ahead, and efforts were repeatedly made during the afternoon to open communication with him; but the scouts who attempted to go through were met and driven back by hostile Indians who were hovering in the front. As evening came on, their numbers increased and large parties could be seen on the bluffs hurrying from place to place and watching every movement of the advancing soldiers.

At 8:40 in the evening the infantry had marched that day about 30 miles. The forks of the Big Horn, the place where Terry had requested Custer to report to him, were many miles behind and the expected messenger from Custer had not arrived. Daylight was fading, the men were fatigued, and the column was therefore halted for the night. The animals were picketed, guards were set, and the weary men, wrapped in their blankets and with their weapons beside them, were soon asleep on the ground.

Early on the morning of the 27th the march up the Little Big Horn was resumed. The smoke cloud was still visible and apparently but a short distance ahead. Soon a dense grove of trees was reached and passed through cautiously, and then the head of the column entered a beautiful level meadow about a mile in width, extending along the west side of the stream and overshadowed east and west by high bluffs. It soon became apparent that this meadow had recently been the site of an immense Indian village, and the great number of temporary brushwood and willow huts indicated that many Indians beside the usual inhabitants had rendezvoused there. It was also evident that it had been hastily deserted. Hundreds of lodge-poles, with finely-dressed buffalo-robes and other hides, dried meat, stores, axes, utensils, and Indian trinkets were left behind; and in two tepees or lodges still standing, were the bodies of nine Indians who had gone to the "happy hunting-grounds."

Every step of the march now revealed some evidence that a conflict had taken place not far away. The dead bodies of Indian horses were seen, and cavalry equipments and weapons, bullet-pierced clothing, and blood-stained gloves were picked up; and at last the bodies of soldiers and their horses gave positive proof that a disastrous battle had taken place. The Crow Indians had told the truth.

The head of the column was now met by a breathless scout, who came running up with the intelligence that Major Reno with a body of troops was intrenched on a bluff further on, awaiting relief. The soldiers pushed ahead in the direction pointed out, and soon came in sight of men and horses intrenched on top of a hill on the opposite or east side of the river. Terry and Gibbon immediately forded the stream and rode toward the group. As they approached the top of the hill, they were welcomed by hearty cheers from a swarm of soldiers who came out of their intrenchments to meet their deliverers. The scene was a touching one. Stout-hearted soldiers who had kept bravely up during the hours of conflict and danger now cried like children, and the pale faces of the wounded lighted up as hope revived within them.

The story of the relieved men briefly told was as follows: After separating from Custer about noon, June 25th . . . Reno proceeded to the river, forded it, and charged down its west bank toward the village, meeting at first with but little resistance. Soon however he was attacked by such numbers as to be obliged to dismount his men, shelter his horses in a strip of woods, and fight on foot. Finding that they would soon be surrounded and defeated, he again mounted his men, and charging upon such of the enemy as obstructed his way, retreated across the river, and reached the top of a bluff followed closely by Indians. Just then Benteen, returning from his detour southward, discovered Reno's perilous position, drove back the Indians, and joined him on the hill. Shortly afterward, the company which was escorting the mule train also joined Reno. The seven companies thus brought together had been subsequently assailed by Indians; many of the men had been killed and wounded, and it was only by obstinate resistance that they had been enabled to defend themselves in an entrenched position. The enemy had retired on the evening of the 26th.

After congratulations to Reno and his brave men for their successful defence enquiries were made respecting Custer, but no one could tell where he was. Neither he or any of his men had been seen since the fight commenced, and the musketry heard from the direction he took had ceased on the afternoon of the 25th. It was supposed by Reno and Benteen that he had been repulsed, and retreated northerly towards Terry's troops.

A search for Custer and his men was immediately began, and it revealed a scene calculated to appal the stoutest heart. Although neither Custer or any of that part of his regiment which he led to combat were found alive to tell the tale, an examination of their trail and the scene of conflict enabled their comrades to form some idea of the engagement in which they perished.

General Custer's trail, from the place where he left Reno's and turned northward, passed along and in the rear of the crest of hills on the east bank of the stream for nearly three miles, and then led, through an opening in the bluff, down to the river. Here Custer had evidently attempted to cross over to attack the village. The trail then turned back on itself, as if Custer had been repulsed and obliged to retreat, and branched to the northward, as if he had been prevented from returning southerly by the way he came, or had determined to retreat in the direction from which Terry's troops were advancing.

Several theories as to the subsequent movements of the troops have been entertained by persons who visited the grounds. One is, that the soldiers in retreating took advantage of two ravines; that two companies under Capt. T. W. Custer and Lieut. A. E. Smith, were led by Gen. Custer up the ravine nearest the river, while the upper ravine furnished a line of retreat for the three companies of Capt. G. W. Yates, Capt. M. W. Keogh, and Lieut. James Calhoun. At the head of this upper ravine, a mile from the river, a stand had been made by Calhoun's company; the skirmish lines were marked by rows of the slain with heaps of empty cartridge shells before them, and Lieuts. Calhoun and Crittenden lay dead just behind the files. Further on, Capt. Keogh had fallen surrounded by his men; and still further on, upon a hill, Capt. Yates' company took its final stand. Here, according to this theory, Yates was joined by what remained of the other two companies, who had been furiously assailed in the lower ravine; and here Gen. Custer and the last survivors of the five companies met their death, fighting bravely to the end.

Another theory of the engagement is, that Custer attempted to retreat up the lower ravine in columns of companies; that the companies of Custer and Smith being first in the advance and last in the retreat, fell first in the slaughter which followed the retrograde movement; that Yates' company took the position on the hill, and perished there with Custer and other officers; and that the two other companies, Keogh's and Calhoun's, perished while fighting their way back towards Reno—a few reaching the place where Custer first struck the high banks of the river.

Still another theory is, that the main line of retreat was by the upper ravine; that Calhoun's company was thrown across to check the Indians, and was the first annihilated. That the two companies of Capt. Custer and Lieut. Smith retreated from the place where Gen. Custer was killed into the lower ravine, and were the last survivors of the conflict.

Near the highest point of the hill lay the body of General Custer, and near by were those of his brother Captain Custer, Lieut. Smith, Capt. Yates, Lieut. W. V. Riley of Yates' company, and Lieut. W. W. Cooke. Some distance away, close together, were found another brother of Gen. Custer—Boston Custer, a civilian, who had accompanied the expedition as forage master of the 7th Cavalry—and his nephew Armstrong Reed, a youth of nineteen, who was visiting the General at the time the expedition started, and accompanied it as a driver of the herd of cattle taken along. The wife of Lieut. Calhoun was a sister of the Custers and she here lost her husband, three brothers, and a nephew.

Other officers of Custer's battalion killed but not already mentioned, were Asst. Surgeon L. W. Lord, and Lieuts. H. M. Harrington, J. E. Porter, and J. G. Sturgis. The last named was a West Point graduate of 1875, and a son of General S. D. Sturgis, the Colonel of the 7th Cavalry, who had been detained by other duties when his regiment started on this expedition. The bodies of the slain were rifled of valuables and all were mutilated excepting Gen. Custer, and Mark Kellogg—a correspondent of the *New York Herald*. Gen. Custer was clad in a buckskin suit; and a Canadian—Mr. Macdonald—was subsequently informed by Indians who were in the fight, that for this reason he was not mangled, as they took him to be some brave hunter accidentally with the troops. Others believe that Custer was passed by from respect for the heroism of one whom the Indians had learned to fear and admire.

The dead were buried June 28th, where they fell, Major Reno and the survivors of his regiment performing the last sad rites over their comrades.

A retreat to the mouth of Big Horn River was now ordered and successfully effected, the wounded being comfortably transported on mule litters to the mouth of the Little Big Horn, where they were placed on a steamboat and taken to Fort Lincoln. Gibbon's Cavalry followed the Indians for about ten miles, and ascertained that they had moved to the south and west by several trails. A good deal of property had been thrown away by them to lighten their march, and was found scattered about. Many of their dead were also discovered secreted in ravines a long distance from the battle field.

At the boat was found one of Custer's scouts, who had been in the fight—a Crow named Curley; his story was as follows:

"Custer kept down the river on the north bank four miles, after Reno had crossed to the south side above. He thought Reno would drive down the valley, to attack the village at the upper end, while he (Custer) would go in at the lower end. Custer had to go further down the river and further away from Reno than he wished on account of the steep bank along the north side; but at last he found a ford and dashed for it. The Indians met him and poured in a heavy fire from across the narrow river. Custer dismounted to fight on foot, but could not get his skirmishers over the stream. Meantime hundreds of Indians, on foot and on ponies, poured over the river, which was only about three feet deep, and filled the ravine on each side of Custer's men. Custer then fell back to some high ground behind him and seized the ravines in his immediate vicinity. The Indians completely surrounded Custer and poured in a terrible fire on all sides. They charged Custer on foot in vast numbers, but were again and again driven back.

"The fight began about 2 o'clock, and lasted almost until the sun went down over the hills. The men fought desperately, and after the ammunition in their belts was exhausted went to their saddlebags, got more and continued the fight. Custer lived until nearly all of his men had been killed or wounded, and went about encouraging his soldiers to fight on. He got a shot in the left side and sat down, with his pistol in his hand. Another shot struck Custer in the breast, and he fell over. The last officer killed was a man who rode a white horse—believed to be Lieut. Cooke, as Cooke and Calhoun were the only officers who rode white horses.

"When he saw Custer hopelessly surrounded he watched his opportunity, got a Sioux blanket, put it on, and worked up a ravine, and when the Sioux charged, he got among them and they did not know him from one of their own men. There were some mounted Sioux, and seeing one fall, he ran to him, mounted his pony, and galloped down as if going towards the white men, but went up a ravine and got away. As he rode off he saw, when nearly a mile from the battle field, a dozen or more soldiers in a ravine, fighting with Sioux all around them. He thinks all were killed, as they were outnumbered five to one, and apparently dismounted. The battle was desperate in the extreme, and more Indians than white men must have been killed."

The following extract is from a letter written to Gen. Sheridan by Gen. Terry at his camp on the Big Horn, July 2d:

"We calculated it would take Gibbon's command until the 26th to reach the mouth of the Little Big Horn, and that the wide sweep I had proposed Custer should make would require so much time that Gibbon would be able to co-operate with him in attacking any Indians that might be found on the stream. I asked Custer how long his marches would be. He said they would be at the rate of about 30 miles a day. Measurements were made and calculations based on that rate of progress. I talked with him about his strength, and at one time suggested that perhaps it would be well for me to take Gibbon's cavalry and go with him. To the latter suggestion he replied: that, without reference to the command, he would prefer his own regiment alone. As a homogeneous body, as much could be done with it as with the two combined. He expressed the utmost confidence that he had all the force that he could need, and I shared his confidence. The plan adopted was the only one which promised to bring the infantry into action, and I desired to make sure of things by getting up every available man. I offered Custer the battery of Gatling guns, but he declined it, saying that it might embarrass him, and that he was strong enough without it. The movements proposed by General Gibbon's column were carried out to the letter, and had the attack been deferred until it was up, I cannot doubt that we should have been successful."

As the foregoing biography of Gen. Custer has been confined chiefly to his military career, it may be well in conclusion to give some account of his personal characteristics; and this can be best done in the language of those who knew him well. A gentleman who accompanied Gen. Custer on the Yellowstone and Black Hills expeditions, contributed to the *New York Tribune* the following:

"Gen. Custer was a born cavalryman. He was never more in his element than when mounted on Dandy, his favorite horse, and riding at the head of his regiment. He once said to me, 'I would rather be a private in the cavalry than a line officer in the infantry.' He was the personification of bravery and dash. If he had only added discretion to his valor he would have been a perfect soldier. His impetuosity very often ran away with his judgment.

He was impatient of control. He liked to act independently of others, and take all the risk and all the glory to himself. He frequently got himself into trouble by assuming more authority than really belonged to his rank. It was on the Yellowstone expedition where he came into collision with Gen. Stanley, his superior officer, and was placed under arrest and compelled to ride at the rear of his column for two or three days, until Gen. Rosser, who fought against Custer in the Shenandoah Valley during the war but was then acting as engineer of the Northern Pacific Railroad, succeeded in effecting a reconciliation. Custer and Stanley afterward got on very well, and perhaps the quarrel would never have occurred if the two generals had been left alone to themselves without the intervention of camp gossips, who sought to foster the traditional jealousy between infantry and cavalry. For Stanley was the soul of generosity, and Custer did not really mean to be arrogant; but from the time when he entered West Point to the day when he fell on the Big Horn, he was accustomed to take just as much liberty as he was entitled to.

"For this reason, Custer worked most easily and effectively when under general orders, when not hampered by special instructions, or his success made dependent on anybody else. Gen. Terry understood his man when, in the order directing him to march up the Rosebud, he very liberally said: 'The Department Commander places too much confidence in your zeal, energy, and ability to wish to impose upon you precise orders which might hamper your action when nearly in contact with the enemy.' But Gen. Terry did not understand Custer if he thought he would wait for Gibbon's support before attacking an Indian camp. Undoubtedly he ought to have done this; but with his native impetuosity, his reckless daring, his confidence in his own regiment, which had never failed him, and his love of public approval, Custer could no more help charging this Indian camp, than he could help charging just so many buffaloes. He had never learned to spell the word 'defeat'; he knew nothing but success, and if he had met the Indians on the open plains, success would undoubtedly have been his; for no body of Indians could stand the charge of the 7th Cavalry when it swept over the Plains like a whirlwind. But in the Mauvaises Terres and the narrow valley of the Big Horn he did it at a fearful risk.

"With all his bravery and self-reliance, his love of independent action, Custer was more dependent than most men on the kind approval of his fellow. He was even vain; he loved display in dress and in action. He would pay $40 for a pair of troop boots to wear on parade, and have everything else in keeping. On the Yellowstone expedition he wore a bright red shirt, which made him the best mark for a rifle of any man in the regiment. I remonstrated with him for this reckless exposure, but found an appeal to his wife more effectual, and on the next campaign he wore a buckskin suit. He formerly wore his hair very long, letting it fall in a heavy mass upon his shoulders, but cut it off before going out on the Black Hills, producing quite a change in his appearance. But if vain and ambitious, Custer had none of those great vices which are so common and so distressing in the army. He never touched liquor in any form; he did not smoke, or chew, or gamble. He could outride almost any man in his regiment, I believe, if it were put to a test. When he set out to reach a certain point at a certain time, you could be sure that he would be there if he killed every horse in the command. He was sometimes too severe in forcing marches, but he never seemed to get tired himself, and he never expected his men to be so. In cutting our way through the forest of the Black Hills, I have often seen him take an ax and work as hard as any of the pioneers. He was never idle when he had a pretext for doing anything, whatever he did he did thoroughly. He would overshoot the mark, but never fall short. He fretted in garrison sometimes, because it was too inactive; but he found an outlet here for his energies in writing articles for the press.

"He had a remarkable memory. He could recall in its proper order every detail of any action, no matter how remote, of which he was participant. He was rather verbose in writing, and had no gifts as a speaker; but his writings interested the masses from their close attention to details, and from his facility with the pen as with the sword in bringing a thing to a climax. As he was apt to overdo in action, so he was apt to exaggerate in statement, not from any willful disregard of the truth, but because he saw things bigger than they really were. He did not distort the truth; he magnified it. He was a natural optimist. He took rose-colored views of everything, even of the miserable lands of the Northern Pacific Railroad. He had a historical memory, but not a historical mind. He was no philosopher; he could reel off facts from his mind better than he could analyze or mass them. He was not a student, or a deep thinker. He loved to take part in events rather than to brood over them. He was fond of fun, genial and pleasant in his manner; a loving and devoted husband. It was my privilege to spend two weeks in his family at one time, and I know how happy he was in his social relations."

The following rambling remarks are accredited to a general, who name is not given:

"The truth about Custer is, that he was a pet soldier, who had risen not above his merit, but higher than men of equal merit. He fought with Phil Sheridan, and through the patronage of Sheridan he rose; but while Sheridan liked his valor and dash he never trusted his judgment. He was to Sheridan what Murat was to Napoleon. While Sheridan is always cool, Custer was always aflame. Rising to high command early in life, he lost the reposed necessary to success in high command. . . . Then Custer must rush into politics, and went swinging around the circle with Johnson. He wanted to be a statesman, and but for Sheridan's influence with Grant, the republicans would have thrown him; but you see we all liked Custer, and did not mind his little freaks in that way any more than we would have minded temper in a woman. Sheridan, to keep Custer in his place, kept him out on the Plains at work. He gave him a fine command—one of the best cavalry regiments in the service. The colonel, Sturgis, was allowed to bask in the sunshine in a large city, while Custer was the real commander. In this service Custer did well, and vindicated the partiality of Sheridan as well as the kind feelings of his friends. . . . The old spirit which sent Custer swinging around the circle revived in him. He came East and took a prominent part in reforming the army. This made feeling, and drew upon Custer the anger of the inside forces of the administration.

"Then he must write his war memoirs. Well, in these memoirs he began to write recklessly about the army. He took to praising McClellan as the greatest man of the war, and, coming as it did when the democrats began to look lively, it annoyed the administration. Grant grew so much annoyed that even Sheridan could do no good, and Custer was disgraced. Technically it was not a disgrace. All that Grant did was to put Terry, a general, over Custer, a lieutenant-colonel, who had his regiment all the same; but all things considered, it was a disgrace."

The following is from an article by Gen. A. B. Nettleton, published in the *Philadelphia Times*:

"It must be remembered that in fighting with cavalry, which was Custer's forte, instantaneous quickness of eye—that is the lightning-like formation and execution of successive correct judgments on a rapidly-shifting situation—is the first thing, and the second is the power of inspiring the troopers with that impetuous yet intelligent ardor with which a mounted brigade becomes a thunderbolt, and without which it remains a useless mass of horses and riders. These qualities Gen. Custer seemed to me to manifest, throughout the hard fighting of the last year of the war, to a degree that was simply astounding, and in a manner that marked him as one of the few really great cavalry commanders developed by the wars of the present century. Of fear, in the sense of dread of death or of bodily harm, he was absolutely destitute, yet his love of life and family and home was keen and constant, leaving no room in his nature for desperation, recklessness, or conscious rashness. In handling his division under Sheridan's general oversight, he seemed to act always on the belief that in campaigning with cavalry, when a certain work must be done, audacity is the truest caution. In action, when all was going well and success was only a question of time or of steady 'pounding,' Gen. Custer did not unnecessarily expose himself, but until the tide of battle had been turned in the right direction, and especially when disaster threatened, the foremost point in our division's line was almost invariably marked by the presence of Custer, his waving division tri-color and his plucky staff.

"A major-general of wide and splendid fame at twenty-five, and now slain at thirty-six, the gallant Custer had already lived long if life be measured by illustrious deeds."

The following is from a sketch of Gen. Custer published in the *Army and Navy Journal*:

"Custer was passionately addicted to active and exciting sports as the turf and hunting. He was a splendid horseman and a lover of the horse; he attended many American race-meetings and ran his own horses several times in the West. His greyhounds and staghounds went with him at the head of his regiment, to be let slip at antelope or buffalo. With rifle or shotgun he was equally expert, and had killed his grizzly bear in the most approved fashion. . . . Bold to rashness; feverish in camp, but cool in action; with the personal vanity of a carpet knight, and the endurance and insensibility to fatigue of the hardiest and boldest rough rider a prince of scouts; a chief of guides, threading a trackless prairie with unerring eye of a native and the precision of the needle to the star; by no means a martinet, his men were led by the golden chain of love, admiration and confidence. He had the proverbial assurance of a hussar, but his personal appearance varied with occasion. During the war he was 'Custer of the golden locks, his broad sombrero turned up from his hard-bronzed face, the ends of his crimson cravat floating over his shoulder, gold galore spangling his jacket sleeves, a pistol in his boot, jangling spurs on his heels, and a ponderous claymore swinging at his side.' And long after, when he roamed a great Indian fighter on the Plains, the portrait was only slightly changed. The cavalry jacket was exchanged for the full suit of buckskin, beautifully embroidered by Indian maidens; across his saddle rested a modern sporting rifle, and at his horse's feet demurely walked hounds of unmixed breed. Again, within a few months, he appears in private society as an honored guest; scrupulously avoiding anything like display, but in a quiet conventional suit of blue, with the 'golden locks' closely shorn, and the bronzed face pale from recent indisposition, he moves almost unnoticed in the throng."

The faithful correspondent who perished with Gen. Custer on the Little Big Horn portrayed him thus:

"A man of strong impulses, of great hearted friendships and bitter enmities; of quick, nervous temperament, undaunted courage, will, and determination; a man possessing electric mental capacity, and of iron frame and constitution; a brave, faithful, gallant soldier, who has warm friends and bitter enemies; the hardest rider, the greatest pusher; with the most untiring vigilance overcoming seeming impossibilities, and with an ambition to succeed in all things he undertakes; a man to do right, as he construes right, in every case; one respected and beloved by his followers, who would freely follow him into the 'jaws of hell.'"

Gen. Custer's last battle "will stand in history as one of the most heroic engagements ever fought, and his name will be respected so long as chivalry is applauded and civilization battles against barbarism."

CHAPTER ELEVEN

The Battle of Trenton
By Henry Cabot Lodge

Another story from the book Hero Tales from American History, *by Henry Cabot Lodge and Theodore Roosevelt, published in 1895 by the Century Company.*
—LAMAR UNDERWOOD

IN DECEMBER, 1776, THE AMERICAN REVOLUTION WAS AT ITS LOWEST EBB. THE FIRST burst of enthusiasm, which drove the British back from Concord and met them hand to hand at Bunker Hill, which forced them to abandon Boston and repulsed their attack at Charleston, had spent its force. The undisciplined American forces called suddenly from the workshop and the farm had given way, under the strain of a prolonged contest, and had been greatly scattered, many of the soldiers returning to their homes. The power of England, on the other hand, with her disciplined army and abundant resources, had begun to tell. Washington, fighting stubbornly, had been driven during the summer and autumn from Long Island up the Hudson, and New York had passed into the hands of the British. Then Forts Lee and Washington had been lost, and finally the Continental army had retreated to New Jersey. On the second of December Washington was at Princeton with some three thousand ragged soldiers, and had escaped destruction only by the rapidity of his movements. By the middle of the month General Howe felt that the American army, unable as he believed either to fight or to withstand the winter, must soon dissolve, and, posting strong detachments at various points, he took up his winter quarters in New York. The British general had under his command in his various divisions twenty-five thousand well-disciplined soldiers, and the conclusion he had reached was not an unreasonable one; everything, in fact, seemed to confirm his opinion. Thousands of the colonists were coming in and accepting his amnesty. The American militia had left the field, and no more would turn out, despite Washington's earnest appeals. All that remained of the American Revolution was the little Continental army and the man who led it.

Yet even in this dark hour Washington did not despair. He sent in every direction for troops. Nothing was forgotten. Nothing that he could do was left undone. Unceasingly he urged action upon Congress, and at the same time with indomitable fighting spirit he planned to attack the British. It was a desperate undertaking in the face of such heavy odds, for in all his divisions he had only some six thousand men, and even these were scattered. The single hope was that by his own skill and courage he could snatch victory from a situation where victory seemed impossible. With the instinct of a great commander he saw that his only chance was to fight the British detachments suddenly, unexpectedly, and separately, and to do this not only required secrecy and perfect judgment, but also the cool, unwavering courage of which, under such circumstances, very few men have proved themselves capable. As Christmas approached his plans were ready. He determined to fall upon the British detachment of Hessians, under Colonel Rahl, at Trenton, and there strike his first blow. To each division of his little army a part in the attack was assigned with careful forethought. Nothing was overlooked and nothing omitted, and then, for some reason good or bad, every one of the division commanders failed to do his part. As the general plan was arranged, Gates was to march from Bristol with two thousand men; Ewing was to cross at Trenton; Putnam was to come up from Philadelphia; and Griffin was to make a diversion against Donop. When the moment came, Gates, who disapproved the plan, was on his way to Congress; Griffin abandoned New Jersey and fled before Donop; Putnam did not attempt to leave Philadelphia; and Ewing made no effort to cross at Trenton. Cadwalader came down from Bristol, looked at the river and the floating ice, and then gave it up as desperate. Nothing remained except Washington himself with the main army, but he neither gave up, nor hesitated, nor stopped on account of the ice, or the river, or the perils which lay beyond. On Christmas Eve, when all the Christian world was feasting and rejoicing, and while the British were enjoying themselves in their comfortable quarters, Washington set out. With twenty-four hundred men he crossed the Delaware through the floating ice, his boats managed and rowed by the sturdy fishermen of Marblehead from Glover's regiment. The crossing was successful, and he landed about nine miles from Trenton. It was bitter cold, and the sleet and snow drove sharply in the faces of the troops. Sullivan, marching by the river, sent word that the arms of his soldiers were wet. "Tell your general," was Washington's reply to the message, "to use the bayonet, for the town must be taken." When they reached Trenton it was broad daylight. Washington, at the front and on the right of the line, swept down the Pennington road, and, as he drove back the Hessian pickets, he heard the shout of Sullivan's men as, with Stark leading the van, they charged in from the river. A company of jaegers and of light dragoons slipped away. There was some fighting in the streets, but the attack was so strong and well calculated that resistance was useless. Colonel Rahl, the British commander, aroused from his revels, was killed as he rushed out to rally his men, and in a few moments all was over. A thousand prisoners fell into Washington's hands, and this important detachment of the enemy was cut off and destroyed.

The news of Trenton alarmed the British, and Lord Cornwallis with seven thousand of the best troops started at once from New York in hot pursuit of the American army. Washington, who had now rallied some five thousand men, fell back, skirmishing heavily, behind the Assunpink, and when Cornwallis reached the river he found the American army awaiting him on the other side of the stream. Night was falling, and Cornwallis, feeling sure of his prey, decided that he would not risk an assault until the next morning. Many lessons had not yet taught him that it was a fatal business to give even twelve hours to the great soldier opposed to him. During the night Washington, leaving his fires burning and taking a roundabout road which he had already reconnoitered, marched to Princeton. There he struck another British detachment. A sharp fight ensued, the British division was broken and defeated, losing some five hundred men, and Washington withdrew after this second victory to the highlands of New Jersey to rest and recruit.

Frederick the Great is reported to have said that this was the most brilliant campaign of the century. With a force very much smaller than that of the enemy, Washington had succeeded in striking the British at two places with superior forces at each point of contact. At Trenton he had the benefit of a surprise, but the second time he was between two hostile armies. He was ready to fight Cornwallis when the latter reached the Assunpink, trusting to the strength of his position to make up for his inferiority of numbers. But when Cornwallis gave him the delay of a night, Washington, seeing the advantage offered by his enemy's mistake, at once changed his whole plan, and, turning in his tracks, fell upon the smaller of the two forces opposed to him, wrecking and defeating it before the outgeneraled Cornwallis could get up with the main army. Washington had thus shown the highest form of military skill, for there is nothing that requires so much judgment and knowledge, so much certainty of movement and quick decision, as to meet a superior enemy at different points, force the fighting, and at each point to outnumber and overwhelm him.

But the military part of this great campaign was not all. Many great soldiers have not been statesmen, and have failed to realize the political necessities of the situation. Washington presented the rare combination of a great soldier and a great statesman as well. He aimed not only to win battles, but by his operations in the field to influence the political situation and affect public opinion. The American Revolution was going to pieces. Unless some decisive victory could be won immediately, it would have come to an end in the winter of 1776–77. This Washington knew, and it was this which nerved his arm. The results justified his forethought. The victories of Trenton and Princeton restored the failing spirits of the people, and, what was hardly less important, produced a deep impression in Europe in favor of the colonies. The country, which had lost heart, and become supine and almost hostile, revived. The militia again took the field. Outlying parties of the British were attacked and cut off, and recruits once more began to come in to the Continental army. The Revolution was saved. That the English colonies in North America would have broken away from the mother country sooner or later cannot be doubted, but that particular

Revolution of 1776 would have failed within a year, had it not been for Washington. It is not, however, merely the fact that he was a great soldier and statesman which we should remember. The most memorable thing to us, and to all men, is the heroic spirit of the man, which rose in those dreary December days to its greatest height, under conditions so adverse that they had crushed the hope of every one else. Let it be remembered, also, that it was not a spirit of desperation or of ignorance, a reckless daring which did not count the cost. No one knew better than Washington—no one, indeed, so well—the exact state of affairs; for he, conspicuously among great men, always looked facts fearlessly in the face, and never deceived himself. He was under no illusions, and it was this high quality of mind as much as any other which enabled him to win victories.

How he really felt we know from what he wrote to Congress on December 20, when he said: "It may be thought that I am going a good deal out of the line of my duty to adopt these measures or to advise thus freely. A character to lose, an estate to forfeit, the inestimable blessing of liberty at stake, and a life devoted, must be my excuse." These were the thoughts in his mind when he was planning this masterly campaign. These same thoughts, we may readily believe, were with him when his boat was making its way through the ice of the Delaware on Christmas Eve. It was a very solemn moment, and he was the only man in the darkness of that night who fully understood what was at stake; but then, as always, he was calm and serious, with a high courage which nothing could depress.

The familiar picture of a later day depicts Washington crossing the Delaware at the head of his soldiers. He is standing up in the boat, looking forward in the teeth of the storm. It matters little whether the work of the painter is in exact accordance with the real scene or not. The daring courage, the high resolve, the stern look forward and onward, which the artist strove to show in the great leader, are all vitally true. For we may be sure that the man who led that well-planned but desperate assault, surrounded by darker conditions than the storms of nature which gathered about his boat, and carrying with him the fortunes of his country, was at that moment one of the most heroic figures in history.

CHAPTER TWELVE

The Fourteenth at Gettysburg

While the general citizenry of the South faced the terrors of the war on a daily basis, comparatively few battles were waged north of the Mason-Dixon line. One exception, and one of the most famous battles in American history, took place in Gettysburg, Pennsylvania. The account of that battle included here, "The Fourteenth at Gettysburg," first appeared in Harper's Weekly *in 1863.*

—LISA PURCELL

"COME, FRED, TELL ME ALL ABOUT THAT GLORIOUS FIGHT WHICH, YOU KNOW, IT WAS just my ill-luck to miss. If it had been such another shipping as we had at Fredericksburg, the Fates would probably have let me be there. I have heard several accounts, and know the regiment did nobly; but the boys all get so excited telling about it that I have not yet a clear idea of the fight."

"Here goes, then," said the Adjutant, lighting a fresh cigar. "It will serve to pass away time, which hangs so heavy on our hands in this dreary hospital."

"We were not engaged on the first day of the fight, July 1, 1863, but were on the march for Gettysburg that day. All the afternoon we heard the cannonading growing more and more distinct as we approached the town, and as we came on the field at night learned that the First and Eleventh corps had fought hard, suffered much, and been driven back outside the town with the loss of Major-General Reynolds, who, it was generally said, brought on an engagement too hastily with Lee's whole army. We bivouacked on the field that night.

"About nine o'clock the next morning we moved up to the front, and by ten o'clock the enemy's shells were falling around us. Captain Coit had a narrow escape here. We had just stacked arms and were resting, when a runaway horse, frightened by the shelling, came full tilt at him; 'twas 'heavy cavalry' against 'light infantry'; but Coit had presence of mind enough to draw his sword and bringing it to a point it entered the animal's belly.

The shock knocked Coit over, and he was picked up senseless with a terribly battered face, and carried to the rear."

"By-the-way, Fred, is it not singular that he should have recovered so quickly and completely from such a severe blow?"

"Indeed it is. He is as handsome as ever; but to go on. At four o'clock in the afternoon we moved up to support a battery, and here we lay all night. About dark Captain Broatch went out with the pickets. Though under artillery fire all day we were not really engaged, as we did not fire a gun. Some of our pickets, unfortunately going too far to the front, were taken prisoners during the night.

"At about five o'clock on the morning of the 3d Captain Townsend went out with companies B and D and relieved Broatch. As soon as he got out Townsend advanced his men as skirmishers some three hundred yards beyond the regiment, which moved up to the impromptu rifle-pits, which were formed partially by a stone-wall and partially by a rail fence. Just as soon as our skirmishers were posted they began firing at the rebel skirmishers, and kept it up all day, until the grand attack in the afternoon. Before they had been out twenty minutes, Corporal Huxham, of Company B, was instantly killed by a rebel bullet. It was not discovered until another of our skirmishers, getting out of ammunition, went up to him, saying, 'Sam, let me have some cartridges?' Receiving no answer, he stooped down and discovered that a bullet had entered the poor fellow's mouth and gone out at the back of his head, killing the brave, Chancellorsville-scarred, corporal so quickly that he never knew what hurt him. Presently Captain Moore was ordered down with four companies into a lot near by, to drive the rebel sharp-shooters out of a house and barn from whence they were constantly picking off our men. Moore went down on a double-quick, and, as usual, ahead of his men; he was first man in the barn, and as he entered the Butternuts were already jumping out. Moore and his men soon cleared the barn and then started for the house. Here that big sergeant in Company J (Norton) sprang in at the front door just in time to catch a bullet in his thigh, from a reb watching at the back; but that reb did not live long to brag of it, one of our boys taking him 'on the wing.' Moore soon cleared the house out and went back with his men. Later in the day rebs again occupied the house, and Major Ellis took the regiment and drove them out, burning the house, so as not to be bothered by any more concealed sharp-shooters in it."

"Yes, I know the Major don't like to do a thing but once, so he always does it thoroughly the first."

"It was in these charges for the possession of that house we lost more officers and men than in all the rest of the fight.

"About one o'clock in the afternoon the enemy, who had been silent so long that the boys were cooking coffee, smoking, sleeping, etc., suddenly opened all their batteries of reserve artillery upon the position held by our corps (the Second). First one great gun spoke, then, as if it had been the signal for the commencement of an artillery conversation, the whole hundred and twenty or more opened their mouths at once and poured out their thunder. A perfect storm of shot and shell rained around and among us. The boys quickly jumped to their rifles and lay down behind the wall and rail barricade. For two hours this storm of shot and shell continued, and seemed to increase in fury. Good God! I never hear any thing like it, and our regiment has been under fire 'somewhat,' as you know. The ground trembled like an aspen leaf; the air was full of small fragments of lead and iron from the shells. Then the sounds: there was the peculiar *'whoo?—whoo?—whoo-oo?'* of the round shot; the *'which-one?—'which-one?'* of that fiendish Whitworth projectile, and the demoniac shriek of shells. It seemed as if all the devils in hell were holding high carnival. But, strange as it may seem, it was like many other 'sensation doings,' 'great cry and little wool,' as our regiment, and, in fact, the whole corps lost very few men by it, the missiles passing over beyond our position, save the Whitworth projectiles which did not quite reach us, as their single gun of that description was two miles off. Had the enemy had better artillerists at their guns, or a better view of our position, I can not say what would have been the final result; but certain it is, nothing mortal could have stood that fire long, had it been better directed, and if our corps had broken that day, Gettysburg would have been a lost battle, and General Lee, instead of Heintzelman, the commanding officer in this District of Columbia today.

"About three p.m. the enemy's fire slackened, died away, and the smoke lifted to disclose a corps of the rebel 'Grand Army of Northern Virginia,' advancing across the long level plain in our front, in three magnificent lines of battle, with the troops massed in close column by division on both flanks. How splendidly they looked! Our skirmishers, who had staid at their posts through all, gave them volley after volley as they came on, until Captain Townsend was ordered to bring his men in, which he did in admirable order; his men, loading and firing all the way, came in steadily and coolly—all that were left of them, for a good half of them were killed or wounded before they reached the regiment.

"On, on came the rebels, with colors flying and bayonets gleaming in the sunlight, keeping their lines as straight as if on parade: over fences and ditches they come, but still their lines never break, and still they come. For a moment all is hush along our lines, as we gaze in silent admiration at these brave rebs; then our division commander, 'Aleck Hayes,' rides up, and, pointing to the last fence the enemy must cross before reaching us, says, 'Don't fire till they get to that fence; then let 'em have it.'

"On, on, come the rebs, till we can see the whites of their eyes, and hear their officers command, 'Steady, boys, steady!' They reach the fence, some hundred yards in front of us, when suddenly the command 'Fire!' rings down our line; and, rising as one man, the rifles of the old Second Army Corps ring a death-knell for many a brave heart, in butternut dress, worthy of a better cause—a knell that will ring in the hearts of many mothers, sister, and wives, on many a plantation in the once fair and sunny South, where there will be weeping and wailing for the soldier who never returns, who sleeps at Gettysburg. 'Load and fire at will!' Oh Heaven! How we poured our fire into them then—a merciless hail of lead! Their first line wavers, breaks, and runs; some of their color sergeants halt and plant their standards firmly in the ground: they are too well disciplined to leave their colors yet. But they stop only for a moment; then fall back, colors and all. They fall back, but rally, and dress on the other lines, under a tremendous fire from our advancing rifles: rally, and come on again to meet their death. Line after line of rebels come up, deliver their fire, one volley, and they are mown down like the grass of the field. They fall back, form, and come up again, with their battle-flags still waving; but again they are driven back.

"On our right is a break in the line, where a battery has been in position, but, falling short of ammunition, and unable to move it off under such a heavy fire, the gunners have abandoned it to its fate. Some of the rebels gain a footing here. One daring fellow leaps upon the gun, and waves his rebel flag. In an instant a right oblique fire from 'ours,' and a left oblique from the regiment on the left of the position, rolls the ragged rebel and rebel rag in the dust, rolls the determined force back from the gun, and it is ours.

"By-and-by the enemy's lines come up smaller and thinner, break quicker, and are longer in forming. Our boys are wild with excitement, and grow reckless. Lieutenant John Tibbetts stands up yelling like mad, 'Give it to 'em! Give it to 'em!' A bullet enters his arm—that same arm in which he caught two bullets at Antietam; Johnny's game arm drops by his side; he turns quickly to his First Lieutenant, saying, 'I have got another bullet in the same old arm, but I don't care a d—n!' Heaven forgive Johnny! Rebel lead will sometimes bring rebel words with it. All of 'Ours' are carried away with excitement; the Sergeant-Major leaps a wall, dashes down among the rebs, and brings back a battle-flag; others follow our Sergeant-Major; and before the enemy's repulse becomes a rout we of the Fourteenth have six of their battle-flags.

"Prisoners are brought in by hundreds, officers and men. We pay no attention to them, being too busy sending our leaden messengers after the now flying hosts. One of our prisoners, a rebel officer, turns to me, saying, 'Where are the men we've been fighting?' 'Here,' I answer, pointing down our short thin line. 'Good God!' says he, 'Is that all? I wish I could get back.'"

"Yes," I interrupted, "Townsend told me that when he fell back with his skirmishers and saw the whole length of our one small, thin, little line pitted against those then full lines of the rebels, his heart almost sank within him; but Meade had planned that battle well, and every one of our soldiers told."

"Yes," said Fred, "Meade planned the fight well, and Hancock, Hayes, and in fact all of them fought it well. All through the fight General Hancock might be seen galloping up and down the lines of our bully corps, regardless of the leaden hail all about him; and when finally severely wounded in the hip he was carried a little to the rear, where he lay on his stretcher and still gave his orders.

"The fight was now about over; there was only an occasional shot exchanged between the retreating rebel sharp-shooters and our own men, and I looked about me and took an account of stock. We had lost about seventy killed and wounded and taken prisoners, leaving only a hundred men fit for duty. We had killed treble that number, and taken nearly a brigade of prisoners; six stands of colors, and guns, swords, and pistols without number. For the first time we had been through an action without having an officer killed or fatally wounded, though Tibbetts, Seymour, Stoughton, Snagg, Seward, and Dudley were more or less seriously wounded, and Coit disabled.

"Hardly a man in the regiment had over two or three cartridges left. Dead and wounded rebels were piled up in heaps in front of us, especially in front of Companies A and B, where Sharpe's rifles had done effective work.

"It was a great victory. 'Fredericksburg on the other leg,' as the boys said. The rebel prisoners told us their leaders assured them that they would only meet the Pennsylvania militia; but when they saw that d—d ace of clubs (the trefoil badge of the Second Corps), a cry went through their lines—'the Army of the Potomac, by Heaven!'

"So ended the battle of Gettysburg, and the sun sank to rest that night on a battle-field that had proved that the Army of the Potomac could and would save the people of the North from invasion whenever and wherever they may be assailed.

> "'Long shall the tale be told,
> Yea, when our babes are old.'"
> "Pshaw, Fred! you are getting sentimental.
> Let's go out in the air and have another cigar."

CHAPTER THIRTEEN

The Brigade Classics
By Alfred, Lord Tennyson

The Charge of the Light Brigade

I
Half a league, half a league
Half a league onward,
All in the valley of Death
Rode the six hundred.
Forward the Light Brigade!
Charge for the guns!' he said.
Into the valley of Death
Rode the six hundred.

II
'Forward, the Light Brigade!'
Was there a man dismay'd?
Not tho' the soldier knew
Some one had blunder'd.
Theirs not to make reply,
Theirs not to reason why,
Theirs but to do and die.
Into the valley of Death
Rode the six hundred.

III
Cannon to right of them,
Cannon to left of them,
Cannon in front of them
Volley'd and thunder'd;

Storm'd at with shot and shell,
Boldly they rode and well,
Into the jaws of Death,
Into the mouth of hell
Rode the six hundred.

IV

Flash'd all their sabres bare,
Flash'd as they turn'd in air
Sabring the gunners there,
Charging an army, while
All the world wonder'd.
Plunged in the battery-smoke
Right thro' the line they broke;
Cossack and Russian
Reel'd from the sabre-stroke
Shatter'd and sunder'd.
Then they rode back, but not,
Not the six hundred.

V

Cannon to right of them,
Cannon to left of them,
Cannon behind them
Volley'd and thunder'd;
Storm'd at with shot and shell,
While horse and hero fell,
They that had fought so well
Came thro' the jaws of Death,
Back from the mouth of hell,
All that was left of them,
Left of six hundred.

VI

When can their glory fade?
O the wild charge they made!
All the world wonder'd.
Honor the charge they made!
Honor the Light Brigade,
Noble six hundred!

The Charge of the Heavy Brigade at Balaclava

I

The charge of the gallant three hundred, the Heavy Brigade!
Down the hill, down the hill, thousands of Russians,

Thousands of horsemen, drew to the valley—and stay'd;
For Scarlett and Scarlett's three hundred were riding by
When the points of the Russian lances arose in the sky;
And he call'd, "Left wheel into line!" and they wheel'd and obey'd.
Then he look'd at the host that had halted he knew not why,
And he turn'd half round, and he bade his trumpeter sound
To the charge, and he rode on ahead, as he waved his blade
To the gallant three hundred whose glory will never die—
"Follow," and up the hill, up the hill, up the hill,
Follow'd the Heavy Brigade.

II

The trumpet, the gallop, the charge, and the might of the fight!
Thousands of horsemen had gather'd there on the height,
With a wing push'd out to the left and a wing to the right,
And who shall escape if they close? but he dash'd up alone
Thro' the great gray slope of men,
Sway'd his sabre, and held his own
Like an Englishman there and then.
All in a moment follow'd with force
Three that were next in their fiery course,
Wedged themselves in between horse and horse,
Fought for their lives in the narrow gap they had made—
Four amid thousands! and up the hill, up the hill,
Gallopt the gallant three hundred, the Heavy Brigade.

III

Fell like a cannon-shot,
Burst like a thunderbolt,
Crash'd like a hurricane,
Broke thro' the mass from below,
Drove thro' the midst of the foe,
Plunged up and down, to and fro,
Rode flashing blow upon blow,
Brave Inniskillens and Greys
Whirling their sabres in circles of light!
And some of us, all in amaze,
Who were held for a while from the fight,
And were only standing at gaze,
When the dark-muffled Russian crowd
Folded its wings from the left and the right,
And roll'd them around like a cloud,—
O, mad for the charge and the battle were we,
When our own good redcoats sank from sight,
Like drops of blood in a dark-gray sea,

And we turn'd to each other, whispering, all dismay'd,
"Lost are the gallant three hundred of Scarlett's Brigade!"
IV
"Lost one and all" were the words
Mutter'd in our dismay;
But they rode like victors and lords
Thro' the forest of lances and swords
In the heart of the Russian hordes,
They rode, or they stood at bay—
Struck with the sword-hand and slew,
Down with the bridle-hand drew
The foe from the saddle and threw
Underfoot there in the fray—
Ranged like a storm or stood like a rock
In the wave of a stormy day;
Till suddenly shock upon shock
Stagger'd the mass from without,
Drove it in wild disarray,
For our men gallopt up with a cheer and a shout,
And the foeman surged, and waver'd, and reel'd
Up the hill, up the hill, up the hill, out of the field,
And over the brow and away.
V
Glory to each and to all, and the charge that they made!
Glory to all the three hundred, and all the Brigade!

Note: The "three hundred" of the "Heavy Brigade" who made this famous charge were the Scots Greys and the 2d squadron of Inniskillens; the remainder of the "Heavy Brigade" subsequently dashing up to their support.

The "three" were Scarlett's aide-de-camp, Elliot, and the trumpeter, and Shegog the orderly, who had been close behind him.

CHAPTER FOURTEEN

The Air War Over the Trenches
By Eddie Rickenbacker

The battlefield horrors of World War I are described in scores of great books and stories, such as Alden Brooks's "The Parisian" in chapter 9 of this volume. The battles that raged in the skies over the bitter fighting in France have been described less frequently than the infantry fighting. The autobiography of one of America's first decorated "Aces," Captain Eddie Rickenbacker, takes us into the cockpits of airmen who fought their battles where few men had ever gone.

—Lamar Underwood

AMERICAN ACE OF ACES

ON SEPTEMBER 15TH THE WEATHER WAS IDEAL FOR FLYING. I LEFT THE AERODROME at 8:30 in the morning on a voluntary patrol, taking the nearest air route to the lines.

I had reached an altitude of 16,000 feet by the time I had reached the trenches. The visibility was unusually good. I could see for miles and miles in every direction. I was flying alone, with no idea as to whether other planes of our own were cruising about the sector or not. But barely had I reached a position over No Man's Land when I noticed a formation of six enemy Fokkers at about my altitude coming towards me from the direction of Conflans.

I turned and began the usual tactics of climbing into the sun. I noticed the Fokkers alter their direction and still climbing move eastward towards the Moselle. I did not see how they could help seeing me, as scarcely half a mile separated us. However, they did not attack nor did they indicate that they suspected my presence beyond continuing steadily their climb for elevation. Three complete circles they made on their side of the lines. I did the same on my side.

Just at this moment I discovered four Spad machines far below the enemy planes and some three miles inside the German lines. I decided at once they must belong to the

American Second Fighting Group, at that time occupying the aerodrome at Souilly. They appeared to be engaged in bombing the roads and strafing enemy infantry from a low altitude. The Spads of the Second Pursuit Group had but recently been equipped with bomb racks for carrying small bombs.

The leader of the Fokker Formation saw the Spads at about the same moment I did. I saw him dip his wings and stick down his nose. Immediately the six Fokkers began a headlong pique directly down at the Spads. Almost like one of the formation I followed suit.

Inside the first thousand feet I found I was rapidly overtaking the enemy machines. By the time we had reached 5,000 feet I was in a position to open fire upon the rear man. Not once had any of them looked around. Either they had forgotten me in their anxiety to get at their prey or else had considered I would not attempt to take them all on single-handed. At all events I was given ample time to get my man dead into my sights before firing.

I fired one long burst. I saw my tracer bullets go straight home into the pilot's seat. There came a sudden burst of fire from his fuel tank and the Fokker continued onwards in its mad flight—now a fiery furnace. He crashed a mile inside his own lines.

His five companions did not stay to offer battle. I still held the upper hand and even got in a few bursts at the next nearest machine before he threw himself into a vrille and escaped me. The sight of one of their members falling in flames evidently quite discouraged them. Abandoning all their designs on the unsuspecting Spads below they dived away for Germany and left me the field.

I returned to my field, secured a car and drove immediately up to the lines to our Balloon Section. I wanted to get my victories confirmed—both this one of to-day and the Fokker that I had brought down yesterday in the same sector. For no matter how many pilots may have witnessed the bringing down of an enemy plane, official confirmation of their testimony must be obtained from outside witnesses on the ground. Often these are quite impossible to get. In such a case the victory is not credited to the pilot.

Upon the tragic death of Major Lufbery, who at that time was the leading American Ace, with 18 victories, the title of American Ace of Aces fell to Lieutenant Paul Frank Baer of Fort Wayne, Ind., a member of the Lafayette Escadrille 103. Baer then had 9 victories and had never been wounded.

Baer is a particularly modest and lovable boy, and curiously enough he is one of the few fighting pilots I have met who felt a real repugnance in his task of shooting down enemy aviators.

When Lufbery fell, Baer's Commanding Officer, Major William Thaw, called him into the office and talked seriously with him regarding the opportunity before him as America's leading Ace. He advised Baer to be cautious and he would go far. Two days later Baer was shot down and slightly wounded behind the German lines!

Thereafter, Lieutenant Frank Bayliss of New Bedford, Mass., a member of the crack French Escadrille of the Cigognes, Spad 3, held the American title until he was killed in action on June 12th, 1918. Bayliss had 13 victories to his credit.

Then David Putnam, another Massachusetts boy, took the lead with 12 victories over enemy aeroplanes. Putnam, as I have said, was, like Lufbery, shot down in flames but a day or two before my last victory.

Lieutenant Tobin of San Antonio, Texas, and a member of the third Pursuit Group (of which Major William Thaw was the Commanding Officer), now had six official victories. He led the list. I for my part had five victories confirmed. But upon receiving confirmation for the two Fokkers I had vanquished yesterday and to-day, I would have my seven and would lead Tobin by one. So it was with some little interest and impatience that I set off to try to find ground witnesses of my last two battles about St. Mihiel.

Mingled with this natural desire to become the leading fighting Ace of America was a haunting superstition that did not leave my mind until the very end of the war. It was that the very possession of this title—Ace of Aces—brought with it the unavoidable doom that had overtaken all its previous holders. I wanted it and yet I feared to learn that it was mine! In later days I began to feel that this superstition was almost the heaviest burden that I carried with me into the air. Perhaps it served to redouble my caution and sharpened my fighting senses. But never was I able to forget that the life of a title-holder is short.

Eating my sandwiches in the car that day I soon ran though St. Mihiel and made my way on the main road east to Apremont and then north to Thiaucourt. I knew that there had been a balloon up near there both days and felt certain that their observers must have seen my two combats overhead.

Unfortunately the road from Apremont to Thiaucourt was closed, owing to the great number of shell-holes and trenches which criss-crossed it. After being lost for two hours in the forest which lies between St. Mihiel and Vigneulles, I was finally able to extricate myself and found I had emerged just south of Vigneulles. I was about one mile south of our trenches. And standing there with map in hand wondering where to go next to find our balloons, I got an unexpected clue.

A sudden flare of flames struck my sight off to the right. Running around the trees I caught a view of one of our balloons between me and Thiaucourt completely immersed in flames! Half-way down was a graceful little parachute, beneath which swung the observer as he settled slowly to Mother Earth!

And as I gazed I saw a second balloon two or three miles further east towards Pont-à-Mousson perform the same maneuver. Another of our observers was making the same perilous jump! A sly Heinie had slipped across our lines and had made a successful attack upon the two balloons and had made a clean getaway. I saw him climbing up away from the furious gale of anti-aircraft fire which our gunners were speeding after him. I am afraid my sympathies were almost entirely with the airman as I watched the murderous bursting of Archy all around his machine. At any rate I realized exactly how he was feeling, with his mixture of satisfaction over the success of his undertaking and of panic over the deadly mess of shrapnel about him.

In half an hour I arrived at the balloon site and found them already preparing to go aloft with a second balloon. And at my first question they smiled and told me they had seen my Fokker of this morning's combat crash in flames. They readily signed the necessary papers to this effect, thus constituting the required confirmation for my last victory. But for the victory of yesterday that I claimed they told me none of the officers were present who had been there on duty at that time. I must go to the 3rd Balloon Company just north of Pont-à-Mousson and there I would find the men I wanted to see.

After watching the new balloon get safely launched with a fresh observer in the basket, a process which consumed some ten or fifteen minutes, I retraced my steps and made my way back to my motor. The observer whom I had seen descending under his parachute had in the meantime made his return to his company headquarters. He was unhurt and quite enthusiastic over the splendid landing he had made in the trees. Incidentally I learned that but two or three such forced descents by parachute from a flaming balloon are permitted any one observer. These jumps are not always so simple and frequently very serious if not fatal injuries are received in the parachute jump. Seldom does one officer care to risk himself in a balloon basket after his third jump. And this fear for his own safety limits very naturally his service and bravery in that trying business. The American record in this perilous profession is held, I believe, by Lieutenant Phelps of New York, who made five successive jumps from a flaming balloon.

On my way to the 3rd Balloon Company I stopped to enquire the road from a group of infantry officers whom I met just north of Pont-à-Mousson. As soon as I stated my business, they unanimously exclaimed that they had all seen my flight above them yesterday and had seen my victim crash near them. After getting them to describe the exact time and place and some of the incidents of the fight I found that it was indeed my combat they had witnessed. This was a piece of real luck for me. It ended my researches on the spot. As they were very kindly signing their confirmation I was thinking to myself, "Eddie! You are the American Ace of Aces!" And so I was for the minute.

Returning home, I lost no time in putting in my reports. Reed Chambers came up to me and hit me a thump on the back.

"Well, Rick!" he said, "how does it feel?"

"Very fine for the moment, Reed," I replied seriously, "but any other fellow can have the title any time he wants it, so far as I am concerned."

I really meant what I was saying. A fortnight later when Frank Luke began his marvelous balloon strafing he passed my score in a single jump. Luke, as I have said, was on the same aerodrome with me, being a member of 27 Squadron. His rapid success even brought 27 Squadron ahead of 95 Squadron for a few days.

The following day I witnessed a typical expedition of Luke's from our own aerodrome. Just about dusk on September 16th Luke left the Major's headquarters and walked over to his machine. As he came out of the door he pointed out the two German observation balloons to the east of our field, both of which could be plainly seen with the naked eye. They were suspended in the sky about two miles back of the Boche lines and were perhaps four miles apart.

"Keep you eyes on these two balloons," said Frank as he passed us. "You will see that first one there go up in flames exactly at 7:15 and the other will do likewise at 7:19."

We had little idea he would really get either of them, but we all gathered together out in the open as the time grew near and kept our eyes glued to the distant specks in the sky. Suddenly Major Hartney exclaimed, "There goes the first one!" It was true! A tremendous flare of flame lighted up the horizon. We all glanced at our watches. It was exactly on the dot!

The intensity of our gaze towards the location of the second Hun balloon may be imagined. It had grown too dusk to distinguish the balloon itself, but we well knew the exact point in the horizon where it hung. Not a word was spoken as we alternately glanced at the second-hands of our watches and then at the eastern skyline. Almost upon the second our watching group yelled simultaneously. A small blaze first lit up the point at which we were gazing. Almost instantaneously another gigantic burst of flames announced to us that the second balloon had been destroyed! It was a most spectacular exhibition.

We all stood by on the aerodrome in front of Luke's hangar until fifteen minutes later we heard through the darkness the hum of his returning motor. His mechanics were shooting up red Very lights with their pistols to indicate to him the location of our field. With one short circle above the aerodrome he shut off his motor and made a perfect landing just in front of our group. Laughing and hugely pleased with his success, Luke jumped out and came running over to us to receive our heartiest congratulations. Within a half hour's absence from the field Frank Luke had destroyed a hundred thousand dollars' worth of enemy property! He had returned absolutely unscratched.

A most extraordinary incident had happened just before Luke had left the ground. Lieutenant Jeffers of my Squadron had been out on patrol with the others during the afternoon and did not return with them. I was becoming somewhat anxious about him when I saw a homing aeroplane coming from the lines towards our field. It was soon revealed as a Spad and was evidently intending to land at our field, but its course appeared to be very peculiar. I watched it gliding steeply down with engine cut off. Instead of making for the field, the pilot, whoever he was, seemed bent upon investigating the valley to the north of us before coming in. If this was Jeff he was taking a foolish chance, since he had already been out longer than the usual fuel supply could last him.

Straight down at the north hillside the Spad continued its way. I ran out to see what Jeff was trying to do. I had a premonition that everything was not right with him.

Just as his machine reached the skyline I saw him make a sudden effort to redress the plane. It was too late. He slid off a little on his right wing, causing his nose to turn back towards the field—and then he crashed in the fringe of bushes below the edge of the hill. I hurried over to him.

Imagine my surprise when I met him walking towards me, no bones broken, but wearing a most sheepish expression on his face. I asked him what in the world was the matter.

"Well," he replied, "I might as well admit the truth! I went to sleep coming home, and didn't wake up until I was about ten feet above the ground. I didn't have time to switch on my engine or even flatten out! I'm afraid I finished the little 'bus!"

Extraordinary as this tale seemed, it was nevertheless true. Jeffers had set his course for home at a high elevation over the lines and cutting off his engine had drifted smoothly along. The soft air and monotonous luxury of motion had lulled him to sleep. Subconsciously his hand controlled the joystick or else the splendid equilibrium of the Spad had kept it upon an even keel without control. Like the true old coach-horse it was, it kept the stable door in sight and made directly for it. Jeff's awakening might have been in another world, however, if he had not miraculously opened his eyes in the very nick of time!

The next day, September 18th, our group suffered a loss that made us feel much vindictiveness as well as sorrow. Lieutenant Heinrichs and Lieutenant John Mitchell, both of 95 Squadron, were out together on patrol when they encountered six Fokker machines. They immediately began an attack.

Mitchell fired one burst from each gun and then found them both hopelessly jammed. He signaled to Heinrichs that he was out of the battle and started for home. But at the same moment Heinrichs received a bullet through his engine which suddenly put it out of action. He was surrounded by enemy planes and some miles back of the German lines. He broke through the enemy line and began his slow descent. Although it was evident he could not possibly reach our lines, the furious Huns continued swooping upon him, firing again and again as he coasted down.

Ten different bullets struck his body in five different attacks. He was perfectly defenseless against any of them. He did not lose consciousness, although one bullet shattered his jawbone and bespattered his goggles so that he could not see through the blood. Just before he reached the ground he managed to push up his goggles with his unwounded arm. The other was hanging limp and worthless by his side.

He saw he was fairly into a piece of woodland and some distance within the German lines. He swung away and landed between the trees, turning his machine over as he crashed, but escaping further injury himself. Within an hour or two he was picked up and taken to a hospital in Metz.

After the signing of the Armistice we saw Heinrichs again at the Toul Hospital. He was a mere shell of himself. Scarcely recognizable even by his old comrades, a first glance at his shrunken form indicated that he had been horribly neglected by his captors. His story quickly confirmed this suspicion.

For the several weeks that he had lain in the Metz hospital he told us that the Germans had not reset either his jaw or his broken arm. In fact he had received no medical attention whatsoever. The food given him was bad and infrequent. It was a marvel that he had survived this frightful suffering!

In all fairness to the Hun I think it is his due to say that such an experience as Heinrichs suffered rarely came to my attention. In the large hospital in which he was confined there were but six nurses and two doctors. They had to care for several scores of wounded. Their natural inclination was to care first for their own people. But how any people calling themselves human could have permitted Heinrichs' suffering to go uncared for during all those weeks passes all understanding. Stories of this kind which occasionally came to our ears served to steel our hearts against any mercy towards the enemy pilots in our vicinity.

And thus does chivalry give way before the horrors of war—even in aviation!

CAPTAIN OF THE HAT-IN-THE-RING SQUADRON

The Three-Fingered Lake is a body of water well known to the American pilots who have flown over the St. Mihiel front. It lies four or five miles directly north of Vigneulles and is quite the largest body of water to be seen in this region. The Germans have held it well within their lines ever since the beginning of the war.

At the conclusion of the American drive around St. Mihiel, which terminated victoriously twenty-two hours after it began, the lines were pushed north of Vignuelles until they actually touched the southern arm of Three-Fingered Lake. Our resistless doughboys pushing in from both directions, met each other in the outskirts of Vigneulles at two o'clock in the morning. Some fifteen thousand Boches and scores of guns were captured within the territory that had thus been pinched out.

With this lake barrier on the very edge of their lines, the Huns had adroitly selected two vantage points on their end of the water from which to hoist their observation balloons. From this position their observers had a splendid view of our lines and noted every movement in our rear. They made themselves a tremendous nuisance to the operations of our Staff Officers.

Frank Luke, the star Balloon Strafer of our group, was, as I have said, a member of the 27th Squadron. On the evening of September 18th he announced that he was going up to get those two balloons that swung above the Three-Fingered Lake. His pal, Lieutenant Wehrner, of the same squadron accompanied Luke as usual.

There was a curious friendship between Luke and Wehrner. Luke was an excitable, high-strung boy, and his impetuous courage was always getting him into trouble. He was extremely daring and perfectly blind and indifferent to the enormous risks he ran. His superior officers and his friends would plead with him to be more cautious, but he was deaf to their entreaties. He attacked like a whirlwind, with absolute coolness but with never a thought of his own safety. We all predicted that Frank Luke would be the greatest air-fighter in the world if he would only learn to save himself unwise risks. Luke came from Phoenix, Arizona.

Wehrner's nature, on the other hand, was quite different. He had just one passion, and that was his love for Luke. He followed him about the aerodrome constantly. When Luke went up, Wehrner usually managed to go along with him. On these trips Wehrner acted as an escort or guard, despite Luke's objections. On several occasions he had saved Luke's life. Luke would come back to the aerodrome and excitedly tell every one about it, but no word would Wehrner say on the subject. In fact Wehrner never spoke except in monosyllables on any subject. After a successful combat he would put in the briefest possible report and sign his name. None of us ever heard him describe how he brought the enemy machine down.

Wehrner hovered in the air above Luke while the latter went in for the balloon. If hostile aeroplanes came up, Wehrner intercepted them and warded off the attack until Luke had finished his operations. These two pilots made an admirable pair for this work and over a score of victories were chalked up for 27 Squadron through the activities of this team.

On the evening of the 18th, Luke and Wehrner set off at five o'clock. It was just getting dark. They flew together at a medium level until they reached the lake. There they separated, Luke diving straight at the balloon which lay to the west, Wehrner staying aloft to guard the sky against a surprise attack from Hun aeroplanes.

Luke's balloon rose out of the swampy land that borders the upper western edge of Three-Fingered Lake. The enemy defenses saw his approach and began a murderous fire through which Luke calmly dived as usual. Three separate times he dived and fired, dived and fired. Constantly surrounded with a hail of bullets and shrapnel, flaming onions and incendiary bullets, Luke returned to the attack the third time and finally completed his errand of destruction. The huge gas-bag burst into flames. Luke zoomed up over the balloon and looked about for his friend. He was not in view at the moment, but another sight struck Luke's searching eyes. A formation of six Fokkers was bearing down upon him from out of Germany. Perhaps Wehrner had fired the red signal light which had been the warning agreed upon, and he had failed to see it in the midst of all that Archy fire. At any rate he was in for it now.

The German Fokkers were to the west of him. The second balloon was to the east. With characteristic foolhardiness Luke determined to withdraw by way of the other balloon and take one burst at it before the Huns reached him. He accordingly continued straight on east, thus permitting the pursuing formation of Fokkers to cut him off at the south.

With his first dive Luke shot down the second balloon. It burst into towering flames, which were seen for miles around. Again he passed through a living stream of missiles fired at him from the ground, and escaped unhurt!

As he began his flight towards home he discovered that he was completely cut off by the six Fokkers. He must shoot his way through single-handed. To make it worse, three more Fokkers were rapidly coming upon him from the north. And then Luke saw his pal, Wehrner.

Wehrner had all this time been patrolling the line to the north of Luke's balloons. He had seen the six Fokkers, but had supposed that Luke would keep ahead of them and abandon his attempt at the second enemy balloon. He therefore fired his signal light, which was observed by our balloon observers but not by Luke, and immediately set off to patrol a parallel course between the enemy planes and Luke's road home. When he saw Luke dart off to the second balloon, Wehrner realized at once that Luke had not seen his signal and was unaware of the second flight of Fokkers coming directly upon him. He quickly sheered off and went forward to meet them.

What Luke saw was the aeroplane of his devoted pal receiving a direct fire from all three of the approaching Fokker pilots. The next instant it fell over in the air and slowly began to fall. Even as it hesitated in its flight, a burst of flames issued from the Spad's tank. Wehrner was shot down in flames while trying to save his comrade! It was a deliberate sacrifice of himself for his friend!

Completely consumed with fury, Luke, instead of seeking safety in flight, turned back and hurled himself upon the three Fokkers. He was at a distinct disadvantage, for they had the superiority both in altitude and position, not to mention numbers. But regardless as ever of what the chances were, Luke climbed upwards at them, firing as he advanced.

Picking out the pilot on the left, Luke kept doggedly on his track firing at him until he suddenly saw him burst into flame. The other two machines were in the meantime on Luke's tail and their tracer bullets were flashing unnoticed by his head. But as soon as he saw the end of his first enemy he made a quick renversement on number two and, firing as he came about, he shot down the second enemy machine with the first burst. The third piqued for Germany and Luke had to let him go.

All this fighting had consumed less time than it takes to tell it. The two Fokkers had fallen in flames within ten seconds of each other. With rage still in his heart Luke looked about him to discover where the six enemy machines had gone. They had apparently been satisfied to leave him with their three comrades, for they were now disappearing back towards the east. And just ahead of them Luke discerned fleecy white clouds of Archy smoke breaking north of Verdun. This indicated that our batteries were firing at enemy aeroplanes in that sector.

As he approached Verdun Luke found that five French Spads were hurrying up to attack an L.V.G. machine of the Huns, the same target at which our Archy had been firing. The six Fokkers had seen them coming and had gone to intercept them. Like a rocket Luke set his own Spad down at the L.V.G. It was a two-seater machine and was evidently taking photographs at a low altitude.

Our Archy ceased firing as Luke drew near. He hurled himself directly down at the German observer, firing both guns as he dove. The enemy machine fell into a vrille and crashed just a few hundred yards from our old Verdun aerodrome. In less than twenty minutes Lieutenant Luke had shot down two balloons, two fighting Fokkers and one enemy photographing machine—a feat that is almost unequaled in the history of this war!

Luke's first question when he arrived at our field was, "Has Wehrner come back?"

He knew the answer before he asked the question, but he was hoping against hope that he might find himself mistaken. But Wehrner had indeed been killed. The joy of Luke over his marvelous victories vanished instantly. He was told that with these five victories he had a total of eleven, thus passing me and making Luke the American Ace of Aces. But this fact did not interest him. He said he would like to go up to the front in a car and see if anything had been heard from Wehrner.

The following morning Major Hartney, Commanding Officer of our Group, took Luke and myself up to Verdun to make inquiries. Shortly after lunch the officer in charge of confirmations came to us and told Lieutenant Luke that not only had his five victories of yesterday been officially confirmed, but that three old victories had likewise been that morning confirmed, making Luke's total fourteen instead of eleven. And these fourteen victories had been gained by Frank Luke in *eight days!* The history of war aviation, I believe, has not a similar record. Not even the famous Guynemer, Fonck, Ball, Bishop or the noted German Ace of Aces, Baron von Richthofen, ever won fourteen victories in a single fortnight at the front. Any air-craft, whether balloon or aeroplane, counts as one victory, and only one, with all the armies.

In my estimation there has never during the four years of war been an aviator at the front who possessed the confidence, ability and courage that Frank Luke had shown during that remarkable two weeks.

In order to do this boy honor and show him that every officer in the Group appreciated his wonderful work, he was given a complimentary dinner that night by the Squadrons. Many interesting speeches were made. When it came Luke's turn to respond he got up laughing, said he was having a bully time—and sat down! Major Hartney came over to him and presented him with a seven days' leave in Paris—which at that time was about the highest gift at the disposal of commanding officers at the front.

Among all the delightful entertainers who came over to the front from the United States to help cheer up the fighting men, none except our own Elsie Janis, who is an honorary member of our Squadron, were quite so highly appreciated by our fellows as the Margaret Mayo Y.M.C.A. troup, which gave us an entertainment just a night or two after this. The players included such well known talent as Elizabeth Brice, Lois Meredith, Bill Morrisey, Tommy Gray and Mr. Walker—all of New York. After a hurried preparation, we cleaned up one of the hangars, prepared a stage and made a dressing room by hanging a curtain over a truck and trailer. After a merry dinner in 94's mess hall everybody crowded into the "theater," and the way the boys laughed and shouted there, during the performance, must have sounded hysterical to the actors; but to my mind this hysteria was only an outlet for the pent-up emotion and an indication of the tension and strain under which we had so long been living. At any rate it was the best show I have ever seen at the front, barring always the one evening Miss Janis appeared on our aerodrome for an entertainment.

The night of September 24th, Major Marr returned from Paris and announced that he had received orders to return to America. Shortly afterward Major Hartney handed me an order promoting me to the Command of the 94 Squadron!

My pride and pleasure at receiving this great honor I cannot put into words. I had been with 94 since its first day at the front. I was a member of this, the very first organization to go over the lines. I had seen my old friends disappear and be replaced by other pilots whom I had learned to admire and respect. And many of these had in turn disappeared!

Now but three members of the original organization were left—Reed Chambers, Thorn Taylor and myself. And I had been given the honor of leading this distinguished Squadron! It had had Lufbery, Jimmy Hall and Dave Peterson as members. And it led all the rest in number of victories over the Huns.

But did it? I walked over to the Operations Office and took a look at the records. I had a suspicion that Frank Luke's wonderful run of the past few days had put 27 Squadron ahead of us.

My suspicions were quite correct. The sober fact was that this presumptuous young 27 had suddenly taken a spurt, thanks to their brilliant Luke, and now led the Hat-in-the-Ring Squadron by six victories! I hurried over to 94 quarters and called together all my pilots.

The half hour we had together that evening firmly fixed a resolve in the aspirations of 94's members. No other American Squadron at the front would ever again be permitted to approach so near our margin of supremacy. From that hour every man in 94 Squadron, I believe, felt that the honor of his Squadron was at stake in this matter of bringing down Huns. At all events, within a week my pilots had overtaken 27's lead and never again did any American Squadron even threaten to overtop our lead.

After a talk that night with the pilots, I went over and called the mechanics to a caucus. We had half an hour's talk together and I outlined to them just what our pilots proposed to do with their help. And they understood that it was only by their whole-souled help that their Squadron's success would be possible. How nobly these boys responded to our appeal was well proved in the weeks that followed. Rarely indeed was a dud motor found in 94 Squadron henceforward. Never did a squadron of pilots receive more faithful attendance from their helpers in the hangar than was given us by these enthusiastic air mechanics of the Hat-in-the-Ring Squadron. I honestly believe that they felt the disgrace of being second more keenly than did we pilots.

Finally, I had a long and serious conference with myself that night. After I had gone to bed I lay awake for several hours, thinking over the situation. I was compelled to believe that I had been chosen Squadron Commander because, first, I had been more successful than the other pilots in bringing down enemy aeroplanes; and second, because I had the power to make a good leader over other pilots. That last proposition caused me infinite thought. Just how and wherein could I do the best by my followers?

I suppose every squadron leader has this same problem to decide, and I cannot help but believe that on his decision as to how he shall lead his pilots depends in a great measure the extent of his success—and his popularity.

To my mind there was but one procedure. I should never ask any pilot under me to go on a mission that I myself would not undertake. I would lead them by example as well as precept. I would accompany the new pilots and watch their errors and help them to feel more confidence by sharing their dangers. Above all, I would work harder than ever I did as mere pilot. There was no question about that. My days of loafing were over!

To avoid the red-tape business at the aerodrome—the making out of reports, ordering materials and seeing that they came in on time, looking after details of the mess, the hangars and the comfort of the enlisted men—all this work must be put under competent men, if I expected to stay in the air and lead patrols. Accordingly I gave this important matter my attention early next morning. And the success of my appointments was such that from that day to this I have never spent more than thirty minutes a day upon the ground business connected with 94's operations.

Full of this early enthusiasm I went up on a lone patrol the very first morning of my new responsibility, to see how much I had changed for the better or the worse.

Within half an hour I returned to the aerodrome with two more victories to my credit—the first double-header I had so far won!

AN EVENTFUL "D" DAY

September 25th, 1918, was my first day as Captain of the 94 Squadron. Early that forenoon I started for the lines alone, flew over Verdun and Fort Douaumont, then turned east towards Etain. Almost immediately I picked up a pair of L.V.G. two-seater machines below me. They were coming out of Germany and were certainly bent upon a expedition over our lines. Five Fokker machines were above them and somewhat behind, acting as protection for the photographers until the lines were reached.

Climbing for the sun for all I was worth, I soon had the satisfaction of realizing that I had escaped their notice and was now well in their rear. I shut down my motor, put down my head and made a bee line for the nearest Fokker.

I was not observed by the enemy until it was too late for him to escape. I had him exactly in my sights when I pulled both triggers for a long burst. He made a sudden attempt to pull away, but my bullets were already ripping through his fusilage and he must have been killed instantly. His machine fell wildly away and crashed just south of Etain.

It had been my intention to zoom violently upwards and protect myself against the expected attack from the four remaining Fokkers as soon as I had finished the first man.

But when I saw the effect of my attack upon the four dumbfounded Boches I instantly changed my tactics and plunged straight on through their formation to attack the photographing L.V.G.'s ahead. For the Heinies were so surprised by finding a Spad in their midst and seeing one of their number suddenly drop that the remaining three viraged to right and left. Their one idea was to escape and save their own skins. Though they did not actually pique for home, they cleared a space large enough for me to slip through and continue my dive upon the two-seaters before they could recover their formation.

The two-seaters had seen my attack and had already put down their heads to escape. I plunged along after them, getting the rear machine in my sights as I drew nearer to him. A glance back over my shoulder showed me that the four Fokkers had not yet reformed their line and were even now circling about with the purpose of again solidifying their formation. I had a few seconds yet before they could begin their attack.

The two L.V.G. machines began to draw apart. Both observers in the rear seats were firing at me, although the range was still too long for accurate shooting. I dove more steeply, passed out of the gunner's view under the nearest machine and zoomed quickly up at him from below. But the victory was not to be an easy one. The pilot suddenly kicked his tail around, giving the gunner another good aim at me. I had to postpone shooting until I had more time for my own aiming. And in the meantime the second photographing machine had stolen up behind me and I saw tracer bullets go whizzing and streaking past my face. I zoomed up diagonally out of range, made a renversement and came directly back at my first target.

Several times we repeated these maneuvers, the four Fokkers still wrangling among themselves about their formation. And all the time we were getting farther and farther back into Germany. I decided upon one bold attack and if this failed I would get back to my own lines before it was too late.

Watching my two adversaries closely, I suddenly found an opening between them. They were flying parallel to each other and not fifty yards apart. Dropping down in a sideslip until I had one machine between me and the other I straightened out smartly, leveled my Spad and began firing. The nearest Boche passed directly through my line of fire and just as I ceased firing I had the infinite satisfaction of seeing him gush forth flames. Turning over and over as he fell the L.V.G. started a blazing path to earth just as the Fokker escort came tearing up to the rescue. I put on the gas and piqued for my own lines.

Pleased as I was over this double-header, the effect it might have upon my pilots was far more gratifying to me.

Arriving at the aerodrome at 9:30 I immediately jumped into a motorcar, called to Lieutenant Chambers to come with me and we set off at once to get official confirmation for this double victory. We took the main road to Verdun, passed through the town and gained the hills beyond the Meuse, towards Etain. Taking the road up to Fort de Tavannes we passed over that bloody battlefield of 1916 where so many thousand German troops fell before French fire in the memorable Battle for Verdun. At the very crest of the hill we were halted by a French poilu, who told us the rest of the road was in full view of the Germans and that we must go no farther.

We asked him as to whether he had seen my combat overhead this morning. He replied in the affirmative and added that the officers in the adjacent fort too had witnessed the whole fight through their field glasses. We thanked him and leaving our car under his care took our way on foot to the Fort.

Two or three hundred yards of shell-holes sprinkled the ground between us and the Fort. We made our way through them, gained admittance to the interior of the Fort and in our best Pidgin French stated our errand to M. le Commandant. He immediately wrote out full particulars of the combat I had had with the L.V.G., signed it and congratulated me upon my victory with a warm shake of the hand. Having no further business at this place, we made our adieus and hastened back to our car.

Plunging through the shallowest shell-holes we had traversed about half the distance to our car, which stood boldly out on the top of the road, when a shrill whining noise made us pause and listen. The next instant a heavy explosion announced that a shell had landed about fifty yards short of us. Simultaneously with the shower of gravel and dirt which headed our way we dropped unceremoniously on our faces in the bottom of the deepest shell-hole in our vicinity.

The Huns had spotted our car and were actually trying to get its range!

Two or three times we crawled out of our hole, only to duck back at the signal of the next coming shell. After six or eight shots the Boche gunners evidently considered their target too small, for they ceased firing long enough for us to make a bolt across the intervening holes and throw ourselves into the waiting automobile. I most fervently wished that I had turned the car around before leaving it, and I shall never forget the frightful length of time it took me to get our car backed around and headed in the right direction. We lost no time in getting down that hill.

Next day was to be an important one for us and for the whole American Army. Officially it was designated as "D" day and the "Zero hour," by the same code, was set for four o'clock in the morning. At that moment the artillery barrage would begin and forty thousand doughboys who were posted along the front line trenches from the Meuse to the Argonne Forest would go over the top. It was the 26th day of September, 1918.

Precisely at four o'clock I was awakened by my orderly who informed me that the weather was good. Hastily getting out of doors, I looked over the dark sky, wondering as I did so how many of our boys it would claim before this day's work was done! For we had an important part to play in this day's operations. Headquarters had sent us orders to attack all the enemy observation balloons along that entire front this morning and to continue the attacks until the infantry's operations were completed. Accordingly every fighting squadron had been assigned certain of these balloons for attack and it was our duty to see that they were destroyed. The safety of thousands of our attacking soldiers depended upon our success in eliminating these all-watching eyes of the enemy. Incidentally, it was the first balloon strafing party that 94 Squadron had been given since I had been made its leader and I desired to make a good showing on this first expedition.

Just here it may be well to point out the difficulties of balloon strafing, which make this undertaking so unattractive to the new pilot.

German "Archy" is terrifying at first acquaintance. Pilots affect a scorn for it, and indeed at high altitudes the probabilities of a hit are small. But when attacking a balloon which hangs only 1,500 feet above the guns (and this altitude is of course known precisely to the anti-aircraft gunner) Archy becomes far more dangerous.

So when a pilot begins his first balloon attacking expeditions, he knows that he runs a gauntlet of fire that may be very deadly. His natural impulse is to make a nervous plunge into the zone of danger, fire his bullets, and get away. Few victories are won with this method of attack.

The experienced balloon strafers, particularly such daring airmen as Coolidge and Luke, do not consider the risks or terrors about them. They proceed in the attack as calmly as though they were sailing through a stormless sky. Regardless of flaming missiles from the ground, they pass through the defensive barrage of fire, and often return again and again, to attack the target, until it finally bursts into flame from their incendiary bullets.

The office charts informed me that day would break this morning at six o'clock. Consequently we must be ready to leave the ground in our machines at 5:20, permitting us thirty minutes in which to reach our objectives, and ten minutes in which to locate our individual balloons. For it is essential to strike at these well defended targets just at the edge of dawn. Then the balloons are just starting aloft, and our attacking aeroplanes are but scantily visible from below. Moreover enemy aeroplanes are not apt to be about so early in the morning, unless the enemy has some inkling of what is going on.

I routed out five of my best pilots, Lieutenants Cook, Chambers, Taylor, Coolidge and Palmer; and as we gathered together for an early breakfast, we went over again all the details of our pre-arranged plans. We had two balloons assigned to our Squadron, and three of us were delegated to each balloon. Both lay along the Meuse between Brabant and Dun. Every one of us had noted down the exact location of his target on the evening before. It would be difficult perhaps to find them before daylight if they were still in their nests, but we were to hang about the vicinity until we did find them, if it took all day. With every man fully posted on his course and objective, we put on our coats and walked over to the hangars.

I was the last to leave the field, getting off the ground at exactly 5:20. It was still dark and we had to have the searchlights turned onto the field for a moment to see the ground while we took off. As soon as we lifted into the darkness the lights were extinguished. And then I saw the most marvelous sight that my eyes have ever seen.

A terrific barrage of artillery fire was going on ahead of me. Through the darkness the whole western horizon was illuminated with one mass of sudden flashes. The big guns were belching out their shells with such rapidity that there appeared to be millions of them shooting at the same time. Looking back I saw the same scene in my rear. From Luneville on the east to Rheims on the west there was not one spot of darkness along the whole front. The French were attacking along both our flanks at the same time with us in order to help demoralize the weakening Boche. The picture made me think of a giant switchboard which emitted thousands of electric flashes as invisible hands manipulated the plugs.

So fascinated did I become over this extraordinary fireworks display that I was startled upon peering over the side of my machine to discover the city of Verdun below my aeroplane's wings. Fastening my course above the dim outline of the Meuse River I followed its windings down stream, occasionally cutting across little peninsulas which I recognized along the way. Every inch of this route was as familiar to me as was the path around the corner of my old home. I knew exactly the point in the Meuse Valley where I would leave the river and turn left to strike the spot where my balloon lay last night. I did not know what course the other pilots had taken. Perhaps they had already—

Just as these thoughts were going through my mind I saw directly ahead of me the long snaky flashes of enemy tracer bullets from the ground piercing the sky. There was the location of my balloon and either Cook or Chambers was already attacking it. The enemy had discovered them and were putting up the usual hail of flaming projectiles around the balloon site. But even as the flaming bullets continued streaming upwards I saw a gigantic flame burst out in their midst! One of the boys had destroyed his gas-bag!

Even before the glare of the first had died I saw our second enemy balloon go up in flames. My pilots had succeeded beyond my fondest expectations. Undoubtedly the enemy would soon be swinging new balloons up in their places, but we must wait awhile for that. I resolved to divert my course and fly further to the north where I knew of the nest of another German observation balloon near Damvillers.

Dawn was just breaking as I headed more to the east and tried to pick out the location of Damvillers. I was piercing the gloom with my eyes when again—straight in front of my revolving propeller I saw another gush of flame which announced the doom of another enemy balloon—the very one I had determined to attack. While I was still jubilating over the extraordinary good luck that had attended us in this morning's expedition, I glanced off to my right and was almost startled out of my senses to discover that a German Fok-ker was flying alongside me not a hundred yards away! Not expecting any of the enemy aeroplanes to be abroad at this early hour, I was naturally upset for the moment. The next instant I saw that he had headed for me and was coming straight at my machine. We both began firing at the same time. It was still so dark that our four streams of flaming bullets cut brilliant lines of fire through the air. For a moment it looked as though our two machines were tied together with four ropes of fire. All my ammunition was of the incendiary variety for use against gas-bags. The Hun's ammunition was part tracer, part incendiary and part regular chunks of lead.

As we drew nearer and nearer I began to wonder whether this was to be a collision or whether he would get out of my way. He settled the question by tipping down his head to dive under me. I instantly made a renversement which put me close behind him and in a most favorable position for careful aim. Training my sights into the center of his fusilage I pulled both triggers. With one long burst the fight was over. The Fokker fell over onto one wing and dropped aimlessly to earth. It was too dark to see the crash, and moreover I had all thoughts of my victory dissipated by a sudden ugly jerk to my motor which immediately developed into a violent vibration. As I turned back towards Verdun, which was the nearest point to our liens, I had recurring visions of crashing down into Germany to find myself a prisoner. This would be a nice ending to our glorious balloon expedition!

Throttling down to reduce the pounding I was able just to maintain headway. If my motor failed completely I was most certainly doomed, for I was less than a thousand feet above ground and could glide but a few hundred yards without power. Providence was again with me, for I cleared the lines and made our Verdun aerodrome where one flight of the 27th Squadron was housed. I landed without damage and hastily climbed out of my machine to investigate the cause of my trouble.

Imagine my surprise when I discovered that one blade of my propeller had been shot in two by my late adversary! He had evidently put several holes through it when he made his head-on attack. And utterly unconscious of the damage I had received, I had reversed my direction and shot him down before the weakened blade gave way! The heavy jolting of my engine was now clear to me—only half of the propeller caught the air.

Lieutenant Jerry Vasconceles of Denver, Colorado, was in charge of the Verdun field on which I had landed. He soon came out and joined me as I was staring at my broken propeller. And then I learned that he had just landed himself from a balloon expedition. A few questions followed and then we shook hands spontaneously. He had shot down the Damvillers balloon himself—the same one for which I had been headed. And as he was returning he had seen me shoot down my Fokker! This was extremely lucky for both of us, for we were able each to verify the other's victory for him, although of course corroboration from ground witnesses was necessary to make these victories official.

His mechanics placed a new propeller on my Spad, and none the worse for its recent rough usage the little 'bus took me rapidly home. I landed at 8:30 on my own field. And there I heard great news. Our Group had that morning shot down ten German balloons! My victory over the Fokker made it eleven victories to be credited us for this hour's work. And we had not lost a single pilot!

As the jubilant and famished pilots crowded into the mess hall one could not hear a word through all the excited chatter. Each one had some strange and fearful adventure to relate about his morning's experiences. But the tale which aroused howls of laughter was the droll story told by Lieutenant White of the 147th Squadron.

White had searched long and earnestly for the balloon that he desired to attack. He thought himself hopelessly lost in the darkness, when off to one side he distinguished the dark outline of what he thought was his balloon. Immediately redressing his machine he tipped downwards and began plugging furious streams of flaming bullets into his target.

He made a miscalculation in his distance and before he could swerve away from the dark mass ahead of him his machine had plunged straight through it!

And then he discovered that he had been piquing upon a round puff of black smoke that had just been made by a German Archy!

Frank Luke Strafes His Last Balloon

Neither side could afford to leave its lines undefended by observation balloons for a longer period than was necessary for replacements. Our onslaught of the early morning had destroyed so many of the Huns' Drachen, however, that it was quite impossible for them to get new balloons up at once, along their entire sector.

That same afternoon I flew along their lines to see what progress they were making in replacements of their observation posts. The only balloon I could discover in our sector was one which lifted its head just behind the town of Sivry-sur-Meuse. I made a note of its position and decided to try to bring in down early next morning.

Accordingly I was up again at the same hour the following day and again found the sky promised clear weather. Leaving the field at 5:30, I again took a course over Verdun in order to pick up the Meuse River there and follow it as a guide.

On this occasion I caught a grand view of No Man's Land as seen from the air by night. It was not yet daylight when I reached the lines and there I caught a longitudinal view of the span of ground that separated the two opposing armies. For upon both sides of this span of ground a horizontal line of flashes could be seen issuing from the mouth of rival guns. The German batteries were drawn up along their front scarcely a mile back of their line. And on our side a vastly more crowded line of flashes indicated the overwhelming superiority in numbers of guns that the American artillerymen were using to belabor the already vanquished Huns. So far as my eye could reach, this dark space lay outlined between the two lines of living fire. It was a most spectacular sight. I followed down its course for a few miles, then turned again to the north and tried to find the Meuse River.

After ten minutes' flight into Germany, I realized I had crossed the river before I began to turn north and that I must be some distance inside the enemy's lines. I dropped down still lower as I saw the outlines of a town in front of me and circling above it I discovered that I had penetrated some 25 miles inside Hunland and was now over the village of Stenay. I had overshot Sivry by about twenty miles.

I lost no time in heading about towards France. Opening up the throttle, I first struck west and followed this course until I had the Meuse River again under my nose. Then turning up the river, I flew just above the road which follows along its banks. It was now getting light enough to distinguish objects on the ground below.

This Meuse River highway is a lovely drive to take in the daytime, for it passes through a fertile and picturesque country. The little city of Dun-sur-Meuse stands out on a small cliff which juts into a bend of the river, making a most charming picture of what a medieval town should look like. I passed directly down Main Street over Dun-sur-Meuse and again picked up the broad highway that clung to the bank of the river. Occasional vehicles were now abroad below me. Day had broken and the Huns were up and ready for work.

It occurred to me that I might as well fly a bit lower and entertain the passing Huns with a little bullet-dodging as we met each other. My morning's work was spoiled anyway. It was becoming too late to take on a balloon now. Perhaps I might meet a general in his automobile and it would be fun to see him jump for the ditch and throw himself down on his face at the bottom. If I was fortunate enough to get him that would surely be helping along the war!

Ahead of me I saw a truck moving slowly in the same direction I was going. "Here goes for the first one!" I said to myself. I tipped down the nose of my machine and reached for my triggers.

As my nose went down something appeared over my top wing which took away my breath for an instant. There directly in my path was a huge enemy observation balloon! It was swaying in the breeze and the cable which held it to earth ran straight down until it reached the moving truck ahead of me. Then it became clear as daylight to me. The Huns were towing a new balloon up the road to its position for observation! They had just received a replacement from the supply station of Dun-sur-Meuse, and after filling it with gas were now getting it forward as rapidly as possible. It was just the target I had been searching for!

Forgetting the truck and crew, I flattened out instantly and began firing at the sway-ing monster in the air. So close to it had I come before I saw it that I had only time to fire a burst of fifty shots when I was forced to make a vertical virage, to avoid crashing through it. I was then but four or five hundred feet above ground.

Just as I began the virage I heard the rat-tat-tat-tat of a machine-gun fire from the truck on the road beneath me. And mingled with this drum fire I heard the sound of an explosion in the fusilage just behind my ear! One of their explosive bullets had come very close to my head and had exploded against a longeron or wire in the tail of the aeroplane! There was nothing I could do about that however, except to fly along as steadily as possible until I reached a place of safety and could make an investigation of the damage received. I cleared the side of the gas-bag and then as I passed I turned and looked behind me.

The enemy balloon was just at the point of exploding and the observer had already leaped from his basket and was still dropping through air with his parachute not yet opened. It was a very short distance to Mother Earth, and sometimes a parachute needs two or three hundred feet fall in which to fully open and check the swiftness of the falling body. I wondered whether this poor chap had any chance for his life in that short distance and just what bones he was likely to break when he landed. And then came a great burst of fire, as the whole interior of the big balloon became suddenly ignited. I couldn't resist one shout of exultation at the magnificent display of fireworks I had thus set off, hoping in the meantime that its dull glare would reach the eyes of some of our own balloon observers across the lines who would thus be in a position to give me the confirmation of my eleventh victory.

Again I decided to pay a call at Jerry Vasconcelle's field at Verdun and there get out and ascertain the extent of the damage in the tail of my Spad. Jerry welcomed me with some amusement and wanted to know whether this dropping in on him was to be a daily occurrence. Yesterday it had been a broken prop and to-day a broken tail. Before answering him I got out, and together we made a minute examination of my machine.

A neat row of bullet holes ran back down the tail of my machine. They were as nicely spaced as if they had been put in by careful measurement. The first hole was about four inches back of the pad on which my head rests when I am in the seat. The others were directly back of it at regular intervals. One, the explosive bullet, had struck the longeron that runs the length of the fusilage, and this had made the sharp explosion that I had heard at the time. The gunners on the truck had done an excellent bit of shooting!

None of the holes were in a vital part of the machine. I took off the field after a short inspection and soon covered the fifteen or sixteen miles that lay between the Verdun field and our own.

Upon landing I found very bad news awaiting me.

On the previous afternoon Lieutenant Sherry and Lieutenant Nutt, both of 94 Squadron, had gone out on patrol and had failed to come in. Long after dark their mechanics remained on the field pooping up Very lights, in the hope that they might still be searching about, trying to find their way. At last we abandoned all hope ourselves and waited for the morning's news from outside sources.

Now it had arrived and to my great joy it was in the form of a telephone call from old "Madam" Sherry himself. But his next message informed us that Nutt had been killed in combat! And Sherry himself had been through an experience that might easily have turned one's hair gray. Just before lunch time Sherry came in by automobile and told us the story of his experiences.

He and Nutt had attacked an overwhelming formation of eight Fokker machines. They had stolen up on the Heinies and counted upon getting one or two victims before the others were aware of their presence. But the attack failed and suddenly both American pilots were having the fight of their lives. The Hun pilots were not only skilful and experienced, but they worked together with such nicety that Sherry and Nutt were unable either to hold their own or to escape.

Soon each was fighting a separate battle against four enemy machines. Sherry saw Nutt go crashing down and later learned that he had been shot through the heart and killed in air. A moment later Sherry's machine received several bullets in the motor which put it immediately out of commission. Dropping swiftly to earth, Sherry saw that the Hun pilots were not taking any chances but were determined to kill him as he fell.

He was two miles and more in the air when he began his forced descent. All the way down the enemy pilots pursued him, firing through his machine continuously as it glided smoothly towards earth. Only by miracles a dozen times repeated did he escape death from their bullets. He saw the lines below him and made desperate efforts to glide his machine to our side of the fence despite the furious attempts of the Boches to prevent this escape. At last he crashed in one of the million shell-holes that covered No Man's Land of last week. His machine turned over and broke into a score of fragments, Sherry being thrown some yards away where he landed unhurt at the bottom of another shell-hole.

While he was still pinching himself to make sure he was actually unhurt he discovered his implacable enemies piquing upon him with their Fokkers and firing long bursts of bullets into his shell-hole with their machine-guns!

Sherry clung as closely to the sides of his hole as he could and watched the dirt fly up all around him as the Fokkers made dive after dive at him. It must have been like watching a file of executioners leveling their guns at one and firing dozens of rounds without hitting one. Except that in Sherry's case, it was machine-guns that were doing the firing!

Finally the Fokkers made off for Germany. Crawling out of his hole, Sherry discovered that a formation of Spads had come to his rescue and had chased the Germans homewards. And then he began to wonder on which side of the trenches he had fallen. For he had been too busy dodging Fokkers to know where his crippled machine was taking him.

One can imagine Sherry's joy when he heard a doughboy in perfectly good United States yell from a neighboring shell-hole:

"Hey guy! Where the h—'s your gas-mask?"

Madam didn't care for the moment whether he had a gas-mask or not, so glad was he to learn that he had fallen among friends and was still in the land of the living.

He quickly tumbled into the next shell-hole, where he found his new friend. The latter informed him that he was still in No Man's Land, that the German infantry were but a hundred yards away and that gas shells had been coming across that space all the afternoon. He even gave Madam his own gas-mask and his pistol, saying he guessed he was more used to gas than an aviator would be! He advised Sherry to lay low where he was until nightfall, when he would see him back into our lines. And thus Lieutenant Sherry spent the next few hours reviewing the strange episodes that flavor the career of an aviator.

Sherry finished his story with a grim recital of what had occurred when they went out next morning to recover Nutt's body. It too had fallen in No Man's Land, but the Americans had advanced a few hundred yards during the night and now covered the spot where Nutt's body lay. Sherry accompanied a squad of doughboys out to the spot where Nutt's smashed machine had lain during the night. They found poor Nutt, as I have said, with several bullets through the heart.

They extricated the body from the wreckage and were beginning to dig a grave when a shot from a hidden Hun sniper struck one of the burial party in the foot. The others jumped to their guns and disappeared through the trees. They soon returned with a look of savage satisfaction on their faces, although Sherry had not heard a shot fired. While they continued their work he strolled off in the direction from which they had returned.

Behind a trench dugout he found the German sniper who had had the yellowness to fire upon a burial party. The man's head was crushed flat with the butts of the doughboys' guns!

—⁓—

"Frank Luke, the marvelous balloon strafer of the 27th, did not return last night!"

So reads the last entry in my flight diary of September 29, 1918. Re-reading that line brings back to me the common anxiety of the whole Group over the extraordinary and prolonged absence of their most popular member. For Luke's very mischievousness and irresponsibility made every one of us feel that he must be cared for and nursed back into a more disciplined way of fighting—and flying—and living. His escapades were the talk of the camp and the despair of his superior officers. Fully a month after his disappearance his commanding officer, Alfred Grant, Captain of the 27th Squadron, told me that if Luke ever did come back he would court-martial him first and then recommend him for the Legion of Honor!

In a word, Luke mingled with his disdain for bullets a very similar distaste for the orders of his superior officers. When imperative orders were given him to come immediately home after a patrol Luke would unconcernedly land at some French aerodrome miles away, spend the night there and arrive home after dark the next night. But as he almost invariably landed with one or two more enemy balloons to his credit, which he had destroyed on the way home, he was usually let off with a reprimand and a caution not to repeat the offense.

As blandly indifferent to reprimands as to orders, Luke failed to return again the following night. This studied disobedience to orders could not be ignored, and thus Captain Grant had stated that if Luke ever did return he must be disciplined for his insubordination. The night of September 27th Luke spent the night with the French Cigognes on the Toul aerodrome.

The last we had heard from Luke was that at six o'clock on the night of September 28th he left the French field where he had spent the night, and flying low over one of the American Balloon Headquarters he circled over their heads until he had attracted the attention of the officers, then dropped them a brief note which he had written in his aeroplane. As may well be imagined, Luke was a prime favorite with our Balloon Staff. All the officers of that organization worshiped the boy for his daring and his wonderful successes against the balloon department of their foes. They appreciated the value of balloon observation to the enemy and knew the difficulties and dangers in attacking these well-defended posts.

Running out and picking up the streamer and sheet of paper which fell near their office they unfolded the latter and read:

"Look out for enemy balloon at D-2 and D-4 positions.—Luke."

Already Luke's machine was disappearing in the direction of the first balloon which lay just beyond the Meuse. It was too dark to make out its dim outline at this distance, but as they all gathered about the front of their "office" they glued their eyes to the spot where they knew it hung. For Luke had notified them several times previously as to his intended victims and every time they had been rewarded for their watching.

Two minutes later a great read glow lit up the northwestern horizon and before the last of it died away the second German balloon had likewise burst into flames! Their intrepid hero had again fulfilled his promise! They hastened into their headquarters and called up our operations officer and announced Frank Luke's last two victories. Then we waited for Luke to make his dramatic appearance.

But Luke never came! That night and the next day we rather maligned him for his continued absence, supposing naturally enough that he had returned to his French friends for the night. But when no news of him came to us, when repeated inquiries elicited no information as to his movements after he had brought down his last balloon, every man in the Group became aware that we had lost the greatest airman in our army. From that day to this not one word of reliable information has reached us concerning Luke's disappearance. Not a single clue to his death and burial was ever obtained from the Germans! Like Guynemer, the miraculous airman of France, Frank Luke was swallowed by the skies and no mortal traces of him remain!

CHAPTER FIFTEEN

Nathan Hale

By James Parton

Like your editor, you probably have been hearing about Nathan Hale and his courage since your earliest school years. Here James Parton provides details you may not know about the man whose picture should be beside the word "patriot" in the dictionary.
— LAMAR UNDERWOOD

GENERAL WASHINGTON WANTED A MAN. IT WAS IN SEPTEMBER, 1776, AT THE CITY OF New York, a few days after the battle of Long Island. The swift and deep East River flowed between the two hostile armies, and General Washington had as yet no system established for getting information of the enemy's movements and intentions. He never needed such information so much as at that crisis.

What would General Howe do next? If he crossed at Hell Gate, the American army, too small in numbers, and defeated the week before, might be caught on Manhattan Island as in a trap, and the issue of the contest might be made to depend upon a single battle; for in such circumstances defeat would involve the capture of the whole army. And yet General Washington was compelled to confess:

"We cannot learn, nor have we been able to procure the least information of late."

Therefore he wanted a man. He wanted an intelligent man, cool-headed, skillful, brave, to cross the East River to Long Island, enter the enemy's camp, and get information as to his strength and intentions. He went to Colonel Knowlton, commanding a remarkably efficient regiment from Connecticut, and requested him to ascertain if this man, so sorely needed, could be found in his command. Colonel Knowlton called his officers together, stated the wishes of General Washington, and, without urging the enterprise upon any individual, left the matter to their reflections.

Captain Nathan Hale, a brilliant youth of twenty-one, recently graduated from Yale College, was one of those who reflected upon the subject. He soon reached a conclusion. He was of the very flower of the young men of New England, and one of the best of the younger soldiers of the patriot army. He had been educated for the ministry, and his motive in adopting for a time the profession of arms was purely patriotic. This we know from the familiar records of his life at the time when the call to arms was first heard.

In addition to his other gifts and graces, he was handsome, vigorous, and athletic, all in an extraordinary degree. If he had lived in our day he might have pulled the stroke-oar at New London, or pitched for the college nine.

The officers were conversing in a group. No one had as yet spoken the decisive word. Colonel Knowlton appealed to a French sergeant, an old soldier of former wars, and asked him to volunteer.

"No, no," said he. "I am ready to fight the British at any place and time, but I do not feel willing to go among them to be hung up like a dog."

Captain Hale joined the group of officers. He said to Colonel Knowlton:

"I will undertake it."

Some of his best friends remonstrated. One of them, afterwards the famous general William Hull, then a captain in Washington's army, has recorded Hale's reply to his own attempt to dissuade him.

"I think," said Hale, "I owe to my country the accomplishment of an object so important. I am fully sensible of the consequences of discovery and capture in such a situation. But for a year I have been attached to the army, and have not rendered any material service, while receiving a compensation for which I make no return. I wish to be useful, and every kind of service necessary for the public good becomes honorable by being necessary."

He spoke, as General Hull remembered, with earnestness and decision, as one who had considered the matter well, and had made up his mind.

Having received his instructions, he traveled fifty miles along the Sound as far as Norwalk in Connecticut. One who saw him there made a very wise remark upon him, to the effect that he was "too good-looking" to go as a spy. He could not deceive. "Some scrubby fellow ought to have gone." At Norwalk he assumed the disguise of a Dutch schoolmaster, putting on a suit of plain brown clothes, and a round, broad-brimmed hat. He had no difficulty in crossing the Sound, since he bore an order from General Washington which placed at his disposal all the vessels belonging to Congress. For several days everything appears to have gone well with him, and there is reason to believe that he passed through the entire British army without detection or even exciting suspicion.

Finding the British had crossed to New York, he followed them. He made his way back to Long Island, and nearly reached the point opposite Norwalk where he had originally landed. Rendered perhaps too bold by success, he went into a well-known and popular tavern, entered into conversation with the guests, and made himself very agreeable. The tradition is that he made himself too agreeable. A man present suspecting or knowing that he was not the character he had assumed, quietly left the room, communicated his suspicions to the captain of a British ship anchored near, who dispatched a boat's crew to capture and bring on board the agreeable stranger. His true character was immediately revealed. Drawings of some of the British works, with notes in Latin, were found hidden in the soles of his shoes. Nor did he attempt to deceive his captors, and the English captain, lamenting, as he said, that "so fine a fellow had fallen into his power," sent him to New York in one of his boats, and with him the fatal proofs that he was a spy.

September twenty-first was the day on which he reached New York—the day of the great fire which laid one-third of the little city in ashes. From the time of his departure from General Washington's camp to that of his return to New York was about fourteen days. He was taken to General Howe's headquarters at the Beekman mansion, on the East River, near the corner of the present Fifty-first Street and First Avenue. It is a strange coincidence that this house to which he was brought to be tried as a spy was the very one from which Major Andre departed when he went to West Point. Tradition says that Captain Hale was examined in a greenhouse which then stood in the garden of the Beekman mansion.

Short was his trial, for he avowed at once his true character. The British general signed an order to his provost-marshal directing him to receive into his custody the prisoner convicted as a spy, and to see him hanged by the neck "to-morrow morning at daybreak."

Terrible things are reported of the manner in which this noble prisoner, this admirable gentleman and hero, was treated by his jailer and executioner. There are savages in every large army, and it is possible that this provost-marshal was one of them. It is said that he refused him writing-materials, and afterwards, when Captain Hale had been furnished them by others, destroyed before his face his last letters to his mother and to the young lady to whom he was engaged to be married. As those letters were never received this statement may be true. The other alleged horrors of the execution it is safe to disregard, because we know that it was conducted in the usual form and in the presence of many spectators and a considerable body of troops. One fact shines out from the distracting confusion of that morning, which will be cherished to the latest posterity as a precious ingot of the moral treasure of the American people. When asked if he had anything to say, Captain Hale replied:

"I only regret that I have but one life to lose for my country."

The scene of his execution was probably an old graveyard in Chambers Street, which was then called Barrack Street. General Howe formally notified General Washington of his execution. In recent years, through the industry of investigators, the pathos and sublimity of these events have been in part revealed.

In 1887 a bronze statue of the young hero was unveiled in the State House at Hartford. Mr. Charles Dudley Warner delivered a beautiful address suitable to the occasion, and Governor Lounsberry worthily accepted the statue on behalf of the State. It is greatly to be regretted that our knowledge of this noble martyr is so slight; but we know enough to be sure that he merits the veneration of his countrymen.

CHAPTER SIXTEEN

Okinawa: The Fight for Sugar Loaf Hill
By George Feifer

In the summer of 1945, more people died in the battle of Okinawa than in both the Hiroshima and Nagaski atomic bomb attacks combined. That stunning loss of Okinawa civilians, Japanese military, and American military may surprise many people, knowing as we do now that the end of the war would come in August 1945. The Okinawa campaign has inspired many books, but none surpass George Feifer's The Battle of Okinawa: The Blood and the Bomb. *The critically acclaimed, highly detailed and voluminous account of the savage fighting on the island closest to the Japanese mainland is a masterpiece of living military history. This excerpt from one of the most savage fights of the battle is typical of the reader reward in the full book. The leading Marine in the fighting is Platoon Sergeant Edmund De Mar, called "Mommy" by fellow Marines in G Company, 2nd Battalion, 22nd Regiment.*

—LAMAR UNDERWOOD

THE "PROMINENT HILL," AS THE AMERICANS REFERRED TO IT, STOOD BEYOND A SLIGHT draw that formed a corridor leading up to it. A similar rise called Charlie Hill had fallen the day before to the 1st Battalion, after a day and a half of tank and infantry assault supported by naval gunfire. There was no reason to expect the new hill, barren except for a few scrubby trees, would be more difficult. De Mar, studying it again from a few hundred yards north, saw it as "just another lump, a brownish incline with a little knoll on top."

G Company's return to combat had been hard. After suffering only two battle-fatigue casualties during its weeks in the north, it lost nine men to exceptionally heavy artillery, mortar, and small-arms fire in just two days in the south, including five killed on the first day alone. De Mar's 3rd Platoon had escaped from one action only with the aid of a smoke screen. But the company would soon look back to those two days pushing south to here as almost easy going. At least everyone could still keep track of the killed and wounded.

Actually, De Mar was reassigning the functions of the missing men in his weakened platoon when the runner arrived with the order to meet with Lieutenant Bair for coordination. De Mar had twenty-eight men left of a full complement of forty. According to the plan, they would be joined by nineteen men still fit for action from dead Ed Ruess's 1st Platoon and be supported by the tank platoon. The hill had to be taken quickly, because its machine guns and mortars were badly chewing up everything in sight, including other companies.

The tanks were waiting in a depression not visible from the hill. When Lieutenant Bair gave platoon Sergeant De Mar and the replacement for Ed Ruess the plan of attack, they took the usual precaution of squatting far enough apart so that one mortar round couldn't hit them all. They were eager to learn one another's names to avoid calling out "Lieutenant!" or "Sergeant!"—another way of making themselves priority targets for snipers. The plan was straightforward: De Mar and his men on the left, Bair and the reduced 1st Platoon on the right, and the tanks moving out at the same time, while a machine-gun section would give additional fire support as they advanced.

The tank commander wanted assurance that he wouldn't be left "high and dry." Tanks were a great advantage to the infantry they supported, and the American 10th Army had vastly more of them than the Japanese 32nd Army. But enemy fire of such intensity and accuracy turned even the best American Shermans into a danger too, as targets for concentrated salvos. Veterans learned to control their first instinct to crouch behind them for protection and to mistrust the false sense of security they provided. Especially when antitank guns and other armament zeroed in on their whistling and clanking, the instinct of troops at their sides was to scramble as far from them as quickly as possible, leaving them vulnerable to dreaded Japanese infantrymen with satchel charges.

Against powerful defenses, therefore, tanks needed the protection of infantrymen as much as infantrymen needed the extra punch from tanks. De Mar urged the lieutenant in command of those four Shermans not to worry: "We'll stick to you like flies on shit." They synchronized watches. Jump-off time would be 1600 hours on a signal from Lieutenant Bair.

～～

De Mar returned to his platoon and gave the word. Final preparations were made for the attack. Waiting was a miniature prelanding limbo, the men hoping the moment would come soon and that it never would. De Mar worried about them, about the steady Japanese fire from both flanks, and about communications because his radio had been knocked out. It would be nice, he mused, to be somewhere else. At 1600 hours, the lead Sherman's hatch cover closed and it started off with the 3rd Platoon.

It was only minutes to the hill. Starting the climb, De Mar and the others suddenly saw it was thick with guns. Tank fire had ripped down camouflage, exposing dozens, maybe hundreds, of emplacements now showing gun barrels and muzzle flashes. They didn't yet know that some of the most damaging fire pouring down on them was from other hills. De Mar had no time to look at anything other than his men, some of whom were already down. The tanks were being hit just as fast by concealed, expertly placed mines and antitank guns. Two were put out of action almost immediately.

The crest was only a few hundred yards away. Hoping audacity would compensate for their lack of deception, the two platoons charged straight up and reached it, but with a much-reduced complement. Bair spread his remaining dozen-odd men into shell holes, but the Japanese fire was so intense and the American already so diminished that the lieutenant, his radio communications also out, sent a man back to report that G needed help to hold the summit. Racing and dodging down, that messenger could see little movement among De Mar's group, which was "getting the hell beaten out of them."

Nothing De Mar had seen in combat, let alone in films, had prepared him for such concentration of incoming fire. It very quickly killed many of his men and left others unable to function as fire teams. Soon only a handful remained unhit, most prominently Bair. The big, burly first lieutenant was a man of few words who, like Ed Ruess, had been among the noncommissioned officers selected for officer training as the Marines' need for more officers to replace casualties grew. He presented a fine target—but also served as an inspiration to the men—as he tried to see to the wounded and rally the others. He motioned to De Mar: something about one of the disabled tanks. Then he was violently spun around and De Mar saw a large chunk had been ripped from his upper leg. But powerful Bair picked up a .30-caliber light machine gun from alongside its two dead operators, threw a belt of ammunition over his shoulder, and, like a John Wayne character, laid out lead in the enemy's direction—one of the directions. It wasn't long before he took a second hit, this time in the arm cradling his machine gun. The lieutenant continued producing covering fire so that some men could crawl to help others who'd been wounded going up the hill until his third hit, in the buttocks, sent him spinning out of sight.

De Mar quickly threw some grenades and started crawling toward Bair. Then he felt as if someone had taken a log from a fire and slammed it with all his might into his leg. He went down flat and couldn't get up. Still down, he saw one of his 3rd Platoon men spring up and bang on a disabled tank with his rifle, after which the crew fired furiously for a moment—against what looked like "thousands of Japanese coming at us," as a crew member would later put it—until they ran out of ammunition and escaped through the tank's emergency hatch. Other tank crews continued firing although their vehicles were burning, then leaped out to help wounded riflemen.

There was no place anywhere to make a stand. Much later, in the sweet luxury of being alive to remember, De Mar would quip it was a situation from which General Custer would have cut and run. Dirt had jammed his rifle. He had no cover or protection. Knowing a sniper was poised somewhere on his left, maybe the one who'd already hit him, all he could do was hug the ground for all he was worth. He heard cries—from about ten yards away, he guessed—from a private named James Davis, whose size had earned him the nickname "Little Bit." Strong and tough nevertheless, Davis was only eighteen years old and his wounds were obviously very bad; he was crying for his parents to come get him. De Mar grunted for him to shut up: Any noise there would probably be a fatal noise. When Davis eventually did fall silent, De Mar hoped it was because he'd heard him.

Disabled in the extremely precarious position on the crest, De Mar thought of his own parents. He looked at his watch. It was 1645 hours. Forty-five days, not minutes, seemed to have passed. Now no Americans at all seemed still to be firing, and he could see none except dead and wounded. "What am I going to do?" he asked himself, trying to stay calm. He decided to wait, head as flat on the ground as he could push it. It would soon be dark. His leg was numb and he'd lost a lot of blood, but he knew he could crawl. A figure slithering down the hill in the dark would most likely be finished off by his own troops, who would take him for a Jap, especially at night when they were the only ones to move. He didn't even have that night's password. But those were problems for later; now he could only lie where he was, still surprised and dismayed by the dense, accurate Japanese fire from big guns, small arms, hand grenades, and mortars.

Some time later, he heard a whisper. "De Mar, you hit bad? Can you crawl?" Although he didn't recognize the voice of the man risking his own life for his, the sense of comradeship gave him an incredible lift.* "Can I crawl?" he whispered back, his head still half buried in the mud. "I can crawl back to the States."

A good smoke screen was laid down—from smoke shells fired by the surviving tanks, De Mar would later learn. He started down. Someone joined him from behind and cut off his pack to ease his crawling. Finding a little ditch, he squeezed into it for cover and kept crawling until his hand touched the body of a rifleman from his platoon—who had a bullet hole between the eyes. He tried to pull the body with him, but the helper behind urged him to just get down off the hill for now. Although it would have been a four-minute stroll from summit to bottom, the incomprehensibly intense enemy fire made their progress painfully slow.

Soon he came upon Lieutenant Bair, badly bleeding from his wounds but trying to get his machine gun operating. De Mar tossed him his pistol because he believed he had some hand grenades left for any Japanese who might try to hurl satchel charges against the tank he hoped would take him back. Reaching it, he saw Little Bit's body lying alongside, where it had been pulled by Jim Chaisson, the man who'd run to the command post for reinforcements, then run back up the murderous hill to help his buddies. A tank man quickly dressed De Mar's wound, but Mommy refused to move until all known wounded had been brought down from the hill.

---

* That was too common among Marines to deserve mention except to restate that their training's most important product was a sacred sense of comradeship. Medical corpsmen who tended the Marines developed the same sense of obligation and almost never failed to respond to calls from the wounded except when ordered not to because the fire was too intense. In many such instances, the officers and noncommissioned officers who issued those orders themselves went out into the killing zone to reach the wounded.

Then he was hoisted up onto the turret, where another wounded man was soon placed beside him. Recognizing the youthful voice of the "tanker" who'd rescued him from the hill, De Mar took out his battle dressing, leaned toward him, and asked where he'd been hit. Five fast rounds cracked out. Four hit the "expeditionary can"—five gallons of spare water or oil on the turret inches from De Mar's head. The fifth hit his savior behind the ear, splattering blood and brains all over De Mar. Gripping the now grievously wounded boy as the tank roared off, he reached for his grenades and found he had none; his pouch had been shot off.

When the tank made it back to Fox Company's command post, the young tank driver was dead. A sergeant asked how things were going. "Pretty rough on that goddamn hill," answered Mommy, not suspecting how much rougher it would become. The full strength of the defenses was still beyond his imagination—or that of any American, including General Buckner.

—❦—

Those were the first assaults on Sugar Loaf Hill, as it would be christened two days later (when Lieutenant Colonel Woodhouse would call it by a name he'd used for objectives during training exercises on Guadalcanal). No more were made that day, for the battalion commander, now aware that the objective was far more difficult than originally believed, withdrew G Company and called for air strikes. Starting the next day, the sequence of attacks became so confused, with so many Americans cut off from their units, that it was impossible to keep track of who reached the summit before he fell.

Besides, holes from both sides' shelling were so large that men who crouched in them couldn't see members of other units yards away. What was known for certain was that five of De Mar's 3rd Platoon were killed and ten wounded on May 12, a casualty rate of 50 percent. Other platoons lost even more men. On May 14, G Company's three rifle platoons with their machine-gun sections had to be consolidated into a single platoon—whose lieutenant would be killed that night. Sustained losses like this would quickly prostrate the 6th Division.

—❦—

The hated hill looked to most Americans less like anything involving sugar than a rectangular loaf of coral and volcanic rock. Stebbins and De Mar weren't alone in wondering how such an object, seemingly less significant than the Kakazu Ridge finally taken by the Army, could cause such slaughter. To the 6th Division staff, it was merely a minor midway station wanted as a platform for fire support against a higher hill called Kokuba about a mile farther south.

Sugar Loaf's three hundred or so yards of frontage rose abruptly to a height of sixty feet from an area of plain before it, an unhappy feature to those who had to cross that open country, about the size of six football fields. The hill itself was low enough, especially in relation to the others in view of it, including the Shuri heights, to appear almost negligible—a "pimple of a hill," as one Marine would call it forty years later, still trying to fathom how it could have been so evil. A young man in the good shape of all infantrymen could run to its crest in three or four minutes. Yet it would cost more casualties than any other single Pacific battle, on Iwo Jima or elsewhere.

CHAPTER SEVENTEEN

An Occurrence at Owl Creek Bridge
By Ambrose Bierce

In the first story in this book, Lisa Purcell introduced one of America's most talented writers of the Civil War era turning his great prose to historical events. For Ambrose Bierce, the Battle of Shiloh was an event observed first-hand, and he was writing in an auto-biographical mode. Here, we see Bierce turning his talents to fiction, with a Civil War short story that has been rewarding readers for ages. Bierce was a lieutenant in the 9th Indiana Infantry Regiment. His life of observing and writing about whatever interested him ended in 1913 when he travelled to Mexico to observe rebel troops during the Mexican Revolution. He was never seen again.

—LAMAR UNDERWOOD

I

A MAN STOOD UPON A RAILROAD BRIDGE IN NORTHERN ALABAMA, LOOKING DOWN INTO the swift water twenty feet below. The man's hands were behind his back, the wrists bound with a cord. A rope closely encircled his neck. It was attached to a stout cross-timber above his head and the slack fell to the level of his knees. Some loose boards laid upon the sleepers supporting the metals of the railway supplied a footing for him and his executioners—two private soldiers of the Federal army, directed by a sergeant who in civil life may have been a deputy sheriff. At a short remove upon the same temporary platform was an officer in the uniform of his rank, armed. He was a captain. A sentinel at each end of the bridge stood with his rifle in the position known as "support," that is to say, vertical in front of the left shoulder, the hammer resting on the forearm thrown straight across the chest—a formal and unnatural position, enforcing an erect carriage of the body. It did not appear to be the duty of these two men to know what was occurring at the centre of the bridge; they merely blockaded the two ends of the foot planking that traversed it.

Beyond one of the sentinels nobody was in sight; the railroad ran straight away into a forest for a hundred yards, then, curving, was lost to view. Doubtless there was an outpost farther along. The other bank of the stream was open ground—a gentle activity topped with a stockade of vertical tree trunks, loopholed for rifles, with a single embrasure through which protruded the muzzle of a brass cannon commanding the bridge. Midway of the slope between bridge and fort were the spectators—a single company of infantry in line, at "parade rest," the butts of the rifles on the ground, the barrels inclining slightly backward against the right shoulder, the hands crossed upon the stock. A lieutenant stood at the right of the line, the point of his sword upon the ground, his left hand resting upon his right. Excepting the group of four at the centre of the bridge, not a man moved. The company faced the bridge, staring stonily, motionless. The sentinels, facing the banks of the stream, might have been statues to adorn the bridge. The captain stood with folded arms, silent, observing the work of his subordinates, but making no sign. Death is a dignitary who when he comes announced is to be received with formal manifestations of respect, even by those most familiar with him. In the code of military etiquette silence and fixity are forms of deference.

The man who was engaged in being hanged was apparently about thirty-five years of age. He was a civilian, if one might judge from his habit, which was that of a planter. His features were good—a straight nose, firm mouth, broad forehead, from which his long, dark hair was combed straight back, falling behind his ears to the collar of his well-fitting frock-coat. He wore a mustache and pointed beard, but no whiskers; his eyes were large and dark gray, and had a kindly expression which one would hardly have expected in one whose neck was in the hemp. Evidently this was no vulgar assassin. The liberal military code makes provision for hanging many kinds of persons, and gentlemen are not excluded.

The preparations being complete, the two private soldiers stepped aside and each drew away the plank upon which he had been standing. The sergeant turned to the captain, saluted and placed himself immediately behind that officer, who in turn moved apart one pace. These movements left the condemned man and the sergeant standing on the two ends of the same plank, which spanned three of the cross-ties of the bridge. The end upon which the civilian stood almost, but not quite, reached a fourth. This plank had been held in place by the weight of the captain; it was now held by that of the sergeant. At a signal from the former the latter would step aside, the plank would tilt and the condemned man go down between two ties. The arrangement commended itself to his judgment as simple and effective. His face had not been covered nor his eyes bandaged. He looked a moment at his "unsteadfast footing," then let his gaze wander to the swirling water of the stream racing madly beneath his feet. A piece of dancing driftwood caught his attention and his eyes followed it down the current. How slowly it appeared to move! What a sluggish stream!

He closed his eyes in order to fix his last thoughts upon his wife and children. The water, touched to gold by the early sun, the brooding mists under the banks at some distance down the stream, the fort, the soldiers, the piece of drift—all had distracted him. And now he became conscious of a new disturbance. Striking through the thought of his dear ones was a sound which he could neither ignore nor understand, a sharp, distinct, metallic percussion like the stroke of a blacksmith's hammer upon the anvil; it had the same ringing quality. He wondered what it was, and whether immeasurably distant or near by—it seemed both. Its recurrence was regular, but as slow as the tolling of a death knell. He awaited each stroke with impatience and—he knew not why—apprehension. The intervals of silence grew progressively longer; the delays became maddening. With their greater infrequency the sounds increased in strength and sharpness. They hurt his ear like the thrust of a knife; he feared he would shriek. What he heard was the ticking of his watch.

He unclosed his eyes and saw again the water below him. "If I could free my hands," he thought, "I might throw off the noose and spring into the stream. By diving I could evade the bullets and, swimming vigorously, reach the bank, take to the woods and get away home. My home, thank God, is as yet outside their lines; my wife and little ones are still beyond the invader's farthest advance."

As these thoughts, which have here to be set down in words, were flashed into the doomed man's brain rather than evolved from it the captain nodded to the sergeant. The sergeant stepped aside.

II

Peyton Farquhar was a well-to-do planter, of an old and highly respected Alabama family. Being a slave owner and like other slave owners a politician he was naturally an original secessionist and ardently devoted to the Southern cause. Circumstances of an imperious nature, which it is unnecessary to relate here, had prevented him from taking service with the gallant army that had fought the disastrous campaigns ending with the fall of Corinth, and he chafed under the inglorious restraint, longing for the release of his energies, the larger life of the soldier, the opportunity for distinction. That opportunity, he felt, would come, as it comes to all in war time. Meanwhile he did what he could. No service was too humble for him to perform in aid of the South, no adventure too perilous for him to undertake if consistent with the character of a civilian who was at heart a soldier, and who in good faith and without too much qualification assented to at least a part of the frankly villainous dictum that all is fair in love and war.

One evening while Farquhar and his wife were sitting on a rustic bench near the entrance to his grounds, a gray-clad soldier rode up to the gate and asked for a drink of water. Mrs. Farquhar was only too happy to serve him with her own white hands. While she was fetching the water her husband approached the dusty horseman and inquired eagerly for news from the front.

"The Yanks are repairing the railroads," said the man, "and are getting ready for another advance. They have reached the Owl Creek bridge, put it in order and built a stockade on the north bank. The commandant has issued an order, which is posted everywhere, declaring that any civilian caught interfering with the railroad, its bridges, tunnels or trains will be summarily hanged. I saw the order."

"How far is it to the Owl Creek bridge?" Farquhar asked.

"About thirty miles."

"Is there no force on this side the creek?"

"Only a picket post half a mile out, on the railroad, and a single sentinel at this end of the bridge."

"Suppose a man—a civilian and student of hanging—should elude the picket post and perhaps get the better of the sentinel," said Farquhar, smiling, "what could he accomplish?"

The soldier reflected. "I was there a month ago," he replied. "I observed that the flood of last winter had lodged a great quantity of driftwood against the wooden pier at this end of the bridge. It is now dry and would burn like tow."

The lady had now brought the water, which the soldier drank. He thanked her ceremoniously, bowed to her husband and rode away. An hour later, after nightfall, he repassed the plantation, going northward in the direction from which he had come. He was a Federal scout.

III

As Peyton Farquhar fell straight downward through the bridge he lost consciousness and was as one already dead. From this state he was awakened—ages later, it seemed to him—by the pain of a sharp pressure upon his throat, followed by a sense of suffocation. Keen, poignant agonies seemed to shoot from his neck downward through every fibre of his body and limbs. These pains appeared to flash along well-defined lines of ramification and to beat with an inconceivably rapid periodicity. They seemed like streams of pulsating fire heating him to an intolerable temperature. As to his head, he was conscious of nothing but a feeling of fulness—of congestion. These sensations were unaccompanied by thought. The intellectual part of his nature was already effaced; he had power only to feel, and feeling was torment. He was conscious of motion. Encompassed in a luminous cloud, of which he was now merely the fiery heart, without material substance, he swung through unthinkable arcs of oscillation, like a vast pendulum. Then all at once, with terrible suddenness, the light about him shot upward with the noise of a loud plash; a frightful roaring was in his ears, and all was cold and dark. The power of thought was restored; he knew that the rope had broken and he had fallen into the stream. There was no additional strangulation; the noose about his neck was already suffocating him and kept the water from his lungs. To die of hanging at the bottom of a river!—the idea seemed to him ludicrous. He opened his eyes in the darkness and saw above him a gleam of light, but how distant, how inaccessible! He was still sinking, for the light became fainter and fainter until it was a mere glimmer. Then it began to grow and brighten, and he knew that he was rising toward the surface—knew it with reluctance, for he was now very comfortable. "To be hanged and drowned," he thought, "that is not so bad; but I do not wish to be shot. No; I will not be shot; that is not fair."

He was not conscious of an effort, but a sharp pain in his wrist apprised him that he was trying to free his hands. He gave the struggle his attention, as an idler might observe the feat of a juggler, without interest in the outcome. What splendid effort!— what magnificent, what superhuman strength! Ah, that was a fine endeavor! Bravo! The cord fell away; his arms parted and floated upward, the hands dimly seen on each side in the growing light. He watched them with a new interest as first one and then the other pounced upon the noose at his neck. They tore it away and thrust it fiercely aside, its undulations resembling those of a water-snake. "Put it back, put it back!" He thought he shouted these words to his hands, for the undoing of the noose had been succeeded by the direst pang that he had yet experienced. His neck ached horribly; his brain was on fire; his heart, which had been fluttering faintly, gave a great leap, trying to force itself out at his mouth. His whole body was racked and wrenched with an insupportable anguish! But his disobedient hands gave no heed to the command. They beat the water vigorously with quick, downward strokes, forcing him to the surface. He felt his head emerge; his eyes were blinded by the sunlight; his chest expanded convulsively, and with a supreme and crowning agony his lungs engulfed a great draught of air, which instantly he expelled in a shriek!

He was now in full possession of his physical senses. They were, indeed, preternaturally keen and alert. Something in the awful disturbance of his organic system had so exalted and refined them that they made record of things never before perceived. He felt the ripples upon his face and heard their separate sounds as they struck. He looked at the forest on the bank of the stream, saw the individual trees, the leaves and the veining of each leaf—saw the very insects upon them: the locusts, the brilliant-bodied flies, the gray spiders stretching their webs from twig to twig. He noted the prismatic colors in all the dewdrops upon a million blades of grass. The humming of the gnats that danced above the eddies of the stream, the beating of the dragon-flies' wings, the strokes of the water-spiders' legs, like oars which had lifted their boat—all these made audible music. A fish slid along beneath his eyes and he heard the rush of its body parting the water.

He had come to the surface facing down the stream; in a moment the visible world seemed to wheel slowly round, himself the pivotal point, and he saw the bridge, the fort, the soldiers upon the bridge, the captain, the sergeant, the two privates, his executioners. They were in silhouette against the blue sky. They shouted and gesticulated, pointing at him. The captain had drawn his pistol, but did not fire; the others were unarmed. Their movements were grotesque and horrible, their forms gigantic.

Suddenly he heard a sharp report and something struck the water smartly within a few inches of his head, spattering his face with spray. He heard a second report, and saw one of the sentinels with his rifle at his shoulder, a light cloud of blue smoke rising from the muzzle. The man in the water saw the eye of the man on the bridge gazing into his own through the sights of the rifle. He observed that it was a gray eye and remembered having read that gray eyes were keenest, and that all famous marksmen had them. Nevertheless, this one had missed.

A counter-swirl had caught Farquhar and turned him half round; he was again looking into the forest on the bank opposite the fort. The sound of a clear, high voice in a monotonous singsong now rang out behind him and came across the water with a distinctness that pierced and subdued all other sounds, even the beating of the ripples in his ears. Although no soldier, he had frequented camps enough to know the dread significance of that deliberate, drawling, aspirated chant; the lieutenant on shore was taking a part in the morning's work. How coldly and pitilessly—with what an even, calm intonation, presaging, and enforcing tranquillity in the men—with what accurately measured intervals fell those cruel words:

"Attention, company! . . . Shoulder arms! . . . Ready! . . . Aim! . . . Fire!"

Farquhar dived—dived as deeply as he could. The water roared in his ears like the voice of Niagara, yet he heard the dulled thunder of the volley and, rising again toward the surface, met shining bits of metal, singularly flattened, oscillating slowly downward. Some of them touched him on the face and hands, then fell away, continuing their descent. One lodged between his collar and neck; it was uncomfortably warm and he snatched it out.

As he rose to the surface, gasping for breath, he saw that he had been a long time under water; he was perceptibly farther down stream—nearer to safety. The soldiers had almost finished reloading; the metal ramrods flashed all at once in the sunshine as they were drawn from the barrels, turned in the air, and thrust into their sockets. The two sentinels fired again, independently and ineffectually.

The hunted man saw all this over his shoulder; he was now swimming vigorously with the current. His brain was as energetic as his arms and legs; he thought with the rapidity of lightning.

"The officer," he reasoned, "will not make that martinet's error a second time. It is as easy to dodge a volley as a single shot. He has probably already given the command to fire at will. God help me, I cannot dodge them all!"

An appalling plash within two yards of him was followed by a loud, rushing sound, *diminuendo*, which seemed to travel back through the air to the fort and died in an explosion which stirred the very river to its deeps! A rising sheet of water curved over him, fell down upon him, blinded him, strangled him! The cannon had taken a hand in the game. As he shook his head free from the commotion of the smitten water he heard the deflected shot humming through the air ahead, and in an instant it was cracking and smashing the branches in the forest beyond.

"They will not do that again," he thought; "the next time they will use a charge of grape. I must keep my eye upon the gun; the smoke will apprise me—the report arrives too late; it lags behind the missile. That is a good gun."

Suddenly he felt himself whirled round and round—spinning like a top. The water, the banks, the forests, the now distant bridge, fort and men—all were commingled and blurred. Objects were represented by their colors only; circular horizontal streaks of color—that was all he saw. He had been caught in a vortex and was being whirled on with a velocity of advance and gyration that made him giddy and sick. In a few moments he was flung upon the gravel at the foot of the left bank of the stream—the southern bank—and behind a projecting point which concealed him from his enemies. The sudden arrest of his motion, the abrasion of one of his hands on the gravel, restored him, and he wept with delight. He dug his fingers into the sand, threw it over himself in handfuls and audibly blessed it. It looked like diamonds, rubies, emeralds; he could think of nothing beautiful which it did not resemble. The trees upon the bank were giant garden plants; he noted a definite order in their arrangement, inhaled the fragrance of their blooms. A strange, roseate light shone through the spaces among their trunks and the wind made in their branches the music of æolian harps. He had no wish to perfect his escape—was content to remain in that enchanting spot until retaken.

A whiz and rattle of grapeshot among the branches high above his head roused him from his dream. The baffled cannoneer had fired him a random farewell. He sprang to his feet, rushed up the sloping bank, and plunged into the forest.

All that day he traveled, laying his course by the rounding sun. The forest seemed interminable; nowhere did he discover a break in it, not even a woodman's road. He had not known that he lived in so wild a region. There was something uncanny in the revelation.

By night fall he was fatigued, footsore, famishing. The thought of his wife and children urged him on. At last he found a road which led him in what he knew to be the right direction. It was as wide and straight as a city street, yet it seemed untraveled. No fields bordered it, no dwelling anywhere. Not so much as the barking of a dog suggested human habitation. The black bodies of the trees formed a straight wall on both sides, terminating on the horizon in a point, like a diagram in a lesson in perspective. Overhead, as he looked up through this rift in the wood, shone great golden stars looking unfamiliar and grouped in strange constellations. He was sure they were arranged in some order which had a secret and malign significance. The wood on either side was full of singular noises, among which—once, twice, and again, he distinctly heard whispers in an unknown tongue.

His neck was in pain and lifting his hand to it he found it horribly swollen. He knew that it had a circle of black where the rope had bruised it. His eyes felt congested; he could no longer close them. His tongue was swollen with thirst; he relieved its fever by thrusting it forward from between his teeth into the cold air. How softly the turf had carpeted the untraveled avenue—he could no longer feel the roadway beneath his feet!

Doubtless, despite his suffering, he had fallen asleep while walking, for now he sees another scene—perhaps he has merely recovered from a delirium. He stands at the gate of his own home. All is as he left it, and all bright and beautiful in the morning sunshine. He must have traveled the entire night. As he pushes open the gate and passes up the wide white walk, he sees a flutter of female garments; his wife, looking fresh and cool and sweet, steps down from the veranda to meet him. At the bottom of the steps she stands waiting, with a smile of ineffable joy, an attitude of matchless grace and dignity. Ah, how beautiful she is! He springs forward with extended arms. As he is about to clasp her he feels a stunning blow upon the back of the neck; a blinding white light blazes all about him with a sound like the shock of a cannon—then all is darkness and silence!

Peyton Farquhar was dead; his body, with a broken neck, swung gently from side to side beneath the timbers of the Owl Creek bridge.

Chapter Eighteen

The Battle at Fort William Henry
By Francis Parkman

Francis Parkman (1823–1893) not only lived the adventures he is most famous for writing about—The Oregon Trail, Sketches of Prairie and Rocky Mountain Life—*he was a historian of the first rank. His seven-volume* France and England in North America *is an important work in North American historical literature. The siege of Fort William Henry in 1757 on the southern end of Lake George by French general Montcalm was one of the most notorious events of the French and Indian War.*

—Lamar Underwood

"I am going on the ninth to sing the war-song at the Lake of Two Mountains, and on the next day at Saut St. Louis,—a long, tiresome ceremony. On the twelfth I am off; and I count on having news to tell you by the end of this month or the beginning of next." Thus Montcalm wrote to his wife from Montreal early in July. All doubts had been solved. Prisoners taken on the Hudson and despatches from Versailles had made it certain that Loudon was bound to Louisbourg, carrying with him the best of the troops that had guarded the New York frontier. The time was come, not only to strike the English on Lake George, but perhaps to seize Fort Edward and carry terror to Albany itself. Only one difficulty remained, the want of provisions. Agents were sent to collect corn and bacon among the inhabitants; the curés and militia captains were ordered to aid in the work; and enough was presently found to feed twelve thousand men for a month.

The emissaries of the Governor had been busy all winter among the tribes of the West and North; and more than a thousand savages, lured by the prospect of gifts, scalps, and plunder, were now encamped at Montreal. Many of them had never visited a French settlement before. All were eager to see Montcalm, whose exploit in taking Oswego had inflamed their imagination; and one day, on a visit of ceremony, an orator from Michillimackinac addressed the General thus: "We wanted to see this famous man who tramples the English under his feet. We thought we should find him so tall that his head would be lost in the clouds. But you are a little man, my Father. It is when we look into your eyes that we see the greatness of the pine-tree and the fire of the eagle."

It remained to muster the Mission Indians settled in or near the limits of the colony; and it was to this end that Montcalm went to sing the war-song with the converts of the Two Mountains. Rigaud, Bougainville, young Longueuil, and others were of the party; and when they landed, the Indians came down to the shore, their priests at their head, and greeted the General with a volley of musketry; then received him after dark in their grand council-lodge, where the circle of wild and savage visages, half seen in the dim light of a few candles, suggested to Bougainville a midnight conclave of wizards. He acted vicariously the chief part in the ceremony. "I sang the war-song in the name of M. de Montcalm, and was much applauded. It was nothing but these words: 'Let us trample the English under our feet,' chanted over and over again, in cadence with the movements of the savages." Then came the war-feast, against which occasion Montcalm had caused three oxen to be roasted. On the next day the party went to Caughnawaga, or Saut St. Louis, where the ceremony was repeated; and Bougainville, who again sang the war-song in the name of his commander, was requited by adoption into the clan of the Turtle. Three more oxen were solemnly devoured, and with one voice the warriors took up the hatchet.

Meanwhile troops, Canadians and Indians, were moving by detachments up Lake Champlain. Fleets of bateaux and canoes followed each other day by day along the capricious lake, in calm or storm, sunshine or rain, till, towards the end of July, the whole force was gathered at Ticonderoga, the base of the intended movement. Bourlamaque had been there since May with the battalions of Béarn and Royal Roussillon, finishing the fort, sending out war parties, and trying to discover the force and designs of the English at Fort William Henry.

Ticonderoga is a high rocky promontory between Lake Champlain on the north and the mouth of the outlet of Lake George on the south. Near its extremity and close to the fort were still encamped the two battalions under Bourlamaque, while bateaux and canoes were passing incessantly up the river of the outlet. There were scarcely two miles of navigable water, at the end of which the stream fell foaming over a high ledge of rock that barred the way. Here the French were building a saw-mill; and a wide space had been cleared to form an encampment defended on all sides by an abattis, within which stood the tents of the battalions of La Reine, La Sarre, Languedoc, and Guienne, all commanded by Lévis. Above the cascade the stream circled through the forest in a series of beautiful rapids, and from the camp of Lévis a road a mile and a half long had been cut to the navigable water above. At the end of this road there was another fortified camp, formed of colony regulars, Canadians, and Indians, under Rigaud. It was scarcely a mile farther to Lake George, where on the western side there was an outpost, chiefly of Canadians and Indians; while advanced parties were stationed at Bald Mountain, now called Rogers Rock, and elsewhere on the lake, to watch the movements of the English. The various encampments just mentioned were ranged along a valley extending four miles from Lake Champlain to Lake George, and bordered by mountains wooded to the top.

Here was gathered a martial population of eight thousand men, including the brightest civilization and the darkest barbarism: from the scholar soldier Montcalm and his no less accomplished aide-de-camp; from Lévis, conspicuous for graces of person; from a throng of courtly young officers, who would have seemed out of place in that wilderness had they not done their work so well in it; from these to the foulest man-eating savage of the uttermost northwest.

Of Indian allies there were nearly two thousand. One of their tribes, the Iowas, spoke a language which no interpreter understood; and they all bivouacked where they saw fit: for no man could control them. "I see no difference," says Bougainville, "in the dress, ornaments, dances, and songs of the various western nations. They go naked, excepting a strip of cloth passed through a belt, and paint themselves black, red, blue, and other colors. Their heads are shaved and adorned with bunches of feathers, and they wear rings of brass wire in their ears. They wear beaver-skin blankets, and carry lances, bows and arrows, and quivers made of the skins of beasts. For the rest they are straight, well made, and generally very tall. Their religion is brute paganism. I will say it once for all, one must be the slave of these savages, listen to them day and night, in council and in private, whenever the fancy takes them, or whenever a dream, a fit of the vapors, or their perpetual craving for brandy, gets possession of them; besides which they are always wanting something for their equipment, arms, or toilet, and the general of the army must give written orders for the smallest trifle,—an eternal, wearisome detail, of which one has no idea in Europe."

It was not easy to keep them fed. Rations would be served to them for a week; they would consume them in three days, and come for more. On one occasion they took the matter into their own hands, and butchered and devoured eighteen head of cattle intended for the troops; nor did any officer dare oppose this "St. Bartholomew of the oxen," as Bougainville calls it. "Their paradise is to be drunk," says the young officer. Their paradise was rather a hell; for sometimes, when mad with brandy, they grappled and tore each other with their teeth like wolves. They were continually "making medicine," that is, consulting the Manitou, to whom they hung up offerings, sometimes a dead dog, and sometimes the belt-cloth which formed their only garment.

The Mission Indians were better allies than these heathen of the west; and their priests, who followed them to the war, had great influence over them. They were armed with guns, which they well knew how to use. Their dress, though savage, was generally decent, and they were not cannibals; though in other respects they retained all their traditional ferocity and most of their traditional habits. They held frequent war feasts, one of which is described by Roubaud, Jesuit missionary of the Abenakis of St. Francis, whose flock formed a part of the company present.

"Imagine," says the father, "a great assembly of savages adorned with every ornament most suited to disfigure them in European eyes, painted with vermilion, white, green, yellow, and black made of soot and the scrapings of pots. A single savage face combines all these different colors, methodically laid on with the help of a little tallow, which serves for pomatum. The head is shaved except at the top, where there is a small tuft, to which are fastened feathers, a few beads of wampum, or some such trinket. Every part of the head has its ornament. Pendants hang from the nose and also from the ears, which are split in infancy and drawn down by weights till they flap at last against the shoulders. The rest of the equipment answers to this fantastic decoration: a shirt bedaubed with vermilion, wampum collars, silver bracelets, a large knife hanging on the breast, moose-skin moccasons, and a belt of various colors always absurdly combined. The sachems and war-chiefs are distinguished from the rest: the latter by a gorget, and the former by a medal, with the King's portrait on one side, and on the other Mars and Bellona joining hands, with the device, *Virtus et Honor*."

Thus attired, the company sat in two lines facing each other, with kettles in the middle filled with meat chopped for distribution. To a dignified silence succeeded songs, sung by several chiefs in succession, and compared by the narrator to the howling of wolves. Then followed a speech from the chief orator, highly commended by Roubaud, who could not help admiring this effort of savage eloquence. "After the harangue," he continues, "they proceeded to nominate the chiefs who were to take command. As soon as one was named he rose and took the head of some animal that had been butchered for the feast. He raised it aloft so that all the company could see it, and cried: 'Behold the head of the enemy!' Applause and cries of joy rose from all parts of the assembly. The chief, with the head in his hand, passed down between the lines, singing his war-song, bragging of his exploits, taunting and defying the enemy, and glorifying himself beyond all measure. To hear his self-laudation in these moments of martial transport one would think him a conquering hero ready to sweep everything before him. As he passed in front of the other savages, they would respond by dull broken cries jerked up from the depths of their stomachs, and accompanied by movements of their bodies so odd that one must be well used to them to keep countenance. In the course of his song the chief would utter from time to time some grotesque witticism; then he would stop, as if pleased with himself, or rather to listen to the thousand confused cries of applause that greeted his ears. He kept up his martial promenade as long as he liked the sport; and when he had had enough, ended by flinging down the head of the animal with an air of contempt, to show that his warlike appetite craved meat of another sort." Others followed with similar songs and pantomime, and the festival was closed at last by ladling out the meat from the kettles, and devouring it.

Roubaud was one day near the fort, when he saw the shore lined with a thousand Indians, watching four or five English prisoners, who, with the war-party that had captured them, were approaching in a boat from the farther side of the water. Suddenly the whole savage crew broke away together and ran into the neighboring woods, whence they soon emerged, yelling diabolically, each armed with a club. The wretched prisoners were to be forced to "run the gauntlet," which would probably have killed them. They were saved by the chief who commanded the war party, and who, on the persuasion of a French officer, claimed them as his own and forbade the game; upon which, according to rule in such cases, the rest abandoned it. On this same day the missionary met troops of Indians conducting several bands of English prisoners along the road that led through the forest from the camp of Lévis. Each of the captives was held by a cord made fast about the neck; and the sweat was starting from their brows in the extremity of their horror and distress. Roubaud's tent was at this time in the camp of the Ottawas. He presently saw a large number of them squatted about a fire, before which meat was roasting on sticks stuck in the ground; and, approaching, he saw that it was the flesh of an Englishman, other parts of which were boiling in a kettle, while near by sat eight or ten of the prisoners, forced to see their comrade devoured. The horror-stricken priest began to remonstrate; on which a young savage fiercely replied in broken French: "You have French taste; I have Indian. This is good meat for me;" and the feasters pressed him to share it.

Bougainville says that this abomination could not be prevented; which only means that if force had been used to stop it, the Ottawas would have gone home in a rage. They were therefore left to finish their meal undisturbed. Having eaten one of their prisoners, they began to treat the rest with the utmost kindness, bringing them white bread, and attending to all their wants,—a seeming change of heart due to the fact that they were a valuable commodity, for which the owners hoped to get a good price at Montreal. Montcalm wished to send them thither at once, to which after long debate the Indians consented, demanding, however, a receipt in full, and bargaining that the captives should be supplied with shoes and blankets.

These unfortunates belonged to a detachment of three hundred provincials, chiefly New Jersey men, sent from Fort William Henry under command of Colonel Parker to reconnoitre the French outposts. Montcalm's scouts discovered them; on which a band of Indians, considerably more numerous, went to meet them under a French partisan named Corbière, and ambushed themselves not far from Sabbath Day Point. Parker had rashly divided his force; and at daybreak of the twenty-sixth of July three of his boats fell into the snare, and were captured without a shot. Three others followed, in ignorance of what had happened, and shared the fate of the first. When the rest drew near, they were greeted by a deadly volley from the thickets, and a swarm of canoes darted out upon them. The men were seized with such a panic that some of them jumped into the water to escape, while the Indians leaped after them and speared them with their lances like fish. "Terrified," says Bougainville, "by the sight of these monsters, their agility, their firing, and their yells, they surrendered almost without resistance." About a hundred, however, made their escape. The rest were killed or captured, and three of the bodies were eaten on the spot. The journalist adds that the victory so elated the Indians that they became insupportable;

"but here in the forests of America we can no more do without them than without cavalry on the plain."

Another success at about the same time did not tend to improve their manners. A hundred and fifty of them, along with a few Canadians under Marin, made a dash at Fort Edward, killed or drove in the pickets, and returned with thirty-two scalps and a prisoner. It was found, however, that the scalps were far from representing an equal number of heads, the Indians having learned the art of making two or three out of one by judicious division.

Preparations were urged on with the utmost energy. Provisions, camp equipage, ammunition, cannon, and bateaux were dragged by gangs of men up the road from the camp of Lévis to the head of the rapids. The work went on through heat and rain, by day and night, till, at the end of July, all was done. Now, on the eve of departure, Montcalm, anxious for harmony among his red allies, called them to a grand council near the camp of Rigaud. Forty-one tribes and sub-tribes, Christian and heathen, from the east and from the west, were represented in it. Here were the mission savages,—Iroquois of Caughnawaga, Two Mountains, and La Présentation; Hurons of Lorette and Detroit; Nipissings of Lake Nipissing; Abenakis of St. Francis, Becancour, Missisqui, and the Penobscot; Algonkins of Three Rivers and Two Mountains; Micmacs and Malecites from Acadia: in all eight hundred chiefs and warriors. With these came the heathen of the west,—Ottawas of seven distinct bands; Ojibwas from Lake Superior, and Mississagas from the region of Lakes Erie and Huron; Pottawattamies and Menomonies from Lake Michigan; Sacs, Foxes, and Winnebagoes from Wisconsin; Miamis from the prairies of Illinois, and Iowas from the banks of the Des Moines: nine hundred and seventy-nine chiefs and warriors, men of the forests and men of the plains, hunters of the moose and hunters of the buffalo, bearers of steel hatchets and stone war-clubs, of French guns and of flint-headed arrows. All sat in silence, decked with ceremonial paint, scalp-locks, eagle plumes, or horns of buffalo; and the dark and wild assemblage was edged with white uniforms of officers from France, who came in numbers to the spectacle. Other officers were also here, all belonging to the colony. They had been appointed to the command of the Indian allies, over whom, however, they had little or no real authority. First among them was the bold and hardy Saint-Luc de la Corne, who was called general of the Indians; and under him were others, each assigned to some tribe or group of tribes,—the intrepid Marin; Charles Langlade, who had left his squaw wife at Michillimackinac to join the war; Niverville, Langis, La Plante, Hertel, Longueuil, Herbin, Lorimier, Sabrevois, and Fleurimont; men familiar from childhood with forests and savages. Each tribe had its interpreter, often as lawless as those with whom he had spent his life; and for the converted tribes there were three missionaries,—Piquet for the Iroquois, Mathevet for the Nipissings, who were half heathen, and Roubaud for the Abenakis.

There was some complaint among the Indians because they were crowded upon by the officers who came as spectators. This difficulty being removed, the council opened,

Montcalm having already explained his plans to the chiefs and told them the part he expected them to play.

Pennahouel, chief of the Ottawas, and senior of all the Assembly, rose and said: "My father, I, who have counted more moons than any here, thank you for the good words you have spoken. I approve them. Nobody ever spoke better. It is the Manitou of War who inspires you."

Kikensick, chief of the Nipissings, rose in behalf of the Christian Indians, and addressed the heathen of the west. "Brothers, we thank you for coming to help us defend our lands against the English. Our cause is good. The Master of Life is on our side. Can you doubt it, brothers, after the great blow you have just struck? It covers you with glory. The lake, red with the blood of Corlaer [the English] bears witness forever to your achievement. We too share your glory, and are proud of what you have done." Then, turning to Montcalm: "We are even more glad than you, my father, who have crossed the great water, not for your own sake, but to obey the great King and defend his children. He has bound us all together by the most solemn of ties. Let us take care that nothing shall separate us."

The various interpreters, each in turn, having explained this speech to the Assembly, it was received with ejaculations of applause; and when they had ceased, Montcalm spoke as follows: "Children, I am delighted to see you all joined in this good work. So long as you remain one, the English cannot resist you. The great King has sent me to protect and defend you; but above all he has charged me to make you happy and unconquerable, by establishing among you the union which ought to prevail among brothers, children of one father, the great Onontio." Then he held out a prodigious wampum belt of six thousand beads: "Take this sacred pledge of his word. The union of the beads of which it is made is the sign of your united strength. By it I bind you all together, so that none of you can separate from the rest till the English are defeated and their fort destroyed."

Pennahouel took up the belt and said: "Behold, brothers, a circle drawn around us by the great Onontio. Let none of us go out from it; for so long as we keep in it, the Master of Life will help all our undertakings." Other chiefs spoke to the same effect, and the council closed in perfect harmony. Its various members bivouacked together at the camp by the lake, and by their carelessness soon set it on fire; whence the place became known as the Burned Camp. Those from the missions confessed their sins all day; while their heathen brothers hung an old coat and a pair of leggings on a pole as tribute to the Manitou. This greatly embarrassed the three priests, who were about to say Mass, but doubted whether they ought to say it in presence of a sacrifice to the devil. Hereupon they took counsel of Montcalm. "Better say it so than not at all," replied the military casuist. Brandy being prudently denied them, the allies grew restless; and the greater part paddled up the lake to a spot near the place where Parker had been defeated. Here they encamped to wait the arrival of the army, and amused themselves meantime with killing rattlesnakes, there being a populous "den" of those reptiles among the neighboring rocks.

Montcalm sent a circular letter to the regular officers, urging them to dispense for a while with luxuries, and even comforts. "We have but few bateaux, and these are so filled with stores that a large division of the army must go by land"; and he directed that everything not absolutely necessary should be left behind, and that a canvas shelter to every two officers should serve them for a tent, and a bearskin for a bed. "Yet I do not forbid a mattress," he adds. "Age and infirmities may make it necessary to some; but I shall not have one myself, and make no doubt that all who can will willingly imitate me."

The bateaux lay ready by the shore, but could not carry the whole force; and Lévis received orders to march by the side of the lake with twenty-five hundred men, Canadians, regulars, and Iroquois. He set out at daybreak of the thirtieth of July, his men carrying nothing but their knapsacks, blankets, and weapons. Guided by the unerring Indians, they climbed the steep gorge at the side of Rogers Rock, gained the valley beyond, and marched southward along a Mohawk trail which threaded the forest in a course parallel to the lake. The way was of the roughest; many straggled from the line, and two officers completely broke down. The first destination of the party was the mouth of Ganouskie Bay, now called Northwest Bay, where they were to wait for Montcalm, and kindle three fires as a signal that they had reached the rendezvous.

Montcalm left a detachment to hold Ticonderoga; and then, on the first of August, at two in the afternoon, he embarked at the Burned Camp with all his remaining force. Including those with Lévis, the expedition counted about seven thousand six hundred men, of whom more than sixteen hundred were Indians. At five in the afternoon they reached the place where the Indians, having finished their rattlesnake hunt, were smoking their pipes and waiting for the army. The red warriors embarked, and joined the French flotilla; and now, as evening drew near, was seen one of those wild pageantries of war which Lake George has often witnessed. A restless multitude of birch canoes, filled with painted savages, glided by shores and islands, like troops of swimming waterfowl. Two hundred and fifty bateaux came next, moved by sail and oar, some bearing the Canadian militia, and some the battalions of Old France in trim and gay attire: first, La Reine and Languedoc; then the colony regulars; then La Sarre and Guienne; then the Canadian brigade of Courtemanche; then the cannon and mortars, each on a platform sustained by two bateaux lashed side by side, and rowed by the militia of Saint-Ours; then the battalions of Béarn and Royal Roussillon; then the Canadians of Gaspé, with the provision-bateaux and the field-hospital; and, lastly, a rear guard of regulars closed the line. So, under the flush of sunset, they held their course along the romantic lake, to play their part in the historic drama that lends a stern enchantment to its fascinating scenery. They passed the Narrows in mist and darkness; and when, a little before dawn, they rounded the high promontory of Tongue Mountain, they saw, far on the right, three fiery sparks shining through the gloom. These were the signal-fires of Lévis, to tell them that he had reached the appointed spot.

Lévis had arrived the evening before, after his hard march through the sultry midsummer forest. His men had now rested for a night, and at ten in the morning he marched again. Montcalm followed at noon, and coasted the western shore, till, towards evening, he found Lévis waiting for him by the margin of a small bay not far from the English fort, though hidden from it by a projecting point of land. Canoes and bateaux were drawn up on the beach, and the united forces made their bivouac together.

The earthen mounds of Fort William Henry still stand by the brink of Lake George; and seated at the sunset of an August day under the pines that cover them, one gazes on a scene of soft and soothing beauty, where dreamy waters reflect the glories of the mountains and the sky. As it is to-day, so it was then; all breathed repose and peace. The splash of some leaping trout, or the dipping wing of a passing swallow, alone disturbed the summer calm of that unruffled mirror.

About ten o'clock at night two boats set out from the fort to reconnoitre. They were passing a point of land on their left, two miles or more down the lake, when the men on board descried through the gloom a strange object against the bank; and they rowed towards it to learn what it might be. It was an awning over the bateaux that carried Roubaud and his brother missionaries. As the rash oarsmen drew near, the bleating of a sheep in one of the French provision-boats warned them of danger; and turning, they pulled for their lives towards the eastern shore. Instantly more than a thousand Indians threw themselves into their canoes and dashed in hot pursuit, making the lake and the mountains ring with the din of their war whoops. The fugitives had nearly reached land when their pursuers opened fire. They replied; shot one Indian dead, and wounded another; then snatched their oars again, and gained the beach. But the whole savage crew was upon them. Several were killed, three were taken, and the rest escaped in the dark woods. The prisoners were brought before Montcalm, and gave him valuable information of the strength and position of the English.

The Indian who was killed was a noted chief of the Nipissings; and his tribesmen howled in grief for their bereavement. They painted his face with vermilion, tied feathers in his hair, hung pendants in his ears and nose, clad him in a resplendent war-dress, put silver bracelets on his arms, hung a gorget on his breast with a flame colored ribbon, and seated him in state on the top of a hillock, with his lance in his hand, his gun in the hollow of his arm, his tomahawk in his belt, and his kettle by his side. Then they all crouched about him in lugubrious silence. A funeral harangue followed; and next a song and solemn dance to the booming of the Indian drum. In the gray of the morning they buried him as he sat, and placed food in the grave for his journey to the land of souls.

As the sun rose above the eastern mountains the French camp was all astir. The column of Lévis, with Indians to lead the way, moved through the forest towards the fort, and Montcalm followed with the main body; then the artillery boats rounded the point that had hid them from the sight of the English, saluting them as they did so with musketry and cannon; while a host of savages put out upon the lake, ranged their canoes abreast in a line from shore to shore, and advanced slowly, with measured paddle strokes and yells of defiance.

The position of the enemy was full in sight before them. At the head of the lake, towards the right, stood the fort, close to the edge of the water. On its left was a marsh; then the rough piece of ground where Johnson had encamped two years before; then a low, flat, rocky hill, crowned with an entrenched camp; and, lastly, on the extreme left, another marsh. Far around the fort and up the slopes of the western mountain the forest had been cut down and burned, and the ground was cumbered with blackened stumps and charred carcasses and limbs of fallen trees, strewn in savage disorder one upon another. This was the work of Winslow in the autumn before. Distant shouts and war-cries, the clatter of musketry, white puffs of smoke in the dismal clearing and along the scorched edge of the bordering forest, told that Lévis' Indians were skirmishing with parties of the English, who had gone out to save the cattle roaming in the neighborhood, and burn some outbuildings that would have favored the besiegers. Others were taking down the tents that stood on a plateau near the foot of the mountain on the right, and moving them to the entrenchment on the hill. The garrison sallied from the fort to support their comrades, and for a time the firing was hot.

Fort William Henry was an irregular bastioned square, formed by embankments of gravel surmounted by a rampart of heavy logs, laid in tiers crossed one upon another, the interstices filled with earth. The lake protected it on the north, the marsh on the east, and ditches with chevaux de frise on the south and west. Seventeen cannon, great and small, besides several mortars and swivels, were mounted upon it; and a brave Scotch veteran, Lieutenant Colonel Monro, of the thirty-fifth regiment, was in command.

General Webb lay fourteen miles distant at Fort Edward, with twenty-six hundred men, chiefly provincials. On the twenty-fifth of July he had made a visit to Fort William Henry, examined the place, given some orders, and returned on the twenty-ninth. He then wrote to the Governor of New York, telling him that the French were certainly coming, begging him to send up the militia, and saying: "I am determined to march to Fort William Henry with the whole army under my command as soon as I shall hear of the farther approach of the enemy." Instead of doing so he waited three days, and then sent up a detachment of two hundred regulars under Lieutenant Colonel Young, and eight hundred Massachusetts men under Colonel Frye. This raised the force at the lake to two thousand and two hundred, including sailors and mechanics, and reduced that of Webb to sixteen hundred, besides half as many more distributed at Albany and the intervening forts. If, according to his spirited intention, he should go to the rescue of Monro, he must leave some of his troops behind him to protect the lower posts from a possible French inroad by way of South Bay. Thus his power of aiding Monro was slight, so rashly had Loudon, intent on Louisbourg, left this frontier open to attack. The defect, however, was as much in Webb himself as in his resources. His conduct in the past year had raised doubts of his personal courage; and this was the moment for answering them. Great as was the disparity of numbers, the emergency would have justified an attempt to save Monro at any risk. That officer sent him a hasty note, written at nine o'clock on the morning of the third, telling him that the French were in sight on the lake; and, in the next night, three rangers came to Fort Edward, bringing another short note, dated at six in the evening, announcing that the firing had begun, and closing with the words: "I believe you will think it proper to send a reinforcement as soon as possible." Now, if ever, was the time to move, before the fort was invested and access cut off. But Webb lay quiet, sending expresses to New England for help which could not possibly arrive in time. On the next night another note came from Monro to say that the French were upon him in great numbers, well supplied with artillery, but that the garrison were all in good spirits. "I make no doubt," wrote the hard-pressed officer, "that you will soon send us a reinforcement"; and again on the same day: "We are very certain that a part of the enemy have got between you and us upon the high road, and would therefore be glad (if it meets with your approbation) the whole army was marched." But Webb gave no sign.

When the skirmishing around the fort was over, La Corne, with a body of Indians, occupied the road that led to Fort Edward, and Lévis encamped hard by to support him, while Montcalm proceeded to examine the ground and settle his plan of attack. He made his way to the rear of the entrenched camp and reconnoitred it, hoping to carry it by assault; but it had a breastwork of stones and logs, and he thought the attempt too hazardous. The ground where he stood was that where Dieskau had been defeated; and as the fate of his predecessor was not of flattering augury, he resolved to besiege the fort in form.

He chose for the site of his operations the ground now covered by the village of Caldwell. A little to the north of it was a ravine, beyond which he formed his main camp, while Lévis occupied a tract of dry ground beside the marsh, whence he could easily move to intercept succors from Fort Edward on the one hand, or repel a sortie from Fort William Henry on the other. A brook ran down the ravine and entered the lake at a small cove protected from the fire of the fort by a point of land; and at this place, still called Artillery Cove, Montcalm prepared to debark his cannon and mortars.

Having made his preparations, he sent Fontbrune, one of his aides-de-camp, with a letter to Monro. "I owe it to humanity," he wrote, "to summon you to surrender. At present I can restrain the savages, and make them observe the terms of a capitulation, as I might not have power to do under other circumstances; and an obstinate defence on your part could only retard the capture of the place a few days, and endanger an unfortunate garrison which cannot be relieved, in consequence of the dispositions I have made. I demand a decisive answer within an hour." Monro replied that he and his soldiers would defend themselves to the last. While the flags of truce were flying, the Indians swarmed over the fields before the fort; and when they learned the result, an Abenaki chief shouted in broken French: "You won't surrender, eh! Fire away then, and fight your best; for if I catch you, you shall get no quarter." Monro emphasized his refusal by a general discharge of his cannon.

The trenches were opened on the night of the fourth,—a task of extreme difficulty, as the ground was covered by a profusion of half-burned stumps, roots, branches, and fallen trunks. Eight hundred men toiled till daylight with pick, spade, and axe, while the cannon from the fort flashed through the darkness, and grape and round-shot whistled and screamed over their heads. Some of the English balls reached the camp beyond the ravine, and disturbed the slumbers of the officers off duty, as they lay wrapped in their blankets and bear-skins. Before daybreak the first parallel was made; a battery was nearly finished on the left, and another was begun on the right. The men now worked under cover, safe in their burrows; one gang relieved another, and the work went on all day.

The Indians were far from doing what was expected of them. Instead of scouting in the direction of Fort Edward to learn the movements of the enemy and prevent surprise, they loitered about the camp and in the trenches, or amused themselves by firing at the fort from behind stumps and logs. Some, in imitation of the French, dug little trenches for themselves, in which they wormed their way towards the rampart, and now and then picked off an artillery-man, not without loss on their own side. On the afternoon of the fifth, Montcalm invited them to a council, gave them belts of wampum, and mildly remonstrated with them. "Why expose yourselves without necessity? I grieve bitterly over the losses that you have met, for the least among you is precious to me. No doubt it is a good thing to annoy the English; but that is not the main point. You ought to inform me of everything the enemy is doing, and always keep parties on the road between the two forts." And he gently hinted that their place was not in his camp, but in that of Lévis, where missionaries were provided for such of them as were Christians, and food and ammunition for them all. They promised, with excellent docility, to do everything he wished, but added that there was something on their hearts. Being encouraged to relieve themselves of the burden, they complained that they had not been consulted as to the management of the siege, but were expected to obey orders like slaves. "We know more about fighting in the woods than you," said their orator; "ask our advice, and you will be the better for it."

Montcalm assured them that if they had been neglected, it was only through the hurry and confusion of the time; expressed high appreciation of their talents for bush-fighting, promised them ample satisfaction, and ended by telling them that in the morning they should hear the big guns. This greatly pleased them, for they were extremely impatient for the artillery to begin. About sunrise the battery of the left opened with eight heavy cannon and a mortar, joined, on the next morning, by the battery of the right, with eleven pieces more. The fort replied with spirit. The cannon thundered all day, and from a hundred peaks and crags the astonished wilderness roared back the sound. The Indians were delighted. They wanted to point the guns; and to humor them, they were now and then allowed to do so. Others lay behind logs and fallen trees, and yelled their satisfaction when they saw the splinters fly from the wooden rampart.

Day after day the weary roar of the distant cannonade fell on the ears of Webb in his camp at Fort Edward. "I have not yet received the least reinforcement," he writes to Loudon; "this is the disagreeable situation we are at present in. The fort, by the heavy firing we hear from the lake, is still in our possession; but I fear it cannot long hold out against so warm a cannonading if I am not reinforced by a sufficient number of militia to march to their relief." The militia were coming; but it was impossible that many could reach him in less than a week. Those from New York alone were within call, and two thousand of them arrived soon after he sent Loudon the above letter. Then, by stripping all the forts below, he could bring together forty-five hundred men; while several French deserters assured him that Montcalm had nearly twelve thousand. To advance to the relief of Monro with a force so inferior, through a defile of rocks, forests, and mountains, made by nature for ambuscades,—and this too with troops who had neither the steadiness of regulars nor the bush-fighting skill of Indians,—was an enterprise for firmer nerve than his.

He had already warned Monro to expect no help from him. At midnight of the fourth, Captain Bartman, his aide-de-camp, wrote: "The General has ordered me to acquaint you he does not think it prudent to attempt a junction or to assist you till reinforced by the militia of the colonies, for the immediate march of which repeated expresses have been sent." The letter then declared that the French were in complete possession of the road between the two forts, that a prisoner just brought in reported their force in men and cannon to be very great, and that, unless the militia came soon, Monro had better make what terms he could with the enemy.

The chance was small that this letter would reach its destination; and in fact the bearer was killed by La Corne's Indians, who, in stripping the body, found the hidden paper, and carried it to the General. Montcalm kept it several days, till the English rampart was half battered down; and then, after saluting his enemy with a volley from all his cannon, he sent it with a graceful compliment to Monro. It was Bougainville who carried it, preceded by a drummer and a flag. He was met at the foot of the glacis, blindfolded, and led through the fort and along the edge of the lake to the entrenched camp, where Monro was at the time. "He returned many thanks," writes the emissary in his Diary, "for the courtesy of our nation, and protested his joy at having to do with so generous an enemy. This was his answer to the Marquis de Montcalm. Then they led me back, always with eyes blinded; and our batteries began to fire again as soon as we thought that the English grenadiers who escorted me had had time to re-enter the fort. I hope General Webb's letter may induce the English to surrender the sooner."

By this time the sappers had worked their way to the angle of the lake, where they were stopped by a marshy hollow, beyond which was a tract of high ground, reaching to the fort and serving as the garden of the garrison. Logs and fascines in large quantities were thrown into the hollow, and hurdles were laid over them to form a causeway for the cannon. Then the sap was continued up the acclivity beyond, a trench was opened in the garden, and a battery begun, not two hundred and fifty yards from the fort. The Indians, in great number, crawled forward among the beans, maize, and cabbages, and lay there ensconced. On the night of the seventh, two men came out of the fort, apparently to reconnoitre, with a view to a sortie, when they were greeted by a general volley and a burst of yells which echoed among the mountains; followed by responsive whoops pealing through the darkness from the various camps and lurking-places of the savage warriors far and near.

The position of the besieged was now deplorable. More than three hundred of them had been killed and wounded; small-pox was raging in the fort; the place was a focus of infection, and the casemates were crowded with the sick. A sortie from the entrenched camp and another from the fort had been repulsed with loss. All their large cannon and mortars had been burst, or disabled by shot; only seven small pieces were left fit for service; and the whole of Montcalm's thirty-one cannon and fifteen mortars and howitzers would soon open fire, while the walls were already breached, and an assault was imminent. Through the night of the eighth they fired briskly from all their remaining pieces. In the morning the officers held a council, and all agreed to surrender if honorable terms could be had. A white flag was raised, a drum was beat, and Lieutenant Colonel Young, mounted on horseback, for a shot in the foot had disabled him from walking, went, followed by a few soldiers, to the tent of Montcalm.

It was agreed that the English troops should march out with the honors of war, and be escorted to Fort Edward by a detachment of French troops; that they should not serve for eighteen months; and that all French prisoners captured in America since the war began should be given up within three months. The stores, munitions, and artillery were to be the prize of the victors, except one field-piece, which the garrison were to retain in recognition of their brave defence.

Before signing the capitulation Montcalm called the Indian chiefs to council, and asked them to consent to the conditions, and promise to restrain their young warriors from any disorder. They approved everything and promised everything. The garrison then evacuated the fort, and marched to join their comrades in the entrenched camp, which was included in the surrender. No sooner were they gone than a crowd of Indians clambered through the embrasures in search of rum and plunder. All the sick men unable to leave their beds were instantly butchered. "I was witness of this spectacle," says the missionary Roubaud; "I saw one of these barbarians come out of the casemates with a human head in his hand, from which the blood ran in streams, and which he paraded as if he had got the finest prize in the world." There was little left to plunder; and the Indians, joined by the more lawless of the Canadians, turned their attention to the entrenched camp, where all the English were now collected.

The French guard stationed there could not or would not keep out the rabble. By the advice of Montcalm the English stove their rum-barrels; but the Indians were drunk already with homicidal rage, and the glitter of their vicious eyes told of the devil within. They roamed among the tents, intrusive, insolent, their visages besmirched with war-paint; grinning like fiends as they handled, in anticipation of the knife, the long hair of cowering women, of whom, as well as of children, there were many in the camp, all crazed with fright. Since the last war the New England border population had regarded Indians with a mixture of detestation and horror. Their mysterious warfare of ambush and surprise, their midnight onslaughts, their butcheries, their burnings, and all their nameless atrocities, had been for years the theme of fire-side story; and the dread they excited was deepened by the distrust and dejection of the time. The confusion in the camp lasted through the afternoon. "The Indians," says Bougainville, "wanted to plunder the chests of the English; the latter resisted; and there was fear that serious disorder would ensue. The Marquis de Montcalm ran thither immediately, and used every means to restore tranquillity: prayers, threats, caresses, interposition of the officers and interpreters who have some influence over these savages." "We shall be but too happy if we can prevent a massacre. Detestable position! of which nobody who has not been in it can have any idea, and which makes victory itself a sorrow to the victors. The Marquis spared no efforts to prevent the rapacity of the savages and, I must say it, of certain persons associated with them, from resulting in something worse than plunder. At last, at nine o'clock in the evening, order seemed restored. The Marquis even induced the Indians to promise that, besides the escort agreed upon in the capitulation, two chiefs for each tribe should accompany the English on their way to Fort Edward." He also ordered La Corne and the other Canadian officers attached to the Indians to see that no violence took place. He might well have done more. In view of the disorders of the afternoon, it would not have been too much if he had ordered the whole body of regular troops, whom alone he could trust for the purpose, to hold themselves ready to move to the spot in case of outbreak, and shelter their defeated foes behind a hedge of bayonets.

Bougainville was not to see what ensued; for Montcalm now sent him to Montreal, as a special messenger to carry news of the victory. He embarked at ten o'clock. Returning daylight found him far down the lake; and as he looked on its still bosom flecked with mists, and its quiet mountains sleeping under the flush of dawn, there was nothing in the wild tranquillity of the scene to suggest the tragedy which even then was beginning on the shore he had left behind.

The English in their camp had passed a troubled night, agitated by strange rumors. In the morning something like a panic seized them; for they distrusted not the Indians only, but the Canadians. In their haste to be gone they got together at daybreak, before the escort of three hundred regulars had arrived. They had their muskets, but no ammunition; and few or none of the provincials had bayonets. Early as it was, the Indians were on the alert; and, indeed, since midnight great numbers of them had been prowling about the skirts of the camp, showing, says Colonel Frye, "more than usual malice in their looks." Seventeen wounded men of his regiment lay in huts, unable to join the march. In the preceding afternoon Miles Whitworth, the regimental surgeon, had passed them over to the care of a French surgeon, according to an agreement made at the time of the surrender; but, the Frenchman being absent, the other remained with them attending to their wants. The French surgeon had caused special sentinels to be posted for their protection. These were now removed, at the moment when they were needed most; upon which, about five o'clock in the morning, the Indians entered the huts, dragged out the inmates, and tomahawked and scalped them all, before the eyes of Whitworth, and in presence of La Corne and other Canadian officers, as well as of a French guard stationed within forty feet of the spot; and, declares the surgeon under oath, "none, either officer or soldier, protected the said wounded men." The opportune butchery relieved them of a troublesome burden.

A scene of plundering now began. The escort had by this time arrived, and Monro complained to the officers that the capitulation was broken; but got no other answer than advice to give up the baggage to the Indians in order to appease them. To this the English at length agreed; but it only increased the excitement of the mob. They demanded rum; and some of the soldiers, afraid to refuse, gave it to them from their canteens, thus adding fuel to the flame. When, after much difficulty, the column at last got out of the camp and began to move along the road that crossed the rough plain between the entrenchment and the forest, the Indians crowded upon them, impeded their march, snatched caps, coats, and weapons from men and officers, tomahawked those that resisted, and, seizing upon shrieking women and children, dragged them off or murdered them on the spot. It is said that some of the interpreters secretly fomented the disorder. Suddenly there rose the screech of the war-whoop. At this signal of butchery, which was given by Abenaki Christians from the mission of the Penobscot, a mob of savages rushed upon the New Hampshire men at the rear of the column, and killed or dragged away eighty of them. A frightful tumult ensued, when Montcalm, Lévis, Bourlamaque, and many other French officers, who had hastened from their camp on the first news of disturbance, threw themselves among the Indians, and by promises and threats tried to allay their frenzy. "Kill me, but spare the English who are under my protection," exclaimed Montcalm. He took from one of them a young officer whom the savage had seized; upon which several other Indians immediately tomahawked their prisoners, lest they too should be taken from them. One writer says that a French grenadier was killed and two wounded in attempting to restore order; but the statement is doubtful.

The English seemed paralyzed, and fortunately did not attempt a resistance, which, without ammunition as they were, would have ended in a general massacre. Their broken column straggled forward in wild disorder, amid the din of whoops and shrieks, till they reached the French advance guard, which consisted of Canadians; and here they demanded protection from the officers, who refused to give it, telling them that they must take to the woods and shift for themselves. Frye was seized by a number of Indians, who, brandishing spears and tomahawks, threatened him with death and tore off clothing, leaving nothing but breeches, shoes, and shirt. Repelled by the officers of the guard, he made for the woods. A Connecticut soldier who was present says of him that he leaped upon an Indian who stood in his way, disarmed and killed him, and then escaped; but Frye himself does not mention the incident. Captain Burke, also of the Massachusetts regiment, was stripped, after a violent struggle, of all his clothes; then broke loose, gained the woods, spent the night shivering in the thick grass of a marsh, and on the next day reached Fort Edward. Jonathan Carver, a provincial volunteer, declares that, when the tumult was at its height, he saw officers of the French army walking about at a little distance and talking with seeming unconcern. Three or four Indians seized him, brandished their tomahawks over his head, and tore off most of his clothes, while he vainly claimed protection from a sentinel, who called him an English dog, and violently pushed him back among his tormentors. Two of them were dragging him towards the neighboring swamp, when an English officer, stripped of everything but his scarlet breeches, ran by. One of Carver's captors sprang upon him, but was thrown to the ground; whereupon the other went to the aid of his comrade and drove his tomahawk into the back of the Englishman. As Carver turned to run, an English boy, about twelve years old, clung to him and begged for help. They ran on together for a moment, when the boy was seized, dragged from his protector, and, as Carver judged by his shrieks, was murdered. He himself escaped to the forest, and after three days of famine reached Fort Edward.

The bonds of discipline seem for the time to have been completely broken; for while Montcalm and his chief officers used every effort to restore order, even at the risk of their lives, many other officers, chiefly of the militia, failed atrociously to do their duty. How many English were killed it is impossible to tell with exactness. Roubaud says that he saw forty or fifty corpses scattered about the field. Lévis says fifty; which does not include the sick and wounded before murdered in the camp and fort. It is certain that six or seven hundred persons were carried off, stripped, and otherwise maltreated. Montcalm succeeded in recovering more than four hundred of them in the course of the day; and many of the French officers did what they could to relieve their wants by buying back from their captors the clothing that had been torn from them. Many of the fugitives had taken refuge in the fort, whither Monro himself had gone to demand protection for his followers; and here Roubaud presently found a crowd of half-frenzied women, crying in anguish for husbands and children. All the refugees and redeemed prisoners were afterwards conducted to the entrenched camp, where food and shelter were provided for them and a strong guard set for their protection until the fifteenth, when they were sent under an escort to Fort Edward. Here cannon had been fired at intervals to guide those who had fled to the woods, whence they came dropping in from day to day, half dead with famine.

On the morning after the massacre the Indians decamped in a body and set out for Montreal, carrying with them their plunder and some two hundred prisoners, who, it is said, could not be got out of their hands. The soldiers were set to the work of demolishing the English fort; and the task occupied several days. The barracks were torn down, and the huge pine-logs of the rampart thrown into a heap. The dead bodies that filled the casemates were added to the mass, and fire was set to the whole. The mighty funeral pyre blazed all night. Then, on the sixteenth, the army reimbarked. The din of ten thousand combatants, the rage, the terror, the agony, were gone; and no living thing was left but the wolves that gathered from the mountains to feast upon the dead.

CHAPTER NINETEEN

The Pass of Thermopylae
430 B.C.
By Charlotte Yonge

"Stranger, bear this message to the Spartans, that we lie here obedient to their laws."

THERE WAS TREMBLING IN GREECE. "THE GREAT KING," AS THE GREEKS CALLED THE chief potentate of the East, whose domains stretched from the Indian Caucasus to the Aegaeus, from the Caspian to the Red Sea, was marshalling his forces against the little free states that nestled amid the rocks and gulfs of the Eastern Mediterranean. Already had his might devoured the cherished colonies of the Greeks on the eastern shore of the Archipelago, and every traitor to home institutions found a ready asylum at that despotic court, and tried to revenge his own wrongs by whispering incitements to invasion. "All people, nations, and languages," was the commencement of the decrees of that monarch's court; and it was scarcely a vain boast, for his satraps ruled over subject kingdoms, and among his tributary nations he counted the Chaldean, with his learning and old civilization, the wise and steadfast Jew, the skilful Phoenician, the learned Egyptian, the wild, free-booting Arab of the desert, the dark-skinned Ethiopian, and over all these ruled the keen-witted, active native Persian race, the conquerors of all the rest, and led by a chosen band proudly called the Immortal. His many capitals— Babylon the great, Susa, Persepolis, and the like—were names of dreamy splendor to the Greeks, described now and then by Ionians from Asia Minor who had carried their tribute to the king's own feet, or by courtier slaves who had escaped with difficulty from being all too serviceable at the tyrannic court. And the lord of this enormous empire was about to launch his countless host against the little cluster of states, the whole of which together would hardly equal one province of the huge Asiatic realm! Moreover, it was a war not only on the men but on their gods. The Persians were zealous adorers of the sun and of fire, they abhorred the idol worship of the Greeks, and defiled and plundered every temple that fell in their way. Death and desolation were almost the best that could be looked for at such hands—slavery and torture from cruelly barbarous masters would only too surely be the lot of numbers, should their land fall a prey to the conquerors.

True it was that ten years back the former Great King had sent his best troops to be signally defeated upon the coast of Attica; but the losses at Marathon had but stimulated the Persian lust of conquest, and the new King Xerxes was gathering together such myriads of men as should crush down the Greeks and overrun their country by mere force of numbers.

The muster place was at Sardis, and there Greek spies had seen the multitudes assembling and the state and magnificence of the king's attendants. Envoys had come from him to demand earth and water from each state in Greece, as emblems that land and sea were his, but each state was resolved to be free, and only Thessaly, that which lay first in his path, consented to yield the token of subjugation. A council was held at the Isthmus of Corinth, and attended by deputies from all the states of Greece to consider of the best means of defense. The ships of the enemy would coast round the shores of the Aegean sea, the land army would cross the Hellespont on a bridge of boats lashed together, and march southwards into Greece. The only hope of averting the danger lay in defending such passages as, from the nature of the ground, were so narrow that only a few persons could fight hand to hand at once, so that courage would be of more avail than numbers.

The first of all these passes was called Tempe, and a body of troops was sent to guard it; but they found that this was useless and impossible, and came back again. The next was at Thermopylae. Look in your map of the Archipelago, or Aegean Sea, as it was then called, for the great island of Negropont, or by its old name, Euboea. It looks like a piece broken off from the coast, and to the north is shaped like the head of a bird, with the beak running into a gulf, that would fit over it, upon the main land, and between the island and the coast is an exceedingly narrow strait. The Persian army would have to march round the edge of the gulf. They could not cut straight across the country, because the ridge of mountains called Ceta rose up and barred their way. Indeed, the woods, rocks, and precipices came down so near the seashore, that in two places there was only room for one single wheel track between the steeps and the impassable morass that formed the border of the gulf on its south side. These two very narrow places were called the gates of the pass, and were about a mile apart. There was a little more width left in the intervening space; but in this there were a number of springs of warm mineral water, salt and sulphurous, which were used for the sick to bathe in, and thus the place was called Thermopylae, or the Hot Gates. A wall had once been built across the western-most of these narrow places, when the Thessalians and Phocians, who lived on either side of it, had been at war with one another; but it had been allowed to go to decay, since the Phocians had found out that there was a very steep narrow mountain path along the bed of a torrent, by which it was possible to cross from one territory to the other without going round this marshy coast road.

This was, therefore, an excellent place to defend. The Greek ships were all drawn up on the farther side of Euboea to prevent the Persian vessels from getting into the strait and landing men beyond the pass, and a division of the army was sent off to guard the Hot Gates. The council at the Isthmus did not know of the mountain pathway, and thought that all would be safe as long as the Persians were kept out of the coast path.

The troops sent for this purpose were from different cities, and amounted to about 4,000, who were to keep the pass against two millions. The leader of them was Leonidas, who had newly become one of the two kings of Sparta, the city that above all in Greece trained its sons to be hardy soldiers, dreading death infinitely less than shame. Leonidas had already made up his mind that the expedition would probably be his death, perhaps because a prophecy had been given at the Temple of Delphi that Sparta should be saved by the death of one of her kings of the race of Hercules. He was allowed by law to take with him 300 men, and these he chose most carefully, not merely for their strength and courage, but selecting those who had sons, so that no family might be altogether destroyed. These Spartans, with their helots or slaves, made up his own share of the numbers, but all the army was under his generalship. It is even said that the 300 celebrated their own funeral rites before they set out, lest they should be deprived of them by the enemy, since, as we have already seen, it was the Greek belief that the spirits of the dead found no rest till their obsequies had been performed. Such preparations did not daunt the spirits of Leonidas and his men, and his wife, Gorgo, who was not a woman to be faint-hearted or hold him back. Long before, when she was a very little girl, a word of hers had saved her father from listening to a traitorous message from the King of Persia; and every Spartan lady was bred up to be able to say to those she best loved that they must come home from battle "with the shield or on it"—either carrying it victoriously or borne upon it as a corpse.

When Leonidas came to Thermopylae, the Phocians told him of the mountain path through the chestnut woods of Mount Ceta, and begged to have the privilege of guarding it on a spot high up on the mountainside, assuring him that it was very hard to find at the other end, and that there was every probability that the enemy would never discover it. He consented, and encamping around the warm springs, caused the broken wall to be repaired, and made ready to meet the foe.

The Persian army were seen covering the whole country like locusts, and the hearts of some of the southern Greeks in the pass began to sink. Their homes in the Peloponnesus were comparatively secure—had they not better fall back and reserve themselves to defend the Isthmus of Corinth? But Leonidas, though Sparta was safe below the Isthmus, had no intention of abandoning his northern allies, and kept the other Peloponnesians to their posts, only sending messengers for further help.

Presently a Persian on horseback rode up to reconnoitre the pass. He could not see over the wall, but in front of it, and on the ramparts, he saw the Spartans, some of them engaged in active sports, and others in combing their long hair. He rode back to the king, and told him what he had seen. Now, Xerxes had in his camp an exiled Spartan Prince, named Demaratus, who had become a traitor to his country, and was serving as counsellor to the enemy. Xerxes sent for him, and asked whether his countrymen were mad to be thus employed instead of fleeing away; but Demaratus made answer that a hard fight was no doubt in preparation, and that it was the custom of the Spartans to array their hair with special care when they were about to enter upon any great peril. Xerxes would, however, not believe that so petty a force could intend to resist him, and waited four days, probably expecting his fleet to assist him, but as it did not appear, the attack was made.

The Greeks, stronger men and more heavily armed, were far better able to fight to advantage than the Persians, with their short spears and wicker shields, and beat them off with great ease. It is said that Xerxes three times leapt off his throne in despair at the sight of his troops being driven backwards; and thus for two days it seemed as easy to force a way through the Spartans as through the rocks themselves. Nay, how could slavish troops, dragged from home to spread the victories of an ambitious king, fight like freemen who felt that their strokes were to defend their homes and children!

But on that evening a wretched man, named Ephialtes, crept into the Persian camp, and offered, for a great sum of money, to show the mountain path that would enable the enemy to take the brave defenders in the rear! A Persian general, named Hydarnes, was sent off at nightfall with a detachment to secure this passage, and was guided through the thick forests that clothed the hillside. In the stillness of the air, at daybreak, the Phocian guards of the path were startled by the crackling of the chestnut leaves under the tread of many feet. They started up, but a shower of arrows was discharged on them, and forgetting all save the present alarm, they fled to a higher part of the mountain, and the enemy, without waiting to pursue them, began to descend.

As day dawned, morning light showed the watchers of the Grecian camp below a glittering and shimmering in the torrent bed where the shaggy forests opened; but it was not the sparkle of water, but the shine of gilded helmets and the gleaming of silvered spears! Moreover, a Cimmerian crept over to the wall from the Persian camp with tidings that the path had been betrayed, that the enemy were climbing it, and would come down beyond the Eastern Gate. Still, the way was rugged and circuitous, the Persians would hardly descend before midday, and there was ample time for the Greeks to escape before they could be shut in by the enemy.

There was a short council held over the morning sacrifice. Megistias, the seer, on inspecting the entrails of the slain victim, declared, as well he might, that their appearance boded disaster. Him Leonidas ordered to retire, but he refused, though he sent home his only son. There was no disgrace to an ordinary tone of mind in leaving a post that could not be held, and Leonidas recommended all the allied troops under his command to march away while yet the way was open. As to himself and his Spartans, they had made up their minds to die at their post, and there could be no doubt that the example of such a resolution would do more to save Greece than their best efforts could ever do if they were careful to reserve themselves for another occasion.

All the allies consented to retreat, except the eighty men who came from Mycenae and the 700 Thespians, who declared that they would not desert Leonidas. There were also 400 Thebans who remained; and thus the whole number that stayed with Leonidas to confront two million of enemies were fourteen hundred warriors, besides the helots or attendants on the 300 Spartans, whose number is not known, but there was probably at least one to each. Leonidas had two kinsmen in the camp, like himself, claiming the blood of Hercules, and he tried to save them by giving them letters and messages to Sparta; but one answered that "he had come to fight, not to carry letters"; and the other, that "his deeds would tell all that Sparta wished to know." Another Spartan, named Dienices, when told that the enemy's archers were so numerous that their arrows darkened the sun, replied, "So much the better, we shall fight in the shade." Two of the 300 had been sent to a neighboring village, suffering severely from a complaint in the eyes. One of them, called Eurytus, put on his armor, and commanded his helot to lead him to his place in the ranks; the other, called Aristodemus, was so overpowered with illness that he allowed himself to be carried away with the retreating allies. It was still early in the day when all were gone, and Leonidas gave the word to his men to take their last meal. "To-night," he said, "we shall sup with Pluto."

Hitherto, he had stood on the defensive, and had husbanded the lives of his men; but he now desired to make as great a slaughter as possible, so as to inspire the enemy with dread of the Grecian name. He therefore marched out beyond the wall, without waiting to be attacked, and the battle began. The Persian captains went behind their wretched troops and scourged them on to the fight with whips! Poor wretches, they were driven on to be slaughtered, pierced with the Greek spears, hurled into the sea, or trampled into the mud of the morass; but their inexhaustible numbers told at length. The spears of the Greeks broke under hard service, and their swords alone remained; they began to fall, and Leonidas himself was among the first of the slain. Hotter than ever was the fight over his corpse, and two Persian princes, brothers of Xerxes, were there killed; but at length word was brought that Hydarnes was over the pass, and that the few remaining men were thus enclosed on all sides. The Spartans and Thespians made their way to a little hillock within the wall, resolved to let this be the place of their last stand; but the hearts of the Thebans failed them, and they came towards the Persians holding out their hands in entreaty for mercy. Quarter was given to them, but they were all branded with the king's mark as untrustworthy deserters. The helots probably at this time escaped into the mountains; while the small desperate band stood side by side on the hill still fighting to the last, some with swords, others with daggers, others even with their hands and teeth, till not one living man remained amongst them when the sun went down. There was only a mound of slain, bristled over with arrows.

Twenty thousand Persians had died before that handful of men! Xerxes asked Demaratus if there were many more at Sparta like these, and was told there were 8,000. It must have been with a somewhat failing heart that he invited his courtiers from the fleet to see what he had done to the men who dared to oppose him! and showed them the head and arm of Leonidas set up upon a cross; but he took care that all his own slain, except 1,000, should first be put out of sight. The body of the brave king was buried where he fell, as were those of the other dead. Much envied were they by the unhappy Aristodemus, who found himself called by no name but the "Coward," and was shunned by all his fellow-citizens. No one would give him fire or water, and after a year of misery, he redeemed his honor by perishing in the forefront of the battle of Plataea, which was the last blow that drove the Persians ingloriously from Greece.

The Greeks then united in doing honor to the brave warriors who, had they been better supported, might have saved the whole country from invasion. The poet Simonides wrote the inscriptions that were engraved upon the pillars that were set up in the pass to commemorate this great action. One was outside the wall, where most of the fighting had been. It seems to have been in honor of the whole number who had for two days resisted—

> "Here did four thousand men from Pelops' land
> Against three hundred myriads bravely stand."

In honor of the Spartans was another column—

> "Go, traveler, to Sparta tell
> That here, obeying her, we fell."

On the little hillock of the last resistance was placed the figure of a stone lion, in memory of Leonidas, so fitly named the lion-like, and Simonides, at his own expense, erected a pillar to his friend, the seer Megistias—

> "The great Megistias' tomb you here may view,
> Who slew the Medes, fresh from Spercheius fords;
> Well the wise seer the coming death foreknew,
> Yet scorn'd he to forsake his Spartan lords."

The names of the 300 were likewise engraven on a pillar at Sparta.

Lions, pillars, and inscriptions have all long since passed away, even the very spot itself has changed; new soil has been formed, and there are miles of solid ground between Mount Ceta and the gulf, so that the Hot Gates no longer exist. But more enduring than stone or brass—nay, than the very battlefield itself—has been the name of Leonidas. Two thousand three hundred years have sped since he braced himself to perish for his country's sake in that narrow, marshy coast road, under the brow of the wooded crags, with the sea by his side. Since that time how many hearts have glowed, how many arms have been nerved at the remembrance of the Pass of Thermopylae, and the defeat that was worth so much more than a victory!

CHAPTER TWENTY

A Woman's Wartime Journal
By Dolly Sumner Lunt

Women such as Alcott, Pember, and Edmonds chose to work in the thick of things, but staying at home was no guarantee of security for women, especially those of the South. With so many men away fighting the war, women were left on their own to run businesses, farms, and entire plantations without help from their husbands, fathers, or sons. Dolly Sumner Lunt, a widow who kept a plantation in Georgia with her small daughter, Sadai, and what was left of her slaves, details the terrifying days of Sherman's march to the sea that took the army through her hometown and her home.

—LISA PURCELL

NOVEMBER 17, 1864

HAVE BEEN UNEASY ALL DAY. AT NIGHT SOME OF THE NEIGHBORS WHO HAD BEEN TO town called. They said it was a large force moving very slowly. What shall I do? Where go?

NOVEMBER 18, 1864

Slept very little last night. Went out doors several times and could see large fires like burning buildings. Am I not in the hands of a merciful God who has promised to take care of the widow and orphan?

Sent off two of my mules in the night. Mr. Ward and Frank took them away and hid them. In the morning took a barrel of salt, which had cost me two hundred dollars, into one of the black women's gardens, put a paper over it, and then on the top of that leached ashes. Fixed it on a board as a leach tub, daubing it with ashes. Had some few pieces of meat taken from my smoke-house carried to the Old Place and hidden under some fodder. Bid them hide the wagon and gear and then go on plowing. Went to packing up mine and Sadai's clothes. I fear that we shall be homeless.

The boys came back and wished to hide their mules. They say that the Yankees camped at Mr. Gibson's last night and are taking all the stock in the county. Seeing them so eager, I told them to do as they pleased. They took them off, and Elbert took his forty fattening hogs to the Old Place Swamp and turned them in.

We have done nothing all day—that is, my people have not. I made a pair of pants for Jack. Sent Nute up to Mrs. Perry's on an errand. On his way back, he said, two Yankees met him and begged him to go with them. They asked if we had livestock, and came up the road as far as Mrs. Laura Perry's. I sat for an hour expecting them, but they must have gone back. Oh, how I trust I am safe! Mr. Ward is very much alarmed.

November 19, 1864

Slept in my clothes last night, as I heard that the Yankees went to neighbor Montgomery's on Thursday night at one o'clock, searched his house, drank his wine, and took his money and valuables. As we were not disturbed, I walked after breakfast, with Sadai, up to Mr. Joe Perry's, my nearest neighbor, where the Yankees were yesterday. Saw Mrs. Laura in the road surrounded by her children, seeming to be looking for someone. She said she was looking for her husband, that old Mrs. Perry had just sent her word that the Yankees went to James Perry's the night before, plundered his house, and drove off all his stock, and that she must drive hers into the old fields. Before we were done talking, up came Joe and Jim Perry from their hiding-place. Jim was very much excited. Happening to turn and look behind, as we stood there, I saw some blue-coats coming down the hill. Jim immediately raised his gun, swearing he would kill them anyhow.

"No, don't!" said I, and ran home as fast as I could, with Sadai.

I could hear them cry, "Halt! Halt!" and their guns went off in quick succession. Oh Clod, the time of trial has come!

A man passed on his way to Covington. I hallooed to him, asking him if he did not know the Yankees were coming.

"No—are they?"

"Yes," said I; "they are not three hundred yards from here."

"Sure enough," said he. "Well, I'll not go. I don't want them to get my horse." And although within hearing of their guns, he would stop and look for them. Blissful ignorance! Not knowing, not hearing, he has not suffered the suspense, the fear, that I have for the past forty-eight hours. I walked to the gate. There they came filing up.

I hastened back to my frightened servants and told them that they had better hide, and then went back to the gate to claim protection and a guard. But like demons they rush in! My yards are full. To my smoke-house, my dairy, pantry, kitchen, and cellar, like famished wolves they come, breaking locks and whatever is in their way. The thousand pounds of meat in my smoke-house is gone in a twinkling, my flour, my meat, my lard, butter, eggs, pickles of various kinds—both in vinegar and brine—wine, jars, and jugs are all gone. My eighteen fat turkeys, my hens, chickens, and fowls, my young pigs, are shot down in my yard and hunted as if they were rebels themselves. Utterly powerless I ran out and appealed to the guard.

"I cannot help you, Madam; it is orders."

As I stood there, from my lot I saw driven, first, old Dutch, my dear old buggy horse, who has carried my beloved husband so many miles, and who would so quietly wait at the block for him to mount and dismount, and who at last drew him to his grave; then came old Mary, my brood mare, who for years had been too old and stiff for work, with her three-year-old colt, my two-year-old mule, and her last little baby colt. There they go! There go my mules, my sheep, and, worse than all, my boys!

Alas! little did I think while trying to save my house from plunder and fire that they were forcing my boys from home at the point of the bayonet. One, Newton, jumped into bed in his cabin, and declared himself sick. Another crawled under the floor,—a lame boy he was,—but they pulled him out, placed him on a horse, and drove him off. Mid, poor Mid! The last I saw of him, a man had him going around the garden, looking, as I thought, for my sheep, as he was my shepherd. Jack came crying to me, the big tears coursing down his cheeks, saying they were making him go. I said:

"Stay in my room."

But a man followed in, cursing him and threatening to shoot him if he did not go; so poor Jack had to yield. James Arnold, in trying to escape from a back window, was captured and marched off. Henry, too, was taken; I know not how or when, but probably when he and Bob went after the mules. . . .

My poor boys! My poor boys! What unknown trials are before you! How you have clung to your mistress and assisted her in every way you knew.

Never have I corrected them; a word was sufficient. Never have they known want of any kind. Their parents are with me, and how sadly they lament the loss of their boys. Their cabins are rifled of every valuable, the soldiers swearing that their Sunday clothes were the white people's, and that they never had money to get such things as they had. Poor Frank's chest was broken open, his money and tobacco taken. He has always been a money-making and saving boy; not infrequently has his crop brought him five hundred dollars and more. All of his clothes and Rachel's clothes, which dear Lou gave before her death and which she had packed away, were stolen from her. Ovens, skillets, coffee-mills, of which we had three, coffee-pots—not one have I left. Sifters all gone!

Seeing that the soldiers could not be restrained, the guard offered me to have their remaining possessions brought into my house, which I did, and they all, poor things, huddled together in my room, fearing every movement that the house would be burned.

A Captain Webber from Illinois came into my house. Of him I claimed protection from the vandals who were forcing themselves into my room. He said that he knew my brother Orrington. At that name I could not restrain my feelings, but, bursting into tears, implored him to see my brother and let him know my destitution. I saw nothing before me but starvation. He promised to do this, and comforted me with the assurance that my dwelling-house would not be burned, though my out-buildings might. Poor little Sadai went crying to him as to a friend and told him that they had taken her doll, Nancy. He begged her to come and see him, and he would give her a fine waxen one.

He felt for me, and I give him and several others the character of gentlemen. I don't believe they would have molested women and children had they had their own way. He seemed surprised that I had not laid away in my house, flour and other provisions. I did not suppose I could secure them there, more than where I usually kept them, for in last summer's raid houses were thoroughly searched. In parting with him; I parted as with a friend.

Sherman himself and a greater portion of his army passed my house that day. All day, as the sad moments rolled on, were they passing not only in front of my house, but from behind; they tore down my garden palings, made a road through my back-yard and lot field, driving their stock and riding through, tearing down my fences and desolating my home—wantonly doing it when there was no necessity for it.

Such a day, if I live to the age of Methuselah, may God spare me from ever seeing again!

As night drew its sable curtains around us, the heavens from every point were lit up with flames from burning buildings. Dinnerless and supperless as we were, it was nothing in comparison with the fear of being driven out homeless to the dreary woods. Nothing to eat! I could give my guard no supper, so he left us. I appealed to another, asking him if he had wife, mother, or sister, and how he should feel were they in my situation. A colonel from Vermont left me two men, but they were Dutch, and I could not understand one word they said.

My Heavenly Father alone saved me from the destructive fire. My carriage-house had in it eight bales of cotton, with my carriage, buggy, and harness. On top of the cotton were some carded cotton rolls, a hundred pounds or more. These were thrown out of the blanket in which they were, and a large twist of the rolls taken and set on fire, and thrown into the boat of my carriage, which was close up to the cotton bales. Thanks to my God, the cotton only burned over, and then went out. Shall I ever forget the deliverance?

To-night, when the greater part of the army had passed, it came up very windy and cold. My room was full, nearly, with the negroes and their bedding. They were afraid to go out, for my women could not step out of the door without an insult from the Yankee soldiers. They lay down on the floor; Sadai got down and under the same cover with Sally, while I sat up all night, watching every moment for the flames to burst out from some of my buildings. The two guards came into my room and laid themselves by my fire for the night. I could not close my eyes, but kept walking to and fro, watching the fires in the distance and dreading the approaching day, which, I feared, as they had not all passed, would be but a continuation of horrors.

NOVEMBER 20, 1864

This is the blessed Sabbath, the day upon which He who came to bring peace and good will upon earth rose from His tomb and ascended to intercede for us poor fallen creatures. But how unlike this day to any that have preceded it in my once quiet home. I had watched all night, and the dawn found me watching for the moving of the soldiery that was encamped about us. Oh, how I dreaded those that were to pass, as I supposed they would straggle and complete the ruin that the others had commenced, for I had been repeatedly told that they would burn everything as they passed.

Some of my women had gathered up a chicken that the soldiers shot yesterday, and they cooked it with some yams for our breakfast, the guard complaining that we gave them no supper. They gave us some coffee, which I had to make in a tea-kettle, as every coffeepot is taken off. The rear-guard was commanded by Colonel Carlow, who changed our guard, leaving us one soldier while they were passing. They marched directly on, scarcely breaking ranks. Once a bucket of water was called for, but they drank without coming in.

About ten o'clock they had all passed save one, who came in and wanted coffee made, which was done, and he, too, went on. A few minutes elapsed, and two couriers riding rapidly passed back. Then, presently, more soldiers came by, and this ended the passing of Sherman's army by my place, leaving me poorer by thirty thousand dollars than I was yesterday morning. And a much stronger Rebel!

After the excitement was a little over, I went up to Mrs. Laura's to sympathize with her, for I had no doubt but that her husband was hanged. She thought so, and we could see no way for his escape. We all took a good cry together. While there, I saw smoke looming up in the direction of my home, and thought surely the fiends had done their work ere they left. I ran as fast as I could, but soon saw that the fire was below my home. It proved to be the gin house belonging to Colonel Pitts.

My boys have not come home. I fear they cannot get away from the soldiers. Two of my cows came up this morning, but were driven off again by the Yankees.

I feel so thankful that I have not been burned out that I have tried to spend the remainder of the day as the Sabbath ought to be spent. Ate dinner out of the oven in Julia's house, some stew, no bread. She is boiling some corn. My poor servants feel so badly at losing what they have worked for; meat, the hog meat that they love better than anything else, is all gone.

NOVEMBER 21, 1864

We had the table laid this morning, but no bread or butter or milk. What a prospect for delicacies! My house is a perfect fright. I had brought in Saturday night some thirty bushels of potatoes and ten or fifteen bushels of wheat poured down on the carpet in the ell. Then the few gallons of syrup saved was daubed all about. The backbone of a hog that I had killed on Friday, and which the Yankees did not take when they cleaned out my smokehouse, I found and hid under my bed, and this is all the meat I have. Major Lee came down this evening, having heard that I was burned out, to proffer me a home. Mr. Dorsett was with him. The army lost some of their beeves in passing. I sent to-day and had some driven into my lot, and then sent to Judge Glass to come over and get some. Had two killed. Some of Wheeler's men came in, and I asked them to shoot the cattle, which they did.

About ten o'clock this morning Mr. Joe Perry called. I was so glad to see him that I could scarcely forbear embracing him. I could not keep from crying, for I was sure the Yankees had executed him, and I felt so much for his poor wife. The soldiers told me repeatedly Saturday that they had hung him and his brother James and George Guise. They had a narrow escape, however, and only got away by knowing the country so much better than the soldiers did. They lay out until this morning. How rejoiced I am for his family! All of his negroes are gone, save one man that had a wife here at my plantation. They are very strong Secesh. When the army first came along they offered a guard for the house, but Mrs. Laura told them she was guarded by a Higher Power, and did not thank them to do it. She says that she could think of nothing else all day when the army was passing but of the devil and his hosts. She had, however, to call for a guard before night or the soldiers would have taken everything she had.

NOVEMBER 22, 1864

After breakfast this morning I went over to my grave-yard to see what had befallen that. To my joy, I found it had not been disturbed. As I stood by my dead, I felt rejoiced that they were at rest. Never have I felt so perfectly reconciled to the death of my husband as I do to-day, while looking upon the ruin of his lifelong labor. How it would have grieved him to see such destruction! Yes, theirs is the lot to be envied. At rest, rest from care, rest from heartaches, from trouble. . . .

Found one of my large hogs killed just outside the grave-yard.

Walked down to the swamp, looking for the wagon and gear that Henry hid before he was taken off. Found some of my sheep; came home very much wearied, having walked over four miles.

Mr. and Mrs. Rockmore called. Major Lee came down again after some cattle, and while he was here the alarm was given that more Yankees were coming. I was terribly alarmed and packed my trunks with clothing, feeling assured that we should be burned out now. Major Lee swore that he would shoot, which frightened me, for he was intoxicated enough to make him ambitious. He rode off in the direction whence it was said they were coming, Soon after, however, he returned, saying it was a false alarm, that it was some of our own men. Oh, dear! Are we to be always living in fear and dread! Oh, the horrors, the horrors of war!

CHAPTER TWENTY-ONE

Andrey and Bagration: A Rearguard Action
By Leo Tolstoy

Is War and Peace *the greatest war novel of them all? Many think so, and this excerpt may inspire you to tackle reading the book itself, if you have not already done so.*
　　　　　　　　　　　　　　　　　　　　　　　　　　—LAMAR UNDERWOOD

PRINCE ANDREY MOUNTED HIS HORSE BUT LINGERED AT THE BATTERY, LOOKING AT THE smoke of the cannon from which the ball had flown. His eyes moved rapidly over the wide plain. He only saw that the previously immobile masses of the French were heaving to and fro, and that it really was a battery on the left. The smoke still clung about it. Two Frenchmen on horseback, doubtless adjutants, were galloping on the hill. A small column of the enemy, distinctly visible, were moving downhill, probably to strengthen the line. The smoke of the first shot had not cleared away, when there was a fresh puff of smoke and another shot. The battle was beginning. Prince Andrey turned his horse and galloped back to Grunte to look for Prince Bagration. Behind him he heard the cannonade becoming louder and more frequent. Our men were evidently beginning to reply. Musket shots could be heard below at the spot where the lines were closest. Lemarrois had only just galloped to Murat with Napoleon's menacing letter, and Murat, abashed and anxious to efface his error, at once moved his forces to the centre and towards both flanks, hoping before evening and the arrival of the Emperor to destroy the insignificant detachment before him.

"It has begun! here it comes!" thought Prince Andrey, feeling the blood rush to his heart. "But where? What form is my Toulon to take?" he wondered.

Passing between the companies that had been eating porridge and drinking vodka a quarter of an hour before, he saw everywhere nothing but the same rapid movements of soldiers forming in ranks and getting their guns, and on every face he saw the same eagerness that he felt in his heart. "It has begun! here it comes! Terrible and delightful!"

said the face of every private and officer. Before he reached the earthworks that were being thrown up, he saw in the evening light of the dull autumn day men on horseback crossing towards him. The foremost, wearing a cloak and an Astrachan cap, was riding on a white horse. It was Prince Bagration. Prince Andrey stopped and waited for him to come up. Prince Bagration stopped his horse, and recognizing Prince Andrey nodded to him. He still gazed on ahead while Prince Andrey told him what he had been seeing.

The expression: "It has begun! it is coming!" was discernible even on Prince Bagration's strong, brown face, with his half-closed, lustreless, sleepy-looking eyes. Prince Andrey glanced with uneasy curiosity at that impassive face, and he longed to know: Was that man thinking and feeling, and what was he thinking and feeling at that moment? "Is there anything at all there behind that impassive face?" Prince Andrey wondered, looking at him. Prince Bagration nodded in token of his assent to Prince Andrey's words, and said: "Very good," with an expression that seemed to signify that all that happened, and all that was told him, was exactly what he had foreseen. Prince Andrey, panting from his rapid ride, spoke quickly. Prince Bagration uttered his words in his Oriental accent with peculiar deliberation, as though impressing upon him that there was no need of hurry. He did, however, spur his horse into a gallop in the direction of Tushin's battery. Prince Andrey rode after him with his suite. The party consisted of an officer of the suite, Bagration's private adjutant, Zherkov, an orderly officer, the staff-officer on duty, riding a beautiful horse of English breed, and a civilian official, the auditor, who had asked to be present from curiosity to see the battle. The auditor, a plump man with a plump face, looked about him with a naïve smile of amusement, swaying about on his horse, and cutting a queer figure in his cloak on his saddle among the hussars, Cossacks, and adjutants.

"This gentleman wants to see a battle," said Zherkov to Bolkonsky, indicating the auditor, "but has begun to feel queer already."

"Come, leave off," said the auditor, with a beaming smile at once naïve and cunning, as though he were flattered at being the object of Zherkov's jests, and was purposely trying to seem stupider than he was in reality.

"It's very curious, *mon Monsieur Prince*," said the staff-officer on duty. (He vaguely remembered that the title *prince* was translated in some peculiar way in French, but could not get it quite right.) By this time they were all riding up to Tushin's battery, and a ball struck the ground before them.

"What was that falling?" asked the auditor, smiling naïvely.

"A French pancake," said Zherkov.

"That's what they hit you with, then?" asked the auditor. "How awful!" And he seemed to expand all over with enjoyment. He had hardly uttered the words when again there was a sudden terrible whiz, which ended abruptly in a thud into something soft, and flop—a Cossack, riding a little behind and to the right of the auditor, dropped from his horse to the ground. Zherkov and the staff-officer bent forward over their saddles and turned their horses away. The auditor stopped facing the Cossack, and looking with curiosity at him. The Cossack was dead, the horse was still struggling.

Prince Bagration dropped his eyelids, looked round, and seeing the cause of the delay, turned away indifferently, seeming to ask, "Why notice these trivial details?" With the ease of a first-rate horseman he stopped his horse, bent over a little and disengaged his sabre, which had caught under his cloak. The sabre was an old-fashioned one, unlike what are worn now. Prince Andrey remembered the story that Suvorov had given his saber to Bagration in Italy, and the recollection was particularly pleasant to him at that moment. They had ridden up to the very battery from which Prince Andrey had surveyed the field of battle.

"Whose company?" Prince Bagration asked of the artilleryman standing at the ammunition boxes.

He asked in words: "Whose company?" but what he was really asking was, "You're not in a panic here?" And the artilleryman understood that.

"Captain Tushin's, your excellency," the red-haired, freckled artilleryman sang out in a cheerful voice, as he ducked forward.

"To be sure, to be sure," said Bagration, pondering something, and he rode by the platforms up to the end cannon. Just as he reached it, a shot boomed from the cannon, deafening him and his suite, and in the smoke that suddenly enveloped the cannon the artillerymen could be seen hauling at the cannon, dragging and rolling it back to its former position. A broad-shouldered, gigantic soldier, gunner number one, with a mop, darted up to the wheel and planted himself, his legs wide apart; while number two, with a shaking hand, put the charge into the cannon's mouth; a small man with stooping shoulders, the officer Tushin, stumbling against the cannon, dashed forward, not noticing the general, and looked out, shading his eyes with his little hand.

"Another two points higher, and it will be just right," he shouted in a shrill voice, to which he tried to give a swaggering note utterly out of keeping with his figure. "Two!" he piped. "Smash away, Medvyedev!"

Bagration called to the officer, and Tushin went up to the general, putting three fingers to the peak of his cap with a timid and awkward gesture, more like a priest blessing some one than a soldier saluting. Though Tushin's guns had been intended to cannonade the valley, he was throwing shells over the village of Schöngraben, in part of which immense masses of French soldiers were moving out.

No one had given Tushin instructions at what or with what to fire, and after consulting his sergeant, Zaharchenko, for whom he had a great respect, he had decided that it would be a good thing to set fire to the village. "Very good!" Bagration said, on the officer's submitting that he had done so, and he began scrutinizing the whole field of battle that lay unfolded before him. He seemed to be considering something. The French had advanced nearest on the right side. In the hollow where the stream flowed, below the eminence on which the Kiev regiment was stationed, could be heard a continual roll and crash of guns, the din of which was overwhelming. And much further to the right, behind the dragoons, the officer of the suite pointed out to Bagration a column of French outflanking our flank. On the left the horizon was bounded by the copse close by. Prince Bagration gave orders for two battalions from the center to go to the right to reinforce the flank. The officer of the suite ventured to observe to the prince that the removal of these battalions would leave the cannon unprotected. Prince Bagration turned to the officer of the suite and stared at him with his lustreless eyes in silence. Prince Andrey thought that the officer's observation was a very just one, and that really there was nothing to be said in reply. But at that instant an adjutant galloped up with a message from the colonel of the regiment in the hollow that immense masses of the French were coming down upon them, that his men were in disorder and retreating upon the Kiev grenadiers, Prince Bagration nodded to signify his assent and approval. He rode at a walking pace to the right, and sent an adjutant to the dragoons with orders to attack the French. But the adjutant returned half an hour later with the news that the colonel of the dragoons had already retired beyond the ravine, as a destructive fire had been opened upon him, and he was losing his men for nothing, and so he had concentrated his men in the wood.

"Very good!" said Bagration.

Just as he was leaving the battery, shots had been heard in the wood on the left too; and as it was too far to the left flank for him to go himself, Prince Bagration despatched Zherkov to tell the senior general—the general whose regiment had been inspected by Kutuzov at Braunau—to retreat as rapidly as possible beyond the ravine, as the right flank would probably not long be able to detain the enemy. Tushin, and the battalion that was to have defended his battery, was forgotten. Prince Andrey listened carefully to Prince Bagration's colloquies with the commanding officers, and to the orders he gave them, and noticed, to his astonishment, that no orders were really given by him at all, but that Prince Bagration confined himself to trying to appear as though everything that was being done of necessity, by chance, or at the will of individual officers, was all done, if not by his orders, at least in accordance with his intentions. Prince Andrey observed, however, that, thanks to the tact shown by Prince Bagration, notwithstanding that what was done was due to chance, and not dependent on the commander's will, his presence was of the greatest value. Commanding officers, who rode up to Bagration looking distraught, regained their composure; soldiers and officers greeted him cheerfully, recovered their spirits in his presence, and were unmistakably anxious to display their pluck before him.

After riding up to the highest point of our right flank, Prince Bagration began to go downhill, where a continuous roll of musketry was heard and nothing could be seen for the smoke. The nearer they got to the hollow the less they could see, and the more distinctly could be felt the nearness of the actual battlefield. They began to meet wounded men. Two soldiers were dragging one along, supporting him on each side. His head was covered with blood; he had no cap, and was coughing and spitting. The bullet had apparently entered his mouth or throat. Another one came towards them, walking pluckily alone without his gun, groaning aloud and wringing his hands from the pain of a wound from which the blood was flowing, as though from a bottle, over his greatcoat. His face looked more frightened than in pain. He had been wounded only a moment before. Crossing the road, they began going down a deep descent, and on the slope they saw several men lying on the ground. They were met by a crowd of soldiers, among them some who were not wounded. The soldiers were hurrying up the hill, gasping for breath, and in spite of the general's presence, they were talking loudly together and gesticulating with their arms. In the smoke ahead of them they could see now rows of grey coats, and the commanding officer, seeing Bagration, ran after the group of retreating soldiers, calling upon them to come back. Bagration rode up to the ranks, along which there was here and there a rapid snapping of shots drowning the talk of the soldiers and the shouts of the officers. The whole air was reeking with smoke. The soldiers' faces were all full of excitement and smudged with powder. Some were plugging with their ramrods, others were putting powder on the touch-pans, and getting charges out of their pouches, others were firing their guns. But it was impossible to see at whom they were firing from the smoke, which the wind did not lift. The pleasant hum and whiz of the bullets was repeated pretty rapidly. "What is it?" wondered Prince Andrey, as he rode up to the crowd of soldiers. "It can't be the line, for they are all crowded together; it can't be an attacking party, for they are not moving; it can't be a square, they are not standing like one."

A thin, weak-looking colonel, apparently an old man, with an amiable smile, and eyelids that half-covered his old-looking eyes and gave him a mild air, rode up to Prince Bagration and received him as though he were welcoming an honoured guest into his house. He announced to Prince Bagration that his regiment had had to face a cavalry attack of the French, that though the attack had been repulsed, the regiment had lost more than half of its men. The colonel said that the attack had been repulsed, supposing that to be the proper military term for what had happened; but he did not really know himself what had been taking place during that half hour in the troops under his command, and could not have said with any certainty whether the attack had been repelled or his regiment had been beaten by the attack. All he knew was that at the beginning of the action balls and grenades had begun flying all about his regiment, and killing men, that then some one had shouted "cavalry," and our men had begun firing. And they were firing still, though not now at the cavalry, who had disappeared, but at the French infantry, who had made their appearance in the hollow and were firing at our men. Prince Bagration nodded his head to betoken that all this was exactly what he had desired and expected. Turning to an adjutant, he commanded him to bring down from the hill the two battalions of the Sixth Chasseurs, by whom they had just come. Prince Andrey was struck at that instant by the change that had come over Prince Bagration's face. His face wore the look of concentrated and happy determination, which may be seen in a man who in a hot day takes the final run before a header into the water. The lustreless, sleepy look in the eyes, the affectation of profound thought had gone. The round, hard, eagle eyes looked ecstatically and rather disdainfully before him, obviously not resting on anything, though there was still the same deliberation in his measured movements.

The colonel addressed a protest to Prince Bagration, urging him to go back, as there it was too dangerous for him. "I beg of you, your excellency, for God's sake!" he kept on saying, looking for support to the officer of the suite, who only turned away from him.

"Only look, your excellency!" He called his attention to the bullets which were continually whizzing, singing, and hissing about them. He spoke in the tone of protest and entreaty with which a carpenter speaks to a gentleman who has picked up a hatchet. "We are used to it, but you may blister your fingers." He talked as though these bullets could not kill him, and his half-closed eyes gave a still more persuasive effect to his words. The staff-officer added his protests to the colonel, but Bagration made them no answer. He merely gave the order to cease firing, and to form so as to make room for the two battalions of reinforcements. Just as he was speaking the cloud of smoke covering the hollow was lifted as by an unseen hand and blown by the rising wind from right to left, and the opposite hill came into sight with the French moving across it. All eyes instinctively fastened on that French column moving down upon them and winding in and out over the ups and downs of the ground. Already they could see the fur caps of the soldiers, could distinguish officers from privates, could see their flag flapping against its staff.

"How well they're marching," said some one in Bagration's suite.

The front part of the column was already dipping down into the hollow. The engagement would take place then on the nearer side of the slope . . .

The remnants of the regiment that had already been in action, forming hurriedly, drew off to the right; the two battalions of the Sixth Chasseurs marched up in good order, driving the last stragglers before them. They had not yet reached Bagration, but the heavy, weighty tread could be heard of the whole mass keeping step. On the left flank, nearest of all to Bagration, marched the captain, a round-faced imposing-looking man, with a foolish and happy expression of face. It was the same infantry officer who had run out of the shanty after Tushin. He was obviously thinking of nothing at the moment, but that he was marching before his commander in fine style. With the complacency of a man on parade, he stepped springing on his muscular legs, drawing himself up without the slightest effort, as though he were swinging, and this easy elasticity was a striking contrast to the heavy tread of the soldiers keeping step with him. He wore hanging by his leg an unsheathed, slender, narrow sword (a small bent sabre, more like a toy than a weapon), and looking about him, now at the commander, now behind, he turned his whole powerful frame round without getting out of step. It looked as though all the force of his soul was directed to marching by his commander in the best style possible. And conscious that he was accomplishing this, he was happy. "Left . . . left . . . left . . ." he seemed to be inwardly repeating at each alternate step. And the wall of soldierly figures, weighed down by their knapsacks and guns, with their faces all grave in different ways, moved by in the same rhythm, as though each of the hundreds of soldiers were repeating mentally at each alternate step, "Left . . . left . . . left . . ." A stout major skirted a bush on the road, puffing and shifting his step. A soldier, who had dropped behind, trotted after the company, looking panic-stricken at his own defection. A cannon ball, whizzing through the air, flew over the heads of Prince Bagration and his suite, and in time to the same rhythm, "Left . . . left . . ." it fell into the column.

"Close the ranks!" rang out the jaunty voice of the captain. The soldiers marched in a half circle round something in the place where the ball had fallen, and an old cavalryman, an under officer, lingered behind near the dead, and overtaking his line, changed feet with a hop, got into step, and looked angrily about him. "Left . . . left . . . left . . ." seemed to echo out of the menacing silence and the monotonous sound of the simultaneous tread of the feet on the ground.

"Well done, lads!" said Prince Bagration.

"For your ex . . . slen, slen, slency!" rang out along the ranks. A surly-looking soldier, marching on the left, turned his eyes on Bagration as he shouted, with an expression that seemed to say, "We know that without telling." Another, opening his mouth wide, shouted without glancing round, and marched on, as though afraid of letting his attention stray. The order was given to halt and take off their knapsacks.

Bagration rode round the ranks of men who had marched by him, and then dismounted from his horse. He gave the reins to a Cossack, took off his cloak and handed it to him, stretched his legs and set his cap straight on his head. The French column with the officers in front came into sight under the hill.

"With God's help!" cried Bagration in a resolute, sonorous voice. He turned for one instant to the front line, and swinging his arms a little with the awkward, lumbering gait of a man always on horseback, he walked forward over the uneven ground. Prince Andrey felt that some unseen force was drawing him forward, and he had a sensation of great happiness.*

The French were near. Already Prince Andrey, walking beside Bagration, could distinguish clearly the sashes, the red epaulettes, even the faces of the French. (He saw distinctly one bandy-legged old French officer, wearing Hessian boots, who was getting up the hill with difficulty, taking hold of the bushes.) Prince Bagration gave no new command, and still marched in front of the ranks in the same silence. Suddenly there was the snap of a shot among the French, another and a third . . . and smoke rose and firing rang out in all the broken-up ranks of the enemy. Several of our men fell, among them the round-faced officer, who had been marching so carefully and complacently. But at the very instant of

---

*This was the attack of which Thiers says: "The Russians behaved valiantly and, which is rare in warfare, two bodies of infantry marched resolutely upon each other, neither giving way before the other came up." And Napoleon on St. Helena said: "Some Russian battalions showed intrepidity."

the first shot, Bagration looked round and shouted, "Hurrah!" "Hura . . . a . . . a . . . ah!" rang out along our lines in a prolonged roar, and out-stripping Prince Bagration and one another, in no order, but in an eager and joyous crowd, our men ran downhill after the routed French.

⌁

The attack of the Sixth Chasseurs covered the retreat of the right flank. In the centre Tushin's forgotten battery had succeeded in setting fire to Schöngraben and delaying the advance of the French. The French stayed to put out the fire, which was fanned by the wind, and this gave time for the Russians to retreat. The retreat of the centre beyond the ravine was hurried and noisy; but the different companies kept apart. But the left flank, which consisted of the Azovsky and Podolsky infantry and the Pavlograd hussars, was simultaneously attacked in front and surrounded by the cream of the French army under Lannes, and was thrown into disorder. Bagration had sent Zherkov to the general in command of the left flank with orders to retreat immediately.

Zherkov, keeping his hand still at his cap, had briskly started his horse and galloped off. But no sooner had he ridden out of Bagration's sight than his courage failed him. He was overtaken by a panic he could not contend against, and he could not bring himself to go where there was danger.

After galloping some distance towards the troops of the left flank, he rode not forward where he heard firing, but off to look for the general and the officers in a direction where they could not by any possibility be; and so it was that he did not deliver the message.

The command of the left flank belonged by right of seniority to the general of the regiment in which Dolohov was serving—the regiment which Kutuzov had inspected before Braunau. But the command of the extreme left flank had been entrusted to the colonel of the Pavlograd hussars, in which Rostov was serving. Hence arose a misunderstanding. Both commanding officers were intensely exasperated with one another, and at a time when fighting had been going on a long while on the right flank, and the French had already begun their advance on the left, these two officers were engaged in negotiations, the sole aim of which was the mortification of one another. The regiments—cavalry and infantry alike—were by no means in readiness for the engagement. No one from the common soldier to the general expected a battle; and they were all calmly engaged in peaceful occupations—feeding their horses in the cavalry, gathering wood in the infantry.

"He is my senior in rank, however," said the German colonel of the hussars, growing very red and addressing an adjutant, who had ridden up. "So let him do as he likes. I can't sacrifice my hussars. Bugler! Sound the retreat!"

But things were becoming urgent. The fire of cannon and musketry thundered in unison on the right and in the centre, and the French tunics of Lannes's sharpshooters had already passed over the milldam, and were forming on this side of it hardly out of musket-shot range.

The infantry general walked up to his horse with his quivering strut, and mounting it and drawing himself up very erect and tall, he rode up to the Pavlograd colonel. The two officers met with affable bows and concealed fury in their hearts.

"Again, colonel," the general said, "I cannot leave half my men in the wood. I *beg* you, I *beg* you," he repeated, "to occupy the position, and prepare for an attack."

"And I beg you not to meddle in what's not your business," answered the colonel, getting hot. "If you were a cavalry officer . . ."

"I am not a cavalry officer, colonel, but I am a Russian general, and if you are unaware of the fact . . ."

"I am fully aware of it, your excellency," the colonel screamed suddenly, setting his horse in motion and becoming purple in the face. "If you care to come to the front, you will see that this position cannot be held. I don't want to massacre my regiment for your satisfaction."

"You forget yourself, colonel. I am not considering my own satisfaction, and I do not allow such a thing to be said."

Taking the colonel's proposition as a challenge to his courage, the general squared his chest and rode scowling beside him to the front line, as though their whole difference would inevitably be settled there under the enemy's fire. They reached the line, several bullets flew by them, and they stood still without a word. To look at the front line was a useless proceeding, since from the spot where they had been standing before, it was clear that the cavalry could not act, owing to the bushes and the steep and broken character of the ground, and that the French were outflanking the left wing. The general and the colonel glared sternly and significantly at one another, like two cocks preparing for a fight, seeking in vain for a symptom of cowardice. Both stood the test without flinching. Since there was nothing to be said, and neither was willing to give the other grounds for asserting that he was the first to withdraw from under fire, they might have remained a long while standing there, mutually testing each other's pluck, if there had not at that moment been heard in the copse, almost behind them, the snap of musketry and a confused shout of voices. The French were attacking the soldiers gathering wood in the copse. The hussars could not now retreat, nor could the infantry. They were cut off from falling back on the left by the French line. Now, unfavourable as the ground was, they must attack to fight a way through for themselves.

The hussars of the squadron in which Rostov was an ensign had hardly time to mount their horses when they were confronted by the enemy. Again, as on the Enns bridge, there was no one between the squadron and the enemy, and between them lay that terrible border-line of uncertainty and dread, like the line dividing the living from the dead. All the soldiers were conscious of that line, and the question whether they would cross it or not, and how they would cross it, filled them with excitement.

The colonel rode up to the front, made some angry reply to the questions of the officers, and, like a man desperately insisting on his rights, gave some command. No one said anything distinctly, but through the whole squadron there ran a vague rumour of attack.

The command to form in order rang out, then there was the clank of sabres being drawn out of their sheaths. But still no one moved. The troops of the left flank, both the infantry and the hussars, felt that their commanders themselves did not know what to do, and the uncertainty of the commanders infected the soldiers.

"Make haste, if only they'd make haste," thought Rostov, feeling that at last the moment had come to taste the joys of the attack, of which he had heard so much from his comrades.

"With God's help, lads," rang out Denisov's voice, "forward, quick, gallop!"

The horses' haunches began moving in the front line. Rook pulled at the reins and set off of himself.

On the right Rostov saw the foremost lines of his own hussars, and still further ahead he could see a dark streak, which he could not distinguish clearly, but assumed to be the enemy. Shots could be heard, but at a distance.

"Quicker!" rang out the word of command, and Rostov felt the drooping of Rook's hindquarters as he broke into a gallop. He felt the joy of the gallop coming, and was more and more lighthearted. He noticed a solitary tree ahead of him. The tree was at first in front of him, in the middle of that border-land that had seemed so terrible. But now they had crossed it and nothing terrible had happened, but he felt more lively and excited every moment. "Ah, won't I slash at him!" thought Rostov, grasping the hilt of his sabre tightly. "Hur . . . r . . . a . . . a!" roared voices.

"Now, let him come on, whoever it may be," thought Rostov, driving the spurs into Rook, and outstripping the rest, he let him go at full gallop. Already the enemy could be seen in front. Suddenly something swept over the squadron like a broad broom. Rostov lifted his sabre, making ready to deal a blow, but at that instant the soldier Nikitenko galloped ahead and left his side, and Rostov felt as though he were in a dream being carried forward with supernatural swiftness and yet remaining at the same spot. An hussar, Bandartchuk, galloped up from behind close upon him and looked angrily at him. Bandartchuk's horse started aside, and he galloped by.

"What's the matter? I'm not moving? I've fallen, I'm killed . . ." Rostov asked and answered himself all in one instant. He was alone in the middle of the field. Instead of the moving horses and the hussars' backs, he saw around him the motionless earth and stubblefield. There was warm blood under him.

"No, I'm wounded, and my horse is killed." Rook tried to get up on his forelegs, but he sank again, crushing his rider's leg under his leg. Blood was flowing from the horse's head. The horse struggled, but could not get up. Rostov tried to get up, and fell down too. His sabretache had caught in the saddle. Where our men were, where were the French, he did not know. All around him there was no one.

Getting his leg free, he stood up. "Which side, where now was that line that had so sharply divided the two armies?" he asked himself, and could not answer. "Hasn't something gone wrong with me? Do such things happen, and what ought one to do in such cases?" he wondered as he was getting up. But at that instant he felt as though something superfluous was hanging on his benumbed left arm. The wrist seemed not to belong to it. He looked at his hand, carefully searching for blood on it. "Come, here are some men," he thought joyfully, seeing some men running towards him. "They will help me!" In front of these men ran a single figure in a strange shako and a blue coat, with a swarthy sunburnt face and a hooked nose. Then came two men, and many more were running up behind. One of them said some strange words, not Russian. Between some similar figures in similar shakoes behind stood a Russian hussar. He was being held by the arms; behind him they were holding his horse too.

"It must be one of ours taken prisoner. . . . Yes. Surely they couldn't take me too? What sort of men are they?" Rostov was still wondering, unable to believe his own eyes. "Can they be the French?" He gazed at the approaching French, and although only a few seconds before he had been longing to get at these Frenchmen and to cut them down, their being so near seemed to him now so awful that he could not believe his eyes. "Who are they? What are they running for? Can it be to me? Can they be running to me? And what for? To kill me? *Me*, whom every one's so fond of?" He recalled his mother's love, the love of his family and his friends, and the enemy's intention of killing him seemed impossible. "But they may even kill me." For more than ten seconds he stood, not moving from the spot, nor grasping his position. The foremost Frenchman with the hook nose was getting so near that he could see the expression of his face. And the excited, alien countenance of the man, who was running so lightly and breathlessly towards him, with his bayonet lowered, terrified Rostov. He snatched up his pistol, and instead of firing with it, flung it at the Frenchman and ran to the bushes with all his might. Not with the feeling of doubt and conflict with which he had moved at the Enns bridge, did he now run, but with the feeling of a hare fleeing from the dogs. One unmixed feeling of fear for his young, happy life took possession of his whole being. Leaping rapidly over the hedges with the same impetuosity with which he used to run when he played games, he flew over the field, now and then turning his pale, good-natured, youthful face, and a chill of horror ran down his spine. "No, better not to look," he thought, but as he got near to the bushes he looked round once more. The French had given it up, and just at the moment when he looked round the foremost man was just dropping from a run into a walk, and turning round to shout something loudly to a comrade behind. Rostov stopped. "There's some mistake," he thought; "it can't be that they meant to kill me." And meanwhile his left arm was as heavy as if a hundred pound weight were hanging on it. He could run no further. The Frenchman stopped too and took aim. Rostov frowned and ducked. One bullet and then another flew hissing by him; he took his left hand in his right, and with a last effort ran as far as the bushes. In the bushes there were Russian sharpshooters.

The infantry, who had been caught unawares in the copse, had run away, and the different companies all confused together had retreated in disorderly crowds. One soldier in a panic had uttered those words—terrible in war and meaningless: "Cut off!" and those words had infected the whole mass with panic.

"Outflanked! Cut off! Lost!" they shouted as they ran.

When their general heard the firing and the shouts in the rear he had grasped at the instant that something awful was happening to his regiment; and the thought that he, an exemplary officer, who had served so many years without ever having been guilty of the slightest shortcoming, might be held responsible by his superiors for negligence or lack of discipline, so affected him that, instantly oblivious of the insubordinate cavalry colonel and his dignity as a general, utterly oblivious even of danger and of the instinct of self-preservation, he clutched at the crupper of his saddle, and spurring his horse, galloped off to the regiment under a perfect hail of bullets that luckily missed him. He was possessed by the one desire to find out what was wrong, and to help and correct the mistake whatever it might be, if it were a mistake on his part, so that after twenty-two years of exemplary service, without incurring a reprimand for anything, he might avoid being responsible for this blunder.

Galloping successfully between the French forces, he reached the field behind the copse across which our men were running downhill, not heeding the word of command. That moment had come of moral vacillation which decides the fate of battles. Would these disorderly crowds of soldiers hear the voice of their commander, or, looking back at him, run on further? In spite of the despairing yell of the commander, who had once been so awe-inspiring to his soldiers, in spite of his infuriated, purple face, distorted out of all likeness to itself, in spite of his brandished sword, the soldiers still ran and talked together, shooting into the air and not listening to the word of command. The moral balance which decides the fate of battle was unmistakably falling on the side of panic.

The general was choked with screaming and gunpowder-smoke, and he stood still in despair. All seemed lost; but at that moment the French, who had been advancing against our men, suddenly, for no apparent reason, ran back, vanished from the edge of the copse, and Russian sharpshooters appeared in the copse. This was Timohin's division, the only one that had retained its good order in the copse, and hiding in ambush in the ditch behind the copse, had suddenly attacked the French. Timohin had rushed with such a desperate yell upon the French, and with such desperate and drunken energy had he dashed at the enemy with only a sword in his hand, that the French flung down their weapons and fled without pausing to recover themselves. Dolohov, running beside Timohin, killed one French soldier at close quarters, and was the first to seize by the collar an officer who surrendered. The fleeing Russians came back; the battalions were brought together; and the French, who had been on the point of splitting the forces of the left flank into two parts, were for the moment held in check. The reserves had time to join the main forces, and the runaways were stopped. The general stood with Major Ekonomov at the bridge, watching the retreating companies go by, when a soldier ran up to him, caught hold of his stirrup and almost clung on to it. The soldier was wearing a coat of blue fine cloth, he had no knapsack nor shako, his head was bound up, and across his shoulders was slung a French cartridge case. In his hand he held an officer's sword. The soldier was pale, his blue eyes looked impudently into the general's face, but his mouth was smiling. Although the general was engaged in giving instructions to Major Ekonomov, he could not help noticing this soldier.

"Your excellency, here are two trophies," said Dolohov, pointing to the French sword and cartridge case. "An officer was taken prisoner by me. I stopped the company." Dolohov breathed hard from weariness; he spoke in jerks. "The whole company can bear me witness. I beg you to remember me, your excellency!"

"Very good, very good," said the general, and he turned to Major Ekonomov. But Dolohov did not leave him; he undid the bandage, and showed the blood congealed on his head.

"A bayonet wound; I kept my place in the front. Remember me, your excellency."

Tushin's battery had been forgotten, and it was only at the very end of the action that Prince Bagration, still hearing the cannonade in the centre, sent the staff-officer on duty and then Prince Andrey to command the battery to retire as quickly as possible. The force which had been stationed near Tushin's cannons to protect them had by somebody's orders retreated in the middle of the battle. But the battery still kept up its fire, and was not taken by the French simply because the enemy could not conceive of the reckless daring of firing from four cannons that were quite unprotected. The French supposed, on the contrary, judging from the energetic action of the battery, that the chief forces of the Russians were concentrated here in the centre, and twice attempted to attack that point, and both times were driven back by the grapeshot fired on them from the four cannons which stood in solitude on the heights. Shortly after Prince Bagration's departure, Tushin had succeeded in setting fire to Schöngraben.

"Look, what a fuss they're in! It's flaming! What a smoke! Smartly done! First-rate! The smoke! the smoke!" cried the gunners, their spirits reviving.

All the guns were aimed without instructions in the direction of the conflagration. The soldiers, as though they were urging each other on, shouted at every volley: "Bravo! That's something like now! Go it! . . . First-rate!" The fire, fanned by the wind, soon spread. The French columns, who had marched out beyond the village, went back, but as though in revenge for this mischance, the enemy stationed ten cannons a little to the right of the village, and began firing from them on Tushin.

In their childlike glee at the conflagration of the village, and the excitement of their successful firing on the French, our artillerymen only noticed this battery when two cannon-balls and after them four more fell among their cannons, and one knocked over two horses and another tore off the foot of a gunner. Their spirits, however, once raised, did not flag; their excitement simply found another direction. The horses were replaced by others from the ammunition carriage; the wounded were removed, and the four cannons were turned facing the ten of the enemy's battery. The other officer, Tushin's comrade, was killed at the beginning of the action, and after an hour's time, of the forty gunners of the battery, seventeen were disabled, but they were still as merry and as eager as ever. Twice they noticed the French appearing below close to them, and they sent volleys of grapeshot at them.

The little man with his weak, clumsy movements, was continually asking his orderly *for just one more pipe for that stroke*, as he said, and scattering sparks from it, he kept running out in front and looking from under his little hand at the French.

"Smash away, lads!" he was continually saying, and he clutched at the cannon wheels himself and unscrewed the screws. In the smoke, deafened by the incessant booming of the cannons that made him shudder every time one was fired, Tushin ran from one cannon to the other, his short pipe never out of his mouth. At one moment he was taking aim, then reckoning the charges, then arranging for the changing and unharnessing of the killed and wounded horses, and all the time shouting in his weak, shrill, hesitating voice. His face grew more and more eager. Only when men were killed and wounded he knitted his brows, and turning away from the dead man, shouted angrily to the men, slow, as they always are, to pick up a wounded man or a dead body. The soldiers, for the most part fine, handsome fellows (a couple of heads taller than their officer and twice as broad in the chest, as they mostly are in the artillery), all looked to their commanding officer like children in a difficult position, and the expression they found on his face was invariably reflected at once on their own.

Owing to the fearful uproar and noise and the necessity of attention and activity, Tushin experienced not the slightest unpleasant sensation of fear; and the idea that he might be killed or badly wounded never entered his head. On the contrary, he felt more and more lively. It seemed to him that the moment in which he had first seen the enemy and had fired the first shot was long, long ago, yesterday perhaps, and that the spot of earth on which he stood was a place long familiar to him, in which he was quite at home. Although he thought of everything, considered everything, did everything the very best officer could have done in his position, he was in a state of mind akin to the delirium of fever or the intoxication of a drunken man.

The deafening sound of his own guns on all sides, the hiss and thud of the enemy's shells, the sight of the perspiring, flushed gunners hurrying about the cannons, the sight of the blood of men and horses, and of the puffs of smoke from the enemy on the opposite side (always followed by a cannon-ball that flew across and hit the earth, a man, a horse, or a cannon)—all these images made up for him a fantastic world of his own, in which he found enjoyment at the moment. The enemy's cannons in his fancy were not cannons, but pipes from which an invisible smoker blew puffs of smoke at intervals.

"There he's puffing away again," Tushin murmured to himself as a cloud of smoke rolled downhill, and was borne off by the wind in a wreath to the left. "Now, your ball— throw it back."

"What is it, your honour?" asked a gunner who stood near him, and heard him muttering something.

"Nothing, a grenade . . ." he answered. "Now for it, our Matvyevna," he said to himself. Matvyevna was the name his fancy gave to the big cannon, cast in an old-fashioned mould, that stood at the end. The French seemed to be ants swarming about their cannons. The handsome, drunken soldier, number one gunner of the second cannon, was in his dream-world "uncle"; Tushin looked at him more often than at any of the rest, and took delight in every gesture of the man. The sound—dying away, then quickening again—of the musketry fire below the hill seemed to him like the heaving of some creature's breathing. He listened to the ebb and flow of these sounds.

"Ah, she's taking another breath again," he was saying to himself. He himself figured in his imagination as a mighty man of immense stature, who was flinging cannon-balls at the French with both hands.

"Come, Matvyevna, old lady, stick by us!" he was saying, moving back from the cannon, when a strange, unfamiliar voice called over his head. "Captain Tushin! Captain!"

Tushin looked round in dismay. It was the same staff-officer who had turned him out of the booth at Grunte. He was shouting to him in a breathless voice:

"I say, are you mad? You've been commanded twice to retreat, and you . . ."

"Now, what are they pitching into me for?" . . . Tushin wondered, looking in alarm at the superior officer.

"I . . . don't . . ." he began, putting two fingers to the peak of his cap. "I . . ."

But the staff-officer did not say all he had meant to. A cannon-ball flying near him made him duck down on his horse. He paused, and was just going to say something more, when another ball stopped him. He turned his horse's head and galloped away.

"Retreat! All to retreat!" he shouted from a distance.

The soldiers laughed. A minute later an adjutant arrived with the same message. This was Prince Andrey. The first thing he saw, on reaching the place where Tushin's cannons were stationed, was an unharnessed horse with a broken leg, which was neighing beside the harnessed horses. The blood was flowing in a perfect stream from its leg. Among the platforms lay several dead men. One cannon-ball after another flew over him as he rode up, and he felt a nervous shudder running down his spine. But the very idea that he was afraid was enough to rouse him again. "I can't be frightened," he thought, and he deliberately dismounted from his horse between the cannons. He gave his message, but he did not leave the battery. He decided to stay and assist in removing the cannons from the position and getting them away. Stepping over the corpses, under the fearful fire from the French, he helped Tushin in getting the cannons ready.

"The officer that came just now ran off quicker than he came," said a gunner to Prince Andrey, "not like your honour."

Prince Andrey had no conversation with Tushin. They were both so busy that they hardly seemed to see each other. When they had got the two out of the four cannons that were uninjured on to the platforms and were moving downhill (one cannon that had been smashed and a howitzer were left behind), Prince Andrey went up to Tushin.

"Well, good-bye till we meet again," said Prince Andrey, holding out his hand to Tushin.

"Good-bye, my dear fellow," said Tushin, "dear soul! good-bye, my dear fellow," he said with tears, which for some unknown reason started suddenly into his eyes.

The wind had sunk, black storm-clouds hung low over the battlefield, melting on the horizon into the clouds of smoke from the powder. Darkness had come, and the glow of conflagrations showed all the more distinctly in two places. The cannonade had grown feebler, but the snapping of musketry-fire in the rear and on the right was heard nearer and more often. As soon as Tushin with his cannons, continually driving round the wounded and coming upon them, had got out of fire and were descending the ravine, he was met by the staff, among whom was the staff-officer and Zherkov, who had twice been sent to Tushin's battery, but had not once reached it. They all vied with one another in giving him orders, telling him how and where to go, finding fault and making criticisms. Tushin gave no orders, and in silence, afraid to speak because at every word he felt, he could not have said why, ready to burst into tears, he rode behind on his artillery nag. Though orders were given to abandon the wounded, many of them dragged themselves after the troops and begged for a seat on the cannons. The jaunty infantry-officer—the one who had run out of Tushin's shanty just before the battle—was laid on Matvyevna's carriage with a bullet in his stomach. At the bottom of the hill a pale ensign of hussars, holding one arm in the other hand, came up to Tushin and begged for a seat.

"Captain, for God's sake. I've hurt my arm," he said timidly. "For God's sake. I can't walk. For God's sake!" It was evident that this was not the first time the ensign had asked for a lift, and that he had been everywhere refused. He asked in a hesitating and piteous voice. "Tell them to let me get on, for God's sake!"

"Let him get on, let him get on," said Tushin. "Put a coat under him, you, Uncle." He turned to his favourite soldier. "But where's the wounded officer?"

"We took him off; he was dead," answered some one.

"Help him on. Sit down, my dear fellow, sit down. Lay the coat there, Antonov."

The ensign was Rostov. He was holding one hand in the other. He was pale, and his lower jaw was trembling as though in a fever. They put him on Matvyevna, the cannon from which they had just removed the dead officer. There was blood on the coat that was laid under him, and Rostov's riding-breeches and arm were smeared with it.

"What, are you wounded, my dear?" said Tushin, going up to the cannon on which Rostov was sitting.

"No; it's a sprain."

"How is it there's blood on the frame?" asked Tushin.

"That was the officer, your honour, stained it," answered an artillery-man, wiping the blood off with the sleeve of his coat, and as it were apologising for the dirty state of the cannon.

With difficulty, aided by the infantry, they dragged the cannon uphill, and halted on reaching the village of Guntersdorf. It was by now so dark that one could not distinguish the soldiers' uniforms ten paces away, and the firing had begun to subside. All of a sudden there came the sound of firing and shouts again close by on the right side. The flash of the shots could be seen in the darkness. This was the last attack of the French. It was met by the soldiers in ambush in the houses of the village. All rushed out of the village again, but Tushin's cannons could not move, and the artillerymen, Tushin, and the ensign looked at one another in anticipation of their fate. The firing on both sides began to subside, and some soldiers in lively conversation streamed out of a side street.

"Not hurt, Petrov?" inquired one.

"We gave it them hot, lads. They won't meddle with us now," another was saying.

"One couldn't see a thing. Didn't they give it to their own men! No seeing for the darkness, mates. Isn't there something to drink?"

The French had been repulsed for the last time. And again, in the complete darkness, Tushin's cannons moved forward, surrounded by the infantry, who kept up a hum of talk.

In the darkness they flowed on like an unseen, gloomy river always in the same direction, with a buzz of whisper and talk and the thud of hoofs and rumble of wheels. Above all other sounds, in the confused uproar, rose the moans and cries of the wounded, more distinct than anything in the darkness of the night. Their moans seemed to fill all the darkness surrounding the troops. Their moans and the darkness seemed to melt into one. A little later a thrill of emotion passed over the moving crowd. Some one followed by a suite had ridden by on a white horse, and had said something as he passed.

"What did he say? Where we are going now? To halt, eh? Thanked us, what?" eager questions were heard on all sides, and the whole moving mass began to press back on itself (the foremost, it seemed, had halted), and a rumour passed through that the order had been given to halt. All halted in the muddy road, just where they were.

Fires were lighted and the talk became more audible. Captain Tushin, after giving instructions to his battery, sent some of his soldiers to look for an ambulance or a doctor for the ensign, and sat down by the fire his soldiers had lighted by the roadside. Rostov too dragged himself to the fire. His whole body was trembling with fever from the pain, the cold, and the damp. He was dreadfully sleepy, but he could not go to sleep for the agonising pain in his arm, which ached and would not be easy in any position. He closed his eyes, then opened them to stare at the fire, which seemed to him dazzling red, and then at the stooping, feeble figure of Tushin, squatting in Turkish fashion near him. The big, kindly, and shrewd eyes of Tushin were fixed upon him with sympathy and commiseration. He saw that Tushin wished with all his soul to help him, but could do nothing for him.

On all sides they heard the footsteps and the chatter of the infantry going and coming and settling themselves round them. The sound of voices, of steps, and of horses' hoofs tramping in the mud, the crackling firewood far and near, all melted into one fluctuating roar of sound.

It was not now as before an unseen river flowing in the darkness, but a gloomy sea subsiding and still agitated after a storm. Rostov gazed vacantly and listened to what was passing before him and around him. An infantry soldier came up to the fire, squatted on his heels, held his hands to the fire, and turned his face.

"You don't mind, your honour?" he said, looking inquiringly at Tushin. "Here I've got lost from my company, your honour; I don't know myself where I am. It's dreadful!"

With the soldier an infantry officer approached the fire with a bandaged face. He asked Tushin to have the cannon moved a very little, so as to let a store wagon pass by. After the officer two soldiers ran up to the fire. They were swearing desperately and fighting, trying to pull a boot from one another.

"No fear! you picked it up! that's smart!" one shouted in a husky voice. Then a thin, pale soldier approached, his neck bandaged with a blood-stained rag. With a voice of exasperation he asked the artillerymen for water.

"Why, is one to die like a dog?" he said.

Tushin told them to give him water. Next a good-humoured soldier ran up, to beg for some red-hot embers for the infantry.

"Some of your fire for the infantry! Glad to halt, lads. Thanks for the loan of the firing; we'll pay it back with interest," he said, carrying some glowing firebrands away into the darkness.

Next four soldiers passed by, carrying something heavy in an overcoat. One of them stumbled.

"Ay, the devils, they've left firewood in the road," grumbled one.

"He's dead; why carry him?" said one of them.

"Come on, you!" And they vanished into the darkness with their burden.

"Does it ache, eh?" Tushin asked Rostov in a whisper.

"Yes, it does ache."

"Your honour's sent for to the general. Here in a cottage he is," said a gunner, coming up to Tushin.

"In a minute, my dear." Tushin got up and walked away from the fire, buttoning up his coat and setting himself straight.

In a cottage that had been prepared for him not far from the artillery-men's fire, Prince Bagration was sitting at dinner, talking with several commanding officers, who had gathered about him. The little old colonel with the half-shut eyes was there, greedily gnawing at a mutton-bone, and the general of twenty-two years' irreproachable service, flushed with a glass of vodka and his dinner, and the staff-officer with the signet ring, and Zherkov, stealing uneasy glances at every one, and Prince Andrey, pale with set lips and feverishly glittering eyes.

In the corner of the cottage room stood a French flag, that had been captured, and the auditor with the naïve countenance was feeling the stuff of which the flag was made, and shaking his head with a puzzled air, possibly because looking at the flag really interested him, or possibly because he did not enjoy the sight of the dinner, as he was hungry and no place had been laid for him. In the next cottage there was the French colonel, who had been taken prisoner by the dragoons. Our officers were flocking in to look at him. Prince Bagration thanked the several commanding officers, and inquired into details of the battle and of the losses. The general, whose regiment had been inspected at Braunau, submitted to the prince that as soon as the engagement began, he had fallen back from the copse, mustered the men who were cutting wood, and letting them pass by him, had made a bayonet charge with two battalions and repulsed the French.

"As soon as I saw, your excellency, that the first battalion was thrown into confusion, I stood in the road and thought, 'I'll let them get through and then open fire on them'; and that's what I did."

The general had so longed to do this, he had so regretted not having succeeded in doing it, that it seemed to him now that this was just what had happened. Indeed might it not actually have been so? Who could make out in such confusion what did and what did not happen?

"And by the way I ought to note, your excellency," he continued, recalling Dolohov's conversation with Kutuzov and his own late interview with the degraded officer, "that the private Dolohov, degraded to the ranks, took a French officer prisoner before my eyes and particularly distinguished himself."

"I saw here, your excellency, the attack of the Pavlograd hussars," Zherkov put in, looking uneasily about him. He had not seen the hussars at all that day, but had only heard about them from an infantry officer. "They broke up two squares, your excellency."

When Zherkov began to speak, several officers smiled, as they always did, expecting a joke from him. But as they perceived that what he was saying all redounded to the glory of our arms and of the day, they assumed a serious expression, although many were very well aware that what Zherkov was saying was a lie utterly without foundation. Prince Bagration turned to the old colonel.

"I thank you all, gentlemen; all branches of the service behaved heroically—infantry, cavalry, and artillery. How did two cannons come to be abandoned in the centre?" he inquired, looking about for some one. (Prince Bagration did not ask about the cannons of the left flank; he knew that all of them had been abandoned at the very beginning of the action.) "I think it was you I sent," he added, addressing the staff-officer.

"One had been disabled," answered the staff-officer, "but the other, I can't explain; I was there all the while myself, giving instructions, and I had scarcely left there. . . . It was pretty hot, it's true," he added modestly.

Some one said that Captain Tushin was close by here in the village, and that he had already been sent for.

"Oh, but you went there," said Prince Bagration, addressing Prince Andrey.

"To be sure, we rode there almost together," said the staff-officer, smiling affably to Bolkonsky.

"I had not the pleasure of seeing you," said Prince Andrey, coldly and abruptly. Every one was silent.

Tushin appeared in the doorway, timidly edging in behind the generals' backs. Making his way round the generals in the crowded hut, embarrassed as he always was before his superior officers, Tushin did not see the flag-staff and tumbled over it. Several of the officers laughed.

"How was it a cannon was abandoned?" asked Bagration, frowning, not so much at the captain as at the laughing officers, among whom Zherkov's laugh was the loudest. Only now in the presence of the angry-looking commander, Tushin conceived in all its awfulness the crime and disgrace of his being still alive when he had lost two cannons. He had been so excited that till that instant he had not had time to think of that. The officers' laughter had bewildered him still more. He stood before Bagration, his lower jaw quivering, and could scarcely articulate:

"I don't know . . . your excellency . . . I hadn't the men, your excellency."

"You could have got them from the battalions that were covering your position!" That there were no battalions there was what Tushin did not say, though it was the fact. He was afraid of getting another officer into trouble by saying that, and without uttering a word he gazed straight into Bagration's face, as a confused schoolboy gazes at the face of an examiner.

The silence was rather a lengthy one. Prince Bagration, though he had no wish to be severe, apparently found nothing to say; the others did not venture to intervene. Prince Andrey was looking from under his brows at Tushin and his fingers moved nervously.

"Your excellency," Prince Andrey broke the silence with his abrupt voice, "you sent me to Captain Tushin's battery. I went there and found two-thirds of the men and horses killed, two cannons disabled and no forces near to defend them."

Prince Bagration and Tushin looked now with equal intensity at Bolkonsky, as he went on speaking with suppressed emotion.

"And if your excellency will permit me to express my opinion," he went on, "we owe the success of the day more to the action of that battery and the heroic steadiness of Captain Tushin and his men than to anything else," said Prince Andrey, and he got up at once and walked away from the table, without waiting for a reply.

Prince Bagration looked at Tushin and, apparently loath to express his disbelief in Bolkonsky's off-handed judgment, yet unable to put complete faith in it, he bent his head and said to Tushin that he could go. Prince Andrey walked out after him.

"Thanks, my dear fellow, you got me out of a scrape," Tushin said to him.

Prince Andrey looked at Tushin, and walked away without uttering a word. Prince Andrey felt bitter and melancholy. It was all so strange, so unlike what he had been hoping for.

CHAPTER TWENTY-TWO

A Buffalo Bill Episode
By William F. Cody

A character as flamboyant and colorful as William Frederick "Buffalo Bill" Cody cannot be fully described in the space we have here. Cody (1846–1917) was an American frontier icon in newspapers, magazines, books and film. He was a rider for the Pony Express at age 14, served for the Union in the Civil War, was a scout for the US Army during the Indian Wars, and was awarded the Medal of Honor for bravery in 1872. Cody was tagged with the name "Buffalo Bill" because of his legendary prowess as a buffalo hunter. Here, we see him in his own words as he describes setting out from Fort Laramie in Wyoming, headed into hostile Indian country.

—LAMAR UNDERWOOD

THE SCOUTS AT FORT LARNED [LARAMIE] WHEN I ARRIVED THERE, WERE COMMANDED by Dick Curtis—an old guide, frontiersman and Indian interpreter. There were some three hundred lodges of Kiowa and Comanche Indians camped near the fort. These Indians had not as yet gone upon the warpath, but were restless and discontented, and their leading chiefs, Satanta, Lone Wolf, Kicking Bird, Satank, Sittamore, and other noted warriors, were rather saucy. The post at the time was garrisoned by only two companies of infantry and one of cavalry.

General Hazen, who was at the post, was endeavoring to pacify the Indians and keep them from going on the warpath. I was appointed as his special scout, and one morning he notified me that he was going to Fort Harker, and wished me to accompany him as far as Fort Zarah, thirty miles distant. The General usually traveled in an ambulance, but this trip he was to make in a six-mule wagon, under the escort of a squad of twenty infantrymen. So, early one morning in August, we started; arriving safely at Fort Zarah at twelve o'clock. General Hazen thought it unnecessary that we should go farther, and he proceeded on his way to Fort Harker without an escort, leaving instructions that we should return to Fort Larned the next day.

After the General had gone I went to the sergeant in command of the squad, and told him that I was going back that very afternoon, instead of waiting till the next morning; and I accordingly saddled up my mule and set out for Fort Larned. I proceeded uninterruptedly until I got about half-way between the two posts, when at Pawnee Rock I was suddenly "jumped" by about forty Indians, who came dashing up to me, extending their hands and saying, "How! How!" They were some of the same Indians who had been hanging around Fort Larned in the morning. I saw that they had on their war-paint, and were evidently now out on the war-path.

My first impulse was to shake hands with them, as they seemed so desirous of it. I accordingly reached out my hand to one of them, who grasped it with a tight grip, and jerked me violently forward; another pulled my mule by the bridle, and in a moment I was completely surrounded. Before I could do anything at all, they had seized my revolvers from the holsters, and I received a blow on the head from a tomahawk which nearly rendered me senseless. My gun, which was lying across the saddle, was snatched from its place, and finally the Indian, who had hold of the bridle, started off towards the Arkansas River, leading the mule, which was being lashed by the other Indians who were following.

The savages were all singing, yelling, and whooping, as only Indians can do, when they are having their little game all their own way. While looking towards the river I saw, on the opposite side, an immense village moving down along the bank, and then I became convinced that the Indians had left the post and were now starting out on the war-path. My captors crossed the stream with me, and as we waded through the shallow water they continued to lash the mule and myself. Finally they brought me before an important looking body of Indians, who proved to be the chiefs and principal warriors. I soon recognized old Satanta among them, as well as others whom I knew, and I supposed it was all over with me.

The Indians were jabbering away so rapidly among themselves that I could not understand what they were saying. Satanta at last asked me where I had been; and, as good luck would have it, a happy thought struck me. I told him I had been after a herd of cattle or "whoa-haws," as they called them. It so happened that the Indians had been out of meat for several weeks, as the large herd of cattle which had been promised them had not yet arrived, although expected by them.

The moment that I mentioned that I had been searching for the "whoa-haws," old Satanta began questioning me in a very eager manner. He asked me where the cattle were, and I replied that they were back only a few miles, and that I had been sent by General Hazen to inform him that the cattle were coming, and that they were intended for his people. This seemed to please the old rascal, who also wanted to know if there were any soldiers with the herd, and my reply was that there were. Thereupon the chiefs held a consultation, and presently Satanta asked me if General Hazen had really said that they should have the cattle. I replied in the affirmative, and added that I had been directed to bring the cattle to them. I followed this up with a very dignified inquiry, asking why his young men had treated me so. The old wretch intimated that it was only "a freak of the boys"; that the young men had wanted to see if I was brave; in fact, they had only meant to test my bravery, and that the whole thing was a joke.

The veteran liar was now beating me at my own game of lying; but I was very glad of it, as it was in my favor. I did not let him suspect that I doubted his veracity, but I remarked that is a rough way to treat friends. He immediately ordered his young men to give me back my arms, and scolded them for what they had done. Of course, the sly old dog was now playing it very fine, as he was anxious to get possession of the cattle, with which he believed "there was a heap of soldiers coming." He had concluded it was not best to fight the soldiers if he could get the cattle peaceably.

Another council was held by the chiefs, and in a few minutes old Satanta came and asked me if I would go over and bring the cattle down to the opposite side of the river, so that they could get them. I replied, "Of course; that's my instruction from General Hazen."

Satanta said I must not feel angry at his young men, for they had only been acting in fun. He then inquired if I wished any of his men to accompany me to the cattle herd. I replied that it would be better for me to go alone, and then the soldiers could keep right on to Fort Larned, while I could drive the herd down on the bottom. So, wheeling my mule around, I was soon re-crossing the river, leaving old Satanta in the firm belief that I had told him a straight story, and was going for the cattle, which only existed in my imagination.

I hardly knew what to do, but thought that if I could get the river between the Indians and myself I would have a good three-quarters of a mile the start of them, and could then make a run for Fort Larned, as my mule was a good one.

Thus far my cattle story had panned out all right; but just as I reached the opposite bank of the river, I looked behind and saw that ten or fifteen Indians who had begun to suspect something crooked, were following me. The moment that my mule secured a good foothold on the bank, I urged him into a gentle lope towards the place where, according to my statement, the cattle were to be brought. Upon reaching a little ridge, and riding down the other side out of view, I turned my mule and headed him westward for Fort Larned. I let him out for all that he was worth, and when I came out on a little rise of ground, I looked back, and saw the Indian village in plain sight. My pursuers were now on the ridge which I had passed over, and were looking for me in every direction.

Presently they spied me, and seeing that I was running away, they struck out in swift pursuit, and in a few minutes it became painfully evident that they were gaining on me. They kept up the chase as far as Ash Creek, six miles from Fort Larned. I still led them half a mile, as their horses had not gained much during the last half of the race. My mule seemed to have gotten his second wind, and as I was on the old road I had played the whip and spurs on him without much cessation. The Indians likewise had urged their steeds to the utmost.

Finally, upon reaching the dividing ridge between Ash Creek and Pawnee Fork, I saw Fort Larned only four miles away. It was now sundown, and I heard the evening gun at the fort. The troops of the garrison little dreamed that there was a man flying for his life from the Indians and trying to reach the post. The Indians were once more gaining on me, and when I crossed the Pawnee Fork, two miles from the post, two or three of them were only a quarter of a mile behind me. Just as I had gained the opposite bank of the stream I was overjoyed to see some soldiers in a government wagon, only a short distance off. I yelled at the top of my voice, and riding up to them, told them that the Indians were after me.

Denver Jim, a well-known scout, asked how many there were, and upon my informing him that there were about a dozen, he said: "Let's drive the wagon into the trees, and we'll lay for 'em." The team was hurriedly driven in among the trees and low box-elder bushes, and there secreted.

We did not have to wait long for the Indians, who came dashing up, lashing their horses, which were panting and blowing. We let two of them pass by, but we opened a lively fire on the next three or four, killing two at the first crack. The others following, discovered that they had run into an ambush, and whirling off into the brush they turned and ran back in the direction whence they had come. The two who had passed heard the firing and made their escape. We scalped the two that we had killed, and appropriated their arms and equipments; and then catching their horses, we made our way into the post. The soldiers had heard us firing, and as we were approaching the fort the drums were being beaten, and the buglers were sounding the call to fall in. The officers had thought that Satanta and his Indians were coming in to capture the fort.

It seems that on the morning of that day, two hours after General Hazen had taken his departure, old Satanta drove into the post in an ambulance, which he had received some months before as a present from the government. He appeared to be angry and bent on mischief. In an interview with Captain Parker, the commanding officer, he asked why General Hazen had left the post without supplying the beef cattle which had been promised to him. The Captain told him that the cattle were surely on the road, but he could not explain why they were detained.

The interview proved to be a stormy one, and Satanta made numerous threats, saying that if he wished, he could capture the whole post with his warriors. Captain Parker, who was a brave man, gave Satanta to understand that he was reckoning beyond his powers, and would find it a more difficult undertaking than he had any idea of, as they were prepared for him at any moment. The interview finally terminated, and Satanta angrily left the officer's presence. Going over to the sutler's store he sold his ambulance to Mr. Tappan the past trader, and with a portion of the proceeds he secretly managed to secure some whisky from some bad men around the fort. There are always to be found around every frontier post some men who will sell whisky to the Indians at any time and under any circumstances, notwithstanding it is a flagrant violation of both civil and military regulations.

Satanta mounted his horse, and taking the whisky with him, he rode rapidly away and proceeded straight to his village. He had not been gone over an hour, when he returned to the vicinity of the post accompanied by his warriors who came in from every direction, to the number of seven or eight hundred. It was evident that the irate old rascal was "on his ear," so to speak, and it looked as if he intended to carry out his threat of capturing the fort. The garrison at once turned out and prepared to receive the red-skins, who, when within half a mile, circled around the fort and fired numerous shots into it, instead of trying to take it by assault.

While this circular movement was going on, it was observed that the Indian village in the distance was packing up, preparatory to leaving, and it was soon under way. The mounted warriors remained behind some little time, to give their families an opportunity to get away, as they feared that the troops might possibly in some manner intercept them. Finally, they encircled the post several times, fired some farewell rounds, and then galloped away over the prairie to overtake their fast departing village. On their way thither, they surprised and killed a party of wood-choppers down on the Pawnee Fork, as well as some herders who were guarding beef cattle; some seven or eight men in all, were killed, and it was evident that the Indians meant business.

The soldiers with the wagon—whom I had met at the crossing of the Pawnee Fork—had been out for the bodies of the men. Under the circumstances it was no wonder that the garrison, upon hearing the reports of our guns when we fired upon the party whom we ambushed, should have thought the Indians were coming back to give them another "turn."

We found that all was excitement at the post; double guards had been put on duty, and Captain Parker had all the scouts at his headquarters. He was endeavoring to get some one to take some important dispatches to General Sheridan at Fort Hays. I reported to him at once, and stated where I had met the Indians and how I had escaped from them.

"You was very fortunate, Cody, in thinking of that cattle story; but for that little game your hair would now be an ornament to a Kiowa's lodge," said he.

Just then Dick Curtis spoke up and said: "Cody, the Captain is anxious to send some dispatches to General Sheridan, at Fort Hays, and none of the scouts here seem to be very willing to undertake the trip. They say they are not well enough acquainted with the country to find the way at night."

As a storm was coming up it was quite dark, and the scouts feared that they would lose the way; besides it was a dangerous ride, as a large party of Indians were known to be camped on Walnut Creek, on the direct road to Fort Hays. It was evident that Curtis was trying to induce me to volunteer. I made some evasive answer to Curtis, for

I did not care to volunteer after my long day's ride. But Curtis did not let the matter drop. Said he:

"I wish, Bill, that you were not so tired by your chase of to-day, for you know the country better than the rest of the boys, and I am certain that you could go through."

"As far as the ride to Fort Hays is concerned, that alone would matter but little to me," I said, "but it is a risky piece of work just now, as the country is full of hostile Indians; still if no other scout is willing to volunteer, I will chance it. I'll go, provided I am furnished with a good horse. I am tired of being chased on a government mule by Indians." At this Captain Nolan, who had been listening to our conversation, said:

"Bill, you may have the best horse in my company. You can take your choice if you will carry these dispatches. Although it is against regulations to dismount an enlisted man, I have no hesitancy in such a case of urgent necessity as this is, in telling you that you may have any horse you may wish."

"Captain, your first sergeant has a splendid horse, and that's the one I want. If he'll let me ride that horse, I'll be ready to start in one hour, storm or no storm," said I.

"Good enough, Bill; you shall have the horse; but are you sure you can find your way on such a dark night as this?"

"I have hunted on nearly every acre of ground between here and Fort Hays, and I can almost keep my route by the bones of the dead buffaloes," I confidently replied.

"Never fear, Captain, about Cody not finding the way; he is as good in the dark as he is in the daylight," said Curtis.

An orderly was sent for the horse, and the animal was soon brought up, although the sergeant "kicked" a little against letting him go. After eating a lunch and filling a canteen with brandy, I went to headquarters and put my own saddle and bridle on the horse I was to ride. I then got the dispatches, and by ten o'clock was on the road to Fort Hays, which was sixty-five miles distant across the country. The scouts had all bidden me a hearty good-bye, and wished me success, not knowing when, if ever, they would again gaze upon "my warlike form," as the poet would say.

It was dark as pitch, but this I rather liked, as there was little probability of any of the red-skins seeing me unless I stumbled upon them accidentally. My greatest danger was that my horse might run into a hole and fall down, and in this way get away from me. To avoid any such accident, I tied one end of my rawhide lariat to the bridle and the other end to my belt. I didn't propose to be left on foot, alone out on the prairie.

It was, indeed, a wise precaution that I had taken, for within the next three miles the horse, sure enough, stepped into a prairie-dog's hole, and down he went, throwing me clear over his head. Springing to his feet, before I could catch hold of the bridle, he galloped away into the darkness; but when he reached the full length of the lariat, he found that he was picketed to Bison William. I brought him up standing, and after finding my gun, which had dropped to the ground, I went up to him and in a moment was in the saddle again, and went on my way rejoicing keeping straight on my course until I came to the ravines leading into Walnut Creek, twenty-five miles from Fort Larned, where the country became rougher, requiring me to travel slower and more carefully, as I feared the horse might fall over the bank, it being difficult to see anything five feet ahead. As a good horse is not very apt to jump over a bank, if left to guide himself, I let mine pick his own way. I was now proceeding as quietly as possible, for I was in the vicinity of a band of Indians who had recently camped in that locality. I thought that I had passed somewhat above the spot, having made a little circuit to the west with that intention; but as bad luck would have it this time, when I came up near the creek I suddenly rode in among a herd of horses. The animals became frightened and ran off in every direction.

I knew at once that I was among Indian horses, and had walked into the wrong pew; so without waiting to apologize, I backed out as quickly as possible. At this moment a dog, not fifty yards away, set up a howl, and then I heard some Indians engaged in con-versation;—they were guarding the horses and had been sleeping. Hearing my horse's retreating footsteps toward the hills, and thus becoming aware that there had been an enemy in their camp, they mounted their steeds and started for me.

I urged my horse to his full speed, taking the chances of his falling into holes, and guided him up the creek bottom. The Indians followed me as fast as they could by the noise I made, but I soon distanced them; and then crossed the creek.

When I had traveled several miles in a straight course, as I supposed, I took out my compass and by the light of a match saw that I was bearing two points to the east of north. At once changing my course to the direct route, I pushed rapidly on through the darkness towards Smoky Hill River. At about three o'clock in the morning I began traveling more cautiously, as I was afraid of running into another band of Indians. Occasionally I scared up a herd of buffaloes, or antelopes, or coyotes, or deer, which would frighten my horse for a moment, but with the exception of these slight alarms I got along all right.

After crossing Smoky Hill River, I felt comparatively safe as this was the last stream I had to cross. Riding on to the northward I struck the old Santa Fe trail, ten miles from Fort Hays, just at break of day.

My horse did not seem much fatigued, and being anxious to make good time and get as near the post as possible before it was fairly daylight as there might be bands of Indians camped along Big Creek, I urged him forward as fast as he could go. As I had not "lost" any Indians, I was not now anxious to make their acquaintance, and shortly after *reveille* rode into the post. I proceeded directly to General Sheridan's headquarters, and was met at the door, by Colonel Moore, *aid-de-camp* on General Sheridan's staff who asked me on what business I had come.

"I have dispatches for General Sheridan, and my instructions from Captain Parker, commanding Fort Larned, are that they shall be delivered to the General as soon as pos-sible," said I.

Colonel Moore invited me into one of the offices, and said he would hand the dispatches to the General as soon as he got up.

"I prefer to give these dispatches to General Sheridan myself, and at once," was my reply.

The General, who was sleeping in the same building, hearing our voices, called out, "Send the man in with the dispatches." I was ushered into the General's presence, and as we had met before he recognized me and said:

"Hello, Cody, is that you?"

"Yes, sir; I have some dispatches here for you, from Captain Parker," said I, as I handed the package over to him.

He hurriedly read them, and said they were important; and then he asked me all about General Hazen and where he had gone, and about the breaking out of the Kiowas and Comanches. I gave him all the information that I possessed, and related the events and adventures of the previous day and night.

"Bill," said he, "you must have had a pretty lively ride. You certainly had a close call when you ran into the Indians on Walnut Creek. That was a good joke that you played on old Satanta. I suppose you're pretty tired after your long journey?"

"I am rather weary, General, that's a fact, as I have been in the saddle since yesterday morning;" was my reply, "but my horse is more tired than I am, and needs attention full as much if not more," I added. Thereupon the General called an orderly and gave instructions to have my animal well taken care of, and then he said, "Cody, come in and have some breakfast with me."

"No, thank you, General," said I, "Hays City is only a mile from here, and I prefer riding over there, as I know about every one in the town, and want to see some of my friends."

"Very well; do as you please, and come to the post afterwards as I want to see you," said he.

Bidding him good-morning, and telling him that I would return in a few hours, I rode over to Hays City, and at the Perry House I met many of my old friends who were of course all glad to see me. I took some refreshments and a two hours nap, and afterward returned to Fort Hays, as I was requested.

As I rode up to the headquarters I noticed several scouts in a little group, evidently engaged in conversation on some important matter. Upon inquiry I learned that General Sheridan had informed them that he was desirous of sending a dispatch to Fort Dodge, a distance of ninety-five miles.

The Indians had recently killed two or three men while they were carrying dispatches between Fort Hays and Fort Dodge, and on this account none of the scouts seemed at all anxious to volunteer, although a reward of several hundred dollars was offered to any one who would carry the dispatches. They had learned of my experiences of the previous day, and asked me if I did not think it would be a dangerous trip. I gave it as my opinion that a man might possibly go through without seeing an Indian, but that the chances were ten to one that he would have an exceedingly lively run and a hard time before he reached his destination, if he ever got there at all.

Leaving the scouts to decide among themselves as to who was to go, I reported to General Sheridan, who also informed me that he wished some one to carry dispatches to Fort Dodge. While we were talking, his chief of scouts Dick Parr, entered and stated that none of the scouts had yet volunteered. Upon hearing that I got my "brave" up a little, and said:

"General, if there is no one ready to volunteer, I'll carry your dispatches myself."

"I had not thought of asking you to do this duty, Cody, as you are already pretty hard worked. But it is really important that these dispatches should go through," said the General.

"Well, if you don't get a courier by four o'clock this afternoon, I'll be ready for business at that time. All I want is a fresh horse," said I; "meantime I'll take a little more rest."

It was not much of a rest, however, that I got, for I went over to Hays City again and had "a time with the boys."

I came back to the post at the appointed hour, and finding that no one had volunteered, I reported to General Sheridan. He had selected an excellent horse for me, and on handing me the dispatches he said:

"You can start as soon as you wish—the sooner the better; and good luck go with you, my boy."

In about an hour afterwards I was on the road, and just before dark I crossed Smoky Hill River. I had not yet urged my horse much, as I was saving his strength for the latter end of the route, and for any run that I might have to make in the case the "wild-boys" should "jump" me. So far I had not seen a sign of Indians, and as evening came on I felt comparatively safe.

I had no adventures worth relating during the night, and just before daylight I found myself approaching Saw-log Crossing, on the Pawnee Fork, having then ridden about seventy miles.

A company of colored cavalry, commanded by Major Cox, was stationed at this point, and I approached their camp cautiously, for fear that the pickets might fire upon me—as the darkey soldiers were liable to shoot first and cry "halt" afterwards. When within hearing distance I yelled out at the top of my voice, and was answered by one of the pickets. I told him not to shoot, as I was a scout from Fort Hays; and then, calling the sergeant of the guard, I went up to the vidette of the post, who readily recognized me. I entered the camp and proceeded to the tent of Major Cox, to whom I handed a letter from General Sheridan requesting him to give me a fresh horse. He at once complied with the request.

After I had slept an hour and had eaten a lunch, I again jumped into the saddle, and before sunrise I was once more on the road. It was twenty-five miles to Fort Dodge, and I arrived there between nine and ten o'clock, without having seen a single Indian.

After delivering the dispatches to the commanding officer, I met Johnny Austin, chief of scouts at this post, who was an old friend of mine. Upon his invitation I took a nap at his house, and when I awoke, fresh for business once more, he informed me that the Indians had been all around the post for the past two or three days, running off cattle and horses, and occasionally killing a stray man. It was a wonder to him that I had met with none of the red-skins on the way there. The Indians, he said, were also very thick on the Arkansas River, between Fort Dodge and Fort Larned, and making considerable trouble. Fort Dodge was located sixty-five miles west of Fort Larned, the latter post being on the Pawnee Fork, about five miles from its junction with the Arkansas River.

The commanding officer at Fort Dodge was anxious to send some dispatches to Fort Larned, but the scouts, like those at Fort Hays, were rather backward about volunteering, as it was considered a very dangerous undertaking to make the trip. As Fort Larned was my post, and as I wanted to go there anyhow, I said to Austin that I would carry dispatches, and if any of the boys wished to go along, I would like to have them for company's sake. Austin reported my offer to the commanding officer, who sent for me and said he would be happy to have me take his dispatches, if I could stand the trip on top of all that I had already done.

"All I want is a good fresh horse, sir," said I.

"I am sorry to say that we haven't a decent horse here, but we have a reliable and honest government mule, if that will do you," said the officer.

"Trot out your mule," said I, "that's good enough for me. I am ready at any time, sir."

The mule was forthcoming, and at dark I pulled out for Fort Larned, and proceeded uninterruptedly to Coon Creek, thirty miles out from Dodge. I had left the main wagon road some distance to the south, and had traveled parallel with it, thinking this to be a safer course, as the Indians might be lying in wait on the main road for dispatch bearers and scouts.

At Coon Creek I dismounted and led the mule by the bridle down to the water, where I took a drink, using my hat for a dipper. While I was engaged in getting the water, the mule jerked loose and struck out down the creek. I followed him in hopes that he would catch his foot in the bridle rein and stop, but this he seemed to have no idea of doing. He was making straight for the wagon road, and I did not know what minute he might run into a band of Indians. He finally got on the road, but instead of going back toward Fort Dodge, as I naturally expected he would do, he turned eastward toward Fort Larned, and kept up a little jog trot just ahead of me, but would not let me come up to him, although I tried it again and again. I had my gun in my hand, and several times I was strongly tempted to shoot him, and would probably have done so had it not been for fear of bringing Indians down upon me, and besides he was carrying the saddle for me. So I trudged on after the obstinate "critter," and if there ever was a government mule that deserved and received a good round cursing it was that one. I had neglected the precaution of tying one end of my lariat to his bit and the other to my belt, as I had done a few nights before, and I blamed myself for this gross piece of negligence.

Mile after mile I kept on after that mule, and every once in a while I indulged in strong language respecting the whole mule fraternity. From Coon Creek to Fort Larned it was thirty-five miles, and I finally concluded that my prospects were good for "hoofing" the whole distance. We—that is to say, the confounded mule and myself—were making pretty good time. There was nothing to hold the mule, and I was all the time trying to catch him—which urged him on. I made every step count, for I wanted to reach Fort Larned before daylight, in order to avoid if possible the Indians, to whom it would have been "pie" to have caught me there on foot.

The mule stuck to the road and kept on for Larned, and I did the same thing. Just as day was beginning to break, we—that is the mule and myself—found ourselves on a hill looking down into the valley of the Pawnee Fork, in which Fort Larned was located, only four miles away; and when the morning gun belched forth we were within half a mile of the post.

"Now," said I, "Mr. Mule, it is my turn," and raising my gun to my shoulder, in "dead earnest" this time, I blazed away, hitting the animal in the hip. Throwing a second cartridge into the gun, I let him have another shot, and I continued to pour the lead into him until I had him completely laid out. Like the great majority of government mules, he was a tough one to kill, and he clung to life with all the tenaciousness of his obstinate nature. He was, without doubt, the toughest and meanest mule I ever saw, and he died hard.

The troops, hearing the reports of the gun, came rushing out to see what was the matter. They found that the mule had passed in his chips, and when they learned the cause they all agreed that I had served him just right. Taking the saddle and bridle from the dead body, I proceeded into the post and delivered the dispatches to Captain Parker. I then went over to Dick Curtis' house, which was headquarters for the scouts, and there put in several hours of solid sleep.

During the day General Hazen returned from Fort Harker, and he also had some important dispatches to send to General Sheridan. I was feeling quite elated over my big ride; and seeing that I was getting the best of the other scouts in regard to making a record, I volunteered to carry General Hazen's dispatches to Fort Hays. The General accepted my services, although he thought it was unnecessary for me to kill myself. I told him that I had business at Fort Hays, and wished to go there anyway, and it would make no difference to the other scouts, for none of them appeared willing to undertake the trip.

Accordingly, that night I left Fort Larned on an excellent horse, and next morning at daylight found myself once more in General Sheridan's headquarters at Fort Hays. The General was surprised to see me, and still more so when I told him of the time I had made in riding to Fort Dodge, and that I had taken dispatches from Fort Dodge to Fort Larned; and when, in addition to this, I mentioned my journey of the night previous, General Sheridan thought my ride from post to post, taken as a whole, was a remarkable one, and he said that he did not know of its equal. I can safely say that I have never heard of its being beaten in a country infested with hostile Indians.

To recapitulate: I had ridden from Fort Larned to Fort Zarah (a distance of sixty-five miles) and back in twelve hours, including the time when I was taken across the Arkansas by the Indians. In the succeeding twelve hours I had gone from Fort Larned to Fort Hays, a distance of sixty-five miles. In the next twenty-four hours I had gone from Fort Hays to Fort Dodge, a distance of ninety-five miles. The following night I had traveled from Fort Dodge thirty miles on muleback and thirty-five miles on foot to Fort Larned; and the next night sixty-five miles more to Fort Hays. Altogether I had ridden (and walked) 355 miles in fifty-eight riding hours, or an average of over six miles an hour. Of course, this may not be regarded as very fast riding, but taking into consideration the fact that it was mostly done in the night and over a wild country, with no roads to follow, and that I had to be continually on the look out for Indians, it was thought at the time to be a big ride, as well as a most dangerous one.

CHAPTER TWENTY-THREE

A Night Ride of the Wounded
By Randall Parrish

During the Civil War, chances of a wounded soldier surviving, even after treatment, were slight. "A Night Ride of the Wounded" from Randall Parrish vividly captures the trauma of being transported from the battlefield to one of the makeshift hospitals, where facilities were primitive at best, medical treatments still crude, and conditions unsanitary.

—LISA PURCELL

IT WAS A WILD, RUDE SCENE WITHOUT, YET IN ITS WAY TYPICAL OF A LITTLE-UNDERSTOOD chapter of Civil War. Moreover it was one with which I was not entirely unacquainted. Years of cavalry scouting, bearing me beyond the patrol lines of the two great armies, had frequently brought me into contact with those various independent, irregular forces which, co-operating with us, often rendered most efficient service by preying on the scattered Federal camps and piercing their lines of communication. Seldom risking an engagement in the open, their policy was rather to dash down upon some outpost or poorly guarded wagon train, and retreat with a rapidity rendering pursuit hopeless. It was partisan warfare, and appealed to many ill-adapted to abide the stricter discipline of regular service. These border rangers would rendezvous under some chosen leader, strike an unexpected blow where weakness had been discovered, then disappear as quickly as they came, oftentimes scattering widely until the call went forth for some fresh assault. It was service not dissimilar to that performed during the Revolutionary struggle by Sumter and Marion in the Carolinas, and added in the aggregate many a day to the contest of the Confederacy.

Among these wild, rough riders between the lines no leader was more favorably known of our army, nor more dreaded by the enemy, than Mosby. Daring to the point of recklessness, yet wary as a fox, counting opposing numbers nothing when weighed against the advantage of surprise, tireless in saddle, audacious in resource, quick to plan and equally quick to execute, he was always where least expected, and it was seldom he failed to win reward for those who rode at his back. Possessing regular rank in the Confederate Army, making report of his operations to the commander-in-chief, his peculiar talent as a partisan leader had won him what was practically an independent command. Knowing him as I did, I was not surprised that he should now have swept suddenly out of the black night upon the very verge of the battle to drive his irritating sting into the hard-earned Federal victory.

An empty army wagon, the "U. S. A." yet conspicuous upon its canvas cover, had been overturned and fired in front of the hospital tent to give light to the raiders. Grouped about beneath the trees, and within the glow of the flames, was a picturesque squad of horsemen, hardy, tough-looking fellows the most of them, their clothing an odd mixture of uniforms, but every man heavily armed and admirably equipped for service. Some remained mounted, lounging carelessly in their saddles, but far the larger number were on foot, their bridle-reins wound about their wrists. All alike appeared alert and ready for any emergency. How many composed the party I was unable to judge with accuracy, as they constantly came and went from out the shadows beyond the circumference of the fire. As all sounds of firing had ceased, I concluded that the work planned had been already accomplished. Undoubtedly, surprised as they were, the small Federal force left to guard this point had been quickly overwhelmed and scattered.

The excitement attendant upon my release had left me for the time being utterly forgetful as to the pain of my wounds, so that weakness alone held me to the blanket upon which I had been left. The night was decidedly chilly, yet I had scarcely begun to feel its discomfort, when a man strode forward from out the nearer group and stood looking down upon me. He was a young fellow, wearing a gray artillery jacket, with high cavalry boots coming above the knees. I noticed his firm-set jaw, and a pearl-handled revolver stuck carelessly in his belt, but observed no symbol of rank about him.

"Is this Captain Wayne?" he asked, not unpleasantly, I answered by an inclination of the head, and he turned at once toward the others.

"Cass, bring three men over here, and carry this officer to the same wagon you did the others," he commanded briefly. "Fix him comfortably, but be in a hurry about it."

They lifted me in the blanket, one holding tightly at either corner, and bore me tenderly out into the night. Once one of them tripped over a projecting root, and the sudden jar of his stumble shot a spasm of pain through me, which caused me to cry out even through my clinched teeth.

"Pardon me, lads," I panted, ashamed of the weakness, "but it slipped out before I could help it."

"Don't be after a mentionin' av it, yer honor," returned a rich brogue. "Sure an me feet got so mixed oup that I wondher I didn't drap ye entoirely."

"If ye had, Clancy," said the man named Cass, grimly, "I reckon as how the Colonel would have drapped you."

At the foot of a narrow ravine, leading forth into the broader valley, we came to a covered army wagon, to which four mules had been already attached. The canvas was drawn aside, and I was lifted up and carefully deposited in the hay that thickly covered the bottom. It was so intensely dark within I could see nothing of my immediate surroundings, but a low moan told me there must be at least one other wounded man present. Outside I heard the tread of horses' hoofs, and then the sound of Mosby's voice.

"Jake," he said, "drive rapidly, but with as much care as possible. Take the lower road after you cross the bridge, and you will meet with no patrols. We will ride beside you for a couple of miles."

Then a hand thrust aside the canvas, and a face peered in. I caught a faint glimmer of stars, but could distinguish little else.

"Boys," said the leader, kindly, "I wish I might give you better transportation, but this is the only form of vehicle we can find. I reckon you'll get pretty badly bumped over the road you are going, but I'm furnishing you all the chance to get away in my power."

"For one I am grateful enough," I answered, after waiting for someone else to speak. "A little pain is preferable to imprisonment."

"After you pass the bridge you will be perfectly safe on that score," he said heartily. "Anything more I can do for any of you?"

"How many of us are there?" asked someone faintly from out the darkness.

"Oh, yes," returned Mosby, with a laugh, "I forgot; you will want to know each other. There are three of you—Colonel Colby of North Carolina, Major Wilkins of Thome's Battery, and Captain Wayne, ———th Virginia. Let that answer for an introduction, gentlemen, and now good-night. We shall guard you as long as necessary, and then must leave you to the kindly ministrations of the driver."

He reached in, leaning down from his saddle to do so, drew the blanket somewhat closer about me, and was gone. I caught the words of a sharp, short order, and the heavy wagon lurched forward, its wheels bumping over the irregularities in the road, each jolt sending a fresh spasm of pain through my tortured body.

May the merciful God ever protect me from such a ride again! It seemed interminable, while each long mile we travelled brought with it new and greater agony of mind and body. That I did not suffer alone was early evident from the low moans borne to me from out the darkness. Once a weak, trembling voice prayed for release,—a short, fervent prayer, which so impressed me in the weakness of my own anguish that I added to it "Amen," spoken unconsciously aloud.

"Who spoke?" asked the same voice, faintly.

"I am Captain Wayne," I answered, almost glad to break the terrible silence by speech of any kind; "and I merely echoed your prayer. Death would indeed prove a welcome relief from such intensity of suffering."

"Yes," he acquiesced gently. "I fear I have not sufficient strength to bear mine for long; yet I am a Christian, and there are wife and child waiting for me at home. God knows I am ready when He calls, but my duty is to live, if possible, for their sake. They will have nothing left if I pass on."

"The road must grow smoother as we come down into the valley. Are your wounds serious?"

"I was struck by fragments of a shell," he answered, and I could tell he spoke the words through his clinched teeth, "and am wounded in the head as well as the body—oh, my God!" The cry was wrung from him by a sudden tilting of the wagon, and for a moment my own pain prevented utterance.

"I hear nothing from the other man," I managed to say at last. "Colonel Mosby said there were three of us; surely the third man cannot be already dead?"

"Mercifully unconscious, I think; at least he has made no sound since I was placed in here."

"No, friends," spoke another and deeper voice from farther back within the jolting wagon, "I am not unconscious, but less noticeably in pain. I have lost a leg, yet the stump seems seared and dead, hurting me little unless I touch it."

We lapsed into solemn silence, it was such an effort to talk, and we had so little to say. Each man, no doubt, was struggling, as I know I was, to withhold expression of his agony for the sake of the others. I lay racked in every nerve, my teeth tightly clinched, my temples beaded with perspiration. I could hear the troopers riding without, the jingling of their accoutrements, and the steady beat of their horses' feet being easily distinguishable above the deeper rumble of the wheels. Then there came a quick order in Mosby's familiar voice, a calling aloud of some further directions to the driver, and afterwards nothing was distinguishable excepting the noise of our own rapid progress.

Jake drove, it seemed to me, most recklessly. I could hear the almost constant crack of his lash and the rough words of goading hurled at the straining mules. The road appeared to be filled with roots, while occasionally the wheels would strike a stone, coming down again with a jar that nearly drove me frantic. The chill night air swept in through the open front of the hood, and made me feel as if my veins were filled with ice, even while the inflammation of my wounds burned and throbbed as with fire. The pitiful moaning of the man who lay next me grew gradually fainter, and finally ceased altogether. Tortured as I was, yet I could not but think of the wife and child far away praying for his safe return. For their sake I forced back the intensity of my own sufferings and spoke into the darkness.

"The man who prayed," I said, not knowing which of my two companions it might be. "Are you suffering less, that you have ceased to moan?"

There was no answer. Then the loose hay rustled, as though someone was slowly dragging his helpless body through it. A moment later the deep voice spoke:

"He is dead," solemnly. "God has answered his prayer. His hand already begins to feel cold."

"Dead?" I echoed, inexpressibly shocked. "Do you know his name?"

"As I am Major Wilkins, it must be Colonel Colby who has died. May God be merciful to the widow and the orphan."

The hours that followed were all but endless. I knew we had reached the lower valley, for the road became more level, yet the slightest jolting now was sufficient to render me crazed with pain, and I had lost all power of restraint. My tortured nerves throbbed; the fever gripped me, and my mind began to wander. Visions of delirium came, and I dreamed dreams too terrible for record: demons danced on the drifting clouds before me, while whirling savages chanting in horrid discord stuck my frenzied body full of blazing brands. At times I was awake, calling in vain for water to quench a thirst which grew maddening, then I lapsed into a semi-consciousness that drove me wild with its delirious fancies. I knew vaguely that the Major had crept back through the darkness and passed his strong arm gently beneath my head. I heard him shouting in his deep voice to the driver for something to drink, but was unaware of any response. All became blurred, confused, bewildering. I thought it was my mother comforting me. The faint gray daylight stole in at last through the cracks of the wagon cover; I could dimly distinguish a dark face bending over me, framed by a heavy gray beard, and then, merciful unconsciousness came, and I rested as one dead beside the corpse of the Colonel.

CHAPTER TWENTY-FOUR

The Battle of Hastings
By Charles Oman

As the last great example of an endeavour to use the old infantry tactics of the Teutonic races against the now fully-developed cavalry of feudalism, we have to describe the battle of Hastings, a field which has been fought over by modern critics almost as fiercely as by the armies of Harold Godwineson and William the Bastard.

About the political and military antecedents of the engagement we have no need to speak at length. Suffice it to say that the final defeat of the old English thegnhood was immediately preceded by its most striking victory. In the summer of 1066 the newly-chosen King Harold was forced to watch two enemies at once. The Norman Duke William had openly protested against the election that had taken place in January, and was known to be gathering a great army and fleet at St. Valery. Harold knew him well, and judged him a most formidable enemy; he had called out the available naval strength of his realm, and a strong squadron was waiting all through June, July, and August, ranging between the Isle of Wight and Dover, ready to dispute the passage of the Channel. At the same time the earls and sheriffs had been warned to have the land forces of the realm ready for mobilisation, and the king with his house-carles lay by the coast in Sussex waiting for news. Duke William came not, for many a week; his host took long to gather, and when his ships were ready, August turned out a month of persistent storm and northerly winds, unsuited for the sailing of a great armament.

Meanwhile there was danger from the North also. King Harold's rebel brother, Earl Tostig, had been hovering off the coast with a small squadron, and had made a descent on the Humber in May, only to be driven away by the Northumbrian Earl Edwin. But Tostig had leagued himself with Harald Hardrada, the warlike and greedy King of Norway, and a Norse invasion was a possibility, though it seemed a less immediate danger than the Norman threat to the South Coast. September had arrived before either of the perils materialised.

By a most unlucky chance the crisis came just when the English fleet had run out of provisions, after keeping the sea for three months. On September 8, Harold ordered it round to London to revictual, and to refit, for it had suffered in the hard weather. It was to resume its cruising as soon as possible. Seven days later came the news that a Norwegian fleet of three hundred sail had appeared off the Yorkshire coast, and had ravaged Cleveland and taken Scarborough. Harold was compelled to commit the guard of the Channel to the winds, which had hitherto served him well, and to fly north with his house-carles to face Hardrada's invasion. On his way he got the disastrous message that the two Earls Edwin of Northumbria and Morkar of Mercia had been beaten in a pitched battle at Fulford, in front of York (September 20), and that the city was treating for surrender. Pressing on with all possible speed, the English king arrived at York in time to prevent this disaster, and the same afternoon he brought the Norsemen to action at Stamford Bridge on the Derwent, seven miles from the city. Here he inflicted on them an absolutely crushing defeat—Hardrada was slain, so was the rebel Earl Tostig, and the invading host was so nearly exterminated that the survivors fled on only twenty-four ships, though they had brought three hundred into the Humber.

The details of the fight are absolutely lost—we cannot unfortunately accept one word of the spirited narrative of the *Heimskringla*, for all the statements in it that can be tested are obviously incorrect. Harold *may* have offered his rebel brother pardon and an earldom, and have promised his Norse ally no more than the famous "seven feet of English earth, since his stature is greater than that of other men." The Vikings *may* have fought for long hours in their shieldring, and have failed at evening only, when their king had been slain by a chance arrow. But we cannot trust a saga which says that Morkar was King Harold Godwineson's brother, and fell at Fulford; that Earl Waltheof (then a child) took part in the fight, and that the English army was mostly composed of cavalry and archers. The whole tale of the *Heimskringla* reads like a version of the battle of Hastings transported to Stamford Bridge by some incredible error. The one detail about it recorded in the Anglo-Saxon Chronicle, namely, that the fighting included a desperate defence of a bridge against the pursuing English, does *not* appear in the Norse narrative at all. We can only be sure that both sides must have fought on foot in the old fashion of Viking and Englishman, "hewing at each other across the war-linden" till the beaten army was well-nigh annihilated.

Meanwhile, on September 28—two days after Stamford Bridge—William of Normandy had landed at Pevensey, unhindered either by the English fleet, which was refitting at London, or by the king's army, which had gone north to repel the Norwegians. The invaders began to waste the land, and met with little resistance, since the king and his chosen warriors were absent. Only at Romney, as we are told, did the landsfolk stand to their arms and beat off the raiders.

Meanwhile, the news of William's landing was rapidly brought to Harold at York, and reached him—as we are told—at the very moment when he was celebrating by a banquet his victory over the Northmen. The king received the message on October 1 or October 2: he immediately hurried southward to London with all the speed that he could make. The victorious army of Stamford Bridge was with him, and the North Country levies of Edwin and Morkar were directed to follow as fast as they were able. Harold reached London on the 7th or 8th of October, and stayed there a few days to gather in the fyrd of the neighbouring shires of the South Midlands. On the 11th he marched forth from the city to face Duke William, though his army was still incomplete. The slack or treacherous earls of the North had not yet brought up their contingents, and the men of the western shires had not been granted time enough to reach the mustering place. But Harold's heart had been stirred by the reports of the cruel ravaging of Kent and Sussex by the Normans, and he was resolved to put his cause to the arbitrament of battle as quickly as possible, though the delay of a few days would perhaps have doubled his army. A rapid march of two days brought him to the outskirts of the Andredsweald, within touch of the district on which William had for the last fortnight been exercising his cruelty.

Harold took up his position at the point where the road from London to Hastings first leaves the woods, and comes forth into the open land of the coast. The chosen ground was the lonely hill above the marshy bottom of Senlac, on which the ruins of Battle Abbey stand, but then marked to the chronicler only by "the hoar apple tree" on its ridge, just as Ashdown had been marked two centuries before by its aged thorn.

The Senlac position consists of a hill some 1,100 yards long and 150 yards broad, joined to the main bulk of the Wealden Hills by a sort of narrow isthmus with steep descents on either side. The road from London to Hastings crosses the isthmus, bisects the hill at its highest point, and then sinks down into the valley, to climb again the opposite ridge of Telham Hill. The latter is considerably the higher of the two, reaching 441 feet above the sea-level, while Harold's hill is but 275 at its summit. The English hill has a fairly gentle slope towards the south, the side which looked towards the enemy, but on the north the fall on either side of the isthmus is so steep as to be almost precipitous. The summit of the position, where it is crossed by the road, is the highest point. Here it was that King Harold fixed his two banners, the Dragon of Wessex, and his own standard of the Fighting Man.

The position was very probably one that had served before for some army of an older century, for we learn from the best authorities that there lay about it, especially on its rear, ancient banks and ditches, in some places scarped to a precipitous slope. Perhaps it may have been the camp of some part of Alfred's army in 893–894, when, posted in the east end of the Andredsweald, between the Danish fleet which had come ashore at Lymne and the other host which had camped at Middleton, he endeavoured from his central position to restrain their ravages in Kent and Sussex. No place indeed could have been more suited for a force observing newly-landed foes. It covers the only road from London which then pierced the Andredsweald, and was so close to its edge that the defenders could seek shelter in the impenetrable woods if they wished to avoid a battle.

The hill above the Senlac bottom, therefore, being the obvious position to take, for an army whose tactics compelled it to stand upon the defensive, Harold determined to offer battle there. We need not believe the authorities who tell us that the King had been thinking of delivering a night attack upon the Normans, if he should chance to find them scattered abroad on their plundering, or keeping an inefficient lookout. It was most unlikely that he should dream of groping in the dark through eight miles of rolling ground, to assault a camp whose position and arrangements must have been unknown. His army had marched hard from London, had apparently only reached Senlac at nightfall, and must have been tired out. Moreover, Harold knew William's capacities as a general, and could not have thought it likely that he would be caught unprepared. It must have seemed to him a much more possible event that the Norman might refuse to attack the strong Senlac position, and offer battle in the open and nearer the sea. It was probably in anticipation of some such chance that Harold ordered his fleet, which had run back into the mouth of the Thames in very poor order some four weeks back, to refit itself and sail round the North Foreland, to threaten the Norman vessels now drawn ashore under the cover of a wooden castle at Hastings. He can scarcely have thought it likely that William would retire over seas on the news of his approach, so the bringing up of the fleet must have been intended either to cut off the Norman retreat in the event of a great English victory on land, or to so molest the invader's stranded vessels that he would be forced to return to the shore in order to defend them.

The English position is said by one narrator of the battle to have been entrenched. According to Wace, the latest and the most diffuse of our authorities, Harold ordered his men to rear a fence of plaited woodwork from the timber of the forest which lay close at their backs. But the earlier chroniclers, without exception, speak only of the shield-wall of the English, of their dense mass covering the crest of the hill, and of relics of ancient fortifications, the *antiquus agger* and *frequentia fossarum*, and *fovea magna* mentioned above. There is nothing inconceivable in the idea of Harold's having used the old Danish device of palisading a camp, save that he had arrived only on the preceding night, and that his army was weary. In the morning hours of October 14 little could have been done, though between daybreak and the arrival of the Norman host there were certainly three long hours. But it is difficult to suppose that if any serious entrenching had been carried out, the earlier Norman narrators of the fight would have refrained from mentioning it, since the more formidable the obstacles opposed to him, the more notable and creditable would have been the triumph of their duke. And the Bayeux Tapestry, which (despite all destructive criticism) remains a primary authority for the battle, appears to show no traces of any breastwork covering the English front. Probably Wace, writing from oral tradition ninety years after the battle, had heard something of the *frequentia fossarum* by William of Poictiers, and the *agger* described by Orderic, and translated them into new entrenchments, which he described as works of the best military type of his day.

From end to end of the crest of the hill the English host was ranged in one great solid mass. Probably its line extended from the high road, which crosses the summit nearer to its eastern than to its western side, for some 200 yards to the left, as far as the head of the small steep combe (with a rivulet at its bottom) which lies 200 yards to the due east of the modern parish church; while on the other, or western, side of the high road, the battle-front was much longer, running from the road as far as the upper banks of the other ravine (with a forked brook flowing out of it from two sources) which forms the western flank of the hill. From the road to this ravine there must have been a front of 800 or 850 yards. Harold's two standards were, as we know, set up on the spot which was afterwards marked by the high altar of Battle Abbey. His standing-place must therefore have been in the left-centre rather than in the absolute middle-front of the line. But the spot was dictated by the lie of the ground—here is the actual highest point of the hill, 275 feet above sea-level, while the greater part of the position is along the 250 feet contour. It was the obvious place for the planting of standards to be visible all around, and a commander standing by them could look down from a slight vantage-ground on the whole front of his host.

In this array, the English centre being slightly curved forward, its flank slightly curved back, the army looked to the Normans more like a circular mass than a deployed line. Although the Northumbrian and west-country levies were still missing, the army must have numbered many thousands, for the fyrd of south and central England and was present in full force, and stirred to great wrath by the ravages of the Normans. It is impossible to guess at the strength of the host: the figures of the chroniclers, which sometimes swell up to hundreds of thousands, are wholly useless. As the position was about 1,100 yards long, and the space required by a single warrior swinging his axe or hurling his javelin was some three feet, the front rank must have been at least some eleven hundred or twelve hundred strong. The hilltop was completely covered by the English, whose spear-shafts appeared to the Normans like a wood, so that they cannot have been a mere thin line: if they were some eight or ten deep, the total must have reached ten or eleven thousand men. Of these the smaller part must have been composed of the fully-armed warriors, the king's house-carles, the thegnhood, and the wealthier and better-equipped freemen, the class owning some five hides of land. The rudely-armed levies of the fyrd must have constituted the great bulk of the army: they bore, as the Bayeux Tapestry shows, the most miscellaneous arms—swords, javelins, clubs, axes, a few bows, and probably even rude instruments of husbandry turned to warlike uses. Their only defensive armour was the round or kite-shaped shield: body and head were clothed only in the tunic and cap of everyday wear.

In their battle array we know that the well-armed house-carles—perhaps two thousand chosen and veteran troops—were grouped in the centre around the king and the royal standards. The fyrd, divided no doubt according to its shires, was ranged on either flank. Presumably the thegns and other fully-armed men formed its front ranks, while the peasantry stood behind and backed them up, though at first only able to hurl their weapons at the advancing foe over the heads of their more fully-equipped fellows.

We must now turn to the Normans. Duke William had undertaken his expedition not as the mere feudal head of the barons of Normandy, but rather as the managing director of a great joint-stock company for the conquest of England and, in which not only his own subjects, but hundreds of adventurers, poor and rich, from all parts of western Europe had taken shares. At the assembly of Lillebonne the Norman baronage had refused in their corporate capacity to undertake the vindication of their duke's claims on England. But all, or nearly all, of them had consented to serve under him as volunteers, bringing not merely their usual feudal contingent, but as many men as they could get together. In return they were to receive the spoils of the island kingdom if the enterprise went well. On similar terms William had accepted offers of help from all quarters: knights and sergeants flocked in, ready, "some for land and some for pence," to back his claim. It seems that, though the native Normans were the core of the invading army, yet the strangers considerably outnumbered them on the muster-rolls. Great nobles like Eustace Count of Boulogne, the Breton Count Alan Fergant, and Haimar of Thouars were ready to risk their lives and resources on the chance of an ample profit. French, Bretons, Flemings, Angevins, knights from the more distant regions of Aquitaine and Lotharingia, even—if Guy of Amiens speaks truly—stray fighting men from among the Norman conquerors of Naples and Sicily, joined the host.

Many months had been spent in the building of a fleet at the mouth of the Dive. Its numbers, exaggerated to absurd figures by many chroniclers, may possibly have reached the six hundred and ninety-six vessels given to the duke by the most moderate estimate. What was the total of the warriors which it carried is as uncertain as its own numbers. If any analogies may be drawn from contemporary hosts, the cavalry must have formed a very heavy proportion of the whole. In continental armies the foot-soldiery were so despised that an experienced general devoted all his attention to increasing the numbers of his horse. If we guess that there may have been three thousand or even four thousand mounted men, and eight thousand or nine thousand foot-soldiers, we are going as far as probability carries us, and must confess that our estimate is wholly arbitrary. The most modest figure given by the chroniclers is sixty thousand fighting men; but, considering their utter inability to realise the meaning of high numbers, we are dealing liberally with them if we allow a fifth of that estimate.

After landing at Pevensey on September 28, William had moved to Hastings and built a wooden castle there for the protection of his fleet. It was then in his power to have moved on London unopposed, for Harold was only starting on his march from York. But the duke had resolved to fight near his base, and spent the fortnight which was at his disposal in the systematic harrying of Kent and Sussex. When his scouts told him that Harold was at hand, and had pitched his camp by Senlac hill, he saw that his purpose was attained; he would be able to fight at his own chosen moment, and at only a few miles' distance from his ships. At daybreak on the morning of October 14, William bade his host get in array, and marched over the eight miles of rolling ground which separate Hastings and Senlac. When they reached the summit of the hill at Telham, the English position came in sight, on the opposite hill, not much more than a mile away.

On seeing the hour of conflict at hand, the duke and his knights drew on their mail-shirts, which, to avoid fatigue, they had not yet assumed, and the host was arrayed in battle order. The form which William had chosen was that of three parallel corps, each containing infantry and cavalry. The centre was composed of the native contingents of Normandy; the left mainly of Bretons and men from Maine and Anjou; the right, of French and Flemings. But there seem to have been some Normans in the flanking divisions also. The duke himself, as was natural, took command in the centre, the wings fell respectively to the Breton Count Alan Fergant and to Eustace of Boulogne: with the latter was associated Roger of Montgomery, a great Norman baron.

In each division there were three lines: the first was composed of bowmen mixed with arbalesters: the second was composed of foot-soldiery armed not with missile weapons but with pike and sword. Most of them seem to have worn mail-shirts, unlike the infantry of the English fyrd. In the rear was the really important section of the army, the mailed knights. We may presume that William intended to harass and thin the English masses with his archery, to attack them seriously with his heavy infantry, who might perhaps succeed in getting to close quarters and engaging the enemy hand to hand; but evidently the crushing blow was to be given by the great force of horsemen who formed the third line of each division.

The Normans deployed on the slopes of Telham, and then began their advance over the rough valley which separated them from the English position.

When they came within range, the archery opened upon the English, and not without effect; at first there must have been little reply to the showers of arrows, since Harold had but very few bowmen in his ranks. The shieldwall, moreover, can have given but a partial protection, though it no doubt served its purpose to some extent. When, however, the Normans advanced farther up the slope, they were received with a furious discharge of missiles of every kind, javelins, lances, taper-axes, and even—if William of Poictiers is to be trusted—rude weapons more appropriate to the neolithic age than to the eleventh century, great stones bound to wooden handles and launched in the same manner that was used for the casting-axe. The archers were apparently swept back by the storm of missiles, but the heavy armed foot pushed up to the front of the English line and got to hand-to-hand fighting with Harold's men. They could, however, make not the least impression on the defenders, and were perhaps already recoiling when William ordered up his cavalry. The horsemen rode up the slope already strewn with corpses, and dashed into the fight. Foremost among them was a minstrel named Taillefer, who galloped forward cheering on his comrades, and playing like a *jougleur* with his sword, which he kept casting into the air and then catching again. He burst right through the shieldwall and into the English line, where he was slain after cutting down several opponents. Behind him came the whole Norman knighthood, chanting their battle-song, and pressing their horses up the slope as hard as they could ride. The foot-soldiery dropped back—through the intervals between the three divisions, as we may suppose—and the duke's cavalry dashed against the long front of the shield-wall, whose front rank men they may have swept down by their mere impetus. Into the English mass, however, they could not break: there was a fearful crash, and a wild interchange of blows, but the line did not yield at any point. Nay, more, the assailants were ere long abashed by the fierce resistance that they met; the English axes cut through shield and mail, lopping off limbs and felling even horses to the ground. Never had the continental horsemen met such infantry before. After a space the Bretons and Angevins of the left wing felt their hearts fail, and recoiled down the hill in wild disorder, many men unhorsed and overthrown in the marshy bottom at the foot of the slope. All along the line the onset wavered, and the greater part of the host gave back, though the centre and right did not fly in wild disorder like the Bretons. A rumour ran along the front that the duke had fallen, and William had to bare his head and to ride down the ranks, crying that he lived, and would yet win the day, before he could check the retreat of his warriors. His brother Odo aided him to rally the waverers, and the greater part of the host was soon restored to order.

As it chanced, the rout of the Norman left wing was destined to bring nothing but profit to William. A great mass of the shire-levies on the English right, when they saw the Bretons flying, came pouring after them down the hill. They had forgotten that their sole chance of victory lay in keeping their front firm till the whole strength of the assailant should be exhausted. It was mad to pursue when two-thirds of the hostile army was intact, and its spirit still unbroken. Seeing the tumultuous crowd rushing after the flying Bretons, William wheeled his centre and threw it upon the flank of the pursuers. Caught in disorder, with their ranks broken and scattered, the rash peasantry were ridden down in a few moments. Their light shields, swords, and javelins availed them nothing against the rush of the Norman horse, and the whole horde, to the number of several thousands, were cut to pieces. The great bulk of the English host, however, had not followed the routed Bretons, and the duke saw that his day's work was but begun. Forming up his disordered squadrons, he ordered a second general attack on the line. Then followed an encounter even more fierce than the first. It would appear that the fortune of the Normans was somewhat better in this than in the earlier struggle: one or two temporary breaches were made in the English mass, probably in the places where it had been weakened by the rash onset of the shire-levies an hour before. Gyrth and Leofwine, Harold's two brothers, fell in the forefront of the fight, the former by William's own hand, if we may trust one good contemporary authority. Yet, on the whole, the duke had got little profit by his assault: the English had suffered severe loss, but their long line of shields and axes still crowned the slope, and their cries of "Out! out!" and "Holy Cross!" still rang forth in undaunted tones.

A sudden inspiration then came to William, suggested by the disaster which had befallen the English right in the first conflict. He determined to try the expedient of a feigned flight, a stratagem not unknown to Bretons and Normans of earlier ages. By his orders a considerable portion of the assailants suddenly wheeled about and retired in seeming disorder. The English thought, with more excuse on this occasion than on the last, that the enemy was indeed routed, and for the second time a great body of them broke the line and rushed after the retreating squadrons. When they were well on their way down the slope, William repeated his former procedure. The intact portion of his host fell upon the flanks of the pursuers, while those who had simulated flight faced about and attacked them in front. The result was again a foregone conclusion: the disordered men of the fyrd were hewn to pieces, and few or none of them escaped back to their comrades on the height. But the slaughter in this period of the fight did not fall wholly on the English; a part of the Norman troops who had carried out the false flight suffered some loss by falling into a deep ditch,—perhaps the remains of old entrenchments, perhaps the "rhine" which drained the Senlac bottom,—and were there smothered or trodden down by the comrades who rode over them. But the loss at this point must have been insignificant compared with that of the English.

Harold's host was now much thinned and somewhat shaken, but, in spite of the disasters which had befallen them, they drew together their thinned ranks, and continued the fight. The struggle was still destined to endure for many hours, for the most daring onsets of the Norman chivalry could not yet burst into the serried mass around the standards. The bands which had been cut to pieces were mere shire-levies, and the well-armed house-carles had refused to break their ranks, and still formed a solid core for the remainder of the host.

The fourth act of the battle consisted of a series of vigorous assaults by the duke's horsemen, alternating with volleys of arrows poured in during the intervals between the charges. The Saxon mass was subjected to exactly the same trial which befell the British squares in the battle of Waterloo—incessant charges by a gallant cavalry mixed with a destructive hail of missiles. Nothing could be more maddening than such an ordeal to the infantry-soldier, rooted to the spot by the necessities of his formation. The situation was frightful: the ranks were filled with wounded men unable to retire to the rear through the dense mass of their comrades, unable even to sink to the ground for the hideous press. The enemy was now attacking on both flanks: shields and mail had been riven: the supply of missile spears had given out: the English could but stand passive, waiting for the night or for the utter exhaustion of the enemy. The cavalry onsets must have been almost a relief compared with the desperate waiting between the acts, while the arrow-shower kept beating in on the thinning host. We have indications that, in spite of the disasters of the noon, some of the English made yet a third sally to beat off the archery. Individuals worked to frenzy by the weary standing still, seem to have occasionally burst out of the line to swing axe or sword freely in the open and meet a certain death. But the mass held firm—"a strange manner of battle," says William of Poictiers, "where the one side works by constant motion and ceaseless charges, while the other can but endure passively as it stands fixed to the sod. The Norman arrow and sword worked on: in the English ranks the only movement was the dropping of the dead: the living stood motionless." Desperate as was their plight, the English still held out till evening; though William himself led charge after charge against them, and had three horses killed beneath him, they could not be scattered while their king still survived and their standards still stood upright. It was finally the arrow rather than the sword that settled the day: the duke is said to have bade his archers shoot not point-blank, but with a high trajectory, so that the shafts fell all over the English host, and not merely on its front ranks. One of these chance shafts struck Harold in the eye and gave him a mortal wound. The arrow-shower, combined with the news of the king's fall, at last broke up the English host: after a hundred ineffective charges, a band of Norman knights burst into the midst of the mass, hewed Harold to pieces as he lay wounded at the foot of his banners, and cut down both the Dragon of Wessex and the Fighting Man.

The remnant of the English were now at last constrained to give ground: the few thousands—it may rather have been the few hundreds—who still clung to the crest of the bloodstained hill turned their backs to the foe and sought shelter in the friendly forest in their rear. Some fled on foot through the trees, some seized the horses of the thegns and house-carles from the camp and rode off upon them. But even in retreat they took some vengeance on the conquerors. The Normans, following in disorder, swept down the steep slope at the back of the hill, scarped like a glacis and impassable for horsemen,—the back defence, as we have conjectured, of some ancient camp of other days. Many of the knights, in the confused evening light, plunged down this trap, lost their footing, and lay floundering, man and horse, in the ravine at the bottom. Turning back, the last of the English swept down on them and cut them to pieces before resuming their flight. The Normans thought for a moment that succours had arrived to join the English—and, indeed, Edwin and Morkar's Northern levies were long overdue. The duke himself had to rally them, and to silence the fainthearted counsels of Eustace of Boulogne, who bade him draw back when the victory was won. When the Normans came on more cautiously, following, no doubt, the line of the isthmus and not plunging down the slopes, the last of the English melted away into the forest and disappeared. The hard day's work was done.

The stationary tactics of the phalanx of axemen had failed decisively before William's combination of archers and cavalry, in spite of the fact that the ground had been favourable to the defensive. The exhibition of desperate courage on the part of the English had only served to increase the number of the slain. Of all the chiefs of the army, only Esegar the Staller and Leofric, Abbot of Bourne, are recorded to have escaped, and both of them were dangerously wounded. The king and his brothers, the stubborn house-carles, and the whole thegnhood of Southern England had perished on the field. The English loss was never calculated; practically it amounted to the entire army. Nor is it possible to guess that of the Normans: one chronicle gives twelve thousand,—the figure is absurd, and the authority is not a good or a trustworthy one for English history. But whatever was the relative slaughter on the two sides, the lesson of the battle was unmistakable. The best of infantry, armed only with weapons for close fight and destitute of cavalry support, were absolutely helpless before a capable general who knew how to combine the horseman and the archer. The knights, if unsupported by the bowmen, might have surged forever against the impregnable shield-wall. The archers, unsupported by the knights, could easily have been driven off the field by a general charge. United by the skilful hand of William, they were invincible.

CHAPTER TWENTY-FIVE

A Grey Sleeve
By Stephen Crane

Divided loyalties is a recurring theme in Civil War fiction. Stephen Crane, who wrote one of the most famous Civil War novels, The Red Badge of Courage, *offers his version in "A Grey Sleeve." Here, a feisty young Southern woman steps up against a Northern captain in order to protect her home and family—and enchants her would-be enemy in the process. Both of them must then face the consequences of a nation divided.*

—LISA PURCELL

I

IT LOOKS AS IF IT MIGHT RAIN THIS AFTERNOON," REMARKED THE LIEUTENANT OF artillery.

"So it does," the infantry captain assented. He glanced casually at the sky. When his eyes had lowered to the green-shadowed landscape before him, he said fretfully: "I wish those fellows out yonder would quit pelting at us. They've been at it since noon."

At the edge of a grove of maples, across wide fields, there occasionally appeared little puffs of smoke of a dull hue in this gloom of sky which expressed an impending rain. The long wave of blue and steel in the field moved uneasily at the eternal barking of the far-away sharpshooters, and the men, leaning upon their rifles, stared at the grove of maples. Once a private turned to borrow some tobacco from a comrade in the rear rank, but, with his hand still stretched out, he continued to twist his head and glance at the distant trees. He was afraid the enemy would shoot him at a time when he was not looking.

Suddenly the artillery officer said: "See what's coming!"

Along the rear of the brigade of infantry a column of cavalry was sweeping at a hard gallop. A lieutenant, riding some yards to the right of the column, bawled furiously at the four troopers just at the rear of the colors. They had lost distance and made a little gap, but at the shouts of the lieutenant they urged their horses forward. The bugler, careering along behind the captain of the troop, fought and tugged like a wrestler to keep his frantic animal from bolting far ahead of the column.

On the springy turf the innumerable hoofs thundered in a swift storm of sound. In the brown faces of the troopers their eyes were set like bits of flashing steel.

The long line of the infantry regiments standing at ease underwent a sudden movement at the rush of the passing squadron. The foot soldiers turned their heads to gaze at the torrent of horses and men.

The yellow folds of the flag fluttered back in silken, shuddering waves, as if it were a reluctant thing. Occasionally a giant spring of a charger would rear the firm and sturdy figure of a soldier suddenly head and shoulders above his comrades. Over the noise of the scudding hoofs could be heard the creaking of leather trappings, the jingle and clank of steel, and the tense, low-toned commands or appeals of the men to their horses; and the horses were mad with the headlong sweep of this movement. Powerful under jaws bent back and straightened, so that the bits were clamped as rigidly as vices upon the teeth, and glistening necks arched in desperate resistance to the hands at the bridles. Swinging their heads in rage at the granite laws of their lives, which compelled even their angers and their ardors to chosen directions and chosen faces, their flight was as a flight of harnessed demons.

The captain's bay kept its pace at the head of the squadron with the lithe bounds of a thoroughbred, and this horse was proud as a chief at the roaring trample of his fellows behind him. The captain's glance was calmly upon the grove of maples whence the sharp-shooters of the enemy had been picking at the blue line. He seemed to be reflecting. He stolidly rose and fell with the plunges of his horse in all the indifference of a deacon's figure seated plumply in church. And it occurred to many of the watching infantry to wonder why this officer could remain imperturbable and reflective when his squadron was thundering and swarming behind him like the rushing of a flood.

The column swung in a saber-curve toward a break in a fence, and dashed into a roadway. Once a little plank bridge was encountered, and the sound of the hoofs upon it was like the long roll of many drums. An old captain in the infantry turned to his first lieutenant and made a remark, which was a compound of bitter disparagement of cavalry in general and soldierly admiration of this particular troop.

Suddenly the bugle sounded, and the column halted with a jolting upheaval amid sharp, brief cries. A moment later the men had tumbled from their horses and, carbines in hand, were running in a swarm toward the grove of maples. In the road one of every four of the troopers was standing with braced legs, and pulling and hauling at the bridles of four frenzied horses.

The captain was running awkwardly in his boots. He held his saber low, so that the point often threatened to catch in the turf. His yellow hair ruffled out from under his faded cap. "Go in hard now!" he roared, in a voice of hoarse fury. His face was violently red.

The troopers threw themselves upon the grove like wolves upon a great animal. Along the whole front of woods there was the dry crackling of musketry, with bitter, swift flashes and smoke that writhed like stung phantoms. The troopers yelled shrilly and spanged bullets low into the foliage.

For a moment, when near the woods, the line almost halted. The men struggled and fought for a time like swimmers encountering a powerful current. Then with a supreme effort they went on again. They dashed madly at the grove, whose foliage from the high light of the field was as inscrutable as a wall.

Then suddenly each detail of the calm trees became apparent, and with a few more frantic leaps the men were in the cool gloom of the woods. There was a heavy odor as from burned paper. Wisps of grey smoke wound upward. The men halted and, grimy, perspiring, and puffing, they searched the recesses of the woods with eager, fierce glances. Figures could be seen flitting afar off. A dozen carbines rattled at them in an angry volley.

During this pause the captain strode along the line, his face lit with a broad smile of contentment. "When he sends this crowd to do anything, I guess he'll find we do it pretty sharp," he said to the grinning lieutenant.

"Say, they didn't stand that rush a minute, did they?" said the subaltern. Both officers were profoundly dusty in their uniforms, and their faces were soiled like those of two urchins.

Out in the grass behind them were three tumbled and silent forms.

Presently the line moved forward again. The men went from tree to tree like hunters stalking game. Some at the left of the line fired occasionally, and those at the right gazed curiously in that direction. The men still breathed heavily from their scramble across the field.

Of a sudden a trooper halted and said: "Hello! there's a house!" Every one paused. The men turned to look at their leader.

The captain stretched his neck and swung his head from side to side. "By George, it is a house!" he said.

Through the wealth of leaves there vaguely loomed the form of a large white house. These troopers, brown-faced from many days of campaigning, each feature of them telling of their placid confidence and courage, were stopped abruptly by the appearance of this house. There was some subtle suggestion—some tale of an unknown thing—which watched them from they knew not what part of it.

A rail fence girded a wide lawn of tangled grass. Seven pines stood along a drive-way which led from two distant posts of a vanished gate. The blue-clothed troopers moved forward until they stood at the fence peering over it.

The captain put one hand on the top rail and seemed to be about to climb the fence, when suddenly he hesitated, and said in a low voice: "Watson, what do you think of it?"

The lieutenant stared at the house. "Derned if I know!" he replied.

The captain pondered. It happened that the whole company had turned a gaze of profound awe and doubt upon this edifice which confronted them. The men were very silent.

At last the captain swore and said: "We are certainly a pack of fools. Derned old deserted house halting a company of Union cavalry, and making us gape like babies!"

"Yes, but there's something—something—" insisted the subaltern in a half stammer.

"Well, if there's 'something—something' in there, I'll get it out," said the captain. "Send Sharpe clean around to the other side with about twelve men, so we will sure bag your 'something—something,' and I'll take a few of the boys and find out what's in the d——d old thing!"

He chose the nearest eight men for his "storming party," as the lieutenant called it. After he had waited some minutes for the others to get into position, he said "Come ahead" to his eight men, and climbed the fence.

The brighter light of the tangled lawn made him suddenly feel tremendously apparent, and he wondered if there could be some mystic thing in the house which was regarding this approach. His men trudged silently at his back. They stared at the windows and lost themselves in deep speculations as to the probability of there being, perhaps, eyes behind the blinds—malignant eyes, piercing eyes.

Suddenly a corporal in the party gave vent to a startled exclamation, and half threw his carbine into position. The captain turned quickly, and the corporal said: "I saw an arm move the blinds—an arm with a grey sleeve!"

"Don't be a fool, Jones, now," said the captain sharply.

"I swear t'—" began the corporal, but the captain silenced him.

When they arrived at the front of the house, the troopers paused, while the captain went softly up the front steps. He stood before the large front door and studied it. Some crickets chirped in the long grass, and the nearest pine could be heard in its endless sighs. One of the privates moved uneasily, and his foot crunched the gravel. Suddenly the captain swore angrily and kicked the door with a loud crash. It flew open.

II

The bright lights of the day flashed into the old house when the captain angrily kicked open the door. He was aware of a wide hallway, carpeted with matting and extending deep into the dwelling. There was also an old walnut hat-rack and a little marble-topped table with a vase and two books upon it. Farther back was a great, venerable fireplace containing dreary ashes.

But directly in front of the captain was a young girl. The flying open of the door had obviously been an utter astonishment to her, and she remained transfixed there in the middle of the floor, staring at the captain with wide eyes.

She was like a child caught at the time of a raid upon the cake. She wavered to and fro upon her feet, and held her hands behind her. There were two little points of terror in her eyes, as she gazed up at the young captain in dusty blue, with his reddish, bronze complexion, his yellow hair, his bright saber held threateningly.

These two remained motionless and silent, simply staring at each other for some moments.

The captain felt his rage fade out of him and leave his mind limp. He had been violently angry, because this house had made him feel hesitant, wary. He did not like to be wary. He liked to feel confident, sure. So he had kicked the door open, and had been prepared, to march in like a soldier of wrath.

But now he began, for one thing, to wonder if his uniform was so dusty and old in appearance. Moreover, he had a feeling that his face was covered with a compound of dust, grime, and perspiration. He took a step forward and said: "I didn't mean to frighten you." But his voice was coarse from his battle-howling. It seemed to him to have hempen fibers in it.

The girl's breath came in little, quick gasps, and she looked at him as she would have looked at a serpent.

"I didn't mean to frighten you," he said again.

The girl, still with her hands behind her, began to back away.

"Is there any one else in the house?" he went on, while slowly following her. "I don't wish to disturb you, but we had a fight with some rebel skirmishers in the woods, and I thought maybe some of them might have come in here. In fact, I was pretty sure of it. Are there any of them here?"

The girl looked at him and said, "No!" He wondered why extreme agitation made the eyes of some women so limpid and bright.

"Who is here besides yourself?"

By this time his pursuit had driven her to the end of the hall, and she remained there with her back to the wall and her hands still behind her. When she answered this question, she did not look at him but down at the floor. She cleared her voice and then said: "There is no one here."

"No one?"

She lifted her eyes to him in that appeal that the human being must make even to falling trees, crashing boulders, the sea in a storm, and said, "No, no, there is no one here." He could plainly see her tremble.

Of a sudden he bethought him that she continually kept her hands behind her. As he recalled her air when first discovered, he remembered she appeared precisely as a child detected at one of the crimes of childhood. Moreover, she had always backed away from him. He thought now that she was concealing something which was an evidence of the presence of the enemy in the house.

"What are you holding behind you?" he said suddenly.

She gave a little quick moan, as if some grim hand had throttled her.

"What are you holding behind you?"

"Oh, nothing—please. I am not holding anything behind me; indeed I'm not."

"Very well. Hold your hands out in front of you, then."

"Oh, indeed, I'm not holding anything behind me. Indeed I'm not."

"Well," he began. Then he paused, and remained for a moment dubious. Finally, he laughed. "Well, I shall have my men search the house, anyhow. I'm sorry to trouble you, but I feel sure that there is some one here whom we want." He turned to the corporal, who with the other men was gaping quietly in at the door, and said: "Jones, go through the house."

As for himself, he remained planted in front of the girl, for she evidently did not dare to move and allow him to see what she held so carefully behind her back. So she was his prisoner.

The men rummaged around on the ground floor of the house. Sometimes the captain called to them, "Try that closet," "Is there any cellar?" But they found no one, and at last they went trooping toward the stairs which led to the second floor.

But at this movement on the part of the men the girl uttered a cry—a cry of such fright and appeal that the men paused. "Oh, don't go up there! Please don't go up there!—ple-ease! There is no one there! Indeed—indeed there is not! Oh, ple-ease!"

"Go on, Jones," said the captain calmly.

The obedient corporal made a preliminary step, and the girl bounded toward the stairs with another cry.

As she passed him, the captain caught sight of that which she had concealed behind her back, and which she had forgotten in this supreme moment. It was a pistol.

She ran to the first step, and standing there, faced the men, one hand extended with perpendicular palm, and the other holding the pistol at her side. "Oh, please, don't go up there! Nobody is there—indeed, there is not! P-l-e-a-s-e!" Then suddenly she sank swiftly down upon the step, and, huddling forlornly, began to weep in the agony and with the convulsive tremors of an infant. The pistol fell from her fingers and rattled down to the floor.

The astonished troopers looked at their astonished captain. There was a short silence.

Finally, the captain stooped and picked up the pistol. It was a heavy weapon of the army pattern. He ascertained that it was empty.

He leaned toward the shaking girl, and said gently: "Will you tell me what you were going to do with this pistol?"

He had to repeat the question a number of times, but at last a muffled voice said, "Nothing."

"Nothing!" He insisted quietly upon a further answer. At the tender tones of the captain's voice, the phlegmatic corporal turned and winked gravely at the man next to him.

"Won't you tell me?"

The girl shook her head.

"Please tell me!"

The silent privates were moving their feet uneasily and wondering how long they were to wait.

The captain said: "Please, won't you tell me?"

Then this girl's voice began in stricken tones half coherent, and amid violent sobbing: "It was grandpa's. He—he—he said he was going to shoot anybody who came in here—he didn't care if there were thousands of 'em. And—and I know he would, and I was afraid they'd kill him. And so—and—so I stole away his pistol—and I was going to hide it when you—you—you kicked open the door."

The men straightened up and looked at each other. The girl began to weep again.

The captain mopped his brow. He peered down at the girl. He mopped his brow again. Suddenly he said: "Ah, don't cry like that."

He moved restlessly and looked down at his boots. He mopped his brow again.

Then he gripped the corporal by the arm and dragged him some yards back from the others. "Jones," he said, in an intensely earnest voice, "will you tell me what in the devil I am going to do?"

The corporal's countenance became illuminated with satisfaction at being thus requested to advise his superior officer. He adopted an air of great thought, and finally said: "Well, of course, the feller with the grey sleeve must be upstairs, and we must get past the girl and up there somehow. Suppose I take her by the arm and lead her—"

"What!" interrupted the captain from between his clinched teeth. As he turned away from the corporal, he said fiercely over his shoulder: "You touch that girl and I'll split your skull!"

III

The corporal looked after his captain with an expression of mingled amazement, grief, and philosophy. He seemed to be saying to himself that there unfortunately were times, after all, when one could not rely upon the most reliable of men. When he returned to the group he found the captain bending over the girl and saying: "Why is it that you don't want us to search upstairs?"

The girl's head was buried in her crossed arms. Locks of her hair had escaped from their fastenings, and these fell upon her shoulder.

"Won't you tell me?"

The corporal here winked again at the man next to him.

"Because," the girl moaned, "because—there isn't anybody up there."

The captain at last said timidly: "Well, I'm afraid—I'm afraid we'll have to—"

The girl sprang to her feet again, and implored him with her hands. She looked deep into his eyes with her glance, which was at this time like that of the fawn when it says to the hunter, "Have mercy upon me!"

These two stood regarding each other. The captain's foot was on the bottom step, but he seemed to be shrinking. He wore an air of being deeply wretched and ashamed. There was a silence!

Suddenly the corporal said in a quick, low tone: "Look out, captain!"

All turned their eyes swiftly toward the head of the stairs. There had appeared there a youth in a grey uniform. He stood looking coolly down at them. No word was said by the troopers. The girl gave vent to a little wail of desolation, "O Harry!"

He began slowly to descend the stairs. His right arm was in a white sling, and there were some fresh blood-stains upon the cloth. His face was rigid and deathly pale, but his eyes flashed like lights. The girl was again moaning in an utterly dreary fashion, as the youth came slowly down toward the silent men in blue.

Six steps from the bottom of the flight he halted and said: "I reckon it's me you're looking for."

The troopers had crowded forward a trifle and, posed in lithe, nervous attitudes, were watching him like cats. The captain remained unmoved. At the youth's question he merely nodded his head and said, "Yes."

The young man in grey looked down at the girl, and then, in the same even tone which now, however, seemed to vibrate with suppressed fury, he said: "And is that any reason why you should insult my sister?"

At this sentence, the girl intervened, desperately, between the young man in grey and the officer in blue. "Oh, don't, Harry, don't! He was good to me! He was good to me, Harry—indeed he was!"

The youth came on in his quiet, erect fashion, until the girl could have touched either of the men with her hand, for the captain still remained with his foot upon the first step. She continually repeated: "O Harry! O Harry!"

The youth in grey maneuvered to glare into the captain's face, first over one shoulder of the girl and then over the other. In a voice that rang like metal, he said: "You are armed and unwounded, while I have no weapons and am wounded; but—"

The captain had stepped back and sheathed his saber. The eyes of these two men were gleaming fire, but otherwise the captain's countenance was imperturbable. He said: "You are mistaken. You have no reason to—"

"You lie!"

All save the captain and the youth in grey started in an electric movement. These two words crackled in the air like shattered glass. There was a breathless silence.

The captain cleared his throat. His look at the youth contained a quality of singular and terrible ferocity, but he said in his stolid tone: "I don't suppose you mean what you say now."

Upon his arm he had felt the pressure of some unconscious little fingers. The girl was leaning against the wall as if she no longer knew how to keep her balance, but those fingers—he held his arm very still. She murmured: "O Harry, don't! He was good to me—indeed he was!"

The corporal had come forward until he in a measure confronted the youth in grey, for he saw those fingers upon the captain's arm, and he knew that sometimes very strong men were not able to move hand nor foot under such conditions.

The youth had suddenly seemed to become weak. He breathed heavily and clung to the rail. He was glaring at the captain, and apparently summoning all his will power to combat his weakness. The corporal addressed him with profound straightforwardness: "Don't you be a derned fool!" The youth turned toward him so fiercely that the corporal threw up a knee and an elbow like a boy who expects to be cuffed.

The girl pleaded with the captain. "You won't hurt him, will you? He don't know what he's saying. He's wounded, you know. Please don't mind him!"

"I won't touch him," said the captain, with rather extraordinary earnestness; "don't you worry about him at all. I won't touch him!"

Then he looked at her, and the girl suddenly withdrew her fingers from his arm.

The corporal contemplated the top of the stairs, and remarked without surprise: "There's another of 'em coming!"

An old man was clambering down the stairs with much speed. He waved a cane wildly. "Get out of my house, you thieves! Get out! I won't have you cross my threshold! Get out!" He mumbled and wagged his head in an old man's fury. It was plainly his intention to assault them.

And so it occurred that a young girl became engaged in protecting a stalwart captain, fully armed, and with eight grim troopers at his back, from the attack of an old man with a walking-stick!

A blush passed over the temples and brow of the captain, and he looked particularly savage and weary. Despite the girl's efforts, he suddenly faced the old man.

"Look here," he said distinctly, "we came in because we had been fighting in the woods yonder, and we concluded that some of the enemy were in this house, especially when we saw a grey sleeve at the window. But this young man is wounded, and I have nothing to say to him. I will even take it for granted that there are no others like him upstairs. We will go away, leaving your d——d old house just as we found it! And we are no more thieves and rascals than you are!"

The old man simply roared: "I haven't got a cow nor a pig nor a chicken on the place! Your soldiers have stolen everything they could carry away. They have torn down half my fences for firewood. This afternoon some of your accursed bullets even broke my window panes!"

The girl had been faltering: "Grandpa! O grandpa!"

The captain looked at the girl. She returned his glance from the shadow of the old man's shoulder. After studying her face a moment, he said: "Well, we will go now." He strode toward the door, and his men clanked docilely after him.

At this time there was the sound of harsh cries and rushing footsteps from without. The door flew open, and a whirlwind composed of blue-coated troopers came in with a swoop. It was headed by the lieutenant. "Oh, here you are!" he cried, catching his breath. "We thought—Oh, look at the girl!"

The captain said intensely: "Shut up, you fool!"

The men settled to a halt with a clash and a bang. There could be heard the dulled sound of many hoofs outside of the house.

"Did you order up the horses?" inquired the captain.

"Yes. We thought—"

"Well, then, let's get out of here," interrupted the captain morosely.

The men began to filter out into the open air. The youth in grey had been hanging dismally to the railing of the stairway. He now was climbing slowly up to the second floor. The old man was addressing himself directly to the serene corporal.

"Not a chicken on the place!" he cried.

"Well, I didn't take your chickens, did I?"

"No, maybe you didn't, but—"

The captain crossed the hall and stood before the girl in rather a culprit's fashion. "You are not angry at me, are you?" he asked timidly.

"No," she said. She hesitated a moment, and then suddenly held out her hand. "You were good to me—and I'm—much obliged."

The captain took her hand, and then he blushed, for he found himself unable to formulate a sentence that applied in any way to the situation.

She did not seem to heed that hand for a time.

He loosened his grasp presently, for he was ashamed to hold it so long without saying anything clever. At last, with an air of charging an entrenched brigade, he contrived to say: "I would rather do anything than frighten or trouble you."

His brow was warmly perspiring. He had a sense of being hideous in his dusty uniform and with his grimy face.

She said, "Oh, I'm so glad it was you instead of somebody who might have—might have hurt brother Harry and grandpa!"

He told her, "I wouldn't have hurt 'em for anything!"

There was a little silence.

"Well, good-bye!" he said at last.

"Good-bye!"

He walked toward the door past the old man, who was scolding at the vanishing figure of the corporal. The captain looked back. She had remained there watching him.

At the bugle's order, the troopers standing beside their horses swung briskly into the saddle. The lieutenant said to the first sergeant:

"Williams, did they ever meet before?"

"Hanged if I know!"

"Well, say—"

The captain saw a curtain move at one of the windows. He cantered from his position at the head of the column and steered his horse between two flower-beds.

"Well, good-bye!"

The squadron trampled slowly past.

"Good-bye!"

They shook hands.

He evidently had something enormously important to say to her, but it seems that he could not manage it. He struggled heroically. The bay charger, with his great mystically solemn eyes, looked around the corner of his shoulder at the girl.

The captain studied a pine tree. The girl inspected the grass beneath the window. The captain said hoarsely: "I don't suppose—I don't suppose—I'll ever see you again!"

She looked at him affrightedly and shrank back from the window. He seemed to have woefully expected a reception of this kind for his question. He gave her instantly a glance of appeal.

She said: "Why, no, I don't suppose you will."

"Never?"

"Why, no, 'tain't possible. You—you are a—Yankee!"

"Oh, I know it, but—" Eventually he continued: "Well, some day, you know, when there's no more fighting, we might—" He observed that she had again withdrawn suddenly into the shadow, so he said: "Well, good-bye!"

When he held her fingers she bowed her head, and he saw a pink blush steal over the curves of her cheek and neck.

"Am I never going to see you again?"

She made no reply.

"Never?" he repeated.

After a long time, he bent over to hear a faint reply: "Sometimes—when there are no troops in the neighborhood—grandpa don't mind if I—walk over as far as that old oak tree yonder—in the afternoons."

It appeared that the captain's grip was very strong, for she uttered an exclamation and looked at her fingers as if she expected to find them mere fragments. He rode away.

The bay horse leaped a flowerbed. They were almost to the drive, when the girl uttered a panic-stricken cry.

The captain wheeled his horse violently, and upon his return journey went straight through a flowerbed.

The girl had clasped her hands. She beseeched him wildly with her eyes. "Oh, please, don't believe it! I never walk to the old oak tree. Indeed I don't! I never—never—never walk there."

The bridle drooped on the bay charger's neck. The captain's figure seemed limp. With an expression of profound dejection and gloom he stared off at where the leaden sky met the dark green line of the woods. The long-impending rain began to fall with a mournful patter, drop and drop. There was a silence.

At last a low voice said, "Well—I might—sometimes I might—perhaps—but only once in a great while—I might walk to the old tree—in the afternoons."

CHAPTER TWENTY-SIX

Gunga Din
By Rudyard Kipling

You may talk o' gin and beer
When you're quartered safe out 'ere,
An' you're sent to penny-fights an' Aldershot it;
But when it comes to slaughter
You will do your work on water,
An' you'll lick the bloomin' boots of 'im that's got it.
Now in Injia's sunny clime,
Where I used to spend my time
A-servin' of 'Er Majesty the Queen,
Of all them blackfaced crew
The finest man I knew
Was our regimental bhisti, Gunga Din.

He was "Din! Din! Din!
"You limpin' lump o' brick-dust, Gunga Din!
"Hi! Slippy *hitherao!*
"Water, get it! *Panee lao,**
"You squidgy-nosed old idol, Gunga Din."

The uniform 'e wore
Was nothin' much before,
An' rather less than 'arf o' that be'ind,
For a piece o' twisty rag
An' a goatskin water-bag
Was all the field-equipment 'e could find.

---

*Bring water swiftly.

When the sweatin' troop-train lay
In a sidin' through the day,
Where the 'eat would make your bloomin' eyebrows crawl,
We shouted "Harry By!"*
Till our throats were bricky-dry,
Then we wopped 'im 'cause 'e couldn't serve us all.

It was "Din! Din! Din!
"You 'eathen, where the mischief 'ave you been?
"You put some *juldee*† in it
"Or I'll *marrow*‡ you this minute
"If you don't fill up my helmet, Gunga Din!"

'E would dot an' carry one
Till the longest day was done;
An' 'e didn't seem to know the use o' fear.
If we charged or broke or cut,
You could bet your bloomin' nut,
'E'd be waitin' fifty paces right flank rear.
With 'is mussick§ on 'is back,
'E would skip with our attack,
An' watch us till the bugles made "Retire,"
An' for all 'is dirty 'ide
'E was white, clear white, inside
When 'e went to tend the wounded under fire!

It was "Din! Din! Din!"
With the bullets kickin' dust-spots on the green.
When the cartridges ran out,
You could hear the front-ranks shout,
"Hi! ammunition-mules an' Gunga Din!"

I shan't forgit the night
When I dropped be'ind the fight
With a bullet where my belt-plate should 'a' been.
I was chokin' mad with thirst,
An' the man that spied me first
Was our good old grinnin', gruntin' Gunga Din.

---

*O brother.
†Be quick.
‡Hit you.
§Water-skin.

'E lifted up my 'ead,
An' he plugged me where I bled,
An' 'e guv me 'arf-a-pint o' water green.
It was crawlin' and it stunk,
But of all the drinks I've drunk,
I'm gratefullest to one from Gunga Din.

It was "Din! Din! Din!
"'Ere's a beggar with a bullet through 'is spleen;
"'E's chawin' up the ground,
"An' 'e's kickin' all around:
"For Gawd's sake git the water, Gunga Din!"

'E carried me away
To where a dooli lay,
An' a bullet come an' drilled the beggar clean.
'E put me safe inside,
An' just before 'e died,
"I 'ope you liked your drink," sez Gunga Din.
So I'll meet 'im later on
At the place where 'e is gone—
Where it's always double drill and no canteen.
'E'll be squattin' on the coals
Givin' drink to poor damned souls,
An' I'll get a swig in hell from Gunga Din!

Yes, Din! Din! Din!
You Lazarushian-leather Gunga Din!
Though I've belted you and flayed you,
By the livin' Gawd that made you,
You're a better man than I am, Gunga Din!

CHAPTER TWENTY-SEVEN

The Saga of Crazy Horse
By Charles A. Eastman

The memorial that commemorates the life of this native American is cut into the side of a mountain in South Dakota's Black Hills, in much the same manner of the Presidents in the Mount Rushmore National Memorial. Many consider the sculpture to represent all native Americans; some native Americans have voiced displeasure with the Memorial, claiming it is a form of pollution on the natural countryside. It is doubtful that Crazy Horse—perhaps the most famous of all native Americans—would like the monument. He was violently opposed to having a photograph of himself taken, and several authorities today claim that all photographs of Crazy Horse are fakes. Who was this interesting man, now an American icon? Read on, and you'll learn.

—LAMAR UNDERWOOD

CRAZY HORSE WAS BORN ON THE REPUBLICAN RIVER ABOUT 1845. HE WAS KILLED AT Fort Robinson, Nebraska, in 1877, so that he lived barely thirty-three years. He was an uncommonly handsome man. While not the equal of Gall in magnificence and imposing stature, he was physically perfect, an Apollo in symmetry. Furthermore he was a true type of Indian refinement and grace. He was modest and courteous as Chief Joseph; the difference is that he was a born warrior, while Joseph was not. However, he was a gentle warrior, a true brave, who stood for the highest ideal of the Sioux. Notwithstanding all that biased historians have said of him, it is only fair to judge a man by the estimate of his own people rather than that of his enemies.

The boyhood of Crazy Horse was passed in the days when the western Sioux saw a white man but seldom, and then it was usually a trader or a soldier. He was carefully brought up according to the tribal customs. At that period the Sioux prided themselves on the training and development of their sons and daughters, and not a step in that development was overlooked as an excuse to bring the child before the public by giving a feast in its honor. At such times the parents often gave so generously to the needy that they almost impoverished themselves, thus setting an example to the child of self-denial for the general good. His first step alone, the first word spoken, first game killed, the attainment of manhood or womanhood, each was the occasion of a feast and dance in his honor, at which the poor always benefited to the full extent of the parents' ability.

Big-heartedness, generosity, courage, and self-denial are the qualifications of a public servant, and the average Indian was keen to follow this ideal. As every one knows, these characteristic traits become a weakness when he enters a life founded upon commerce and gain. Under such conditions the life of Crazy Horse began. His mother, like other mothers, tender and watchful of her boy, would never once place an obstacle in the way of his father's severe physical training. They laid the spiritual and patriotic foundations of his education in such a way that he early became conscious of the demands of public service.

He was perhaps four or five years old when the band was snowed in one severe winter. They were very short of food, but his father was a tireless hunter. The buffalo, their main dependence, were not to be found, but he was out in the storm and cold every day and finally brought in two antelopes. The little boy got on his pet pony and rode through the camp, telling the old folks to come to his mother's teepee for meat. It turned out that neither his father nor mother had authorized him to do this. Before they knew it, old men and women were lined up before the teepee home, ready to receive the meat, in answer to his invitation. As a result, the mother had to distribute nearly all of it, keeping only enough for two meals.

On the following day the child asked for food. His mother told him that the old folks had taken it all, and added: "Remember, my son, they went home singing praises in your name, not my name or your father's. You must be brave. You must live up to your reputation."

Crazy Horse loved horses, and his father gave him a pony of his own when he was very young. He became a fine horseman and accompanied his father on buffalo hunts, holding the pack horses while the men chased the buffalo and thus gradually learning the art. In those days the Sioux had but few guns, and the hunting was mostly done with bow and arrows.

Another story told of his boyhood is that when he was about twelve he went to look for the ponies with his little brother, whom he loved much, and took a great deal of pains to teach what he had already learned. They came to some wild cherry trees full of ripe fruit, and while they were enjoying it, the brothers were startled by the growl and sudden rush of a bear. Young Crazy Horse pushed his brother up into the nearest tree and himself sprang upon the back of one of the horses, which was frightened and ran some distance before he could control him. As soon as he could, however, he turned him about and came back, yelling and swinging his lariat over his head. The bear at first showed fight but finally turned and ran. The old man who told me this story added that young as he was, he had some power, so that even a grizzly did not dare to tackle him. I believe it is a fact that a silver-tip will dare anything except a bell or a lasso line, so that accidentally the boy had hit upon the very thing which would drive him off.

It was usual for Sioux boys of his day to wait in the field after a buffalo hunt until sundown, when the young calves would come out in the open, hungrily seeking their mothers. Then these wild children would enjoy a mimic hunt, and lasso the calves or drive them into camp. Crazy Horse was found to be a determined little fellow, and it was settled one day among the larger boys that they would "stump" him to ride a good-sized bull calf. He rode the calf, and stayed on its back while it ran bawling over the hills, followed by the other boys on their ponies, until his strange mount stood trembling and exhausted.

At the age of sixteen he joined a war party against the Gros Ventres. He was well in the front of the charge, and at once established his bravery by following closely one of the foremost Sioux warriors, by the name of Hump, drawing the enemy's fire and circling around their advance guard. Suddenly Hump's horse was shot from under him, and there was a rush of warriors to kill or capture him while down. But amidst a shower of arrows the youth leaped from his pony, helped his friend into his own saddle, sprang up behind him, and carried him off in safety, although they were hotly pursued by the enemy. Thus he associated himself in his maiden battle with the wizard of Indian warfare, and Hump, who was then at the height of his own career, pronounced Crazy Horse the coming warrior of the Teton Sioux.

At this period of his life, as was customary with the best young men, he spent much time in prayer and solitude. Just what happened in these days of his fasting in the wilderness and upon the crown of bald buttes, no one will ever know; for these things may only be known when one has lived through the battles of life to an honored old age. He was much sought after by his youthful associates, but was noticeably reserved and modest; yet in the moment of danger he at once rose above them all—a natural leader! Crazy Horse was a typical Sioux brave, and from the point of view of our race an ideal hero, living at the height of the epical progress of the American Indian and maintaining in his own character all that was most subtle and ennobling of their spiritual life, and that has since been lost in the contact with a material civilization.

He loved Hump, that peerless warrior, and the two became close friends, in spite of the difference in age. Men called them "the grizzly and his cub." Again and again the pair saved the day for the Sioux in a skirmish with some neighboring tribe. But one day they undertook a losing battle against the Snakes. The Sioux were in full retreat and were fast being overwhelmed by superior numbers. The old warrior fell in a last desperate charge; but Crazy Horse and his younger brother, though dismounted, killed two of the enemy and thus made good their retreat.

It was observed of him that when he pursued the enemy into their stronghold, as he was wont to do, he often refrained from killing, and simply struck them with a switch, showing that he did not fear their weapons nor care to waste his upon them. In attempting this very feat, he lost this only brother of his, who emulated him closely. A party of young warriors, led by Crazy Horse, had dashed upon a frontier post, killed one of the sentinels, stampeded the horses, and pursued the herder to the very gate of the stockade, thus drawing upon themselves the fire of the garrison. The leader escaped without a scratch, but his young brother was brought down from his horse and killed.

While he was still under twenty, there was a great winter buffalo hunt, and he came back with ten buffaloes' tongues which he sent to the council lodge for the councilors' feast. He had in one winter day killed ten buffalo cows with his bow and arrows, and the unsuccessful hunters or those who had no swift ponies were made happy by his generosity. When the hunters returned, these came chanting songs of thanks. He knew that his father was an expert hunter and had a good horse, so he took no meat home, putting in practice the spirit of his early teaching.

He attained his majority at the crisis of the difficulties between the United States and the Sioux. Even before that time, Crazy Horse had already proved his worth to his people in Indian warfare. He had risked his life again and again, and in some instances it was considered almost a miracle that he had saved others as well as himself. He was no orator nor was he the son of a chief. His success and influence was purely a matter of personality. He had never fought the whites up to this time, and indeed no "coup" was counted for killing or scalping a white man.

Young Crazy Horse was twenty-one years old when all the Teton Sioux chiefs (the western or plains dwellers) met in council to determine upon their future policy toward the invader. Their former agreements had been by individual bands, each for itself, and every one was friendly. They reasoned that the country was wide, and that the white traders should be made welcome. Up to this time they had anticipated no conflict. They had permitted the Oregon Trail, but now to their astonishment forts were built and garrisoned in their territory.

Most of the chiefs advocated a strong resistance. There were a few influential men who desired still to live in peace, and who were willing to make another treaty. Among these were White Bull, Two Kettle, Four Bears, and Swift Bear. Even Spotted Tail, afterward the great peace chief, was at this time with the majority, who decided in the year 1866 to defend their rights and territory by force. Attacks were to be made upon the forts within their country and on every trespasser on the same.

Crazy Horse took no part in the discussion, but he and all the young warriors were in accord with the decision of the council. Although so young, he was already a leader among them. Other prominent young braves were Sword (brother of the man of that name who was long captain of police at Pine Ridge), the younger Hump, Charging Bear, Spotted Elk, Crow King, No Water, Big Road, He Dog, the nephew of Red Cloud, and Touch-the-Cloud, intimate friend of Crazy Horse.

The attack on Fort Phil Kearny was the first fruits of the new policy, and here Crazy Horse was chosen to lead the attack on the woodchoppers, designed to draw the soldiers out of the fort, while an army of six hundred lay in wait for them. The success of this stratagem was further enhanced by his masterful handling of his men. From this time on a general war was inaugurated; Sitting Bull looked to him as a principal war leader, and even the Cheyenne chiefs, allies of the Sioux, practically acknowledged his leadership. Yet during the following ten years of defensive war he was never known to make a speech, though his teepee was the rendezvous of the young men. He was depended upon to put into action the decisions of the council, and was frequently consulted by the older chiefs.

Like Osceola, he rose suddenly; like Tecumseh he was always impatient for battle; like Pontiac, he fought on while his allies were suing for peace, and like Grant, the silent soldier, he was a man of deeds and not of words. He won from Custer and Fetterman and Crook. He won every battle that he undertook, with the exception of one or two occasions when he was surprised in the midst of his women and children, and even then he managed to extricate himself in safety from a difficult position.

Early in the year 1876, his runners brought word from Sitting Bull that all the roving bands would converge upon the upper Tongue River in Montana for summer feasts and conferences. There was conflicting news from the reservation. It was rumored that the army would fight the Sioux to a finish; again, it was said that another commission would be sent out to treat with them.

The Indians came together early in June, and formed a series of encampments stretching out from three to four miles, each band keeping separate camp. On June 17, scouts came in and reported the advance of a large body of troops under General Crook. The council sent Crazy Horse with seven hundred men to meet and attack him. These were nearly all young men, many of them under twenty, the flower of the hostile Sioux. They set out at night so as to steal a march upon the enemy, but within three or four miles of his camp they came unexpectedly upon some of his Crow scouts. There was a hurried exchange of shots; the Crows fled back to Crook's camp, pursued by the Sioux. The soldiers had their warning, and it was impossible to enter the well-protected camp. Again and again Crazy Horse charged with his bravest men, in the attempt to bring the troops into the open, but he succeeded only in drawing their fire. Toward afternoon he withdrew, and returned to camp disappointed. His scouts remained to watch Crook's movements, and later brought word that he had retreated to Goose Creek and seemed to have no further disposition to disturb the Sioux. It is well known to us that it is Crook rather than Reno who is to be blamed for cowardice in connection with Custer's fate. The latter had no chance to do anything, he was lucky to save himself; but if Crook had kept on his way, as ordered, to meet Terry, with his one thousand regulars and two hundred Crow and Shoshone scouts, he would inevitably have intercepted Custer in his advance and saved the day for him, and war with the Sioux would have ended right there. Instead of this, he fell back upon Fort Meade, eating his horses on the way, in a country swarming with game, for fear of Crazy Horse and his braves!

The Indians now crossed the divide between the Tongue and the Little Big Horn, where they felt safe from immediate pursuit. Here, with all their precautions, they were caught unawares by General Custer, in the midst of their midday games and festivities, while many were out upon the daily hunt.

On this twenty-fifth of June, 1876, the great camp was scattered for three miles or more along the level river bottom, back of the thin line of cottonwoods—five circular rows of teepees, ranging from half a mile to a mile and a half in circumference. Here and there stood out a large, white, solitary teepee; these were the lodges or "clubs" of the young men. Crazy Horse was a member of the "Strong Hearts" and the "Tokala" or Fox lodge. He was watching a game of ring-toss when the warning came from the southern end of the camp of the approach of troops.

The Sioux and the Cheyennes were "minute men," and although taken by surprise, they instantly responded. Meanwhile, the women and children were thrown into confusion. Dogs were howling, ponies running hither and thither, pursued by their owners, while many of the old men were singing their lodge songs to encourage the warriors, or praising the "strong heart" of Crazy Horse.

That leader had quickly saddled his favorite war pony and was starting with his young men for the south end of the camp, when a fresh alarm came from the opposite direction, and looking up, he saw Custer's force upon the top of the bluff directly across the river. As quick as a flash, he took in the situation—the enemy had planned to attack the camp at both ends at once; and knowing that Custer could not ford the river at that point, he instantly led his men northward to the ford to cut him off. The Cheyennes followed closely. Custer must have seen that wonderful dash up the sage-bush plain, and one wonders whether he realized its meaning. In a very few minutes, this wild general of the plains had outwitted one of the most brilliant leaders of the Civil War and ended at once his military career and his life.

In this dashing charge, Crazy Horse snatched his most famous victory out of what seemed frightful peril, for the Sioux could not know how many were behind Custer. He was caught in his own trap. To the soldiers it must have seemed as if the Indians rose up from the earth to overwhelm them. They closed in from three sides and fought until not a white man was left alive. Then they went down to Reno's stand and found him so well intrenched in a deep gully that it was impossible to dislodge him. Gall and his men held him there until the approach of General Terry compelled the Sioux to break camp and scatter in different directions.

While Sitting Bull was pursued into Canada, Crazy Horse and the Cheyennes wandered about, comparatively undisturbed, during the rest of that year, until in the winter the army surprised the Cheyennes, but did not do them much harm, possibly because they knew that Crazy Horse was not far off. His name was held in wholesome respect. From time to time, delegations of friendly Indians were sent to him, to urge him to come in to the reservation, promising a full hearing and fair treatment.

For some time he held out, but the rapid disappearance of the buffalo, their only means of support, probably weighed with him more than any other influence. In July, 1877, he was finally prevailed upon to come in to Fort Robinson, Nebraska, with several thousand Indians, most of them Ogallala and Minneconwoju Sioux, on the distinct understanding that the government would hear and adjust their grievances.

At this juncture General Crook proclaimed Spotted Tail, who had rendered much valuable service to the army, head chief of the Sioux, which was resented by many. The attention paid Crazy Horse was offensive to Spotted Tail and the Indian scouts, who planned a conspiracy against him. They reported to General Crook that the young chief would murder him at the next council, and stampede the Sioux into another war. He was urged not to attend the council and did not, but sent another officer to represent him. Meanwhile the friends of Crazy Horse discovered the plot and told him of it. His reply was, "Only cowards are murderers."

His wife was critically ill at the time, and he decided to take her to her parents at Spotted Tail agency, whereupon his enemies circulated the story that he had fled, and a party of scouts was sent after him. They overtook him riding with his wife and one other but did not undertake to arrest him, and after he had left the sick woman with her people he went to call on Captain Lea, the agent for the Brules, accompanied by all the warriors of the Minneconwoju band. This volunteer escort made an imposing appearance on horseback, shouting and singing, and in the words of Captain Lea himself and the missionary, the Reverend Mr. Cleveland, the situation was extremely critical. Indeed, the scouts who had followed Crazy Horse from Red Cloud agency were advised not to show themselves, as some of the warriors had urged that they be taken out and horsewhipped publicly.

Under these circumstances Crazy Horse again showed his masterful spirit by holding these young men in check. He said to them in his quiet way: "It is well to be brave in the field of battle; it is cowardly to display bravery against one's own tribesmen. These scouts have been compelled to do what they did; they are no better than servants of the white officers. I came here on a peaceful errand."

The captain urged him to report at army headquarters to explain himself and correct false rumors, and on his giving consent, furnished him with a wagon and escort. It has been said that he went back under arrest, but this is untrue. Indians have boasted that they had a hand in bringing him in, but their stories are without foundation. He went of his own accord, either suspecting no treachery or determined to defy it.

When he reached the military camp, Little Big Man walked arm-in-arm with him, and his cousin and friend, Touch-the-Cloud, was just in advance. After they passed the sentinel, an officer approached them and walked on his other side. He was unarmed but for the knife which is carried for ordinary uses by women as well as men. Unsuspectingly he walked toward the guardhouse, when Touch-the-Cloud suddenly turned back exclaiming: "Cousin, they will put you in prison!"

"Another white man's trick! Let me go! Let me die fighting!" cried Crazy Horse. He stopped and tried to free himself and draw his knife, but both arms were held fast by

Little Big Man and the officer. While he struggled thus, a soldier thrust him through with his bayonet from behind. The wound was mortal, and he died in the course of that night, his old father singing the death song over him and afterward carrying away the body, which they said must not be further polluted by the touch of a white man. They hid it somewhere in the Bad Lands, his resting place to this day.

Thus died one of the ablest and truest American Indians. His life was ideal; his record clean. He was never involved in any of the numerous massacres on the trail, but was a leader in practically every open fight. Such characters as those of Crazy Horse and Chief Joseph are not easily found among so-called civilized people. The reputation of great men is apt to be shadowed by questionable motives and policies, but here are two pure patriots, as worthy of honor as any who ever breathed God's air in the wide spaces of a new world.

CHAPTER TWENTY-EIGHT

Bull Run
By Joseph A. Altsheler

By the late 1800s and early 1900s, with the war a respectable distance in the past, it had become easy to romanticize soldiers' lives—especially those of the South. Joseph A. Altsheler was one of many turn-of-the-century authors who set his tales in the midst of the war. Altsheler, a prolific writer, turned out several novels featuring a company of Southern soldiers, the "Invincibles," who in the selection here from The Guns of Bull Run *face the first decisive battle of the war.*

—LISA PURCELL

HARRY ROSE TO HIS FEET AND SHOOK ST. CLAIR AND LANGDON. "UP, BOYS!" HE SAID. "The enemy will soon be here. I can see their bayonets glittering on the hills."

The Invincibles sprang to their feet almost as one man, and soon all the troops of Evans were up and humming like bees. Food and coffee were served to them hastily, but, before the last cup was thrown down, a heavy crash came from one of the hills beyond Bull Run, and a shell, screaming over their heads, burst beyond them. It was quickly followed by another, and then the round shot and shells came in dozens from batteries which had been posted well in the night.

The Southern batteries replied with all their might and the riflemen supported them, sending the bullets in sheets across Bull Run. The battle flamed in fifteen minutes into extraordinary violence. Harry had never before heard such a continuous and terrific thunder. It seemed that the drums of his ears would be smashed in, but over his head he heard the continuous hissing and whirring of steel and lead. The Northern riflemen were at work, too, and it was fortunate for the Invincibles that they were able to lie down, as they poured their fire into the bushes and woods on the opposite bank.

The volume of smoke was so great that they could no longer see the position of the enemy, but Harry believed that so much metal must do great damage. Although he was a lieutenant he had snatched up a rifle dropped by some fallen soldier, and he loaded and fired it so often that the barrel grew hot to his hand. Lying so near the river, most of the hostile fire went over the heads of the Invincibles, but now and then a shell or a cluster of bullets struck among them, and Harry heard groans. But he quickly forgot these sounds as he watched the clouds of smoke and the blaze of fire on the other side of Bull Run.

"They are not trying to force the passage of the bridge! Everything is for the best!" shouted Langdon.

"No, they dare not," shouted St. Clair in reply. "No column could live on that bridge in face of our fire."

It seemed strange to Harry that the Northern troops made no attempt to cross. Why did all this tremendous fire go on so long, and yet not a foe set foot upon the bridge? It seemed to him that it had endured for hours. The sun was rising higher and higher and the day was growing hotter and hotter. It lay with the North to make the first movement to cross Bull Run, and yet no attempt was made.

Colonel Talbot came repeatedly along the line of the Invincibles, and Harry saw that he was growing uneasy. Such a great volume of fire, without any effort to take advantage of it, made the veteran suspicious. He knew that those old comrades of his on the other side of Bull Run would not waste their metal in a mere cannonade and long range rifle fire. There must be something behind it. Presently, with the consent of the commander, he drew the Invincibles back from the river, where they were permitted to cease firing, and to rest for a while on their arms.

But as they drew long breaths and tried to clear the smoke from their throats, a rumor ran down the lines. The attack at the bridge was but a feint. Only a minor portion of the hostile army was there. The greater mass had gone on and had already crossed the river in face of the weak left flank of the Southern army. Beauregard had been outwitted. The Yankees were now in great force on his own side of Bull Run, and it would be a pitched battle, face to face.

The whole line of the Invincibles quivered with excitement, and then Harry saw that the rumor was true, or that their commander at least believed it to be so. The firing stopped entirely and the bugles blew the retreat. All the brigades gathered themselves up and, wild with anger and chagrin, slowly withdrew.

"Why are we retreating?" exclaimed Langdon, angrily. "Not a Yankee set his foot on the bridge! We're not whipped!"

"No," said Harry, "we're not whipped, but if we don't retreat we will be. If fifteen or twenty thousand Yankees struck us on the flank while those fellows are still in front everything would go."

These were young troops, who considered a retreat equivalent to a beating, and fierce murmurs ran along the line. But the officers paid no attention, marching them steadily on, while the artillery rumbled by their side. Both to right and left they heard the sound of firing, and they saw the smoke floating against both horizons, but they paid little attention to it. They were wondering what was in store for them.

"Cheer up, you lads!" cried Colonel Talbot. "You'll get all the fighting you can stand, and it won't be long in coming, either."

They marched only half an hour and then the troops were drawn up on a hill, where the officers rapidly formed them into position. It was none too soon. A long blue line, bristling with cannon on either flank, appeared across the fields. It was Burnside with the bulk of the Northern army moving down upon them. Harry was standing beside Colonel Talbot, ready to carry his orders, and he heard the veteran say, between his teeth:

"The Yankees have fooled us, and this is the great battle at last."

The two forces looked at each other for a few moments. Elsewhere great guns and rifles were already at work, but the sounds came distantly. On the hill and in the fields there was silence, save for the steady tramp of the advancing Northern troops. Then from the rear of the marching lines suddenly came a burst of martial music. The Northern bands, by a queer inversion, were playing Dixie:

> "In Dixie's land
> I'll take my stand,
> To live and die for Dixie.
> Look away! Look away!
> Down South in Dixie."

Harry's feet beat to the tune, the wild and thrilling air played for the first time to troops going into battle.

"We must answer that," he said to St. Clair.

"Here comes the answer," said St. Clair, and the Southern bands began to play "The Girl I Left Behind Me." The music entered Harry's veins. He could not look without a quiver upon the great mass of men bearing down upon them, but the strains of fife and drum put courage in him and told him to stand fast. He saw the face of Colonel Talbot grow darker and darker, and he had enough experience himself to know that the odds were heavily against them.

The intense burning sun poured down a flood of light, lighting up the opposing ranks of blue and gray, and gleaming along swords and bayonets. Nearer and nearer came the piercing notes of Dixie.

"They march well," murmured Colonel Talbot, "and they will fight well, too."

He did not know that McDowell himself, the Northern commander, was now before them, driving on his men, but he did know that the courage and skill of his old comrades were for the present in the ascendant. Burnside was at the head of the division and it seemed long enough to wrap the whole Southern command in its folds and crush it.

Scattered rifle shots were heard on either flank, and the young Invincibles began to breathe heavily. Millions of black specks danced before them in the hot sunshine, and their nervous ears magnified every sound tenfold.

"I wish that tune the Yankees are playing was ours," said Tom Langdon. "I think I could fight battles by it."

"Then we'll have to capture it," said Harry.

Now the time for talking ceased. The rifle fire on the flanks was rising to a steady rattle, and then came the heavy boom of the cannon on either side. Once more the air was filled with the shriek of shells and the whistling of rifle bullets. Men were falling fast, and through the rising clouds of smoke Harry saw the blue lines still coming on. It seemed to him that they would be overwhelmed, trampled under foot, routed, but he heard Colonel Talbot shouting:

"Steady, Invincibles! Steady!"

And Lieutenant-Colonel St. Hilaire, walking up and down the lines, also uttered the same shout. But the blue line never ceased coming. Harry could see the faces dark with sweat and dust and powder still pressing on. It was well for the Southerners that nearly all of them had been trained in the use of the rifle, and it was well for them, too, that most of their officers were men of skill and experience. Recruits, they stood fast nevertheless and their rifles sent the bullets in an unceasing bitter hail straight into the advancing ranks of blue. There was no sound from the bands now. If they were playing somewhere in the rear no one heard. The fire of the cannon and rifles was a steady roll, louder than thunder and more awful.

The Northern troops hesitated at last in face of such a resolute stand and such accurate firing. Then they retreated a little and a shout of triumph came from the Southern lines, but the respite was only for a moment. The men in blue came on again, walking over their dead and past their wounded.

"If they keep pressing in, and it looks as if they would, they will crush us," murmured Colonel Talbot, but he did not let the Invincibles hear him say it. He encouraged them with voice and example, and they bent forward somewhat to meet the second charge of the Northern army, which was now coming. The smoke lifted a little and Harry saw the green fields and the white house of the Widow Henry standing almost in the middle of the battlefield, but unharmed. Then his eyes came back to the hostile line, which, torn by shot and shell, had closed up, nevertheless, and was advancing again in overwhelming force.

Harry now had a sudden horrible fear that they would be trodden under foot. He looked at St. Clair and saw that his face was ghastly. Langdon had long since ceased to smile or utter words of happy philosophy.

"Open up and let the guns through!" someone suddenly cried, and a wild cheer of relief burst from the Invincibles as they made a path. The valiant Bee and Bartow, rushing to the sound of the great firing, had come with nearly three thousand men and a whole battery. Never were men more welcome. They formed instantly along the Southern front, and the battery opened at once with all its guns, while the three thousand men sent a new fire into the Northern ranks. Yet the Northern charge still came. McDowell, Burnside, and the others were pressing it home, seeking to drive the Southern army from its hill, while they were yet able to bring forces largely superior to bear upon it.

The thunder and crash of the terrible conflict rolled over all the hills and fields for miles. It told the other forces of either army that here was the center of the battle, and here was its crisis. The sounds reached an extraordinary young-old man, bearded and awkward, often laughed at, but never to be laughed at again, one of the most wonderful soldiers the world has ever produced, and instantly gathering up his troops he rushed them toward the very heart of the combat. Stonewall Jackson was about to receive his famous nickname.

Jackson's burning eyes swept proudly over the ranks of his tall Virginians, who mourned every second they lost from the battle. An officer retreating with his battery glanced at him, opened his mouth to speak, but closed it again without saying a word, and infused with new hope, turned his guns afresh toward the enemy. Already men were feeling the magnetic current of energy and resolution that flowed from Jackson like water from a fountain.

A message from Colonel Talbot, which he was to deliver to Jackson himself, sent Harry to the rear. He rode a borrowed horse and he galloped rapidly until he saw a long line of men marching forward at a swift but steady pace. At their head rode a man on a sorrel horse. His shoulders were stooped a little, and he leaned forward in the saddle, gazing intently at the vast bank of smoke and flame before him. Harry noticed that the hands upon the bridle reins did not twitch nor did the horseman seem at all excited. Only his burning eyes showed that every faculty was concentrated upon the task. Harry was conscious even then that he was in the presence of General Jackson.

The boy delivered his message. Jackson received it without comment, never taking his eyes from the battle, which was now raging so fiercely in front of them. Behind came his great brigade of Virginians, the smoke and flame of the battle entering their blood and making their hearts pound fast as they moved forward with increasing speed.

Harry rode back with the young officers of his staff, and now they saw men dash out of the smoke and run toward them. They cried that everything was lost. The lip of Jackson curled in contempt. The long line of his Virginians stopped the fugitives and drove them back to the battle. It was evident to Harry, young as he was, that Jackson would be just in time.

Then they saw a battery galloping from that bank of smoke and flame, and, its officer swearing violently, exclaimed that he had been left without support. The stern face and somber eyes of Jackson were turned upon him.

"Unlimber your guns at once," he said. "Here is your support."

Then the valiant Bee himself came, covered with dust, his clothes torn by bullets, his horse in a white lather. He, too, turned to that stern brown figure, as unflinching as death itself, and he cried that the enemy in overwhelming numbers were beating them back.

"Then," said Jackson, "we'll close up and give them the bayonet."

His teeth shut down like a vise. Again the electric current leaped forth and sparkled through the veins of Bee, who turned and rode back into the Southern throng, the Virginians following swiftly. Then Jackson looked over the field with the eye and mind of genius, the eye that is able to see and the mind that is able to understand amid all the thunder and confusion and excitement of battle.

He saw a stretch of pines on the edge of the hill near the Henry house. He quickly marched his troops among the trees, covering their front with six cannon, while the great horseman, Stuart, plumed and eager, formed his cavalry upon the left. Harry felt instinctively that the battle was about to be restored for the time at least, and he turned back to Colonel Talbot and the Invincibles. A shell burst near him. A piece struck his horse in the chest, and Harry felt the animal quiver under him. Then the horse uttered a terrible neighing cry, but Harry, alert and agile, sprang clear, and ran back to his own command.

On the other side of Bull Run was the Northern command of Tyler, which had been rebuffed so fiercely three days before. It, too, heard the roar and crash of the battle, and sought a way across Bull Run, but for a time could find none. An officer named Sherman, also destined for a mighty fame, saw a Confederate trooper riding across the river further down, and instantly the whole command charged at the ford. It was defended by only two hundred Southern skirmishers whom they brushed out of the way. They were across in a few minutes, and then they advanced on a run to swell McDowell's army. The forces on both sides were increasing and the battle was rising rapidly in volume. But in the face of repeated and furious attacks the Southern troops held fast to the little plateau. Young's Branch flowed on one side of it and protected them in a measure; but only the indomitable spirit of Jackson and Evans, of Bee and Bartow, and others kept them in line against those charges which threatened to shiver them to pieces.

"Look!" cried Bee to some of his men who were wavering. "Look at Jackson, standing there like a stone wall!"

The men ceased to waver and settled themselves anew for a fresh attack.

But in spite of everything the Northern army was gaining ground. Sherman at the very head of the fresh forces that had crossed Bull Run hurled himself upon the Southern army, his main attack falling directly upon the Invincibles. The young recruits reeled, but Colonel Talbot and Lieutenant-Colonel St. Hilaire still ran up and down the lines begging them to stand. They took fresh breath and planted their feet deep once more. Harry raised his rifle and took aim at a flitting figure in the smoke. Then he dropped the muzzle. Either it was reality or a powerful trick of the fancy. It was his own cousin, Dick Mason, but the smoke closed in again, and he did not see the face.

The rush of Sherman was met and repelled. He drew back only to come again, and along the whole line the battle closed in once more, fiercer and more deadly than ever. Upon all the combatants beat the fierce sun of July, and clouds of dust rose to mingle with the smoke of cannon and rifles.

The advantage now lay distinctly with the Northern army, won by its clever passage of Bull Run and surprise. But the courage and tenacity of the Southern troops averted defeat and rout in detail. Jackson, in his strong position near the Henry house, in the cellars of which women were hiding, refused to give an inch of ground. Beauregard, called by the cannon, arrived upon the field only an hour before noon, meeting on the way many fugitives, whom he and his officers drove back into the battle. Hampton's South Carolina Legion, which reached Richmond only that morning, came by train and landed directly upon the battlefield about noon. In five minutes it was in the thick of the battle, and it alone stemmed a terrific rush of Sherman, when all others gave way.

Noon had passed and the heart of McDowell swelled with exultation. The Northern troops were still gaining ground, and at many points the Southern line was crushed. Some of the recruits in gray, their nerves shaken horribly, were beginning to run. But fresh troops coming up met them and turned them back to the field. Beauregard and Johnston, the two senior generals, both experienced and calm, were reforming their ranks, seizing new and strong positions, and hurrying up every portion of their force. Johnston himself, after the first rally, hurried back for fresh regiments, while Jackson's men not only held their ground but began to drive the Northern troops before them.

The Invincibles had fallen back somewhat, leaving many dead behind them. Many more were wounded. Harry had received two bullets through his clothing, and St. Clair was nicked on the wrist. Colonel Talbot and Lieutenant-Colonel St. Hilaire were still unharmed, but a deep gloom had settled over the Invincibles. They had not been beaten, but certainly they were not winning. Their ranks were seamed and rent. From the place where they now stood they could see the place where they formerly stood, but Northern troops occupied it now. Tears ran down the faces of some of the youngest, streaking the dust and powder into hideous, grinning masks.

Harry threw himself upon the ground and lay there for a few moments, panting. He choked with heat and thirst, and his heart seemed to have swollen so much within him that it would be a relief to have it burst. His eyes burned with the dust and smoke, and all about him was a fearful reek. He could see from where he lay most of the battlefield. He saw the Northern batteries fire, move forward, and then fire again. He saw the Northern infantry creeping up, ever creeping, and far behind he beheld the flags of fresh regiments coming to their aid. The tears sprang to his eyes. It seemed in very truth that all was lost. In another part of the field the men in blue had seized the Robinson house, and from points near it their artillery was searching the Southern ranks. A sudden grim humor seized the boy.

"Tom," he shouted to Langdon, "what was that you said about sleeping in the White House at Washington with your boots on?"

"I said it," Langdon shouted back, "but I guess it's all off! For God's sake, Harry, give me a drink of water! I'll give anybody a million dollars and a half dozen states for a single drink!"

A soldier handed him a canteen, and he drank from it. The water was warm, but it was nectar, and when he handed it back, he said:

"I don't know you and you don't know me, but if I could I'd give you a whole lake in return for this. Harry, what are our chances?"

"I don't know. We've lost one battle, but we may have time to win another. Jackson and those Virginians of his seem able to stand anything. Up, boys, the battle is on us again!"

The charge swept almost to their feet, but it was driven back, and then came a momentary lull, not a cessation of the battle, but merely a sinking, as if the combatants were gathering themselves afresh for a new and greater effort. It was two o'clock in the afternoon, and the fierce July sun was at its zenith, pouring its burning rays upon both armies, alike upon the living and upon the dead who were now so numerous.

The lull was most welcome to the men in gray. Some fresh regiments sent by Johnston had come already, and they hoped for more, but whether they came or not, the army must stand. The brigades were massed heavily around the Henry house with that of Jackson standing stern and indomitable, the strongest wall against the foe. His fame and his spirit were spreading fast over the field.

The lull was brief, the whole Northern army, its lines reformed, swept forward in a half curve, and the Southern army sent forth a stream of shells and bullets to meet it. The brigades of Jackson and Sherman, indomitable foes, met face to face and swept back and forth over the ground, which was littered with their fallen. Everywhere the battle assumed a closer and fiercer phase. Hampton, who had come just in time with his guns, went down wounded badly. Beauregard himself was wounded slightly, and so was Jackson, hit in the hand. Many distinguished officers were killed.

The whole Northern army was driven back four times, and it came a fifth time to be repulsed once more. In the very height of the struggle Harry caught a glimpse in front of them of a long horizontal line of red, like a gleaming ribbon.

"It's those Zouaves!" cried Langdon. "Shoot their pants!"

He did not mean it as a jest. The words just jumped out, and true to their meaning the Invincibles fired straight at that long line of red, and then reloading fired again. The Zouaves were cut to pieces, the field was strewed with their brilliant uniforms. A few officers tried to bring on the scattered remnants, but two regiments of regulars, sweeping in between and bearing down on the Invincibles, saved them from extermination.

The Invincibles would have suffered the fate they had dealt out to the Zouaves, but fresh regiments came to their help and the regulars were driven back. Sherman and Jackson were still fighting face to face, and Sherman was unable to advance. Howard hurled a fresh force on the men in gray. Bee and Bartow, who had done such great deeds earlier in the day, were both killed. A Northern force under Heintzelman, converging for a flank attack, was set upon and routed by the Southerners, who put them all to flight, captured three guns and took the Robinson house.

Fortune, nevertheless, still seemed to favor the North. The Southerners had barely held their positions around the Henry house. Most of their cannon were dismounted. Hundreds had dropped from exhaustion. Some had died from heat and excessive exertion. The mortality among the officers was frightful. There were few hopeful hearts in the Southern army.

It was now three o'clock in the afternoon and Beauregard, through his glasses, saw a great column of dust rising above the tops of the trees. His experience told him that it must be made by marching troops, but what troops were they, Northern or Southern? In an agony of suspense he appealed to the generals around him, but they could tell nothing. He sent off aides at a gallop to see, but meanwhile he and his generals could only wait, while the column of dust grew broader and broader and higher and higher. His heart sank like a plummet in a pool. The cloud was on the Federal flank and everything indicated that it was the army of Patterson, marching from the Valley of Virginia.

Harry and his comrades had also seen the dust, and they regarded it anxiously. They knew as well as any general present that their fate lay within that cloud.

"It's coming fast, and it's growing faster," said Harry. "I've got so used to the roar of this battle that it seems to me alien sounds are detached from it, and are heard easily. I can hear the rumble of cannon wheels in that cloud."

"Then tell us, Harry," said Langdon, "is it a Northern rumble or a Southern rumble that you hear?"

Harry laughed.

"I'll admit it's a good deal of a fancy," he said.

Arthur St. Clair suddenly leaped high in the air, and uttered at the very top of his voice the wild note of the famous rebel yell.

"Look at the flags aloft in that cloud of dust! It's the Stars and Bars! God bless the Bonnie Blue Flag! They are our own men coming, and coming in time!"

Now the battle flags appeared clearly through the dust, and the great rebel yell, swelling and triumphant, swept the whole Southern line. It was the remainder of Johnston's Army of the Shenandoah. It had slipped away from Patterson, and all through the burning day it had been marching steadily toward the battlefield, drummed on by the thudding guns. Johnston, the silent and alert, was himself with them now, and aflame with zeal they were advancing on the run straight for the heart of the Northern army.

Kirby Smith, one of Harry's own Kentucky generals, was in the very van of the relieving force. A man after Stonewall Jackson's own soul, he rushed forward with the leading regiments and they hurled themselves bodily upon the Northern flank.

The impact was terrible. Smith fell wounded, but his men rushed on and the men behind also threw themselves into the battle. Almost at the same instant Jubal Early, who had made a circuit with a strong force, hurled it upon the side of the Northern army. The brave troops in blue were exhausted by so many hours of fierce fighting and fierce heat. Their whole line broke and began to fall back. The Southern generals around the Henry house saw it and exulted. Swift orders were sent and the bugles blew the charge for the men who had stood so many long and bitter hours on the defense.

"Now, Invincibles, now!" cried Colonel Leonidas Talbot. "Charge home, just once, my boys, and the victory is ours!"

Covered with dust and grime, worn and bleeding with many wounds, but every heart beating triumphantly, what was left of the Invincibles rose up and followed their leader. Harry was conscious of a flame almost in his face and of whirling clouds of smoke and dust. Then the entire Southern army burst upon the confused Northern force and shattered it so completely that it fell to pieces.

The bravest battle ever fought by men, who, with few exceptions, had not smelled the powder of war before, was lost and won.

As the Southern cannon and rifles beat upon them, the Northern army, save for the regulars and the cavalry, dissolved. The generals could not stem the flood. They rushed forward in confused masses, seeking only to save themselves. Whole regiments dashed into the fords of Bull Run and emerged dripping on the other side. A bridge was covered with spectators come out from Washington to see the victory, many of them bringing with them baskets of lunch. Some were Members of Congress, but all joined in the panic and flight, carrying to the capital many untrue stories of disaster.

A huge mass of fleeing men emerged upon the Warrenton turnpike, throwing away their weapons and ammunition that they might run the faster. It was panic pure and simple, but panic for the day only. For hours they had fought as bravely as the veterans of twenty battles, but now, with weakened nerves, they thought that an overwhelming force was upon them. Every shell that the Southern guns sent among them urged them to greater speed. The cavalry and little force of regulars covered the rear, and with firm and unbroken ranks retreated slowly, ready to face the enemy if he tried pursuit.

But the men in gray made no real pursuit. They were so worn that they could not follow, and they yet scarcely believed in the magnitude of their own victory, snatched from the very jaws of defeat. Twenty-eight Northern cannon and ten flags were in their hands, but thousands of dead and wounded lay upon the field, and night was at hand again, close and hot.

Harry turned back to the little plateau where those that were left of the Invincibles were already kindling their cooking fires. He looked for his two comrades and recognized them both under their masks of dust and powder.

"Are you hurt, Tom?" he said to Langdon.

"No, and I'm going to sleep in the White House at Washington after all."

"And you, Arthur?"

"There's a red line across my wrist, where a bullet passed, but it's nothing. Listen, what do you think of that, boys?"

A Southern band had gathered in the edge of the wood and was playing a wild thrilling air, the words of which meant nothing, but the tune everything:

"In Dixie's land
I'll take my stand,
To live and die for Dixie.
Look away! Look away!
Look away down South in Dixie."

"So we have taken their tune from them and made it ours!" St. Clair exclaimed jubilantly. "After all, it really belonged to us! We'll play it through the streets of Washington." But Colonel Leonidas Talbot, who stood close by, raised his hand warningly.

"Boys," he said, "this is only the beginning."

Chapter Twenty-Nine

Eight Survived

By Douglas A. Campbell

Like many another war and history buff, your editor is captivated by submarine stories. This harrowing story is an excerpt from a book on the only submarine crew in WW II to survive a sinking and evade capture. It's from the book of the same title, published by Lyons Press in 2010.

—Lamar Underwood

It was also in 1943 that the navy perfected a new method of decoding Japanese radio messages and relaying the information to submarines. Called Ultra, this system allowed the subs to find convoys crossing the vast southern seas rather than waiting for a lucky break outside a port.

Statistics showed the effectiveness of these changes. In 1942, United States submarines conducted about 350 patrols in the Pacific, sinking 180 ships rated at a total of 725,000 tons. In 1943, the same number of patrols recorded about 335 Japanese ships sunk, or 1.5 million tons.

"In one sense it could be said that the U.S. submarine war against Japan did not truly begin until the opening days of 1944," wrote Clay Blair Jr. in *Silent Victory*. "What had come before had been a learning period, a time of testing, of weeding out, of fixing defects in weapons, strategy, and tactics, of waiting for sufficient numbers of submarines and workable torpedoes. Now that all was set, the contribution of the submarine force would be more than substantial: it would be decisive."

Even the most successful boats were dangerous homes for sailors. In part, this was due to the brazenness with which some submarine skippers attacked the enemy, firing from extremely close range or taking up positions with no escape route.

In the seven months since the October 18 commissioning of *Flier*, nine submarines had been lost, along with 647 men. In seven of those cases, all hands were lost.

Wahoo was the first in that span, disappearing sometime in October, on its seventh patrol. In its first five patrols beginning in August 1942, the boat sank 27 Japanese ships, or 119,100 tons, the measurement that counted as much as any. On its third patrol, *Wahoo* sank two large freighters, a transport, a tanker, and an escort vessel, and, after slipping into a harbor on the Japanese-held north coast of New Guinea, seriously damaged a destroyer. On its sixth patrol, *Wahoo* ran into a drought—not of targets, but of victims. Prowling the Sea of Japan, the boat fired again and again on Japanese ships—nine attacks in all. But in each case, malfunctioning torpedoes caused no damage. A frustrated skipper, Commander Dudley W. Morton—known to his men as Mush—returned to Pearl Harbor from that patrol and vented his anger by pounding Admiral Lockwood's desk.

"Well, Mush, what do you want to do?" Lockwood asked.

"Admiral, I want to go right back to the Sea of Japan, with a load of live fish this time."

Each of the torpedoes delivered to *Wahoo* was carefully examined and then loaded into the submarine. The boat steamed from Pearl Harbor on September 9, stopped at Midway for fuel a few days later, and then headed west, for the Sea of Japan. *Wahoo* apparently reached its destination. Japanese records of the war say that four Japanese ships were sunk in *Wahoo*'s patrol area. The records also show that an antisubmarine attack was made in the same area on October 11. *Wahoo* and the eighty men aboard were never heard from again.

About three weeks later, *Corvina*, with a crew of eighty-two, left Pearl Harbor with an assignment to patrol as close to the island of Truk as possible. Japanese records indicate that a Japanese submarine found *Corvina* on the surface on November 16, 1943, and fired a torpedo, sinking the American boat with all hands.

Sculpin left Pearl Harbor on November 5 and stopped at Johnston Island to refuel before heading for its assignment: intercepting Japanese ships responding to an Allied attack on the Gilbert Islands. The boat and its crew of seventy-four were never heard from again, and were presumed lost. At the end of the war, twenty-one survivors were released from Japanese prison camps—half of the men who had survived a depth-charge attack on *Sculpin* on November 19.

Japanese records show that on November 23, an American submarine was attacked in the area in the Celebes Sea, in northern Indonesia, by Japanese ships. There was little evidence that the submarine was damaged. *Capelin*, with seventy-eight men aboard, was assigned to that area, but another American submarine, *Bonefish*, saw an American submarine nine days later in a region that was also included in *Capelin*'s assignment. The boat and its crew were never seen again, and the navy included among the possible causes for the loss that *Capelin* had struck a mine.

On January 3, thirteen days before *Flier* grounded on the Midway reef, *Scorpion*—which had suffered the same fate five months earlier—had left Midway for its fourth patrol. Two days later, the boat attempted to rendezvous with another submarine returning to Midway to transfer a crewman with a broken arm. The transfer was impossible in heavy seas, so *Scorpion* went on toward its assigned patrol area in the East China and Yellow seas. Mines had been laid recently across the entrance to the Yellow Sea, a fact unknown to the navy. Nor had any of several submarines that had crossed that water encountered mines. The boat and its crew of seventy-six, who had sunk ten ships in their first three patrols, were never heard from again, and in February were listed as presumed lost.

Grayback had completed a remarkable nine patrols in the Pacific when it left Pearl Harbor in late January 1944 for its tenth patrol. Since the war started, the boat had sunk twenty-two ships and damaged another nine, one of them a coveted Japanese destroyer. Four weeks after beginning the tenth patrol, the skipper, Commander J. A. Moore, reported by radio that the crew had sunk two enemy ships and damaged another two. *Grayback* had six torpedoes remaining. The next day, Moore reported having fired four torpedoes, three of which had hit two enemy freighters. The skipper was told to return to Midway. Japanese records show that a day later, a Japanese airplane saw a surfaced submarine and sank it with a direct hit. Moore and his crew of sixty-nine were lost.

On February 4, when the inquiry into the grounding of the *Flier* was in its fourth day in Pearl Harbor, the submarine *Trout* left that port for its eleventh patrol, sailing northwest for a fuel stop at Midway. The day after *Macaw* sank in tumultuous surf on the Midway reef, *Trout* and the seventy-one men aboard sailed out of Brooks Inlet past the wreck and resumed their westward trek, never to be heard from again. Japanese records suggest that the boat was lost in a battle after sinking one ship and badly damaging another on February 29.

In early March, while *Flier* was still at Mare Island, *Tullibee* left Hawaii with sixty-nine men aboard. One survivor later told how a torpedo running in a circle had sunk his boat.

One week before *Flier*'s May departure from Pearl Harbor, the submarine *Gudgeon* had been given orders to return to Midway from its twelfth patrol. Then on May 11, Headquarters had radioed the boat again, altering *Gudgeon*'s assignment. The message required that the skipper call back to Headquarters by radio, but he failed to reply.

Gudgeon was built at Mare Island and was named for a small, freshwater fish, but the submarine was quite at home in the salty sea. Its achievements during the war had been anything but small. In eleven prior patrols, the boat had amassed an incredible record, sinking twenty-five Japanese ships and damaging another eight, ranking it fifteenth in kills among all American submarines. *Gudgeon*'s first patrol had begun in Hawaii four days after the attack on Pearl Harbor. A month later, *Gudgeon* earned the distinction of being the first United States submarine in history to sink an enemy warship when the boat's torpedoes destroyed a Japanese submarine. By May of 1944, *Gudgeon* had been in the battle for two and a half years and had few equals in the navy's submarine fleet. The boat's seventy-eight-man crew had begun its twelfth patrol in April when it left Johnston Island, a tiny refueling depot west of Hawaii. Those men were never heard from again.

Gudgeon was not reported as presumed lost until June 7, 1944, so as *Flier* headed for the front, its captain and crew were unaware of the latest loss. As events would later prove, such information would likely have played little part in tempering the aggressiveness with which *Flier* pursued enemy ships. Finally, John "Cautious" Crowley had a boat and some sailors with whom he could make a dent in the Japanese war machinery. After the Midway debacle, he also had something to prove, and his men had something to learn. In battle, Crowley was anything but cautious.

Welcome to the War

Crowley wasted no time on his way to the war zone. The stop at Johnston Island for refueling, two days after leaving Pearl Harbor, took less than three hours. That included time for a pilot to board the boat outside the Johnston inlet and to guide the submarine up to the fuel dock. As the diesel fuel was loaded, the pilot asked, then begged, Crowley to take him along on the patrol. There was nothing for the man to do on the tiny island, and he felt he was going mad. Crowley patted the man on the back but left without him, and at 6:30 p.m. on May 23, *Flier* was on its way west once more. Two days later, as the submarine submerged, the crew took note that they were passing the International Date Line. They threw away the May 26 page from the calendar—a date in which they spent almost no time.

Memorial Day, Al Jacobson's birthday, was uneventful except that he was fed first among the officers, a tradition on the submarine. And the next day, a few hundred miles east of the Philippine archipelago, lookouts saw a Japanese airplane and *Flier* dove, successfully avoiding notice. In the ten days since they had left Pearl Harbor, the crew of *Flier* had seen Jacobson, the newest officer on board, crawling around their boat on hands and knees, inspecting every square inch. After all the schooling he had endured, the young ensign was still learning the nuts and bolts of a submarine. To become a qualified submarine officer, he would have to pass an extensive examination sometime after his first patrol. To prepare for the test, he frequently followed the engineering officer, Ensign Herbert A. "Teddy" Behr. Although the same rank as Jacobson, Behr was an old salt. He already had many years in the navy as a chief petty officer, one who got his hands dirty fixing engines. The navy, apparently recognizing Behr's talents, took the extraordinary step of elevating him to the status of commissioned officer, the equal of Annapolis graduates. Unlike most officers, however, Behr was a mechanic capable of fixing almost anything on the boat. Al, the mechanical engineer with the smell of the foundry still in his nose, and Teddy liked each other almost immediately.

Officers and crewmen alike were on duty for two eight-hour shifts every day, with four hours off between shifts. Meals came during a shift. The floating cribbage game—a no-betting diversion shared by officers, and learned aboard by Jacobson—was played between shifts in the wardroom, a small room with a fixed steel table in its center, covered with green linoleum. The wardroom was the officers' gathering place, separated from the forward torpedo room by the mess steward's pantry. Sitting at the table playing cribbage, every officer from the skipper to the fresh ensign could watch, through an open pass-through to the pantry, as John Clyde Turner, their steward, made the coffee and heated their meals, adding special touches to the plain grub the rest of the crew was eating. Some of the officers smoked, and although Al didn't, he was comfortable with his colleagues' fumes. If the boat was on the surface charging batteries, smoking was prohibited here and in the crew's mess. A spark could set off an explosion in the batteries, which were mounted under the flooring. It was at the wardroom table that Jacobson would sit with his mentor, Lieutenant John Edward Casey, reviewing the latest part of the submarine that young Al had studied.

Flier was a fleet-type submarine, designated *SS-250* for its place in the chronology of submarine construction. Almost identical to every other fleet submarine, *Flier* had a pressure hull—designed to withstand the extreme forces of seawater at a depth of 300 feet—surrounded by a steel superstructure that gave the boat its long, sleek appearance. It was the superstructure that had suffered the cracks and distortions when *Flier* was ground by the surf on the Midway reef. The pressure hull—a series of eight welded-steel cylindrical compartments joined end to end like sausage links, the links connected by watertight doors—had not been damaged, a testimony to the boat's robust construction.

The forward torpedo room with its six tubes for firing those weapons—often called "fish"—occupied the first sausage link. Stepping high through the watertight door at the torpedo room's rear, a sailor entered the next link in the pressure hull, with the steward's pantry and the officers' wardroom on the port side—the right side as you walked toward the boat's rear. Next came the officers' and chief petty officers' quarters on both port and starboard. Al Jacobson and another officer shared a cramped room with a double bunk on the port side. Under all these rooms was a bank of 126 huge batteries that powered the submarine when it was submerged. The third pressurized link contained the control room, where the crew managed most of the functions of the boat. Here were the two big spoked wheels that sailors turned to tilt the diving planes—pairs of wings on the front and rear of the submarine that, by the angle of their tilt, caused the vessel to rise or dive. Here also were a congestion of brass and glass gauges, long-handled levers, valve wheels, tubes, cables, phones, and bells, all mounted on the inner side of the pressure hull where it curved from the steel deck on one side, overhead and down to the deck on the other side.

Welded to the top of the control-room pressure hull—like another, small sausage link somehow out of sync with the rest of the submarine—was the conning tower, where the skipper would stay for most of his duty when the boat was submerged. The helmsman stood at the big steering wheel at the front of the conning tower, taking directions directly from the officer of the deck, either the skipper or the executive officer. The two periscopes were manned in the conning tower, and the radar and sonar operators were among the half-dozen men crammed into this little space. A watertight hatch opened in the conning-tower floor, and a steel ladder descended to the control room. Another hatch in the conning-tower ceiling led to the bridge, where Commander Crowley spent his time when *Flier* was on the surface.

To the rear of the control room in the row of links came the after battery compartment, where the crew's galley, mess hall, and sleeping quarters were aligned above another bank of 126 batteries. The fifth and sixth links in the pressure hull housed four enormous diesel engines, which ran when the submarine was surfaced, generating electricity both to run the motors that propelled the boat and to charge the batteries. The seventh pressurized link contained the maneuvering room, where two sailors sat at two panels, each with a bank of ten levers the size of—and resembling—shovel handles. Above the levers were two dozen gauges, all used to monitor and control the four powerful electric motors that turned the two propeller shafts.

Finally, the after torpedo room was in the eighth pressurized link. Here were four more torpedo tubes through which *Flier*'s weapons could be fired.

In all, there were tens of thousands of parts that, when pieced together, comprised the submarine, a lot of details for a young ensign to memorize. For Jacobson, being on shift might mean he was inspecting these parts. Frequently, it meant he was sitting in the control room, almost below the hatch that led up to the conning tower. Here his job involved plotting the submarine's course. Jacobson was assistant navigating officer, and he and the navigating officer, Jim Liddell, were solely responsible for recording *Flier*'s path across the ocean. When it was his time to plot the course, Jacobson would lower a rectangular table, hinged against the periscope tube, from its stowed position to its horizontal position on top of a thigh-high, egg-shaped gyro compass. Then he would spread a chart on the table. As the skipper or Liddell called out course changes, the ensign would record them, finding the boat's location on the chart and entering that information in an ongoing log that traced *Flier*'s course.

Two days after *Flier* dove to avoid the Japanese airplane, the boat changed course, having received word that the submarine *Silversides* had located an enemy convoy ripe for attack. At four the next morning, Jacobson calculated *Flier*'s position as being latitude 22 degrees 27 minutes north, longitude 138 degrees 7 minutes east, or roughly northeast of Luzon, the northernmost major Philippine island. Crowley held the position for the next ten hours until, through the magnification of the periscope, he spotted smoke—the telltale sign of a ship at sea—almost due north. He estimated that the ship was thirty miles away. By recording the movement of the smoke, he calculated that it was on a southeasterly course. The convoy that *Silversides* had reported was heading in the opposite direction. *Flier* had found its own prey.

On a glassy calm day at sea, as was June 3, 1944, any object on the surface is visible from miles away. A floating log can appear, at a distance, to be the size of a freighter, and a seagull might seem to be a navigational buoy. The slender periscope of a submarine might well be a mid-oceanic telephone pole, or even a tall building. Consequently, great care had to be taken by the skipper of a submarine on such a day, particularly when he knew that enemy vessels were within sight. Crowley and Liddell discussed the situation, and both concluded that while making a successful surface approach on this convoy was impossible, an approach at periscope depth during daylight was also improbable. Jacobson, sitting on a small stool before his chart table and looking toward the port side and the two planes-men, listened as the two ranking officers weighed their options. These were the first words he had heard in a real combat situation, and, like the quarterback's words in the huddle before the big play, they were the sort that could quicken any young man's pulse.

Crowley decided to dive and sneak toward the target ship, hoping to gather enough information to launch a nighttime attack. Two short blasts from the diving alarm—a claxon bell—rang throughout *Flier*, and a ritual aboard the submarine began to unfold. The diesel engines stopped running, and power from the battery banks began turning the electric motors. The huge air vents that brought fresh air to both the crew and the engines were closed, as were the engine exhaust valves. From above Jacobson's head came the sound of the conning-tower hatch to the bridge closing. Looking ahead over his chart, Al could see the bow and stern planesmen—one on each side of the ladder leading up to the conning tower—standing at their huge wheels. The bow planesman began turning his wheel clockwise, to the full-dive position. The stern planesman to his left turned his wheel counterclockwise. To the right of the bow planesman, a board of red and green lights blinked from red to green. When this "Christmas tree" was all green, air was bled into the boat, and one man watched a pressure gauge that showed whether the sub was watertight.

Chiefs were passing orders to crewmen in an everyday voice. If they felt any excite-ment, the men aboard *Flier* showed only the calm intensity of well-trained confidence.

The dive began just before two o'clock in the afternoon. At 3:30 p.m., with the smoke of the enemy ship still the only visible assurance of its presence, the men aboard *Flier* heard a series of twenty-two distant depth charges. Three hours later, a look through the periscope revealed a vessel—either a submarine or an escort ship—steaming north at high speed, off to the west of *Flier*. Thirty minutes later, at 7:18 p.m., Crowley gave orders to turn away from the target ship and to prepare to surface. Just then, smoke was sighted to the southwest. This was a different target than the first, which by now had moved from its original position to the north and, by traveling southeast, was steaming to the east of the submarine. Crowley decided to go after the more recently spotted ship because *Flier* was in a better position to make a successful attack than it was on the first, and because, having heard the depth charges, he assumed the first ship was already under attack by another submarine.

At 8:20 p.m., *Flier* surfaced beneath a black sky but on an ocean surface brightly lit by the moon. Crowley and Liddell, conferring with some of the other senior officers, decided to work ahead on the starboard flank of the new ship, which was heading northwest toward Japan at about eight knots, around nine miles per hour. Looking west from the bridge, Crowley could clearly see the smoke rising above the silvery sea—eight columns of smoke from as many ships, a convoy ripe for attack by an eager submarine crew. Looking to the east, the skipper could see that, about thirty miles away, the convoy that he had spotted first was under heavy attack as it headed south. There, the sky was lit again and again by gunfire.

Then to the west, there was gunfire from the second convoy that *Flier* was shadowing. Perhaps they too were under attack.

In order to avoid exposing their broad sides to torpedo attacks, ships of all navies followed zigzag courses, even when in convoy. The challenge for a submarine crew was to calculate, by observing the progress of a convoy over time, what the baseline of its course was—where, in other words, it was headed. At 10:20 p.m., the convoy that now was *Flier*'s target zigzagged directly toward the submarine, a little more than ten miles away. Al Jacobson, who had spent two hours on plot and two hours on the bridge, alternating with ensign Teddy Behr, looked toward the approaching convoy and was amazed at what he saw—every ship in the convoy silhouetted in the moonlight, each ship's zigs and zags obvious from this many miles away. He could even see when someone on the deck of one of those ships lit a match. Heading directly for *Flier*, though, the enemy skippers could not see the submarine due to its low profile and the distance it stayed away.

Crowley and his officers quickly concluded that the ships had changed their baseline because they were under attack. If they were running away from their tormentors, the skipper believed, these Japanese ships were in for a surprise. He gave the order to dive and begin a radar approach. But a half-hour before midnight, Crowley changed his mind. He had been unable to get *Flier* any closer than about four miles. He gave the order to surface and resume the chase. Making twice the speed of the convoy, the boat circled ahead to the east, intent on finding a spot in the ocean where it could lay in wait for its prey.

The moon set at 3:20 a.m. that morning, leaving the Pacific in near total darkness. A half-hour later, having maneuvered the submarine so that it was almost directly ahead of the convoy, Crowley gave the order to sound the dive alarm once again. With the lead ship of the group again about ten miles away, *Flier* once more began a radar approach. An hour later, the distance between the stalker and its victims had shrunk to just over a mile.

It was 4:47 a.m. when Al Jacobson heard the order passed.

"Periscope depth," Crowley said in an even voice.

Fourteen minutes later, six torpedoes were blasted from the forward tubes, three at each of two large freighters in a column of three ships passing before the submarine like soldiers on review.

Crowley spun the periscope in the opposite direction now, because another column of ships was passing behind *Flier*. The nearest ship was too close for Crowley to fire. A torpedo had to travel a certain distance before its explosives were armed—a distance that was greater than the space between *Flier* and its target. More important, two escort vessels, armed with depth charges and other weapons, were turning toward the submarine. Crowley ordered a deep dive, and the bow planesman cranked his wheel hard. The skipper took one more look around through the periscope. He saw smoke billowing from the first ship. A torpedo had found its mark. The second freighter had turned away and was apparently stopped. By the timing of the explosions that had by now been heard aboard *Flier*, the crew knew that two torpedoes had hit the first ship and another had hit the second.

Now it was payback time. The first depth charges began exploding over *Flier* soon after the five o'clock torpedo attack. Inside the submarine, everything was silent. The boat could not move because movement meant noise, and the slightest sound could be heard by sensitive sonar equipment on the Japanese military escort ships up on the surface. Silence meant no air-conditioning inside *Flier*. The air became thick with humidity, and following the lead of the senior men, Al began peeling off his clothing until he was down to his undershorts. The lights were off, and the only sounds were those of the depth charges. To Al, it was as if he had his head inside a metal oil drum on which someone was beating with a sledgehammer. The closer the explosions, the more chunks of cork insulation fell from the inside surface of the pressure hull.

The last of thirty-four depth charges exploded at 6:34 that morning, just under two hours after Crowley had initiated the conflict. Just before seven o'clock, Jacobson heard the last of the propeller sounds from the escort ships. *Flier*'s men had survived the retaliation. Crowley gave the order to surface, and the submarine's motors began to turn the two big propellers at its rear. When the periscope broke the surface, the skipper saw smoke on the horizon. Crowley ordered another deep dive to load torpedoes in the six empty forward tubes.

The tension had been felt by everyone aboard *Flier*, not just by the green ensign. And the men needed a little humor just now to let off some steam. Someone looked at John Clyde Turner, the officers' black mess steward, and concluded that he had been scared white. All the white men laughed. Someone said it was a good thing the rest of them were white already.

An escort had apparently lagged behind the convoy after the depth-charge attack, because sometime after ten o'clock on the morning of June 4, the menacing ship was spotted racing toward *Flier*. Crowley turned his boat south and fled the scene, waiting another hour before returning to the hunt. Spotting the escort again, he decided to try circling to the west. But after eighteen hours of searching, he was unable to find the convoy. At daybreak the next morning, he decided to return to the scene of the attack. Arriving four hours later, *Flier* slipped through a floating maritime junkyard. There were six lifeboats and the wooden pilothouse of a ship. When Crowley sent some men over the side to inspect the wreckage, they returned with a packet of documents from one of the lifeboats and said they had seen compass equipment in the pilothouse that was made in New York.

Looking down from the bridge at the *Flier*'s handiwork, Al Jacobson saw not just wood and metal. The bodies of hundreds of Japanese men, buoyed by life jackets, were scattered throughout the debris. At least one of the two ships struck by *Flier*'s torpedoes was a troopship. *Flier* had killed 1,200 men on that darkened ocean.

———

Crowley pointed *Flier* west once more, and three days later, after steaming across the Philippine Sea, the boat reached the Balintang Channel, the central passage through the Luzon Strait, which separates Taiwan to the north from the Philippines to the south. Later that day, with the submarine running submerged, the smoke and mast of a fast-moving ship was spotted ten miles ahead, moving north toward Japan. Its speed was equal to the best *Flier* could make, and it got away. For the next four days, June 9 through June 12, Crowley kept the boat underwater all day long as he steered ten miles north of Calayan Island, one of the Babuyan Islands—among the northernmost specks of land in the Philippines—and then five miles off Cape Bojeador, the northwestern tip of Luzon. On June 12, *Flier* slipped past Cape Bolinao, a hook of land that reaches out from the peninsula that forms the western side of Lingayen Gulf, where Japanese troops first landed on December 21, 1941, to complete the occupation of the Philippines.

Flier was truly deep in the heart of enemy territory.

The ocean off the western shores of Luzon fills some of the deepest voids on the Earth's surface. Only five miles off the beaches, *Flier* was also miles above the ocean floor, a graveyard where boats and the bones of their sailors could perhaps lie untouched forever. This was not on the minds of John Crowley and his men. They fully expected to send as many Japanese men and ships as they could down to this burying ground.

The next day, June 13, promised to be a lucky one. At one o'clock in the afternoon, *Flier*'s crew saw, through the periscope, the smoke from ships following the submarine from the north as it skirted the shore. Crowley ordered the helmsman to turn the submarine around and, with the boat still submerged, the crew began preparations for its second battle. Ahead of them lay a military bonanza, a convoy of eleven ships and at least six escorts. As they drew closer, it was clear that this big flotilla was hugging the coast, its escorts keeping offshore from the transport ships, like a gentleman walking a lady down a sidewalk, protecting her from being splashed from the gutter.

Again the sea was as smooth as a pool of oil. Crowley remained in the conning tower as he pressed *Flier* in on the convoy, but he kept his periscope observations brief. In the control room below the skipper, and throughout the submarine, there was silence as the men anticipated the coming attack, each sailor poised in position, the whole crew a jungle cat suspended in the moment before the pounce. In the control room, the planesmen turned their wheels without a word, synchronized in the effort to hold the boat level and keep it at the depth that Crowley had dictated. Waiting for the next course change, Jacobson gazed across the control room, watching the depth gauge and the dials that showed the angle of the boat and of the two sets of planes. He saw the competence he had grown to expect, a comforting order in the quiet.

And then he saw trouble. The stern planesman was struggling with his wheel. Calling out a warning to the control-room chief, the planesman grabbed a crank handle mounted near his wheel and, bracing himself, strained to move the planes as the submarine went into an unintended dive.

The bow planesman spun his wheel to counteract the tilt that the stern planes had already given to the boat, and the chief, his voice urgent, ordered all hands to the rear. Men from the forward torpedo room began hustling one after another past Jacobson's chart table, stepping through the high, oval, watertight door at the forward end of the compartment and climbing out through the similar door at the rear. Those who couldn't leave their posts—men like the green ensign—froze in anticipation. Miles of pitch-dark ocean lay beneath them, and *Flier*, with no help from the enemy, was headed there.

Among those moving to the rear was one sailor who raced around the rest. His job was to find out what was wrong in the after torpedo room. The planes, attached to the boat outside that final sausage link, were operated by a hydraulic system. A pump might have gone or a hose might have ruptured. Whatever the problem, it needed to be fixed immediately.

In the control room, the chief waited for his man's report. But without any explanation, the hydraulics suddenly began working. Then, just as quickly, they once again failed, and the stern planesman strained at his crank. Behind him, young Jacobson had a ringside seat to the struggle, but no immediate job to do. It was clear to the ensign that this was a serious matter, but if he felt fear, he also felt confidence in the boat, its crew, and the skipper—a sense of the rightness of things, an assurance, perhaps connected to his god, in the outcome. Finally, at 2:18 p.m., power mysteriously returned to the stern-plane controls. After six minutes of uncertainty, the stern planesman returned from his crank to his wheel, and *Flier* resumed a steady, level course.

Crowley now discussed strategy with Liddell, Ed Casey, and the other senior officers. The convoy they were stalking was within a mile of the lush jungle coast of Luzon, and between those ships and the submarine were the half-dozen escorts. An attack clearly would not be successful if launched from offshore. There were too many escorts protecting the convoy's flank. The alternative, Jacobson heard the officers say, was to speed across the convoy's path ahead of the lead ship and, a half-mile from the coast, launch an attack on the long, unprotected steel of the cargo ships. There would be no escorts on that side . . . until the first torpedo hit.

Crowley was cautious no more. Bristling with a warrior's courage, he gave the order to race across the convoy's path, the naval equivalent of running down a dead-end alley.

At just before three o'clock, with *Flier* facing toward shore, Crowley ordered all four stern torpedo tubes fired. One by one, the fish were blown out of the tubes by compressed air and began running toward the 10,000-ton tanker that was just passing on its southern voyage. As soon as the torpedoes were fired, Crowley ordered the ship turned around so that the forward torpedoes could be aimed. A small freighter was less than 100 yards off

Flier's bow when the sub completed its turn. That was too close for an attack, so Crowley shifted his aim to a ship less than a mile away in the convoy column closest to shore. Before the skipper, using the periscope to aim, could give a bearing to the sailor manning the torpedo arming and aiming device, the sonar man in the conning tower, wearing headphones, heard two hits on the tanker, followed immediately by a huge explosion. The word was relayed throughout the submarine—*Score!*

In the haste to get set up for the next target ship, the diving officer, misunderstanding an order, ducked the periscope. Blind under the ocean's waves, Crowley ordered a deep dive without firing the bow torpedoes. He knew that the escorts would be heading to where *Flier* was backed against the shore, and he knew there were not even seconds to spare. Behind him in the conning tower, Crowley heard the voice of the sonar (or sound-) man. Escorts were approaching from several angles. Then more bad news. The stern planes had failed again. Down in the control room, the stern planesman wrenched his crank, struggling to pull the boat from its dive as the first depth charges fell. By the sounds coming from the propellers of the escorts, the soundman could tell that all six vessels were in on the attack, like a pack of dogs against one lonely cat.

The cat had to move, but it needed camouflage. The escort ships on the surface could tell where the submarine was only if it made sounds. There were no devices for "looking" at the ocean floor, only the sonar that could, like radar, read the echo from a sound wave and microphones that could listen for ship noises.

Crowley needed to keep moving and keep the stalking escorts guessing where *Flier* was. But this required running the boat's motors, and that could be done only when the attacking ships were also moving, because their own movement would hide the sound of the submarine. The deadly game had begun, and once again the heat started to build inside *Flier*. The escorts would fall silent and every movement aboard *Flier* would cease. No one walked or talked. They closed their eyes and simply breathed in the thick air. Then the escorts, apparently having decided that the submarine was in a certain location, all began moving toward that point. Crowley would quietly call out orders for a course and speed, and in the bottomless ocean, *Flier* would make a right-angle turn and glide to a new location. At his chart table, Jacobson recorded each new course, the speed, and the length of time the boat moved, and then plotted on the chart where they stopped. He gave this information to Crowley so that when the next move came, the skipper would know how to avoid the rocks of shore, and where to head for safe, deep water.

Twenty minutes after the torpedoes had been fired, everyone on the boat heard a loud rumbling explosion from the general direction of the Japanese tanker. Jacobson listened to the conversations coming from the conning tower. The soundman reported that he heard noises similar to those of a ship breaking up, but these sounds came between continuing blasts from depth charges. Again and again the Japanese escorts—probably destroyers— swung toward *Flier* and rolled off another batch of barrels that sank to a predetermined depth before exploding. Sometimes they were nowhere near the submarine. Other times, they seemed to be directly overhead. Cork rained down from the ceiling then, and in each of the segments of the pressure hull—each one now sealed from the rest by closed, watertight doors on which the locking levers, called dogs, had been jammed in place—trickles of sweat, driven both by heat and fear, fell from eighty-six nearly naked men. The sweat on Crowley's chest streamed around a chain necklace from which hung a small crucifix, etched with the words JESUS NAZARENUS, REX JUDAEORUM.

One of the men appeared to be unmoved by the dangers that now preoccupied the rest of the crew. John Clyde Turner needed to keep the officers fed, so he busied himself in his pantry, between the officers' quarters and the forward torpedo room, working as if the next meal was the most crucial concern on board the submarine. In the course of his chores, Turner decided he needed something from the refrigerator. *Flier* happened to be motionless at the time, waiting for the next rush of the escorts. You could have heard the breath of a mouse. The sound of a refrigerator door opening was, to the men in the forward torpedo room, as loud as if the claxon had been tripped. Several of them—no doubt driven by their own inexpressible fears—opened and vaulted through the watertight door, tackling Turner. His life was theirs to take, and their intentions were obvious. Officers raced from the wardroom to restrain the attackers, whose own scrambling had probably made more noise than the opening of several refrigerator doors. In moments, everyone returned to his place to wait for the next round of depth charges that he knew would come.

The pounding continued all afternoon. Each man inside *Flier* could keep his own score as the number of depth-charge runs rose past twenty, thirty, forty—with no end in sight. At one point, an escort was heard directly overhead, as if running straight up the submarine's spine. The ship unleashed its explosives only after it had passed the boat, but there was no spontaneous sigh of relief because the next swing could be the lethal one.

At 7:15 p.m., Crowley grew impatient. *Flier* had a dummy torpedo stored in the after torpedo room. It was filled with explosives, set to detonate after the torpedo had traveled a specific distance. It also held a tank of oil. At the skipper's command, the crew fired the torpedo from a stern tube and the fish ran out a thousand yards before its blast was heard inside *Flier*. The concussion and the huge oil slick that soon appeared on the surface looked and sounded to ships on the surface like evidence of a sinking submarine.

In minutes, the depth-charge attack ceased. It had been five hours since Crowley had started this engagement. Now the skipper was convinced the escorts were finished, and he gave the order to surface. Once the hatch to the bridge was opened and the commander had climbed the ladder, Jacobson followed, eager to escape the stuffy confines and stinking perspiration odor of the control room. To his surprise, he found that now the scent of fresh air was actually offensive.

June 13 had ended okay. None of the 105 depth charges dropped by the Japanese escorts had found its mark.

———

Night fell off Luzon, and later, *Flier* headed south once more, hoping to pick up the convoy, which was probably headed for Subic Bay, the main shipping port near Manila. In the middle of the night, as *Flier* ran on the surface, lookouts above the bridge spotted smoke on the horizon. But a patrol plane flew over and *Flier* turned away, unwilling to risk the continued pursuit.

For the next four days, the submarine prowled around the islands near Manila, submerged during the day and then surfacing at night. Young Jacobson was thrilled to see the silhouettes of Corregidor, Bataan, and Manila's shoreline, knowing that the enemy soldiers there had no idea *Flier* was so close. He hoped with a youthful eagerness that some vessel would stray out on the water and present the submarine with a target. Having tasted the kill, he wanted to sink another ship.

He would have to wait five days.

———

Ed Casey was officer of the deck on June 22, standing watch in the conning tower as *Flier*, following its daytime routine, ran submerged. Around dinnertime, Casey spotted five columns of smoke in the southwest, about fifteen miles ahead. This was the eighth time on its first patrol that *Flier* had encountered enemy ships. The crew had destroyed two enemy ships and damaged another, but there had been many more missed opportunities. Listening to Casey's report was young Jacobson, who had the duty of diving officer—the man responsible for ordering a dive should it become necessary. The ensign hoped, as he heard Casey's description from the periscope, for better luck this time.

Casey, an agreeable family man, slender but athletic and quiet, was Jacobson's mentor. He had bet Jacobson earlier in the day that if he saw any targets, the inexperienced kid would order a dive too quickly, ducking the periscope. Jacobson won that bet, and Casey was able to observe the changing compass bearing of the enemy convoy's smoke. The smoke was heading right for *Flier*. Casey consulted with Crowley, who decided to wait for dark to make a surface attack on the convoy. Soon the soundman heard the sonar "pinging" from the convoy's escorts as they searched for trouble. Now Crowley was handling the periscope, taking regular bearings on the convoy, and Jacobson had moved to the chart table to plot the enemy's course.

Darkness had settled on Apo East Pass when *Flier*—which the day before had been directed to intercept the Japanese fleet as it sailed north from Mindanao—surfaced about seven miles behind the convoy, which was zigging and zagging four miles off the coast of Mindoro Island. On the surface, the submarine began a circular sweep, called an "end-around," up the western side of the convoy, and Jacobson reported to the bridge and took up the post of junior officer of the deck, standing to the rear of the bridge on the after cigarette deck. Looking east, he could see the whole convoy and each of the ships' movements.

Flier raced north, and by eleven o'clock that night had reached a position to attack the convoy, almost in front of it on its left flank, about six miles away. Crowley now turned his boat and, driving toward the leading ships, the submarine slipped inside of the destroyers escorting the convoy. Jacobson's job during the approach was to keep the crosshairs of a set of binoculars, temporarily resting in a deck-mounted stand, trained on the target ships. The cradle supporting the binoculars could be pivoted in any direction, and there was a mechanical connection between the cradle and the "torpedo data computer"—the device that programmed the course for each torpedo. Below the binoculars was a pistol grip with a trigger. As he adjusted the bearing of the crosshairs, Jacobson's finger rested lightly on the trigger. Crowley, standing on the bridge forward of Jacobson, had settled on two freighters out of the nine ships in the convoy—the first one large and the second one medium-size, and both at the lead of the nearest convoy column. Unnoticed, *Flier* moved to within a mile of those ships, scooting in front of the escorting destroyers, and Crowley told Jacobson to fire when he was ready.

If a soldier can be trained to think of the enemy as a target, rather than one or more human beings, the destruction of those lives becomes more of a mathematics problem to be solved than a moral question to be pondered. Admiral I. J. Galantin addressed this phenomenon in his reflections on his World War II submarine service: "Naval warfare had evolved to the point that sailors no longer saw their enemy as people; they saw only the steel or aluminum vehicles in which their enemy sailed or flew, trying to bring their own weapons to bear. The ships or aircraft were the enemy of one's own ship; *they* were the enemy . . .

"Submarine war was even more detached, its special horror comparatively new to history, its action generally remote from human experience. Though our sinkings of enemy combat and cargo ships sent thousands of men to their deaths, this was but incidental to the real purpose—the strangling of an empire through cutting off its oil, its food, its raw materials."

On that black night off Mindoro, Al Jacobson pulled the trigger once. A torpedo shot silently underwater from *Flier*'s bow. He pulled again. Another torpedo followed the first, speeding toward the larger freighter. Again he squeezed his hand and a third torpedo was on its way.

Now he turned the binoculars slightly south. The smaller freighter was in the cross-hairs. He pulled the trigger once, twice, a third time, and *Flier* swung sharply away to return to the safety of the open ocean. Looking back at the convoy, Jacobson saw geysers of water rise in the blackness—two from the big ship and one from the medium-size one. The sound of a second torpedo hitting the second ship came through the warm night air. With each hit, the orange flash of an explosion lit the target ship, and, at this close range, Jacobson could see objects flying up into the air—all of it junk to his eyes.

The shooting had begun at 11:23 that night. In only a few minutes, the two target ships were dropping out of the convoy, and then the smaller one sank. Although but one part of a coordinated team, the ensign at the trigger could take direct credit for the steel and flesh that disappeared before his eyes under the waves.

The escorts, now with only seven ships in their convoy, began hunting *Flier*, dropping depth charges where they thought the boat was submerged. But the submarine was on the surface, stealing away in the night at high speed, just far enough away to keep the convoy in sight but not close enough to be spotted by the escorts. Having fallen to the stern of the convoy, Crowley wanted another shot, and so he did another end-around up the western flank of the seven ships and their escorts, and at one minute after midnight, the convoy zigged right toward *Flier*. The saltwater waves splashed over the submarine's bow as the skipper ordered full speed ahead and the predator raced in for another kill. Jacobson was still on deck, hands on the binoculars, a wad of gum in his mouth. When the boat approached an escort, he heard Crowley order the engines slowed so *Flier* could sneak by. Once inside all the escorts, Crowley poured on the power and the submarine went for its next target.

There were only four torpedoes left in the forward torpedo room, and the skipper dedicated these to the ship that now led the convoy, a medium-size freighter. From the bridge, Crowley relayed the compass bearing to the freighter. At the same time, the radar operator relayed his own observations on the distance to the ship. When the submarine was in a firing position, Crowley gave Jacobson the order to fire, and the ensign squeezed his trigger four times. Jacobson knew how long it should take the torpedoes to reach the ship, and he timed their invisible progress with the rhythm of his gum chewing.

There was silence, and like a gunslinger who learns he has fired blanks in a shootout, Jacobson began to worry. A few tense seconds passed before the flash of two explosions lit the rear of the target ship and the sound of a third blast was heard.

By incalculable luck, *Flier* had inflicted damage on two ships. While the skipper had been giving bearings on the lead ship, the radar operator was figuring the distance to a second, closer vessel. All of the torpedoes might well have missed the target, but two had followed a course that found the rear of that ship. The third torpedo had passed behind the ship, but here the luck came in for *Flier*. Seen from the submarine, another ship in the convoy overlapped the first and had the misfortune to be directly in front of that third torpedo.

Crowley swung the boat around, hoping to do more damage to the convoy with torpedoes from the stern tubes. But by now, the escorts had located *Flier*. Crowley called down to Liddell in the conning tower, asking where on the radar the widest space was between the escorts.

"I think course 205 degrees," Liddell yelled back.

"Put on all the power we have and head out on course 205," Crowley shouted.

The escorts were searching wildly as *Flier* raced toward them. From the deck of the surfaced submarine, Jacobson saw one looming out of the darkness, on a course almost parallel to the submarine but headed in the opposite direction. Both boats were moving at full speed, and when they passed, there was no hint that the escort had seen the submarine. *Flier* plowed ahead into the safety of a dark sea, and the ensign looked back to see the ships at which he had fired, smoking heavily and apparently sinking.

It was about two hours after midnight when *Flier* made another dash between two Japanese escort vessels for a second attack on a still-floating but burning freighter two miles closer to shore. When they cleared the escorts, the men on *Flier's* deck saw their target ship sink—their fourth victim, if they were counting ships. If they were counting men, no one could guess the score.

By now, the rest of the convoy was many miles to the north. Two hours later, the submarine dove so that the crew could take a rest after the long night of fighting. Although the boat remained submerged all day on June 23, the crew knew they were being hunted. Pinging could be heard from several directions, and at two o'clock that afternoon, several patrol planes were seen through the periscope, circling. Later, a group of antisubmarine ships were up there, searching. After dinner, a destroyer headed toward *Flier*, and it was clear the Japanese believed a submarine was still in the neighborhood. Crowley turned the boat away from the destroyer so that the stern tubes, which held *Flier's* four remaining torpedoes, were aimed at the destroyer. But the menace never came within range of the torpedoes, and eventually turned away.

One young ensign had had enough and sighed with relief.

CHAPTER THIRTY

Vicksburg During the Trouble
By Mark Twain

There seem to be few subjects about which Mark Twain did not take up pen, and the Civil War was no exception. In his classic Life on the Mississippi, *as he steams past Vicksburg, Mississippi—well known for its famous caves—he recounts the story of a couple who lived through the city's shelling between May and July of 1863.*

—LISA PURCELL

WE USED TO PLOW PAST THE LOFTY HILL-CITY, VICKSBURG, DOWN-STREAM; BUT WE cannot do that now. A cut-off has made a country town of it, like Osceola, St. Genevieve, and several others. There is currentless water—also a big island—in front of Vicksburg now. You come down the river the other side of the island, then turn and come up to the town; that is, in high water: in low water you can't come up, but must land some distance below it.

Signs and scars still remain, as reminders of Vicksburg's tremendous war experiences; earthworks, trees crippled by the cannon balls, cave-refuges in the clay precipices, etc. The caves did good service during the six weeks' bombardment of the city—May 8 to July 4, 1863. They were used by the non-combatants—mainly by the women and children; not to live in constantly, but to fly to for safety on occasion. They were mere holes, tunnels, driven into the perpendicular clay bank, then branched Y shape, within the hill. Life in Vicksburg, during the six weeks was perhaps—but wait; here are some materials out of which to reproduce it:

Population, twenty-seven thousand soldiers and three thousand non-combatants; the city utterly cut off from the world—walled solidly in, the frontage by gunboats, the rear by soldiers and batteries; hence, no buying and selling with the outside; no passing to and fro; no God-speeding a parting guest, no welcoming a coming one; no printed acres of world-wide news to be read at breakfast, mornings—a tedious dull absence of such matter, instead; hence, also, no running to see steamboats smoking into view in the distance up or down, and plowing toward the town—for none came, the river lay vacant and undisturbed; no rush and turmoil around the railway station, no struggling over bewildered swarms of passengers by noisy mobs of hackmen—all quiet there; flour two hundred dollars a barrel, sugar thirty, corn ten dollars a bushel, bacon five dollars a pound, rum a hundred dollars a gallon; other things in proportion: consequently, no roar and racket of drays and carriages tearing along the streets; nothing for them to do, among that handful of non-combatants of exhausted means; at three o'clock in the morning, silence; silence so dead that the measured tramp of a sentinel can be heard a seemingly impossible distance; out of hearing of this lonely sound, perhaps the stillness is absolute: all in a moment come ground-shaking thunder-crashes of artillery, the sky is cobwebbed with the crisscrossing red lines streaming from soaring bomb-shells, and a rain of iron fragments descends upon the city; descends upon the empty streets: streets which are not empty a moment later, but mottled with dim figures of frantic women and children scurrying from home and bed toward the cave dungeons—encouraged by the humorous grim soldiery, who shout "Rats, to your holes!" and laugh.

The cannon-thunder rages, shells scream and crash overhead, the iron rain pours down, one hour, two hours, three, possibly six, then stops; silence follows, but the streets are still empty; the silence continues; by-and-by a head projects from a cave here and there and yonder, and reconnoitres, cautiously; the silence still continuing, bodies follow heads, and jaded, half smothered creatures group themselves about, stretch their cramped limbs, draw in deep draughts of the grateful fresh air, gossip with the neighbors from the next cave; maybe straggle off home presently, or take a lounge through the town, if the stillness continues; and will scurry to the holes again, by-and-by, when the war-tempest breaks forth once more.

There being but three thousand of these cave-dwellers—merely the population of a village—would they not come to know each other, after a week or two, and familiarly; insomuch that the fortunate or unfortunate experiences of one would be of interest to all?

Those are the materials furnished by history. From them might not almost anybody reproduce for himself the life of that time in Vicksburg? Could you, who did not experience it, come nearer to reproducing it to the imagination of another non-participant than could a Vicksburger who did experience it? It seems impossible; and yet there are reasons why it might not really be. When one makes his first voyage in a ship, it is an experience which multitudinously bristles with striking novelties; novelties which are in such sharp contrast with all this person's former experiences that they take a seemingly deathless grip upon his imagination and memory. By tongue or pen he can make a landsman live that strange and stirring voyage over with him; make him see it all and feel it all. But if he wait? If he make ten voyages in succession—what then? Why, the thing has lost color, snap, surprise; and has become commonplace. The man would have nothing to tell that would quicken a landsman's pulse.

Years ago, I talked with a couple of the Vicksburg non-combatants—a man and his wife. Left to tell their story in their own way, those people told it without fire, almost without interest.

A week of their wonderful life there would have made their tongues eloquent forever perhaps; but they had six weeks of it, and that wore the novelty all out; they got used to being bomb-shelled out of home and into the ground; the matter became commonplace. After that, the possibility of their ever being startlingly interesting in their talks about it was gone. What the man said was to this effect:

"It got to be Sunday all the time. Seven Sundays in the week—to us, anyway. We hadn't anything to do, and time hung heavy. Seven Sundays, and all of them broken up at one time or another, in the day or in the night, by a few hours of the awful storm of fire and thunder and iron. At first we used to shin for the holes a good deal faster than we did afterwards. The first time, I forgot the children, and Maria fetched them both along. When she was all safe in the cave she fainted. Two or three weeks afterwards, when she was running for the holes, one morning, through a shell-shower, a big shell burst near her, and covered her all over with dirt, and a piece of the iron carried away her game-bag of false hair from the back of her head. Well, she stopped to get that game-bag before she shoved along again! Was getting used to things already, you see. We all got so that we could tell a good deal about shells; and after that we didn't always go under shelter if it was a light shower. Us men would loaf around and talk; and a man would say, 'There she goes!' and name the kind of shell it was from the sound of it, and go on talking—if there wasn't any danger from it. If a shell was bursting close over us, we stopped talking and stood still;—uncomfortable, yes, but it wasn't safe to move. When it let go, we went on talking again, if nobody hurt—maybe saying, 'That was a ripper!' or some such commonplace comment before we resumed; or, maybe, we would see a shell poising itself away high in the air overhead. In that case, every fellow just whipped out a sudden, 'See you again, gents!' and shoved. Often and often I saw gangs of ladies promenading the streets, looking as cheerful as you please, and keeping an eye canted up watching the shells; and I've seen them stop still when they were uncertain about what a shell was going to do, and wait and make certain; and after that they sa'ntered along again, or lit out for shelter, according to the verdict. Streets in some towns have a litter of pieces of paper, and odds and ends of one sort or another lying around. Ours hadn't; they had iron litter. Sometimes a man would gather up all the iron fragments and unbursted shells in his neighborhood, and pile them into a kind of monument in his front yard—a ton of it, sometimes. No glass left; glass couldn't stand such a bombardment; it was all shivered out. Windows of the houses vacant—looked like eye-holes in a skull. Whole panes were as scarce as news.

"We had church Sundays. Not many there, along at first; but by-and-bye pretty good turnouts. I've seen service stop a minute, and everybody sit quiet—no voice heard, pretty funeral-like then—and all the more so on account of the awful boom and crash going on outside and overhead; and pretty soon, when a body could be heard, service would go on again. Organs and church-music mixed up with a bombardment is a powerful queer combination—along at first. Coming out of church, one morning, we had an accident—the only one that happened around me on a Sunday. I was just having a hearty handshake with a friend I hadn't seen for a while, and saying, 'Drop into our cave to-night, after bombardment; we've got hold of a pint of prime wh—.' Whiskey, I was going to say, you know, but a shell interrupted. A chunk of it cut the man's arm off, and left it dangling in my hand. And do you know the thing that is going to stick the longest in my memory, and outlast everything else, little and big, I reckon, is the mean thought I had then? It was 'the whiskey is saved.' And yet, don't you know, it was kind of excusable; because it was as scarce as diamonds, and we had only just that little; never had another taste during the siege.

"Sometimes the caves were desperately crowded, and always hot and close. Sometimes a cave had twenty or twenty-five people packed into it; no turning-room for anybody; air so foul, sometimes, you couldn't have made a candle burn in it. A child was born in one of those caves one night, Think of that; why, it was like having it born in a trunk.

"Twice we had sixteen people in our cave; and a number of times we had a dozen. Pretty suffocating in there. We always had eight; eight belonged there. Hunger and misery and sickness and fright and sorrow, and I don't know what all, got so loaded into them that none of them were ever rightly their old selves after the siege. They all died but three of us within a couple of years. One night a shell burst in front of the hole and caved it in and stopped it up. It was lively times, for a while, digging out. Some of us came near smothering. After that we made two openings—ought to have thought of it at first.

"Mule meat. No, we only got down to that the last day or two. Of course it was good; anything is good when you are starving."

This man had kept a diary during—six weeks? No, only the first six days. The first day, eight close pages; the second, five; the third, one—loosely written; the fourth, three or four lines; a line or two the fifth and sixth days; seventh day, diary abandoned; life in terrific Vicksburg having now become commonplace and matter of course.

The war history of Vicksburg has more about it to interest the general reader than that of any other of the river-towns. It is full of variety, full of incident, full of the picturesque. Vicksburg held out longer than any other important river-town, and saw warfare in all its phases, both land and water—the siege, the mine, the assault, the repulse, the bombardment, sickness, captivity, famine.

The most beautiful of all the national cemeteries is here. Over the great gateway is this inscription:

"Here Rest In Peace 16,600 Who Died For Their Country In The Years 1861 To 1865"

CHAPTER THIRTY-ONE

Intensification of Suffering and Hatred
By Phoebe Yates Pember

Like Louisa May Alcott, many Northern and Southern women volunteered for duty in army hospitals as a way to serve their cause. Often inexperienced, many times from pampered backgrounds, they nonetheless rose to the challenge of this backbreaking—and heartbreaking—work. Phoebe Yates Levy Pember was a well-educated woman from a prosperous Jewish family in Charleston, South Carolina. A widow by 1861, she accepted the offer to serve as matron at the largest military hospital in the country at that time, Chimborazo Hospital in Richmond, Virginia. Even in this large and established facility, casualties were greatly compounded by severe shortages of personnel, food, medicine, and equipment. As did Alcott, Pember began her service in December 1862, but her stint lasted far longer. She remained at Chimborazo even after the fall of Richmond, until Union troops took it over. During that time, she did whatever she could to relieve her patients' miseries—from playing cards with recovering patients to holding the hands of dying young men. During her time at Chimborazo, she noticed the regard her Southern boys felt for their Northern counterparts. Yet, as the suffering in the South intensified, so did the hatred toward the foe. "Intensification of Suffering and Hatred" is an excerpt from Pember's A Southern Woman's Story, *which takes place in 1864 as the war was grinding to a close.*

—SARA PURCELL

NOW DURING THE SUMMER OF 1864 BEGAN WHAT IS REALLY MEANT BY "WAR," FOR privations had to be endured which tried body and soul, and which temper and patience had to meet unflinchingly day and night. A growing want of confidence was forced upon the mind; and with doubts which though unexpressed were felt as to the ultimate success of our cause, there came into play the antagonistic qualities of human nature.

The money worthless, and a weak Congress and weaker financier failing to make it much more valuable than the paper it was printed on; the former refusing to the last to raise the hospital fund to meet the depreciation. Everything furnished through government contracts of the very poorest description, perhaps necessarily so from the difficulty of finding any supply.

The railroads were cut so constantly that what had been carefully collected in the country in the form of poultry and vegetables by hospital agents would be rendered unfit for use by the time the connection would be restored. The inducements for theft were great in this season of scarcity of food and clothing. The pathetic appeals made for the coarsest meal by starving men all wore upon the health and strength of those exposed to the strain, and made life weary and hopeless.

The rations became so small about this time that every ounce of flour was valuable, and there were days when it was necessary to refuse with aching heart and brimming eyes the request of decent, manly-looking fellows for a piece of dry corn-bread. If given it would have robbed the rightful owner of part of his scanty rations. After the flour or meal had been made into bread, it was almost ludicrous to see with what painful solicitude Miss G. and myself would count the rolls, or hold a council over the pans of corn-bread, measuring with a string how large we could afford to cut the squares, to be apportioned to a certain number.

Sometimes when from the causes above stated, the supplies were not issued as usual, invention had to be taxed to an extreme, and every available article in our pantry brought into requisition. We had constantly to fall back upon dried apples and rice for convalescing appetites, and herb-tea and arrowroot for the very ill. There was only one way of making the last at all palatable, and that was by drenching it with whiskey.

Long abstinence in the field from everything that could be considered, even then, a delicacy, had exaggerated the fancy of sick men for any particular article of food they wanted into a passion; and they begged for such peculiar dishes that surgeons and nurses might well be puzzled. The greatest difficulty in granting these desires was that tastes became contagious, and whatever one patient asked for, his neighbor and the one next to him, and so on throughout the wards, craved also, and it was impossible to decide upon whom to draw a check.

No one unacquainted with our domestic relations can appreciate the difficulties under which we labored. Stoves in any degree of newness or usefulness we did not have; they were rare and expensive luxuries. As may be supposed, they were not the most convenient articles in the world to pack away in blockade-running vessels; and the trouble and expense of land transportation also seriously affected the quality of the wood for fuel furnished us. Timber which had been condemned heretofore as unfit for use, light, soggy and decayed, became the only quality available. The bacon, too, cured the first two years of the war, when salt commanded an enormous price, in most cases was spoilt, from the economy used in preparing that article; and bacon was one of the sinews of war.

We kept up brave hearts, and said we could eat the simplest fare, and wear the coarsest clothing, but there was absolutely nothing to be bought that did not rank as a luxury. It was wasting time and brain to attempt to economize, so we bent to the full force of that wise precept, "Sufficient for the day is the evil thereof."

There really was a great deal of heroism displayed when looking back, at the calm courage with which I learned to count the number of mouths to be fed daily, and then contemplating the food, calculate not how much but how little each man could be satisfied with. War may be glorious in all its panoply and pride, when in the field opposing armies meet and strive for victory; but battles fought by starving the sick and wounded—by crushing in by main force day by day all the necessities of human nature, make victories hardly worth the name.

Another of my local troubles were the rats, who felt the times, and waxed strong and cunning, defying all attempts to entrap them, and skillfully levying blackmail upon us day by day, and night after night. Hunger had educated their minds and sharpened their reasoning faculties. Other vermin, the change of seasons would rid us of, but the coldest day in winter, and the hottest in summer, made no apparent difference in their vivacious strategy.

They examined traps with the air of connoisseurs, sometimes springing them from a safe position, and kicked over the bread spread with butter and strychnine to show their contempt for such underhand warfare. The men related wonderful rat-stories not well enough authenticated to put on record, but their gourmands ate all the poultices applied during the night to the sick, and dragged away the pads stuffed with bran from under the arms and legs of the wounded.

They even performed a surgical operation which would have entitled any of them to pass the board. A Virginian had been wounded in the very center of the instep of his left foot. The hole made was large, and the wound sloughed fearfully around a great lump of proud flesh which had formed in the center like an island. The surgeons feared to remove this mass, as it might be connected with the nerves of the foot, and lockjaw might ensue. Poor Patterson would sit on his bed all day gazing at his lame foot and bathing it with a rueful face, which had brightened amazingly one morning when I paid him a visit. He exhibited it with great glee, the little island gone, and a deep hollow left, but the wound washed clean and looking healthy. Some skillful rat surgeon had done him this good service while in the search for luxuries, and he only knew that on awaking in the morning he had found the operation performed.

I never had but one personal interview with any of them. An ancient gray gentleman, who looked a hundred years old, both in years and depravity, would eat nothing but butter, when that article was twenty dollars a pound; so finding all means of getting rid of him fail through his superior intelligence, I caught him with a fish-hook, well baited with a lump of his favorite butter, dropped into his domicile under the kitchen floor.

Epicures sometimes managed to entrap them and secure a nice broil for supper, declaring that their flesh was superior to squirrel meat; but never having tasted it, I cannot add my testimony to its merits. They staid with us to the last, nor did I ever observe any signs of a desire to change their politics. Perhaps some curious gourmet may wish a recipe for the best mode of cooking them. The rat must be skinned, cleaned, his head cut off and his body laid open upon a square board, the legs stretched to their full extent and secured upon it with small tacks, then baste with bacon fat and roast before a good fire quickly like canvas-back ducks.

One of the remarkable features of the war was the perfect good nature with which the rebels discussed their foes. In no instance up to a certain period did I hear of any remark that savored of personal hatred. They fought for a cause and against a power, and would speak in depreciation of a corps or brigade; but "they fit us, and we fit them," was the whole story generally, and till the blowing up of the mine at Petersburg there was a gay, insouciant style in their descriptions of the war scenes passing under their observation.

But after that time the sentiment changed from an innate feeling the Southern soldiers had that mining was "a mean trick," as they expressed it. They were not sufficiently versed in military tactics to recognize that stratagem is fair in war ... The men had heretofore been calm and restrained, particularly before a woman, never using oaths or improper language, but the wounded that were brought in from that fight emulated the talents of Uncle Toby's army in Flanders, and eyes gleamed, and teeth clenched as they showed me the locks of their muskets to which the blood and hair still clung, when after firing, without waiting to re-load, they had clenched the barrels and fought hand to hand. If their accounts could be relied upon, it was a gallant strife and a desperate one, and ghastly wounds bore testimony of the truth of many a tale then told.

Once again the bitter blood showed itself, when, after a skirmish, the foe cut the rail track, so that the wounded could not be brought to the city. Of all the monstrous crimes that war sanctions, this is surely the most sinful. Wounded soldiers without the shelter of a roof, or the comfort of a bed of straw, left exposed to sun, dew, and rain, with hardly the prospect of a warm drink or decent food for days, knowing that comfortable quarters awaited them, all ready prepared, but rendered useless by what seems an unnecessarily cruel act. Was it any wonder that their habitual indifference to suffering gave way, and the soldier cursed loud and deep at a causeless inhumanity, which, if practiced habitually, is worse than savage! When the sufferers at last reached the hospital, their wounds had not been attended to for three days, and the sight of them was shocking.

Busy in my kitchen, seeing that the supply of necessary food was in preparation, I was spared the sight of much of the suffering, but on passing among the ambulances going in and out of the wards I descried seated up on one of them a dilapidated figure, both hands holding his head which was tied up with rags of all descriptions. He appeared to be incapable of talking, but nodded and winked and made motions with head and feet. In the general confusion he had been forgotten, so I took him under my especial charge. He was taken into a ward, seated on a bed, while I stood on a bench to be able to unwind rag after rag from around his head. There was no sensitiveness on his part, for his eye was merry and bright, but when the last came off, what a sight!

Two balls had passed through his cheek and jaw within half an inch of each other, knocking out the teeth on both sides and cutting the tongue in half. The inflammation caused the swelling to be immense, and the absence of all previous attendance, in consequence of the detention of the wounded until the road could be mended, had aggravated the symptoms. There was nothing fatal to be apprehended, but fatal wounds are not always the most trying.

The sight of this was the most sickening my long experience had ever seen. The swollen lips turned out, and the mouth filled with blood, matter, fragments of teeth from amidst all of which the maggots in countless numbers swarmed and writhed, while the smell generated by this putridity was unbearable. Castile soap and soft sponges soon cleansed the offensive cavity, and he was able in an hour to swallow some nourishment he drew through a quill.

The following morning I found him reading the newspaper, and entertaining every one about him by his abortive attempts to make himself understood, and in a week he actually succeeded in doing so. The first request distinctly enunciated was that he wanted a looking-glass to see if his sweetheart would be willing to kiss him when she saw him. We all assured him that she would not be worthy of the name if she would not be delighted to do so.

An order came about this time to clear out the lower wards for the reception of improperly vaccinated patients, who soon after arrived in great numbers. They were dreadfully afflicted objects, many of them with sores so deep and thick upon arms and legs that amputation had to be resorted to, to preserve life. As fast as the eruption would be healed in one spot, it would break out in another, for the blood seemed entirely poisoned. The unfortunate victims bore the infliction as they had borne everything else painful—with calm patience and indifference to suffering. Sometimes a favorable comparison would be made between this and the greater loss of limbs.

No one who was a daily witness to their agonies from this cause, can help feeling indignant at charges made of inhumanity to Federal prisoners of war, who were vaccinated with the same virus; and while on this subject, though it may be outside of the recollections of hospital life, I cannot help stating that on no occasion was the question of rations and medicines to be issued for Federal prisoners discussed in my presence; and circumstances placed me where I had the best opportunity of hearing the truth (living with the wife of a cabinet officer); that good evidence was not given, that the Confederate commissary-general, by order of the government issued to them the same rations it gave its soldiers in the field, and only when reductions of food had to be made in our army, were they also made in the prisons. The question of supplies for them was an open and a vexed one among the people generally, and angry and cruel things were said; but every one cognizant of facts in Richmond knows that even when General Lee's army lived on corn-meal at times that the prisoners still received their usual rations.

At a cabinet meeting when the Commissary-General Northrop advocated putting the prisoners on the half rations which our soldiers had been obliged to content themselves with for some time, General Lee opposed him on the ground that men animated by companionship and active service could be satisfied with less than prisoners with no hope and leading an inactive life. Mr. Davis sided with him, and the question was settled that night, although in his anger Mr. Northrop accused General Lee of showing this consideration because his son was a prisoner in the enemy's lines.

CHAPTER THIRTY-TWO

The Flag-Bearer

By Theodore Roosevelt

Politician, hunter, naturalist, explorer, soldier—all these words can describe our 26th president. He was also a prodigious writer, producing scores of volumes. This gem is from the book Hero Tales from American History, *which he co-authored with the distinguished senator and historian Henry Cabot Lodge.*

—LAMAR UNDERWOOD

> Mine eyes have seen the glory of the coming of the Lord;
> He is trampling out the vintage where the grapes of wrath are stored;
> He hath loosed the fateful lightning of His terrible swift sword;
> His truth is marching on.
>
> I have seen Him in the watch-fires of a hundred circling camps;
> They have builded Him an altar in the evening dews and damps;
> I can read his righteous sentence by the dim and flaring lamps;
> His day is marching on.
>
> He has sounded forth the trumpet that shall never beat retreat;
> He is sifting out the hearts of men before his judgment seat;
> Oh! be swift, my soul, to answer him! be jubilant, my feet!
> Our God is marching on.
> —Julia Ward Howe.

IN NO WAR SINCE THE CLOSE OF THE GREAT NAPOLEONIC STRUGGLES HAS THE FIGHTING been so obstinate and bloody as in the Civil War. Much has been said in song and story of the resolute courage of the Guards at Inkerman, of the charge of the Light Brigade, and of the terrible fighting and loss of the German armies at Mars La Tour and Gravelotte.

The praise bestowed, upon the British and Germans for their valor, and for the loss that proved their valor, was well deserved; but there were over one hundred and twenty regiments, Union and Confederate, each of which, in some one battle of the Civil War, suffered a greater loss than any English regiment at Inkerman or at any other battle in the Crimea, a greater loss than was suffered by any German regiment at Gravelotte or at any other battle of the Franco-Prussian war. No European regiment in any recent struggle has suffered such losses as at Gettysburg befell the 1st Minnesota, when 82 per cent. of the officers and men were killed and wounded; or the 141st Pennsylvania, which lost 76 per cent.; or the 26th North Carolina, which lost 72 per cent.; such as at the second battle of Manassas befell the 101st New York, which lost 74 per cent., and the 21st Georgia, which lost 76 per cent. At Cold Harbor the 25th Massachusetts lost 70 per cent., and the 10th Tennessee at Chickamauga 68 per cent.; while at Shiloh the 9th Illinois lost 63 per cent., and the 6th Mississippi 70 per cent.; and at Antietam the 1st Texas lost 82 per cent. The loss of the Light Brigade in killed and wounded in its famous charge at Balaklava was but 37 per cent.

These figures show the terrible punishment endured by these regiments, chosen at random from the head of the list which shows the slaughter-roll of the Civil War. Yet the shattered remnants of each regiment preserved their organization, and many of the severest losses were incurred in the hour of triumph, and not of disaster. Thus, the 1st Minnesota, at Gettysburg, suffered its appalling loss while charging a greatly superior force, which it drove before it; and the little huddle of wounded and unwounded men who survived their victorious charge actually kept both the flag they had captured and the ground from which they had driven their foes.

A number of the Continental regiments under Washington, Greene, and Wayne did valiant fighting and endured heavy punishment. Several of the regiments raised on the northern frontier in 1814 showed, under Brown and Scott, that they were able to meet the best troops of Britain on equal terms in the open, and even to overmatch them in fair fight with the bayonet. The regiments which, in the Mexican war, under the lead of Taylor, captured Monterey, and beat back Santa Anna at Buena Vista, or which, with Scott as commander, stormed Molino Del Rey and Chapultepec, proved their ability to bear terrible loss, to wrest victory from overwhelming numbers, and to carry by open assault positions of formidable strength held by a veteran army. But in none of these three wars was the fighting so resolute and bloody as in the Civil War.

Countless deeds of heroism were performed by Northerner and by Southerner, by officer and by private, in every year of the great struggle. The immense majority of these deeds went unrecorded, and were known to few beyond the immediate participants. Of those that were noticed it would be impossible even to make a dry catalogue in ten such volumes as this. All that can be done is to choose out two or three acts of heroism, not as exceptions, but as examples of hundreds of others. The times of war are iron times, and bring out all that is best as well as all that is basest in the human heart. In a full recital of the civil war, as of every other great conflict, there would stand out in naked relief feats of wonderful daring and self-devotion, and, mixed among them, deeds of cowardice, of treachery, of barbarous brutality. Sadder still, such a recital would show strange contrasts in the careers of individual men, men who at one time acted well and nobly, and at another time ill and basely. The ugly truths must not be blinked, and the lessons they teach should be set forth by every historian, and learned by every statesman and soldier; but, for our good fortune, the lessons best worth learning in the nation's past are lessons of heroism.

From immemorial time the armies of every warlike people have set the highest value upon the standards they bore to battle. To guard one's own flag against capture is the pride, to capture the flag of one's enemy the ambition, of every valiant soldier. In consequence, in every war between peoples of good military record, feats of daring performed by color-bearers are honorably common. The Civil War was full of such incidents. Out of very many two or three may be mentioned as noteworthy.

One occurred at Fredericksburg on the day when half the brigades of Meagher and Caldwell lay on the bloody slope leading up to the Confederate entrenchments. Among the assaulting regiments was the 5th New Hampshire, and it lost one hundred and eighty-six out of three hundred men who made the charge. The survivors fell sullenly back behind a fence, within easy range of the Confederate rifle-pits. Just before reaching it the last of the color guard was shot, and the flag fell in the open. A Captain Perry instantly ran out to rescue it, and as he reached it was shot through the heart; another, Captain Murray, made the same attempt and was also killed; and so was a third, Moore. Several private soldiers met a like fate. They were all killed close to the flag, and their dead bodies fell across one another. Taking advantage of this breastwork, Lieutenant Nettleton crawled from behind the fence to the colors, seized them, and bore back the blood-won trophy.

Another took place at Gaines' Mill, where Gregg's 1st South Carolina formed part of the attacking force. The resistance was desperate, and the fury of the assault unsurpassed. At one point it fell to the lot of this regiment to bear the brunt of carrying a certain strong position. Moving forward at a run, the South Carolinians were swept by a fierce and searching fire. Young James Taylor, a lad of sixteen, was carrying the flag, and was killed after being shot down three times, twice rising and struggling onward with the colors. The third time he fell the flag was seized by George Cotchet, and when he, in turn, fell, by Shubrick Hayne. Hayne was also struck down almost immediately, and the fourth lad, for none of them were over twenty years old, grasped the colors, and fell mortally wounded across the body of his friend. The fifth, Gadsden Holmes, was pierced with no less than seven balls. The sixth man, Dominick Spellman, more fortunate, but not less brave, bore the flag throughout the rest of the battle.

Yet another occurred at Antietam. The 7th Maine, then under the command of Major T. W. Hyde, was one of the hundreds of regiments that on many hard-fought fields established a reputation for dash and unyielding endurance. Toward the early part of the day at Antietam it merely took its share in the charging and long-range firing, together with the New York and Vermont regiments which were its immediate neighbors in the line. The fighting was very heavy. In one of the charges, the Maine men passed over what had been a Confederate regiment. The gray-clad soldiers were lying, both ranks, privates and officers, as they fell, for so many had been killed or disabled that it seemed as if the whole regiment was prone in death.

Much of the time the Maine men lay on the battle-field, hugging the ground, under a heavy artillery fire, but beyond the reach of ordinary musketry. One of the privates, named Knox, was a wonderful shot, and had received permission to use his own special rifle, a weapon accurately sighted for very long range. While the regiment thus lay under the storm of shot and shell, he asked leave to go to the front; and for an hour afterward his companions heard his rifle crack every few minutes. Major Hyde finally, from curiosity, crept forward to see what he was doing, and found that he had driven every man away from one section of a Confederate battery, tumbling over gunner after gunner as they came forward to fire. One of his victims was a general officer, whose horse he killed. At the end of an hour or so, a piece of shell took off the breech of his pet rifle, and he returned disconsolate; but after a few minutes he gathered three rifles that were left by wounded men, and went back again to his work.

At five o'clock in the afternoon the regiment was suddenly called upon to undertake a hopeless charge, owing to the blunder of the brigade commander, who was a gallant veteran of the Mexican war, but who was also given to drink. Opposite the Union lines at this point were some haystacks, near a group of farm buildings. They were right in the center of the Confederate position, and sharpshooters stationed among them were picking off the Union gunners. The brigadier, thinking that they were held by but a few skirmishers, rode to where the 7th Maine was lying on the ground, and said: "Major Hyde, take your regiment and drive the enemy from those trees and buildings." Hyde saluted, and said that he had seen a large force of rebels go in among the buildings, probably two brigades in all. The brigadier answered, "Are you afraid to go, sir?" and repeated the order emphatically. "Give the order, so the regiment can hear it, and we are ready, sir," said Hyde. This was done, and "Attention" brought every man to his feet. With the regiment were two young boys who carried the marking guidons, and Hyde ordered these to the rear. They pretended to go, but as soon as the regiment charged came along with it. One of them lost his arm, and the other was killed on the field. The colors were carried by the color corporal, Harry Campbell.

Hyde gave the orders to left face and forward and the Maine men marched out in front of a Vermont regiment which lay beside them; then, facing to the front, they crossed a sunken road, which was so filled with dead and wounded Confederates that Hyde's horse had to step on them to get over.

Once across, they stopped for a moment in the trampled corn to straighten the line, and then charged toward the right of the barns. On they went at the double-quick, fifteen skirmishers ahead under Lieutenant Butler, Major Hyde on the right on his Virginia thoroughbred, and Adjutant Haskell to the left on a big white horse. The latter was shot down at once, as was his horse, and Hyde rode round in front of the regiment just in time to see a long line of men in gray rise from behind the stone wall of the Hagerstown pike, which was to their right, and pour in a volley; but it mostly went too high. He then ordered his men to left oblique.

Just as they were abreast a hill to the right of the barns, Hyde, being some twenty feet ahead, looked over its top and saw several regiments of Confederates, jammed close together and waiting at the ready; so he gave the order left flank, and, still at the double quick, took his column past the barns and buildings toward an orchard on the hither side, hoping that he could get them back before they were cut off, for they were faced by ten times their number. By going through the orchard he expected to be able to take advantage of a hollow, and partially escape the destructive flank fire on his return.

To hope to keep the barns from which they had driven the sharpshooters was vain, for the single Maine regiment found itself opposed to portions of no less than four Confederate brigades, at least a dozen regiments all told. When the men got to the orchard fence, Sergeant Benson wrenched apart the tall pickets to let through Hyde's horse. While he was doing this, a shot struck his haversack, and the men all laughed at the sight of the flying hardtack.

Going into the orchard there was a rise of ground, and the Confederates fired several volleys at the Maine men, and then charged them. Hyde's horse was twice wounded, but was still able to go on.

No sooner were the men in blue beyond the fence than they got into line and met the Confederates, as they came crowding behind, with a slaughtering fire, and then charged, driving them back. The color corporal was still carrying the colors, though one of his arms had been broken; but when half way through the orchard, Hyde heard him call out as he fell, and turned back to save the colors, if possible.

The apple-trees were short and thick, and he could not see much, and the Confederates speedily got between him and his men. Immediately, with the cry of "Rally, boys, to save the Major," back surged the regiment, and a volley at arm's length again destroyed all the foremost of their pursuers; so they rescued both their commander and the flag, which was carried off by Corporal Ring.

Hyde then formed the regiment on the colors, sixty-eight men all told, out of two hundred and forty who had begun the charge, and they slowly marched back toward their place in the Union line, while the New Yorkers and Vermonters rose from the ground cheering and waving their hats. Next day, when the Confederates had retired a little from the field, the color corporal, Campbell, was found in the orchard, dead, propped up against a tree, with his half-smoked pipe beside him.

CHAPTER THIRTY-THREE

We Die Alone
By David Howarth

With a foreword by noted historian Stephen E. Ambrose, the book We Die Alone: A
World War II Epic of Escape and Endurance *has lived up to its title's distinctions
in several editions since being originally published in 1955. This excerpt from the Lyons
Press edition, 1999, focuses on a small Norwegian commando raiding party in an
attack on Nazi units that had been occupying and terrorizing their native land since
the early days of the war. The leader is Sigurd Eskeland, in charge of three other men,
including Jan Baalsrud, who will play a key role in the story to come.*

—LAMAR UNDERWOOD

ON THAT SORT OF EXPEDITION IT WAS USELESS TO MAKE A DETAILED PLAN, BECAUSE
nobody could foresee exactly what was going to happen. The leader always had a degree of
responsibility which few people are called upon to carry in a war. The orders he was given
were in very general terms, and in carrying them out he had nobody whatever to advise
him. His success, and his own life and the lives of his party, were in his own hands alone.

As leader of this party in north Norway, Eskeland had a specially heavy load to carry.
From the south, or from any country from which a lot of refugees had escaped to England,
a fund of information had been collected about German dispositions and the characters
and politics of innumerable people, and the information was always being renewed. The
leader of an expedition could be told, in more or less detail, whom he could trust and
whom he should avoid, and where he was most likely to meet enemy sentries or patrols.
But information about north Norway was scanty. A good many people had escaped from
there, but the only route they could follow was across the mountains into Sweden, where
they were interned. Many of them were content to stay in internment and wait for better
times; and even those who made the effort to escape again, and managed to pass on what
they knew to the British intelligence services, had usually been held by the Swedes for a

matter of months, so that all that they could tell was out of date. Eskeland had been given the names of a few people who were known to be sound, but beyond that very little could be done to help him. Once he left Britain, he could only depend on his own training and wit and skill.

He had been as thorough as he possibly could be in his preparations. Ever since he had known he was to lead a landing from a fishing-boat, he had pondered in a quiet way over every emergency he could foresee. On the high seas, the skipper of the boat was in command, and out there the problems had been comparatively simple.

The boat might have been overcome by stress of weather, which was a matter of seamanship; or its one single-cylinder engine might have broken down, which was a job for the engineers; or it might have been attacked by aircraft, which would have been fought with the boat's own "Q-ship" armament. But now that it had closed the coast, he had to take charge, and now anything might happen and an instantaneous decision might be needed. For the present, the boat's first line of defence was for its guns to be kept hidden, so that it seemed to be innocently fishing. But once they got into the constricted waters of the sounds among the islands, they might meet a larger ship with heavier armament at short range at any moment, and then the boat's armament would be nothing but a hindrance.

They might still bluff their way out as a fishing-boat, but they could not hope to fight an action at two or three hundred yards. Apart from anything else, a single shot in their cargo might blow them all to pieces. The only way they could prepare for that kind of encounter, as Eskeland foresaw it, was to hide every vestige of war-like equipment and to lure the enemy ship to within pistol shot. Then, by surprise, there was a chance of boarding it and wiping out its crew.

During the past night, as *Brattholm* approached the coast, Eskeland and his three men had begun to prepare for this possible crisis. They had cleaned and loaded their short-range weapons, Sten guns and carbines and pistols; and they had primed hand-grenades and stowed them in convenient places, in the wheelhouse and galley, and along the inside of the bulwarks, where they could be thrown without warning on board a ship alongside. In case it came to close quarters, he and his three men had all put on naval uniform, although they were soldiers, so that the Germans would not be able to identify them as a landing party.

But even while they made these preparations, they all knew that although with luck they might be successful in that sort of hand-to-hand action, they had very little chance of getting away with their lives. Between themselves and safety there were the thousand miles of sea which they had crossed. They might hope to kill or capture the entire crew of even a larger ship; but unless they could do it so quickly that no radio signal could be sent, and unless it happened in such a remote place that nobody heard the gunshots, all the German defences would be alerted; and then, it was obvious, *Brattholm* at eight knots would not get very far. The only hope of escape then, and it was a small one, was to scuttle the ship and get ashore.

Eskeland had provided for this too. The three radio transmitters in their cargo were a new type still graded top secret, and they also had a few important papers: ciphers, maps, and notes about trustworthy people and German defences. They all understood quite clearly that they had to defend these things with their lives. It went without saying. It was one of the basic rules which they had been taught. Ever since they had entered enemy waters, the papers had been stowed in an accessible place with matches and a bottle of petrol; and a primer, detonators and fuses had been laid in the eight tons of high explosives in the hold. The transmitters were on top of the primer. There were three fuses. One had a five-minute delay, for use if there seemed to be a chance to destroy the ship and cargo and then to get away. The next was thirty seconds, and the last was instantaneous. Each of the twelve men on board was able to contemplate soberly the prospect of lighting the instantaneous fuse, and they understood the circumstances in which they were to do it; if they had tried a hand-to-hand fight with a German ship, for example, and been defeated. The main point was that the Germans should not get the cargo.

Eskeland should have felt satisfied with these preparations as he approached the coast; they were intelligently conceived, and carefully carried out. But on that very day a change of plan was forced upon him, and he was reminded, if there had been any doubt about it, how sketchy his information was. They had intended to land on an island called Senja, about forty miles south-west of the town of Tromsö; but as they approached it, steaming peacefully through the fishing zone, they sighted a trawler coming out towards them. They altered course to the eastward, waiting to see what was going to happen. The trawler reached the open sea at the outer edge of the islands, and then it turned back on its track and went into the sounds again. As it turned, they saw a gun on its foredeck. It was a patrol ship, where no patrol ship had been reported.

At the stage of the expedition, it was their job to avoid trouble rather than look for it, and there was no sense in trying to land their cargo on the one island, from all the hundreds in the district which they now knew for certain was patrolled. Their disguise had worked so far. They had been seen, and passed as a fishing-boat. The sensible thing to do was to choose another island; and after a discussion, they agreed upon one a little farther north. It is called Ribbenesöy. It is due north of Tromsö, thirty miles from the town. On the chart of it, they found a little bay on the north-east side which seemed to offer good shelter, and one of the men who had been in that district before remembered the bay as a remote and deserted spot. At about midday on the 29th of March, they set course towards it. Its name is Toftefjord.

It was late in the afternoon by the time they reached the skerries which lie scattered in the sea for seven miles off the shore of Ribbenesöy, and began to pick their way among them. In bad weather the passage which they used is impassable. There are thousands of rocks awash on either side, and the whole area becomes a mass of spray in which no marks are visible. But on that day the sea was calm and the air was clear. They sighted the stone cairns which are built as seamarks on some of the biggest rocks, and passed through into sheltered water. They steamed below a minute island called Fuglö, which rises sheer on every side to a black crag a thousand feet high; they skirted the north shore of Ribbenesöy, a steep, smooth, gleaming sheet of snow which sweeps upwards to the curved ice-cornice of a hill called Helvedestind, which means Hell's Peak; and as the light began to fade they crept slowly into Toftefjord, and let go an anchor into clear ice-blue water.

When the engine stopped, Toftefjord seemed absolutely silent. After six days of the racket and vibration of a Norwegian fishing-boat under way, the mere absence of noise was unfamiliar; but there is always a specially noticeable silence in sheltered places when the land is covered thickly with snow. All familiar sounds are muted and unresonant. There are no footfalls, no sounds of birds or running water, no hum of insects or rustle of animals or leaves. Even one's own voice seems altered. Even without reason, in places hushed by snow, the deadening of sound seems menacing. Yet the appearance of Toftefjord was reassuring. They stood on deck when the work of coming to anchor was finished and looked round them, talking involuntarily in quiet voices. It was almost a perfect hiding-place. To the south and west and east it was shut in by low rounded hills. The tops of the hills were bare; but in the hollows by the shore, the twigs of stunted arctic birch showed black against the snow. To the north was the entrance of the bay, but it was blocked by a little island, so that one could not see into it from outside. *Brattholm* was quite safe there from observation from the sea, and she could not be seen from the air unless an aircraft flew almost overhead.

The beaches showed that the bay was always calm. On the rocks and islands which are exposed to the sea, there is always a broad bare strip of shore where the waves have washed the snow away; but there in the land-locked fjord the snow lay smooth and thick down to the tidemark. There were no tracks in it. Close inshore, the sea itself had been frozen, but the ice had broken up and was floating in transparent lumps around the ship. The air was cold and crisp.

Yet the place was not quite deserted. At the head of the bay, below the hill, there was a barn and a very small wooden house. Close by, on the beach, there were racks for drying fish. There was nobody to be seen, but there was smoke from the cottage chimney.

The first thing to be done, when the ship was at anchor, was to find out who lived in that cottage, and whether they were likely to cause any difficulties or danger. Eskeland and the skipper changed out of their naval uniforms into fishermen's clothes and rowed ashore. Perhaps they wanted to be the first to land in Norway. It was always a moment of unexpressed emotion.

They soon came back, saying there was nothing to worry about. There was a middle-aged woman with her two children, a boy of about sixteen and a girl who was younger. Her husband was away at the cod fishing in the Lofoten islands, and she did not expect him back for several weeks. Eskeland had told her that they had stopped to make some engine repairs. There was no reason why she should be suspicious, and there was no telephone in the house. It would be quite easy to keep an eye on her and the children. She had told him, incidentally, that no Germans had ever been in Toftefjord. In fact, she herself had never seen a German. Her husband had had to hand in his radio set to the authorities, and her nearest neighbours were two miles away. She was quite out of touch with the world and with the war.

The landing party and crew had dinner in relays, leaving a watch on deck. They were very cheerful. For one thing, it was the first good dinner they had had on board, not only because it is difficult to do much cooking in a fishing-boat at sea, but also because the cook had been seasick and Jan Baalsrud, who had deputised for him, had had rather limited ideas. The landing party was happy also because the voyage was successfully ended, and they could really get to work. For soldiers, a sea voyage is always tedious; they are usually pleased to get out of the hands of sailors.

While they ate, they discussed the coming night. When the four men of the sabotage group had started to prepare themselves for the expedition, they had divided among them the enormous territory they were to cover, and each of them had studied his own part of it in detail. But by changing the landing place from Senja, they had put themselves farther north than any of the districts they knew best.

However, Eskeland remembered a little about Ribbenesöy from his days as a postal inspector, and he had taken the precaution of learning the names of a few reliable people in the neighbourhood. One of these was a merchant who kept a small general store on the south side of the island. Eskeland had never met him, but his name was on a list in London of men who could be trusted. His shop was only a few miles away and they decided to make a start that night by going to see him and asking him about hiding their cargo. Experience in the southern part of Norway had shown that shopkeepers were often more adept than anyone else at providing a temporary hiding-place for stores. Most shops had outhouses and back premises which in war-time were nearly empty. Cases of weapons had often been stacked among cases of groceries. A shopkeeper was also a likely man to tell them where they could get a local boat to take them into Tromsö, where they would find their principal "contacts."

So Eskeland set off, as soon as it was dark, in *Brattholm*'s motor dinghy. He took the ship's engineer with him to look after the motor, and another man who had been added to the crew as an extra hand because he knew the district. They steered out of the bay and followed the shore of Ribbenesöy to the eastward, through the sound which separates it from the south side of the island. They saw the shop and a few buildings near it, and a wooden jetty, silhouetted against the afterglow in the western sky. There was a light in the shop, and another on board a boat which was lying, with its engine running, a few yards off the end of the jetty.

As they approached the jetty, they passed close to the boat. It was a small fishing craft with two or three men on board. It would have seemed strange to pass it without a word, and besides, a small local fishing craft was one of the things they wanted. So they hailed it and told the men the story they had prepared: that they had engine trouble and wanted a lift to Tromsö to get some spare parts.

The men were sympathetic, and only mildly inquisitive, as fishermen would naturally be. They talked all round the subject, in the infinitely leisurely manner of people who live on islands. They asked what make of engine it was, and what horse-power, and what spare parts were needed. They recommended a dealer in Tromsö, and suggested ringing him up in the morning and getting him to send the parts out in the mail-boat, which would probably be as quick as going to fetch them, and certainly cheaper. They asked what the herring fishing was like, and where the *Brattholm* was bound for.

Everyone who lives under false pretences gets used to receiving perfectly useless advice with patience and cunning. Eskeland and the engineer, in the unrealistic conversation across the dark water, answered the questions carefully one by one, until a chance came for them to put the one question in which they were interested.

"I suppose you couldn't take us into Tromsö?"

This started a long explanation about how they were waiting there for a man to bring them some bait which they had paid for already, so that they could not afford to miss him, and they said all over again that they could not see any sense in going all the way to Tromsö for spares when there was a telephone up in the shop. But they told Eskeland that if he was really set on wasting money by going there, the shopkeeper had a boat and might take him in.

Eskeland thanked them and left them, understanding perhaps that to a man who lives in the outer islands Tromsö is a very distant city, and a journey there is not a thing to be undertaken lightly. At least, he had learned that the shop at the head of the jetty was really the one he wanted.

The shopkeeper was in bed when they got to the house; but when they knocked he came downstairs in his underclothes and took them to the kitchen. They apologised for coming so late, and told the same story again. But with him, they only told it as a means of introduction, to make conversation till he felt at ease with them and they could tell him the true reason for their visit. While they were talking, they slipped in questions about the Germans. No, he said when they asked him, the Germans had really been no trouble out there on the islands. They had never been ashore. He saw their convoys passing in the channel south of Ribbenesöy, and they had been out laying minefields. And of course they sent out notices which had to be stuck up everywhere: "Contact with the enemy is punished by death." There was one downstairs in the shop. He had heard stories about how they behaved in Tromsö, but as for himself, he had never had anything to do with them.

Carefully feeling his way, Eskeland began to broach the subject of his cargo, and his need to go to Tromsö. The shopkeeper was willing to take one or two men to town in his boat. Eskeland offered to pay him a substantial sum of money for his help. It was the size of this sum which first impressed on the shopkeeper that he was being asked to do more than hire out a boat. He looked puzzled; and then, because it would be unjust to involve a man in what they were doing without giving him an idea of the risks he was running, and because the man had such an excellent reputation, Eskeland told him that they had come from England.

At this, his expression changed. At first he was incredulous. One of them gave him a cigarette, and he took it and lit it; and the English tobacco seemed to convince him that what they said was true. Then, to their surprise, they saw that he was frightened.

He began to make excuses. He couldn't leave the shop. It wasn't fair to leave his wife alone in the house these days. There were the animals to attend to. Fuel for the boat was difficult to come by.

Slowly and reluctantly, they had to admit to themselves that it was useless to try to persuade him. An unwilling nervous helper would be a danger and a liability. Yet they could not understand how a man who had been so highly recommended could be so cowardly in practice. The vast majority of Norwegians, as everybody knew, would have been delighted by a chance to do something against the Germans. They puzzled over his behaviour, and told him they were disappointed in him.

"But why did you come to me?" he asked, plaintively. "What made you think I'd do a thing like that?"

They told him they had heard he was a patriot; and then the truth came out, too late, and they saw the mistake which they had made. The man told them he had only been running the shop for a few months. Its previous owner had died. His name was the same, so there had been no need to change the name of the business.

There was nothing left to do then except to impress on him as clearly as they could that he must never tell anyone what they had told him. He promised this willingly, glad to see that they had accepted his refusal. In his relief, he even recommended two other men who he thought would give them the help they needed. Their names were Jenberg Kristiansen and Sedolf Andreasson. They were both fishermen, and they lived on the north shore of the island, beyond Toftefjord. He felt sure they would be willing.

Eskeland and his two companions left him then, with a final warning that he must never mention what he had heard that night. They went back to their dinghy, annoyed and slightly uneasy. There was no reason to think that the shopkeeper was hostile, or that he would do anything active to harm them. Not one man in a thousand would go out of his way to help the Germans. But many Norwegians of the simpler sort were prone to gossip, and any man whose own safety was not at stake was potentially the nucleus of a rumour. It was a pity, but the risk, so far as they could see, was small, and without entirely recasting their own plans there was nothing much they could do about it. It was sheer bad luck that the one man they had selected from the lists in London should have died, and even worse luck that another man with the same name should have taken his house and business. But it could not be helped. At least, he had given them new contacts.

They set off back towards Toftefjord, to tell the rest of the party what had happened. On the way, they were overtaken by the fishing-boat which had been lying off the jetty of the shop. Its crew had got their bait and were on their way to the fishing-grounds. They took the dinghy in tow; but just before they came to the mouth of Toftefjord the skipper shouted that they had forgotten a rope, some part of their fishing gear, and that they had to go back to the shop to fetch it. He cast the dinghy off. Eskeland went on into Toftefjord, and saw the fishing-boat turn round and steam away.

What happened when the skipper and crew of the fishing-boat got back to the shop will never exactly be known. The shopkeeper had gone back to bed, but they called him out again, and this time his wife joined them to hear what was going on. He said he was feeling sick and giddy. He thought it was due to the cigarettes the strangers had given him. His brother was one of the crew, and he and the skipper plied him with questions about the strange boat and the three unknown men. Before very long, the shopkeeper had told them everything.

It was probably during this conversation that a new and appalling fear struck him. Was it possible that the three men were German agents sent to test him? He had heard people say that the Germans sent men about in the islands, dressed in civilian clothes, to do that very thing: to say that they came from England, and then to report anyone who offered to help them. What was more likely than that they should pick on him, a merchant, a man with a certain standing in the community, and one who had only recently set up in business?

He was thankful, now he came to think of it, that he had refused to help them. And yet, had he been careful enough? He racked his brains to remember exactly what he had said about Germans. He felt sure he had been indiscreet. There had been something about minefields. That was probably secret. Of course, he said to the others, the only way to make sure of his position, the only safe thing to do, was to report what the men had told him. Supposing they were German agents, it would not be enough only to have refused to help them. They would be waiting now to see if he reported them. If he didn't, they would get him anyhow.

The three men discussed this dilemma for an hour. The shopkeeper's wife listened in distress at his agitation. His brother was in favour of doing nothing. It would be a bad business, he admitted, if the men were Germans; but on the other hand, if he reported them and it turned out that they had really come from England, it would be far worse. The trouble was, it was impossible to be sure; but on the whole, he thought it was right to take the chance.

With this decision, after a long confusing argument, the skipper and the shopkeeper's brother left for the fishing again. The shopkeeper himself went back to bed, still feeling sick and dizzy. He could not sleep. He knew what it meant to be disloyal to the Germans, or rather, to be caught at it: the concentration camp for himself and perhaps for his wife as well; the end of the little business he had begun to build up; the end of his safety was so easy. There was the telephone downstairs in the shop. And yet, if they were really Norwegians, and had really come from England, and the neighbours got to know he had told the Germans, he knew very well what they would say, and he knew very well what his customers would do.

Those men had sounded like Norwegians: not local men, but they spoke Norwegian perfectly. But of course there might be Norwegian Nazis, for all he knew, who would do a job like that for the Germans. And was it possible to come in a fishing-boat in March all the way from England? That sounded an unlikely story. Perhaps the best thing would be to get up and go over to Toftefjord and speak to them again and see if they could prove it. But then the Germans were too clever to do anything by halves; they would have their proofs all ready. How could he tell? How could he possibly find out?

The shopkeeper lay all night, sick with fear and confusion. Towards the morning, the last of his courage ebbed away. About seven, he crept down to the shop, and picked up the telephone. He had thought of a compromise. He asked for a man he knew who had an official post in the Department of Justice.

In Toftefjord, when Eskeland had told the others about the two merchants with the same name, they agreed that there was nothing to be done. The man had promised not to talk, and short of murder they could not think of any way of making more sure of him than that. So Eskeland set off again, not very much discouraged, to see the two fishermen the shopkeeper had recommended.

This time he got the answer he expected. There was no point in telling these men the story about spare parts. By then, it was about three o'clock in the morning, and even in the Arctic, where nobody takes much notice of the time of day, people would not expect to be woken up at such an hour with any ordinary request. He did not ask them to go to Tromsö either. Most of the first night was already gone, and the most urgent need was to get the cargo ashore so that *Brattholm* could sail again for Shetland.

The two fishermen agreed at once, enthusiastically, to hide it in some caves which they knew. Eskeland did not tell them the whole story. He did not mention England, but left them with the impression that he had brought the cargo from the south of Norway, and that it contained food and equipment for the home forces to use when the tide began to turn. But the two men did not want to be told any more about it. If it was anti-German, that seemed to be good enough for them. They said they would come to Toftefjord at half-past four on the following afternoon to pilot *Brattholm* out to their hiding place, so that everything would be ready for unloading as soon as it was dark.

It was daylight by the time the dinghy got back to Toftefjord. Eskeland and then men who were with him were tired, not merely by being out all night, but by the long hours of careful conversation.

When they came aboard, they found that Jan Baalsrud, the only one of the landing party who had not been either to the shop or the fishermen, had been at work all night checking over their small arms again. As an instrument maker, Jan loved the mechanism of guns and always took particular care of them; and like Eskeland, he had been a little worried about the shopkeeper.

They made breakfast, and talked about the shop again. It was only two hours' steaming from Tromsö, somebody pointed out, for any kind of warship; so if they had really had the bad luck to hit upon a Nazi and he had reported them, they would surely have been attacked by then. Dawn would have been the obvious time for the Germans to choose. But dawn was past, and Toftefjord was as quiet and peaceful as before. They agreed in the end that the landing party should stay on watch till ten o'clock. If nothing had happened by then, it really would look as if that particular danger was over; and then the landing party would turn in and leave some of the crew on watch till the fishermen came at half-past four.

The morning passed. The only thing which was at all unusual was the number of aircraft they could hear. There was the sound of machine-gun fire too, from time to time. It was all out at sea. But none of the aircraft flew over Toftefjord. It sounded as though there was a practice target somewhere beyond the islands, and that seemed a possible explanation. The air forces at Bardufoss must have somewhere for training, and the sea or the outer skerries would be a likely place. As the day went by, the men began to relax. By noon, they were reassured. Eskeland and his party went below to sleep leaving half of the crew on deck.

A shout awoke them: "Germans! Germans!" They rushed for the hatch. The men on watch stood there appalled. Two hundred yards away, coming slowly into the fjord, there was a German warship. As the last of the men reached the deck, it opened fire. At once they knew that the aircraft were on patrol stopping the exits from the sounds. There was no escape for *Brattholm*. Eskeland shouted "Abandon ship! Abandon ship!"

That was the only order. They knew what to do. Somebody ran up the naval flag to the mizen head. The crew leaped down into one of the boats and cast off and rowed for shore. The German ship stopped and lowered two boats. Troops piled into them and made for the shore a little farther north. Jan Baalsrud and Salvesen poured petrol on the cipher books and set them all on fire, and cast off the second dinghy and held it ready in the lee of the ship out of sight of the Germans. Eskeland and Blindheim tore off the hatch covers and climbed down among the cargo and lit the five-minute fuse.

With her boats away the German ship began to approach again. It was firing with machine-guns and a three-pounder, but the shots were going overhead. The Germans meant to capture them alive: they were not expecting much resistance. Eskeland called from the hold: "Jan, hold them off!" Jan took a sub-machine gun and emptied the magazine at the German's bridge. The ship stopped for a moment, and then came on again. Eskeland jumped up from the hold, calling to the others "It's burning," and all of them climbed down into the dinghy, and waited. They knew the drill: to wait till the last possible minute hidden in *Brattholm*'s lee before they started to try to row away.

Eskeland sat looking at his wrist-watch, with his arm held steadily in front of him. One of the others held on to the side of *Brattholm*'s hull. Two were ready at oars. One minute had gone already. They could not see the German ship from there. They could hear it approaching the other side of the *Brattholm*, firing in bursts at *Brattholm* and at the crew in the other dinghy. Per Blindheim said: "Well, we've had a good time for twenty-six years, Jan." Eskeland said: "Two minutes." Jan could see the crew. They had got to the shore.

Two were still in the dinghy with their hands up. Three were on the beach. One was lying on the edge of the water. One was trying to climb the rocks, and machine-gun bullets were chipping the stones above him and ricocheting across the fjord. Eskeland said: "Three minutes." The German landing party came into sight, running along the shore towards the place where the crew had landed, jumping from rock to rock. When they got near, the firing stopped, and for a few seconds there was no sound but the shouts of German orders.

"Three and a half," Eskeland said. "Cast off." They began to row, keeping *Brattholm* between them and the Germans. In that direction, towards the head of the fjord, it was two hundred yards to shore. But the German ship was very close, and it was much bigger than *Brattholm*. Before they had gone fifty yards they were sighted, and at this point-blank range the Germans opened fire. The dinghy was shot full of holes and began to sink. But the German ship was slowly drawing alongside *Brattholm*, and the last quarter of a minute of the fuse was burning down, and the fascination of watching the trap being sprung blinded them to the miracle that so far they had not been wounded.

The ship and *Brattholm* touched, and at that very moment the explosion came. But it was nothing, only a fraction of what it should have been. Only the primer exploded. The hatch covers were blown off and the front of the wheelhouse was wrecked, but the German ship was undamaged. There were shouts and confusion on deck and for a few seconds the firing stopped. The ship went full speed astern. *Brattholm* was burning fiercely. In that momentary respite, the men in the dinghy rowed for their lives, but the ship swung round till its three-pounder came to bear. Its first shot missed the dinghy. And then the whole cargo exploded. *Brattholm* vanished, in the crack of the shock wave, the long roar in the hills, the mushroom of smoke streaked with debris and blazing petrol. Eskeland was blown overboard. Jan leaned out and got him under the arms and hauled him on to the gunwale, and the German gunner recovered and a shot from the three-pounder smashed the dinghy into pieces. They were all in the water, swimming. There were seventy yards to go. The Germans brought all their guns to bear on the heads in the water.

The men swam on, through water foaming with bullets, thrusting the ice aside with their heads and hands. All of them reached the shore. Jan Baalsrud stumbled through the shallows with his friend Per Blindheim beside him. As they reached the water's edge Per was hit in the head and fell forward half out of the water. With a last effort, Jan climbed a rocky bank and found cover behind a stone. As he climbed he had been aware that his leader Eskeland had fallen on the beach and that Salvesen, either wounded or exhausted, had sunk down there unable to make the climb. He shouted to them all to follow him, but there was no answer. A bullet hit the stone above his head and whined across the fjord.

He was under fire from both sides. He looked behind him, and saw the Germans who had landed. Four of them had worked round the shore and crossed the hillside fifty yards above him to cut off his retreat. He was surrounded.

At the head of the fjord there is a little mound, covered with small birch trees. Behind it the hills rise steeply for about two hundred feet. A shallow gully divides them. Within the gully the snow lies deeply, a smooth steep slope only broken by two large boulders. The patrol came floundering down the hill, pausing to kneel in the snow and snipe at Jan with rifles. Caught between them and the fire from the ship he could find no cover. But to reach him the patrol had to cross the little dip behind the mound, and there for a moment they were out of sight. He got up and ran towards them. He could not tell whether they would come over the mound, through the birches, or skirt round it to the left. He crept round it to the right. He had been wearing rubber sea-boots, but had lost one of them when he was swimming, and one of his feet was bare. He heard the soldiers crashing through the brittle bushes. Soon, as he and the patrol each circled round the mound, he come upon their tracks and crossed them. It could only be seconds before they came to his. But now the foot of the gully was near, and he broke cover and ran towards it.

They saw him at once, and they were even closer than before. An officer called on him to halt. He struggled up the first part of the gully, through the soft sliding snow. The officer fired at him with a revolver and missed, and he got to cover behind the first boulder in the gully and drew his automatic.

Looking back down the snow slope, he watched the officer climbing up towards him with the three soldiers following close behind. The officer was in Gestapo uniform. They came on with confidence, and Jan remembered that so far he had not fired a shot, so they possibly did not know that he was armed. He waited, not to waste his fire. Beyond the four figures close below him, he was aware of uproar and confusion, shouting and stray shots in the fjord. As he climbed, the officer called to Jan to surrender. He was out of breath. Jan fixed on a spot in the snow six yards below him. When they reached there, he would shoot.

The officer reached it first. Jan squeezed the trigger. The pistol clicked. It was full of ice. Twice more he tried, but it would not work, and the men were within three paces. He ejected to cartridges and it fired. He shot the Gestapo officer twice and he fell dead in the snow and his body rolled down the slope over and over towards the feet of his men. Jan fired again and the next man went down, wounded. The last two turned and ran, sliding down the snow to find cover. Jan jumped to his feet and began the long climb up the gully.

For a little while, it was strangely quiet. He was hidden from the fjord by one side of the gully. The snow was soft and deep and difficult, and he often slipped with his rubber boot. With all his strength, he could only climb slowly.

Above the second boulder, for the last hundred feet, the gully opened out into a wide snow slope, perfectly clean and white and smooth, and as soon as he set foot on it he came into sight of the German ship behind him.

In his dark naval uniform against the gleaming snow up there he was exposed as a perfect target for every gun on the warship and the rifles of the soldiers on the beaches. He struggled in desperation with the powdery snow, climbing a yard and slipping back, clawing frantically with his hands at the yielding surface which offered no hold.

The virgin slope was torn to chaos by the storm of bullets from behind him. Three-pounder shells exploding in it blew clouds of snow powder in the air. He could feel with sickening expectation the thud and the searing pain in his back which would be the end of it all. The impulse to hide, to seek any refuge from this horror, was overwhelming. But there was nowhere to hide, no help, no escape from the dreadful thing that was happening to him. He could only go on and on and on, choking as his lungs filled with ice crystals, sobbing with weariness and rage and self-pity, kicking steps which crumbled away beneath him, climbing and falling, exhausting the last of his strength against the soft deep cushion of the snow.

He got to the top. There were rocks again, hard windswept snow, the crest of the hill, and shelter just beyond it. He dropped in his tracks, and for the first time he dared to look behind him. The firing died. There below him he could see the whole panorama of the fjord.

Smoke hung above it in the sky. The German ship was at the spot where *Brattholm* had been anchored. On the far shore, a knot of soldiers were gathered around the crew. Nearer, where he had landed, his companions were lying on the beach, not moving, and he thought they were all dead. All round the fjord there were parties of Germans, some staring towards him at the spot where he had reached the ridge and disappeared, and others beginning to move in his direction. In his own tracks before his eyes the snow was red, and that brought him to full awareness of a pain in his foot, and he looked at it. His only injury was almost ludicrous. It was his right foot, the bare one, and half of his big toe had been shot away. It was not bleeding much, because the foot was frozen. He got up and turned his back on Toftefjord and began to try to run. It was not much more then ten minutes since he had been sleeping in the cabin with his friends, and now he was alone.

CHAPTER THIRTY-FOUR

The Trojan Horse
By Virgil

THE GRECIAN LEADERS, NOW DISHEARTENED BY THE WAR, AND BAFFLED BY THE FATES, after a revolution of so many years, build a horse to the size of a mountain, and interweave its ribs with planks of fir. This they pretend to be an offering, in order to procure a safe return; which report spread. Hither having secretly conveyed a select band, chosen by lot, they shut them up into the dark sides, and fill its capacious caverns and womb with armed soldiers. In sight of Troy lies Tenedos, an island well known by fame, and flourishing while Priam's kingdom stood: now only a bay, and a station unfaithful for ships. Having made this island, they conceal themselves in that desolate shore. We imagined they were gone, and that they had set sail for Mycenae. In consequence of this, all Troy is released from its long distress: the gates are thrown open; with joy we issue forth, and view the Grecian camp, the deserted plains, and the abandoned shore. Some view with amazement that baleful offering of the virgin Minerva, and wonder at the stupendous bulk of the horse; and Thymoetes first advises that it be dragged within the walls and lodged in the tower, whether with treacherous design, or that the destiny of Troy now would have it so. But Capys, and all whose minds had wiser sentiments, strenuously urge either to throw into the sea the treacherous snare and suspected oblation of the Greeks; or by applying flames consume it to ashes; or to lay open and ransack the recesses of the hollow womb. The fickle populace is split into opposite inclinations. Upon this, Laocoön, accompanied with numerous troop, first before all, with ardour hastens down from the top of the citadel; and while yet a great way off cries out, "O, wretched countrymen, what desperate infatuation is this? Do you believe the enemy gone? or think you any gifts of the Greeks can be free from deceit? Is Ulysses thus known to you? Either the Greeks lie concealed within this wood, or it is an engine framed against our walls, to overlook our houses, and to come down upon our city; or some mischievous design lurks beneath it. Trojans, put no faith in this horse. Whatever it be, I dread the Greeks, even when they bring gifts." Thus said, with valiant strength he hurled his massive spear against the sides and belly of the monster, where it swelled out with its jointed timbers; the weapon stood quivering, and the womb being shaken, the hollow caverns rang, and sent forth a groan. And had not the decrees of heaven been adverse, if our minds had not been infatuated, he had prevailed on us to mutilate with the sword this dark recess of the Greeks; and thou, Troy, should still have stood, and thou, lofty tower of Priam, now remained!

In the meantime, behold, Trojan shepherds, with loud acclamations, came dragging to the king a youth, whose hands were bound behind him; who, to them a mere stranger, had voluntarily thrown himself in the way, to promote this same design, and open Troy to the Greeks; a resolute soul, and prepared for either event, whether to execute his perfidious purpose, or submit to inevitable death. The Trojan youth pour tumultuously around from every quarter, from eagerness to see him, and they vie with one another in insulting the captive. Now learn the treachery of the Greeks, and from one crime take a specimen of the whole nation. For as he stood among the gazing crowds perplexed, defenceless, and threw his eyes around the Trojan bans, "Ah!" says he, "what land, what seas can now receive me? or to what further extremity can I, a forlorn wretch, be reduced, for whom there is no shelter anywhere among the Greeks? and to complete my misery the Trojans too, incensed against me, sue for satisfaction with my blood." By which mournful accents our affections at once were moved towards him, and all our resentment suppressed.

At these tears we grant him his life, and pity him from our hearts. Priam himself first gives orders that the manacles and strait bonds be loosened from the man, then thus addresses him in the language of a friend: "Whoever you are, now henceforth forget the Greeks you have lost; ours you shall be: and give me an ingenuous reply to these questions: To what purpose raised they this stupendous bulk of a horse? Who was the contriver? or what do they intend? what was the religious motive? or what warlike engine is it?" he said. The other, practised in fraud and Grecian artifice, lifted up to heaven his hands, loosed from the bonds: "Troy can never be razed by the Grecian sword, unless they repent the omens at Argos, and carry back the goddess whom they had conveyed in their curved ships. And now, that they have sailed for their native Mycenae with the wind, they are providing themselves with arms; and, they will come upon you unexpected." For he declared that "if your hands should violate this offering sacred to Minerva, then signal ruin awaited Priam's empire and the Trojans. But, if by your hands it mounted into the city, that Asia, without further provocation given, would advance with a formidable war to the very walls, and our posterity be doomed to the same fate." By such treachery and artifice of perjured Sinon, the story was believed: and we, whom neither Diomede, nor Achilles, nor a siege of ten years, nor a thousand ships, had subdued, were ensnared by guile and constrained tears.

Meanwhile they urge with general voice to convey the statue to its proper seat, and implore the favour of the goddess. We make a breach in the walls, and lay open the bulwarks of the city. All keenly ply the work; and under the feet apply smooth-rolling wheels;

stretch hempen ropes from the neck. The fatal machine passes over our walls, pregnant with arms. It advances, and with menacing aspect slides into the heart of the city. O country, O Ilium, the habitation of gods, and ye walls of Troy by war renowned! Four times it stopped in the very threshold of the gate, and four times the arms resounded in its womb: yet we, heedless, and blind with frantic zeal, urge on, and plant the baneful monster in the sacred citadel. Unhappy we, to whom that day was to be the last, adorn the temples of the gods throughout the city with festive boughs. Meanwhile, the heavens change, and night advances rapidly from the ocean, wrapping in her extended shade both earth and heaven, and the wiles of the Myrmidons. The Trojans, dispersed about the walls, were hushed: deep sleep fast binds them weary in his embraces. And now the Grecian host, in their equipped vessels, set out for Tenedos, making towards the well-known shore, by the friendly silence of the quiet moonshine, as soon as the royal galley stern had exhibited the signal fire; and Sinon, preserved by the will of the adverse gods, in a stolen hour unlocks the wooden prison to the Greeks shut up in its tomb: the horse, from his expanded caverns, pours them forth to the open air. They assault the city buried in sleep, and wine. The sentinels are beaten down; and with opened gates they receive all their friends, and join the conquering bands.

Meanwhile the city is filled with mingled scenes of woe; and though my father's house stood retired and enclosed with trees, louder and louder the sounds rise on the ear, and the horrid din of arms assails. I start from sleep and, by hasty steps, gain the highest battlement of the palace, and stand with erect ears: as when a flame is driven by the furious south winds on standing corn; or as a torrent impetuously bursting in a mountain-flood desolates the fields, desolates the rich crops of corn and the labours of the ox.

Then, indeed, the truth is confirmed and the treachery of the Greeks disclosed. Now Deiphosus' spacious house tumbles down, overpowered by the conflagration; now, next to him, Ucalegon blazes: the straits of Sigaeum shine far and wide with the flames. The shouts of men and clangour of trumpets arise. My arms I snatch in mad haste: nor is there in arms enough of reason: but all my soul burns to collect a troop for the war and rush into the citadel with my fellows: fury and rage hurry on my mind, and it occurs to me how glorious it is to die in arms.

The towering horse, planted in the midst of our streets, pours forth armed troops; and Sinon victorious, with insolent triumph scatters the flames. Others are pressing at our wide-opened gates, as many thousands as ever came from populous Mycenae: others with arms have blocked up the lanes to oppose our passage; the edged sword, with glittering point, stands unsheathed, ready for dealing death: hardly the foremost wardens of the gates make an effort to fight and resist in the blind encounter. By the impulse of the gods, I hurry away into flames and arms, whither the grim Fury, whither the din and shrieks that rend the skies, urge me on. Ripheus and Iphitus, mighty in arms, join me; Hypanis and Dymas come up with us by the light of the moon, and closely adhere to my side. Whom, close united, soon as I saw resolute to engage, to animate them the more I thus begin: "Youths, souls magnanimous in vain! If it is your determined purpose to follow me in this last attempt, you see what is the situation of our affairs. All the gods, by whom this empire stood, have deserted their shrines and altars to the enemy: you come to the relief of the city in flames: let us meet death, and rush into the thickest of our armed foes. The only safety for the vanquished is to throw away all hopes of safety." Thus the courage of each youth is kindled into fury. Then, like ravenous wolves in a gloomy fog, whom the fell rage of hunger hath driven forth, blind to danger, and whose whelps left behind long for their return with thirsting jaws; through arms; through enemies, we march up to imminent death, and advance through the middle of the city: sable Night hovers around us with her hollow shade.

Who can describe in words the havoc, who the death of that night? or who can furnish tears equal to the disasters? Our ancient city, having borne sway for many years, falls to the ground: great numbers of sluggish carcasses are strewn up and down, both in the streets, in the houses, and the sacred thresholds of the gods. Nor do the Trojans alone pay the penalty with their blood: the vanquished too at times resume courage in their hearts, and the victorious Grecians fall: everywhere is cruel sorrow, everywhere terror and death in a thousand shapes.

We march on, mingling with the Greeks, but not with heaven on our side; and in many a skirmish we engage during the dark night: many of the Greeks we send down to Hades. Some fly to the ships, and hasten to the trusty shore; some through dishonest fear, scale once more the bulky horse, and lurk within the well-known womb.

Ye ashes of Troy, ye expiring flames of my country! witness, that in your fall I shunned neither darts nor any deadly chances of the Greeks. Thence we are forced away, forthwith to Priam's palace called by the outcries. Here, indeed, we beheld a dreadful fight, as though this had been the only seat of the war, as though none had been dying in all the city besides; with such ungoverned fury we see Mars raging and the Greeks rushing forward to the palace, and the gates besieged by an advancing testudo. Scaling ladders are fixed against the walls, and by their steps they mount to the very door-posts, and protecting themselves by their left arms, oppose their bucklers to the darts, while with their right hands they grasp the battlements. On the other hand, the Trojans tear down the turrets and roofs of their houses; with these weapons, since they see the extremity, they seek to defend themselves now in their last death-struggle, and tumble down the gilded rafters; others with drawn swords beset the gates below; these they guard in a firm, compact body . . . I mount up to the roof of the highest battlement, whence the distressed Trojans were hurling unavailing darts. With our swords assailing all around a turret, situated on a precipice, and shooting up its towering top to the stars (whence we were wont to survey all Troy, the fleet of Greece, and all the Grecian camp), where the topmost story made the joints more apt to give way, we tear it from its deep foundation, and push it on our foes. Suddenly tumbling down, it brings thundering desolation with it, and falls with wide havoc on the Grecian troops. But others succeed: meanwhile, neither stones, nor any sort of missile weapons, cease to fly. Just before the vestibule, and at the outer gate, Pyrrhus exults, glittering in arms and gleamy brass. At the same time, all the youth from Scyros advance to the wall, and toss brands to the roof. Pyrrhus himself in the front, snatching up a battleaxe, beats through the stubborn gates, and labours to tear the brazen posts from the hinges; and now, having hewn away the bars, he dug through the firm boards, and made a large, wide-mouthed breach. The palace within is exposed to view, and the long galleries are discovered: the sacred recesses of Priam and the ancient kings are exposed to view; and they see armed men standing at the gate.

As for the inner palace, it is filled with mingled groans and doleful uproar, and the hollow rooms all throughout howl with female yells: their shrieks strike the golden stars. Then the trembling matrons roam through the spacious halls, and in embraces hug the door-posts, and cling to them with their lips. Pyrrhus presses on with all his father's violence: nor bolts, nor guards themselves, are able to sustain. The gate, by repeated battering blows, gives way, and the door-posts, torn from their hinges, tumble to the ground. The Greeks make their way by force, burst a passage, and, being admitted, butcher the first they meet, and fill the places all about with their troops. Those fifty bedchambers, those doors, that proudly shone with barbaric gold and spoils, were leveled to the ground: where the flames relent, the Greeks take their place.

Perhaps, too, you are curious to hear what was Priam's fate. As soon as he beheld the catastrophe of the taken city, and his palace gates broken down, and the enemy planted in the middle of his private apartments, the aged monarch, with unavailing aim, buckles on his shoulders (trembling with years) arms long disused, girds himself with his useless sword, and rushes into the thickest of the foes, resolute on death. And lo! Polites, one of Priam's sons, who had escaped from the sword of Pyrrhus, through darts, through foes, flies along the long galleries, and wounded traverses the waste halls. Pyrrhus, all afire, pursues him with the hostile weapon, is just grasping him with his hand, and presses on him with the spear. Soon as he at length got into the sight and presence of his parents, he dropped down, and poured out his life with a stream of blood. Upon this, Priam, though now held in the very midst of death, yet did not forbear, nor spared his tongue and passion; and, without any force, threw a feeble dart: which was instantly repelled by the hoarse brass, and hung on the highest boss of the buckler without any execution. Pyrrhus made answer and dragged him to the very altar, trembling and sliding in the streaming gore of his son: and with his left hand grasped his twisted hair, and with his right unsheathed his glittering sword, and plunged it into his side up to the hilt. Such was the end of Priam's fate: this was the final doom allotted to him, having before his eyes Troy consumed, and its towers laid in ruins; once the proud monarch over so many nations and countries of Asia: now his mighty trunk lies extended on the shore, the head torn from the shoulders, and a nameless corpse.

Chapter Thirty-Five

The View from a Hill
By John Buchan

British novelist John Buchan (1875–1940) is renowned for his prolific works embracing outdoor action and adventure, intrigue, and historical details. Scottish-born and very much an adventurer in real life, Buchan experienced the air war of World War 1 and brought it to the pages of fiction in his book Mr. Standfast, *which is excerpted here. His great fondness of Canada and its people resulted in his being appointed Governor General of Canada by King George V in 1935. The full list of Buchan titles will reveal great opportunities for reader reward.*

—Lamar Underwood

We were standing by the crumbling rails of what had once been the farm sheepfold. I looked at Archie and he smiled back at me, for he saw that my face had changed. Then he turned his eyes to the billowing clouds.

I felt my arm clutched.

"Look there!" said a fierce voice, and his glasses were turned upward.

I looked, and far up in the sky saw a thing like a wedge of wild geese flying towards us from the enemy's country. I made out the small dots which composed it, and my glasses told me they were planes. But only Archie's practised eye knew that they were enemy.

"Boche?" I asked.

"Boche," he said. "My God, we're for it now."

My heart had sunk like a stone, but I was fairly cool. I looked at my watch and saw that it was ten minutes to eleven.

"How many?"

"Five," said Archie. "or there may be six—no, only five."

"Listen!" I said. "Get on to your headquarters. Tell them that it's all up with us if a single plane gets back. Let them get well over the line, the deeper in the better, and tell them to send up every machine they possess and down them all. Tell them it's life or death. Not one single plane goes back. Quick!"

Archie disappeared, and as he went our anti-aircraft guns broke out. The formation above opened and zigzagged, but they were too high to be in much danger. But they were not too high to see that which we must keep hidden or perish.

The roar of our batteries died down as the invaders passed westwards. As I watched their progress they seemed to be dropping lower. Then they rose again and a bank of cloud concealed them.

I had a horrid certainty that they must beat us, that some at any rate would get back. They had seen our thin lines and the roads behind us empty of supports. They would see, as they advanced, the blue columns of the French coming up from the south-west, and they would return and tell the enemy that a blow now would open the road to Amiens and the sea. He had plenty of strength for it, and presently he would have overwhelming strength. It only needed a spearpoint to burst the jerry-built dam and let the flood through. . . . They would return in twenty minutes, and by noon we would be broken. Unless—unless the miracle of miracles happened, and they never returned.

Archie reported that his skipper would do his damnedest and that our machines were now going up. "We've a chance, sir," he said, "a good sportin' chance." It was a new Archie, with a hard voice, a lean face, and very old eyes.

Behind the jagged walls of the farm buildings was a knoll which had once formed part of the highroad. I went up there alone, for I didn't want anybody near me. I wanted a view-point, and I wanted quiet, for I had a grim time before me. From that knoll I had a big prospect of country. I looked east to our lines on which an occasional shell was falling, and where I could hear the chatter of machine-guns. West there was peace, for the woods closed down on the landscape. Up to the north, I remember, there was a big glare as from a burning dump, and heavy guns seemed to be at work in the Ancre valley. Down in the south there was the dull murmur of a great battle. But just around me, in the gap, the deadliest place of all, there was an odd quiet. I could pick out clearly the different sounds. Somebody down at the farm had made a joke and there was a short burst of laughter. I envied the humorist his composure. There was a clatter and jingle from a battery changing position. On the road a tractor was jolting along—I could hear its driver shout and the screech of its un-oiled axle.

My eyes were glued to my glasses, but they shook in my hands so that I could scarcely see. I bit my lip to steady myself, but they still wavered. From time to time I glanced at my wrist-watch. Eight minutes gone—ten—seventeen. If only the planes would come into sight! Even the certainty of failure would be better than this harrowing doubt. They should be back by now unless they had swung north across the salient, or unless the miracle of miracles—

Then came the distant yapping of an anti-aircraft gun, caught up the next second by others, while smoke patches studded the distant blue of the sky. The clouds were banking in mid-heaven, but to the west there was a big clear space now woolly with shrapnel bursts. I counted them mechanically—one—three—five—nine—with despair beginning to take the place of my anxiety. My hands were steady now, and through the glasses I saw the enemy.

Five attenuated shapes rode high above the bombardment, now sharp against the blue, now lost in a film of vapour. They were coming back, serenely, contemptuously, having seen all they wanted.

The quiet had gone now and the din was monstrous. Anti-aircraft guns, singly and in groups, were firing from every side. As I watched it seemed a futile waste of ammunition. The enemy didn't give a tinker's curse for it. . . . But surely there was one down. I could only count four now. No, there was the fifth coming out of a cloud. In ten minutes they would be all over the line. I fairly stamped in my vexation. Those guns were no more use than a sick headache. Oh, where in God's name were our own planes?

At that moment they came, streaking down into sight, four fighting scouts with the sun glinting on their wings and burnishing their metal cowls. I saw clearly the rings of red, white, and blue. Before their downward drive the enemy instantly spread out.

I was watching with bare eyes now, and I wanted companionship, for the time of waiting was over. Automatically I must have run down the knoll, for the next instant I knew I was staring at the heavens with Archie by my side. The combatants seemed to couple instinctively. Diving, wheeling, climbing, a pair would drop out of the melee or disappear behind a cloud. Even at that height I could hear the methodical rat-tat-tat of the machine-guns. Then there was a sudden flare and wisp of smoke. A plane sank, turning and twisting, to earth.

"Hun!" said Archie, who had his glasses on it.

Almost immediately another followed. This time the pilot recovered himself while still a thousand feet from the ground, and started gliding for the enemy lines. Then he wavered, plunged sickeningly, and fell headlong into the wood behind La Bruyère.

Farther east, almost over the front trenches, a two-seater Albatross and a British pilot were having a desperate tussle. The bombardment had stopped, and from where we stood every movement could be followed. First one, then another, climbed uppermost, and dived back, swooped out and wheeled in again, so that the two planes seemed to clear each other only by inches. Then it looked as if they closed and interlocked. I expected to see both go crashing, when suddenly the wings of one seemed to shrivel up, and the machine dropped like a stone.

"Hun," said Archie. "That makes three. Oh, good lads! Good lads!"

Then I saw something which took away my breath. Sloping down in wide circles came a German machine, and, following, a little behind and a little above, a British. It was the first surrender in mid-air I had seen. In my amazement I watched the couple right down to the ground, till the enemy landed in a big meadow across the highroad and our own man in a field nearer the river.

When I looked back into the sky, it was bare. North, south, east, and west, there was not a sign of aircraft, British or German.

A violent trembling took me. Archie was sweeping the heavens with his glasses and muttering to himself. Where was the fifth man? He must have fought his way through, and it was too late.

But was it? From the toe of a great rolling cloud bank a flame shot earthwards, followed by a V-shaped trail of smoke. British or Boche? British or Boche? I didn't wait long for an answer. For, riding over the far end of the cloud, came two of our fighting scouts.

I tried to be cool, and snapped my glasses into their case, though the reaction made me want to shout. Archie turned to me with a nervous smile and a quivering mouth. "I think we have won on the post," he said.

He reached out a hand for mine, his eyes still on the sky, and I was grasping it when it was torn away. He was staring upwards with a white face.

We were looking at a sixth enemy plane.

It had been behind the others and much lower, and was making straight at a great speed for the east. The glasses showed me a different type of machine—a big machine with short wings, which looked menacing as a hawk in a covey of grouse. It was under the cloud bank, and above, satisfied, easing down after their fight, and unwitting of this enemy, rode the two British craft.

A neighbouring anti-aircraft gun broke out into a sudden burst, and I thanked Heaven for its inspiration. Curious as to this new development, the two British turned, caught sight of the Boche, and dived for him.

What happened in the next minutes I cannot tell. The three seemed to be mixed up in a dogfight, so that I could not distinguish friend from foe. My hands no longer trembled; I was too desperate. The patter of machine-guns came down to us, and then one of the three broke clear and began to climb. The others strained to follow, but in a second he had risen beyond their fire, for he had easily the pace of them. Was it the Hun?

Archie's dry lips were talking.

"It's Lensch," he said.

"How d'you know?" I gasped angrily.

"Can't mistake him. Look at the way he slipped out as he banked. That's his patent trick."

In that agonizing moment hope died in me. I was perfectly calm now, for the time for anxiety had gone. Farther and farther drifted the British pilots behind, while Lensch in the completeness of his triumph looped more than once as if to cry an insulting fare-well. In less than three minutes he would be safe inside his own lines, and he carried the knowledge which for us was death.

———

Some one was bawling in my ear, and pointing upward. It was Archie and his face was wild. I looked and gasped—seized my glasses and looked again.

A second before Lensch had been alone; now there were two machines.

I heard Archie's voice. "My God, it's the Gladas—the little Gladas." His fingers were digging into my arm and his face was against my shoulder. And then his excitement sobered into an awe which choked his speech, as he stammered, "It's old—"

But I did not need him to tell me the name, for I had divined it when I first saw the new plane drop from the clouds. I had that queer sense that comes sometimes to a man that a friend is present when he cannot see him. Somewhere up in the void two heroes were fighting their last battle—and one of them had a crippled leg.

I had never any doubt about the result. Lensch was not aware of his opponent till he was almost upon him, and I wonder if by any freak of instinct he recognized his greatest antagonist. He never fired a shot, nor did Peter.... I saw the German twist and side-slip as if to baffle the fate descending upon him. I saw Peter veer over vertically and I knew that the end had come. He was there to make certain of victory and he took the only way.... The machines closed, there was a crash which I felt though I could not hear it, and next second both were hurtling down, over and over, to the earth.

They fell in the river just short of the enemy lines, but I did not see them, for my eyes were blinded and I was on my knees.

———

After that it was all a dream. I found myself being embraced by a French General of Division, and saw the first companies of the cheerful bluecoats for whom I had longed. With them came the rain, and it was under a weeping April sky that early in the night I marched what was left of my division away from the battlefield. The enemy guns were starting to speak behind us, but I did not heed them. I knew that now there were warders at the gate, and I believed that by the grace of God that gate was barred for ever.

———

They took Peter from the wreckage with scarcely a scar except his twisted leg. Death had smoothed out some of the age in him, and left his face much as I remembered it long ago in the Mashonaland hills. In his pocket was his old battered *Pilgrim's Progress*. It lies before me as I write, and beside it—for I was his only legatee—the little case which came to him weeks later, containing the highest honour that can be bestowed upon a soldier of Britain.

It was from the *Pilgrim's Progress* that I read next morning, when in the lee of an apple orchard Mary and Blenkiron and I stood in the soft spring rain beside his grave. And what I read was the tale of the end, not of Mr. Standfast whom he had singled out for his counterpart, but of Mr. Valiant-for-Truth whom he had not hoped to emulate. I set down the words as a salute and a farewell:

"*Then said he, 'I am going to my Father's; and though with great difficulty I am got hither, yet now I do not repent me of all the trouble I have been at to arrive where I am. My sword I give to him that shall succeed me in my pilgrimage, and my courage and skill to him that can get it. My marks and scars I carry with me, to be a witness for me that I have fought His battles who now will be my rewarder.'*

"*So he passed over, and all the trumpets sounded for him on the other side.*"

CHAPTER THIRTY-SIX

A Horseman in the Sky
By Ambrose Bierce

Newspaper columnist, satirist, essayist, short-story writer, and novelist Ambrose Bierce also chose to illustrate the consequences of divided loyalties in the haunting short story "A Horseman in the Sky." Bierce was himself a veteran of the war, fighting for the Union at several major battles, including Shiloh and Chickamauga, before he was severely wounded in the head at Kennesaw Mountain. "A Horseman in the Sky" is the tale of Carter Druse, a young Virginian whose conscience tells him he must fight for the Union. This is a heartbreaking decision for his proud Southern father, who can only tell him, "Well, go, sir, and whatever may occur do what you conceive to be your duty. . . ." For this one young man, however, following that advice costs him that which is most precious to him.

—LISA PURCELL

I

ONE SUNNY AFTERNOON IN THE AUTUMN OF THE YEAR 1861 A SOLDIER LAY IN A CLUMP of laurel by the side of a road in western Virginia. He lay at full length upon his stomach, his feet resting upon the toes, his head upon the left forearm. His extended right hand loosely grasped his rifle. But for the somewhat methodical disposition of his limbs and a slight rhythmic movement of the cartridge-box at the back of his belt he might have been thought to be dead. He was asleep at his post of duty. But if detected he would be dead shortly afterward, death being the just and legal penalty of his crime.

The clump of laurel in which the criminal lay was in the angle of a road which after ascending southward a steep acclivity to that point turned sharply to the west, running on the summit for perhaps one hundred yards. There it turned southward again and went zig-zagging downward through the forest. At the salient of that second angle was a large flat rock, jutting out northward, overlooking the deep valley from which the road ascended.

The rock capped a high cliff; a stone dropped from its outer edge would have fallen sheer downward one thousand feet to the tops of the pines. The angle where the soldier lay was on another spur of the same cliff. Had he been awake he would have commanded a view, not only of the short arm of the road and the jutting rock, but of the entire profile of the cliff below it. It might well have made him giddy to look.

The country was wooded everywhere except at the bottom of the valley to the northward, where there was a small natural meadow, through which flowed a stream scarcely visible from the valley's rim. This open ground looked hardly larger than an ordinary door-yard, but was really several acres in extent. Its green was more vivid than that of the enclosing forest. Away beyond it rose a line of giant cliffs similar to those upon which we are supposed to stand in our survey of the savage scene, and through which the road had somehow made its climb to the summit. The configuration of the valley, indeed, was such that from this point of observation it seemed entirely shut in, and one could but have wondered how the road which found a way out of it had found a way into it, and whence came and whither went the waters of the stream that parted the meadow more than a thousand feet below.

No country is so wild and difficult but men will make it a theatre of war; concealed in the forest at the bottom of that military rat-trap, in which half a hundred men in possession of the exits might have starved an army to submission, lay five regiments of Federal infantry. They had marched all the previous day and night and were resting. At nightfall they would take to the road again, climb to the place where their unfaithful sentinel now slept, and descending the other slope of the ridge fall upon a camp of the enemy at about midnight. Their hope was to surprise it, for the road led to the rear of it. In case of failure, their position would be perilous in the extreme; and fall they surely would should accident or vigilance apprise the enemy of the movement.

II

The sleeping sentinel in the clump of laurel was a young Virginian named Carter Druse. He was the son of wealthy parents, an only child, and had known such ease and cultivation and high living as wealth and taste were able to command in the mountain country of western Virginia. His home was but a few miles from where he now lay. One morning he had risen from the breakfast-table and said, quietly but gravely: "Father, a Union regiment has arrived at Grafton. I am going to join it."

The father lifted his leonine head, looked at the son a moment in silence, and replied: "Well, go, sir, and whatever may occur do what you conceive to be your duty. Virginia, to which you are a traitor, must get on without you. Should we both live to the end of the war, we will speak further of the matter. Your mother, as the physician has informed you, is in a most critical condition; at the best she cannot be with us longer than a few weeks, but that time is precious. It would be better not to disturb her."

So Carter Druse, bowing reverently to his father, who returned the salute with a stately courtesy that masked a breaking heart, left the home of his childhood to go soldiering. By conscience and courage, by deeds of devotion and daring, he soon commended himself to his fellows and his officers; and it was to these qualities and to some knowledge of the country that he owed his selection for his present perilous duty at the extreme outpost. Nevertheless, fatigue had been stronger than resolution and he had fallen asleep. What good or bad angel came in a dream to rouse him from his state of crime, who shall say? Without a movement, without a sound, in the profound silence and the languor of the late afternoon, some invisible messenger of fate touched with unsealing finger the eyes of his consciousness—whispered into the ear of his spirit the mysterious awakening word which no human lips ever have spoken, no human memory ever has recalled. He quietly raised his forehead from his arm and looked between the masking stems of the laurels, instinctively closing his right hand about the stock of his rifle.

His first feeling was a keen artistic delight. On a colossal pedestal, the cliff,—motionless at the extreme edge of the capping rock and sharply outlined against the sky,—was an equestrian statue of impressive dignity. The figure of the man sat the figure of the horse, straight and soldierly, but with the repose of a Grecian god carved in the marble which limits the suggestion of activity. The gray costume harmonized with its aerial background; the metal of accoutrement and caparison was softened and subdued by the shadow; the animal's skin had no points of high light. A carbine strikingly foreshortened lay across the pommel of the saddle, kept in place by the right hand grasping it at the "grip"; the left hand, holding the bridle rein, was invisible. In silhouette against the sky the profile of the horse was cut with the sharpness of a cameo; it looked across the heights of air to the confronting cliffs beyond. The face of the rider, turned slightly away, showed only an outline of temple and beard; he was looking downward to the bottom of the valley. Magnified by its lift against the sky and by the soldier's testifying sense of the formidableness of a near enemy the group appeared of heroic, almost colossal, size.

For an instant Druse had a strange, half-defined feeling that he had slept to the end of the war and was looking upon a noble work of art reared upon that eminence to commemorate the deeds of an heroic past of which he had been an inglorious part. The feeling was dispelled by a slight movement of the group: the horse, without moving its feet, had drawn its body slightly backward from the verge; the man remained immobile as before. Broad awake and keenly alive to the significance of the situation, Druse now brought the butt of his rifle against his cheek by cautiously pushing the barrel forward through the bushes, cocked the piece, and glancing through the sights covered a vital spot of the horseman's breast. A touch upon the trigger and all would have been well with Carter Druse. At that instant the horseman turned his head and looked in the direction of his concealed foeman—seemed to look into his very face, into his eyes, into his brave, compassionate heart.

Is it then so terrible to kill an enemy in war—an enemy who has surprised a secret vital to the safety of one's self and comrades—an enemy more formidable for his knowledge than all his army for its numbers? Carter Druse grew pale; he shook in every limb, turned faint, and saw the statuesque group before him as black figures, rising, falling, moving unsteadily in arcs of circles in a fiery sky. His hand fell away from his weapon, his head slowly dropped until his face rested on the leaves in which he lay. This courageous gentleman and hardy soldier was near swooning from intensity of emotion.

It was not for long; in another moment his face was raised from earth, his hands resumed their places on the rifle, his forefinger sought the trigger; mind, heart, and eyes were clear, conscience and reason sound. He could not hope to capture that enemy; to alarm him would but send him dashing to his camp with his fatal news. The duty of the soldier was plain: the man must be shot dead from ambush—without warning, without a moment's spiritual preparation, with never so much as an unspoken prayer, he must be sent to his account. But no—there is a hope; he may have discovered nothing—perhaps he is but admiring the sublimity of the landscape. If permitted, he may turn and ride carelessly away in the direction whence he came. Surely it will be possible to judge at the instant of his withdrawing whether he knows. It may well be that his fixity of attention— Druse turned his head and looked through the deeps of air downward, as from the surface to the bottom of a translucent sea. He saw creeping across the green meadow a sinuous line of figures of men and horses—some foolish commander was permitting the soldiers of his escort to water their beasts in the open, in plain view from a dozen summits!

Druse withdrew his eyes from the valley and fixed them again upon the group of man and horse in the sky, and again it was through the sights of his rifle. But this time his aim was at the horse. In his memory, as if they were a divine mandate, rang the words of his father at their parting: "Whatever may occur, do what you conceive to be your duty." He was calm now. His teeth were firmly but not rigidly closed; his nerves were as tranquil as a sleeping babe's—not a tremor affected any muscle of his body; his breathing, until suspended in the act of taking aim, was regular and slow. Duty had conquered; the spirit had said to the body: "Peace, be still." He fired.

III

An officer of the Federal force, who in a spirit of adventure or in quest of knowledge had left the hidden bivouac in the valley, and with aimless feet had made his way to the lower edge of a small open space near the foot of the cliff, was considering what he had to gain by pushing his exploration further. At a distance of a quarter-mile before him, but apparently at a stone's throw, rose from its fringe of pines the gigantic face of rock, towering to so great a height above him that it made him giddy to look up to where its edge cut a sharp, rugged line against the sky. It presented a clean, vertical profile against a background of blue sky to a point half the way down, and of distant hills, hardly less blue, thence to the tops of the trees at its base. Lifting his eyes to the dizzy altitude of its summit the officer saw an astonishing sight—a man on horseback riding down into the valley through the air!

Straight upright sat the rider, in military fashion, with a firm seat in the saddle, a strong clutch upon the rein to hold his charger from too impetuous a plunge. From his bare head his long hair streamed upward, waving like a plume. His hands were concealed in the cloud of the horse's lifted mane. The animal's body was as level as if every hoof-stroke encountered the resistant earth. Its motions were those of a wild gallop, but even as the officer looked they ceased, with all the legs thrown sharply forward as in the act of alighting from a leap. But this was a flight!

Filled with amazement and terror by this apparition of a horseman in the sky—half believing himself the chosen scribe of some new Apocalypse, the officer was overcome by the intensity of his emotions; his legs failed him and he fell. Almost at the same instant he heard a crashing sound in the trees—a sound that died without an echo—and all was still.

The officer rose to his feet, trembling. The familiar sensation of an abraded shin recalled his dazed faculties. Pulling himself together he ran rapidly obliquely away from the cliff to a point distant from its foot; thereabout he expected to find his man; and thereabout he naturally failed. In the fleeting instant of his vision his imagination had been so wrought upon by the apparent grace and ease and intention of the marvelous performance that it did not occur to him that the line of march of aerial cavalry is directly downward, and that he could find the objects of his search at the very foot of the cliff. A half-hour later he returned to camp.

This officer was a wise man; he knew better than to tell an incredible truth. He said nothing of what he had seen. But when the commander asked him if in his scout he had learned anything of advantage to the expedition he answered:

"Yes, sir; there is no road leading down into this valley from the southward."

The commander, knowing better, smiled.

IV

After firing his shot, Private Carter Druse reloaded his rifle and resumed his watch. Ten minutes had hardly passed when a Federal sergeant crept cautiously to him on hands and knees. Druse neither turned his head nor looked at him, but lay without motion or sign of recognition.

"Did you fire?" the sergeant whispered.

"Yes."

"At what?"

"A horse. It was standing on yonder rock—pretty far out. You see it is no longer there. It went over the cliff."

The man's face was white, but he showed no other sign of emotion. Having answered, he turned away his eyes and said no more. The sergeant did not understand.

"See here, Druse," he said, after a moment's silence, "it's no use making a mystery. I order you to report. Was there anybody on the horse?"

"Yes."

"Well?"

"My father."

The sergeant rose to his feet and walked away. "Good God!" he said.

CHAPTER THIRTY-SEVEN

A Night

By Louisa May Alcott

The battlefield combatants in the Civil War were men (with a few exceptions), but women were no less affected by the war. Many women volunteered as nurses, cooks, and even spies. In 1863 Louisa May Alcott, most famous for Little Women, *published* Hospital Sketches, *which chronicles her wartime experiences as a nurse in Washington, D.C. Although written with humor and a light touch, there is no disguising the pain of trying to save the lives of the shattered young soldiers who poured regularly into the wards, or of watching helplessly as one of them dies. Alcott's stint as a nurse was brief—only six weeks. While on duty, Alcott contracted typhoid pneumonia, from which she nearly died and never fully recovered; nurses were no less susceptible to the diseases that swept through hospital wards than were the patients.*

—LISA PURCELL

BEING FOND OF THE NIGHT SIDE OF NATURE, I WAS SOON PROMOTED TO THE POST OF night nurse, with every facility for indulging in my favorite pastime of "owling." My colleague, a black-eyed widow, relieved me at dawn, we two taking care of the ward, between us, like the immortal Sairy and Betsey, "turn and turn about." I usually found my boys in the jolliest state of mind their condition allowed; for it was a known fact that Nurse Periwinkle objected to blue devils, and entertained a belief that he who laughed most was surest of recovery. At the beginning of my reign, dumps and dismals prevailed; the nurses looked anxious and tired, the men gloomy or sad; and a general "Hark!-from-the-tombs-a-doleful-sound" style of conversation seemed to be the fashion: a state of things which caused one coming from a merry, social New England town, to feel as if she had got into an exhausted receiver; and the instinct of self-preservation, to say nothing of a philanthropic desire to serve the race, caused a speedy change in Ward No. 1.

More flattering than the most gracefully turned compliment, more grateful than the most admiring glance, was the sight of those rows of faces, all strange to me a little while ago, now lighting up, with smiles of welcome, as I came among them, enjoying that moment heartily, with a womanly pride in their regard, a motherly affection for them all. The evenings were spent in reading aloud, writing letters, waiting on and amusing the men, going the rounds with Dr. P., as he made his second daily survey, dressing my dozen wounds afresh, giving last doses, and making them cozy for the long hours to come, till the nine o'clock bell rang, the gas was turned down, the day nurses went off duty, the night watch came on, and my nocturnal adventure began.

My ward was now divided into three rooms; and, under favor of the matron, I had managed to sort out the patients in such a way that I had what I called, "my duty room," my "pleasure room," and my "pathetic room," and worked for each in a different way. One, I visited, armed with a dressing tray, full of rollers, plasters, and pins; another, with books, flowers, games, and gossip; a third, with teapots, lullabies, consolation, and sometimes, a shroud.

Wherever the sickest or most helpless man chanced to be, there I held my watch, often visiting the other rooms, to see that the general watchman of the ward did his duty by the fires and the wounds, the latter needing constant wetting. Not only on this account did I meander, but also to get fresher air than the close rooms afforded; for, owing to the stupidity of that mysterious "somebody" who does all the damage in the world, the windows had been carefully nailed down above, and the lower sashes could only be raised in the mildest weather, for the men lay just below. I had suggested a summary smashing of a few panes here and there, when frequent appeals to headquarters had proved unavailing, and daily orders to lazy attendants had come to nothing. No one seconded the motion, however, and the nails were far beyond my reach; for, though belonging to the sisterhood of "ministering angels," I had no wings, and might as well have asked for Jacob's ladder, as a pair of steps, in that charitable chaos.

One of the harmless ghosts who bore me company during the haunted hours, was Dan, the watchman, whom I regarded with a certain awe; for, though so much together, I never fairly saw his face, and, but for his legs, should never have recognized him, as we seldom met by day. These legs were remarkable, as was his whole figure, for his body was short, rotund, and done up in a big jacket, and muffler; his beard hid the lower part of his face, his hat-brim the upper; and all I ever discovered was a pair of sleepy eyes, and a very mild voice. But the legs!—very long, very thin, very crooked and feeble, looking like gray sausages in their tight coverings, without a ray of pegtopishness about them, and finished off with a pair of expansive, green cloth shoes, very like Chinese junks, with the sails down. This figure, gliding noiselessly about the dimly lighted rooms, was strongly suggestive of the spirit of a beer barrel mounted on corkscrews, haunting the old hotel in search of its lost mates, emptied and staved in long ago.

Another goblin who frequently appeared to me, was the attendant of the pathetic room, who, being a faithful soul, was often up to tend two or three men, weak and wandering as babies, after the fever had gone. The amiable creature beguiled the watches of the night by brewing jorums of a fearful beverage, which he called coffee, and insisted on sharing with me; coming in with a great bowl of something like mud soup, scalding hot, guiltless of cream, rich in an all-pervading flavor of molasses, scorch and tin pot. Such an amount of good will and neighborly kindness also went into the mess, that I never could find the heart to refuse, but always received it with thanks, sipped it with hypocritical relish while he remained, and whipped it into the slop-jar the instant he departed, thereby gratifying him, securing one rousing laugh in the doziest hour of the night, and no one was the worse for the transaction but the pigs. Whether they were "cut off untimely in their sins," or not, I carefully abstained from inquiring.

It was a strange life—asleep half the day, exploring Washington the other half, and all night hovering, like a massive cherubim, in a red rigolette, over the slumbering sons of man. I liked it, and found many things to amuse, instruct, and interest me. The snores alone were quite a study, varying from the mild sniff to the stentorian snort, which startled the echoes and hoisted the performer erect to accuse his neighbor of the deed, magnanimously forgive him, and wrapping the drapery of his couch about him, lie down to vocal slumber. After listening for a week to this band of wind instruments, I indulged in the belief that I could recognize each by the snore alone, and was tempted to join the chorus by breaking out with John Brown's favorite hymn:

"Blow ye the trumpet, blow!"

I would have given much to have possessed the art of sketching, for many of the faces became wonderfully interesting when unconscious. Some grew stern and grim, the men evidently dreaming of war, as they gave orders, groaned over their wounds, or damned the rebels vigorously; some grew sad and infinitely pathetic, as if the pain borne silently all day, revenged itself by now betraying what the man's pride had concealed so well. Often the roughest grew young and pleasant when sleep smoothed the hard lines away, letting the real nature assert itself; many almost seemed to speak, and I learned to know these men better by night than through any intercourse by day. Sometimes they disappointed me, for faces that looked merry and good in the light, grew bad and sly when the shadows came; and though they made no confidences in words, I read their lives, leaving them to wonder at the change of manner this midnight magic wrought in their nurse. A few talked busily; one drummer boy sang sweetly, though no persuasions could win a note from him by day; and several depended on being told what they had talked of in the morning.

Even my constitutionals in the chilly halls, possessed a certain charm, for the house was never still. Sentinels tramped round it all night long, their muskets glittering in the wintry moonlight as they walked, or stood before the doors, straight and silent, as figures of stone, causing one to conjure up romantic visions of guarded forts, sudden surprises, and daring deeds; for in these war times the hum drum life of Yankeedom had vanished, and the most prosaic feel some thrill of that excitement which stirs the nation's heart, and makes its capital a camp of hospitals.

Wandering up and down these lower halls, I often heard cries from above, steps hurrying to and fro, saw surgeons passing up, or men coming down carrying a stretcher, where lay a long white figure, whose face was shrouded and whose fight was done. Sometimes I stopped to watch the passers in the street, the moonlight shining on the spire opposite, or the gleam of some vessel floating, like a white-winged seagull, down the broad Potomac, whose fullest flow can never wash away the red stain of the land.

The night whose events I have a fancy to record, opened with a little comedy, and closed with a great tragedy; for a virtuous and useful life untimely ended is always tragical to those who see not as God sees. My headquarters were beside the bed of a New Jersey boy, crazed by the horrors of that dreadful Saturday. A slight wound in the knee brought him there; but his mind had suffered more than his body; some string of that delicate machine was over strained, and, for days, he had been reliving in imagination, the scenes he could not forget, till his distress broke out in incoherent ravings, pitiful to hear. As I sat by him, endeavoring to soothe his poor distracted brain by the constant touch of wet hands over his hot forehead, he lay cheering his comrades on, hurrying them back, then counting them as they fell around him, often clutching my arm, to drag me from the vicinity of a bursting shell, or covering up his head to screen himself from a shower of shot; his face brilliant with fever; his eyes restless; his head never still; every muscle strained and rigid; while an incessant stream of defiant shouts, whispered warnings, and broken laments, poured from his lips with that forceful bewilderment which makes such wanderings so hard to overhear.

It was past eleven, and my patient was slowly wearying himself into fitful intervals of quietude, when, in one of these pauses, a curious sound arrested my attention. Looking over my shoulder, I saw a one-legged phantom hopping nimbly down the room; and, going to meet it, recognized a certain Pennsylvania gentleman, whose wound-fever had taken a turn for the worse, and, depriving him of the few wits a drunken campaign had left him, set him literally tripping on the light, fantastic toe "toward home," as he blandly informed me, touching the military cap which formed a striking contrast to the severe simplicity of the rest of his decidedly undress uniform. When sane, the least movement produced a roar of pain or a volley of oaths; but the departure of reason seemed to have wrought an agreeable change, both in the man and his manners; for, balancing himself on one leg, like a meditative stork, he plunged into an animated discussion of the war, the President, lager beer, and Enfield rifles, regardless of any suggestions of mine as to the propriety of returning to bed, lest he be court-martialed for desertion.

Anything more supremely ridiculous can hardly be imagined than this figure, scantily draped in white, its one foot covered with a big blue sock, a dingy cap set rakingly askew on its shaven head, and placid satisfaction beaming in its broad red face, as it flourished a mug in one hand, an old boot in the other, calling them canteen and knapsack, while it skipped and fluttered in the most unearthly fashion. What to do with the creature I didn't know; Dan was absent, and if I went to find him, the perambulator might festoon himself out of the window, set his toga on fire, or do some of his neighbors a mischief. The attendant of the room was sleeping like a near relative of the celebrated Seven, and nothing short of pins would rouse him; for he had been out that day, and whiskey asserted its supremacy in balmy whiffs. Still declaiming, in a fine flow of eloquence, the demented gentleman hopped on, blind and deaf to my graspings and entreaties; and I was about to slam the door in his face, and run for help, when a second and saner phantom, "all in white," came to the rescue, in the likeness of a big Prussian, who spoke no English, but divined the crisis, and put an end to it, by bundling the lively monoped into his bed, like a baby, with an authoritative command to "stay put," which received added weight from being delivered in an odd conglomeration of French and German, accompanied by warning wags of a head decorated with a yellow cotton night cap, rendered most imposing by a tassel like a bell-pull. Rather exhausted by his excursion, the member from Pennsylvania subsided; and, after an irrepressible laugh together, my Prussian ally and myself were returning to our places, when the echo of a sob caused us to glance along the beds. It came from one in the corner—such a little bed!—and such a tearful little face looked up at us, as we stopped beside it! The twelve-year-old drummer boy was not singing now, but sobbing, with a manly effort all the while to stifle the distressful sounds that would break out.

"What is it, Teddy?" I asked, as he rubbed the tears away, and checked himself in the middle of a great sob to answer plaintively:

"I've got a chill, ma'am, but I ain't cryin' for that, 'cause I'm used to it. I dreamed Kit was here, and when I waked up he wasn't, and I couldn't help it, then."

The boy came in with the rest, and the man who was taken dead from the ambulance was the Kit he mourned. Well he might; for, when the wounded were brought from Fredericksburg, the child lay in one of the camps thereabout, and this good friend, though sorely hurt himself, would not leave him to the exposure and neglect of such a time and place; but, wrapping him in his own blanket, carried him in his arms to the transport, tended him during the passage, and only yielded up his charge when Death met him at the door of the hospital which promised care and comfort for the boy. For ten days, Teddy had shivered or burned with fever and ague, pining the while for Kit, and refusing to be comforted, because he had not been able to thank him for the generous protection, which, perhaps, had cost the giver's life. The vivid dream had wrung the childish heart with a fresh pang, and when I tried the solace fitted for his years, the remorseful fear that haunted him found vent in a fresh burst of tears, as he looked at the wasted hands I was endeavoring to warm:

"Oh! if I'd only been as thin when Kit carried me as I am now, maybe he wouldn't have died; but I was heavy, he was hurt worser than we knew, and so it killed him; and I didn't see him, to say good bye."

This thought had troubled him in secret; and my assurances that his friend would probably have died at all events, hardly assuaged the bitterness of his regretful grief.

At this juncture, the delirious man began to shout; the one-legged rose up in his bed, as if preparing for another dart, Teddy bewailed himself more piteously than before: and if ever a woman was at her wit's end, that distracted female was Nurse Periwinkle, during the space of two or three minutes, as she vibrated between the three beds, like an agitated pendulum. Like a most opportune reinforcement, Dan, the bandy, appeared, and devoted himself to the lively party, leaving me free to return to my post; for the Prussian, with a nod and a smile, took the lad away to his own bed, and lulled him to sleep with a soothing murmur, like a mammoth humblebee. I liked that in Fritz, and if he ever wondered afterward at the dainties that sometimes found their way into his rations, or the extra comforts of his bed, he might have found a solution of the mystery in sundry persons' knowledge of the fatherly action of that night.

Hardly was I settled again, when the inevitable bowl appeared, and its bearer delivered a message I had expected, yet dreaded to receive:

"John is going, ma'am, and wants to see you, if you can come."

"The moment this boy is asleep; tell him so, and let me know if I am in danger of being too late."

My Ganymede departed, and while I quieted poor Shaw, I thought of John. He came in a day or two after the others; and, one evening, when I entered my "pathetic room," I found a lately emptied bed occupied by a large, fair man, with a fine face, and the serenest eyes I ever met. One of the earlier comers had often spoken of a friend, who had remained behind, that those apparently worse wounded than himself might reach a shelter first. It seemed a David and Jonathan sort of friendship. The man fretted for his mate, and was never tired of praising John—his courage, sobriety, self-denial, and unfailing kindliness of heart; always winding up with: "He's an out an' out fine feller, ma'am; you see if he ain't."

I had some curiosity to behold this piece of excellence, and when he came, watched him for a night or two, before I made friends with him; for, to tell the truth, I was a little afraid of the stately looking man, whose bed had to be lengthened to accommodate his commanding stature; who seldom spoke, uttered no complaint, asked no sympathy, but tranquilly observed what went on about him; and, as he lay high upon his pillows, no picture of dying statesman or warrior was ever fuller of real dignity than this Virginia blacksmith. A most attractive face he had, framed in brown hair and beard, comely featured and full of vigor, as yet unsubdued by pain; thoughtful and often beautifully mild while watching the afflictions of others, as if entirely forgetful of his own. His mouth was grave and firm, with plenty of will and courage in its lines, but a smile could make it as sweet as any woman's; and his eyes were child's eyes, looking one fairly in the face, with a clear, straightforward glance, which promised well for such as placed their faith in him. He seemed to cling to life, as if it were rich in duties and delights, and he had learned the secret of content. The only time I saw his composure disturbed, was when my surgeon brought another to examine John, who scrutinized their faces with an anxious look, asking of the elder: "Do you think I shall pull through, sir?" "I hope so, my man." And, as the two passed on, John's eye still followed them, with an intentness which would have won a clearer answer from them, had they seen it. A momentary shadow flitted over his face; then came the usual serenity, as if, in that brief eclipse, he had acknowledged the existence of some hard possibility, and, asking nothing yet hoping all things, left the issue in God's hands, with that submission which is true piety.

The next night, as I went my rounds with Dr. P., I happened to ask which man in the room probably suffered most; and, to my great surprise, he glanced at John:

"Every breath he draws is like a stab; for the ball pierced the left lung, broke a rib, and did no end of damage here and there; so the poor lad can find neither forgetfulness nor ease, because he must lie on his wounded back or suffocate. It will be a hard struggle, and a long one, for he possesses great vitality; but even his temperate life can't save him; I wish it could."

"You don't mean he must die, Doctor?"

"Bless you there's not the slightest hope for him; and you'd better tell him so before long; women have a way of doing such things comfortably, so I leave it to you. He won't last more than a day or two, at furthest."

I could have sat down on the spot and cried heartily, if I had not learned the wisdom of bottling up one's tears for leisure moments. Such an end seemed very hard for such a man, when half a dozen worn out, worthless bodies round him, were gathering up the remnants of wasted lives, to linger on for years perhaps, burdens to others, daily reproaches to themselves. The army needed men like John, earnest, brave, and faithful; fighting for liberty and justice with both heart and hand, true soldiers of the Lord. I could not give him up so soon, or think with any patience of so excellent a nature robbed of its fulfillment, and blundered into eternity by the rashness or stupidity of those at whose hands so many lives may be required. It was an easy thing for Dr. P. to say: "Tell him he must die," but a cruelly hard thing to do, and by no means as "comfortable" as he politely suggested. I had not the heart to do it then, and privately indulged the hope that some change for the better might take place, in spite of gloomy prophesies; so, rendering my task unnecessary. A few minutes later, as I came in again, with fresh rollers, I saw John sitting erect, with no one to support him, while the surgeon dressed his back. I had never hitherto seen it done; for, having simpler wounds to attend to, and knowing the fidelity of the attendant, I had left John to him, thinking it might be more agreeable and safe; for both strength and experience were needed in his case. I had forgotten that the strong man might long for the gentle tendance of a woman's hands, the sympathetic magnetism of a woman's presence, as well as the feebler souls about him. The Doctor's words caused me to reproach myself with neglect, not of any real duty perhaps, but of those little cares and kindnesses that solace homesick spirits, and make the heavy hours pass easier. John looked lonely and forsaken just then, as he sat with bent head, hands folded on his knee, and no outward sign of suffering, till, looking nearer, I saw great tears roll down and drop upon the floor. It was a new sight there; for, though I had seen many suffer, some swore, some groaned, most endured silently, but none wept. Yet it did not seem weak, only very touching, and straightway my fear vanished, my heart opened wide and took him in, as, gathering the bent head in my arms, as freely as if he had been a little child, I said, "Let me help you bear it, John."

Never, on any human countenance, have I seen so swift and beautiful a look of gratitude, surprise and comfort, as that which answered me more eloquently than the whispered—

"Thank you, ma'am, this is right good! This is what I wanted!"

"Then why not ask for it before?"

"I didn't like to be a trouble; you seemed so busy, and I could manage to get on alone."

"You shall not want it any more, John."

Nor did he; for now I understood the wistful look that sometimes followed me, as I went out, after a brief pause beside his bed, or merely a passing nod, while busied with those who seemed to need me more than he, because more urgent in their demands; now I knew that to him, as to so many, I was the poor substitute for mother, wife, or sister, and in his eyes no stranger, but a friend who hitherto had seemed neglectful; for, in his modesty, he had never guessed the truth. This was changed now; and, through the tedious operation of probing, bathing, and dressing his wounds, he leaned against me, holding my hand fast, and, if pain wrung further tears from him, no one saw them fall but me. When he was laid down again, I hovered about him, in a remorseful state of mind that would not let me rest, till I had bathed his face, brushed his "bonny brown hair," set all things smooth about him, and laid a knot of heath and heliotrope on his clean pillow. While doing this, he watched me with the satisfied expression I so liked to see; and when I offered the little nosegay, held it carefully in his great hand, smoothed a ruffled leaf or two, surveyed and smelt it with an air of genuine delight, and lay contentedly regarding the glimmer of the sunshine on the green. Although the manliest man among my forty, he said, "Yes, ma'am," like a little boy; received suggestions for his comfort with the quick smile that brightened his whole face; and now and then, as I stood tidying the table by his bed, I felt him softly touch my gown, as if to assure himself that I was there. Anything more natural and frank I never saw, and found this brave John as bashful as brave, yet full of excellencies and fine aspirations, which, having no power to express themselves in words, seemed to have bloomed into his character and made him what he was.

After that night, an hour of each evening that remained to him was devoted to his ease or pleasure. He could not talk much, for breath was precious, and he spoke in whispers; but from occasional conversations, I gleaned scraps of private history which only added to the affection and respect I felt for him. Once he asked me to write a letter, and as I settled pen and paper, I said, with an irrepressible glimmer of feminine curiosity, "Shall it be addressed to wife, or mother, John?"

"Neither, ma'am; I've got no wife, and will write to mother myself when I get better. Did you think I was married because of this?" he asked, touching a plain ring he wore, and often turned thoughtfully on his finger when he lay alone.

"Partly that, but more from a settled sort of look you have; a look which young men seldom get until they marry."

"I didn't know that; but I'm not so very young, ma'am, thirty in May, and have been what you might call settled this ten years; for mother's a widow, I'm the oldest child she has, and it wouldn't do for me to marry until Lizzy has a home of her own, and Laurie's learned his trade; for we're not rich, and I must be father to the children and husband to the dear old woman, if I can."

"No doubt but you are both, John; yet how came you to go to war, if you felt so? Wasn't enlisting as bad as marrying?"

"No, ma'am, not as I see it, for one is helping my neighbor, the other pleasing myself. I went because I couldn't help it. I didn't want the glory or the pay; I wanted the right thing done, and people kept saying the men who were in earnest ought to fight. I was in earnest, the Lord knows! But I held off as long as I could, not knowing which was my duty; mother saw the case, gave me her ring to keep me steady, and said 'Go': so I went."

A short story and a simple one, but the man and the mother were portrayed better than pages of fine writing could have done it.

"Do you ever regret that you came, when you lie here suffering so much?"

"Never, ma'am; I haven't helped a great deal, but I've shown I was willing to give my life, and perhaps I've got to; but I don't blame anybody, and if it was to do over again, I'd do it. I'm a little sorry I wasn't wounded in front; it looks cowardly to be hit in the back, but I obeyed orders, and it don't matter in the end, I know."

Poor John! It did not matter now, except that a shot in the front might have spared the long agony in store for him. He seemed to read the thought that troubled me, as he spoke so hopefully when there was no hope, for he suddenly added:

"This is my first battle; do they think it's going to be my last?"

"I'm afraid they do, John."

It was the hardest question I had ever been called upon to answer; doubly hard with those clear eyes fixed on mine, forcing a truthful answer by their own truth. He seemed a little startled at first, pondered over the fateful fact a moment, then shook his head, with a glance at the broad chest and muscular limbs stretched out before him:

"I'm not afraid, but it's difficult to believe all at once. I'm so strong it don't seem possible for such a little wound to kill me."

Merry Mercutio's dying words glanced through my memory as he spoke: "'Tis not so deep as a well, nor so wide as a church door, but 'tis enough." And John would have said the same could he have seen the ominous black holes between his shoulders; he never had; and, seeing the ghastly sights about him, could not believe his own wound more fatal than these, for all the suffering it caused him.

"Shall I write to your mother, now?" I asked, thinking that these sudden tidings might change all plans and purposes; but they did not; for the man received the order of the Divine Commander to march with the same unquestioning obedience with which the soldier had received that of the human one; doubtless remembering that the first led him to life, and the last to death.

"No, ma'am; to Laurie just the same; he'll break it to her best, and I'll add a line to her myself when you get done."

So I wrote the letter which he dictated, finding it better than any I had sent; for, though here and there a little ungrammatical or inelegant, each sentence came to me briefly worded, but most expressive; full of excellent counsel to the boy, tenderly bequeathing "mother and Lizzie" to his care, and bidding him good bye in words the sadder for their simplicity. He added a few lines, with steady hand, and, as I sealed it, said, with a patient sort of sigh, "I hope the answer will come in time for me to see it"; then, turning away his face, laid the flowers against his lips, as if to hide some quiver of emotion at the thought of such a sudden sundering of all the dear home ties.

These things had happened two days before; now John was dying, and the letter had not come. I had been summoned to many deathbeds in my life, but to none that made my heart ache as it did then, since my mother called me to watch the departure of a spirit akin to this in its gentleness and patient strength. As I went in, John stretched out both hands:

"I know you'd come! I guess I'm moving on, ma'am."

He was; and so rapidly that, even while he spoke, over his face I saw the gray veil falling that no human hand can lift. I sat down by him, wiped the drops from his forehead, stirred the air about him with the slow wave of a fan, and waited to help him die. He stood in sore need of help—and I could do so little; for, as the doctor had foretold, the strong body rebelled against death, and fought every inch of the way, forcing him to draw each breath with a spasm, and clench his hands with an imploring look, as if he asked, "How long must I endure this, and be still!" For hours he suffered dumbly, without a moment's respite, or a moment's murmuring; his limbs grew cold, his face damp, his lips white, and, again and again, he tore the covering off his breast, as if the lightest weight added to his agony; yet through it all, his eyes never lost their perfect serenity, and the man's soul seemed to sit therein, undaunted by the ills that vexed his flesh.

One by one, the men woke, and round the room appeared a circle of pale faces and watchful eyes, full of awe and pity; for, though a stranger, John was beloved by all. Each man there had wondered at his patience, respected his piety, admired his fortitude, and now lamented his hard death; for the influence of an upright nature had made itself deeply felt, even in one little week. Presently, the Jonathan who so loved this comely David, came creeping from his bed for a last look and word. The kind soul was full of trouble, as the choke in his voice, the grasp of his hand, betrayed; but there were no tears, and the farewell of the friends was the more touching for its brevity.

"Old boy, how are you?" faltered the one.

"Most through, thank heaven!" whispered the other.

"Can I say or do anything for you anywheres?"

"Take my things home, and tell them that I did my best."

"I will! I will!"

"Good bye, Ned."

"Good bye, John, good bye!"

They kissed each other, tenderly as women, and so parted, for poor Ned could not stay to see his comrade die. For a little while, there was no sound in the room but the drip of water, from a stump or two, and John's distressful gasps, as he slowly breathed his life away. I thought him nearly gone, and had just laid down the fan, believing its help to be no longer needed, when suddenly he rose up in his bed, and cried out with a bitter cry that broke the silence, sharply startling every one with its agonized appeal:

"For God's sake, give me air!"

It was the only cry pain or death had wrung from him, the only boon he had asked; and none of us could grant it, for all the airs that blew were useless now. Dan flung up the window. The first red streak of dawn was warming the gray east, a herald of the coming sun; John saw it, and with the love of light which lingers in us to the end, seemed to read in it a sign of hope of help, for, over his whole face there broke that mysterious expression, brighter than any smile, which often comes to eyes that look their last. He laid himself gently down; and, stretching out his strong right arm, as if to grasp and bring the blessed air to his lips in a fuller flow, lapsed into a merciful unconsciousness, which assured us that for him suffering was forever past. He died then; for, though the heavy breaths still tore their way up for a little longer, they were but the waves of an ebbing tide that beat unfelt against the wreck, which an immortal voyager had deserted with a smile. He never spoke again, but to the end held my hand close, so close that when he was asleep at last, I could not draw it away. Dan helped me, warning me as he did so that it was unsafe for dead and living flesh to lie so long together; but though my hand was strangely cold and stiff, and four white marks remained across its back, even when warmth and color had returned elsewhere, I could not but be glad that, through its touch, the presence of human sympathy, perhaps, had lightened that hard hour.

When they had made him ready for the grave, John lay in state for half an hour, a thing which seldom happened in that busy place; but a universal sentiment of reverence and affection seemed to fill the hearts of all who had known or heard of him; and when the rumor of his death went through the house, always astir, many came to see him, and I felt a tender sort of pride in my lost patient; for he looked a most heroic figure, lying there stately and still as the statue of some young knight asleep upon his tomb. The lovely expression which so often beautifies dead faces, soon replaced the marks of pain, and I longed for those who loved him best to see him when half an hour's acquaintance with Death had made them friends. As we stood looking at him, the ward master handed me a letter, saying it had been forgotten the night before. It was John's letter, come just an hour too late to gladden the eyes that had longed and looked for it so eagerly! Yet he had it; for, after I had cut some brown locks for his mother, and taken off the ring to send her, telling how well the talisman had done its work, I kissed this good son for her sake, and laid the letter in his hand, still folded as when I drew my own away, feeling that its place was there, and making myself happy with the thought, that, even in his solitary place in the "Government Lot," he would not be without some token of the love which makes life beautiful and outlives death. Then I left him, glad to have known so genuine a man, and carrying with me an enduring memory of the brave Virginia blacksmith, as he lay serenely waiting for the dawn of that long day which knows no night.

Sources

Classic American Hero Stories: Twelve Inspirational Tales of American Heroism, edited Stephen Vincent Brennan.

Classic Civil War Stories: Twenty Extraordinary Tales of the North and South, edited by Lisa Purcell.

Classic War Stories: Thirteen Thrilling Tales from the Battlefield, edited by Lamar Underwood.

"What I Saw of Shiloh," by Ambrose Bierce (1881).

"The Sword of the Lord and of Gideon," by Theodore Roosevelt Jr.

"Poker and Missiles: A Pilot's Life in Vietnam," from *Midair*, by Craig K. Collins (Lyons Press, 2016).

"The Very Real George Washington," by Henry Cabot Lodge, from *Hero Tales from American History*, by Henry Cabot Lodge and Theodore Roosevelt (Century Company, 1895).

"Waterloo," by Victor Hugo, from *Les Misérables* (1862).

The Red Badge of Courage, by Stephen Crane (1895).

"Sniper: American Single-Shot Warriors in Iraq and Afghanistan," by Gina Cavallaro with Matt Larsen, from the book of the same title (Lyons Press, 2010).

"The Parisian," by Alden Brooks, from *The Fighting Men* (1917).

"General Custer," by Francis Fuller Victor, from *A History of the Sioux War* (1881).

"The Battle of Trenton," by Henry Cabot Lodge, from *Hero Tales from American History*, by Henry Cabot Lodge and Theodore Roosevelt (Century Company, 1895).

"The Fourteenth at Gettysburg" from *Harper's Weekly*, November 21, 1863.

"The Brigade Classics," "The Charge of the Light Brigade" and "The Charge of the Heavy Brigade," by Alfred, Lord Tennyson.

"The Air War Over the Trenches," by Eddie Rickenbacker, from *Fighting the Flying Circus* (Frederick A. Stokes, 1919).

"Nathan Hale," by James Parton, from *Captain Nathan Hale, the Martyr-Spy* (1866).

"Okinawa: The Fight for Sugar Loaf Hill," by George Feifer, from *The Battle of Okinawa: The Blood and the Bomb* (Lyons Press, 2001). Originally published as *Tennozna: The Battle of Okinawa and the Atomic Bomb* (Ticknor and Fields, 1992).

"An Occurrence at Owl Creek Bridge," by Ambrose Bierce, from *The Collected Works of Ambrose Bierce* (1911).

"The Battle at Fort William Henry," by Francis Parkman, from *Fort William Henry 1757* (1884).

"The Pass of Thermopylae," by Charlotte Yonge, from *A Book of Golden Deeds* (1864).

"A Woman's Wartime Journal," by Dolly Sumner Lunt, excerpts from *A Woman's Wartime Journal: An Account of the Passage over a Georgia Plantation of Sherman's Army on the March to the Sea, as Recorded in the Diary of Dolly Sumner Lunt (Mrs. Thomas Burge)* (1918).

"Andrey and Bagration: A Rearguard Action," by Leo Tolstoy, from *War and Peace* (1868).

"A Buffalo Bill Episode," by William F. Cody, from *The Life of the Hon. William F. Cody* (Frank E. Bliss, 1879).

"A Night Ride of the Wounded," by Randall Parrish, from *My Lady of the North* (1904).

"The Battle of Hastings," by Charles Oman, from *A History of the Art of War in the Middle Ages* (1898).

"A Grey Sleeve," by Stephen Crane, from *The Little Regiment, and Other Stories of the American Civil War* (1896).

"Gunga Din," by Rudyard Kipling, from *Ballads and Barrack Room Ballads* (1892).

"The Saga of Crazy Horse," by Charles A. Eastman, from *Indian Heroes and Great Chieftains* (Little, Brown, 1918).

"Bull Run," by Joseph A. Altsheler, from *The Guns of Bull Run* (1914).

"Eight Survived," by Douglas A. Campbell, from *Eight Survived: The Harrowing Story of the USS* Flier *and the Only Downed World War II Submariners to Survive and Evade Capture* (Lyons Press, 2010).

"Vicksburg During the Trouble," by Mark Twain, from *Life on the Mississippi* (1883).

"Intensification of Suffering and Hatred," by Phoebe Yates Pember, from *A Southern Woman's Story* (1879).

"The Flag-Bearer," by Theodore Roosevelt, from *Hero Tales from American History*, by Henry Cabot Lodge and Theodore Roosevelt (Century Company, 1895).

"We Die Alone," by David Howarth, from *We Die Alone: A World War II Epic of Escape and Endurance*, by David Howarth (Lyons Press, 1999; originally published by Macmillan Company, 1955).

"The Trojan Horse," by Virgil, from *The Aeneid* (19 BC).

"The View from a Hill," by John Buchan, from *Mr. Standfast* (1919).

"A Horseman in the Sky," by Ambrose Bierce, from *Tales of Soldiers and Civilians* (1891).

"A Night," by Louisa May Alcott, from *Hospital Sketches* (1863).